KU-504-121

THE PILLARS OF CREATION

TERRY GOODKIND

Copyright © 2001 Terry Goodkind
All rights reserved

The right of Terry Goodkind to be identified as
the author of this work has been asserted by him
in accordance with the Copyright, Designs and
Patents Act 1988.

Maps by Terry Goodkind

This edition published in Great Britain in 2002 by

Gollancz
An imprint of the Orion Publishing Group
Orion House, 5 Upper St Martin's Lane, London WC2H 9EA

Second impression 2003

A CIP catalogue record for this book is available
from the British Library

ISBN 0 575 07375 6

Printed in Great Britain by
Clays Ltd, St Ives plc

With a cry, Friedrich scrambled to his feet and took off running as fast as his legs would fly. His age mattered little when powered by such a fright. A quick glance over his shoulder revealed the beast bounding down the trail behind him, easily closing the distance.

Worse yet, in that brief glance back, Friedrich saw more pairs of glowing yellow eyes emerging from the woods to join in the pursuit.

They were coming out for the night's hunt.

Friedrich was their prey.

The howling beast hit his back with such force that it drove the wind from his lungs. He pitched face-first to the ground, hitting with a grunt, sliding through the dirt. As he tried to scramble away, the powerful beast pounced on him. Raging with snarling snapping teeth, it lunged, caught his backpack, tearing it open in a mad effort to get at his bone and muscle.

Friedrich vividly envisioned being torn apart.

He knew he was about to die.

Terry Goodkind lives in the western United States.

Dedicated to the people in the United States Intelligence Community who, for decades, have valiantly fought to preserve life and liberty, while being ridiculed, condemned, demonized, and shackled by the jackals of evil.

Evil thinks not to beguile us by unveiling the terrible truth of its festering intent, but comes, instead, disguised in the diaphanous robes of virtue, whispering sweet-sounding lies intended to seduce us into the dark bed of our eternal graves.

—translated from *Koloblicin's Journal*

THE PILLARS
OF CREATION

Chapter 1

Picking through the dead man's pockets, Jennsen Daggett came across the last thing in the world she would ever have expected to find. Startled, she sat back on her heels. The raw breeze ruffled her hair as she stared wide-eyed at the words written in precise, blocky letters on the small square of paper. The paper had been folded in half twice, carefully, so that the edges had been even. She blinked, half expecting the words to vanish, like some grim illusion. They remained solid and all too real.

Foolish though she knew the thought was, she still felt as if the dead soldier might be watching her for any reaction. Showing none, outwardly, anyway, she stole a look at his eyes. They were dull and filmy. She had heard people say of the deceased that they looked like they were only sleeping. He didn't. His eyes looked dead. His pale lips were taut, his face was waxy. There was a purplish blush at the back of his bull neck.

Of course he wasn't watching her. He was no longer watching anything. With his head turned to the side, toward her, though, it almost seemed as if he might be looking at her. She could imagine he was.

Up on the rocky hill behind her, bare branches clattered together in the wind like bones clacking. The paper in her trembling fingers seemed to be rattling with them. Her heart, already thumping at a brisk pace, started to pound harder.

Jennsen prided herself in her levelheadedness. She knew she was letting her imagination get carried away. But she had never before seen a dead person, a person so grotesquely still. It was dreadful seeing someone who didn't breathe. She swallowed in an attempt to compose her own breathing, if not her nerves.

Even if he was dead, Jennsen didn't like him looking at her, so she stood, lifted the hem of her long skirts, and stepped around the body. She carefully folded the small piece of paper over twice, the way it had been folded when she had found it, and slipped it into her pocket. She would have to worry about that later. Jennsen knew how her mother would react to those two words on the paper.

Determined to be finished with her search, she squatted on the other side of the man. With his face turned away, it almost seemed as if he were looking back up at the trail from where he had fallen, as if he might be wondering what had happened and how he had come to be at the bottom of the steep, rocky gorge with his neck broken.

His cloak had no pockets. Two pouches were secured to his belt. One pouch held oil, whetstones, and a strop. The other was packed with jerky. Neither contained a name.

If he'd known better, as she did, he would have taken the long way along the bottom of the cliff, rather than traverse the trail across the top, where patches of black ice made it treacherous this time of year. Even if he didn't want to retreat the way he had come in order to climb down into the gorge, it would have been wiser for him to have made his way through the woods, despite the thick bramble that made travel difficult up there among the deadfall.

Done was done. If she could find something that would tell her who he was, maybe she could find his kin, or someone who knew him. They would want to know. She clung to the safety of the pretense.

Almost against her will, Jennsen returned to wondering what he had been doing out here. She feared that the carefully folded piece of paper told her only too clearly. Still, there could be some other reason.

If she could just find it.

She had to move his arm a little if she was to look in his other pocket.

'Dear spirits forgive me,' she whispered as she grasped the dead limb.

His unbending arm moved only with difficulty. Jennsen's nose wrinkled with disgust. He was as cold as the ground he lay on, as cold as the sporadic raindrops that fell from the iron sky. This time of year, it was almost always snow driven before such a stiff west wind. The unusual intermittent mist and drizzle had surely made the icy places on the trail at the top even slicker. The dead man only proved it.

She knew that if she stayed much longer she would be caught out in the approaching winter rain. She was well aware that people exposed to such weather risked their lives. Fortunately, Jennsen wasn't terribly far from home. If she didn't get home soon, though, her mother, worried at what could be taking so long, would probably come out after her. Jennsen didn't want her mother getting soaked, too.

Her mother would be waiting for the fish Jennsen had retrieved from baited lines in the lake. For once, the lines they tended through holes in the ice had brought them a full stringer. The fish were lying dead on the other side of the dead man, where she had dropped them after making her grim discovery. He hadn't been there earlier, or she would have seen him on her way out to the lake.

Taking a deep breath to gird her resolve, Jennsen made herself return to her search. She imagined that some woman was probably wondering about her big, handsome soldier, worrying if he was safe, warm, and dry.

He was none of that.

Jennsen would want someone to tell her mother, if it were she who had fallen and broken her neck. Her mother would understand if she delayed a bit to try to find out the man's identity. Jennsen reconsidered. Her mother might understand, but she still wouldn't want Jennsen anywhere near one of these soldiers. But he was dead. He couldn't hurt anyone, now, much less her and her mother.

Her mother would be even more troubled once Jennsen showed her what was written on the little piece of paper.

Jennsen knew that what really drove her search was the hope

3

for some other explanation. She desperately wanted it to be something else. That frantic need kept her beside his dead body when she wanted nothing so much as to run for home.

If she didn't find anything to explain away his presence, then it would be best to cover him and hope that no one ever found him. Even if she had to stay out in the rain, she should cover him over as quickly as possible. She shouldn't wait. Then no one would ever know where he was.

She made herself push her hand down into his trouser pocket, all the way to the end. The flesh of his thigh was stiff. Her fingers hurriedly gathered up the nest of small objects at the bottom. Gasping for breath at the awful task, she pulled it all out in her fist. She bent close in the gathering gloom and opened her fingers for a look.

On top were a flint, bone buttons, a small ball of twine, and a folded handkerchief. With one finger, she pushed the twine and handkerchief to the side, exposing a weighty clutch of coins – silver and gold. She let out a soft whistle at the sight of such wealth. She didn't think that soldiers were rich, but this man had five gold marks among a larger number of silver marks. A fortune by most any standard. All the silver pennies – not copper, silver – seemed insignificant by contrast, even though they alone were probably more than she had spent in the whole of her twenty years.

The thought occurred to her that it was the first time in her life that she had ever held gold – or even silver – marks. The thought occurred to her that it might be plunder.

She found no trinket from a woman, as she had hoped, so as to soften her worry about what sort of man he had been.

Regrettably, nothing in the pocket told her anything of who he might be. Her nose wrinkled as she went about the chore of returning his possessions to his pocket. Some of the silver pennies spilled from her fist. She picked them all up from the wet, frozen ground and forced her hand into his pocket again in order to return them all to their rightful place.

His pack might tell her more, but he was sprawled atop it, and she wasn't sure she wanted to try to have a look, since it was likely to hold only supplies. His pockets would have held anything he considered valuable.

Like the piece of paper.

She supposed all the evidence that she really needed was in plain sight. He wore stiff leather armor under his dark cloak and tunic. At his hip was a simple but ruggedly made and wickedly sharp soldier's sword in a torn utilitarian black leather scabbard. The sword was broken at midlength, no doubt in the long tumble from the trail.

Her eyes glided more carefully over the remarkable knife sheathed at his belt. The hilt of the knife, gleaming in the gloom, was what had riveted her attention from the first instant. The sight of it had held her frozen until she realized its owner was dead. She was sure that no simple soldier would possess a knife that exquisitely crafted. It had to be more expensive than any knife she had ever seen.

On the silver hilt was the ornate letter 'R.' Even so, it was a thing of beauty.

From a young age, her mother had taught her to use a knife. She wished her mother could have a knife as fine as this.

Jennsen.

Jennsen jumped at the whispered word.

Not now. Dear spirits, not now. Not here.

Jennsen.

Jennsen was not a woman who hated much in life, but she hated the voice that sometimes came to her.

She ignored it, now, as always, forcing her fingers to move, to try to discover if there was anything else about the man that she should know. She checked the leather straps for concealed pockets but found none. The tunic was a plain cut, without pockets.

Jennsen, came the voice again.

She gritted her teeth. 'Leave me be,' she said aloud, if under her breath.

Jennsen.

It sounded different, this time. Almost as if the voice wasn't in her head, as it always was.

'Leave me alone,' she growled.

5

Surrender, came the dead murmur.

She glanced up and saw the man's dead eyes staring at her.

The first curtain of cold rain, billowing in the wind, felt like the icy fingers of spirits caressing her face.

Her heart galloped yet faster. Her breath caught against her ragged pulls, like silk catching on dry skin. With her wide-eyed gaze locked on the dead soldier's face, she pushed with her feet, scuttling back across the gravel.

She was being silly. She knew she was. The man was dead. He wasn't looking at her. He couldn't be. His stare was fixed in death, that's all, like her stringer of dead fish – they weren't looking at anything. Neither was he. She was being silly. It only seemed he was looking at her.

But even if the dead eyes were staring at nothing, she would just as soon that they weren't doing it in her direction.

Jennsen.

Beyond, above the sharp rise of granite, the pine trees swayed from side to side in the wind and the bare maple and oak waved their skeletal arms, but Jennsen kept her gaze fixed on the dead man as she listened for the voice. The man's lips were still. She knew they would be. The voice was in her head.

His face was still turned toward the trail from where he had fallen to his death. She had thought his lifeless sight had been turned in that direction, too, but now his eyes seemed to be turned more toward her.

Jennsen curled her fingers around the hilt of her knife.

Jennsen.

'Leave me be. I'll not surrender.'

She never knew what it was that the voice wanted her to surrender. Despite having been with her nearly her whole life, it had never said. She found refuge in that ambiguity.

As if in answer to her thought, the voice came again.

Surrender your flesh, Jennsen.

Jennsen couldn't breathe.

Surrender your will.

She swallowed in terror. It had never said that before – never said anything she could understand.

Often, she would faintly hear it – as if it were too far away to

6

be clearly understood. Sometimes she thought she could hear the words, but they seemed to be in a strange language.

She often heard it when she was falling asleep, calling to her in that distant, dead whisper. It spoke other words to her, she knew, but never so as she could understand more than her name and that frighteningly seductive single-word command to surrender. That word was always more forceful than any other. She could always hear it even when she could hear no other.

Her mother said that the voice was the man who, nearly Jennsen's whole life, had wanted to kill her. Her mother said that he wanted to torment her.

'Jenn,' her mother would often say, 'it's all right. I'm here with you. His voice can't hurt you.' Not wanting to burden her mother, Jennsen often didn't tell her about the voice.

But even if the voice couldn't hurt her, the man could, if he found her. At that moment, Jennsen desperately wished for the protective comfort of her mother's arms.

One day, he would come for her. They both knew he would. Until then, he sent his voice. That's what her mother thought, anyway.

As much as that explanation frightened her, Jennsen preferred it to thinking herself mad. If she didn't have her own mind, she had nothing.

'What's happened here?'

Jennsen gasped in a cry of fright as she spun, pulling her knife. She dropped into a half crouch, feet spread, knife held in a death grip.

It was no disembodied voice, this. A man was walking up the gully toward her. With the wind in her ears, and the distraction of the dead man and the voice, she hadn't heard him coming.

As big as he was, as close as he was, she knew that if she ran, and if he was of a mind, he could easily run her down.

Chapter 2

The man slowed when he saw her reaction, and her knife.

'I didn't mean to give you a scare.'

His voice was pleasant enough.

'Well, you did.'

Although the hood of his cloak was up and she couldn't see his face clearly, he seemed to be taking in her red hair the way most people did when they saw her.

'I can see that. I apologize.'

She didn't slacken her defensive posture in acceptance of the apology, but instead swept her gaze to the sides, checking to see if he was alone, to see if anyone else was with him and might be sneaking up on her.

She felt a fool for being caught by surprise like that. In the back of her mind she knew she couldn't ever really be safe. It didn't necessarily take stealth. Even simple carelessness on her part could at any time bring the end. She felt a sense of forlorn doom at how easily it could happen. If this man could walk up in broad daylight and startle her so easily, what did that say of her hopelessly extravagant dream that one day her life could be her own?

The dark rock wall of the cliff glistened in the wet. The windswept gully was deserted of anyone but her and the two men, the dead one and the one alive. Jennsen was not given to imagining sinister faces lurking in forest shadows, as she had been as a child. The dark places in among the trees were empty.

The man stopped a dozen paces away. By his posture, it wasn't fear of her knife that halted him, but fear of causing her a

8

worse fright. He stared openly at her, seemingly lost in some private thought. He quickly recovered from whatever it was about her face that so held his gaze.

'I can understand why a woman would have cause to be frightened when a stranger suddenly walks up on her. I would have passed on by without alarming you, but I saw that fellow on the ground and you there, bent over him. I thought you might need help, so I rushed over.'

The cold wind pressed his dark green cloak against his sinewy build and lifted the other side away to reveal his well-cut but simple clothes. His cloak's hood covered his head against the first trailers of rain, leaving his face somewhat indistinct in its shadow. His smile was one of courteous intent, no more. He wore the smile well.

'He's dead' was all she could think to say.

Jennsen was unaccustomed to speaking to strangers. She was unaccustomed to speaking to anyone but her mother. She was unsure as to what to say – how to react – especially under the circumstances.

'Oh. I'm sorry.' He stretched his neck a little, without coming any closer, trying to see the man on the ground.

Jennsen thought it a considerate thing to do – not trying to come closer to someone who was clearly nervous. She hated that she was so obvious. She had always hoped she might appear to others somewhat inscrutable.

His gaze lifted from the dead man, to her knife, to her face. 'I suppose you had cause.'

Perplexed for a second, she finally grasped his meaning and blurted out, 'I didn't do it!'

He shrugged. 'Sorry. From over here I can't tell what happened.'

Jennsen felt awkward holding a knife on the man. She lowered the arm with the weapon.

'I didn't mean to . . . to appear a madwoman. You just startled the wits out of me.'

His smile warmed. 'I understand. No harm done. So, what happened?'

Jennsen gestured with her empty hand toward the cliff face. 'I think he fell from the trail up there. His neck's broken. At least I think it is. I only just discovered him. I don't see any other footprints. My guess is that he was killed in a fall.'

As Jennsen returned her knife to its sheath on her belt, he considered the cliff. 'Glad I took the bottom, rather than the trail up there.'

She inclined her head in invitation toward the dead man. 'I was looking for something that might tell me who he was. I thought maybe I should . . . notify someone. But I haven't found anything.'

The man's boots crunched through the coarse gravel as he approached. He knelt on the other side of the body, rather than beside her, perhaps to give the knife-wielding madwoman a precautionary bit of space so she would feel a little less jumpy.

'I'd guess you were right,' he said, after taking in the abnormal cant of the head. 'Looks like he's been here at least part of the day.'

'I was through here earlier. Those are my tracks, there. I don't see any others about.' She gestured toward her catch lying just behind her. 'When I went to the lake to check my lines, earlier, he wasn't here.'

He twisted his head in order to better study the still face. 'Any idea who he was?'

'No. I don't have a clue, other than that he's a soldier.'

The man looked up. 'Any idea what kind of soldier?'

Jennsen's brow drew tight. 'What kind? He's a D'Haran soldier.' She lowered herself to the ground in order to look at the stranger more directly. 'Where are you from that you wouldn't recognize a D'Haran soldier?'

He ran his hand under his cloak's hood and rubbed it along the side of his neck. 'I'm just a traveler, passing through.' He looked as tired as he sounded.

The answer perplexed her. 'I've moved around my whole life and I don't know of anyone who wouldn't know a D'Haran soldier when they saw one. How can you not?'

'I'm new to D'Hara.'

'That's not possible. D'Hara covers most of the world.'

This time, his smile betrayed amusement. 'Is that so?'

She could feel her face heat and she knew it must be going red with how ignorant of the world at large she had shown herself to be. 'Well, doesn't it?'

He shook his head. 'No. I'm from far to the south. Beyond the land that is D'Hara.'

She stared in wonder, her chagrin evaporating in light of the implications that came into her head at such an astonishing notion. Perhaps her dream might not be so extravagant.

'And what are you doing, here, in D'Hara?'

'I told you. Traveling.' He sounded weary. She knew how exhausting it could be to travel. His tone turned more serious. 'I know he's a D'Haran soldier. You misunderstood me. What I meant was, what kind of soldier? A man belonging to a local regiment? A man stationed here? A soldier on his way home for a visit? A soldier going for a drink in town? A scout?'

Her sense of alarm rose. 'A scout? What would he be scouting for in his own homeland?'

The man looked off at the low dark clouds. 'I don't know. I was only wondering if you knew anything of him.'

'No, of course not. I just found him.'

'Are these D'Haran soldiers dangerous? I mean, do they bother folks? Folks just traveling through?'

Her gaze fled his questioning eyes. 'I – I don't know. I guess they could be.'

She feared to say too much, but she wouldn't want him to end up in trouble because she said too little.

'What do you suppose a lone soldier was doing way out here? Soldiers aren't often alone.'

'I don't know. Why do you suppose a simple woman would know more about soldiering than a man of the world who travels about? Don't you have any ideas of your own? Maybe he was just on his way home, for a visit, or something. Maybe he was thinking about a girl back home, and so he wasn't paying attention like he should have been. Maybe that's why he slipped and fell.'

He rubbed his neck again, as if he were in pain.

'I'm sorry. I guess I'm not making much sense. I'm a little

11

tired. Maybe I'm not thinking clearly. Maybe I was only concerned for you.'

'For me? What do you mean?'

'I mean that soldiers belong to units of one sort or another. Other soldiers know them and know where they're supposed to be. Soldiers don't just go off alone when they want to. They aren't like some lone trapper who could vanish and no one would know.'

'Or some lone traveler?'

An easy grin softened his expression. 'Or some lone traveler.' The grin withered. 'The point is, other soldiers will likely look for him. If they come upon his body, here, they'll bring in troops to prevent anyone from leaving the area. Once they gather anyone they can find, they'll start asking questions.

'From what I've heard about D'Haran soldiers, they know how to ask questions. They'll want to know every detail about every person they question.'

Jennsen's middle cramped in sick, churning consternation. The last thing in the world she wanted was D'Haran soldiers asking questions of her or her mother. This dead soldier could end up being the death of them.

'But what are the chances—'

'I'm only saying that I'd not like to have this fellow's friends come along and decide that someone has to pay for his death. They might not see it as an accident. Soldiers get stirred up by the death of a comrade, even if it was an accident. You and I are the only two around. I'd not like to have a bunch of soldiers discover him and decide to blame us.'

'You mean, even if it was an accident, they might seize an innocent person and blame them for it?'

'I don't know, but in my experience that's the way soldiers are. When they're angry they find someone to blame.'

'But they can't blame us. You weren't even here, and I was only going to tend my fishing lines.'

He planted an elbow on his knee and leaned over the dead man toward her. 'And this soldier, going about his business for the great D'Haran Empire, saw a beautiful young woman strutting along and was so distracted by her that he slipped and fell.'

'I wasn't "strutting"!'

'I don't mean to suggest you were. I only meant to show you how people can find blame when they decide they want to.'

She'd not thought of that. They were D'Haran soldiers. Such behavior would hardly be out of the question.

The rest of what he'd said registered in her mind. Jennsen had never before had a man call her beautiful. It flustered her, coming so unexpectedly and out of place, as it did, in the middle of such a worry. Since she didn't have any idea how to react to the compliment, and since there were so many more important thoughts commanding her emotions, she ignored it.

'If they find him,' the man said, 'then, at the least, they're going to collect anyone around and question them long and hard.'

All the ugly implications were becoming all too real. The day of doom was suddenly looming near.

'What do you think we should do?'

He thought it over a moment. 'Well, if they do come by, but don't find him, then they won't have any reason to stop and question the people here. If they don't find him, they'll go somewhere else to keep looking for him.'

He rose and looked around. 'Ground's too hard to dig a grave.' He pulled his hood farther forward to shield his eyes from the mist as he searched. He pointed to a spot near the base of the cliff. 'There. There's a deep cleft that looks big enough. We could put him in there and cover him over with gravel and rocks. Best burial we can manage this time of year.'

And probably more than he deserved. She would just as soon leave him, but that wouldn't be wise. Covering him up was what she had planned on doing before the stranger happened along. This would be a better way to do it. There would be less chance that animals would uncover him for passing soldiers to discover.

Seeing her trying hastily to weigh the various ramifications, and mistaking it for reluctance, he spoke in soft assurance. 'The man is dead. Nothing can be done about it. It was an accident. Why let that accident bring trouble? We didn't do anything

13

wrong. We weren't even here when it happened. I say we bury him and go on with our lives – without D'Haran soldiers becoming unjustly involved.'

Jennsen stood. The man might be right about soldiers coming upon a dead friend and deciding to question people. There was abundant reason to be worried about the dead D'Haran soldier without this new concern. She thought again about the piece of paper she'd found in his pocket. That would be reason enough – without any other.

If the piece of paper was what she thought it might be, then questioning would only be the beginning of the ordeal.

'Agreed,' she said. 'If we're to do it, let's be quick.'

He smiled, more relief than anything, she thought. Then, turning to face her more squarely, he pushed his hood back off his head, the way men did out of respect for a woman.

Jennsen was shocked to see, even though he was at most only six or seven years older than she, that his cropped hair was as white as snow. She gazed at it with much the same sense of wonder as people gazed at her red hair. With the shadows of the hood gone, she saw that his eyes were as blue as hers, as blue as people said her father's had been.

The combination of his short white hair and those blue eyes was arresting. The way they both went with his clean-shaven face was singularly appealing. It all fit together with his features in a way that seemed completely right.

He held his hand out across the dead soldier.

'My name is Sebastian.'

She hesitated a moment, but then offered her hand in return. Even though his was big and no doubt powerful, he didn't squeeze her hand to prove it, the way some men did. The unnatural warmth of the hand surprised her.

'Are you going to tell me your name?'

'I'm Jennsen Daggett.'

'Jennsen.' He smiled his pleasure at the sound of it.

She felt her face going red again. Instead of noticing, he immediately set to the task by grabbing the soldier under his arms and giving him a tug. The body moved only a short distance with each mighty pull. The soldier had been a huge man. Now he was a huge dead weight.

Jennsen seized the soldier's cloak at the shoulder to help. Sebastian moved his hold to the cloak at the other shoulder and together they dragged the weight of the man, who loomed as dangerous to her in death as he would have in life, across the gravel and slick patches of smooth rock.

Still panting from the effort, and before pushing the soldier into the crevice that was to be his final resting place, Sebastian rolled him over. Jennsen saw for the first time that he wore a short sword strapped over his shoulder, under his pack. She hadn't seen it before because he was lying on it. Hooked on the weapons belt around his waist, at the small of his back, hung a crescent-bladed battle-axe. Jennsen's level of apprehension rose at seeing how heavily armed the soldier had been. Regular soldiers didn't carry this many weapons. Or a knife like he had.

Sebastian tugged the straps of the pack down off the arms. He unstrapped the short sword and set it aside. He pulled off the weapons belt and tossed it atop the sword.

'Nothing too unusual in the pack,' he said after a brief inspection. He added the pack to the short sword, the weapons belt, and the axe.

Sebastian started searching the dead man's pockets. Jennsen was about to question what he was doing when she recalled that she had done the same. She was somewhat more disturbed when he returned the other items after picking out the money. She thought it rather cold-blooded, stealing from the dead.

Sebastian held the money out to her.

'What are you doing?' she asked.

'Take it.' He offered the money again, more insistently this time. 'What good is it going to do in the ground? Money is of use to relieve the suffering of the living, not the dead. You think the good spirits will ask him for the price of a bright and pleasant eternity?'

He was a D'Haran soldier. Jennsen expected the Keeper of the underworld would have something somewhat more dark in store for this man's eternity.

'But . . . it's not mine.'

He frowned a reproving look. 'Consider it partial compensation for all you've suffered.'

She felt her flesh go cold. How could he know? They were always so careful.

'What do you mean?'

'The years taken off your life by the fright this fellow gave you today.'

Jennsen finally was able to let her breath go in a silent sigh. She had to stop fearing the worst in what people said.

She allowed Sebastian to put the coins in her hand. 'All right, but I think you should have half for helping me.' She handed three gold marks back.

He grasped her hand with his other and pressed all three coins into her palm. 'Take it. It's yours, now.'

Jennsen thought of what this much money could mean. She nodded. 'My mother has had a hard life. She could use it. I will give it to my mother.'

'I hope it helps you both, then. Let it be this man's last good act – helping you and your mother.'

'Your hands are warm.' By the look in his eyes, she thought she knew why. She said no more.

He nodded and confirmed her suspicion. 'I've got a touch of fever. I came down with it this morning. When we get finished with this business I'm hoping to get to the next town and rest up in a dry room for a while. I just need some rest to regain my strength.'

'Town is too far for you to make today.'

'You sure? I can make good time. I'm used to traveling.'

'So am I,' Jennsen said, 'and it takes me most of a day to make it. There's only a couple of hours of light left – and we have yet to finish with this task. Not even a fast horse would get you near town today.'

Sebastian let out a sigh. 'Well, I guess I'll make do.'

He knelt again and rolled the soldier partway over in order to unstrap the knife. The sheath, fine-grain black leather, was trimmed with silver to match the handle and decorated with the same ornate emblem. On one knee, Sebastian held the gleaming, sheathed knife up to her.

16

'Silly to bury such a fine weapon. Here you go. Better than that piece of junk you showed me before.'

Jennsen stood stunned and confused. 'But, you should keep it.'

'I'll take the others. More to my taste anyway. The knife is yours. Sebastian's rule.'

'Sebastian's rule?'

'Beauty belongs with beauty.'

Jennsen blushed at the intended compliment. But this was not a thing of beauty. He had no idea of the ugliness this represented.

'Any idea what the "R" in the hilt stands for?'

Oh yes, she wanted to say. She knew only too well what it represented. That was the ugliness.

'It stands for the House of Rahl.'

'House of Rahl?'

'Lord Rahl – the ruler of D'Hara,' she said in simple explanation of a nightmare.

Chapter 3

By the time they were finished with the laborious task of covering the troublesome body of the dead D'Haran soldier, Jennsen's arms were weak with fatigue. The damp wind scything through her clothes felt like it cut to the bone. Her ears and nose and fingers were numb.

Sebastian's face was covered in a sheen of sweat.

But the dead man was at last buried under gravel and then rocks that were in abundance at the base of the cliff. Animals were not likely to be able to dig through all the heavy stone to get at the body. The worms would feast undisturbed.

Sebastian had said a few simple words, asking the Creator to welcome the man's soul into eternity. He made no plea for mercy in His judgment, and neither did Jennsen.

As she finished scattering gravel with a heavy branch and her feet, obscuring the marks left by their work, she gave the area a critical examination and was relieved to see that no one would ever suspect that a person lay buried there. If soldiers came through they wouldn't realize that one of their own had met his end here. They would have no reason to question local people, except, perhaps, to ask if anyone had seen him. That would be a simple enough lie to feed them and one easily swallowed.

Jennsen pressed her hand against Sebastian's forehead. It confirmed her fears. 'You're burning with fever.'

'We're done, now. I can rest more easily, not having to worry that soldiers will be rousting me out of my bedroll to ask me questions at the point of a sword.'

She wondered where he was going to sleep. The drizzle was

18

thickening. She expected it would soon be raining. Given the persistence of the darkening clouds, once it started it would likely rain the whole night. Cold rain soaking him to the skin would only further inflame his fever. Such a winter rain could easily kill someone who lacked proper shelter.

She watched as Sebastian strapped the weapons belt around his waist. He didn't place the axe at the small of his back the way the soldier had worn it, but rather positioned it at his right hip. After testing its edge and finding it satisfactory, he fastened the short sword to the left side of the belt. Both weapons were placed so as to come readily to hand.

When he'd finished he flipped his heavy green cloak closed over it all. He seemed again a simple traveler. She suspected he was more. He had his secrets. He wore them casually, almost in the open. She wore hers uneasily, and held close.

He handled the sword with the kind of smooth ease that came only with long acquaintance. She knew because she handled a knife with effortless grace, and such proficiency had come only with experience and continual practice. Some mothers taught their daughters to sew and cook. Jennsen's mother didn't think sewing would save her daughter. Not that a knife would, either, but it was better protection than needle and thread.

Sebastian lifted the dead man's pack and threw back the flap. 'We'll divide the supplies. Do you want the pack?'

'You should keep the supplies and the pack,' Jennsen said as she retrieved her stringer of fish.

He agreed with a nod. He appraised the sky as he cinched the pack closed. 'I'd best be on my way, then.'

'Where?'

His weary eyelids blinked at the question. 'No place special. Traveling. I guess I'll walk for a while and then I suppose I'd better try to find some shelter.'

'Rain is coming,' she said. 'It doesn't take a prophet to tell that.'

He smiled. 'Guess not.' His eyes bore the prospect of what lay ahead with resigned acceptance. He swiped his hand back over his wet spikes of white hair, then pulled up his hood. 'Well, take care of yourself, Jennsen Daggett. Give my best to your mother. She raised a lovely daughter.'

Jennsen smiled and acknowledged his words with a single nod. She stood facing the damp wind as she watched him turn and start off across the flat expanse of gravel. Craggy rock walls rose up all around, their snow-crusted shoulders disappearing into the low gray overcast that concealed the bulk of the mountains and the nearly endless range of high peaks.

It seemed so funny, so freakish, so futile that in all this vast country their paths should cross so briefly, at that instant in time, for such a tragic moment as one life ended, and then that they would both go off again into that infinite oblivion of life.

Jennsen's heart pounded in her ears as she listened to his footsteps crunching across the jagged gravel, watched his long strides carrying him away. With a sense of urgency, she debated what she should do. Was she always to turn away from people? To hide?

Was she always to forfeit even small snatches of what it was to live life because of a crime she did not commit? Dare she risk this?

She knew what her mother would say. But her mother loved her dearly, and so would not say it out of cruelty.

'Sebastian?' He looked back over his shoulder, waiting for her to speak. 'If you don't have shelter, you may not live to see tomorrow. I wouldn't like it if I knew you were out here with a fever getting soaked to the skin.'

He stood watching her, the drizzle drifting between them.

'I wouldn't like that, either. I'll mind your words and do my best to find some shelter.'

Before he could turn away again, she lifted her hand, gesturing off in the other direction. She saw that her fingers were trembling. 'You could come home with me.'

'Would your mother mind?'

Her mother would be in a panic. Her mother would never allow a stranger, despite what help he had been, to sleep in the house. Her mother wouldn't sleep a wink all night with a stranger anywhere near. But if Sebastian stayed out with a fever he could die. Jennsen's mother would not wish that on this man.

Her mother had a kind heart. That loving concern, not malice, was the reason she was so protective of Jennsen.

'The house is small, but there's room in the cave where we keep the animals. If you wouldn't mind, you could sleep there. It's not as bad as it sounds. I've slept there myself, on occasion, when the house felt too confining. I'd make you a fire near the entrance. You'd be warm and could get the rest you need.'

He looked reluctant. Jennsen held up her stringer of fish.

'We could feed you,' she said, sweetening the offer. 'You would at least have a good meal along with a warm rest. I think you need both. You helped me. Let me help you?'

His smile, one of gratitude, returned. 'You're a kind woman, Jennsen. If your mother will allow it, I will accept your offer.'

She lifted her cloak open, displaying the fine knife in its sheath, which she had tucked behind her belt. 'We'll offer her the knife. She will value it.'

His smile, warm and suddenly lighthearted with amusement, was as pleasant a smile as Jennsen had ever seen.

'I don't think two knife-wielding women need lose any sleep over a stranger with a fever.'

That was Jennsen's thought, but she didn't admit it. She hoped her mother would see it that way, too.

'It's settled then. Come along before the rain catches us out.'

Sebastian trotted to catch up with her as she started out. She lifted the pack from his hand and shouldered it. With his own pack, and his new weapons, he had enough to carry in his weakened condition.

Chapter 4

'Wait here,' Jennsen said in a low voice. 'I'll go tell her that we have a guest.'

Sebastian dropped heavily onto a low projection of rock that made a convenient seat. 'You just tell her what I said, that I'll understand if she doesn't want a stranger spending the night at your place. I know it wouldn't be an unreasonable fear.'

Jennsen considered him with a calm and somber demeanor.

'My mother and I have reason not to fear a visitor.'

She was not alluding to common weapons, and by her tone he knew it. For the first time since she had met him, she saw a spark of uncertainty in Sebastian's steady blue eyes – a shadow of uneasiness not elicited by her expertise with a knife.

A hint of a smile came in turn to Jennsen's lips as she watched him considering what manner of dark danger she might represent. 'Don't worry. Only those bringing trouble would have cause to fear being here.'

He lifted his hands in a gesture of surrender. 'Then I'm as safe as a babe in his mother's arms.'

Jennsen left Sebastian to wait on the rock while she made her way up the winding path, through sheltering spruce, using twisted roots as steps up, toward her house set back in a clutch of oak on a small shelf in the side of a mountain. The flat patch of grassy ground was, on a better day, a sunny open spot among the towering old trees. There was room enough to yard their goat along with some ducks and chickens. Steep rock to the back prevented any visitors happening upon them from that direction. Only the path up the front provided an approach.

Should they be threatened, Jennsen and her mother had constructed a well-hidden set of footholds up the back, to a narrow ledge, and out a twisting side way via deer paths that would take them through a ravine and away. The escape route was nearly inaccessible as a way in unless you knew the precise course through the maze of rock walls, fissures, and narrow ledges, and even then they had made certain that key passages were well hidden by strategically placing deadwood and brush they'd planted.

Ever since Jennsen was young they had moved often, never staying in one place too long. Here, though, where they felt safe, they had stayed for over two years. Travelers had never discovered their mountain hideaway, as sometimes had happened in other places they had stayed, and the people in Briarton, the nearest town, never ventured this far into such a dark and forbidding wood.

The seldom-used trail around the lake, from where the soldier had fallen, was as close as any trail came to them. Jennsen and her mother had gone into Briarton only once. It was unlikely that anyone even knew they were living out in the vast trackless mountains far from any farmland or city. Except for the chance encounter with Sebastian down closer to the lake, they'd never seen anyone near their place. This was the most secure spot she and her mother had ever had, and so Jennsen had dared to begin to think of it as home.

Since she was six, Jennsen had been hunted. As careful as her mother always was, several times they had come frighteningly close to being snared. He was no ordinary man, the one who hunted her; he was not bound by ordinary means of searching. For all Jennsen knew, the owl watching her from a high limb as she made her way up the rocky path could be his eyes watching her.

Just as Jennsen reached the house, she met her mother, throwing her cloak around her shoulders as she came out the door. She was the same height as Jennsen, with the same thick hair to just past her shoulders but more auburn than red. She was not yet thirty-five, and the prettiest woman Jennsen had ever seen, with a figure the Creator Himself would marvel at. In different circumstances, her mother's life would have been one of countless suitors, some, no doubt, willing to offer a king's ransom for her hand. Her mother's heart, though, was as loving and beautiful as her face, and she had given up everything to protect her daughter.

When Jennsen sometimes felt sorry for herself, for the normal things in life that she couldn't have, she would then think of her mother, who had willingly given up all those same things and more for the sake of her daughter. Her mother was as close as it came to a guardian spirit in the flesh.

'Jennsen!' Her mother rushed to her and seized her shoulders. 'Oh, Jenn, I was starting to worry so. Where have you been? I was just coming to look for you. I thought you must have had some trouble and I was—'

'I did, Mother,' Jennsen confided.

Her mother paused only momentarily; then, without further question, she embraced Jennsen in protective arms. After such a frightening day, Jennsen openly welcomed the balm of her mother's hug. Finally, with a comforting arm encircling Jennsen's shoulders, her mother urged her toward the door.

'Come inside and get yourself dry. I see you have quite the catch. We'll have a good dinner and you can tell me . . .'

Jennsen was dragging her feet. 'Mother, I have someone with me.'

Her mother halted, suddenly searching her daughter's face for any outward sign of the nature and depth of the trouble. 'What do you mean? Who would you have with you?'

Jennsen flicked a hand back toward the path. 'He's waiting down there. I told him to wait. I told him I'd ask you if he could sleep in the cave with the animals—'

'What? Stay here? Jenn, what were you thinking? We can't—'

'Mother, please, listen to me. Something terrible happened today. Sebastian—'

'Sebastian?'

Jennsen nodded. 'The man I brought with me. Sebastian helped me. I came across a soldier who fell from the path – the high trail around the lake.'

Her mother's face went ashen. She said nothing.

Jennsen took a calming breath and started again. 'I found a D'Haran soldier dead in the gorge below the high trail. There were no other tracks – I looked. He was an extraordinarily big soldier, and he was heavily armed. Battle-axe, sword at his hip, sword strapped over his shoulder.'

Her mother canted her head with an admonishing expression. 'What aren't you telling me, Jenn?'

Jennsen wanted to hold it back until she explained Sebastian, first, but her mother could read it in her eyes, hear it in her voice. The terrible threat of that piece of paper with the two words on it seemed almost to be screaming its presence from her pocket.

'Mother, please, let me tell it my way?'

Her mother cupped a hand to the side of Jennsen's face. 'Tell me, then. Your way, if you must.'

'I was searching the soldier, looking for anything important. And I found something. But then, this man, a traveler, came upon me. I'm sorry, Mother, I was frightened by the soldier being there and by what I found and I wasn't paying attention as I should have. I know I behaved foolishly.'

Her mother smiled. 'No, baby, we all have lapses. None of us can be perfect. We all sometimes make mistakes. That doesn't make you foolish. Don't say that about yourself.'

'Well I felt foolish when he said something and I turned around and there he was. I had my knife out, though.' Her mother was nodding with a smile of approval. 'He saw then that the man had fallen to his death. He – Sebastian, that's his name – he said that if we just left him there, then, more likely than not, other soldiers would find him and start questioning us all and maybe blame us for their fellow soldier being dead.'

'This man, Sebastian, sounds like he knows what he's talking about.'

'I thought so, too. I had intended to cover the dead soldier, to try to hide him, but he was big – I could never have dragged him over to a cranny by myself. Sebastian offered to help me bury the body. Together we were able to drag him over and roll him into a deep split in the rock. We covered him over good. Sebastian put some heavy rocks atop the gravel I scooped in. No one will find him.'

Her mother looked more relieved. 'That was wise.'

'Before we buried him, Sebastian thought we should take anything valuable, rather than let it go to waste in the ground.'

One eyebrow arched. 'Did he, now?'

Jennsen nodded. She pulled the money from her pocket, the pocket that didn't have the piece of paper in it. She dumped all the money in her mother's hand.

'Sebastian insisted that I take it all. There's gold marks there. He didn't want any for himself.'

Her mother took in the fortune in her hand, then glanced briefly to the trail where Sebastian waited. She leaned closer.

'Jenn, if he came with you, then perhaps he thinks he can have the money back at any time of his choosing. That would give him the opportunity to look generous and win your trust – and still be near enough to end up with the money when he chooses.'

'I considered that, too.'

Her mother's tone softened sympathetically. 'Jenn, it's not your fault – I've kept you so sheltered – but you just don't know how men can be.'

Jennsen let her gaze drop from her mother's knowing eyes. 'I suppose it could be true, but I don't think so.'

'And why not?'

Jennsen looked back up, more intently, this time. 'He has a fever, Mother. He's not well. He was leaving, without asking to come with me at all. He bid me a good-bye. As tired and feverish as he is, I feared he'd die out in the rain tonight. I stopped him, told him that if it was all right with you he could sleep in the cave with the animals where he could at least be dry and warm.'

After a moment of silence, Jennsen added, 'He said that if you don't want a stranger near, he will understand and be on his way.'

'Did he? Well, Jenn, this man is either very honest, or very clever.' She fixed Jennsen with an intent look. 'Which do you think it is, hmm?'

Jennsen twined her fingers together. 'I don't know, Mother. I honestly don't. I wondered the same things as you – I really did.'

She remembered, then. 'He said that he wanted you to have this, so you wouldn't have to fear a stranger sleeping nearby.'

Jennsen drew the knife in its sheath from behind her belt and held it out to her mother. The silver handle gleamed in the dim yellow light coming from the small window behind her mother.

Staring in astonishment, her mother slowly lifted the weapon in both hands as she whispered, 'Dear spirits . . .'

'I know,' Jennsen said. 'I nearly yelped in fright when I saw it. Sebastian said that this was a fine weapon, too fine to bury, and he wanted me to keep it. He kept the soldier's short sword and axe for himself. I told him I would give this to you. He said that he hoped it would help you feel safe.'

Her mother slowly shook her head. 'This does not make me feel safe at all – knowing that a man carrying this was near us. Jenn, I don't like that one bit. Not one bit.'

Her mother's eyes showed that she was on to worries bigger than the man Jennsen had brought home with her.

'Mother, Sebastian is sick. Can he stay in the cave? I led him to believe that he has more to fear from us than we from him.'

Her mother glanced up with a sly smile. 'Good girl.' They both knew that in order to survive they had to work as a team, with well-practiced roles they fell into without the need for formal discussion.

She let out a sigh, then, as if with the burden of knowing all the things her daughter was missing in life. She ran a hand tenderly down Jennsen's hair, letting it come to rest on her shoulder.

'All right, baby,' she said at last, 'we'll let him stay the night.'

'And feed him. I told him he would have a hot meal for helping me.'

Her mother's warm smile widened. 'And a meal, then.'

She drew the blade from its sheath, finally. She gave it a critical appraisal, turning it this way and that, inspecting its design. She tested the edge, and then the weight. She spun it between her slender fingers to get the feel of it, the balance.

At last she held it in her open palm, contemplating the ornate letter 'R.' Jennsen could not imagine what terrible thoughts – and memories – must be going through her mother's mind as she silently considered the emblem representing the House of Rahl.

'Dear spirits,' her mother whispered again to herself.

Jennsen didn't say anything. She entirely understood. It was an ugly evil thing.

'Mother,' Jennsen whispered when her mother had looked at the handle for an eternity, 'it's almost dark. May I go get Sebastian and take him back to the cave?'

Her mother slid the blade home into its sheath, looking to put a panorama of painful memories away with it.

'Yes, I suppose you had better go get him. Take him to the cave. Make a fire for him. I'll cook some fish and bring some herbs along to help him sleep with his fever. Wait there with him until I come out. Keep your eye on him. We will eat with him, out there. I don't want him in the house.'

Jennsen nodded. She touched her mother's arm, halting her before she could go into the house. Jennsen had one more thing to tell her mother. She dearly wished she didn't have to. She didn't want to bring her mother such a worry, but she had to.

'Mother,' she said in a voice barely above a whisper, 'we are going to need to go from this place.'

Her mother looked startled.

'I found something on the D'Haran soldier.'

Jennsen pulled the piece of paper from her pocket, unfolded it, and held it out in her open palm.

Her mother's gaze took in the two words on the paper.

'Dear spirits . . .' was all she said, was all she was able to say.

She turned and looked at the house, taking it all in, her eyes suddenly brimming with tears. Jennsen knew that her mother had come to think of it as home, too.

'Dear spirits,' her mother whispered to herself again, at a loss for anything more.

Jennsen thought the weight of it might overcome her, and her mother might break down in helpless tears. That was what Jennsen wanted to do. Neither did.

Her mother wiped a finger under each eye as she looked back at Jennsen. And then she did cry – one brief inhalation of a gasping sob of hopelessness. 'I'm so sorry, baby.'

It broke Jennsen's heart to see her mother in such anguish. Everything that Jennsen had missed in life, her mother had missed twice over. Once for herself, and once for her daughter. On top of it, her mother had to be strong.

'We'll leave at first light,' her mother said in simple pronouncement. 'Traveling at night, and in the rain, will serve us ill. We'll have to find a new place to hide. He's getting too close to this one.'

Jennsen's own eyes overflowed with tears and her voice came only with great difficulty. 'I'm so sorry, Mama, that I'm such trouble.' Her tears flooded forth in a painful torrent. She crushed the piece of paper as her hands fisted. 'I'm so sorry, Mama. I wish you could be free of me.'

Her mother caught her up in her arms then, cradling Jennsen's head to a shoulder as she wept. 'No, no, baby. Don't ever say that. You're my light, my life. This trouble is caused by others. Don't you ever wear a cloak of guilt because they are evil. You're my wonderful life. I would give everything else up a thousand times over for you and then once again and be joyous to do so.'

Jennsen was glad that she would never have any children, for she knew she didn't have her mother's strength. She held on for dear life to the only person in the world who was a comfort to her.

But then she pushed away from her mother's embrace. 'Mama, Sebastian is from far away. He told me. He said that he's from beyond D'Hara. There are other places – other lands. He knows of them. Isn't that wonderful? There is a place that isn't D'Hara.'

'But those places are beyond barriers and boundaries that can't be crossed.'

'Then how can he be here? It must be so, otherwise he could not have traveled here.'

'And Sebastian is from one of these other lands?'

'To the south, he said.'

'The south? I don't see how it could be possible. Are you sure that's what he said?'

'Yes.' Jennsen added a firm nod of confirmation. 'He said the south. He only mentioned it casually. I'm not sure how it's possible, but what if it is? Mother, maybe he could guide us there. Maybe, if we asked, he would guide us out of this nightmare land.'

As levelheaded as her mother was, Jennsen could see that she was considering this wild idea. It wasn't crazy – her mother was thinking it over, so it couldn't be crazy. Jennsen was suddenly filled with a sense of hope that maybe she had come up with something that would save them.

'Why would he do this for us?'

'I don't know. I don't even know if he would consider it, or what he would want in return. I didn't ask him. I didn't dare even to mention it until I talked to you, first. That's part of why I wanted him to stay here – so you could question him. I feared to lose this chance to discover if it really is possible.'

Her mother looked around again at the house. It was tiny, only one room, and it was nothing fancy, built from logs and wood they had shaped themselves, but it was warm and snug and dry. It was frightening to contemplate striking out in the dead of winter. The alternative of being caught, though, was far worse.

Jennsen knew what would happen if they were caught. Death would not come swiftly. If they were caught, death would come only after endless torture.

At last, her mother gathered herself and spoke. 'That's good thinking, Jenn. I don't know if anything can come of such an idea, but we'll talk to Sebastian and see. One thing is for sure. We have to leave. We dare not delay until spring – not if they're this close. We'll leave at dawn.'

'Mother, where will we go, this time, if Sebastian won't lead us away from D'Hara?'

Her mother smiled. 'Baby, the world is a big place. We are only two small people. We will simply vanish again. I know it's hard, but we're together. It will be fine. We'll see some new sights, now won't we? Some more of the world.

'Now, go get Sebastian and take him to the cave. I'll get started on dinner. We'll all need to have a good meal.'

Jennsen quickly kissed her mother's cheek before racing down the trail. The rain was starting, and it was so gloomy among the trees that she could hardly see. The trees were all huge D'Haran soldiers to her, broad, powerful, grim. She knew she would have nightmares after seeing a real D'Haran soldier up close.

Sebastian was still sitting on the rock, waiting. He stood as she rushed up to him.

'My mother said it was all right for you to sleep in the cave with the animals. She's started on cooking up the fish for us. She wants to meet you.'

He looked too tired to be happy, but he managed to show her a small smile. Jennsen seized his wrist and urged him to follow her. He was already shivering with the wet. His arm was warm, though. Fever was like that, she knew. You shivered even though you were burning up. But with some food and herbs and a good night's rest, she was sure he would soon be well.

What she wasn't sure of was if he would help them.

Chapter 5

Betty, their brown goat, watched attentively from her pen, occasionally voicing her displeasure at sharing her home, as Jennsen quickly collected straw to the side for the stranger in Betty's sanctuary. Bleating her distress, Betty finally quieted when Jennsen affectionately scratched the nervous goat's ears, patted the wiry hair covering her round middle, and then gave her half a carrot from the stash up on a high ledge. Betty's short upright tail wagged furiously.

Sebastian shed his cloak and pack, but kept on the belt with his new weapons. He unstrapped his bedroll from under his pack and spread it out over the mat of straw. Despite Jennsen's urging, he wouldn't lie down and rest while she knelt near the cave's entrance and prepared the fire pit.

As he helped her stack dry kindling, she could see by the dim light coming from the window of the house on the other side of the clearing that sweat beaded his face. He repeatedly scraped his knife down the length of a branch, swiftly building a clump of fluffy fibers. He struck a steel to flint several times, sending sparks through the darkness into the tinder he'd made. He cupped the fluff in his hands and with gentle puffs of breath nursed the slow flames until they strengthened, then placed the burning tinder beneath the kindling, where the flames quickly grew and popped to life among the dry twigs. The branches released a pleasing fragrance of balsam as they caught flame.

Jennsen had been planning on running to the house, not far off, to get some hot coals to start the fire, but he had it going before she could even suggest it. By the way he trembled, she imagined he was impatient for heat, even though he was burning with fever. She could smell the aroma of the frying fish coming from the house, and when the wind among the pine boughs died from time to time, she could hear the sizzle.

The chickens retreated from the growing light into the deep shadows at the back of the cave. Betty's ears stood at attention as she watched Jennsen for any signs that another carrot might be forthcoming. Her tail wagged in hopeful fits.

The opening in the mountain was simply a place where, in some distant age past, a slab of rock had tumbled out, like some giant granite tooth come loose, to plunge down the slope and leave a dry socket behind. Now, trees below grew among a collection of such fallen boulders. The cave only ran back about twenty feet, but the overhang of rock at the entrance further sheltered it and helped keep it dry. Jennsen was tall, but the ceiling of the cave was high enough that she could stand in most of it, and since Sebastian was only a little taller than she, his spikes of snow white hair, now a mellow orange in the firelight, didn't brush the top as he went to the back to collect some of the dry wood stacked there. The chickens squawked at being bothered, but then quickly settled back down.

Jennsen squatted on the opposite side of the fire from Sebastian, with her back to the rain that had started, so she could see his face in the firelight as they both warmed their hands in the heat of the crackling flames. After a day in the frigid damp weather, the fire's warmth felt luxurious. She knew that sooner or later winter would return with a vengeance. As cold and uncomfortable as it was now, it would get worse.

She tried not to think about having to leave their snug home, especially at this time of year. She had known from the first instant she saw the piece of paper, though, that they might.

'Are you hungry?' she asked.

'Starving,' he said, looking as eager for the fish as Betty was for a carrot. The wonderful smells were making her stomach grumble, too.

'That's good. My mother always says that if you're ill, and you have an appetite, then it can't be too serious.'

'I'll be fine in a day or two.'

33

'A rest will do you good.'

Jennsen drew her knife from its sheath at her belt. 'We've never allowed anyone to stay here before. You will understand that we will be taking precautions.'

She could see in his eyes that he didn't know what she was talking about, but he shrugged his understanding of her prudence.

Jennsen's knife wasn't anything like the fine weapon the soldier had been carrying. They could afford nothing like that knife. Hers had a simple handle made of antler and the blade wasn't thick, but she kept its edge razor sharp.

Jennsen used the blade to slice a shallow cut across the inside of her forearm. With a frown, Sebastian started to rise, to voice a protest. Her challenging glare stopped him cold before he was halfway up. He sank back down and watched with growing concern as she wiped the sides of the blade through the crimson beads of blood welling up from the cut. She very deliberately looked him in the eye again before turning her back on him and moving out closer to the edge of the cave where the rain dampened the ground.

With the knife wetted in blood, Jennsen first drew a large circle. Feeling Sebastian's eyes on her, she next pulled the tip of the bloody blade through the damp earth in straight lines to make a square, its corners just touching the inside of the circle. With hardly a pause, she drew a smaller circle that touched the insides of the square.

As she worked, she murmured prayers under her breath, asking the good spirits to guide her hand. It seemed the right thing to do. She knew that Sebastian could hear her soft singsong, but not make out the words. It occurred unexpectedly to her that it must be something like the voices she heard in her own head. Sometimes, when she drew the outer circle, she heard the whisper of that dead voice call her name.

Opening her eyes from the prayer, she drew an eight-pointed star, its rays piercing all the way through the inner circle, the square, and then the outer circle. Every other ray bisected a corner of the square.

The rays were said to represent the gift of the Creator, so as she drew the eight-pointed star, Jennsen always whispered a prayer of thanks for the gift of her mother.

When she finished and looked up, her mother was standing before her, as if she had risen from the shadows, or materialized from the edge of the drawing itself, to be lit by the leaping flames of the fire behind Jennsen. In the light of those flames, her mother was like a vision of some impossibly beautiful spirit.

'Do you know what this drawing represents, young man?' Jennsen's mother asked in a voice hardly more than a whisper.

Sebastian stared up at her, the way people often stared when they first saw her, and shook his head.

'It's called a Grace. They have been drawn by those with the gift of magic for thousands of years – some say since the dawn of Creation itself. The outer circle represents the beginning of the eternity of the underworld, the Keeper's world of the dead. The inner circle is the extent of the world of life. The square represents the veil that separates both worlds – life from death. It touches both at times. The star is the light of the gift from the Creator Himself – magic – extending through life and crossing over into the world of the dead.'

The fire crackled and hissed as Jennsen's mother, like some spectral figure, towered over the two of them. Sebastian said nothing. Her mother had spoken the truth, but it was truth used to convey a specific impression that was not true.

'My daughter has drawn this Grace as protection for you as you rest this night, and as protection for us. There is another before the door to the house.' She let the silence drag before adding, 'It would be unwise to cross either without our consent.'

'I understand, Mrs. Daggett.' In the firelight, his face showed no emotion.

His blue eyes turned to Jennsen. A hint of a smile came to his lips, even though his expression remained serious. 'You are a surprising woman, Jennsen Daggett. A woman of many mysteries. I will sleep safely, tonight.'

'And well,' Jennsen's mother said. 'Besides the dinner, I brought some herbs to help you sleep.'

Her mother, holding the bowl full of fried fish in one hand, collected Jennsen with a hand on her shoulder and guided her around to the back of the fire to sit beside her, on the opposite side of her from Sebastian. By the sober look on his face, their demonstration had had the desired effect.

Her mother glanced at Jennsen and gave her a smile Sebastian couldn't see. Jennsen had done well.

Holding the bowl out, her mother offered Sebastian some fish, saying, 'I would like to thank you, young man, for the help you gave Jennsen, today.'

'Sebastian, please.'

'So Jennsen has told me.'

'I was glad to help. It was helping myself, too, really. I'd not like to have D'Haran soldiers chasing me.'

She pointed. 'If you would accept it, this one on top is coated with the herbs that will help you sleep.'

He used his knife to stab the darker piece of fish coated in the herbs. Jennsen took another on her own knife after first wiping the blade clean on her skirts.

'Jennsen tells me that you are from outside D'Hara.'

He glanced up as he chewed. 'That's right.'

'I find that hard to believe. D'Hara is bordered by impassable boundaries. In my lifetime no one has been able to come into, or leave, D'Hara. How is it possible, then, that you have?'

With his teeth, Sebastian pulled the chunk of herb-coated fish off his knife. He inhaled between his teeth to cool the bite. He gestured around with the blade as he chewed. 'How long have you been out here alone in this great wood? Without seeing people? Without news?'

'Several years.'

'Oh. Well, then, I guess it makes sense that you wouldn't know, but since you've been out here, the barriers have come down.'

Jennsen and her mother both took in this staggering, nearly incomprehensible news in silence. In that silence, they both dared to begin to imagine the heady possibilities. For the first time in Jennsen's life, escape seemed conceivable. The impossible dream of a life of their own suddenly seemed only a journey away. They had been traveling and hiding their whole life. Now it seemed the journey might at last be near the end.

'Sebastian,' Jennsen's mother said, 'why did you help Jennsen today?'

'I like to help people. She needed help. I could tell how much that man scared her, even though he was dead.' He smiled at Jennsen. 'She looked nice. I wanted to help her. Besides,' he finally admitted, 'I don't much care for D'Haran soldiers.'

When she gestured by lifting the bowl toward him, he stabbed another piece of fish. 'Mrs. Daggett, I'm liable to fall asleep before long. Why don't you just tell me what's on your mind?'

'We are hunted by D'Haran soldiers.'

'Why?'

'That's a story for another night. Depending on the outcome of this night, you may yet learn it, but for now all that really matters is that we are hunted – Jennsen more so than me. If the D'Haran soldiers catch us, she will be murdered.'

Her mother made it sound simple. He would not let it be so simple. It would be much more grisly than any mere murder. Death would be a reward gained only after inconceivable agony and endless begging.

Sebastian glanced over at Jennsen. 'I'd not like that.'

'Then we three are of a single mind,' her mother murmured.

'That's why the two of you are good friends with those knives you keep at hand,' he said.

'That's why,' her mother confirmed.

'So,' Sebastian said, 'you fear the D'Haran soldiers finding you. D'Haran soldiers aren't exactly a rarity. The one today gave you both a scare. What makes you both fear this one, today, so much?'

Jennsen added a stout stick to the fire, glad to have her mother to do the talking. Betty bleated for a carrot, or at least attention. The chickens grumbled about the noise and light.

'Jennsen,' her mother said, 'show Sebastian the piece of paper you found on the D'Haran soldier.'

Taken aback, Jennsen waited until her mother's eyes turned her way. They shared a look that told Jennsen her mother was determined to take this chance, and if she was to try, then they had to at least tell him some of it.

Jennsen drew the crumpled piece of paper from her pocket and handed it past her mother to Sebastian. 'I found this in that D'Haran soldier's pocket.' She swallowed at the ghastly memory of seeing a dead person. 'Just before you showed up.'

Sebastian pulled the crumpled paper open, smoothing it between a thumb and finger as he cast them both a suspicious look. He turned the paper toward the firelight so he could see the two words.

'Jennsen Lindie,' he said, reading it from the piece of paper. 'I don't get it. Who's Jennsen Lindie?'

'Me,' Jennsen said. 'At least it was for a while.'

'For a while? I don't understand.'

'That was my name,' Jennsen said. 'The name I used, anyway, a few years back, when we lived far to the north. We move around often – to keep from being caught. We change our name each time so it will be harder to track us.'

'Then . . . Daggett is not a real name, either?'

'No.'

'Well, what is your real name, then?'

'That, too, is part of the story for another night.' Her mother's tone said that she didn't mean to discuss it. 'What matters is that the soldier today had that name. That can only mean the worst.'

'But you said it's a name you no longer use. You use a different name, here: Daggett. No one here knows you by that name, Lindie.'

Her mother leaned toward Sebastian. Jennsen knew her mother was giving him a look that he would find uncomfortable. Her mother had a way of making people nervous when she fixed them with that intent, penetrating gaze of hers.

'It may no longer be our name, a name we used only far to the north, but he had that name written down, and he was here, mere miles from where we are now. That means he has somehow connected that name with us – with two women somewhere up in this remote place. Somehow, he connected it, or, more precisely, the man who hunts us connected it, and sent him after us. Now, they search for us here.'

Sebastian broke her gaze and took a thoughtful breath. 'I see what you mean.' He went back to eating the piece of fish skewered on the point of his knife.

'That dead soldier would have others with him,' her mother said. 'By burying him, you bought us time. They won't know what happened to him. We have that much luck. We are still a few steps ahead of them. We must use our advantage to get away before they tighten the noose. We will have to leave in the morning.'

'Are you sure?' He gestured around with his knife. 'You have a life here. Your lives are remote, hidden – I would never have found you had I not seen Jennsen with that dead soldier. How could they find you? You have a house, a good place.'

'"Life" is the word that matters in all that you said. I know the man who hunts us. He has thousands of years of bloody heritage as guidance in hunting us. He will not rest. If we stay, sooner or later he will find us here. We must escape while we can.'

She pulled from her belt the exquisite knife Jennsen had brought her from the dead D'Haran soldier. Still in its sheath, she spun it in her fingers, presenting it, hilt first, to Sebastian.

'This letter "R" on the hilt stands for the House of Rahl. Our hunter. He would only have presented a weapon this fine to a very special soldier. I don't want a weapon which has been presented by that evil man.'

Sebastian glanced down at the knife tendered, but didn't take it. He gave them both a look that unexpectedly chilled Jennsen to the bone. It was a look that burned with ruthless determination.

'Where I come from, we believe in using what is closest to an enemy, or what comes from him, as a weapon against him.'

Jennsen had never heard such a sentiment. Her mother didn't move. The knife still lay in her hand. 'I don't—'

'Do you choose to use what he has inadvertently given you, and turn it against him? Or do you choose instead to be a victim?'

'What do you mean?'

'Why don't you kill him?'

Jennsen's jaw dropped. Her mother seemed less astonished. 'We can't,' she insisted. 'He's a powerful man. He is protected by countless people, from simple soldiers to soldiers of great skill at killing – like the one you buried today – to people with the gift who can call upon magic. We are but two simple women.'

Sebastian was not moved by her plea. 'He won't stop until he kills you.' He lifted the piece of paper, watching her eyes take it in. 'This proves it. He will never stop. Why don't you kill him before he kills you – kills your daughter? Or will you choose to be corpses he has yet to collect?'

Her mother's voice heated. 'And how do you propose we kill the Lord Rahl?'

Sebastian stabbed another piece of fish. 'For starters, you should keep the knife. It's a weapon superior to the one you carry. Use what is his to fight him. Your sentimental objection to taking it only serves him, not you – or Jennsen.'

Her mother sat still as stone. Jennsen had never heard anyone talk like this. His words had a way of making her see things differently than she ever had before.

'I must admit that what you say makes sense,' her mother said. Her voice came softly and laced with pain, or perhaps regret. 'You have opened my eyes. A little, anyway. I don't agree with you that we should try to kill him, for I know him all too well. Such an attempt would be simple suicide at best, or accomplish his goal, at worst. But I will keep the knife and use it to defend myself and my daughter. Thank you, Sebastian, for speaking sense when I didn't want to hear it.'

'I'm glad you're keeping the knife, at least.' Sebastian pulled the bite of fish off his own knife. 'I hope it can help you.' With the back of his hand, he wiped the sweat from his brow. 'If you don't want to try to kill him in order to save yourself, then what do you propose to do? Keep running?'

'You say the barriers are down. I propose to leave D'Hara. We will try to make it to another land, where Darken Rahl cannot hunt us.'

Sebastian looked up as he stabbed another piece of fish. 'Darken Rahl? Darken Rahl is dead.'

Jennsen, having run from the man since she was little, having awakened countless times from nightmares of his blue eyes watching her from every shadow or of him leaping out to snatch her when her feet wouldn't move fast enough, having lived every day wondering if this was the day he would finally catch her, having imagined a thousand times and then another thousand what terrible brutal torturous things he would do to her, having prayed to the good spirits every day for deliverance from her merciless hunter and his implacable minions, was thunderstruck. She realized only then that she had always thought of the man as next to immortal. As immortal as evil itself.

'Darken Rahl . . . dead? . . . It can't be,' Jennsen said as tears of deliverance welled up and ran down her cheeks. She was filled with a wild, heart-pounding sense of expectant hope . . . and at the same time an inexplicable shadow of dark dread.

Sebastian nodded. 'It's true. About two years ago, from what I heard.'

Jennsen gave voice to the hope. 'Then, he is no longer the threat we thought.' She paused. 'But, if Darken Rahl is dead—'

'Darken Rahl's son is Lord Rahl, now,' Sebastian said.

'His son?' Jennsen felt her hope being eclipsed by that dark dread.

'The Lord Rahl hunts us,' her mother said, her voice, calm and enduring, betraying no evidence of even a moment of exalted hope. 'The Lord Rahl is the Lord Rahl. It is now, as it has always been. As it will always be.'

As immortal as evil itself.

'Richard Rahl,' Sebastian put in. 'He's the Lord Rahl, now.'

Richard Rahl. So, now Jennsen knew her hunter's new name.

A terrifying thought washed over her. She had never before heard the voice say anything more than 'Surrender,' and her name, and occasionally those strange foreign words she didn't understand. Now it demanded she surrender her flesh, her very will. If it was the voice of the one who hunted her, as her mother said, then this new Lord Rahl must be even more terrifyingly powerful than his wicked father. Fleeting salvation had left behind grim despair.

'This man, Richard Rahl,' her mother said, searching for understanding amid all the startling news, 'he ascended to rule as the Lord Rahl of D'Hara when his father died, then?'

Sebastian leaned forward, a cloaked rage unexpectedly surfacing in his blue eyes. 'Richard Rahl became the Lord Rahl of

D'Hara when he murdered his father and seized rule. And if you are next going to suggest that perhaps the son is less of a threat than his father, then let me set you straight.

'Richard Rahl is the one who brought down the barriers.'

At that, Jennsen threw up her hands in confusion. 'But, that would only give those who wish to be free their opening to escape D'Hara, to escape him.'

'No. He brought those ancient protective barriers down so he could extend his tyrannical rule to the lands that were beyond the reach of even his father.' Sebastian thumped his chest once with a tight fist. 'My land he wants! Lord Rahl is a madman. D'Hara is not enough for him to rule. He lusts to dominate the entire world.'

Jennsen's mother stared off into the flames, looking dispirited. 'I always thought – hoped, I guess – that if Darken Rahl were dead, then maybe we might have a chance. The piece of paper Jennsen found today with her name on it now tells me that the son is even more dangerous than his father, and that I was only deluding myself. Even Darken Rahl never got this close to us.'

Jennsen felt numb after having been rocked by a turbulent swing of emotions, only to be left more terrified and hopeless than before. But seeing such despair on her mother's face wounded her heart.

'I will keep the knife.' Her mother's decision said how much she feared the new Lord Rahl, and how frightful was their plight.

'Good.'

Dim light coming from the house reflected off the swollen pools of water standing beyond the cave entrance, but the droning rain churned the light into thousands of sparkles, like the tears of the good spirits themselves. In a day or two, the collection of ponds would be ice. Traveling would be easier in that cold than in cold rain.

'Sebastian,' Jennsen asked, 'do you think, well, do you think we could escape D'Hara? Maybe go to your homeland . . . escape the reach of this monster?'

Sebastian shrugged. 'Maybe. But, until this madman is killed, will there be anywhere beyond his ravenous reach?'

Her mother tucked the exquisite knife behind her belt and then folded her fingers together around one bent knee. 'Thank you, Sebastian. You've helped us. Being in hiding has, regrettably, kept us in the dark. You've at least brought us a bit of light.'

'Sorry it wasn't better news.'

'The truth is the truth. It helps us know what to do.' Her mother smiled at her. 'Jennsen always was one who sought to know the truth of things. I've never kept it from her. Truth is the only means of survival; it's as simple as that.'

'If you don't want to try to kill him in order to eliminate the threat, maybe you can think of some way to make the new Lord Rahl lose interest in you – in Jennsen.'

Jennsen's mother shook her head. 'There are more things involved than we can tell you tonight – things you are in the dark about. Because of them, he will never rest, never stop. You don't understand the lengths to which the Lord Rahl – any Lord Rahl – will go in order to kill Jennsen.'

'If that's so, then perhaps you're right. Maybe the two of you should run.'

'And would you help us – help her – to get away from D'Hara?'

He looked from one of them to the other. 'If I can, I guess I could try. But I'm telling you, there is no place to hide. If you ever want to be free, you'll have to kill him.'

'I'm no assassin,' Jennsen said, not so much out of protest as out of acceptance of her own frailty in the face of such brutal strength. 'I want to live, but I just don't have the nature to be an assassin. I will defend myself, but I don't think I could effectively set out to kill someone. The sad fact is, I just wouldn't be any good at it. He's a killer by birth. I'm not.'

Sebastian met her gaze with an icy look. His white hair cast red by the firelight framed cold blue eyes. 'You'd be surprised what a person can do, if they have the proper motivation.'

Her mother lifted a hand to halt such talk. She was a practical woman, not given to wasting valuable time on wild schemes. 'Right now, the important thing is for us to get away. Lord Rahl's minions are too close. That's the simple truth of it. From the description, and this knife, the dead man you found today was probably part of a quad.'

Sebastian looked up with a frown. 'A what?'

'A team of four assassins. On occasion, several quads will work together – if the target has proven particularly elusive or is of inestimable worth. Jennsen is both.'

Sebastian rested an arm over his knee. 'For someone on the run and in hiding all these years, you seem to know a lot about these quads. Are you sure you're right?'

Firelight danced in her mother's eyes. Her voice turned more distant. 'When I was young, I used to live at the People's Palace. I used to see those men, the quads. Darken Rahl used them to hunt people. They are ruthless beyond anything you could imagine.'

Sebastian looked uneasy. 'Well, I guess you would know better than I. In the morning, then, we leave.' He yawned as he stretched. 'Your herbs are already working, and this fever has exhausted me. After a good night's sleep I'll help you both get away from here, away from D'Hara, and on your way to the Old World, if that's your wish.'

'It is.' Her mother stood. 'You two eat the rest of the fish.' As she moved past, her loving fingers trailed along the back of Jennsen's head. 'I'm going to go collect some of our things, get together what we can carry.'

'I'll be right in,' Jennsen said. 'Soon as I bank the fire.'

Chapter 6

The rain was getting worse. Runoff ran in a rippled sheet over the ledge at the brow of the cave. Jennsen scratched Betty behind her ears to try to stop her bleating. The always nervous goat was suddenly inconsolable. Perhaps she sensed that they were going to be leaving. Maybe she was just unhappy that Jennsen's mother had gone into the house. Betty loved that woman, and would often follow her around the yard like a puppy. Betty would be only too happy to sleep in the house with them both, if they would let her.

Sebastian, having had his fill of fish, rolled himself in his cloak. His eyelids drooped as he tried to watch her bank the fire. He lifted his head and frowned over at the pacing goat.

'Betty will settle down when I go in the house,' Jennsen told him.

Sebastian, already half asleep, mumbled something about Betty that Jennsen couldn't even begin to hear over the noise of the rain. She knew it wasn't important enough to ask him to repeat it. He needed sleep. She yawned. Despite her anxiety over everything that had happened that day, and her worry about what the next would bring, the din of the downpour was making her sleepy, too.

As much as she ached to ask him about what was beyond D'Hara, she bid him a good night's sleep, even though she doubted that he heard her over the rain. She would have time enough to ask him all her questions. Her mother would be waiting for help with selecting what to take and packing it. They didn't have much, but they would have to leave some of what they had.

At least the clumsy dead D'Haran soldier had provided them with money just when they would need it most. It was enough money to buy horses and supplies that would help them get out of D'Hara. The new Lord Rahl, the bastard son of a bastard son in an unbroken long line of bastard sons, had inadvertently provided them with the means to escape his grasp.

Life was so precious. She just wanted her and her mother to be able to live their own lives. Somewhere, over the distant dark horizon, lay their new lives.

Jennsen threw her cloak around her shoulders. She pulled the hood up to protect herself from the rain, but as hard as it was coming down she expected she was likely to get wet on the run to the house. She hoped the morning would dawn clear for their first day of travel so they could put distance between them and their pursuers. She was pleased to see that Sebastian looked dead to the world. He needed a good sleep. She was thankful that amid all the torment and injustice, at least he had come into their lives.

Jennsen picked up the bowl with the few remaining pieces of fish, tucked it under her cloak, held her breath, and, lowering her head against the onslaught, dove into the roaring rain. The cold shock of the downpour made her gasp as she splashed through the dark puddles on her dash to the house.

She made the house, her wet lashes turning the dim light of the oil lamps and firelight coming through the window to a blinking blur. Without looking up, she threw the door open as she ran in.

'It's cold as the Keeper's heart!' she called out to her mother as she raced in.

Jennsen's breath left her lungs in a grunt as she crashed into a solid wall that had never been there before.

Rebounding from the collision, she looked up to see a broad back turning, to see a huge hand snatching for her.

The hand caught only her cloak. The heavy wool cloak stripped away from her as she fell back. The bowl thudded to the floor, spinning like a crazy top. The door bounced back from hitting the wall, banging closed behind her, trapping her, just before her back slammed into it.

Gasping, Jennsen reacted.

It was wild instinct, not deliberate thought.

Jennsen.

Terror, not technique.

Surrender.

Desperation, not design.

The man's blocky face was clearly lit by the fire from the hearth. He plunged toward her. A monster with stringy wet hair. Straining sinew and muscle twisted in rage. The knife in her fist whipped around, powered by stark terror.

Her cry was a growl of panicked effort. Her knife slammed into the side of his head. The blade snapped at midlength as it hit his cheekbone. His head twisted from the impact. Blood splashed across his face.

Swinging madly, his meaty hand walloped her face. Her shoulder hit the wall. A shock of pain lanced her arm. She stumbled on something. Thrown off balance, she tumbled past her footing.

Her face smacked the floor beside another of the huge men. He was like the dead soldier she had buried. Her mind grasped at snatches of what she was seeing, trying to make sense of it. Where did they come from? How were they in her house?

Her leg was draped over the man's still legs. She pushed herself up. He was slumped against the wall. His dead eyes stared at her. The handle with the ornate 'R,' sideways below his ear, reflected sparkles of firelight. The point of the knife jutted from the other side of his bull neck. He wore a wet red shirt.

Surrender.

With cold fright, she saw a man coming for her.

Gripping her broken knife, she scrambled to her feet, turning toward the threat. She saw her mother on the floor. A man held her by the hair. There was blood everywhere.

Nothing seemed real.

In a nightmare vision, Jennsen saw her mother's severed arm on the floor, fingers slack and open. Red stab wounds.

Jennsen.

Panic ruled her mind. She heard her own short, choppy screams. Wet blood, splashed across the floor, glistened in the firelight. Whirling movement. A man slammed into her, driving her to the wall. She lost her breath. Pain crushed her chest.

Surrender.

'No!' Her own voice seemed unreal.

She slashed with her broken knife, ripping the man's arm. He bellowed a vile oath.

The man holding Jennsen's mother dropped her and made for Jennsen. She stabbed wildly, frantically, at the men around her. Reaching hands shot toward her from all around. A huge hand clamped her thrashing knife arm.

Surrender.

Jennsen gasped a cry. She struggled savagely. She kicked. She bit. Men cursed. The second man seized her throat in iron fingers.

No breath. No breath. She tried – couldn't breathe – tried desperately – but couldn't draw a breath.

He sneered as he squeezed her throat. Pain shot up through her temples. His cheek, slashed by her knife, laid open from ear to mouth, ran with gouts of blood. She could see glistening red teeth through the gaping wound.

Jennsen struggled, but couldn't pull a breath. A fist slammed her stomach. She kicked him. He seized her ankle before she could kick him again. One was dead. Two had her. Her mother down.

Her vision was narrowing to a black tunnel. Her chest burned. It hurt so much. So much.

Sound was muffled.

She heard a bone-jarring thunk.

The man in front of her, squeezing her throat, staggered once as his head jerked.

It made no sense to her. His grip went slack. She gasped an urgent breath. His head tipped forward. A crescent-bladed axe was embedded in the back of the man's neck, severing his spine.

The axe handle swung in an arc as he dropped. Sebastian, measured fury with white hair, stood behind him.

48

The last man let go of her arm. His other fist brought up a blood-slick sword. Sebastian was quicker than the man.

Jennsen was quicker even than Sebastian.

Surrender.

She cried out, an animal sound, savage, unbridled, terror and fury. Her broken blade slashed across the side of the man's neck.

Her half blade ripped bone-deep, cut the artery, severed muscles. He cried out. Blood seemed to float, suspended in midair, as the man pitched against the far wall on his way down. She'd swung so hard she fell sprawling with him. Sebastian's short sword struck like lightning, slamming through the great barrel chest with bone-cracking power.

Jennsen scrambled over the bodies, slipping on blood. She saw only her mother on the floor, half sitting, leaning against the far wall. Her mother watched her come. Jennsen couldn't stop screaming, couldn't breathe through her hysterical cries.

Her mother, covered in blood, eyelids half closed, looked as if she were falling asleep. But she had that spark of joy at seeing Jennsen. Always that spark in her eyes. Her face had bloody streaks from big fingers down the side. She smiled her beautiful smile at seeing Jennsen.

'Baby . . .' she whispered.

Jennsen couldn't make herself stop screaming, shaking. She didn't look down at the awful red wounds.

She saw only her mother's face.

'Mama, Mama, Mama.'

One arm embraced her. Her other was gone. Her knife arm gone.

The one around Jennsen was love and comfort and shelter.

Her mother smiled a weary smile. 'Baby . . . you did good. Now, listen to me.'

Sebastian was there, working frantically to tie something around what was left of her mother's right arm, trying to stem the tide of blood. Her mother only saw Jennsen.

'I'm here, Mama. Everything will be fine. I'm here. Mama – don't die – don't die. Hold on, Mama. Hold on.'

'Listen.' Her voice was hardly more than a breath.

'I'm listening, Mama,' Jennsen cried. 'I'm listening.'

'I'm gone. I'm crossing to be with the good spirits, now.'

'No, Mama, no, please no.'

'Can't help it, baby . . . It's all right. The good spirits will take good care of me.'

Jennsen held her mother's face in both hands, trying to see it through the helpless flood of tears. Jennsen gasped with frantic sobs.

'Mama – don't leave me alone. Don't leave me. Please oh please don't. Oh, Mama, I love you.'

'Love you, baby. More than anything. I've taught you all I can. Listen, now.'

Jennsen nodded, fearing to miss a single precious word.

'The good spirits are taking me. You must understand that. When I go, this body won't be me any longer. Understand? I don't need it anymore. It doesn't hurt at all. Not at all. Isn't that a wonder? I'm with the good spirits. You must be strong now, and leave what is no longer me.'

'Mama,' Jennsen could only sob in agony as she held the face she loved more than life itself.

'He's coming for you, Jenn. Run. Don't stay with this body that isn't me after I'm with the good spirits. Understand?'

'No, Mama. I can't leave you. I can't.'

'You must. Don't foolishly risk your life just to bury this useless body. It isn't me. I'm in your heart and with the good spirits. This body isn't me. Understand, baby?'

'Yes, Mama. Not you. You'll be with the good spirits. Not here.'

Her mother nodded in Jennsen's hands. 'Good girl. Take the knife. I took one out with it. It's a worthy weapon.'

'Mama, I love you.' Jennsen wished for better words but there were none. 'I love you.'

'I love you . . . that's why you must run, baby. I don't want you to throw your life away over what is no longer me. Your life is too precious. Leave this empty vessel. Run, Jenn. Or he'll get you. Run.' Her eyes turned toward Sebastian. 'Help her?'

Sebastian, right there, nodded. 'I swear I will.'

She looked back at Jennsen and smiled her sweet love. 'I'll always be in your heart, baby. Always. Love you, always.'

'Oh Mama, you know I love you. Always.'

Her mother smiled as she watched her daughter. Jennsen's fingers caressed her mother's beautiful face. For a fleeting eternity her mother watched her.

Until Jennsen realized that her mother was no longer seeing anything in this world.

Jennsen fell against her mother, dissolving in tears and terror. Choking in sobs. Everything had ended. The crazy senseless world had ended.

Her arms stretched out toward her mother as she was pulled away.

'Jennsen.' His mouth was close to her ear. 'We have to do what she wanted.'

'No! Please oh please no,' she wailed.

He gently pulled. 'Jennsen, do as she asked. We must.'

Jennsen pounded her fists against the blood-slicked floor. 'No!' The world had ended. 'Oh please no. No, it can't be.'

'Jenn, we have to go.'

'You go,' she sobbed. 'I don't care. I give up.'

'No, Jenn, you don't. You can't.'

His arm around her middle lifted her, set her on her wobbly legs. Numb, Jennsen couldn't move. Nothing was real. Everything was a dream. The world was crumbling to ash.

Holding her by her upper arms, he shook her. 'Jennsen, we have to get out of here.'

She turned her head and looked at her mother on the floor. 'We have to do something. Please. We have to do something.'

'Yes, we do. We have to leave before more men show up.'

His face was dripping. She wondered if it was rain. As if she were watching herself from some great disconnected distance, her own thoughts seemed crazy to her.

'Jennsen, listen to me.' Her mother had said that. It was important. 'Listen to me. We have to get out of here. Your mother was right. We have to go.'

He turned to the pack beside the lamp on the table at the side of the room. Jennsen slumped to the floor. Her knees hit with a thump. She was empty of everything but the hot coals of agony from which she could not pull away. Why did everything have to be so wrong?

Jennsen crawled toward her sleeping mother. She couldn't die. She couldn't. Jennsen loved her too much for her to die.

'Jennsen! Grieve later! We have to get out of here!'

Out the open door, the rain poured down.

'I won't leave her!'

'Your mother made a sacrifice for you – so you would have a life. Don't throw away her final act of courage.'

He was stuffing whatever he could find in a pack. 'You have to do as she said. She loves you and wants you to live. She told you to run. I swore I'd help you. We have to leave before they catch us here.'

She stared at the door. It had been closed. She remembered crashing into it. Now it stood open. Maybe the latch broke . . .

A huge shadow materialized out of the rain, melting through the doorway into the house.

The brawny man's eyes fixed on her. Feral fright surged through her. He moved toward her. Faster and faster.

Jennsen saw the knife with the ornate 'R' sticking from the side of a dead man's neck. The knife her mother told her to take. It wasn't far. Her mother had lost her arm – her life – to kill him.

The man, seemingly oblivious of Sebastian, dove for Jennsen. She dove for the knife. Her fingers, greasy with blood, seized the handle. The worked metal gave good grip. Art, with purpose. Deadly art. With teeth gritted, she yanked the blade free and rolled.

Before the man reached her, Sebastian growled with the effort of burying his axe in the back of the man's head. The soldier crashed to the floor beside her, his meaty arm falling across her middle.

Jennsen, crying out, wriggled out from under the arm as blood grew in a dark pool beneath his head. Sebastian pulled her up.

'Get whatever you want to take,' he ordered.

She moved through the room, walking in a dream. The world had gone mad. Perhaps it was she who had finally gone mad.

The voice in her head whispered to her, in its strange language. She found herself listening, almost comforted by it.

Tu vash misht. Tu vask misht. Grushdeva du kalt misht.

'We have to go,' Sebastian said. 'Get what you want to take.'

She couldn't think. She didn't know what to do. She blocked the voice and told herself to do as her mother said to do.

She went to the cupboard and rapidly began picking out things that they always took when they traveled – things always at the ready. Traveling clothes were kept in her pack, ready to leave at a moment's notice. She threw herbs, spices, and dried food in on top of them. She pulled other clothes, a brush, a small mirror, from a simple chest of woven branches.

Her hand paused when she started grabbing her mother's clothes for her. She stopped, fingers trembling, focusing on her mother's orders. She couldn't think, so she moved like a trained animal, doing as she had been taught. They'd had to run before.

She scanned the room. Four dead D'Harans. One that morning. That made five. A quad plus one. Where were the other three? In the dark outside the door? In the trees? In the dark woods, waiting? Waiting to take her to Lord Rahl to be tortured to death?

With both hands, Sebastian seized her wrist. 'Jennsen, what are you doing?'

She realized she was stabbing at the empty air.

She watched as he pried the knife from her fist and returned it to its sheath. He tucked it behind her belt. He scooped up her cloak, which the huge D'Haran soldier had ripped off her as she had first fallen into the nightmare.

'Hurry up, Jennsen. Grab anything else you want.'

Sebastian rifled through the dead men's pockets, pulling out money he found, cramming it in his own pockets. He unstrapped all four knives, none as good as the one he'd tucked behind her belt, the one with the ornate letter 'R' on the handle, the one from the fallen dead man, the one her mother had used.

Sebastian slipped the four knives down the side of the pack as he yelled at her again to hurry. While he took the best sword from one of the men, Jennsen went to the table. She scooped up candles and stuffed them in the pack. Sebastian attached the scabbard of the sword to his weapons belt. Jennsen collected small implements – cooking utensils, pots – pushing them in her pack. She wasn't really aware of what she was taking. She was just picking up whatever she saw and putting it in.

Sebastian lifted her pack, took one of her wrists, and stuffed it through the strap, as if he were handling a rag doll. He put her other arm through the other strap he held out for her, then threw her cloak around her shoulders. After he pulled the hood up over her head, he stuffed her red hair in the sides.

He held her mother's pack in one hand. He tugged twice and freed his axe from the soldier's skull. Blood ran down the handle as he hooked the axe on his weapons belt. With the heel of his sword hand against the small of her back, he urged her onward.

'Anything else?' he asked as they moved toward the door. 'Jennsen, do you want anything else from your house before we go?'

Jennsen looked over her shoulder at her mother on the floor.

'She's gone, Jennsen. The good spirits are taking care of her, now. She's smiling down on you, now.'

Jennsen looked up at him. 'Really? You think so?'

'Yes. She's in a better world, now. She told us to go from here. We have to do what she said.'

In a better world. Jennsen clung to that idea. Her world held only anguish.

She moved toward the door, doing as Sebastian said to do. He scanned in every direction. She simply followed, stepping over bodies, over bloody arms and legs. She was too scared to feel anymore, too heartsick to care. Her thoughts seemed completely muddled. She had always prided herself on her clear thinking. Where had her clear thinking gone?

In the rain, he pulled her by her arm toward the path down.

'Betty,' she said, digging in her heels. 'We have to get Betty.'

He gazed at the path, then toward the cave. 'I don't think we need bother with the goat, but I should get my pack, my things.'

She saw he was standing in the downpour without his cloak. He was soaked to the skin. It occurred to her that she wasn't the only one who wasn't thinking clearly. He was so intent on escaping that he almost left his things. That would be the death of him. She couldn't let him die. Betty would help, but there was one other thing that she remembered. Jennsen ran back in the house.

She ignored Sebastian's yells. Inside, she wasted no time rushing to a small wooden chest just inside the door. She looked at nothing else as she pulled out two bundled sheepskin cloaks – one hers, one her mother's. They kept them there, rolled and tied, at the ready, in case they ever had to leave in a hurry. He watched from the doorway, impatient, but silent when he saw what she was doing. Without looking death in the eye, she rushed back out of her house for the last time.

Together, they ran to the cave. The fire was still crackling hot. Betty paced and trembled but was uncharacteristically silent, as if knowing something was terribly wrong.

'Dry yourself a bit, first,' she said.

'We don't have time! We have to get out of here. The others could come at any moment.'

'You'll freeze to death if you don't. Then what good will running do? Dead is dead.' Her own reasoned words surprised her.

Jennsen pulled the two rolled sheepskin cloaks from under her wool cloak and started working loose the knots in the thongs. 'These will help keep the rain out, but you need to get dry, first, otherwise you won't stay warm enough.'

He was nodding as he shivered and rubbed his hands before the fire, the sense of what she said finally overcoming his urgency to be gone. She wondered how she managed to do all he had done with a fever and after having taken herbs. Fear, she guessed. Stark-raving fear. That, she understood.

Her whole body ached. Not only had she been banged around, but she saw now that her shoulder was bleeding. The cut wasn't bad, but it throbbed. The sustained level of terror had left her drained and exhausted.

She wanted only to lie down and cry, but her mother had told her to get away. Only her mother's words motivated her now. Without those last commands, Jennsen would be unable to function. Now she simply did what her mother had told her to do.

Betty was beside herself. The distraught goat tried to climb the pen to get to Jennsen. As Sebastian hovered over the fire,

Jennsen tied a rope around Betty's neck. The goat was as thankful to be going as a goat could be.

They would give Betty a chance to return the favor. When they had gotten away and found at least simple shelter, they would not be able to build a fire on such a wet night. If they could find a dry hole, a spot under a rock ledge, or beneath fallen trees, they would hunker down beside the goat. Betty would keep them both warm so they wouldn't freeze to death.

Jennsen understood the plaintive calls Betty made toward the house. The goat's ears were at attention. Betty was worried for the woman who wasn't going. Jennsen collected all the carrots and acorns off the shelf, stuffing them in pockets and packs.

When Sebastian was as dry as he was going to allow himself to get, they donned their wool cloaks and topped them with the sheepskin. With Jennsen leading Betty by the rope, they started out into the drenching darkness. Sebastian headed for the trail down from the front – the way he had come in.

Jennsen seized his arm, stopping him. 'They might be waiting down there.'

'But we have to get out of here.'

'I have a better way. We made an escape route.'

He gazed at her a moment through the fall of icy rain separating them, then, without further protest, followed her into the unknown.

Chapter 7

Oba Schalk snatched the chicken by the neck and lifted it from the nest box. The chicken's head looked tiny above his meaty fist. With his other hand, he fished a warm brown egg from the bottom of the depression in the straw. He gently placed the egg in the basket with the others.

Oba didn't set the chicken back down.

He grinned as he lifted it closer to his face, watching its head twist from side to side, its beak open and close, open and close. He put his own lips close, so the beak was touching his lips, then, with all his might, he blew in the chicken's open mouth.

The chicken squawked and flapped, madly trying to escape the vise-like fist. A deep laugh rolled up from Oba's throat.

'Oba! Oba, where are you!'

When he heard his mother hollering for him, Oba plopped the chicken back on its nest. His mother's voice had come from the nearby barn. Squawking its terror, the chicken fled the henhouse. Oba followed it out of the coop and then trotted toward the door to the barn.

The week before, they had had a rare winter downpour. By the following day, the standing water had frozen and the rain had turned to snow. Windswept snow now hid the ice, making for treacherous footing. Despite his size, Oba negotiated the icy conditions without much difficulty. Oba prided himself on being light on his feet.

It was important for a person not to let their body or mind become slow and dull. Oba believed it was important to learn new things. He believed it was important to grow. He thought it

57

was important for a person to use what they had learned. That was how people grew.

The barn and house were one small structure made of wattle and daub – woven branches covered with a mixture of clay, straw, and dung. Inside, the house and barn were separated by a stone wall. After he'd built the house, Oba had made the wall inside by stacking flat gray rocks from the field. He had learned the technique from observing a neighbor stack rocks at the side of his field. The wall was a luxury most homes didn't have.

Hearing his mother yell his name again, he tried to think of what he could have done wrong. As he perused his mental list of the chores she'd told him to do, he couldn't recall one in the barn that he'd failed to do. Oba wasn't forgetful, and besides, they were chores he did often. There shouldn't be anything in the barn to have set her off.

True as all that was, none of it shielded him from incurring his mother's ire. She could think of things that needed doing that had never before needed doing.

'Oba! Oba! How many times do I need to call for you!'

In his mind's eye, he could see her mean little mouth all pinched up as she said his name, expecting him to appear the instant she screeched for him. The woman had a voice that could unwind a good rope.

Oba turned sideways to fit his shoulders through the small side door into the barn. Rats squeaked and scurried away at his feet. The barn, with a hayloft above, housed their milk cow, two hogs, and two oxen. The cow was still in the barn. The hogs had been turned loose in the oak stand to rut for acorns under the snow. Oba could see the hind ends of both oxen through the larger barn door out to the yard on the other side.

His mother stood on the low hill of frozen muck, hands on her hips, the cold smoke of her breath rising from her nostrils like a dragon's fiery snort.

Mother was a big-boned woman, broad in the shoulders and hips. Broad everywhere. Even her forehead was broad. He had heard people say that when his mother was younger she had been a handsome woman, and indeed, when he had been a boy, she had had a number of suitors. Year by year, though, the struggles of life had worn away her looks, leaving behind deeply etched lines and sagging folds of flesh. The suitors had long ago stopped coming around.

Oba made his way across the black, icy ground inside the barn and stood before her, hands in his pockets. She walloped the side of his shoulder with a stout stick. 'Oba.' He flinched when she whacked him three times more, each swat punctuating his name. 'Oba. Oba. Oba.'

When he had been young, such a thrashing would have left him black and blue. He was too big and strong, now, for her stick to hurt him. That made her angry, too.

While he wasn't bothered much by the stick now that he was grown, the condemnation in her voice whenever she spoke his name still made his ears burn. She reminded him of a spider with a mean little mouth. A black widow spider.

He hunched, trying not to look so big. 'What is it, Mama?'

'Where are you loafing when your mother calls?' Her face screwed up, a plum long ago turned to a prune. 'Oba the ox. Oba the dimwit. Oba the oaf. Where were you!'

Oba lifted his arm defensively as she cracked him with the stick again. 'I was getting the eggs, Mama. Getting the eggs.'

'Look at this mess! Don't it ever occur to you to do anything round here unless someone with brains tells you to?'

Oba looked around, but didn't see what needed doing – other than the regular work – that would have set her off so. There was always work to do. Rats stuck their noses out from under boards in the stalls, whiskers twitching as they sniffed, watching with beady black eyes, listening with little rat ears.

He looked back at his mother, but had no answer. None would suit her, anyway.

She pointed at the ground. 'Look at this place! Don't you ever think to scoop out the muck? Soon as it thaws it'll be running under the wall and into the house where I sleep. Do you think I feed you for nothing? Don't you think you have to earn your keep, you lazy oaf? Oba the oaf.'

She had already used the last invective. Oba was surprised, sometimes, that she wasn't more creative, didn't learn new things. When he had been little she had seemed to him a mind reader of inscrutable ability, with a talented tongue that could cut him with knowing lashes. Now that he had grown so much larger than her, he sometimes wondered if other aspects of his mother were less formidable than he had once feared, wondered if her power over him wasn't somehow ... artificial. An illusion. A scarecrow with a mean little mouth.

Yet she still had a way about her that could cut him down to nothing. And she was his mother. A person was supposed to mind their mother. That was the most important thing a person could do. She had taught him that lesson well.

Oba didn't think he could do much more to earn his keep. He worked from sunup to sundown. He prided himself on not being lazy. Oba was a man of action. He was strong, and worked as hard as any two men. He could best any man he knew. Men didn't give him any trouble. Women, though, stymied him. He never knew what to do around women. Big as he was, women had a way of making him feel puny.

He scuffed his boot against the dark, rippled, slick mound underfoot, assessing the rock-hard mass. The animals added to it continually, much of it freezing before it could all be scooped out, allowing it to build in layers throughout the long, cold winter. Periodically, Oba scattered straw over the top for better footing. He'd not want his mother to slip and fall. It wasn't long, though, before the layer of straw became slicked over and it was time for another.

'But Mama, the ground's all frozen.'

In the past, he had always scooped it out as it thawed and could be worked. In the spring, when it got warmer and the flies filled the barn with their constant buzzing, it would come off in layers where the straw was. But not now. Now, it was welded together into a solid mass.

'Always an excuse. Isn't that right, Oba? Always an excuse for your mother. You worthless bastard boy.'

She folded her arms, glowering at him. He couldn't hide from the truth, couldn't pretend, and she knew it.

Oba peered around in the dark barn and saw the heavy steel scoop shovel leaning against the wall.

'I'll scoop it, Mama. You go back to your spinning, and I'll scoop the barn good.'

He didn't exactly know how he was going to scoop the solid frozen muck, only that he had to.

'Get started now,' she huffed. 'Use what light is left of the day. When it gets dark, then I want you to go to town to get me some medicine from Lathea.'

Now he knew why she had come to the barn looking for him.

'My knees is aching me again,' she complained, as if she wanted to cut off any objection he might voice, even though he never did. He thought it, though. She always seemed to know what he was thinking. 'Today you can get started in the barn, and tomorrow you can go back to scraping the muck all the way down until you clean it all out. Before the day wears on, though, I want you to go get my medicine.'

Oba pulled on his ear as he cast his gaze toward the ground. He didn't like going to see Lathea, the woman with the cures. He didn't like her. She always looked at him like he was a worm. She was mean as rake. Worse, she was a sorceress.

If Lathea didn't like someone, they suffered for it. Everybody was afraid of Lathea, so Oba didn't feel so singled out. Still, though, he didn't like going to see her.

'I will, Mama. I'll fetch your medicine. And don't you worry, I'll get to work at scraping the muck out, just like you said.'

'I have to tell you every little thing, don't I, Oba?' Her glare burned into him. 'I don't know why I bothered raising such a worthless bastard boy,' she added under her breath. 'Should have done what Lathea told me, in the beginning.'

Oba heard her say this often, when she was feeling sorry for herself, sorry that no suitors came around anymore, sorry that none had wanted to marry her. Oba was a curse she bore with bitter regret. A bastard child who'd brought her trouble from the first. If not for Oba, maybe she would have gotten herself a husband to provide for her.

'And don't you be staying in town with any foolishness.'

'I won't, Mama. I'm sorry that your knees are bad today.'

She whacked him with the stick. 'They wouldn't be so bad if I didn't have to follow around a big dumb ox seeing that he does what he should already be doing.'

'Yes, Mama.'

'Did you get the eggs?'

'Yes, Mama.'

She eyed him suspiciously, then pulled a coin from her flaxen apron. 'Tell Lathea to make up a remedy for you, too, along with my medicine. Maybe we can yet rid you of the Keeper's evil. If we could get the evil out of you, maybe you wouldn't be so worthless.'

His mother, from time to time, sought to purge him of what she believed to be his evil nature. She tried all sorts of potions. When he was little she had often forced him to drink burning powder she mixed with soapy water; then she would lock him in a pen in the barn, hoping the otherworldly evil wouldn't like being burned and locked up both, and would flee his restrained earthly body.

His pen didn't have slats, like the pens for the animals did. It was made of solid boards. In the summer it was an oven. When she made him take burning powder and then dragged him by the arm and locked him in the pen, he near to died of terror that she'd never let him out, or never let him have a drink of water. He welcomed the beatings she would give him to try to silence his screams, just to be let out.

'You buy my medicine from Lathea, and a remedy for you.' His mother held up the small silver coin as her eyes narrowed into a spiteful squint. 'And don't you go wasting any of this on women.'

Oba felt his ears heating. Each time his mother sent him to buy something, whether medicine or leather work or pottery or supplies, she always admonished him not to waste the money on women.

He knew that when she told him not to waste it on women, she was mocking him.

Oba didn't have the courage to say much of anything to women. He always bought what his mother said to buy. He never once wasted it on anything – he feared his mother's wrath.

He hated that she always told him not to waste the money

when he never did. It made him feel like she thought he was intending to do wrong even though he wasn't. It made him guilty even though he had done no wrong. It made what was in his thoughts, even if he didn't have them, a crime.

He tugged on a burning ear. 'I won't waste it, Mama.'

'And dress respectable, not like some dumb ox. You already reflect badly enough on me.'

'I will, Mama. You'll see.'

Oba ran around to the house and fetched his felt cap and brown woolen jacket for his journey to Gretton, a couple miles northwest. She watched him carefully hang them on a peg, where they would stay clean until he was ready to go to town.

With the scoop shovel, he started in on the rock-hard muck. The steel shovel rang like a bell each time he rammed it at the frozen ground. He grunted with each mighty blow. Chips of black ice burst forth, splattering his trousers. Each was but an infinitesimal speck from the dark mountain of muck. It was going to take a long time and a lot of work. He didn't mind hard work, though. Time he had in abundance.

Mother watched from the doorway of the barn for a few minutes to make sure he was working up a sweat as he chipped away at the frozen mound. When she was satisfied, she vanished from the doorway to go back to her own work, leaving him to think about his coming visit to Lathea.

Oba.

Oba paused. The rats, back in the small places, stilled. Their little black rat eyes watched him watching them. The rats went back to their search for food. Oba listened for the familiar voice. He heard the door to the house close. Mother, a spinster, was going back to spinning her wool. Mr. Tuchmann brought her wool, which she spun into thread for him to use on his loom. The meager pay helped support her and her bastard son.

Oba.

Oba knew the voice well. He'd heard it ever since he could remember. He never told his mother about it. She would be angry and think that it was the Keeper's evil calling to him. She would want to force him to swallow even more potions and

63

cures. He was too big to be locked in the pen anymore. But he wasn't too big to drink Lathea's cures.

When one of the fat rats scurried past, Oba stepped on its tail, trapping it.

Oba.

The rat squeaked a little rat squeak. Little rat legs scrambled, trying to get away. Little rat claws scratched against the black ice.

Oba reached down and seized the fat furry body. He peered at the whiskered face. The head twisted futilely. Beady black eyes watched him.

Those eyes were filled with fear.

Surrender.

Oba thought it was vitally important to learn new things.

Quick as a fox, he bit off the rat's head.

Chapter 8

From what seemed to her the least troublesome corner of the room, Jennsen kept an eye on the door as well as the boisterous crowd. Half a room away, Sebastian leaned on the thick wooden plank counter, speaking to the innkeeper. She was a big woman, and with a forbidding scowl that made her look like she was as used to trouble as she was prepared to deal with it.

The roomful of people, mostly men, were a jovial lot. Some of the men played at dice or other table games. Some arm-wrestled. Most were drinking and telling jokes that would set tables of them off in peals of fist-pounding laughter.

Laughter sounded obscene to Jennsen. There was no joy in her world. There could be none.

The past week was a blur. Or was it more than a week? She couldn't recall exactly how long they had been traveling. What did it matter? What did anything matter?

Jennsen was unaccustomed to people. People had always represented danger to her. Groups of them made her nervous – people at an inn, drinking and gambling, even more so.

When men noticed her standing at the end of the counter near the wall, they forgot the jokes, or paused at their dice, and lingered on the sight of her. Meeting their gazes, she pushed the hood of her cloak back, letting her thick rings of red hair fall over the front of her shoulders. That was enough to turn their eyes back to their own business.

Jennsen's red hair spooked people, especially those who were superstitious. Red hair was uncommon enough that it raised suspicion. It gave people a worry that she might be gifted, or perhaps that she might even be a witch. Jennsen, by boldly meeting their gazes, played on such fears. It had in the past helped protect her, oftentimes better than a knife could have.

Back at her house, it hadn't helped one little bit.

After the men turned away from her and went back to their dice and drinks, Jennsen looked back down the counter. The stout innkeeper was staring at her, at her red hair. When Jennsen met her gaze, the woman quickly turned her attention back to Sebastian. He asked her another question. She bent closer as she spoke to him. Jennsen couldn't hear them over the roar of all the talking, joking, betting, cheering, cursing, and laughing. Sebastian nodded to the woman's words spoken close to his ear. She pointed off over the heads of her customers, apparently giving directions.

Sebastian straightened and pulled a coin from his pocket, then slid it across the counter toward the woman. After taking the coin, she traded it for a key from a box behind her. Sebastian scooped the key off the counter worn smooth by countless mugs and hands. He picked up his own mug, and bid the woman a good day.

When he reached the end of the counter, he leaned close to Jennsen so she could hear him and gestured with his mug. 'You sure you wouldn't like a drink?'

Jennsen shook her head.

He kept an eye on the roomful of people. They were all once again engaged in their own business. 'It was a good thing you pushed your hood back. Until the woman of the house saw that red hair of yours, she was playing dumb. After that, her tongue loosened.'

'The woman knows her? She is still living here in Gretton, as my mother said? The innkeeper is sure?'

Sebastian took a long drink, watching a roll of dice bring a cheer for the winner. 'She gave me directions.'

'And you got us rooms?'

'Only one room.' As he took another swig, he saw her reaction. 'Better to be together in case of trouble. I thought it would be safer with us both in one room.'

'I'd rather sleep with Betty.' Realizing how that must have

66

sounded, she looked away in embarrassment and added, 'Than in an inn, I mean. I'd rather be by myself than where there are so many people so close all around. I'd feel safer in the woods than closed in a room, here. I didn't mean—'

'I know what you meant.' Sebastian's blue eyes took up his smile. 'It will do you good to sleep inside – it's going to be a bitter night. And Betty will be better sheltered at the stable.'

The man who ran the stable had been a bit surprised to be asked to stable a goat for the night, but horses enjoyed the company of goats, so he was accommodating.

That first night, Betty had probably saved their lives. Sebastian, with his fever, might not have survived had Jennsen not found a dry place under a jut of ledge. The back of the small cleft beneath the overhang narrowed to a point, but it was big enough for the two of them. Jennsen had cut balsam and fir limbs to line the depression, lest the cold rock sap their bodies of heat. She and Sebastian then wedged themselves into the back. With Jennsen's urging and with the aid of the rope, Betty knelt behind the pine boughs positioned over the opening and then lay down close before them. With Betty's body against them, blocking the cold and providing her warmth, they had a dry, warm bed.

Jennsen quietly wept the long miserable night away. She was at least relieved that Sebastian, feverish, was able to sleep. By morning, his fever had broken. Morning had been the first day of Jennsen's bleak new life without her mother.

Leaving her mother's body there at the house, all alone, constantly haunted Jennsen. The memory of the horrifying bloody sight gave her nightmares. That her mother was gone brought limitless tears and crushed Jennsen with heartache. Life seemed desolate and meaningless.

But Sebastian and Jennsen had escaped. They had survived. That instinct to survive, and knowing all that her mother had done to give Jennsen life, kept her going. At times she wished she were not such a coward and could simply face the end and be done with it. At other times the terror of being pursued kept her putting one foot in front of the other. At yet other moments she felt a sense of fierce commitment to life, to not allowing all her mother's sacrifices to be in vain.

'We should have some supper,' Sebastian said. 'They have lamb stew. Then maybe you should get a good night's sleep in a warm bed before we go see this old acquaintance of yours. I'll stand watch while you sleep.'

Jennsen shook her head. 'No. Let's go see her now. We can sleep later.' She had seen people eating thick stew from wooden bowls. The thought of food held no appeal for her.

Sebastian studied the look on her face and saw that he wasn't going to talk her out of it. He drained the mug and set it on the counter. 'It's not far. We're on the right side of town.'

Outside in the gathering dusk, she asked, 'Why did you want to stay here, at this inn? There were other places much nicer, where the people didn't look so . . . rough.'

His blue-eyed gaze swept the buildings, the dark doorways, the alleys, as his fingers touched his cloak, seeking the reassurance of the hilt of his sword. 'A rough crowd asks fewer questions, especially the kind of questions we don't want to answer.'

He seemed to her a man who was used to avoiding having questions asked of him.

She stepped along the narrow furrow of a frozen rut, following it down the road toward the woman's house, a woman Jennsen only dimly remembered. She held on tightly to the hope that the woman might be able to help. Her mother must have had some reason for not going to this woman again, but Jennsen could think of nothing else to try but to seek her aid.

Without her mother, Jennsen needed help. The other three members of the quad were surely hunting her. Five men dead told her that there were at least two quads. That would mean at least three of those killers were still after her. It was entirely possible there were more. It was probable that even if there were not more, there soon would be.

They had escaped by using the hidden trail away from her house – the men probably wouldn't have been expecting that – so she and Sebastian had gained the temporary safety of distance. The rain would have done a good job of covering any tracks. It was possible that the two of them had gotten away cleanly and were for the time being safe. But since her pursuer was the Lord Rahl himself, it was also possible that the killers were, by some dark and mysterious means, moment by moment, closing in on her.

After the horrifying encounter with the huge soldiers at her house, the terror of that possibility always loomed in Jennsen's fears.

At a deserted corner, Sebastian pointed to the right. 'Down this street.'

They walked past dark buildings, square and windowless, that suggested to her that maybe they were only used for storage. No one seemed to live down the street. Before long, they'd left the buildings behind. Trees, naked before the bitter wind, huddled in clumps. When they came to a narrow road, Sebastian pointed.

'By the directions, it's the house down this road, down at the end, in that stand of trees.'

The road looked to be little used. Weak light from a distant window stole through bare branches of oak and alder. The light, rather than warm invitation, shone more like a glowing warning to stay away.

'Why don't you wait here,' she said. 'It might be better if I went alone.'

She was providing him with an excuse. Most people didn't want anything to do with a sorceress. Jennsen, herself, wished she had some other choice.

'I'll go with you.'

He had shown a distinct distrust of anything to do with magic. The way his eyes watched the dark place off through the branches and brush to the sides, he might have been trying to sound more brave than he was.

Jennsen admonished herself for even thinking such thoughts. He had fought D'Haran soldiers who not only had been much bigger than he, but had outnumbered him. He could have simply stayed out in the cave and not risked his life. He could have left the scene of such carnage and gone on with his life. Fearing magic only proved him of sound mind. She, of all people, could understand fearing magic.

Snow crunched under their boots as the two of them, after reaching the end of the road, made their way along the narrow path through the trees. Sebastian watched off to the sides while her attention was mostly fixed on the house. Behind the small place, the woods marched off up foothills. Jennsen imagined that only those with a strong need dared walk the path toward this door.

Jennsen reasoned that if the sorceress lived this near in to town, then she must be someone who helped people, someone whom people trusted. It was entirely possible that the woman was a valued and respected member of the community – a healer, devoted to helping others. Not someone to fear.

As the wind moaned through the trees looming around her, Jennsen rapped on the door. Sebastian's gaze studied the woods to each side. Off behind them the lights from homes and businesses would at least provide light enough for them to find their way back.

As she waited, Jennsen's gaze, too, was drawn to the gloom all around. She imagined eyes in the darkness watching her. The hairs at the back of her neck lifted.

The door finally drew in, but only as wide as the face of the woman peering out at them. 'Yes?'

Jennsen couldn't clearly make out the shadowed features of the face, but by the light coming out through the partly opened door, the woman could see Jennsen plainly enough.

'Are you Lathea?' she asked. 'Lathea, the . . . sorceress?'

'Why?'

'We were told that Lathea the sorceress lives here. If that's you, may we come in?'

Still the door didn't open any wider. Jennsen pulled her cloak tighter against the cold night air, as well as the chilly reception. The woman's steady look took in Sebastian, then Jennsen's form hidden within a heavy cloak.

'I'm not a midwife. If you want to get yourself out of the trouble you two are in, I can't help with that. Go see a midwife.'

Jennsen was mortified. 'That's not why we're here!'

The woman peered out for a moment, considering the two strangers at her door. 'What sort of medicine do you need, then?'

'No medicine. A . . . spell. I've met you before, once. I need a spell like you once cast for me – when I was little.'

The face in the shadows frowned. 'When? Where?'

Jennsen cleared her throat. 'Back at the People's Palace. When I lived there. You helped me when I was little.'

'Helped you what? Speak up, girl.'

'Helped . . . hide me. With some kind of spell, I believe. I was little at the time, so I don't recall exactly.'

'Hide you?'

'From Lord Rahl.'

There was an awful silence from the house.

'Do you remember? My name is Jennsen. I was very little at the time.' Jennsen pushed her hood back so the woman could see her ringlets of red hair lit in the wedge of light coming through the door.

'Jennsen. Don't recall the name, but the hair I remember. It's not often one sees hair like yours.'

Jennsen's spirits buoyed with relief. 'It has been a while. I'm so glad to hear that—'

'I don't deal in your kind,' the woman said. 'Never have. I cast no spell for you.'

Jennsen was stunned speechless. She didn't know what to say. She was sure the woman had once cast a spell to help her.

'Now, be gone. The both of you.' The door started to close.

'Wait! Please – I can pay.'

Jennsen reached into a pocket and hurriedly brought out a coin. Only after she passed it through the door did she see that it had been gold.

The woman inspected the gold mark for a time, perhaps considering if it was worth becoming involved again in what was sure to be a high crime, even for what amounted to a small fortune.

'Now do you remember?' Sebastian asked.

The woman's eyes turned to him. 'And who are you?'

'Just a friend.'

'Lathea, I need your help again. My mother . . .' Jennsen couldn't bring herself to say it, and started over in a different direction. 'I remember my mother telling me about you, and how you helped us, once. I was very little at the time, but I remember having the spell cast over me. It wore off years ago. I need that help again.'

'Well, you have the wrong person.'

Jennsen's fists tightened on her wool cloak. She had no other ideas. This was the only thing she could think of.

'Lathea, please, I'm at my wits' end. I need help.'

'She's given you a goodly sum,' Sebastian put in. 'If you say that we have the wrong person, and you don't want to help, then I guess we should save the gold for the right person.'

Lathea gave him a sly smile. 'Oh, I said she had the wrong person, but I didn't say I couldn't earn the payment tendered.'

'I don't understand,' Jennsen said, holding her cloak closed at her throat as she shivered with cold.

Lathea gazed out at her for a moment, as if waiting to be sure they were paying close attention. 'You are looking for my sister, Althea. I am La-thea. She is Al-thea. She is the one who helped you, not I. Your mother probably got our names mixed up, or you recalled it wrong. It used to be a common mistake, back when we were together. Althea and I have different talents with the gift. It was she who helped you and your mother, not I.'

Jennsen was dumbfounded and disappointed, but at least not defeated. There was still a thread of hope. 'Please, Lathea, could you help me this time? In your sister's place?'

'No. I can do nothing for you. I am blind to your kind. Only Althea can see the holes in the world. I cannot.'

Jennsen didn't know what that meant – holes in the world. 'Blind . . . to my kind?'

'Yes. I have told you what I can. Now, go away.'

The woman started pulling back from the door.

'Wait! Please! Can you at least tell me where your sister lives, then?'

She looked back at Jennsen's expectant face. 'This is dangerous business—'

'It's business,' Sebastian said, his voice as cold as the night. 'A gold mark's worth. For that price we should at the least have the place where we can find your sister.'

Lathea considered his words, then in a voice as cold as his had been said to Jennsen, 'I don't want nothing to do with your kind.

Understand? Nothing. If Althea does, that's her business. Inquire at the People's Palace.'

Jennsen seemed to remember traveling to a woman not terribly far from the palace. She had thought it was Lathea, but it must have been her sister, Althea. 'But can't you tell me more than that? Where she lives, how I can find her?'

'Last time I saw her she lived near there with her husband. You can inquire there for the sorceress Althea. People will know her – if she still lives.'

Sebastian put his hand against the door before the woman could shut it. 'That's a pretty thin bit of information. We should have more than that for the price offered.'

'For what I have told you the price is paltry. I gave you the information you need. If my sister wants to tempt her doom, that's up to her. What I don't need, for any price, is trouble.'

'We mean no trouble,' Jennsen said. 'We only need the help of a spell. If you can't help with that, then we thank you for your sister's name. We will seek her out. But there are some important things I need to know. If you could tell me—'

'If you had any decency, you'd leave Althea alone. Your kind will only bring us harm. Now go from my door before I set a nightmare upon you.'

Jennsen stared at the face in the shadows.

'Someone already has,' she said as she turned away.

Chapter 9

Oba, feeling fashionable in his cap and brown wool jacket, walked down the sides of the narrow streets, humming a tune he had heard played on a pipe at an inn he'd passed. He had to wait for a rider to go by before he turned down Lathea's road. The horse's ears swiveled toward him as it passed. Oba had had a horse, once, and liked to ride, but his mother had decided that they couldn't afford to keep a horse. Oxen were more useful and did more work, but they weren't as companionable.

As he walked down the dark road, his boots crunching on the crust of snow, a couple came past from the opposite direction, from the direction of Lathea's place. He wondered if they had gone to the sorceress for a cure. The woman cast a wary look his way. On a dark road, such a reaction was not undue, and, too, Oba knew that his size frightened some women. She sidestepped clear of him. The man with her met Oba's gaze – many men didn't.

The way they stared reminded Oba of the rat. He grinned at that memory, at learning new things. Both the man and the woman thought he was grinning at them. Oba tipped his cap to the lady. She returned a weak smile. It was the kind of empty smile Oba had often seen from women. It made him feel a buffoon. The couple melted into the dark streets.

Oba stuffed his hands in his jacket pockets and turned back toward Lathea's place. He hated going there in the dark. The sorceress was fearsome enough without the walk down her dark path. He let out a troubled sigh into the brisk winter air.

He wasn't afraid to confront the strength of men, but he knew he was helpless against the mysteries of magic. He knew how much misery her potions inflicted upon him. They burned him going in and coming out. They not only hurt, they made him lose control of himself, making him seem like he was just an animal. It was humiliating.

He had heard tell of others, though, who had angered the sorceress and suffered worse fates – fevers, blindness, a slow lingering death. One man had gone mad and run off naked into a swamp. People said he must have crossed the sorceress, somehow. They found him snakebit and dead, all puffed up and purple, floating among the slimy weed. Oba couldn't imagine what the man had done to earn such a fate from the sorceress. He should have known better and been more cautious with the old shrew.

Sometimes, Oba had nightmares about what she might do to him with her magic. He imagined Lathea's powers could lance him with a thousand cuts, or even strip the flesh from his bones. Boil his eyes in his head. Or make his tongue swell until he gagged and choked in a slow, agonizing death.

He hurried along the path. The sooner started, the sooner finished. Oba had learned that.

When he reached the house he knocked. 'It's Oba Schalk. My mother sent me for her medicine.'

He watched his breath cloud in the air while he waited. The door finally opened a sliver so she could peer out at him. He thought that, being a sorceress, she should be able to see him without having to open the door for a look, first. Sometimes when he was there waiting for Lathea to mix up medicine, someone would come and she would simply open the door. Whenever Oba came, though, she always peered out first to see it was him.

'Oba.' Her voice was as sour with recognition as her expression.

The door opened to admit him. Cautiously, respectfully, Oba stepped inside. He peered about, even though he knew the place well. He was careful not to act too forward with her. Harboring no fear of him, she swatted his shoulder to spur him to move deeper into the room to give her the leeway to shut the door.

75

'Your mother's knees, again?' the sorceress asked, pushing the door closed against the frigid air.

Oba nodded as he stared at the floor. 'She says they're aching her, and she'd like some of your medicine.' He knew he had to tell her the rest of it. 'She asked for you to ... to send along something for me, as well.'

Lathea smiled in that sly way she had. 'Something for you, Oba?'

Oba knew that she knew very well what he meant. There were only two cures he ever went to her for – one for his mother and the one for him. She liked to make him say it, though. Lathea was as mean as a toothache.

'A remedy for me, too, Mama said.'

Her face floated closer. She peered up at him, the snaky smile still playing across her features. 'A remedy for wickedness?' Her voice came in a hiss. 'That it, Oba? Is that what Mother Schalk wanted you to fetch?'

He cleared his throat and nodded. He felt puny before her thin smile, so he looked back down at the floor.

Lathea's gaze lingered on him. He wondered what was in that clever mind of hers, what devious thoughts, what grim schemes. She finally moved off to fetch the ingredients she kept in the tall cabinet. The rough pine door squeaked as she pulled it open. She set bottles in the crook of her other arm and carried them to the table in the middle of the room.

'She keeps trying, doesn't she, Oba?' Her voice had gone flat, like she was talking to herself. 'Keeps trying even though it never changes what is.'

Oba.

An oil lamp on the trestle table lit the collection of bottles as she set them there, one at a time, her eyes lingering on each. She was thinking about something. Maybe what vile brew she might mix up for him this time, what sort of sickly condition she would inflict upon him in an attempt to purge him of his ever present, unspecified, evil.

The oak logs in the hearth had checkered in the wavering yellow-orange glow of the fire, throwing good heat as well as light into the room. In the middle of their room, Oba and his mother had a pit for a fire. He liked the way the smoke in Lathea's fireplace went right up the chimney and out of the house, rather than hanging in the room before eventually making its way out a small hole in the roof. Oba liked a proper fireplace, and thought that he should make one for him and his mother. Every time he went to Lathea's place, he studied the way her fireplace was built. It was important to learn things.

He also kept an eye on Lathea's back as she poured liquid from bottles into a wide-mouthed jar. She mixed the concoction with a glass rod as each new ingredient was slowly added. When she was satisfied, she poured the medicine in a small bottle and stoppered it with a cork.

She handed him the little bottle. 'For your mother.'

Oba passed her the coin his mother had given him. She watched his eyes as her knobby fingers slipped the coin into a pocket in her dress. Oba finally let his breath go after she turned back to her table, to her work. She lifted a few bottles, studying them in the light of the fire, before she began mixing his cure. His cursed cure.

Oba didn't like speaking with Lathea, but her silence often made him even more uncomfortable, made him itch. He couldn't really think of anything worthy of saying, but he finally decided that he had to say something.

'Mama will be glad for the medicine. She's hoping it will help her knees.'

'And she's hoping for something to cure her son?'

Oba shrugged, regretting his attempt at casual conversation. 'Yes, ma'am.'

The sorceress peered back over her shoulder. 'I've told Mother Schalk that I don't believe it will do any good.'

Oba didn't think so, either, because he didn't really believe there was anything needing curing. When he had been little, he thought that his mother knew best, and wouldn't give him the cure if he didn't need it, but he had since come to doubt that. She no longer seemed to him as smart as he had once believed her to be.

'She must care about me, though. She keeps trying.'

'Maybe she's hoping that the cure might rid her of you,' Lathea said, almost absently, as she worked.

Oba.

Oba's head came up. He stared at the sorceress's back. He had never considered such a thought. Maybe Lathea was hoping that the cure would rid them both of the bastard boy. His mother sometimes went to see Lathea. Maybe they had discussed it.

Had he ignorantly believed the two women were trying to do good for him, to help him, when the opposite was actually true? Maybe both women had hatched a plan. Maybe they had been conniving all along to poison him.

If something happened to him, his mother would no longer have to help support him. She often complained about how much he ate. Time and again she told him that she worked more to feed him than herself, and that because of him she could never put any money away. Maybe if she had instead put away the money she'd spent on his cures over the years, she'd have a comfortable nest egg by now.

But if something happened to him, his mother would have to do all the work.

Maybe both women just wanted to do it out of simple meanness.

Maybe they hadn't thought it all through, as Oba would. His mother often surprised him with her simplemindedness. Maybe both women had been sitting around one day and had just decided to be mean.

Oba watched the flickering light play over the thin strands of the sorceress's straight hair. 'Today Mama said that she should have done what you always told her to do, from the beginning.'

Lathea, pouring thick brown liquid into the jar, glanced back over her shoulder again. 'Did she, now?'

Oba.

'What did you say from the beginning that Mama should do?'

'Isn't it obvious?'

Oba.

Icy realization prickled his flesh.

'You mean that she should have killed me.'

He had never before come out and said anything so bold. He

had never once in any way dared to confront the sorceress – he feared her too much. But, this time, the words had just come into his mind, much like the voice did, and he had spoken them before he had time to consider whether or not it was wise to do so.

He had surprised Lathea even more than he had surprised himself. She hesitated at her bottles, watching him as if he had changed before her very eyes. Maybe he had.

He realized then that he liked the way it felt to speak his mind.

He had never before seen Lathea falter. Maybe it was because she felt safe dancing around the subject, safe in the shadows of the words, without having them brought out into the light of day.

'That what you always wanted her to do, Lathea? That it? Kill her bastard boy?'

A smile pushed its way onto her thin face. 'It wasn't like you make it sound, Oba.' All the low, slow, haughty intonation had evaporated from her voice. 'Not at all.' She addressed him more like a man than she ever had before, rather than an evil bastard boy she tolerated. She sounded almost sweet. 'Women are sometimes better off without a newborn babe. It isn't so bad, when the babe is newborn. They're not such a . . . such a person, yet.'

Oba. Surrender.

'You mean, it would be easier.'

'That's right,' she said, eagerly latching on to his words. 'It would be easier.'

His own voice slowed and took on an edge that he didn't know had been in him. 'You mean it would be easier . . . before they got big enough to fight back.'

The range of his latent talents amazed him. It was a night of new wonders.

'No, no, that's not at all what I mean.' But he thought it was. Her voice, reflecting a fresh respect for him, quickened, became almost urgent. 'I only mean that it's easier before a woman comes to love her child. You know, before the child comes to be a person. A real person, with a mind. It's easier, then, and sometimes it's best for the mother.'

Oba was learning something new, but he hadn't put it all

together, yet. He sensed that all his new learning was profoundly important, that he was on the cusp of true understanding.

'How could it be best?'

Lathea stopped pouring the liquid and set the bottle down. 'Well, sometimes it's a hardship to have a new baby. A hardship on both. It's best for both, really, sometimes . . .'

She walked briskly to the cabinet. When she returned with a new bottle, she stepped around to the other side of the table so her back was no longer to him. Most of the ingredients for his cures were powders or liquids and he didn't know what they were. The bottle she brought back contained one of the few things he recognized, the dried base of mountain fever roses. They looked like brown, shriveled little circles with stars in the centers. She often added one to his cure. This time, she poured a pile in her cupped hand, made a fist to crush them, and dumped the fine brown crumbles in the cure she was mixing.

'Best, for both?' Oba asked.

Her fingers seemed to be looking for something to do. 'Yes, sometimes.' She seemed like she didn't want to talk about it anymore, but couldn't find a way to make it end. 'Sometimes it's more of a hardship than a woman can endure, that's all – a hardship that only endangers her and the rest of her children.'

'But Mama had no other children.'

Lathea went silent for a moment.

Oba. Surrender.

He listened to the voice, the voice that had become somehow different. Somehow vastly more important.

'No, but all the same you was a hardship on her. It's difficult for a woman to raise a child by herself. Especially a child—' She caught herself, then started over. 'I only meant that it would be hard.'

'But she did it. I guess you were wrong. Isn't that so, Lathea? You were wrong. Not Mama – you. Mama wanted me.'

'And she never married,' Lathea snapped. Her flash of anger had put the flame of haughty authority back in her eyes. 'Maybe if she . . . maybe if she'd married she would have had a chance to have a whole family, instead of only . . .'

'A bastard boy?'

Lathea didn't answer this time. She seemed to regret having taken a stand. The spark of anger left her eyes. With slightly trembling fingers, she dumped another pile of the dried flower buds in her palm, hurriedly crushed them in her fist, and dumped them in the cure. She turned and busied herself studying the flames in the hearth through a liquid in a blue glass bottle.

Oba took a step toward the table. Her head came up, her eyes turning to his.

'Dear Creator . . .' she whispered as she looked into his eyes. He realized she was not speaking to him, but to herself. 'Sometimes, when I look into those blue eyes, I can see him . . .'

Oba's brow drew down above his glare.

The bottle slipped from her hand, thumped on the table, and rolled to the floor, where it shattered.

Oba. Surrender. Surrender your will.

This was new. The voice had never before said that.

'You wanted Mama to kill me, didn't you, Lathea?'

He took another step toward the table.

Lathea stiffened. 'Stay where you are, Oba.'

There was fear in her eyes. Little rat eyes. This was definitely new. He was learning new things almost faster than he could note them all.

He saw her hands, the weapons of a sorceress, lifting. Oba paused. He stood cautiously, at attention.

Surrender, Oba, and you will be invincible.

This was not merely new, it was startling.

'I think you want to kill me with your "cures," don't you, Lathea? You want me dead.'

'No. No, Oba. That isn't true. I swear it isn't.'

He took another step, testing what the voice promised.

Her hands rose, a glow of light coming to life around her clawed fingers. The sorceress was conjuring magic.

'Oba' -- her voice was more forceful, more sure—'stay where you are, now.'

Surrender, Oba, and you will be invincible.

Oba felt his thighs bump the table as he advanced. The jars rattled and clanked together. One of them wobbled. Lathea watched it teeter and almost right itself, only to topple and spill its thick red liquid.

Lathea's face abruptly twisted with hatred, with rage, with effort. She cast her clawed hands forward, toward him, cast the full force of her power at him.

With a thunderous clap, light ignited, the flash making everything in the room go white for an instant.

He saw a flare of a yellow-white light knife through the air toward him – deadly lightning sent to kill.

Oba felt nothing.

Behind him, the light blasted a man-sized hole through the wooden wall, scattering flaming splinters out into the night. All the fire fizzled out in the snow.

Oba touched his chest where the full force of her power had been directed. No blood. No torn flesh. He was unharmed.

He thought that Lathea was even more surprised about it than he. Her mouth hung open in astonishment. Her wide eyes stared.

All his life he had feared this scarecrow.

Lathea quickly recovered, and again her face twisted with effort as she drew her hands up. This time an eerie blue hiss of light formed. The air smelled like burning hair. Lathea turned her palms up, sending forth her deadly magic, sending him death. Power no person could withstand shrieked toward him.

The blue light scorched the walls behind, but again he felt nothing. Oba grinned.

Again, Lathea wheeled her arms, but this time she also whispered a chant of clipped words he could not understand – rattling off a menace of magic. A column of light bloomed, undulating in the air before him, a viper of extraordinary might. Beyond doubt, it was meant to kill.

Oba lifted his hands to feel the snaking rope of crackling death she had spawned. He ran his fingers through it, but could feel nothing. It was like looking at something in a different world. There, but not.

It was as if he were . . . invincible.

With a howl of outrage, her hands came up again.

Quick as thought, Oba seized her by the throat.

'Oba!' she screeched. 'Oba, no! Please!'

This was new. He had never before heard Lathea say please.

With her neck in his meaty grip, he dragged her across the table toward him. Bottles scattered, tumbling to the floor. Some thudded and rolled, some broke like eggs.

Oba closed a fist on Lathea's stringy hair. She clawed at him, desperately calling upon her talents. She spoke words that had to be a mystical entreaty to magic, to her gift, to her sorceress power. While he didn't recognize the words, he understood their lethal intent.

Oba had surrendered, though, and he had become invincible.

He had watched her unleash her rage; now he unleashed his.

He slammed her up against her cabinet. Her mouth grew wide with a silent scream.

'Why did you want Mama to get rid of me?'

Her eyes, big and round, were fixed on the object of her terror: Oba. All his life, she had delighted in terrifying others. Now all that terror had returned to haunt her.

'Why did you want Mama to get rid of me?'

A series of small panting cries were her only answer.

'Why! Why!'

Oba ripped her dress from her body. Coins spilled from the pocket, raining across the floor.

'Why!'

He clutched the white shift she wore underneath the dress.

'Why!'

She tried to hold the shift to herself, but he stripped it away, sending her tumbling across the floor, bony arms and legs sprawling. Her wasted breasts hung like shriveled udders. This powerful sorceress was now naked before him, and she was nothing.

Her cries, full and round, came to life at last. Teeth gritted, he snatched her by the hair and hauled her to her feet. Oba rammed her against the cabinet. Wood splintered. Bottles cascaded out. He seized a bottle as it rolled out and broke it against the cabinet.

'Why, Lathea?' He brought the neck of a broken bottle up against her body. 'Why!' She shrieked all the louder. He twisted it against her soft middle. 'Why?'

'Please . . . oh dear Creator . . . please, no.'

'Why, Lathea?'

'Because,' she wailed, 'you are the bastard son of that monster, Darken Rahl.'

Oba hesitated. This was stunning news – if it was true.

'Mama was forced. She told me so. She said it was some man she didn't know who fathered me.'

'Oh, she knew him she did. She worked at the palace when she was younger. Your mother had big breasts and bigger ideas, back then. Poorly conceived ideas. She wasn't smart enough to realize that she was no more than a night's diversion for a man with a limitless supply of women – those eager, like her, and those not.'

This was definitely something new. Darken Rahl had been the most powerful man in the world. Could that noble Rahl blood flow in his veins? The heady implications made his head swim.

If the sorceress was telling the truth.

'My mother would have stayed there at the People's Palace if she carried Darken Rahl's son.'

'You aren't his gifted heir.'

'But still, if I was his son—'

Despite her pain, she managed to give him that smile that said he was but dirt to her. 'You are not gifted. Your kind were vermin to him. He ruthlessly exterminated all he discovered. He would have tortured you and your mother to death if he knew of you. Once she learned this, your mother fled.'

Oba was overwhelmed with new things. They were beginning to become a jumble in his mind.

He pulled the sorceress close. 'Darken Rahl was a powerful wizard. If what you say is true, he would have hunted us.' He slammed her against the cabinet again. 'He would have hunted me!' He shook her to elicit an answer. 'He would have!'

'He did, but he could not see the holes in the world.'

Her eyes were rolling. Her frail body was no match for Oba's strength. Blood ran from her right ear.

'What?' Oba reasoned that Lathea was babbling nonsense now.

'Only Althea can . . .'

She had ceased to make sense. He wondered how much of what she had said was true.

Her head lolled to the side. 'I should have . . . saved us all . . . when I had the chance. Althea was wrong . . .'

He shook her, trying to get her to say more. Red froth bubbled from her nose. Despite his yelling, his demanding, his shaking her, no more words came. He held her close, his heavy, hot breath lifting thin strands of her hair as he glared into her aimless eyes.

He had learned all he would from her.

He remembered all the burning powder he'd had to drink, the potions she had mixed for him, the days he'd spent in the pen. He remembered all the times he'd vomited his guts out and it still wouldn't stop burning his insides.

Oba growled as he lifted the bony woman. With a roar of anger he slammed her against the wall. Her cries were fuel for the fire of his vengeance. He reveled in her helpless agony.

He smashed her down against the heavy trestle table, breaking it, and breaking her. With each crash, she became more limp, bloody, incoherent.

But Oba had only just begun to rage at her.

Chapter 10

Jennsen didn't want to go back to the inn, but it was dark and cold and she didn't know what else to do. It was disheartening that Lathea wouldn't answer their questions. Jennsen had pinned her hopes on the woman's help.

'What shall we do tomorrow?' Sebastian asked.

'Tomorrow?'

'Well, do you still want me to help you leave D'Hara, as you and your mother asked of me?'

She hadn't really thought it out. In view of what little Lathea had told her, Jennsen wasn't sure what to do. She stared absently out into the empty night as they trudged across the crusted snow.

'If we went to the People's Palace, I would have some answers,' she said, thinking out loud. 'And, hopefully, Althea's help.'

Going to the People's Palace was by far the most dangerous alternative. But no matter where she ran, where she hid, Lord Rahl's magic would haunt her. Althea might be able to help. Maybe, somehow, she would be able to conceal Jennsen from him so she could have her own life.

He seemed to give her words serious thought, a long cloud of his breath trailing away in the wind. 'We'll go to the People's Palace, then. Find this Althea woman.'

She felt somehow uneasy when she realized that he wasn't offering any argument, or trying to talk her out of it. 'The People's Palace is the heart of D'Hara. It's not just the heart of D'Hara, but the home of the Lord Rahl.'

'Then he wouldn't be likely to expect you to go there, would he?'

Expected or not, they would still be walking into the enemy's lair. No predator long neglected to notice the prey in his midst. They would be naked before his fangs.

Jennsen glanced over at the shadowed shape walking beside her. 'Sebastian, what are you doing in D'Hara? You seem to have no love for the place. Why would you travel to a place you don't like?'

Beneath his hood, she saw his smile. 'Am I that obvious?'

Jennsen shrugged. 'I've met travelers before. They talk about places they've been, sights they've seen. Wonders. Beautiful valleys. Breathtaking mountains. Fascinating cities. You don't speak of anywhere you've been, or anything you've seen.'

'You want the truth?' he asked, his expression now serious.

Jennsen looked away. She suddenly felt awkward, nosy – especially in light of what she wasn't telling him.

'I'm sorry. I have no right to ask such a thing. Forget I mentioned it.'

'I don't mind.' He looked over at her with a wry smile. 'I don't think you would be one to report me to D'Haran soldiers.'

She was appalled at the very idea. 'Of course not.'

'Lord Rahl and his D'Haran Empire wish to rule the world. I'm trying to help prevent that. I'm from south of D'Hara, as I told you before. I was sent by our leader, the emperor of the Old World, Jagang the Just. I am Emperor Jagang's strategist.'

'Then you're someone of high authority,' she whispered in astonishment. 'A man of high rank.' The astonishment quickly transformed to tingling intimidation. She feared to guess at his importance, his rank. In her mind it rose by the moment, notch by notch. 'How am I to address one such as you?'

'As Sebastian.'

'But, you're an important man. I'm a nobody.'

'Oh, you're somebody, Jennsen Daggett. The Lord Rahl himself does not hunt nobodies.'

Jennsen felt an odd and unexpected sense of uneasiness. She harbored no love for D'Hara, of course, but she still felt somewhat uncomfortable to know that Sebastian was there to help bring about the defeat of her land.

The twinge of loyalty confused her. After all, the Lord Rahl had sent the men who had murdered her mother. The Lord Rahl hunted Jennsen, wanted her dead.

But it was the Lord Rahl who wanted her dead, not necessarily the people of her land. The mountains, the rivers, the vast plains, the trees and plant life had always all sheltered and nurtured her. She'd never really thought it through in that way before – that she could love her homeland, yet hate those who ruled it.

If this Jagang the Just succeeded, though, she would be freed from her pursuer. If D'Hara was defeated, Lord Rahl would be defeated – the rule of evil men would be ended. She would at last be free to live her own life.

In light of how open he was with her, she also felt foolish, even ashamed, for not telling Sebastian who she was and why Lord Rahl hunted her. She didn't know it all, herself, but she knew enough to know that Sebastian would share the same fate as she if they caught him with her.

As she thought about it, it began to make sense why he might not object to going to the People's Palace, why he might be willing to risk such a dangerous journey. As a strategist for the emperor Jagang, perhaps Sebastian would like nothing better than to sneak a look into the enemy's lair.

'Here we are,' he said.

She looked up and saw the white clapboard face of the inn. A metal mug hanging from a bracket overhead squeaked as it swung to and fro in the wind. The sounds of singing and dancing spilled out onto the snow-covered silence of the night. With an arm around her shoulders, Sebastian sheltered her as they made their way through the great room, shielded her from the prying eyes, and led her to the stairs at the far side. If possible, the place was even more crowded and noisy than before.

Without pause, the two of them quickly ascended the stairs. Partway down the dim hall, he unlocked a door to the right. Inside, Sebastian turned the wick up on the oil lamp sitting on a small table. Alongside the lamp was a pitcher and washbasin and near the table a bench. Looming to the side of the room sat a high bed covered crookedly with a dark brown blanket.

The room was better than the home she had left, but Jennsen didn't like it. One wall was overlaid with drab, painted linen. The plastered walls were stained and flyblown. Since the room was on the second floor, the only way down was back through the inn. She hated the stink of the room – a sour mixture of pipe smoke and urine. The chamber pot beneath the bed hadn't been emptied.

As Jennsen pulled a few things from her pack and went to the table to wash her face, Sebastian left her to it and went back downstairs. By the time she had finished washing and had brushed her hair, he returned with two bowls of lamb stew. He had brown bread, too, and mugs of ale. They ate sitting close together on the short bench, hunched over the table, close to the wavering light of the oil lamp.

The stew didn't taste as good as it looked. She picked out the chunks of meat but left the colorless, tasteless, soft vegetables. She sopped up some of the juice with the hard bread. She gave her ale to Sebastian and drank water instead. She wasn't used to drinking ale. To her the ale smelled as unpleasant as the lamp oil. Sebastian seeméd to like it.

When she had finished eating, Jennsen paced in the confining room the way Betty paced in her pen. Sebastian threw a leg to each side of the bench and leaned back against the wall. His blue eyes followed her from the bed to the wall hung with linen and back again, as she began wearing a path in the plank floor.

'Why don't you lie down and get some sleep,' he said in a soft voice. 'I'll watch over you.'

She felt like a trapped animal. She watched him take a long draft of ale from his mug. 'And what will we do tomorrow?'

It wasn't only her dislike of the inn, of the room. Her conscience was eating at her. She didn't let him answer.

'Sebastian, I have to tell you who I am. You were honest with me. I can't stay with you and endanger your mission. I don't know anything about the important things you do, but being with me will only put you at great risk. You've already helped me

89

more than I could have hoped, more than I ever could have asked.'

'Jennsen, I'm already at risk being here. I am in the land of my enemy.'

'And you're someone of high rank. An important man.' She rubbed her hands together, trying to bring some warmth to her icy fingers. 'If they captured you because you were with me . . . well, I couldn't bear it.'

'I took the risk of coming here.'

'But I haven't been honest with you – I haven't lied to you, but I haven't told you what I should have long ago. You're too important a man to chance being with me when you don't even know why I'm hunted, or what that attack back at my house was about.' She swallowed at the painful lump in her throat. 'Why my mother lost her life.'

He said nothing, but simply gave her the time to gather herself and tell him in her own way. From the first moment she had met him, and he hadn't come close when she had been afraid, he always gave her the room she needed in order to feel safe. He deserved more than she gave him in return.

Jennsen finally brought a halt to her pacing and looked down at him, at his blue eyes, blue eyes like hers, like her father's.

'Sebastian, Lord Rahl – the last Lord Rahl, Darken Rahl – was my father.'

He took the news without any outward reaction. She couldn't know what he was thinking. As he gazed up at her, as calmly as he did when she wasn't telling him terrible news, she felt safe in his company.

'My mother worked at the People's Palace. She was part of the palace staff. Darken Rahl . . . he noticed her. It is the Lord Rahl's prerogative to have any woman he wants.'

'Jennsen, you don't—'

She lifted a hand, silencing him. She wanted the whole thing out before she lost her nerve. Having always been with her mother, she feared being alone now. She feared he would abandon her, but she had to tell him what she knew.

'She was fourteen,' Jennsen said, beginning the story as calmly as she could. 'Too young to really understand about the ways of the world, of men. You saw how beautiful she was. At that young age, she was already pretty as could be, growing into a woman sooner than many her age. She had a bright smile and an innocent exuberance for life.

'She was a nobody, though, and to an extent excited to be noticed – desired – by a man of such power, a man who could have any woman he wanted. That was foolish, of course, but at her age and station it was flattering, and, in her innocence, I suppose it might have even seemed glamorous.

'She was bathed and pampered by older women on the palace staff. Her hair done up like a real lady. She was dressed in a beautiful gown for her meeting with the great man himself. When she was brought to him, he bowed and gently kissed the back of her hand – her, a servant in his great palace, and he kissed her hand. From all accounts, he was so handsome that he shamed the finest marble statues.

'She had dinner with him, in a great hall, and ate rare and exotic foods she had never tasted before. Just the two of them at a long dining table with people serving her for the first time in her life.

'He was charming. He complimented her on her beauty, her grace. He poured wine for her – the Lord Rahl himself.

'When she was at last alone with him, she was confronted with the reality of why she was there. She was too frightened to resist. Of course, had she not meekly submitted, he would have done what he wished anyway. Darken Rahl was a powerful wizard. He was easily as cruel as he was charming. He could have handled any woman without the slightest difficulty. He had but to command it, and those who resisted his will were tortured to death.

'But she never gave any thought to resisting. For a brief time, despite her apprehension, that world, at the center of such splendor, such power, had probably seemed exciting. When it turned to terror for her, she bore it silently.

'It wasn't rape in the meaning of being taken against her will, with a knife held to her throat, but it was a crime nonetheless. A savage crime.'

Jennsen looked away from Sebastian's blue eyes. 'He took my

mother to his bed for a period of time before he tired of her and moved on to other women. There were as many women as he could want. Even at that age, my mother didn't hold any foolish illusion that she meant something to him. She knew he was simply taking what he wanted, for as long as he wanted, and that when he was finished with her she would soon be forgotten. She was doing as a servant did. A flattered servant, perhaps, but still a frightened, innocent young servant who knew better than to resist a man above any law but his own.'

She couldn't bear to look at Sebastian. In a small voice, she added the last bit to the tale.

'I was the result of that brief ordeal in her life, and the beginning of a far greater one.'

Jennsen had never before told anyone the awful story, the terrible truth. She felt cold and dirty. She felt sick. Most of all, she felt deep anguish for what her mother must have gone through, for her young life spoiled.

Her mother never told the story all out as Jennsen had just done. Jennsen had pieced snippets and snatches of it together over her whole life, until it was finally a whole picture in her mind. She wasn't telling Sebastian all the snippets, either – the true extent of the horror of the way her mother had been treated by Darken Rahl. Jennsen felt burning shame that she had to be born to remind her mother every day of that terrible memory she could never tell in whole.

When Jennsen looked up through tears, Sebastian was standing close before her. His fingertips gently touched the side of her face. It was as tender a thing as she had ever felt.

Jennsen wiped the tears from under her eyes. 'The women and their children mean nothing to him. The Lord Rahl eliminates all those offspring who are not gifted. Since he takes many women, children of these couplings are not uncommon. He covets only one, his heir, the single child born of his seed who carries the gift.'

'Richard Rahl,' Sebastian said.

'Richard Rahl,' she confirmed. 'My half brother.'

Richard Rahl, her half brother, who hunted her as his father before him had hunted her. Richard Rahl, her half brother, who sent the quads to kill her. Richard Rahl, her half brother, who had sent the quads that had murdered her mother.

But why? She could have been no threat to Darken Rahl, and even less of a threat to the new Lord Rahl. He was a powerful wizard who commanded armies, legions of the gifted, and countless other loyal supporters. And she? She was nothing but one lone woman who knew few people and wanted only to live her own simple life in peace. She was hardly a threat to his rule.

Even the truth of her story would not so much as raise an eyebrow. Everyone knew that any Lord Rahl lived by his own laws. No one was even remotely likely to disbelieve her story, but no one would really care, either. At most, they might wink or give one another a knowing elbow at the lives of powerful men, and Darken Rahl had been the most powerful man alive.

Jennsen's whole life seemed suddenly to come down to that central question: Why would her father, a man she never knew, have wanted so desperately to kill her? And why would his son, Richard Rahl, her own half brother and now the Lord Rahl, also be so intent on killing her? It made no sense.

What could she possibly do that could harm either of them? What threat could she possibly constitute to such power?

Jennsen checked that the knife at her belt – her knife displaying the emblem of the House of Rahl – was secure. She lifted the blade to be sure it was free in its scabbard. The steel made a pleasing metallic click as she pushed it home. She scooped her cloak off the bed and threw it around her shoulders.

Sebastian swiped a hand back across his white spikes of hair as he watched her quickly tie the cloak shut. 'What do you think you're doing?'

'I'll be back in a while. I'm going out.'

He reached for his weapons and cloak. 'All right, I'll—'

'No. Leave me to it, Sebastian. You've put yourself at risk enough on my behalf. I wish to go alone. I'll be back when I've finished.'

'Finished what?'

She hurried to the door. 'What I have to do.'

He stood in the center of the room, fists at his sides, apparently hesitant to go against her explicit wishes. Jennsen quickly pulled the door shut tight behind herself, closing off her view of him. She took the steps two at a time, intent on being quickly out of the inn and gone before he changed his mind and followed.

The crowd downstairs was as rowdy as they had been before. She ignored the men, their gambling, their dancing, their laughter, and headed for the door. Before she made it, though, a bearded man hooked his arm around her middle and jerked her back into the press of people. She let out a small cry that was lost in the gale of revelry. Her left arm was pinned against her waist. He swung her around, catching her right hand, dancing her across the floor.

Jennsen tried to reach up to pull back her hood, to free her red hair in order to give him a scare, but she couldn't liberate her arm. He held her other hand in an iron grip. Not only could she not free her hair, she couldn't reach her knife to defend herself. Her breath came in a frightened pant.

The man laughed with his fellows, and swirled her to the music, holding her tight lest he lose his dance with her. His eyes shone with merriment, not menace, but she knew that was only because she had not yet forcefully resisted. She knew that when he discovered that she was unwilling, his pleasant demeanor was sure to change.

He released her waist and spun her around. With only one hand still entrapped in his callused fingers, she hoped yet to break the hold. With her left hand, she fumbled for her knife, but it was under her cloak, and not handy to her off hand. The crowd clapped in time with the tune of the pipes and drums. As she turned and stepped away, another man caught her up around the waist, bumping against her hard enough to knock the wind from her in a grunt. He captured her hand away from the first fellow. She had wasted her chance to pull back her hood by trying for her knife instead.

She found herself adrift in a sea of men. The few other women, serving girls mostly, were either willing or laughed and were able to alight briefly, and then move away, like bugs that were able to walk on water. Jennsen didn't know how they performed the trick; she was in danger of drowning among waves of men who passed her along from one to another.

When she caught sight of the door, she yanked away suddenly, breaking the hold of the latest man to have her in his grip. He hadn't been expecting her to suddenly break free. The men all laughed at the fellow who had lost hold of her. His merriment, as she had expected, died. The rest of the men were more good-natured about it than she had expected, and sent up a cheer for her escape.

Instead of showing anger, the man from whom she had escaped bowed. 'Thank you, my beautiful lass, for the gracious dance. It was a kindness to a lumbering old soul such as me.'

His grin returned and he winked at her before turning back to clap along with his fellows in time to the music.

Jennsen stood stunned, realizing that it had not been the danger she had expected. The men were having a good time, and not really intent on harm. None had touched her in an unseemly manner, or even spoken any crude words to her. They had only smiled, laughed, and danced with her. Still, Jennsen made a quick line for the door.

Before she went out, another arm caught her around the waist. Jennsen started to fight and pull away.

'I didn't know you liked to dance.'

It was Sebastian. She relaxed, and let him usher her out of the inn.

Out in the dark night, the cold air was a relief. She pulled a long breath, happy to be away from the unfamiliar smell of ale, pipe smoke, and sweaty men, happy to be away from the noise of so many people.

'I told you to leave me to it,' she said.

'Leave you to what?'

'I'm going to Lathea's place. Stay here, Sebastian. Please?'

'If you tell me why you don't want me to go.'

She lifted a hand but let it flop back to her side. 'Sebastian, you're an important man. I feel terrible about the danger you've already been in all because of me. This is my problem, not yours. My life is . . . I don't know. I don't have a life. You do. I don't want to get you all tangled up in my mess.'

She started out across the crusty snow. 'Just wait here.'

He stuffed his hands in his pockets as he strode along beside her. 'Jennsen, I'm a grown man. Don't decide for me what I should be doing, all right?'

She didn't answer as she turned the corner down a deserted street.

'Tell me why you want to go see Lathea, will you?'

She stopped then at the side of the road, close to an uninhabited building not far from the corner of the road that turned down to Lathea's place.

'Sebastian, my whole life I've been running. My mother spent the better part of her life running from Darken Rahl, hiding me. She died running from his son, Richard Rahl. It was me Darken Rahl was after, me Darken Rahl wanted to kill, and now it's Richard Rahl who is after me, who wants to kill me, and I don't know why.

'I'm sick of it. My life is nothing but running, hiding, and being afraid. It's all I do. All I think about. That's all my life is – running from a man trying to kill me. Trying to stay a step ahead of him and stay alive.'

He didn't argue with her. 'So, why do you want to go to the sorceress?'

Jennsen pushed her hands under her cloak, under her arms, to warm them. She gazed down toward the dark road to Lathea's place, at the feathery canopy of bare branches moving in the wind. Some of the limbs creaked and groaned as they rubbed together.

'I even ran from Lathea, earlier. I don't know why Lord Rahl is chasing me, but she does. I was afraid to insist she tell me. I was going to travel all the way to the People's Palace in order to find her sister, Althea, hoping that maybe as I stand meekly before her door she might deign to tell me, to help me.

'What if she doesn't? What if she, too, dismisses me? Then what? What greater danger could there be than for me to go there, to the People's Palace? And for what? The hollow hope that someone will finally volunteer to stoop to help a solitary woman hunted by the mighty force of a nation led by the murderous bastard son of a monster?

'Don't you see? If I would stop taking "no" for an answer, and insist Lathea tell me, then maybe I could save a dangerous journey to the even more dangerous heart of D'Hara, and leave, instead. For the first time in my life, I could be free, then. But I was about to throw away that chance because I was afraid of Lathea, too. I'm sick to death of being afraid.'

In the dim light, he stood considering their options.

'So, let's just leave. Let me take you away from D'Hara, if that's what you want.'

'No. Not until I find out why Lord Rahl wants to kill me.'

'Jennsen, what difference does it make if—'

'No!' Her fists tightened. 'Not until I find out first why my mother had to die!'

She could feel bitter tears turning icy cold as they ran down her cheeks.

Finally, Sebastian nodded. 'I understand. Let's go see Lathea. I'll help you get an answer from her. Maybe then you'll let me take you away from D'Hara, to where you will be safe.'

She brushed back the tears. 'Thank you, Sebastian. But, don't you have some kind of job to do, here? I can't let my problems get in your way any longer. This is my trouble. You must live your own life.'

He smiled then. 'Our people's spiritual guide, Brother Narev, says that our most important job in this life is helping those who need help.'

Such a sentiment lifted her spirits when she didn't think they could be lifted. 'He sounds like a wonderful man.'

'He is.'

'But you are still on a duty from your leader, Jagang the Just, aren't you?'

'Brother Narev is also a close friend and spiritual guide to Emperor Jagang. Both men would want me to help you, I know they would. After all, the Lord Rahl is our enemy, too. Lord Rahl has caused our people untold hardship. Both men, Brother Narev and Emperor Jagang, would insist I help you. That's the truth of it.'

She was choked with emotion, and couldn't speak. She let him put his arm around her waist and lead her down the road. Sharing the quiet darkness with him, Jennsen listened to the soft sound of their boots crunching through the hard crust of snow.

Lathea had to help her. Jennsen intended to see to it.

Chapter 11

Oba hated it to end, but he knew it had to. He would have to get home. His mother would be angry if he stayed too long in town. Besides, he could wring no more enjoyment out of Lathea. She had given him all the satisfaction she was ever going to give him.

It had been fascinating, while it lasted. Boundlessly fascinating. And he had learned many new things. Animals simply did not provide the same kind of sensations as those he had gotten from Lathea. True, watching a person die was in many ways much like watching an animal die, but at the same time it was oh so very different. Oba had learned that.

Who knew what a rat was really thinking – or if rats could even think at all? But people could think. You could see their mind through their eyes, and you knew. To know they were thinking real people thoughts – not some chicken-rabbit-rat thoughts – behind those human eyes, behind that look that said it all, was intoxicating. Witnessing Lathea's ordeal had been rapture. Especially as he waited for that singular inspirational instant of ultimate anguish when her soul fled her human form, and the Keeper of the dead received her into his eternal realm.

Animals did give him a thrill, though, even if they lacked that human element. There was tremendous enjoyment to be had in nailing an animal to a fence, or a barn wall, and skinning them while they were still alive. But he didn't think they had a soul. They just . . . died.

Lathea had died, too, but it had been a whole new experience. Lathea had made him grin like he had never grinned before. Oba unscrewed the top of the lamp, pulled out the woven wick, and dribbled lamp oil across the floor, over the broken pieces of the trestle table, around Lathea's medicine cabinet lying facedown in the center of the room.

As much as he knew he would enjoy it, he couldn't just leave her there to be discovered. There would be questions, if she was found like this. He glanced over at her. Especially if she was found like this.

That idea did hold a certain fascination. He would enjoy listening to all the hysterical talk. He would love to hear people tell him all the macabre details of the monstrous death Lathea had suffered. The very idea of a man who could have taken the powerful sorceress out in such a grisly fashion would cause a sensation. People would want to know who had done it. To some folk, he would be an avenging hero. People everywhere would be abuzz. As word spread about Lathea's ordeal and gruesome end, the gossip would heat to a fever pitch. That would be fun.

As he emptied the last of the lamp oil, he saw his knife, where he'd left it, beside the overturned cabinet. He tossed the empty lamp on the heap of ruin and bent to retrieve his knife. It was a mess. Couldn't have an omelet without breaking eggs, his mother always said. She said it a lot. In this case, Oba thought her tired old saw fit.

With one hand, he took Lathea's favorite chair and tossed it into the center of the room, then began carefully cleaning his blade on the quilted throw from the chair. His knife was a valuable tool, and he kept it razor sharp. He was relieved to see the shine returning when the blood and slop was wiped off. He'd heard that magic could be troublesome in untold ways. Oba had briefly worried that the sorceress might be made up of some kind of dreadful acid sorceress-blood that once spilled would eat through steel.

He looked around. No, just regular blood. Lots of it.

Yes, the sensation this would create would be exciting.

But, he didn't like the idea of soldiers coming around to ask questions. They were a suspicious lot, soldiers. They would poke their noses into it, sure as cows gave milk. They would spoil everything with their suspicion and questions. He didn't think that soldiers appreciated omelets.

No, best if Lathea's house burned down. That wouldn't provide nearly the enjoyment that all the conversation and scandal would, but it also wouldn't be so suspicious. People's houses burned down all the time – especially in winter. Logs rolled out of fireplaces, spilling flaming coals; sparks shot into curtains and set homes ablaze; candles melted down and fell, catching things on fire. Happened all the time. Not really suspicious, a fire in the dead of winter. With all the lightning and sparks the sorceress sent flying willy-nilly, it was a wonder the place hadn't already burned down. The woman was a menace.

Of course, someone might notice the blaze way down at the end of the road, but by then it would be too late. By then the fire would be too hot for anyone to be able to come near the place. Tomorrow, if no one found the place ablaze, there would be nothing but ashes.

He let out a sad sigh for the stillborn gossip, for what might have been, if not for the tragic fire that would be blamed for Lathea's end.

Oba knew about fires. Over the years, several of his homes had burned down. Their animals had been burned alive. That was back when they had lived in other towns, before they moved to the place where they lived now.

Oba liked to watch a place burn, liked to hear the animals scream. He liked it when people came running, all in a panic. They always seemed puny in the face of what he created. People were afraid when there was a fire. The uproar caused by a burning building always swelled him with a sense of power.

Sometimes, as they yelled for more help, men would throw buckets of water on the fire or beat at the roaring flames with blankets, but that never stopped a fire Oba had started. He wasn't slipshod. He always did good work. He knew what he was doing.

Finally finished cleaning and polishing his knife, he threw the bloody quilted throw on the oil-soaked wood beside the overturned cabinet.

What was left of Lathea was nailed to the back of the cabinet that lay facedown on the floor. She stared at the ceiling.

Oba grinned. Soon, there would be no ceiling for her to stare up at. His grin widened. And no eyes to stare with.

Oba saw a glint of light on the floor beside the cabinet. He bent and recovered the small object. It was a gold coin. Oba had never seen a gold mark before that night. It must have fallen from the pocket of Lathea's dress, along with the others. He slipped the gold coin into his own pocket, where he'd put the rest he had collected from the floor. He'd also found a fat purse under her sleeping pallet.

Lathea had made him rich. Who knew that the sorceress had been so wealthy? Some of that money, earned by his mother from her spinning and used for his hated cures, had at last returned to Oba. Justice, finally done.

As Oba started for the fireplace, he heard the soft but unmistakable crunch of footsteps in the snow outside. He froze in midstride.

The footsteps were coming closer. They were approaching the door to Lathea's house.

Who would be coming to Lathea's place this late at night? That was just plain inconsiderate. Couldn't they wait until morning for their cures? Couldn't they let the poor woman get her rest? Some people only thought of themselves.

Oba snatched up the poker leaning against the fireplace and quickly spilled the burning oak logs out of the hearth and across the oil-soaked floor. The oil, the splintered wood, the bedsheets, and the quilted throw caught flame with a woosh. Dense white smoke swirled up around Lathea's pyre.

Quick as a fox, Oba scurried out the hole that the troublesome sorceress had conveniently blown through the back wall when she had tried to kill him with her magic.

She didn't know that he had become invincible.

Jennsen was pulled up short when Sebastian caught her by the arm. She turned to see his face in the dim light coming from the only window. That orange glow danced in his eyes. She knew immediately by his serious expression that she should remain silent.

Sebastian noiselessly drew his sword as he slipped past her on his way to the door. In that smooth, practiced movement, she saw a professional, a man familiar with such business.

He leaned to the side, trying for a look through the window without having to step into the deep snow below it. He turned back and whispered.

'Fire!'

Jennsen rushed to him. 'Hurry. She might be asleep. We have to warn her.'

Sebastian considered for only an instant, then burst through the door. Jennsen was right on his heels. She had difficulty making sense of what she saw inside. The place was washed in whirling orange light that cast monstrous shadows up the walls. In that wavering light, everything seemed surreal, out of scale, and out of place.

When she spotted the debris in the center of the room, it became only too real. She saw a woman's open hand sticking out beyond the top of what looked to be a tall wooden cabinet that had fallen. Jennsen drew a choking gasp of smoke and the smell of lamp oil. Thinking that maybe the cabinet had toppled and hurt the old sorceress, Jennsen rushed to help.

As she raced around the foot of the splintered chest, she caught the full view of what was left of Lathea.

The shock of it stiffened her. She couldn't move, couldn't blink her wide eyes. She gagged on the sickly stench of butchery and blood. As Jennsen stared, her anguished cry was lost in the leaping roar of flames and crackle of burning wood.

Sebastian briefly took in the remains of Lathea nailed to the back of the cabinet, only one detail of many as his gaze scanned the room. By his calculated movements, she surmised that he had seen such things enough that the human element no longer arrested his attention as it did hers.

Jennsen.

Jennsen's fingers tightened around the hilt of her knife. She could feel the ornately worked ridges of metal pressing against her palm, the worked metal peaks and whorls that made up the letter 'R.' As she gasped her breath past the nausea welling up inside, she pulled the blade free.

Surrender.

'They've been here,' she whispered. 'The D'Haran soldiers have been here.'

103

What she detected in his eyes was more like surprise, or confusion, than anything else.

He frowned as he glanced around again. 'Do you really think so?'

Jennsen.

She ignored the echo of the dead voice in her head and thought back to the man they had met out on the road after they had come to see the sorceress the first time. He was big, blond, and good-looking, like most D'Haran soldiers. She hadn't thought at the time that he was a soldier. Could he have been one, though?

No, if anything, he had seemed more intimidated by them than they were of him. Soldiers didn't behave the way that man had.

'Who else? We didn't see all of them, before. It had to be the rest of the quad from back at my house. When we escaped out the back way, they must have somehow followed us.'

He was still peering about as the flames grew, now licking at the ceiling. 'I guess you could be right.'

Surrender.

'Sebastian, we have to get out of here, now, or we'll be next.' Jennsen clutched the cloak at his shoulder, pulling him away. 'They may be near – right now.'

'But, how could they know?'

'Dear spirits, Lord Rahl is a wizard! How does he do anything he does? How did he find my house?'

Sebastian was still looking, prodding at the rubble with his sword. Jennsen tugged again at his cloak, urging him toward the open door.

'Your house . . .' he said, frowning. 'Yes, I see what you mean.'

'We have to get out of here before they catch us!'

He nodded, reassuring her. 'Where do you want to go?'

They both watched the dark doorway over their shoulders as well as the growing conflagration to their other side.

'We've no choice, now,' Jennsen said. 'Lathea was our only hope to find an answer. We have to go to the People's Palace, now. Find her sister, Althea. She's the only one with any

104

answers. She's a sorceress, too, and the only one who can see the holes in the world – whatever that means.'

'Are you sure that's what you want to do?'

She thought about the voice. It sounded so cold and lifeless in her head. It had surprised her. She hadn't heard it since her mother's murder.

'What other choice do we have, now? If I'm ever to know why Lord Rahl wants to kill me, why he murdered my mother, why I'm hunted, and maybe how to escape his clutches for good, then I have to go find this woman, Althea. I have to!'

He hurried with her through the door and out into the bitter night. 'We better go back and get our things together. We can get an early start.'

'With them this close, I fear to be trapped in the inn while we sleep. I have the money from my mother. You have what you took from the men. We can buy horses. We have to leave tonight and hope that no one saw us come here earlier, or again, now.'

Sebastian sheathed his sword. His breath streamed out into the night as he considered their options.

He glanced back through the door. 'With the fire, at least there won't be any evidence of what happened here. We have that much going for us. No one saw us come here earlier, so no one will have cause to ask us questions. No one will know we were here again. They won't have any reason to tell soldiers about us.'

'As long as we get out of here before it's discovered and everyone gets suspicious,' Jennsen said. 'Before soldiers start asking about strangers in town.'

He took her arm. 'All right. Let's be quick, then.'

Chapter 12

Well, wasn't this just something. Stranger and stranger. This night was full of new things, one right after another.

From his hiding place just around the corner of the house, Oba had been able to hear much of the conversation between the two. At first, he had been sure they would run off to get help. Oba didn't think the fire could be extinguished, but for a time he had been concerned, fearing that the man and woman might pull Lathea out of the house – rescue her from the blaze so that people could have a look. It would be just like the troublesome sorceress to find a way to come back to torment him, and after all his work.

But both the man and the woman wanted to leave Lathea to the fire. They, too, hoped the fire would cover the evidence of the sorceress's true end. They almost sounded like thieves, the woman talking about taking money from her mother and him taking money from men. That sounded suspicious.

If they had found gold and silver there, they might have taken it. Had they worked and slaved their whole lives, as he had, to finally recover money that was their due? Or had they been forced to suffer the abuse of swallowing Lathea's cursed cures their whole life? Oba didn't think so. It had been different for him. He had simply recovered money that was rightfully his all along. He felt a little indignant to be almost in the company of common thieves.

This night was just one startling thing after another. It seemed amazing to him how his life had gone along, day after day, month after month, year after year, always the same, same chores, same work, same everything. Now, in one night, all that seemed to have changed.

First, he had become invincible and in so doing unleashed his righteous inner self, only to discover that Rahl blood coursed through his veins, and now this odd pair showed up to help him conceal Lathea's true end. Stranger and stranger.

The startling news that he was in fact the son of Darken Rahl still had him in a state of astonished shock. He, Oba Schalk, as it turned out, was someone quite important, someone of noble blood, someone of noble birth.

He wondered whether or not he should now properly think of himself as Oba Rahl. He wondered if he was, in fact, a prince.

That was an intriguing notion. Unfortunately, his mother had raised him simply, so he didn't know much about such matters, what station or title was rightfully his.

He also realized that his mother was a liar. She had hidden his true identity from her own son, her flesh and blood. Darken Rahl's flesh and blood. She was probably resentful and envious and didn't want Oba to know of his greatness. That would be just like her. She was always trying to beat him down. The bitch.

The smoke coming through the open door no longer smelled of lamp oil. It now carried the aroma of roasting meat. Oba grinned as he peeked through the doorway to see Lathea's hand sticking above the cabinet, blackening in the flames, waving to him from the world of the dead.

Sneaking across the snow to hide behind the fat trunk of an oak, Oba watched as the couple hurried down the path, through the trees, toward the road. When they had passed out of sight, he followed in their tracks, staying hidden. He was a pretty big man to hide behind a tree, but in the darkness it wasn't difficult.

He was puzzled, and troubled, by certain aspects of the encounter. He had been surprised that the couple wouldn't want to call for help, and instead ran away. The woman, especially, was eager to escape, thinking that because of Lathea's death, someone was after them. A quad, she had said. That was part of what troubled him.

Oba had vaguely heard of quads before. Assassins of some sort. Assassins sent by the Lord Rahl himself. Assassins sent after important people. Or people who were especially dangerous. Maybe that was it, they were dangerous people and not common thieves, after all.

Oba had heard her name – Jennsen.

But the thing that had really perked up his ears was that Lathea had a sister named Althea – yet another cursed sorceress – and Althea was the only one who could see the holes in the world. That was most troubling of all, because that was the very same thing that Lathea had said to him. At the time, he had thought the old sorceress was already conversing with the spirits in the world of the dead, or maybe with the Keeper of the underworld himself, but as it turned out, she was speaking the truth.

Somehow, this Jennsen woman and Oba were both what Lathea called holes in the world. That sounded important. This Jennsen was somehow like him. They were somehow connected. That fascinated him.

He wished he had gotten a better look at her. The first meeting had been in darkness. The second time he saw her, just now, the fire had provided only enough light for a dim and shadowed view. As she had turned away, he only had time for a quick glimpse. From that fleeting look, he'd seen that she was a remarkably beautiful young woman.

He paused behind a tree before making his way across the open snow toward the concealment of a more distant tree. These people, like Jennsen, like Oba, who were holes in the world, were important. Quads were sent after important people – people who were especially dangerous to the Lord Rahl. Lathea had said that if he knew of Oba, the Lord Rahl would want to exterminate him.

Oba didn't know if he believed Lathea. She would be jealous of anyone more important than herself. Still, he might be in some kind of danger without even knowing it – hunted because he was an important man. That seemed pretty far-fetched, but in view of all the other new things he had learned this night, he didn't think it was entirely out of the question. An important man, a man interested in learning new things, didn't just dismiss such new information without giving it due consideration.

Oba was still trying to connect together all the things he had learned. It was all very complicated – that much he did know. He had to take everything into account if he was to put it all together.

As he scurried to the next tree, he decided that it might be best if he went to the inn and got a better look at Jennsen and Sebastian, the man with her. His eyes tracked them as they reached the road that headed back into town.

Even though the couple kept looking around, it wasn't difficult in such darkness for Oba to follow them without being seen. Once they were back among the buildings, it was even easier. From around the corner of one building, Oba saw the light spill out into the road when they opened the door below a metal mug swinging in the wind. Laughter and music spilled out, too – like a celebration of the sorceress's demise. Too bad everyone didn't know that Oba was the hero who had done away with the bane of all their lives. If people knew what he had managed to accomplish, he would probably have all the free drinks he could want. He watched as Jennsen and Sebastian were swallowed inside. The door thudded shut. The stillness of the winter night returned.

Oba never got a chance to go to an inn for a drink. He never had any money. He had money, now. He had had a hard night, but he had emerged a new man. A rich man. Wiping his nose on his jacket sleeve, he made for the door. It was time for him to go to a cozy inn and have a drink. If anyone deserved one, it was Oba Rahl.

Jennsen suspiciously scanned the faces at the inn, looking for any that might betray murderous design. She still felt sick from the sight of what had been done to Lathea. This night, there were monsters about. Men looked her way, but the twinkle in their eyes seemed merry, not murderous. But how would she know, before it was too late?

She ached to take the stairs two at a time.

'Easy,' Sebastian whispered, apparently believing she was on the verge of panicked flight. Maybe she was. His grip on her arm tightened. 'Let's not make people suspicious.' They took the stairs one at a time, moving at a measured pace, just a couple going to their room.

In their room, Jennsen burst into motion, gathering the few items they had removed from their packs, replacing them, securing the straps and buckles. Even Sebastian, checking his weapons beneath his cloak, seemed unnerved by what had happened to Lathea. Jennsen made sure that her knife was free in its scabbard.

'You sure you wouldn't like to get some sleep? Lathea couldn't have told them anything – she didn't know we were staying here at the inn. It might be better to start fresh at dawn.'

She shot him a look as she shouldered her pack.

'Right,' he said. He caught her arm. 'Jennsen, slow down. If you run, people will want to know why you're running.'

He was in enemy territory. He would know how to go about the business of not raising suspicion. Jennsen nodded.

'What should I do?'

'Just act like we're going down for a drink, or to listen to the music. If you insist on going directly out, walk. Don't call attention to us by running. Maybe we're just going to visit a friend or relative – who's to say? But we don't want people to wonder if there's something wrong. People forget normal. They remember when things look wrong.'

Abashed, she nodded again. 'I guess I'm not very good at this. Close-up running, I mean. I've been running and hiding my whole life, but not like this, when they're so close I can almost feel their breath on my neck.'

He smiled that warm smile of his, the one that looked so good on him. 'You aren't trained in this kind of thing. I wouldn't expect you to know how to act. Even so, I don't think I've ever met another woman who was as good as you are under such pressure. You're doing fine – you really are.'

Jennsen felt a little better to know that she wasn't acting like a complete fool. He had a way about him that gave her confidence, put her at ease, made her able to do things she didn't think she could. He let her decide on her own what it was she wanted to do, and then he backed up her decision. Not many men would do that for a woman.

Down the steps once again, for the last time, she could feel the door on the other side of the room, as if she were drowning and it was the only air. People so close, brushing against her, still made her uneasy, made her feel the desperate need for that air.

She had learned earlier, though, that the men weren't the threat she had thought. She was somewhat humbled by how wrong she had been about them. Where before she had seen thieves and cutthroats, she now saw farmers, craftsmen, laborers, joining together for company, companionship, and some harmless recreation.

Still, there were killers somewhere close this night. After seeing Lathea, there could be no doubt of that. Jennsen could never have imagined that anyone could be that perverted. She knew that if they caught her, they would eventually do those kinds of things to her, too, before she was allowed to die.

She felt her stomach roil with nausea at the vivid memory of what she had seen. She held back her tears, but she needed the air of outdoors and the solitude of the night.

As she and Sebastian wound their way through the crowd and toward that air, she bumped into a big man as they crossed paths. Stopped by the human wall, she looked up into the handsome face. She remembered him. He was the man they had seen on the road to Lathea's place, earlier.

He lifted his cap in greeting. 'Evening.' He grinned at her.

'Good evening,' she said. She told herself to smile, and make it believable, normal. She wasn't sure if she was doing a good job of it, but he seemed to find it convincing.

He didn't act as shy as she thought he had seemed before. Even the way he carried himself, his movements, were more sure. Maybe it was just that her smile was working as she had hoped.

'You two look like you could use a drink.' When Jennsen frowned, not knowing what the man meant, he gestured at her face, and then at Sebastian. 'Your noses are red with the cold. May I buy you an ale on this chill night?'

Before Sebastian could accept, which she feared he might, she said, 'Thank you, no. We have to go . . . to check on some business. But it was very kind of you to offer.' She made herself smile again. 'Thank you.'

The way the man stared at her made her nervous. The thing was, she found herself staring back into his blue eyes just as intently, and she didn't know why. Finally, she broke the gaze and, after a bow of her head to bid the big man a good night, made her way toward the door.

'Something about him look familiar?' she whispered to Sebastian.

'Yes. We saw him earlier, out on the streets, when we were on our way to Lathea's house.'

She looked back over her shoulder, peering between the milling throng. 'I guess maybe that's all it is, then.'

Before she went out the door, the man, as if he sensed her looking at him, turned. When their eyes met, and he smiled, it was as if no one else existed for either of them. His smile was polite, no more, but it made her go cold and tingly all over, the way the dead voice in her head sometimes did. There was something frighteningly familiar about the feeling she got looking at him, and the way he looked at her. Something about the look in his eyes reminded her of the voice.

It was as if she remembered him from a deep dream she had completely forgotten until that very instant. The sight of him, in her awake life, left her . . . shaken.

She was relieved to make it out into the empty night and be on their way. She bundled her cloak's hood close around her face, against the bitter wind, as they hurried across the snow and down the street. Her thighs stung with the cold. She was glad the stable was not far, but she knew that would be only a brief respite. It was going to be a long cold night, but there was no choice. Lord Rahl's men were too close. They had to run.

While Sebastian went to rouse the stableman, Jennsen squeezed through the barn door. A lantern hanging from a beam provided enough light for her to make her way to the pen where Betty was tied up for the night. The shelter from the wind, along with the warm bodies of the horses and the sweet smell of hay and dusty wood, made the stable a cozy haven.

Betty bleated plaintively when she saw Jennsen, as if she

112

feared she had been abandoned for all time. Betty's upright tail was a happy blur as Jennsen sank to one knee and hugged the goat's neck. Jennsen stood and stroked her hand along the silken ears, a touch Betty mooned over. As the horse in the next stall put her head over the rail to watch her stablemate, Betty stood on her hind legs, joyful to be reunited with her lifelong friend and eager to be closer.

Jennsen patted the wiry hair on Betty's fat middle. 'There's a good girl.' She urged the lovable goat down. 'Glad to see you, too, Betty.'

Jennsen, at ten, had been there for Betty's birth, and had named her. Betty had been Jennsen's only childhood friend, and had listened patiently to any number of worries and fears. When her short horns first began to come in, Betty had in turn rubbed and comforted her head against her faithful friend. Other than her worry of being abandoned by her lifelong companion, Betty's fears in life were few.

Jennsen groped through her pack until her fingers located a carrot for the ever-hungry goat. Betty danced about as she watched, then with her tail wagging in excitement accepted the treat. For reassurance, after the torment of an unusual separation, she rubbed the top of her head against Jennsen's thigh while chewing the carrot.

The horse in the next stall, her bright intelligent eyes watching, neighed softly and tossed her head. Jennsen smiled and gave the horse a carrot along with a rub on her white blaze.

Jennsen heard the jangle of tack as Sebastian returned, along with the stableman, both carrying saddles. Each man, in turn, laid his load over the rail of Betty's stall. Betty, still wary of Sebastian, backed a few steps.

'Sorry to lose the company of your friend, there,' the man said, indicating the goat, as he came up beside Sebastian.

Jennsen scratched Betty's ears. 'I appreciate her care.'

'Not much care. The night isn't over.' The man's gaze shifted from Sebastian to Jennsen. 'Why do you two want to leave in the night, anyway? And why do you want to buy horses? Especially at this hour?'

Jennsen froze in panic. She hadn't expected to have anyone question her and so she had no answer prepared.

'It's my mother,' Sebastian said in a confidential tone. He let out a convincing sigh. 'We just got word that she's taken ill. They don't know if she'll last until we can get there. I wouldn't be able to live with myself if I didn't . . . Well, we'll just have to make it in time, that's all.'

The man's suspicious expression softened with sympathy. Jennsen was surprised at how credible Sebastian sounded. She tried to imitate his look of concern.

'I understand, son. I'm sorry – I didn't realize. What can I do to help?'

'Which two horses can you sell us?' Sebastian asked.

The man scratched his whiskered chin. 'You going to leave the goat?'

Sebastian said 'Yes' at the same time Jennsen said 'No.'

The man's big dark eyes looked from one to the other.

'Betty won't slow us down,' Jennsen said. 'She can keep up. We'll make it to your mother just the same.'

Sebastian leaned a hip against the rail. 'I guess the goat will be leaving with us.'

With a sigh of disappointment, the man gestured to the horse Jennsen was scratching behind the ear. 'Rusty, here, gets on well with that goat of yours. I guess she'd be as good to sell as any of the others. You're a tall girl, so she would fit you well.'

Jennsen nodded her agreement. Betty, as if she had understood every word, bleated hers.

'I have a strong chestnut gelding that would better carry your weight,' he said to Sebastian. 'Pete's down the way, there, on the right. I'd be willing to let you have him along with Rusty, here.'

'Why's she called Rusty?' Jennsen asked.

'Dark as it is in here, you can't see so well, but she's a red roan, about as red as they come, all except that white blaze on her forehead.'

Rusty sniffed Betty. Betty licked Rusty's muzzle. The horse snorted softly in response.

'Rusty it is,' Sebastian said. 'And the other, then.'

The stableman scratched his stubble again and nodded to seal the agreement. 'I'll go get Pete.'

When they returned, Jennsen was pleased to see Pete nuzzle a greeting against Rusty's shoulder. With danger close on their heels, the last thing she wanted to have to worry about was handling bickering horses, but these two were friendly enough. The two men hurried at their work. A mother lay dying, after all.

Riding with a blanket on her lap promised to be a welcome relief from traveling on foot. A horse would help keep her warm and make the night ahead more tolerable. They had a long rope for Betty, who tended to get distracted by things along the way – edible things, especially.

Jennsen didn't know what Sebastian had to pay for the horses and tack, nor did she care. It was money that had come from her mother's killers, and would get them away. Getting away was all that mattered.

With a wave to the stableman as he held the big door open for them, they rode out into the frigid night. Both horses, apparently pleased at the prospect of activity, despite the hour, stepped briskly along the street. Rusty turned her head back, making sure that Betty, at their left, was keeping up.

It wasn't long before they passed the last building on their way out of town. Thin clouds raced before the rising moon, but left enough light to turn the snow-covered road to a silk ribbon between the thick darkness of the woods along each side.

Betty's rope suddenly jerked tight. Jennsen looked over her shoulder, expecting to see the goat trying to nibble at a young branch. Instead, Betty, her legs stiff, had her hooves dug in, resisting any progress.

'Betty,' Jennsen whispered harshly, 'come on! What's wrong with you? Come on.' The goat's weight was no match for the horse, so she was dragged down the snowy road against her will.

When Sebastian's horse stepped over, jostling Rusty, Jennsen saw the trouble. They were overtaking a man walking down the road. In his dark clothing, they hadn't seen him at the right side, against the dark of the trees. Knowing that horses didn't like surprises, Jennsen patted Rusty's neck to assure her that the man wasn't anything to be frightened of. Betty, though, remained unconvinced, and used all the rope available to swing a wide arc.

Jennsen saw then that it was the big blond man from the inn, the man who had offered to buy them a drink – the man she thought, for some reason, should dwell only in her dream life rather than in her waking life.

Jennsen kept an eye on the man as they passed him. As cold as she was, it felt as if a door opened into the infinitely colder eternal night of the underworld.

Sebastian and the stranger exchanged a brief greeting in passing. Once beyond the man, Betty scampered ahead, pulling at her rope, eager to put distance between her and the man.

'*Grushdeva du kalt misht.*'

Jennsen, her breath caught fast at the end of a gasp, turned to stare wide-eyed at the man walking down the road behind. It sounded like it had been he who'd spoken the words. That was impossible; those were the strange words from inside her head.

Sebastian made no notice of it, so she didn't say anything lest he think her crazy.

With Betty's agreement, Jennsen urged her horse to pick up the pace.

Just before they rounded a bend and were away, Jennsen looked back one last time. In the moonlight she saw the man grinning at her.

Chapter 13

Oba was throwing a hay bale down from the loft when he heard his mother's voice.

'Oba! Where are you? Get down here!'

Oba scurried down the ladder. He brushed hay from himself as he straightened before her waiting scowl.

'What is it, Mama?'

'Where's my medicine? And your cure?' Her glare swept across the floor. 'I see you still haven't gotten the mess out of the barn. I didn't hear you come home last night. What took you so long? Look at that stanchion rail! Haven't you fixed that, yet? What have you been doing all this time? Do I have to tell you every little thing?'

Oba wasn't sure which question he was supposed to answer first. She always did that to him, confused him before he could answer her. When he faltered, she would then insult and ridicule him. After all he had learned the night before, and all that had happened, he thought that he might feel more confident when he faced his mother.

In the light of day, standing back in the barn, with his mother gathered before him like a thunderhead, he felt much the same as he always did before her storming onslaught, ashamed, small, worthless. He had felt big when he came home. Important. Now he felt as if he were shrinking. Her words shriveled him.

'Well, I was—'

'You was dawdling! That's what you was doing – dawdling! Here I am waiting for my medicine, my knees aching me, and

117

my son Oba the oaf is kicking a rock down the road, forgetting what I sent him for.'

'I didn't forget—'

'Then where's my medicine? Where is it?'

'Mama, I didn't get it—'

'I knew it! I knew you was spending the money I gave you. I worked my fingers to the bone at spinning to earn that, and you go wasting it on women! Whoring! That's what you was doing, whoring!'

'No, Mama, I didn't waste it on women.'

'Then where's my medicine! Why didn't you get it like I told you to!'

'I couldn't because—'

'You mean you wouldn't, you worthless oaf! You only had to go to Lathea's—'

'Lathea is dead.'

There, he'd said it. It was out and in the light of day.

His mother's mouth hung open, but no words rained out. He had never seen her go silent like that before, seen her so shocked that her jaw just hung. He liked it.

Oba fished a coin from his pocket, one he had set aside to return so she wouldn't think he'd spent her money. Amid the drama of such a rare silence, he handed her the coin.

'Dead . . . Lathea?' She stared at the coin in her palm. 'What do you mean, dead? She went ill?'

Oba shook his head, feeling his confidence build as he thought about what he had done to Lathea, how he'd handled the troublesome sorceress.

'No, Mama. Her house burned down. She was killed in the fire.'

'Her house burned . . .' His mother's brow drew together. 'How do you know she died? Lathea isn't likely to be caught unawares by a fire. The woman is a sorceress.'

Oba shrugged. 'Well, all I know is that when I went to town, I heard a ruckus. People were running toward her house. We all found the place ablaze. A big crowd gathered around, but the fire was so hot that there was no chance of saving the place.'

That last part was, to a degree, true. He had started to leave

118

town, headed home, because he figured that if no one had spotted the fire, maybe they wouldn't until morning. He didn't want to be the one to start yelling 'fire.' In light of history, that might look suspicious, especially to his mother. She was a suspicious woman – one of her many peevish traits. Oba had planned on simply telling his mother the story of what he knew was bound to happen anyway, the blazing ruins, the charred body found.

But as he had been walking home after his visit to the inn, not long after that Jennsen woman and the man with her, Sebastian, passed by leaving town on their journey to find Althea, he heard people yelling that there was a fire down at Lathea's place. Oba ran down the long dark road with the rest of the people, toward the orange glow off in the trees. He was just a bystander, same as everyone else. There was no reason to suspect him of anything.

'Maybe Lathea escaped the flames.' His mother sounded more like she was trying to convince herself than him.

Oba shook his head. 'I stayed, hoping the same as you, Mama. I knew you'd want me to help her if she was hurt. I stayed to do what I could. That's why I was so late.'

That, too, was partly true; he had stayed, along with the crowd, watching the fire, listening to the talk. He had savored the crowd's anticipation. The gossip. The speculation.

'She's a sorceress. Fire isn't likely to catch such a woman.'

His mother was starting to sound suspicious. Oba had figured on this. He leaned a little toward her.

'When the fire burned out enough, some of us men threw snow down so we could get in over the smoking rubble. Inside, we found Lathea's bones.'

Oba pulled a blackened finger bone from his pocket. He held it out, offering it to his mother. She stared down at the grim evidence, but folded her arms without taking it. Pleased with the effect it had, Oba finally returned the treasure to his pocket.

'She was in the middle of the room, with one hand lifted above her head, like she had tried to make it to the door but was overcome by the smoke. The men said that a fire's smoke was what put folks down, and then the fire got at them. That must have been what happened to Lathea. The smoke got her. Then, laying there on the floor, reaching toward the door, the fire burned her to death.'

His mother glared at him, her mean little mouth all pinched up, but silent. For once, she had no words. He found her glare, though, was just as bad. In the daggers of that glare, he could tell that she was thinking he was no good. Her bastard boy.

Darken Rahl's bastard son. Almost royalty.

Her arms slipped from their sullen knot as she turned away. 'I have to get back to my spinning for Mr. Tuchmann. You get this mess scooped off the floor, you hear?'

'I will, Mama.'

'And you had better get that stanchion fixed before I come back and see that you've been loafing away the day.'

For several days Oba worked at the frozen muck on the floor, but made little headway. The weather had stayed bitterly cold, so the frozen mound, if anything, had only hardened. His efforts at wearing it down seemed interminable, like trying to chip away granite ledge. Or his mother's stony disposition.

He had his other chores, of course, and he couldn't let them go. He had fixed the stanchion and a broken hinge on the barn door. The animals had to be attended to, along with a hundred other small things.

In his head, as he worked, he planned the construction of their fireplace. He would use the back wall between the house and barn, since it was already existing. Mentally, he stacked stones against it, creating the shape of the firebox. He already had his eye on a long stone to use for the lintel. He would mortar everything all together properly. When Oba set his mind to doing something, he put his all into it. He didn't do any job he started just halfway.

In his mind's eye, he pictured how surprised and happy his mother would be when she saw what he'd built them. She would recognize his worth, then. She would finally acknowledge his value. But he had other work to do before he could begin to build a fireplace.

One job, in particular, loomed before him. The surface of the mound of frozen muck in the barn showed the scars of the battle.

It was now pocked with holes, places where he had been able to find a weakness, a place with air or dry straw underneath that had allowed him to break out a chunk. Each time a piece went 'pop' and came lose, he was sure that he had at last found a way into the formidable tomb of ice, but each time had been a false hope. Chipping away with the scoop shovel was slow going, but Oba was not a quitter.

The worry had come to him that perhaps a man of his importance should not be wasting his time on such menial labor. Frozen manure hardly seemed the province of a man who was in all likelihood something akin to a prince. At the least, he now knew he was an important man. A man with Rahl blood in his veins. A direct descendant – the son – of the man who had ruled D'Hara, Darken Rahl. There probably wasn't a single person who had not heard of Darken Rahl. Oba's father.

Sooner or later, he would confront his mother with the truth she had been keeping from him – the truth of the man he really was. He just couldn't figure how to do it without her discovering that Lathea had spilled the news before she spilled her blood.

Winded from a particularly spirited attack on the frozen mound, Oba rested his forearms on the shovel's handle while he caught his breath. Despite the cold, sweat trickled down from his matted blond hair.

'Oba the oaf,' said his mother as she strode into the barn. 'Standing around, doing nothing, thinking nothing, worth nothing. That's you, isn't it? Oba the oaf?'

She glided to a stop, her mean little mouth all puckered up as she peered down her nose at him.

'Mama. I was just catching my breath.' He pointed around at the chips of ice littering the floor, evidence of his strenuous efforts. 'I've been working at it, Mama. I have.'

She didn't look. She was glaring at him. He waited, knowing she had something more on her mind than the mound of frozen muck. He always knew when she was on a mission to trouble him, to make him feel like the muck he stood in. From the dark crevices and hidey-holes around the barn, the rats watched with their little black rat eyes.

With her critical gaze locked on him, his mother held out a

coin. She held it between her thumb and first finger, not simply to convey the coin itself, but its importance.

Oba was a little bewildered. Lathea was dead. There was no other sorceress anywhere close, none that he knew of, anyway, who could provide his mother's medicine – or his cure. He obediently turned his palm up, anyway.

'Look at it,' she commanded, dropping the coin into his hand.

Oba held it out to the light of the doorway, scrutinizing it with care. He knew she expected him to find something – what, he didn't know. He turned it over as he cautiously stole a glance at her. He carefully inspected the other side, but still saw nothing out of the ordinary.

'Yes, Mama?'

'Notice anything unusual about it, Oba?'

'No, Mama.'

'It doesn't have a scratch along the edge.'

Oba puzzled that over for a moment, then looked again at the coin, this time carefully inspecting the edge.

'No, Mama.'

'That's the coin you gave back to me.'

Oba nodded, having no reason to doubt her. 'Yes, Mama. The coin you gave me for Lathea. But I told you, Lathea died in the fire, so I couldn't buy your medicine. That's why I gave you your coin back.'

Her hot glare was murderous, but her voice was arrestingly cool and collected. 'It isn't the same coin, Oba.'

Oba grinned. 'Sure it is, Mama.'

'The coin I gave you had a mark on the edge. A mark I put there.'

Oba's grin withered as his mind raced. He tried to think of what to say – what he could say – that she would believe. He couldn't contend that he put the coin in a pocket and then pulled out a different coin when he gave it back to her, because he never had any money of his own. She knew very well that he didn't have any money; she wouldn't allow it. She thought he was no good, and that he might waste it.

But he had money, now. He had all the money from Lathea – a fortune. He remembered hurriedly gathering up all the coins that

122

had spilled from Lathea's pocket, including the coin he'd only just given her. When he later set aside a coin to return to his mother, he hadn't known that she had marked the one she'd given him. Oba had the bad luck of returning a different coin than the one she had originally given him.

'But, Mama . . . are you sure? Maybe you only thought you marked the coin. Maybe you forgot.'

She slowly shook her head. 'No. I marked it so that if you spent it on drinking or on women I would know because I could go look for it if I had to, and see what you had done.'

The conniving bitch. She didn't even trust her own son. What kind of mother was she, anyway?

What proof did she have other than a missing, tiny scratch on the edge of a coin? None. The woman was a lunatic.

'But, Mama, you must be wrong. I don't have any money – you know I don't. Where would I get a different coin?'

'That's what I'd like to know.' Her eyes were frightening. He could hardly breathe under their blistering scrutiny. Her voice, though, remained composed. 'I told you to buy medicine with that money.'

'How could I? Lathea died. I gave you your coin back.'

She looked so broad and powerful standing there before him, like an avenging spirit in the flesh come to speak for the dead. Maybe Lathea's spirit had returned to tell on him. He hadn't considered that possibility. That would be just like the troublesome sorceress. She was sneaky. This might be just what she had done, intent on denying him his importance, his due prestige.

'Do you know why I named you "Oba"?'

'No, Mama.'

'It's an ancient D'Haran name. Did you know that, Oba?'

'No, Mama.' His curiosity got the best of him. 'What does it mean?'

'It means two things. Servant, and king. I named you "Oba," hoping you might someday be a king, and if not, then you would at least be a servant of the Creator. Fools are rarely made kings. You will never be a king. That was just a silly dream of a new mother. That leaves "servant." Who do you serve, Oba?'

Oba knew very well who he served. In so doing, he had become invincible.

'Where did you get this coin, Oba?'

'I told you, Mama, I couldn't get your medicine because Lathea had died in the fire at her place. Maybe the mark on your coin rubbed off against something in my pocket.'

She seemed to consider his words. 'Are you sure, Oba?'

Oba nodded, hoping that maybe he was at last turning her mind away from the coin mix-up. 'Of course, Mama. Lathea died. That's why I gave you your coin back. I couldn't get your medicine.'

His mother lifted an eyebrow. 'Really, Oba?'

She slowly drew her hand from the pocket of her dress. He couldn't see what it was she had, but he was relieved that he was finally bringing her around.

'That's right, Mama. Lathea was dead.' He found he liked saying that.

'Really, Oba? You couldn't get the medicine? You wouldn't lie to your mother, would you, Oba?'

He shook his head emphatically. 'No, Mama.'

'Then what's this?' She turned over her hand and held out the bottle of medicine Lathea had given him before he had dealt with her. 'I found this in your jacket pocket, Oba.'

Oba stared at the cursed bottle, at the troublesome sorceress's revenge. He should have killed the woman right off, before she gave him the telltale bottle of medicine. He had completely forgotten that he had put it in a pocket of his jacket, intending to toss it in the woods on his way home that night. What with all the important new things he had been learning, he had completely forgotten about the cursed bottle of medicine.

'Well, I think ... I think it must be an old bottle—'

'And old bottle? It's full!' Her razor-edged voice was back. 'How did you manage to get a bottle of medicine from a woman who was dead – in her house that had already burned down? How, Oba? And how is it that you gave me back a different coin than the one I gave you to pay with? How!' She took a step closer. 'How, Oba?'

Oba backed a step. He couldn't pull his eyes away from the

cursed cure. He couldn't look up into his mother's fierce eyes. If he did, he just knew she would wither him to tears under her deadly glare.

'Well, I . . .'

'Well I what, Oba? Well I what, you filthy bastard boy? You worthless lazy lying bastard boy. You wretched, scheming, vile bastard boy, Oba Schalk.'

Oba's eyes turned up. He was right, she had him fixed in her deadly glare.

But he had become invincible.

'Oba Rahl,' he said.

She didn't flinch. He realized then that she had been goading him into admitting he knew. It was all part of her scheme. That name, Rahl, screamed out how he had come to know it, betraying everything to his mother. Oba stood frozen, his mind in a wild state of turmoil, like a rat with a foot on his tail.

'The spirits curse me,' she said under her breath, 'I should have done what Lathea always told me. I should have spared us all. You killed her. You loathsome bastard. You contemptible lying—'

Quick as a fox, Oba whipped the shovel around, putting all his weight and strength behind the swing. The steel shovel rang like a bell against her skull.

She dropped like a sack of grain pushed out of the loft – whump.

Oba rapidly retreated a step, fearful she might skitter toward him, spiderlike, and with her mean little mouth bite him on the ankle. He was positive that she was fully capable of it. The conniving bitch.

Lightning quick, he darted forward and whacked her again with the shovel, right on the same place on her broad forehead, then retreated out of range of her teeth, before she could bite him like a spider. He often thought of her as a spider. A black widow.

The ring of steel on skull hung in the otherwise still air of the barn, slowly, slowly, slowly dying away. Silence, like a heavy shroud, settled around him.

Oba stood poised, shovel cocked back over his shoulder, ready to swing again. He watched her carefully. Nearly clear, pinkish fluid leaked from both her ears, out across the frozen muck.

In a frenzy of fear and rage, he ran forward and swung the shovel at her head, over and over. The ringing blows of steel on bone echoed around the barn, creating one long clangorous din. The rats, watching with their little black rat eyes, scurried for their holes.

Oba staggered back, gasping for air after the violent effort of silencing her. He panted as he watched her still form sprawled atop the mound of frozen muck. Her arms were spread out wide to each side, as if asking for a hug. The sneaky bitch. She might be up to something. Trying to make amends, probably. Offering a hug, as if that could make up for the times he'd spent in the pen.

Her face looked different. She had an odd expression. He tiptoed closer for a look. Her skull was all misshapen, like a ripe melon broken on the ground.

This was so new that he couldn't gather his thoughts.

Mama, her melon head, all broke open.

For good measure, he whacked her three more times, quick as he could, then retreated to a safe distance, shovel at the ready, should she suddenly spring up to start yelling at him. That would be just like her. Sneaky. The woman was a lunatic.

The barn remained silent. He saw his breath puffing out in the cold air. No breath came from his mother. Her chest was still. The crimson pool around her head oozed down the muck mound. Some of the holes he'd chopped filled with the runny contents of her curious melon head all broken open on the ground.

Oba began to feel more confident, then, that his mother was not going to say hateful things to him anymore. His mother, not being too smart, had probably gone along with Lathea's nagging, and had been talked into hating him, her only son. The two women had ruled his life. He had been nothing but the helpless servant of the two harpies.

Fortunately, he had finally become invincible and had rescued himself from them both.

'Do you want to know who I serve, Mama? I serve the voice that made me invincible. The voice that rid me of you!'

His mother had nothing more to say. At long last, she had nothing more to say.

Then, Oba grinned.

He pulled out his knife. He was a new man. A man who pursued intellectual interests when they arose. He thought he should have a look at what other odd and curious things might be found inside his lunatic mother.

Oba liked to learn new things.

Oba was eating a nice lunch of eggs cooked in the hearth he had started to build for himself, when he heard a wagon rumbling into the yard. It had been over a week since his sneaky mother had opened her mean little mouth for the last time.

Oba went to the door, opened it a crack, and stood eating his eggs as he peered out to see the rear of a wagon pulled up close by. A man climbed down.

It was Mr. Tuchmann, who regularly brought wool. Oba's mother was a spinster who made thread for Mr. Tuchmann. He used the thread on his loom. With so many new things demanding his attention lately, Oba had forgotten all about Mr. Tuchmann. Oba glanced over to the corner to see how much thread his mother had ready. Not much. Bales of wool sat to the side, waiting to be spun into thread. The least his mother could have done would be to attend to her work before she started in causing trouble.

Oba didn't know what to do. When he looked back to the doorway, Mr. Tuchmann was standing right there, looking in. He was a tall man, thin, with a big nose and ears. His hair was graying and as curly as the wool he dealt in. He was recently widowed. Oba knew that his mother liked Mr. Tuchmann. Maybe he could have leached some of the venom from her fangs. Softened her a bit. It was an interesting theory to contemplate.

'Afternoon, Oba.' His eyes, eyes that Oba had always found curiously liquid, were peering in the crack, searching the house. 'Is your mother about?'

Oba, feeling a little violated by the man's roving eyes, stood holding the plate of eggs, trying to think what to do, what to say. Mr. Tuchmann's gaze settled on the fireplace.

Oba, standing ill at ease behind the door, reminded himself that he was a new man. An important man. Important men weren't unsure of themselves. Important men seized the moment, and created their own greatness.

'Mama?' Oba set down his plate as he glanced to the fireplace. 'Oh, she's about, somewhere.'

Wool-headed Mr. Tuchmann stared stone-faced at Oba's grin for a time.

'You heard about Lathea? What they found at her place?'

Oba thought the man had a mouth kind of like his mother had. Mean. Sneaky.

'Lathea?' Oba sucked at a piece of egg stuck between his teeth. 'She's dead. What could they find?'

'More precisely, what they didn't find, I guess you could say. Money. Lathea had money, everyone knew that. But they found none in her house.'

Oba shrugged. 'Must have burned up. Melted.'

Mr. Tuchmann grunted his skepticism. 'Maybe. Maybe not. Some folks say maybe it was gone before the fire started.'

Oba felt indignant that people just couldn't let a thing go. Didn't they have their own business to mind? Why couldn't they leave well enough alone? They should rejoice that the sorceress was out of their lives and leave it at that. They had to keep picking at it, though. Peck, peck, peck, like a gaggle of geese at the grain. Busybodies, that's what they were.

'I'll tell Mama you were here.'

'I need the thread she's spun. I have another load of wool for her. I need to be on my way. Got other people waiting.'

The man had a whole bevy of women who spun wool for him. Didn't he ever give his poor spinsters a chance to catch their breath?

'Well, I'm afraid that Mama hasn't had time to ...'

Mr. Tuchmann was staring at the fireplace again, only more intently, this time. The look on his face was more than curious; it bordered on anger. The man, accustomed to ordering people around and always more bold than Oba felt comfortable around, stepped through the door and into the house, to the center of the room, still staring at the fireplace. His arm rose, pointing.

'What's . . . what's that? Dear Creator . . .'

Oba looked where he was pointing – at the new fireplace being built against the stone wall that separated the house from the barn. Oba thought his work was quite well done – sturdy and straight. He had studied other fireplaces and learned how they were done. Even though the chimney wasn't built all the way up yet, he was using it. He had put it to good advantage.

Oba saw then, what Mr. Tuchmann was really pointing at. Mama's jawbone.

Well, wasn't this just something. Oba hadn't expected visitors, especially snoopy visitors. What gave this man the right to poke his nose into other people's houses, just because they spun wool for him?

Mr. Tuchmann started backing toward the door. Oba knew that Mr. Tuchmann would talk about what he'd seen. The man was a gossip, already flapping his tongue to anyone who would listen about Lathea's missing money – which, after all, was really Oba's, when you considered the lifetime of trouble he had endured to earn it. Who were all these people coming out of the woodwork to stick up for the troublesome sorceress?

When Mr. Tuchmann started blabbing about what he saw in the fireplace, there were sure to be questions. Everyone would have to stick their noses in it and want to know whose it was. They would probably start fretting over his mother, now, just like they were doing over the sorceress.

Oba, a new man, a man of action, could hardly let that happen. Oba was an important man, he'd learned. Rahl blood coursed through his veins, after all. Important men acted – handled problems as they arose. Quickly. Efficiently. Decisively.

Oba seized Mr. Tuchmann by the back of his neck, halting his retreat. The man struggled fiercely. He was tall and wiry, but he was no match for Oba's strength or speed.

With a grunt of effort, Oba plunged his knife up into Mr. Tuchmann's middle. The man's mouth opened wide. His eyes, always so liquid, always so curious, went wide as well, filled now with a look of terror.

Oba followed the obnoxious Mr. Tuchmann to the ground. They had work to do. Oba was never afraid of hard work. First, there was the struggling wool-headed snoop to deal with. Then, there was the matter of his wagon. People would probably come looking for him. Oba's life was getting complicated.

Mr. Tuchmann called for help. Oba rammed his knife up into the soft part under Mr. Tuchmann's chin. Oba leaned over him, watched the man struggle, knowing he was going to die.

Oba had nothing against Mr. Tuchmann, really – even though the man was impertinent and bossy. This was all that troublesome sorceress's fault. She was still making Oba's life difficult. She had probably sent some message to his mother and then to Mr. Tuchmann from beyond in the underworld. The bitch. Then, his mother had to get all sneaky and suspicious. And now this irksome pest, Mr. Tuchmann. They were like a swarm of locusts, come from nowhere to plague him.

It was because he was important, he knew.

It was probably time for changes. Oba couldn't stay around and keep having people who knew him pestering him with questions. He was too important to be in this little nothing of a place, anyway.

Mr. Tuchmann grunted in his futile effort to escape. It was time for the unhappy widower to join Oba's lunatic mother and the troublesome sorceress with the Keeper of the underworld, the world of the dead.

And then, the time had come for Oba to take up his important life as a new man and to move on to better places.

Just as the realization struck him that he would never again have to go in the barn and see the mound of frozen muck that he hadn't been able to dislodge with the scoop shovel, despite the ranting insistence of his lunatic mother, it occurred to him that if he had used the pickaxe, that would have made quick work of it.

Well, wasn't that just something.

Chapter 14

With an easy but flawlessly precise turn of his wrist, Friedrich Gilder lifted a leaf of gold on the fine hairs of his brush and laid it over. The gold, light enough to float on the gentlest breath of air, drew down onto the wet gesso as if by magic. Leaning over his workbench in concentration, Friedrich used a sheep's-wool pad to carefully rub the freshly gilded surface of the small stylized carving of a bird, checking for any flaws.

Outside, the rain occasionally tink-tink-tinked against the window. Though midday, when the prowling clouds passed bearing fits of rain, it darkened as if to dusk.

From the back room where he worked, Friedrich glanced up, looking out through the doorway into the main room, watching the familiar movements of his wife casting her stones over the Grace. Many years ago he had gilded the lines of her Grace, the eight-sided star within a circle within a square within another circle – after she had properly drawn it all out, of course. The Grace would have been useless had he drawn it. A Grace, to be real, had to be drawn by one with the gift.

He enjoyed doing whatever he could to make the things in her life a little more beautiful. She was what made his life beautiful. He thought that her smile had been gilded by the Creator Himself.

Friedrich saw, too, the woman who had ventured to their home for a telling lean forward expectantly, absorbed in watching the fall of her fate.

If they could really see such things, people would not come to Althea for a telling, yet they always watched intently as the

131

stones rolled from his wife's long slender fingers and out across the board upon which was drawn the Grace.

This woman, middle-aged and widowed, was a pleasant sort, and had been to see Althea twice before, but that had been several years back. As he had concentrated on his own work, he'd absently heard her tell Althea about her several grown children who were married and lived close to her, and that her first grandchild was on the way. Now, though, it was the drop of stones, not a child, that held the woman's interest.

'Again?' she asked. It was not a question so much as astonishment. 'They did it again.'

Althea said nothing. Friedrich burnished the freshly laid gold as he listened to the familiar sounds of his wife gathering up her stones from the board.

'Do they do that, often?' the woman asked, her wide eyes turning from the Grace to Althea's face. Althea didn't answer. The woman rubbed her knuckles so hard that Friedrich thought the skin might come off. 'What does it mean?'

'Hush,' Althea murmured as she rattled the stones.

Friedrich had never heard his wife be so uncommunicative with a customer. The stones clacking in Althea's loose fist seemed to have an urgency to their bony knock. The woman rubbed her knuckles, awaiting her destiny.

Again, the seven stones rolled out across the board, come to divulge the holy secrets of the fates.

From where he sat, Friedrich couldn't see the stones fall, but he could hear the familiar sound of their uneven shapes rolling across the board. After all these years, he rarely watched Althea practice her profession, that is, watched the stones themselves. He did, though, despite the years, savor watching Althea. As he looked out, seeing the side of her strong jaw, her hair still mostly a golden sweep down past her jaw, falling like sunlight over her shoulder, he smiled.

The woman gasped. 'Again!' As if to make the woman's point, thunder in the distance rolled over the house. 'Mistress Althea, what could it mean?' Her voice carried the unmistakable timbre of apprehension.

Althea, on her pillow on the floor, leaning on one arm, her

withered legs out to the side, used the arm against the floor to straighten herself. She finally looked at the woman.

'It means, Margery, that you are a woman of strong spirit—'

'That's one of those two stones? Me? A strong spirit?'

'That's right,' Althea confirmed with a nod.

'And the other, then? It can't be good. Not there. It can only mean the worst.'

'I was about to tell you, that the other stone, which follows with each throw, is also a strong spirit. A man of strong spirit.'

Margery peered again at the stones on the board. She rubbed her knuckles. 'But, but they both . . .' She gestured. 'They both keep going . . . out there. To beyond the outer circle. To the underworld.' Her troubled eyes searched Althea's face.

Althea pulled on her knees, drawing her legs before herself to cross them. Though her legs were withered and nearly useless, crossing them before her pillow on the floor helped her sit up straight.

'No, no, my dear. Not at all. Don't you see? This is good. Both strong spirits going through life together, and together ever after. It's the best possible outcome of a telling.'

Margery cast another worried look at the board. 'Really? Really, Mistress Althea? You think it's good, then, that they keep . . . doing that?'

'Of course, Margery. Good it is. Two strong spirits joining.'

Margery touched a finger to her lower lip as she peered up at Althea. 'Who is it then? Who is this mystery man I'm to meet?'

Althea shrugged. 'Too soon to tell. But the stones say you will meet a man' – she made a show of putting her first and second fingers tight together – 'and you two will be fast with each other. Congratulations, Margery. It looks as if you are close to finding the happiness you seek.'

'When? How soon?'

Again, Althea shrugged. 'Too soon to tell. The stones only say "will," not "when." Maybe tomorrow, maybe next year. But the important thing is that you are near to meeting a man who will be good with you, Margery. You must now keep your eyes open. Don't hide yourself away in your house, or you will miss him.'

'But if the stones say—'

'The stones say he is strong and he is open to you, but they don't fix it sure. That's up to you and the man. Keep yourself open to him when he comes into your life, or he may pass without seeing you.'

'I will, Mistress Althea.' The conviction in her voice strengthened. 'I will. I'll stay prepared so when he happens into my life, I'll see him, and he'll see me, just as the stones foretell.'

'Good.'

The woman fished around in the leather purse hanging from her belt until she found a coin. She handed it over eagerly, pleased with the outcome of her telling.

Friedrich had watched Althea give tellings for nearly four decades. In all that time, he had never before seen her lie to someone.

The woman stood, holding out her hand. 'May I help you, Mistress Althea?'

'Thank you, my dear, but Friedrich will help me, later. I want to stay with my board for now.'

The woman smiled, perhaps daydreaming of the new life waiting for her. 'Well, then, I'd best be on my way before it gets any later in the day . . . before nightfall. And then it's a long ride back.' She leaned to the side and waved through the doorway. 'Good day, Master Friedrich.'

The rain rattled against the window in earnest. The sky, he noticed, had darkened, casting a gray gloom over their place in the swamp. Rising from his bench, Friedrich waved. 'Let me see you to the door, Margery. You do have someone waiting to take you back, don't you?'

'My son-in-law is up at the rim of the canyon, where the path starts down in, waiting with our horses.' She paused in the doorway and gestured to his work on the bench. 'That's a fine piece you've made.'

Friedrich smiled. 'I hope to find a customer at the palace who thinks so, too.'

'You will, you will. You do fine work. Everyone says so. Those who own a piece of your work count themselves as lucky.'

Margery curtsied happily to Althea, thanking her again, before

134

retrieving her lamb's-skin cloak from the hook by the door. She smiled out at the angry sky and donned the cloak, drawing its hood over her head, eager to be on her way to find her new man. It would be a long journey back. Before closing the door, Friedrich warned Margery to be absolutely certain to stay on the path and to watch her step up out of the canyon. She said she remembered the instructions and promised to follow them with care.

He watched her hurry off, disappearing into the shadows and mist, before closing the door tight against the foul weather. Silence settled once more inside the house. Outside, thunder rumbled in a deep voice, as if in discontent.

Friedrich shuffled up behind his wife. 'Here, let me help you to your chair.'

Althea had gathered up her stones. Once again, they rattled in her hand like the bones of spirits. As considerate as she always was, it was unlike her not to acknowledge him when he spoke. It was even more unlike her to cast her stones again after a customer left. Casting her stones for a telling called upon her gift in ways he could not fully understand, but he did understand how it fatigued her. Casting her stones for a telling drew down her strength so that it left her detached from the world and wanting anything but to cast them again for a while.

Now, though, she was in the spell of some tacit need.

She turned her wrist and opened her hand, casting the stones at her board as easily, as gracefully, as he handled his ethereal leaves of gold. Smooth, dark, irregular-shaped stones rolled forth, bouncing on the board, tumbling across the gilded Grace.

In their life together, Friedrich had seen her cast her stones tens of thousands of times. There were times when, much like her customers, he had tried to discern a pattern in the fall of the stones. He never could.

Althea always did.

She saw meaning no mere mortal could see. She saw in the random fall of the stones some obscure omen only a sorceress could decipher. Patterns of magic.

There was no pattern expressed through the act of the throw; it was the fall of the stones that was touched by powers he dared not consider, powers that spoke only to the sorceress through her gift. In that random motif of disorder, she could read the flow of powers through the world of life, and even, he feared, the world of the dead, although she never spoke of it. Despite how close they were in body and soul, this was one thing they could not share in their life together.

This time, as the stones rolled and wobbled across the board, one stopped in the exact center. Two stopped on opposite corners of the square where it touched the outer circle. Two ended up at opposite points where the square and the inner circle touched. The final two stones came to rest beyond the outer circle, which represented the underworld.

Lightning flashed, and seconds later thunder clapped.

Friedrich stared in disbelief. He wondered what the odds were of the stones coming to the end of their tumble at these specific points on the Grace. He had never before seen them end in any discernible pattern.

Althea, too, was staring at her board.

'Have you ever seen anything like that before?' he asked.

'I'm afraid so,' she said under her breath as she raked the stones up with her graceful fingers.

'Really?' He was sure he would have recalled such an unlikely event, such a startling orderliness. 'When was that?'

She rattled the stones in her loose fist. 'The four previous throws. That casting made five, all the same, each individual stone coming to rest in the identical place it had before.'

Again, she cast the stones at the board. At the same time, the sky seemed to open, letting rain roar down on the roof. The noise reverberated through the house. Involuntarily, he glanced toward the ceiling briefly before watching along with Althea as the stones rolled and bounced across the board.

The first stone rolled to a halt in the exact center of the Grace. Lightning flashed. The other stones, rolling in what looked to be a completely natural manner, came to rest in what appeared a perfectly normal way, except that they stopped in the exact same places they had before.

'Six,' Althea said under her breath. Thunder boomed.

Friedrich didn't know if she was speaking to him, or to herself.

'But the first four throws were for that woman, Margery. You were casting them for her. This is for her telling.'

Even to himself, it sounded more like a plea than reason.

'Margery came for a telling,' Althea said. 'That does not mean the stones chose to give her one. The stones have decided that this telling is for me.'

'What does it mean, then?'

'Nothing,' she said. 'Not yet, anyway. At this point it is only potential – a thunderhead on the horizon. The stones may yet say this storm is to pass us by.'

Watching as she gathered up her stones, he was overcome with a sense of dread. 'Enough of this – you need to rest. Why don't you let me help you up, now, Althea? I'll make you something to eat.' He watched her pluck the last stone, the one in the center, off the board. 'Leave your stones for now. I'll make you some nice hot tea.'

He never before thought of the stones as anything sinister. Now he felt as if they were somehow inviting menace into their lives.

He didn't want her to cast the stones again.

He sank down beside her. 'Althea—'

'Hush, Friedrich.' She spoke the words in a flat tone, not in anger or reproach, but simple necessity. The rain drummed against the roof with rabid intensity. Water cascading off the eaves roared. Darkness out the windows faltered in fits of lightning.

He listened to the stones rattle, like the bones of the dead speaking to her. For the first time in their life together, he felt a kind of defensive hatred for the seven stones she held, as if they were some lover come to steal her away from him.

From her seat atop her gold and red pillow on the floor, Althea cast the stones down onto the Grace.

As they tumbled across the board, he watched with resignation as they came to rest, natural as could be, in the exact same places. He would have been surprised only if they had fallen differently.

'Seven,' she whispered. 'Seven times seven stones.'

Thunder rumbled in a deep resonant tone, like the voice of discontent of spirits in the underworld.

Friedrich rested a hand on his wife's shoulder. A presence had come into their home – invaded their lives. He couldn't see it, but he knew it was there. He felt a great weariness, as if all his years had come at once to weigh him down, making him feel very old. He wondered if this was in some small way what she felt all the time when she became so weary from casting a telling. He shuddered to contemplate always swimming in such emotionally turbulent waters. His world, his work of gilding, seemed so simple, so blissful, in its ignorance of the swirl of tempestuous forces all around.

The worst of it, though, was that he could not protect her from this unseen threat. In this, he was helpless.

'Althea, what does it mean?'

She hadn't moved. She was staring at the smooth dark stones setting on her Grace.

'One who hears the voices is coming.'

Lightning ignited in a blinding angry flash, illuminating the room with white incandescence. The scintillating contrast between bright light and smothering shadow was dizzying. The intense strike flickered on as thunder crashed with a boom that shook the ground. A ripping crash followed on its heels, the clamor adding a confusion of sound to match the flashing of light.

Friedrich swallowed. 'Do you know which one?'

She reached up and patted his hand resting on her shoulder. 'Tea, you say? The rain gives me a chill. I'd like some tea.'

He looked from the crinkled smile showing in her eyes to the stones on the Grace. For whatever reason, she wasn't going to answer that question, for now. He asked another, instead.

'Why did your stones fall like that, Althea? What does something like that mean?'

Lightning struck nearby. The crack of thunder felt as if it split air made of solid stone. Fists of rain beat against the window in petulant fits.

Althea finally looked away from the window, from Creation's

fury, and turned back to the board. She reached out and placed her forefinger on the stone in the center.

'The Creator?' he guessed aloud before she could name it.

She shook her head. 'Lord Rahl.'

'But, the star in the center represents the Creator – His gift.'

'It does, in the Grace. But you must not forget, this is a telling. This is different. A telling only uses the Grace, and in this telling the stone in the center represents the one with His gift.'

'Then it could be anyone,' Friedrich said. 'Anyone with the gift.'

'No. The lines coming from the eight points of the star represent the gift as it passes through life, through the veil between the worlds, and beyond the outer circle into the underworld. Thus it represents the gift in a sense that it conveys with no other person: the gift for magic of both worlds, the world of life, and the world of the dead: Additive and Subtractive. This stone in the center touches both.'

He glanced back at the stone in the center of the Grace. 'But why would that mean Lord Rahl?'

'Because he is the only one born in three thousand years with both aspects of the gift. In all that time, until he came into his gift, no stone I have cast has ever landed in that place. None could.

'What has it been? Two years, now, since he succeeded his father? Less, since his gift came to life in him – which in itself leaves questions with only troubling answers.'

'But I recall you telling me years ago that Darken Rahl used both sides of the gift.'

Gazing off into dark memories, Althea shook her head. 'He also used Subtractive powers, but he did not do so by birth. He offered the pure souls of children to the Keeper of the underworld in return for the Keeper's favors. Darken Rahl had to trade for the limited use of such powers. But this man, this Lord Rahl, has been born with both sides of the gift, as those of old were.'

Friedrich wasn't sure what to make of that, what danger it could be that he so strongly felt. He remembered quite distinctly the day the new Lord Rahl had risen to power. Friedrich had been at the palace to sell his small gilded carvings when the great event had taken place. That day, he had seen the new Lord Rahl, Richard.

It had been one of those moments in life never to be forgotten – only the third Rahl to rule in Friedrich's lifetime. He remembered quite clearly the new Lord Rahl, tall, strong, with a raptor gaze, striding through the palace, seeming completely out of place, and at the same time belonging. And then there was the sword he carried, a legendary sword not seen in D'Hara since Friedrich had been a boy, way back before the boundaries had been brought into existence, cutting D'Hara off from the rest of the new world.

The new Lord Rahl had been walking through the corridors of the People's Palace along with an old man – a wizard, people said – and a sublime woman. The woman, with long lush hair, wearing a satiny white dress, made the grandeur and majesty of the palace seem dull and common by comparison.

Richard Rahl and that woman seemed right together. Friedrich recognized the special way they looked at each other. The commitment, loyalty, and bond in the gray eyes of that man and the green eyes of that woman was as profound as it was unmistakable.

'What of the other stones?' he asked.

Althea gestured out past the larger circle of the Grace, where only the gilt rays of the Creator's gift dared go, to the two dark stones sitting in the world of the dead.

'Those who hear the voices,' Althea said.

He nodded at having his suspicions confirmed. In such things dealing with magic, it wasn't often that he was able to guess the truth from what appeared to be obvious.

'And the rest?'

Staring at the four stones resting at the cusps of lines, her voice came softly, mingling with the rain. 'These are protectors.'

'They protect Lord Rahl?'

'They protect us all.'

He saw then the tears rolling down her weathered cheeks.

'Pray,' she whispered, 'that they are enough, or the Keeper will have us all.'

'You mean to say, there are only these four who protect us?'

'There are others, but these four are pivotal. Without them, everything is lost.'

Friedrich licked his lips, fearful of the fate of the four sentinels standing against the Keeper of the dead. 'Althea, do you know who they are?'

She turned then, putting her arms around him, pressing the side of her face to his chest. It was as childlike a gesture as he could imagine, one that touched his heart and made him ache with his love for her. Gently he put protective arms around her, comforting her, in spite of the fact that in truth he could do nothing to protect her from such things as she rightly feared.

'Carry me to my chair, Friedrich?'

He nodded, lifting her in his arms as she hugged his neck. Her withered, useless legs dangled. A woman of such power as could enforce a warm and rain-swept swamp around them in winter, yet she needed him to carry her to a chair. Him, Friedrich, a mere man she loved – a man without the gift. A man who loved her.

'You didn't answer my question, Althea.'

Her arms tightened on his neck.

'One of the four protective stones,' she whispered, 'is me.'

Friedrich's wide eyes turned back to the Grace with the stones upon it. His jaw fell open when he saw that one of the four stones had crumbled to ash.

She had no need to look. 'One was my sister,' Althea said. Cradled in his arms, he felt her grieving sob. 'And now there are three.'

Chapter 15

Jennsen moved out of the way of the flood of people flowing up the road from the south. Huddling close to Sebastian for shelter from the wind, she briefly considered simply curling up on the frozen ground off to the side and going to sleep. Her stomach grumbled with hunger.

When Rusty stepped sideways, Jennsen slid her grip up on the reins, closer to the bit. Betty, her eyes, ears, and tail alert, pressed up against Jennsen's thigh for reassurance. The footsore goat occasionally huffed her annoyance at the passing throngs. When Jennsen patted her fat middle, Betty's upright tail instantly became a wagging blur. She glanced up at Jennsen, swiped her tongue out for a brief lick of Rusty's muzzle, and then folded her legs to lie down at Jennsen's feet.

As his sheltering arm enclosed her shoulders, Sebastian eyed the wagons, carts, and people moving past on their way toward the People's Palace. The sound of the wagons rumbling by, people talking and laughing, feet shuffling, and horses clopping all melted together into a steady drone punctuated by jangling metal and the rhythmic squeaking of axles. The clouds of dust lifted by all the movement carried the aroma of food along with the stink of people and animals and left the taste of dirt on her tongue.

'What do you think?' Sebastian asked in a low voice.

The cold sunrise bathed the distant sheer cliffs of the huge plateau in glowing lavender light. The cliffs themselves rose what seemed thousands of feet from the Azrith Plains, but what man had made atop them rose higher yet. Countless roofs behind imposing walls collected together into the massive structure that was a city founded on the plateau. Low winter sunlight lent the soaring marble walls and columns a warm glow.

Jennsen had been little when her mother had taken her away. Her childhood memory of having lived here had not prepared her adult sensibilities for the actual splendor of the palace. The heart of D'Hara stood noble and proud, triumphant above a barren land. Her awe was dimmed only by the taint of it also being the ancestral home of the Lord Rahl.

Jennsen swiped a hand over her face, closing her eyes briefly against her pounding headache, against what it meant to be the prey of Lord Rahl. It had been a difficult and exhausting journey. After they had stopped each night, Sebastian used the cover of darkness to scout while she started to make camp. A number of times he had rushed back with the horrifying news that their pursuers were closing in. Despite exhaustion and her tears of frustration, they had to pack up and keep running.

'I think we came here for a reason,' she finally answered. 'Now is a poor time to lose courage.'

'Now is the last chance to lose courage.'

She studied the note of caution in his blue eyes for only a moment before answering by wading back into the moving river of people. Betty sprang to her feet, peering up at the strangers as she pressed in close to Jennsen's left leg. Sebastian moved in close on the other side.

An older woman in a cart beside them smiled down at Jennsen. 'Care to sell your goat, dear?'

Jennsen, one hand grasping Betty's rope along with Rusty's reins, her other holding the hood of her cloak closed against a cold gust of wind, smiled, but shook her head firmly to decline. As the woman in the horsedrawn cart returned a disappointed smile and started to move away, Jennsen saw a sign on the cart proclaiming sausages for sale.

'Mistress? Are you here selling your sausages today?'

The woman reached behind, pushed aside a lid, and stretched her hand into one of the kettles nestled snugly in blankets and cloth. She came up holding a fat coil of sausage.

'Fresh cooked this morning. Could I interest you? Only a silver penny and well worth it.'

When Jennsen nodded eagerly, Sebastian passed the woman the coin requested. He cut the sausage in two and handed half to Jennsen. It was wonderfully warm. She quickly devoured a few bites, hardly taking the time to chew. It was a relief to dull the sharp edge of her gnawing hunger. Only after those bites were down did she begin to appreciate the taste.

'It's delicious,' she called up to the woman. The woman smiled, seeming not at all surprised at the compliment. Walking abreast with the cart, Jennsen asked, 'Would you happen to know of a woman by the name of Althea?'

Sebastian swept a furtive gaze around at the people walking within earshot. The woman, not at all shocked by the question, leaned down toward Jennsen.

'You've come for a telling, then?'

Although she couldn't be sure, Jennsen thought it easy enough to guess what the woman meant. 'Yes, that's right. Would you know where I can find her?'

'Well, dear, I don't know her, but I know of her husband, Friedrich. He comes to the palace to sell his gilded carvings.'

Many of the people moving up the road looked to have come to sell their wares. Jennsen dimly recalled when she was very young the palace being a buzz of activity, with throngs coming every day to sell everything from food to jewelry. Many towns near where Jennsen had lived when she was older had a market day. The People's Palace, though, was a city with the buying and selling of goods taking place every day. She recalled her mother taking her to booths to buy food and, once, cloth for a dress.

'Would you know where we can find this man, Friedrich, or someone else who knows the way?'

The woman gestured ahead toward the palace. 'Friedrich has a small booth in the marketplace. Up top. As I hear told, you'll need to be invited out to see Althea. I'd advise you to talk to Friedrich, up top.'

Sebastian put a hand on Jennsen's back as he leaned past her. 'Up top?' he asked the woman.

She nodded. 'You know. Up top, where the palace is. I don't go up there myself.'

'Then where do you sell your sausages?' he asked.

'Oh, I have my cart and horse, so I stay down along the road, selling to those going to and from the palace. They won't let you take those horses of yours up, if it be your intention to go look for Althea's husband. Your goat, neither, for that matter. There are ramps for horses inside for the soldiers and those with official business, but wagons with supplies and such mostly use the cliff road on the east side. They don't let just anyone ride their horses up. Only the soldiers keep horses up top.'

'Well,' Jennsen said, 'I guess we'll need to stable them, if we're to go up to find Althea's husband.'

'Friedrich doesn't come often. You'll be lucky to catch him on a day he's here. Best, though, if you could talk to him.'

Jennsen swallowed another mouthful of sausage. 'Do you know if he would be here today? Or what days he does come to the palace?'

'Sorry, dear, but I don't.' The woman pulled an oversized red scarf over her head and fastened it tight with a knot under her chin. 'I see him now and then, that's all I know. I sold him sausages a time or two to take home to his wife.'

Jennsen glanced up at the looming People's Palace. 'I guess we'll just have to go for a look, then.'

They weren't even inside, yet, and already Jennsen's heart was pounding at a furious pace. She saw Sebastian's fingers glide over his cloak, touching the hilt of his sword. She couldn't resist brushing her forearm against her side, checking for the reassuring presence of her knife under her own cloak. Jennsen hoped not to be in the palace long. When they found out where Althea lived, they could be on their way. The sooner the better.

She wondered if Lord Rahl was at the palace, or off making war on Sebastian's homeland. She felt great empathy for his people being at the mercy of Lord Rahl – a man she knew to be without a shred of mercy.

On their journey to the People's Palace, she had asked Sebastian about his homeland. He had shared with her some of the convictions and beliefs of the people in the Old World, their sensitivity for the plight of their fellow man, and their longings for the blessings of the Creator. Sebastian spoke passionately about the beloved spiritual leader of the Old World, Brother Narev, and his disciples of Order, who taught that the welfare of others was not only the responsibility but also the sacred duty of all people. She had never imagined a place with people who were so compassionate.

Sebastian said that the Imperial Order was fighting back valiantly against Lord Rahl's invaders. She, of all people, understood what it was to fear the man. It was that fear that worried Jennsen about going into the palace. She feared that if Lord Rahl was there, his powers might somehow tell him that she was near.

An orderly column of soldiers in chain mail and dark leather armor rode out, headed in the opposite direction. Their weapons – swords, axes, lances – flashed menacingly in the morning sunlight. Jennsen kept her eyes turned to the ground ahead and tried not to stare at the soldiers. She feared they could pick her out of the throng by sight, as if she were glowing with some mark only they could see. She kept the hood of her cloak pulled up to cover her red hair, fearing that it would attract unwanted attention.

As they drew near the great portals into the plateau the crowds grew thicker. Spread out on the Azrith Plains to the south of the cliffs, vendors had set up their stalls in makeshift streets. Those newly arrived settled in wherever they found room. Despite the cold, everyone seemed in a good mood as they went about setting out their wares. Many were already doing a brisk business.

D'Haran soldiers seemed to be everywhere. They were all big men, all wearing the same orderly leather, chain mail, and wool uniforms. All were armed with at least a sword, but most carried additional weapons – an axe, spiked mace, or knives. While the soldiers were alert and watchful, they didn't appear to be bothering the merchants or hampering their business.

The woman selling sausages waved her good wishes to Jennsen and Sebastian before she pulled her cart off the road at an empty space beside three men setting out casks of wine on a short table. The three men, with the same strong jaws, broad shoulders, and tousled blond hair, were obviously brothers.

'Careful who you leave your animals with,' she called after them.

Many of the people who set up their stands down on the plain had animals and it seemed easy enough to conduct business where they were, rather than go up to the palace. Other people roamed the crowds, hawking items to passersby. Perhaps their simple wares sold better to those come to the open-air market. Some, like the woman with the cart, came to sell food they had cooked, and since there were plenty of people down below they had no need to go up inside. Jennsen suspected that others were content to be away from what was sure to be the greater scrutiny of officials and yet more guards in the palace proper.

Sebastian took it all in without looking obvious. She imagined in his gaze a running tally of troops. To others it would appear he was merely looking about at the merchants, enticed by the variety of wares for sale, but Jennsen saw that his vision focused beyond, to the great portals between towering stone columns.

'What should we do with the horses?' she asked. 'And Betty?'

Sebastian gestured to one of the enclosures where horses were picketed. 'We're going to have to leave them.'

In addition to being so close to the home of the man trying to kill her, Jennsen didn't like being among the press of so many people. She felt so flush with the sense of danger that she couldn't think straight. Leaving Betty at a stable in a town was one thing, but leaving her lifelong friend out here, among all these people, was something else.

She pointed with her chin to the scruffy men minding the livestock enclosure. They were busily engaged in a game of dice.

'Do you think we can trust the animals to people like that? They could be thieves, for all we know. Maybe you could stay with the horses while I go look for Althea's husband.'

Sebastian turned back from his survey of the soldiers near the entrance. 'Jenn, I don't think it's a good idea to separate in a place like this. Besides, I don't want you going in there alone.'

She gauged the concern in his eyes. 'And if we get into trouble? Do you really think we could fight our way out?'

'No. You have to use your head – keep your wits about you. I've brought you this far, I'm not going to abandon you now and let you go in there alone.'

'And if they draw swords on us?'

'If it came to that, fighting wouldn't save us in a place like this. It's more important to give people a worry, make them think twice about how dangerous you might be, so that you don't end up fighting in the first place. You have to bluff.'

'I'm not any good at that kind of thing.'

He grunted a short laugh. 'You do it well enough. You did it with me that first night when you drew the Grace.'

'But that was just with you, and with my mother there. That's different than in a place with so many people.'

'You did it at the inn in the way you showed the innkeeper your red hair. Your manner loosened her tongue. And, you kept the men at bay with nothing but your bearing and a look. All by yourself you gave all those men worry enough that they left you alone.'

She had never thought about it in that way. She viewed it more as simple desperation than calculated deception.

As Betty rubbed the top of her head against Jennsen's leg, she idly stroked the goat's ear and watched as the men left their game of dice to take horses from travelers. She didn't like the rough way the men handled the horses, using switches instead of a steady hand.

Jennsen scanned the crush of people until she spotted the red scarf. She coiled the slack out of Betty's rope and started off, pulling Rusty along with her. Surprised, Sebastian stepped quickly to catch up.

The woman in the red scarf was setting out pots with her sausages when Jennsen reached her. 'Mistress?'

She squinted in the sunlight. 'Yes, dear? Some more sausages?' She lifted a lid. 'They are good, aren't they?'

'Delicious, but I was wondering if you would accept a payment to watch our horses, and my goat.'

The woman replaced the lid. 'The animals? I'm not a stableman, dear.'

Jennsen, holding the rope and the reins in one hand, rested her forearm on the side of the cart. Betty folded her legs and laid down beside the wheel. 'I thought you might like the company of my goat for a while. Betty is a fine goat and wouldn't cause you any trouble.'

The woman smiled as she peered down over the edge of her cart. 'Betty, is it? Well, I could watch your goat, I guess.'

Sebastian handed the woman a silver coin. 'If we could picket our horses with yours, it would put our minds at ease that they were in good hands, and that you were keeping an eye on them.'

The woman carefully inspected the coin, then appraised Sebastian more critically. 'How long will you be? When I sell my sausages I'll want to be heading home, after all.'

'Not long,' Jennsen said. 'We just want to go find the man you told us about – Friedrich.'

Sebastian, in an offhand manner, pointed at the coin the woman was still holding. 'When we get back, I'll give you another to thank you for watching our animals. If we don't get back until after your sausages are all sold, then I'll give you two for your trouble of waiting on us.'

Finally, the woman nodded. 'All right, then. I'll be here selling my sausages. Tie your goat to the wheel, there, and I'll keep my eye on her until you get back.' She gestured over her shoulder. 'And you can put your horses with mine, there. My old girl would enjoy the company.'

Betty eagerly took the small chunk of carrot from Jennsen's fingers. Rusty nudged her shoulder, insistent that she not be left out, so Jennsen let the horse have a piece of the rare treat, then passed a chunk to Sebastian so an ever-eager Pete wouldn't be left out.

'If you lose track of where I am, just ask around for Irma, the sausage lady.'

'Thank you, Irma.' Jennsen smoothed Betty's ears. 'I appreciate your help. We'll be back before you know it.'

As they mingled into the crowd funneling toward the great plateau, Sebastian put his arm around her waist to keep her close beside him as he escorted her into the gaping maw of Lord Rahl's palace.

Jennsen could hear in the distance Betty's plaintive bleating at being abandoned.

Chapter 16

Soldiers in polished breastplates, all carrying upright pikes with razor-sharp edges glinting in the sunlight, silently studied the people entering between the great columns. As their scrutiny turned toward Jennsen and Sebastian, she made sure not to look them in the eye. She kept her head down and moved in step with the other people shuffling past the ranks of soldiers. She didn't know if they paid any particular attention to the two of them, but none reached out to seize her, so she kept moving.

The huge, cavelike entrance was lined in a light-colored stone, giving Jennsen a sense of passing into a grand hall rather than through a tunnel into a plateau the size of a mountain. Hissing torches in iron brackets set into the walls lit the way with a dotted line of light. The air smelled of burning pitch, but it felt warm inside, out of the winter wind.

To the sides, cut into the rock, were rows of rooms. Most were simple openings with a short front wall behind which vendors sold their wares. Walls in many of the small rooms were decorated with brightly colored cloth or painted planks, offering a welcoming touch. It had appeared that anyone outside could set up shop and sell their goods. Jennsen imagined the vendors inside had to pay rent for the rooms, but, in return, they had a warm and dry place in out of the weather to do business, where customers were more willing to linger.

Clumps of chatting people waited near the shoemaker to have their shoes repaired, while others lined up to buy ale, or bread, or steaming bowls of stew. Another man, with a singsong voice that attracted throngs to his booth, sold meat pies. At one jammed and noisy place, women were having their hair pinned up, or curled, or decorated with bits of colored glass set in fine chains. At another, they were having their faces made up, or their nails painted. Other places sold beautiful ribbons, some cut to look just like fresh flowers, to adorn dresses. By the nature of many of the businesses, Jennsen realized that a lot of the people wanted to look their best before going up to the palace, where they meant to be seen, as much as they meant to look.

Sebastian seemed to find it all as astonishing as she did. Jennsen stopped at a booth with no customers, where a small man with a lasting smile was setting out pewter mugs.

'Could you tell me, sir, if you know of a gilder named Friedrich?'

'No man by that name down here. Finer work like that is usually sold up top.'

As they were swallowed deeper into the underground entrance, Sebastian's arm returned to enclose her waist. She found comfort in his close presence, his handsome face, and those times he smiled at her. His spikes of white hair made him different from everyone else – unique, special. His blue eyes seemed to hold so many answers to the mysteries of the larger world she had never seen. He almost made her forget her heartache at missing her mother.

A succession of massive iron doors stood open, admitting the advancing throng. It was intimidating going through such doors, knowing that if they closed she would be trapped inside. Beyond, wide marble stairs, paler than straw and swirled through with white veins, led up to grand landings edged with massive stone balustrades. In contrast to the immense iron doors into the plateau, finely crafted wooden doors closed off some of the rooms. Whitewashed corridors well lit by reflector lamps distracted from the feeling of being inside the plateau.

The stairs seemed endless, in some places branching off in different directions. Some of the landings opened into spacious passageways, the destination for many of the people. It was like a city in eternal night, lit by the wall lanterns with reflectors and pole lamps by the hundreds. Along the way were beautiful stone benches where people could rest. On some levels were more small shops selling bread, cheeses, meats, some with tables and benches set outside. Rather than feeling dark and forbidding, it seemed cozy inside, perhaps even romantic.

Some passageways, barred by huge doors and blocked by guards, appeared as if they might be barracks. In one place Jennsen glimpsed a spiral ramp with troops moving down on horseback.

From her childhood, Jennsen only dimly recalled the city under the palace. Now, with the endless new sights, it was a place of wonder.

As her legs grew weary from the effort of climbing the stairs and traversing passageways, it occurred to her then why many of the people chose to remain down on the plain to do business; it was a long way up, both in distance and in time, and quite the labor. From the conversations she overheard, many of the people who came would lengthen their stay at the palace that was a city by taking rooms.

Jennsen and Sebastian were finally rewarded for their effort when they emerged once again in the daylight. Three tiers of balconies fronted with roped columns supporting arched openings looked down on the marble hall. Overhead, glassed windows let in the light, creating a bright corridor unlike anything she had ever seen. If Jennsen was moved by the marvel of it, Sebastian seemed thunderstruck.

'How could any people build a place such as this?' he whispered. 'Why would they even want to?'

Jennsen didn't have an answer to either question. Yet, in spite of how much she loathed those who ruled her land, the palace still filled her with awe. This was a place built by people with vision and imagination beyond anything she could conceive of.

'With all the need in the world,' he murmured to himself, 'the House of Rahl builds this marble monument to themselves.'

She thought that there seemed to be many thousands other than the Lord Rahl himself who benefited from the People's Palace, those who derived their living from what the palace brought together, people of all kinds, even down to Irma the sausage lady, but Jennsen didn't want to just then break her spell of astonishment to try to explain it.

The corridor, stretching off in both directions, was lined with rows of shops set back under the balconies. Some were open, with a single craftsman, but many were glass-fronted and quite ornate, with doors, signs hung out, and a number of people working inside. The variety was overwhelming. Shopkeepers cut hair, pulled teeth, painted portraits, made clothes, and sold every sort of thing as could be imagined, from common produce and herbs to priceless perfumes and jewels. The aromas from the wide variety of foods were distracting. The sights were dizzying.

As she was taking in those sights while looking for the gilder's place, Jennsen spotted two women in brown leather uniforms. Each wore her long blond hair in a single braid. She clutched Sebastian's arm and hauled him into a side passageway. Without a word, she rushed him along, trying not to go so fast as to make people suspicious, but at the same time get them out of sight as quickly as possible. As soon as she reached the first of the huge pillars lining the side hall, she ducked behind it, pulling Sebastian along with her. When people glanced their way, they both sat down on the stone bench against the wall, trying to look as normal as possible. A statue of a naked man across the way stared down at them as he leaned on a spear.

Cautiously, casually, they both peeked out just enough to see. Jennsen watched the two leather-clad women stroll past the intersection; their gazes, cool, penetrating, intelligent, took in the people to both sides. These were the eyes of women that in an instant and without regret could decide between life and death. When one woman looked toward the side hall, Jennsen sank back behind the pillar, pressing herself up against the wall. She was relieved to finally see the backs of the two as they continued down the main corridor.

'What was that all about?' Sebastian asked as she let out a relieved sigh.

'Mord-Sith.'

'What?'

'Those two women. They were Mord-Sith.'

Sebastian carefully peered out for another look, but the two were gone. 'I don't know much about them, except that they're guards of some kind.'

She realized, then, that being from another land he might not know much about those women. 'Yes, in a way. Mord-Sith are very special guards. They are the Lord Rahl's personal guards, I guess. They protect him, and more. They torture information out of gifted people.'

He gauged the demeanor in her eyes. 'You mean those with simple magic.'

'Any magic. Even a sorceress. Even a wizard.'

He looked skeptical. 'A wizard commands powerful magic. He could simply use his power to crush those women.'

Jennsen's mother had told her about Mord-Sith, how dangerous they were, and that she must avoid them at all cost. Her mother never tried to hide the nature of deadly threats.

'No. Mord-Sith have a power that enables them to appropriate another's magic – even a wizard or a sorceress. They capture not only the person, but their magic, as well. There can be no escape from a Mord-Sith unless she releases the person.'

Sebastian seemed only more confused. 'What do you mean they appropriate another's magic? That makes no sense. What could they do with such magic if it were another's power? That would be like pulling out someone's teeth and trying to eat with them.'

Jennsen swept her hand back over her head, under her hood, replacing the red ringlets that had fallen out. 'I don't know, Sebastian. I've heard that they use the person's own magic against them, to hurt them – to give them pain.'

'Then why should we be afraid of them?'

'They may torture information out of the gifted enemies of Lord Rahl, but they can hurt anyone. Did you see the weapon they carry?'

'No. I saw no weapon on them. They only carried a small, red leather rod.'

'That is their weapon. It's called an Agiel. They keep it on a chain around their wrist so it is always at hand. It's a weapon of magic.'

He considered what she said, but clearly didn't yet understand it. 'What do they do with it, with their Agiel?'

His manner had turned from incredulity to a more calm,

analytical questioning for information. He was once again doing the job Jagang the Just had sent him to do.

'I'm no expert on the subject, but from what I've heard, the mere touch of an Agiel can do anything from causing inconceivable pain, to breaking bones, to instant death. The Mord-Sith decides how much pain, if the bones are to break, and whether or not you are to die by the touch.'

He watched out toward the intersection as he considered what she'd said. 'Why are you so afraid of them? And if you have only heard these things, why do you fear them so?'

Now she was the one who was incredulous. 'Sebastian, Lord Rahl has been hunting me my whole life. These women are his personal killers. Don't you think they would love to bring me to the feet of their master?'

'I suppose.'

'At least they were wearing their brown leather. They wear red leather when they sense a threat, or when they torture someone. In red leather the blood doesn't show so much.'

He slid both hands over his eyes and then back over his white spikes of hair. 'This is a nightmare land you live in, Jennsen Daggett.'

Jennsen Rahl, she almost corrected out of self-pity. Jennsen from her mother, Rahl from her father.

'Do you think I don't know it?'

'And what if this sorceress doesn't want to help you?'

She picked at a thread on her knee. 'I don't know.'

'He will come after you. Lord Rahl will never let you be. You will never be free.'

... unless you kill him were the words she could hear left off.

'Althea must help me . . . I'm so sick of being afraid,' Jennsen said, near tears, 'so sick of running.'

He put a gentle hand on her shoulder. 'I understand.'

No two words could have been more meaningful at that moment. She could only nod her appreciation.

His tone turned more impassioned. 'Jennsen, we have gifted women like Althea. They're from a sect, the Sisters of the Light, that used to live at the Palace of the Prophets in the Old World. Richard Rahl, when he invaded the Old World, destroyed their palace. It was said to be a beautiful and special place, but he destroyed it. Now the Sisters are with Emperor Jagang, helping him. Maybe our sorceresses would be able to help you, too.'

She looked up into his caring eyes. 'Really? Maybe those with the emperor would know a way to hide me from my murderous half brother's wizardry? ... But he's always only a half step behind, waiting for me to stumble so he can pounce. Sebastian, I don't think I could make it that far. Althea helped hide me from Lord Rahl once. I must convince her to help me again. If she won't, I fear I'll have no chance before I'm caught.'

He leaned out again, checking, then gave her a confident smile. 'We'll find Althea. Her magic will hide you and then you can get away.'

Feeling better, she returned the smile.

Judging that the Mord-Sith were gone and it was safe, they returned to the hall to search for Friedrich. They each inquired at several places before Jennsen found someone who knew of the gilder. With fresh hope, she and Sebastian moved deeper into the palace, following the directions they were given, to a juncture of grand passageways.

There, in the center of the intersection of two central corridors, she was surprised to see a quiet plaza with a square pool of dark water. Tiles, rather than the usual marble, surrounded the pool. Four columns at the outer edge of the tiles supported the soaring opening to the sky, covered, since it was winter, by leaded glass panels. The beveled glass gave the light cast down across the tiles a shimmering, liquid quality.

In the pool, off center in a way that seemed right without Jennsen understanding exactly why it felt right, stood a dark pitted rock with a bell atop it. It was a remarkably quiet sanctuary in the center of such a busy place.

Seeing the square with the bell sparked her memory of similar places. When the bell tolled, she recalled, the people came to such squares to bow down and chant a devotion to the Lord Rahl. She suspected that such homage was one price paid for the honor of being allowed in his palace.

People sat on the low wall around the edge, talking in hushed tones, watching orange fish gliding through the dark water. Even Sebastian stared for a few minutes before moving on.

Everywhere, there were alert soldiers. Some seemed to be stationed at key spots. Squads of guards moved through the halls, watching everyone, stopping some people to speak with them. What the soldiers asked, Jennsen didn't know, but it worried her greatly.

'What do we say if they question us?' she asked.

'It's best not to say anything unless you have to.'

'But if you have to, then what?'

'Tell them that we live on a farm to the south. Farmers are isolated and don't know much about anything but life on their farm, so it wouldn't sound suspicious if we say we don't know about anything else. We came to see the palace and perhaps buy a few small things – herbs and such.'

Jennsen had met farmers, and didn't think they were as ignorant of things as Sebastian seemed to think. 'Farmers grow or collect their own herbs,' she said. 'I don't think they would need to come to the palace to buy them.'

'Well, then . . . we came to buy some nice cloth so you could make clothes for the baby.'

'Baby? What baby?'

'Your baby. You are my wife and only recently found yourself pregnant. You are with child.'

Jennsen felt her face flush to red. She couldn't say she was pregnant – that would only lead to more questions.

'All right. We're farmers, here to buy a few small things – herbs and such. Rare herbs we don't grow ourselves.'

His only answer was a sideways glance and a smile. His arm returned to her waist, as if to banish her embarrassment.

Beyond another intersection of wide passageways, following the directions they'd been given, they turned down another hall to the right. It, too, was lined with vendors. Jennsen immediately spotted the booth with a gilded star hanging before it. She didn't know if it was intentional or not, but the gilded star had eight points, like the star in a Grace. She had drawn the Grace often enough to know.

With Sebastian at her side, she rushed over to the booth. Her

158

heart sank when they found the place occupied only by an empty chair, but it was still morning, and she reasoned that maybe he hadn't come in yet. The closest businesses weren't yet open, either.

She stopped several stalls down at a place selling leather mugs. 'Do you know if the gilder is here today?' she asked the man working behind the bench.

'Sorry, don't know,' he said without looking up from his work at cutting decorations with a fine gouge. 'I just started here.'

She hurried down to the next occupied booth, a place that sold hangings with colorful scenes sewn on them. She turned to say something to Sebastian, but saw him inquiring at another booth not far away.

The woman behind the short counter was sewing a blue brook through mountains stitched on a stretched square of coarsely woven cloth. Some of the scenes were made up into pillows displayed on a rack to the back.

'Mistress, would you know if the gilder is here, today?'

The woman smiled up at her. 'Sorry, but far as I know, he won't be in today.'

'Oh, I see.' Thwarted by the disappointing news, Jennsen hesitated, not knowing what to do next. 'Would you know when he will return, at least?'

The woman pushed her needle through, making a blue stitch of water. 'No, can't say as I do. Last time I saw him, over a week ago, he said he may not be back for a while.'

'Why is that? Do you know?'

'Can't say as I do.' She pulled the long thread of the water out taut. 'Sometimes he stays away for a spell, working at his gilding, doing up enough to make it worth his time to travel to the palace.'

'Would you happen to know where he lives?'

The woman glanced up from under a crinkled brow. 'Why do you wish to know?'

Jennsen's mind raced. She said the only thing she could think of – what she had learned from Irma, the sausage lady watching Betty for her. 'I wish to go for a telling.'

'Ah,' The woman said, her suspicion fading as she pulled

another stitch through. 'It's Althea, then, that you really want to see.'

Jennsen nodded. 'My mother took me to Althea when I was young. Since my mother . . . passed away, I'd like to visit Althea again. I thought it might be a comfort if I went for a telling.'

'Sorry about your mother, dear. I know what you mean. When I lost my mother, it was a hard time for me, too.'

'Could you tell me how to find Althea's place?'

She set her sewing down and came to the low wall at the front of her booth. 'It's a goodly ways to Althea's place – to the west, through a desolate land.'

'The Azrith Plains.'

'That's right. Going west, the land turns rugged, with mountains. Around the other side of the largest snowcapped mountain due west of here, if you turn north, staying just the other side of the cliffs you will find, following the low land down lower yet, you will come into a nasty place. A swampy place. Althea and Friedrich live there.'

'In a swamp? But not in the winter.'

The woman leaned close and lowered her voice. 'Yes, even in the winter, people say. Althea's swamp. A vile place it is, too. Some say it isn't a natural place, if you know what I mean.'

'Her . . . magic, you mean?'

She shrugged. 'Some say.'

Jennsen nodded in thanks and repeated the directions. 'Other side of the largest snowcapped peak west of here, stay below the cliffs and go north. Down in a swampy place.'

'A nasty, dangerous, swampy place.' The woman used a long fingernail to scratch her scalp. 'But you don't want to be going there unless you're invited.'

Jennsen glanced around briefly, to signal to Sebastian, but she didn't see him right off. 'How does one get invited?'

'Most people ask Friedrich. I see them come here to talk to him and leave without even looking at his work. I guess he asks Althea if she will see them, and the next time he returns with his gilding, he invites them. Sometimes, people give him a letter to take to his wife.

'Some people travel out there and wait. I hear that sometimes he comes out of the swamp to meet those people and pass along Althea's invitation. Some people return from the edge of the swamp without ever being invited in, their long wait for nothing. None dare venture in uninvited, though. Least, none that did ever came back to tell about it, if you know what I mean.'

'Are you saying I'll have to go there and just wait? Wait until she or her husband comes to invite us in?'

'Guess so. But it won't be Althea who comes out. She never comes out of her swamp, as I hear it. You could come back here each day until Friedrich finally returns to sell his gilding. He's never been away for more than a month. I'd say he'll be back to the palace within a few weeks, at most.'

Weeks. Jennsen couldn't stay in one place, waiting weeks, while Lord Rahl's men hunted her, closing in day by day. From as close as Sebastian said they were, she didn't think she even had days, much less weeks, before they would have her.

'Thank you, then, for all your help. I guess I'll come back another day to see if Friedrich has returned and ask him if I might go for a telling.'

The woman smiled as she sat back down and picked up her sewing. 'That might be best.' She looked up. 'Sorry to hear about your mother, dear. It's hard, I know.'

She nodded, her eyes watery, fearing to test her voice just then. The vivid scene flashed through her mind. The men, the blood everywhere, the terror of them coming for her, seeing her mother slumped on the floor, stabbed, her arm severed. With effort, Jennsen pushed the memory away, lest it consume her in grief and anger.

She had immediate worries. They had made a long and difficult journey in winter to find Althea, to obtain her help. They couldn't wait around, hoping to be invited to visit Althea – Lord Rahl's men were close on their heels. The last time Jennsen had wavered in her determination she had missed her chance – and Lathea had been murdered. The same thing could happen again. She had to get to Althea before those men did, at least to tell her about her sister, to warn her, if nothing else.

Jennsen scanned the vast hallway, searching for Sebastian. He couldn't have gone far. She saw him, then, his back to her, across the broad corridor, just turning away from a place that sold silver jewelry.

Before she took two steps, she saw soldiers swarm in and surround him. Jennsen froze in her tracks. Sebastian did, too. One of the soldiers used his sword to carefully lift back Sebastian's cloak, uncovering his array of weapons. She was too frightened to move, to take another step.

Half a dozen gleaming razor-edged pikes lowered at Sebastian. Swords came out of sheaths. People nearby backed away, others turned to look. In the center of a ring of D'Haran soldiers towering over him, Sebastian held his arms out to the sides in surrender.

Surrender.

Just then a bell, the one back at the square, tolled.

Chapter 17

The single long peal of the bell calling people to the devotion echoed through the cavernous halls as two of the big men seized Sebastian by the arms and started bearing him away. Jennsen watched helplessly as the rest of the D'Haran soldiers surrounded him in a tight formation bristling with steel meant not only to keep their prisoner at bay, but to ward any possible attempt to extricate him. It was immediately clear to her that these guards were prepared for any eventuality and took no chances, not knowing if this one armed man might signify a force about to storm the palace.

Jennsen saw that there were other men, visitors to the palace like Sebastian, also carrying swords. Perhaps it was that Sebastian carried a variety of combat weapons, and they were all concealed, that so raised the soldiers' suspicions. But he wasn't doing anything. It was winter – of course he was wearing a cloak. He was causing no harm. Jennsen's urge was to yell at the soldiers to leave him be, yet she feared that if she did they would take her, too.

The people who had spread back away from the potential trouble, along with everyone else strolling the halls, all began moving toward the square. People in the shops set down their work to join them. No one paid much attention to the soldiers' business. In response to that single chime still hanging in the air, laughter and talking trailed off to respectful whispers.

Panic clawed at Jennsen as she saw the soldiers muscling Sebastian down a hall to the side. She could see his white hair amid the dark armor. She didn't know what to do. This wasn't supposed to happen. They only came to find a gilder. She wanted to scream for the soldiers to stop. She dared not, though.

Jennsen.

Jennsen stood her ground against the current of bodies, trying to keep Sebastian and his captors in sight. The Lord Rahl was after her, and now they had Sebastian. Her mother had been murdered, and now they were taking Sebastian. It wasn't fair.

As she watched, afraid to do anything to stop the soldiers, her own fear shamed her. Sebastian had done so much for her. He had made so many sacrifices for her. He had risked his life to save hers.

Jennsen's breath came in ragged pulls. But what could she do?

Surrender.

It wasn't fair what they were doing to Sebastian, to her, to innocent people. Anger welled up through her fear.

Tu vash misht.

He was only there because of her. She had asked him to come.

Tu vask misht.

Now, he was in trouble.

Grushdeva du kalt misht.

The words sounded so right. They flared through her, carried on flames of igniting rage.

People pushed against her. She growled through gritted teeth as she squeezed her way among the crush of people, trying to follow the soldiers who had Sebastian. It wasn't fair. She wanted them to stop. Just stop. Stop.

Her helplessness frustrated her. She was sick of it. When they wouldn't stop, when they kept going, it only further enraged her.

Surrender.

Jennsen's hand slid inside her cloak. The touch of cold steel welcomed her. Her fingers tightened around the hilt of her knife. She could feel the worked metal of the symbol of the House of Rahl pressing into the flesh of her palm.

A soldier gently pushed her, turning her in the direction of the rest of the crowd. 'The devotion square is that way, ma'am.'

It was spoken as a suggestion, but wrapped around the core of command.

Through the rage, she looked up into his hooded eyes. She saw the dead man's eyes. She saw the soldiers at her house – men on the floor dead, men coming for her, men grabbing her. She saw flashes of movement through a crimson sheen of blood.

As she and the soldier stared into each other's eyes, she felt the blade at her waist coming out of its sheath.

A hand under her arm tugged at her. 'This way, dear. I'll show you where it is.'

Jennsen blinked. It was the lady who had given her directions to Althea's place. The woman who sat in the palace of the murdering bastard Lord Rahl and sewed the peaceful scenes of the mountains and brooks.

Jennsen stared at the woman, at her inexplicable smile, trying to make sense of her. Jennsen found everything around her strangely incomprehensible. She only knew that her hand was on the hilt of her knife and she longed for the blade to be free.

But, for some reason, the knife stubbornly remained where it was.

Jennsen, at first convinced that some malevolent magic had seized her, saw then that the woman had a tight, motherly arm around her. Without realizing it, the woman was keeping Jennsen's blade in its sheath. Jennsen locked her knees, resisting being pulled along.

The woman's eyes, now, were set with warning. 'No one misses a devotion, dear. No one. Let me show you where it is.'

The soldier, his expression grim, watched as Jennsen yielded, allowing herself to be guided by the woman. Jennsen and the woman, swept into the current of people moving toward the square, left the soldier behind. She looked up into the woman's smiling face. The whole world seemed to Jennsen to be swimming in a strange light. The voices around her were a smear of sound that in her mind was pierced by the echoes of screams from her house.

Jennsen.

Through the murmuring around her, the voice, sharp and distinct, caught her attention. Jennsen listened, alert to what it might tell her.

Surrender your will, Jennsen.

It made sense, in a visceral way.

Surrender your flesh.

Nothing else seemed to matter anymore. Nothing she had tried in her whole life had brought her salvation, or safety, or peace. To the contrary, everything seemed lost. There seemed nothing else to lose.

'Here we are, dear,' the woman said.

Jennsen looked around. 'What?'

'Here we are.'

Jennsen felt her knees touch the tiled floor as the woman urged her down. People were all around. Before them was the square with the pool of quiet water at its center. She wanted only the voice.

Jennsen. Surrender.

The voice had grown harsh, commanding. It fanned the flames of her anger, her rage, her wrath.

Jennsen bent forward, trembling, in the grip of rage. Somewhere, in the far corners of her mind, screamed a distant terror. Despite that remote sense of foreboding, it was rage that was carrying her will away.

Surrender!

She saw strings of her saliva hanging, dripping, as she panted through parted lips. Tears dropped to the tiles close beneath her face. Her nose ran. Her breath came in gasps. Her eyes were opened so wide it hurt. She shook all over, as if alone in the coldest darkest winter night. She couldn't make herself stop.

People bowed forward deeply, hands pressed to the tiles. She wanted her knife out.

Jennsen lusted for the voice.

'*Master Rahl guide us.*'

It was not the voice. It was the people all around, in one voice, chanting the devotion. As they began, they all bowed farther forward until their foreheads touched the tile floor. A soldier moved past close behind, patrolling, watching as she knelt, bent over, hands to the floor, quaking uncontrollably.

Inch by halting inch, as she gasped, panted, shook, Jennsen's head lowered until her forehead touched the floor.

'*Master Rahl teach us.*'

That was not what she wanted to hear.

She wanted the voice. She raged for it. She wanted her knife. She wanted blood.

'*Master Rahl protect us*,' the people all chanted in unison.

Jennsen, pulling ragged jerking breaths, consumed with loathing, wanted only the voice, and her blade free. But her palms were flat on the tiles.

She listened for the voice, but heard only the chant of the devotion.

'*In your light we thrive. In your mercy we are sheltered. In your wisdom we are humbled. We live only to serve. Our lives are yours.*'

At first, Jennsen only vaguely remembered it from her youth, from when she had lived at the palace. Hearing it now, that memory came flooding back. She had known the words. She had chanted them when she was little. When they fled the palace, running from Lord Rahl, she had banished the words of the devotion to the man who was trying to kill her and her mother.

Now, hungering for the voice that wanted her to surrender, almost unbeknownst to her, almost as if it were someone else doing it, her trembling lips began moving with the words.

'*Master Rahl guide us. Master Rahl teach us. Master Rahl protect us. In your light we thrive. In your mercy we are sheltered. In your wisdom we are humbled. We live only to serve. Our lives are yours.*'

The cadence of those murmured words filled the great hall, many people but one voice resounding powerfully off the walls. She listened with all her strength for the voice that had been her companion for nearly as long as she could remember, but it wasn't there.

Now, Jennsen was helplessly carried along with all the others. She clearly heard herself speaking the words.

'*Master Rahl guide us. Master Rahl teach us. Master Rahl protect us. In your light we thrive. In your mercy we are sheltered. In your wisdom we are humbled. We live only to serve. Our lives are yours.*'

Over and over Jennsen softly spoke the words of the devotion along with everyone else. Over and over, without pause but for breath. Over and over, yet without haste.

The chant filled her mind. It beckoned to her, spoke to her. It was all that filled her thoughts as she chanted it over and over and over. It filled her so completely that it left no room for anything else.

Somehow, it calmed her.

Time slipped by, incidental, inconspicuous, unimportant.

Somehow, the soft chant brought her a sense of peace. It reminded her of how Betty calmed when having her ears smoothed. Jennsen's rage was being smoothed. She fought against it, but, bit by bit, she was pulled into the chant, into its promise, smoothed and gentled.

She understood, then, why it was called a devotion.

Despite everything, it drained her, and then filled her with a profound calm, a serene sense of belonging.

She no longer fought the words. She allowed herself to whisper them, letting them lift away the shards of pain. For that time, as she knelt, her head to the tiles, with nothing to do but say the words, she was free of anything and everything.

As she chanted along with everyone else, the shadow cast on the floor from the mullions of the leaded glass overhead moved past her, leaving her in the glow of the full sun. It felt warm and protective. It felt like her mother's warm embrace. Her body felt light. The soft radiance all around reminded Jennsen of how she pictured the good spirits.

An instant in time later, the hours of chanting were ended.

Jennsen uncurled, slowly pushing away from the floor, to sit up with the others. Without warning, a sob poured forth.

'Anything wrong, here?'

There was a soldier towering over her.

The woman to the side put an arm around Jennsen's shoulders.

'Her mother passed away recently,' the woman quietly explained.

The soldier shifted his weight, looking ill at ease.

'I'm sorry, ma'am. My heartfelt sympathy to you and your family.'

Jennsen saw in his blue eyes that he meant every word.

Stunned speechless, she watched as he turned, huge and muscular, layered in leather, Lord Rahl's killer continuing on his patrol. Empathy in armor. If he knew who she was, he would deliver her into the hands of those who would see to it that she suffered a long and lingering death.

Jennsen buried her face in the stranger's shoulder and wept for her mother, whose embrace had felt so good.

She missed her mother beyond endurance. And now, she was terrified for Sebastian.

Chapter 18

Jennsen thanked the woman who sewed country scenes and gave directions. Only after Jennsen had started down the hall did she realize that she didn't even know the woman's name. It didn't really matter. They both had mothers. Both understood and shared the same feelings.

Now that the devotion was over, the noise of all the people in the palace rose again to resound off marble walls and columns. Laughter could be heard ringing out across the hall. People had gone back to their own concerns, buying, trading, discussing their wants and needs. Guards patrolled, and palace staff, most in light-colored robes, went about their business, carrying messages, seeing to matters Jennsen could only guess at. In one place, workers were at the task of repairing the hinges on a huge oak double door to a side passageway.

The cleaning staff was back, too, busy at dusting, mopping, polishing. Jennsen's mother had once been one of those women, seeing to the work in the sections of the palace closed off to the public, official rooms where matters of governance were conducted, the sections that housed the officials and palace staff, and, of course, Lord Rahl's rooms.

After chanting the devotion for hours, Jennsen's mind was as clear as if she had had a long and needed rest. In that calm but refreshed and wide-awake state, a solution had come to her. She knew what she had to do.

She moved quickly, back the way she had come. There was no time to lose. On balconies above, people who lived at the People's Palace gazed down on the hall as they went about their work, watching those who had come to marvel at the great place. Jennsen focused on keeping her wits about her as she moved through the throngs.

Sebastian had warned her not to run and cause people to wonder if there was something wrong. He had cautioned her to act normal, lest she give people reason to take note. Yet, so acute was the danger of being at the palace, that he had been captured despite knowing how to act. If she raised suspicion, then soldiers would surely stop her. If the soldiers got ahold of her, and found out who she was . . .

Jennsen ached to have Sebastian back. Her fear for him urged her down the hall. She had to get him away from the D'Haran soldiers before they did something terrible to him. She knew that every minute they had him, he was in mortal danger.

If they tortured him, he might not be able to hold out. If he confessed to who he was, they would put him to death. The thought of Sebastian being executed almost made her knees give out. Under torture, people would confess to anything, whether true or not. If they decided to torture him to make him confess to something, he was doomed. The mental image of Sebastian being tortured made her sick and dizzy.

She had to rescue him.

But to do that, she had to have the sorceress's help. If Althea would help her, cast Jennsen a protective spell, then she could try to get Sebastian back. Althea had to help her. Jennsen would convince her. Sebastian's life hung in the balance.

She reached the stairs where they had come up. People were still emptying up into the hall, some sweating and huffing with the effort of the climb. Few were going down, yet. Standing at the edge, hand on the marble rail, she took a careful look around, making sure she wasn't being followed or observed. Despite her urge to run, she made herself look around casually. Some people looked at her, but no more than they looked at anyone. Patrolling soldiers were a good distance off. Jennsen started down.

She went as quickly as possible without looking like she was running for her life – for Sebastian's life. But she was. If not for Jennsen, he would not be in this trouble.

She thought that going down would be easy, but after

hundreds of steps she found that going down was tiring on the legs. Her legs burned with the effort. She told herself that if she couldn't run, she could at least not stop but keep going and in that way make better time.

On the landings, she cut the corners, saving steps. When no one was looking, she took the stairs two at a time. When she had to traverse passageways, she tried to screen herself behind clumps of people as she went past watchful guards. People sitting on benches, eating bread and meat pies, drinking ale, talking with friends, casually noted her along with everyone else who passed, just another visitor going by.

Lord Rahl's half sister among them.

On the steps again, she went quickly, her legs trembling from the nonstop effort. Her muscles burned with the need of a rest, but she gave them none. Instead, she pushed faster when she had the chance. On an empty flight of stairs between two landings screened from sight because they turned from different directions, Jennsen raced recklessly down. She slowed again when a couple, arm in arm, their heads close together as they giggled over whispered words, reached the landing below and headed up.

The air grew colder as she descended. On one level, with guards thick as flies in a barn in spring, one of the soldiers looked right into her eyes and smiled. Stunned to a stop for an instant, she realized that he was smiling at her as a man smiled at a woman, not as a killer smiled at his victim. She returned the smile, polite, warm, but not so much as to give the impression that she was encouraging him. Jennsen pulled her cloak tight and turned down the next flight of stairs. When she glanced over her shoulder as she turned the corner on a landing, he stood above, one hand on the rail, watching her. He smiled again and waved a farewell before turning back to his duties.

Unable to contain her fear, Jennsen sprinted down the stairs two at a time and ran down the hall, past small stands selling food, brooches, and finely decorated daggers, past visitors sitting on stone benches set before the marble balustrade, on toward the next flight of stairs, until she realized that people were staring at her. She stopped running and fell casually into walking, trying to flounce to make it look as if she had just been dashing from youthful vivacity. The tactic worked. She saw the people who had been eyeing her seem to chalk it up as nothing more than a spirited girl dashing along. They turned back to their own business. Since it worked, Jennsen intermittently used the same trick and was able to make better time.

Breathing hard from the long descent, she finally made it to the cave-like entrance with the hissing torches. Since there were so many soldiers at the portal into the great plateau, she slowed and walked close behind an older couple to make it look as if she might be a daughter with her parents. The couple was engaged in a spirited debate of a friend's chances of making a go of it with his new shop selling wigs up in the palace. The woman thought it a good business. The man thought his friend would run out of willing sellers of their hair and would end up spending too much of his time looking for more.

Jennsen could imagine no more foolish conversation when a man had been taken prisoner and was about to be tortured and probably put to death. To Jennsen, the D'Haran palace was nothing more than a vile death trap. She had to get Sebastian out of there. She would get him out.

Neither one of the couple noticed Jennsen close behind, head bowed, matching their slow pace. The gaze of guards skimmed over the three of them. At the mouth of the opening, cold wind swept in to take the breath from Jennsen's lungs. After being in the lamplit darkness for so long, she had to squint at the expanse of bright daylight. As soon as they were in the open-air market, she turned down one of the makeshift streets, hurrying to find Irma, the sausage lady.

Stretching her neck, she looked about for the red scarf as she rushed down the rows of stalls. The places that before had seemed so splendid now looked shabby after she had been in the palace. In the whole of her life, Jennsen had never seen anything like the People's Palace. She could not imagine how a place of such beauty could hold such ugliness as the House of Rahl.

A hawker pushed in close. 'Charms, for the lady? Good luck for sure.' Jennsen kept walking. His breath stank. 'Special charms with magic. Can't go wrong for a silver penny.'

'No, thank you.'

He walked sideways, right close in front of her but off to the side a bit. 'Just a silver penny, my lady.'

She thought she would trip over the man's feet. 'No, thank you. Please leave me be, now.'

'A copper penny, then.'

'No.' Jennsen shoved him each time he bumped into her as he pushed in close, yammering about his charms. He kept putting his face in front of hers, looking back up at her as he stooped and shuffled along, grinning at her.

'Good charms, they are, my lady.' He kept bumping her as she tried to walk, as she craned her neck, looking for the red scarf. 'Good luck for you.'

'No, I said.' Almost stumbling over the man, she gave him a stiff shove. 'Please, leave me be!'

Jennsen sighed in relief as an older man came past going in the opposite direction and the hawker turned to him. She could hear his voice fade behind, trying to sell the man a magic charm for a silver penny. She thought about the irony that here this man was offering magic, and she turned it down because she was in a hurry to be off to try to get magic from someone else.

Past an empty space, before a table with wine casks, Jennsen halted abruptly. She looked up and saw the three brothers. One was pouring wine into a leather goblet for a customer while the other two were lifting a full cask from the back of their wagon.

Jennsen turned and stared at the empty place. That was where Irma had been. Her heart felt as if it came up in her throat. Irma had their horses. Irma had Betty.

In a panic, she seized the arm of the man behind the table as the customer departed.

'Please, could you tell me where Irma is?'

He looked up, squinting in the sunlight. 'The sausage lady?'

Jennsen nodded. 'Yes. Where is she? She couldn't be gone already. She had her sausages to sell.'

The man grinned. 'She said that being beside us, selling our wine, had helped sell her sausages faster than she ever sold them before.'

Jennsen could only stare. 'She's gone?'

'Too bad, too. Having sausages for sale next to us really

helped sell wine. People ate those spicy goat sausages of hers and had to have some of our wine.'

'Her what?' Jennsen whispered.

The man's smile flagged. 'Her sausages. What's wrong, ma'am? You look as if a spirit from the underworld just tapped you on the shoulder.'

'What did you say she sells? ... Goat sausages?'

He nodded, looking concerned. 'Among others. I tried them all, but I liked the spicy goat sausages best.' He lifted a thumb over his shoulder, indicating his two brothers. 'Joe liked her beef sausages best, and Clayton, well he liked the pork, but I favored her goat sausages.'

Jennsen was shivering and it wasn't the cold. 'Where is she? I have to find her!'

The man scratched his head of disheveled blond hair. 'I'm sorry, but I don't know. She comes here to sell sausages. Most folks around here have seen her before. She's a nice lady, always a smile and a good word.'

Jennsen felt freezing tears run down her cheeks. 'But where is she? Where does she live? I have to find her.'

The man grasped Jennsen's arm, as if fearing she might fall. 'Sorry, ma'am, but I don't know. Why? What's wrong?'

'She has my animals. My horses. And Betty.'

'Betty?'

'My goat. She has them. We paid her to watch them until we got back.'

'Oh.' He looked gloomy to have no better news for her. 'Sorry. Her sausages pretty much sold steady till they were gone. It usually takes her all day long to sell what she cooks up, but sometimes it just goes better, I guess. After her sausages were gone, she sat around and talked to us for a long spell. Finally, she let out a sigh, and said she had to get home.'

Jennsen's mind raced. The world felt as if it were spinning around her. She didn't know what to do. She felt dazed, confused. Jennsen had never felt so alone.

'Please,' she said, her voice choked with tears, 'please, could I rent one of your horses?'

'Our horses? Then how would we get our wagon home?

Besides, they're draft horses. We don't have any saddle or tack for riding or any—'

'Please! I have gold.' Jennsen groped at her belt. 'I can pay.'

Feeling around at her waist, she couldn't find her small leather pouch with her gold and silver coins. Jennsen threw back her cloak, searching. There, on her belt, beside her knife, she found only a small piece of a leather thong, parted cleanly.

'My purse . . . my purse is gone.' She couldn't get her breath. 'My money . . .'

The man's face sagged with sorrow as he watched her pull the remnant of the drawstring from her belt. 'There are wicked people prowling around, looking to steal—'

'But I need it.'

He fell silent. She looked back behind, searching for the hawker selling charms. It all flashed back through her mind. He had bumped into her, jostled her. He was really cutting her purse. She couldn't even recall what he looked like – just that he was scruffy and ill kept. She hadn't wanted to look at his face, meet his eyes. She couldn't seem to get her breath as she frantically looked this way and that, trying to find the man who had stolen her money.

'No . . .' she whined, too overcome to know what to say. 'No, oh please no.' She sank down, sitting on the ground beside the table. 'I need a horse. Dear spirits, I need a horse.'

The man hurriedly poured wine in a cup and squatted down beside her as she sobbed. 'Here, drink this.'

'I have no money,' she managed to get out as she wept.

'No charge,' he said, giving her a sympathetic, lopsided smile of straight white teeth. 'It'll help. Drink it down.'

The other two blond-headed brothers, Joe and Clayton, stood behind the table, hands in their pockets, heads lowered with regret for the woman their brother was tending to.

The man tipped the cup up, trying to get her to drink as she cried. Some spilled down her chin, some went in her mouth and she had to swallow it.

'Why do you need a horse?' the man asked.

'I have to get to Althea's place.'

'Althea? The old sorceress?'

Jennsen nodded as she wiped wine from her chin and tears from her cheeks.

'Have you been invited out there?'

'No,' Jennsen admitted. 'But I have to go.'

'Why?'

'It's a matter of life or death. I need Althea's help or a man could die.'

Crouching beside her, still holding the cup he'd used to give her a drink, his eyes turned from looking into hers to take in her ringlets of red hair under her hood.

The big man put his hands on his knees and stood, going back to his brothers to let her be as she tried but failed to halt her desperate tears. Jennsen wept with worry for Betty, too. Betty was Jennsen's friend and companion, and a connection to her mother. The poor goat probably felt abandoned and unloved. Jennsen would give anything, just then, to see Betty's little upright tail wagging.

She told herself that she couldn't just sit there acting like a child. It would accomplish nothing. She had to do something. There could be no help in the shadow of Lord Rahl's palace, and she had no money to help her. She couldn't depend on anyone – except Sebastian, and he had no hope of help but from her. Now his life depended on her actions alone. She couldn't sit there feeling sorry for herself. If her mother had taught her anything, she had taught Jennsen better than this.

She had no idea what to do to rescue Betty, but she at least knew what she had to attempt in order to help Sebastian. That was what was most important, and what she had to do. She was wasting precious time.

Jennsen stood, angrily wiping the tears from her face, and then put a hand to her brow to shield her eyes from the sun. She had been in the palace a long time, so it was hard to judge, but she figured it to be late afternoon. Taking into account the sun's position in the sky at the time of year, she judged which way was west. If only she had Rusty, she could make better time. If only she had her money, she could rent or buy another horse.

No sense yearning for what was gone and couldn't be recovered. She would have to walk.

'Thank you for the wine,' Jennsen said to the blond-headed man standing there fidgeting as he watched her.

'Not at all,' he said as he cast his gaze downward.

As she started away, he seemed to gather his courage. He stepped out into the dusty road and grabbed her by the arm. 'Hold on there, ma'am. What are you thinking of doing?'

'A man's life depends on my getting out to Althea's place. I've no choice. I have to walk.'

'What man? What's going on that his life would hinge on you seeing Althea?'

Jennsen, looking up into the man's sky blue eyes, gently pulled her arm away. Big and blond, with his strong jaw and muscular build, he reminded her of the men who had murdered her mother.

'I'm sorry, but I can't say.'

Jennsen held the hood of her cloak tight against a bitter gust of wind as she struck out again. Before she had taken a dozen steps, he took several long strides and gently grasped her under her upper arm again to drag her to a halt.

'Look,' he said in a quiet voice when she scowled at him, 'do you even have any supplies?'

Jennsen's scowl withered and she had to fight back the tears of frustration. 'Everything is with our horses. The sausage lady, Irma, has everything. Except my money – the cutpurse has that.'

'So, you have nothing.' It wasn't a question so much as scorn for so simpleminded a plan.

'I have myself and I know what I must do.'

'And you intend to strike out for Althea's, in the winter, on foot, without any supplies?'

'I've lived in the woods my whole life. I can get by.'

She pulled, but his big hand held her arm securely. 'Maybe so, but the Azrith Plains aren't the woods. There's nothing to help you make a shelter. Not a stick of wood to make a fire. After the sun sets it'll get as cold as the Keeper's heart. You don't have any supplies or anything. What are you going to eat?'

This time she more forcefully jerked her arm away and succeeded in freeing it. 'I don't have any other choice. You may not understand that, but there are some things that you have to do, even if it means risking your own life, or else life means nothing and isn't worth living.'

Before he could stop her again, Jennsen ran into the river of people moving along the makeshift streets. She pushed her way through the crowds, past people selling food and drink she could not buy. It all served to remind her that she had not eaten since the sausage that morning. The knowledge that Sebastian might not live to have another meal gave urgency to her steps.

She turned down the first road going west. With the southern winter sun on the left side of her face, she thought about the sunlight in the palace when she had been at the devotion, and how much it felt like her mother's embrace.

Chapter 19

Jennsen wove her way among the people below the plateau, making her way down the haphazard streets, imagining she was stepping among trees, moving through the forests where she felt most at home. That was where she wished she were, in a quiet forest, sheltered among the trees, with her mother, the both of them watching Betty nibble on tender shoots. Some of the people pausing at stalls, or the merchants behind tables, or those strolling along, cast a gaze in Jennsen's direction, but she kept her head bowed and continued along at a brisk pace.

She was worried sick about Betty. The sausage lady, Irma, sold goat meat. That was no doubt why she wanted to buy Betty in the first place. The poor goat was probably heartsick and terrified at being taken away by a stranger. As sick as Jennsen was over Betty, though, and as much as she ached to go find her and have her back, she couldn't put that desire ahead of Sebastian's life.

Passing stands selling food only served to remind her of how hungry she was, especially after the effort of climbing all the stairs up to the palace. She hadn't eaten since that morning and wished she could buy something to eat, now, but there was no hope of that. People cooked over open fires made with wood they no doubt had brought with them. Pans sizzled with butter, garlic, and spices. Smoke from roasting meats drifted past. The aromas were intoxicating and made her hunger nearly unbearable.

When her mind wandered to her hunger, Jennsen thought about Sebastian. Every moment she delayed could mean another lash of a whip for him, another cut, another twist to a limb, another broken bone. Another moment of agony. The thought of it made bile rise in the back of her throat. No wonder he was here to help in the struggle to defeat D'Hara.

A thought even more terrifying abruptly jolted her: Mord-Sith. Wherever Jennsen had traveled with her mother throughout D'Hara, no one feared anything or anyone more than they feared the Mord-Sith. Their ability to inflict pain and suffering was legend. It was said that this side of the Keeper's hand, a Mord-Sith existed without peer.

What if the D'Harans used one of those women to torture Sebastian? Even though he had no magic, that wouldn't matter. With that Agiel of theirs – and who knew what else – the Mord-Sith could hurt anyone. They simply had the added ability to capture a person with magic. A person without magic, like Sebastian, would be nothing but a brief blood sport to a Mord-Sith.

The crowds thinned as she reached the edge of the open-air market. The temporary lane she was on dwindled to nothing as it reached the last stall, occupied by a lanky man selling leather tack and piles of used wagon fittings. There was nothing beyond his heavily loaded wagon full of pieces and parts but desolate open land. An endless file of people moved along the road going south. She could see a haze of dust in the air marking the more distant sections of the road south, along with others branching off to the southwest and southeast. No road went west.

A few people at the fringe of the marketplace glanced her way as she struck out, alone, toward the lowering sun. While some people might have looked her way, none followed into the wasteland that was the Azrith Plains. Jennsen was relieved to be alone. Being around people had proven as dangerous as she had always feared. The market scene was quickly left behind as she marched west.

Jennsen slid her hand in under her cloak, feeling the reassuring presence of her knife. Lying against her body, it was warm to the touch, as if it were a living thing, rather than silver and steel.

At least the thief had taken her money and not her knife. Given a choice of the two, she would rather have the knife. She had lived her whole life without much money, her and her mother providing for themselves. But a knife was vital to that means of survival. If you lived in a palace, you needed money. If you lived out-of-doors, you needed a knife, and she had never seen a better knife than this one, despite its provenience.

Her fingers idly traced the ornate letter 'R' on the silver handle. Some people needed a knife even if they lived in a palace, she guessed.

She turned back to look, and was relieved to see that no one followed her. The plateau had shrunk in the distance, until all the people below it looked like slow little ants moving about. It was good to be away from the place, but she knew she would have to return, after seeing Althea, if she was to rescue Sebastian.

As she walked backward for a spell to gain a reprieve from the icy wind in her face, her gaze rose along the road switching back and forth up the steep cliffs, to the massive stone wall surrounding the palace itself. Coming in from the south, she hadn't seen the road. At one place along its length a bridge spanned a particularly treacherous gap in the rock. The bridge was pulled up. As if the cliff itself were not deterrent enough, the high stone walls around the People's Palace would defeat any attempt to get inside unless you were allowed in.

She hoped it would not be that hard to get in to see Althea.

Somewhere in that vast complex, Sebastian was held prisoner. She wondered if he thought himself forever abandoned, as Betty probably did. She whispered a prayer to the good spirits asking that he not give up hope, and that the good spirits somehow let him know she was going to get him out.

When she tired of walking backward, and of seeing the People's Palace, she turned around. Then, she had to endure the wind buffeting her, sometimes ripping the breath right out of her mouth. Sharp gusts kicked the dry gritty ground up into her eyes.

The land was flat, dry, and featureless, mostly hardpan cut through here and there with a swath of coarse sandy soil. In places, the tawny landscape was stained a darker brown, as if strong tea had been stirred through. There was only occasional vegetation, and that was a low, scruffy plant, now winter brown and brittle.

Gathered to the west lay a ragged line of mountains. The one in the center looked like it might have snow on top, but it was hard to tell against the sun. She had no guess at how far it was. Being unfamiliar with such land, she found it difficult to judge distances out on the plain. It could be hours, or even days, for all she knew. At least she didn't have to trudge through snow, as they often had to do on their way up to the People's Palace.

Jennsen realized that, even in winter, she was going to need water. She guessed that in a swamp there would be water aplenty. She realized, too, that the woman who had given her directions said that it was a long way, but hadn't described what was to her a long way. Maybe to her a long way was what Jennsen would consider only a brisk walk of a few hours. Maybe the woman had meant days. Jennsen whispered a prayer under her breath that it wouldn't be days, even though she didn't at all relish the idea of going into a swamp.

When a sound rose to rattle through the wind, she turned and saw a plume of dust rising in the distance behind her. She squinted, finally recognizing that it was a wagon coming her way.

Jennsen turned all the way around, scanning the barren country trying to see if there was any place she could hide. She didn't like the idea of being caught out in the open all alone. It occurred to her that men from back in the open-air market might have watched her leave, and then planned to wait until she was all alone, with no one around, to come out and attack her.

She started running. Since the wagon was coming from the palace, she ran the direction she had been walking – west – toward the dark slash of mountains. As she ran, she sucked frigid gasps of air so cold it hurt her throat. The plain stretched out before her, without so much as a crack to hide in. She focused on the dark line of mountains, running for them with all her effort, but even as she ran, she knew they were too far.

Before long, Jennsen forced herself to stop. She was acting foolish. She couldn't outrun horses. She bent at her waist, hands on her thighs, catching her breath, watching the wagon come for her. If someone was coming out to attack her, then running, using up her strength, was about as senseless a thing as she could do.

She turned back to face the sun and kept walking, but at a pace that wouldn't wear her out. If she was going to have to fight, she should at least not be winded. Maybe it was only someone going home, and they would turn in a different direction. She had only spotted them because of the noise of the wagon and the dust it raised. They probably didn't even see her walking.

The chilling thought washed through her: maybe a Mord-Sith had already tortured a confession out of Sebastian. Maybe one of those merciless women had already broken him. She feared to think what she would do if someone were methodically going about snapping her bones in two. Jennsen could not honestly say what she would do under such excruciating torture.

Maybe, under unendurable agony, he had given them Jennsen's name. He knew all about her. He knew Darken Rahl was her father. He knew Richard Rahl was her half brother. He knew she wanted to go to the sorceress for help.

Maybe they had promised him they would stop if Sebastian gave her up. Could she blame him for a betrayal under such conditions?

Maybe the wagon racing toward her was full of big, grim, D'Haran soldiers come to capture her. Maybe the nightmare was only about to begin in earnest. Maybe this was the day she lived in fear of.

As tears of fright stung her eyes, Jennsen slipped her hand under her cloak and checked to be sure that her knife was free in its scabbard. She lifted it slightly, then pushed it back down, feeling its reassuring metallic click as it seated in its sheath.

The minutes dragged as she walked, waiting for the wagon to catch her. She fought to keep her fear in check and tried to run through in her mind everything her mother had taught her about using a knife. Jennsen was alone, but she was not helpless. She knew what to do. She told herself to remember that.

If there were too many men, though, nothing would help her. She recalled only too vividly how the men at her house had grabbed her, and how helpless she had then been. They had caught her by surprise, but, of course, it mattered not how, really

– they had caught her. That was all that mattered. If not for Sebastian . . .

When she turned again to check, the wagon was bearing down on her. She planted her feet, keeping her cloak lifted open slightly so she could reach in and snatch her knife, surprising her attacker. Surprise could be her valuable ally, too, and the only one she could hope to summon.

She saw, then, a lopsided grin of straight teeth beaming at her. The big blond man drew his wagon close, scattering gravel and raising dust. As he set the brake, the dust drifted away. It was the man from market, the man beside Irma's place, the man who had given her the drink of wine. He was alone.

Unsure of his intent, Jennsen kept her tone curt and her knife hand at the ready. 'What are you doing out here?'

He still wore the grin. 'I came out to give you a ride.'

'What about your brothers?'

'I left them back at the palace.'

Jennsen didn't trust him. He had no reason to come give her a ride. 'Thank you, but I think you had better go back to your own business.' She started walking.

He hopped down off the wagon, landing with a thud. She turned to be ready, should he come at her.

'Look, I wouldn't feel right about it,' he said.

'About what?'

'I could never forgive myself if I just stood by and let you go out here to your death – which is what it will be with no food, no water, no nothing. I thought about what you said, that there are some things that you have to do, or else life means nothing and isn't worth living. I couldn't live with myself if I knew you were out here going to your death.' His tenacity faltered and his voice turned more pleading. 'Come on, climb up in the wagon and let me give you a ride?'

'What about your brothers? Before I found out I'd lost my money, you wouldn't rent me a horse because you said you had to get back.'

He hooked a thumb behind his belt, resigned to having to explain himself. 'Well, we've been doing so well at selling wine today that we made a goodly sum. Joe and Clayton were wanting to stay at the palace, anyway, and have a little fun for a change. It was that Irma, selling her spicy sausages right beside us, that did it.' He shrugged. 'So, since she helped us do so well, it gives me a chance to come help you. Since she took your horses and supplies, I figure that giving you a ride is the least I can do. Kind of makes it even out a little. It's just a ride. It's not like I'm risking my life or something. Just a bit of help I'm offering someone who I know needs it.'

Jennsen surely could use help, but she feared to trust this stranger.

'I'm Tom,' he said, as if reading her thoughts. 'I'd be grateful if you would let me do this to help you.'

'What do you mean?'

'Like you said – some things you have to do to make life a little more meaningful.' The briefest of glances took in her ringlets of red hair beneath the cloak's hood before turning solemn. 'That's the way it would make me feel . . . grateful to have done something like that.'

She broke the gaze first. 'I'm Jennsen. But I don't—'

'Come along, then. I have some wine—'

'I don't like wine. It only makes me thirsty.'

He shrugged. 'I have plenty of water. I brought along some meat pies, too. They're still hot, I bet, if you hurry and have some now.'

She studied his blue eyes, blue like her bastard father's. Even so, this man's eyes had a simple sincerity about them. His smile wasn't cocky, but modest.

'Don't you have a wife to get back to?'

This time, it was Tom who broke the gaze to look at the ground. 'No, ma'am. I'm not married. I travel around a lot. I don't imagine a woman would much take to that kind of life. Besides, it doesn't afford me much of a chance to come to know anyone well enough to be thinking about marriage. Someday, though, I dearly hope to find a woman who would want to share life with me, a woman who makes me smile, a woman I can live up to.'

Jennsen was surprised to see that the very question made his face go red. It seemed to her as if his boldness in talking to her and offering her this ride might be more forward than was his customary conduct. As affable as he was, he appeared painfully shy. Something about a man that big and strong being intimidated by her, a lone woman in the middle of nowhere, by her question about matters of the heart, put her at ease.

'If I'm not harming you, your business at earning a living—'

'No,' he put in. 'No, you're not – not at all.' He gestured back toward the plateau. 'We made a good profit today and we can afford a short rest. My brothers don't mind at all. We travel all over and buy whatever goods we can find at a reasonable price, everything from wine, to carpets, to spring chickens, and then we haul it back here to sell. It would really be doing my brothers a favor, giving them a break.'

Jennsen nodded. 'I could use the ride, Tom.'

He turned serious. 'I know. A man's life is at stake.'

Tom scrambled up onto the wagon and held down a hand. 'Careful, ma'am.'

She took his big hand and put a boot in the iron rung. 'I'm Jennsen.'

'So you said, ma'am.' He gently drew her up to the seat.

As soon as she was seated, he pulled a blanket from behind and placed it in a pile in her lap, apparently not wanting to be so presumptuous as to spread it out over her. As she arranged it on her lap, she smiled her appreciation for the warm wool cover. Reaching behind again, he rooted around under a pile of well-worn packing blankets and came up with a small bundle. Tom grinned his lopsided smile as he presented her with the pie wrapped in a white cloth. He was as good as his word; it was still warm. He recovered a waterskin, too, and set it on the seat between them.

'If you'd prefer, you can ride in back. I brought plenty of blankets to keep you warm, and they might be more comfortable to sit on than a wooden seat.'

'I'm fine up here for now,' she said. She lifted the pie in gesture. 'When I get my supplies back, and my money, I want to pay you back for everything. You keep a tally, and I'll pay you back for it all.'

He released the brake and flicked the reins. 'If that's your wish, but I don't expect it.'

'I do,' she said as the wagon lurched ahead.

As soon as they were under way, he turned from her westerly course to a more northwest line.

She instantly reverted to her suspicion. 'What are you doing? Where do you think you're going?'

He looked a little startled at her renewed mistrust. 'You said you wanted to go to Althea's, didn't you?'

'Yes, but I was told to go west until I reached the tallest snowcapped mountain, and then on the other side to turn north and follow cliffs—'

'Oh,' he said, realizing then what she was thinking and why. 'That's if you want it to take an extra day.'

'Why would that woman tell me to go a way that would take more time?'

'Probably because that's the way everyone goes to Althea's and she didn't know you were in a hurry.'

'Why send people that way, if it takes more time?'

'People go that way because they fear the swamp. That way puts you in closest to Althea's at the end, meaning you have to go through the least amount of the swamp. It was probably the only way she knew about.'

Jennsen had to grab the rail for support as the wagon bounced over a crease in the rocky ground. He was right, the wooden seat was hard sitting and with a wagon made for hauling heavy loads, it bounced more when empty.

'But, shouldn't I fear the swamp, too?' she finally asked.

'I suppose.'

'Well then, why should I go this other way?'

He looked over, again, taking the briefest glance at her hair. It was a behaviour she was used to. Most people couldn't help but to look.

'You said a man's life was at stake,' he said, his timidity gone. 'It takes a lot less time this way, cutting the corner off the route by going this side of that peak she told you about and not having to go up that twisting canyon beneath the cliffs. The problem is, you have to go in the swamp from the back, so you'll have more of the swamp to go through to get in to Althea's.'

'And that doesn't take more time, going through more swamp?'

'Yes, but even with having to go through more swamp, I'm betting you'll still save a day each way. That's two days saved.'

Jennsen didn't like swamps. More to the point, she didn't like the kinds of things that lived in swamps.

'Is it much more dangerous?'

'You wouldn't strike out alone with no supplies if it wasn't pretty important – a matter of life and death. If you were willing to risk your life to do that, then I figured you'd be looking to save any time you can. If you'd rather, though, I can take you the long way, with less distance through the swamp. Up to you, but if time is important, it's two days more by going that way.'

'No, you're right.' The meat pie on her lap was warm. It felt good to have her fingers around it. He was a thoughtful man for bringing it. 'Thank you, Tom, for thinking to save time.'

'Who is it that's at the other end of life and death?'

'A friend,' she said.

'Must be a good friend.'

'I'd be dead, now, if not for him.'

He was silent as they rolled toward the dark band of mountains in the distance. She brooded about what might lie in the swamp. Worse, she worried about what would happen to Sebastian if she didn't get Althea's help soon enough.

'How long?' Jennsen asked. 'How long till we get to the swamp?'

'Depends on how much snow is in the pass, and on a few other things. I don't go this way often, so I can't say for sure. If we ride all night, though, I'm reasonably sure we can be to the back reaches of the swamp by morning.'

'How long to get to Althea's, then. Through the swamp, I mean.'

He glanced over uneasily. 'Sorry, Jennsen, but I don't know for sure. I've never been in Althea's swamp before.'

'Any guess?'

'Just knowing the lay of the land, I don't think it should take

189

more than a day to go in and come back, but I'm guessing. And that doesn't count how much time you'll be spending in there with Althea.' His uneasiness returned. 'I'll get you in to Althea's as quickly as I can.'

Jennsen had to talk to Althea about the Lord Rahl – both her father, and the present Lord Rahl, Richard, her half brother. It would not be good if Tom were to discover who she was, or her purpose. His helpfulness would evaporate, at the least. She also thought that a reason for him to stay behind might be in order, lest he get suspicious.

She shook her head. 'I think it would be best if you stayed with the wagon and horses. If you drive all night, then you'll need to get some rest to be ready as soon as I come out. It will save us time.'

He nodded as he considered her words. 'That makes sense. But I could still—'

'No. I appreciate the ride, the food and water, and the warm blanket, but I won't let you risk your life in there, too. It would be the most help if you waited with the wagon and were ready to drive back when I come out.'

She watched the wind in his blond hair as he thought it over. 'All right, if those are your wishes. I'm glad you let me help you with my part of it. Where to after you see Althea?'

'Back to the palace,' she said.

'Then, with good fortune, I'll have you back at the palace day after tomorrow.'

That was three days for Sebastian. She didn't know if he had three days, or three hours. Or even three minutes. As long as there was a chance he was still alive, though, she had to go into the swamp.

Despite Jennsen's misgivings about the job ahead of her, the meat pie tasted wonderful. Hungry as she was, nearly anything would have tasted good. She pulled a big piece of meat out of the pie, and, holding it between a finger and thumb, fed it to Tom.

After he chewed, he said, 'The moon will be up not long after sundown, so by the time I reach the pass through the mountains, I should be able to see well enough to keep going. There's plenty of blankets in back. When night comes, you should probably crawl back there and, if you can, get some sleep for tomorrow. You'll be needing the rest. In the morning, I'll catch a nap while you go in to see Althea. When you come back, I'll drive all night and get you right back to the palace. I hope that way we can save enough time for you to help your friend.'

She swayed in the seat along with the big man she had only just met, who was doing all this for a stranger.

'Thank you, Tom. You're a good man.'

He grinned. 'My mama always said so.'

Just as she took another bite, he added, 'I hope Lord Rahl thinks so, too. You'll tell him when you see him, won't you?'

She didn't know what he could possibly mean, and feared to ask him. As her mind raced, she chewed, using her mouthful as an excuse to delay. Saying anything might inadvertently get her into trouble. Sebastian's life was at stake. Jennsen decided to smile and play along. She finally swallowed the mouthful.

'Of course.'

By the slight but sublime smile that lent a curve to the line of his mouth as he tended the reins and watched out ahead, it had been the right answer.

Chapter 20

Light suddenly hurt her eyes. Jennsen held a hand up against the brightness and saw that Tom was pulling the blankets back off her. She stretched and yawned, but then, realizing fully why she was in the back of a wagon, where they were, and why they were there, her yawn cut short. She sat up. The wagon was stopped at the edge of a grassy meadow.

Jennsen put a hand on the side of the wagon, on the coarse plank worn smooth along the top edge, and blinked as she looked about. Behind them, craggy gray rock rose up, holding in its cracks and fissures low stalwart bushes, gnarled and hunkered low, as if against an enduring wind. Her gaze rose up the weathered rock to where it dissolved into mist. Tangled growth lay at the foot of the walls beyond the edges of the meadow and beside the narrow chasm that cut through the rock. Tom had somehow jockeyed the wagon between those steep cliffs. The two big draft horses, still standing in their harnesses, cropped at the shaggy grass.

Ahead, beyond the meadow, the ground descended into the gloom among spreading trees, trailers of vine, and hanging moss. Strange calls, clicks, and whistles came from under the verdant shroud.

'In the middle of winter . . .' was all she could think to say.

Tom lifted the feed bags from the back of the wagon. 'Might be a nice place to spend the winter, too' – he gestured with a nod down the hill, under the tangle of growth – 'were it not for what people say comes out of there. If it weren't true, I'd bet there would be some fool who by now would have tried to give it a go, here. But, if they have, they were pulled in there by some nightmare creature and never made it back out.'

'You mean, you really think there are ... monsters, or something, in there?'

He rested his forearms on the wagon's sides as he leaned in, right over her. 'Jennsen, I don't hold with scaring ladies. When I was a boy, some of the other boys enjoyed waving a wriggling snake at the girls just to hear them scream. I never did. I'm not trying to frighten you.

'But I wouldn't be able to live with myself if I just allowed you to go bounding in there as if it were some lark and then you ended up never coming out. Maybe it's just talk; I don't know; I've never gone in there. I don't know anyone who has ever gone in there without being invited in – and that's from the other side. People say you can't go in the back and live to tell about it. If anyone would insist on attempting it, it would be you. I know you're here for an important reason, so I don't expect you're going to sit around for days, waiting for an invitation.'

Jennsen swallowed. Her tongue tasted sour. She nodded her thanks, not knowing what to say.

Tom swiped back his fall of blond hair. 'I just wanted to tell you the truth of what I know.' He hoisted the feed bags on his way to the horses.

Whatever was in there was in there. She had to go in, that was all there was to it. She didn't have any choice; if she wanted to get Sebastian away from his captors, she had to go in. If she ever wanted to be free of Lord Rahl, she had to go in.

She reached under her cloak and touched the hilt of her knife. She wasn't some town girl, scared of her own shadow, unable to defend herself.

She was Jennsen Rahl.

Jennsen pushed the blankets the rest of the way off her and climbed out of the wagon bed, using a rear wheel spoke for a step. Tom was coming back around carrying a waterskin.

'Drink? It's water – I kept it hooked over the hame so the horses would keep it from freezing.'

The cold had dried her out and she drank eagerly. She saw Tom wipe sweat from his brow and realized only then how warm it really was. She supposed no proper self-respecting swamp full of monsters would allow itself to be frozen over.

Tom pulled back the folds of cloth of something he held in one hand. 'Breakfast?'

She smiled at seeing a meat pie. 'You're a thoughtful man, besides being a good man.'

He grinned as he handed her the pie and then turned to undo the trace chains from the horses. 'Don't forget, you promised to tell Lord Rahl,' he called back to her.

Rather than be pulled into any kind of a conversation having to do with her hunter, she diverted him from the subject. 'You'll be right here, then? When I come back, I mean? You'll be waiting, so we can get back?'

He peered back as he lifted the breaching strap over the horse's rump. 'You have my word, Jennsen. I won't desert you here.'

By his expression, he was swearing an oath. She smiled her appreciation. 'You should get some rest. You've driven all night.'

'I'll try.'

She took another bite of the meat pie. It was cold, but good, and it was filling. As she chewed, she glanced at the wall of green beyond the meadow, at the darkness within, then appraised the iron gray sky.

'Any idea what time of day it is?'

'Sun's been up an hour, at most,' he said as he checked the joints on the leather straps. He gestured back the way they had come in. 'Before we started down into this low place, we were up above this fog and mist. It was sunny up there.'

As somber as it was below the dark overcast, such a notion amazed her. It looked like dawn had yet to arrive. It was hard to believe that the sun was shining not far off, but she had seen such heavy blankets of fog before as she looked down from high places.

After she was finished eating the meat pie and had brushed the crumbs from her palm, Jennsen stood waiting until Tom turned from unbuckling the girth strap from around the deep, powerful chest of one of his horses. Both big, well-kept animals were gray with black manes and tails. They were horses as big as any she had ever seen. They seemed out of scale, until she took in Tom working beside them. He made them seem not quite so imposing, especially as he gave them affectionate strokes. They appeared to welcome his familiar touch.

Both horses looked back occasionally at Tom as he removed all their gear, or rolled a dark eye toward Jennsen, but both kept much closer watch on the shadows beyond the edge of the meadow. Their ears were at attention, and fixed on the swamp.

'I'd better get going. There's no time to waste.' He offered a single nod. 'Thank you, Tom. If I don't get another chance to say it, thank you for helping me. Not many people would have done as you did.'

His shy grin appeared again to show his teeth. 'Most anyone would have helped you. But I'm pleased to be the one who was able to.'

She was sure he meant something that she didn't quite understand. Whatever it was, she had bigger worries.

Her eyes turned toward the echoing calls coming out of the swamp. There was no telling how big the trees were because the tops disappeared up into the mist. As large as they looked, the trunks would have to be enormous. Vines descended out of the mist, along with any number of other twisting climbing plants enshrouding the limbs of the huge trees, as if trying to wrestle them down into the darkness below.

Jennsen searched the rim and found a ridge descending from the edge of the meadow, like the spine of some huge beast beneath the ground. It ran down in under the spreading limbs. It wasn't a path, exactly, but a place to start. She had lived in the woods her whole life and could find a trail others would never know existed. There was no trail into this place. Nothing, it appeared, ever went in. She would have to find her own way. Jennsen turned back from the edge of the meadow and shared a long look with the big man's blue eyes.

He offered her a small smile – respect for what she was doing. 'May the good spirits be with you, and watch over you.'

'And you, Tom. Get some sleep. When I get back, we'll need to ride hard back to the palace.'

He bowed. 'By your command.'

She smiled at his surprising manner, and then turned to the gloom and headed down in.

The swamp held heat gathered under its skirts. The humidity was like a presence waiting to push intruders back. With every step it grew darker. The quiet was as thick as the damp air, and the few calls reverberating through the darkness beyond only accentuated the hush and the vast distance that lay below.

Jennsen followed the spine of the ridge as it twisted this way and that, going ever lower. Branches of trees off to each side drooped with the weight of mosses and vines draped over them. In some places, as she stepped along the exposed rock of the ridge, she had to squat down to duck under the limbs. In other places, she had to push vines aside to make progress. The stink of decay drifted up to her through the dead still air.

Turning, looking back, she saw a tunnel of light back up to the meadow. In the center of the circle of dull light at the end, she could see the silhouette of a big man, standing, hands on hips, watching down at her. As dark as it was, he had no hope of seeing her. She could only see him because he stood against the light. But he stood watching, anyway.

Jennsen couldn't decide what she thought about him. He was difficult to figure out. He seemed a kindhearted man, but she trusted no one. Except Sebastian. She trusted him.

As her eyes adjusted to the dim light, she saw, looking back, that the way she had come in was the only way to enter, at least anywhere close that she could see. There were steep walls where the rock dropped downward. The meadow had been like a mere shelf in the mountainside's descent into the swamp. Below the meadow, the walls held a wealth of plants that used the rock for support as they climbed upward from the swamp below. The ridge she used for her descent was a mere fold of rock that provided a way for her to climb down. Without it, the walls were too steep.

Taking a deep breath for resolve as she gazed about, Jennsen started back down, following the ridge of rock as it twisted its way down, deeper and deeper in among the trees. In places, there were frightening drops to each side of where she walked. In one place, there was only darkness to each side below, as if she were on a thread of stone spanning a rupture in the world. After peering down into the depths, and imagining the Keeper of the underworld below awaiting the unwary, she trod more carefully.

She soon came to realize that many of the trees she had seen up higher had only been the canopy of towering, ancient oaks rising up from ledges in the rock. She realized that she had mistaken some of their upper limbs for trunks. Jennsen had never seen trees so big. Her fear was almost replaced by awe. She gaped at the layer upon layer of massive limbs as she climbed down past them. In the distance she saw nests, large clumps of twigs and stalks draped with downy moss and lichen, perched in the crotch of limbs. If the nests were occupied, she didn't see what sort of bird could have built such imposing havens, but she guessed they had to be raptors.

As she stooped while clambering over rock to squeeze herself under a tightly woven net of limbs drooping down close over the spine of the ridge, the vista opened onto a vast land hidden under the thick leafy layers of the upper canopy. It was like a whole new world hidden away, unvisited by anyone before. Shafts of muted light hardly dared penetrate down this far. Here and there vines hung down out of the dark growth above. Birds drifted silently through the cavernous gloom. An animal she had never heard before called from the distance. A faraway answer returned from another direction.

As primitive and foreboding as the place seemed, she also thought it was darkly beautiful. It put her in mind of being in a garden of the underworld, where plants basked in eternal gloom. The underworld might be the Keeper's cold domain, but the Creator's everlasting light nourished and warmed good souls.

In a way, the swamp reminded her of so much about D'Hara – dark, threatening, and dangerous, but at the same time achingly beautiful. In the same way, her knife embodied the ugliness of the House of Rahl, yet it was undeniably exquisite.

Trees clung to the rocky slope around her with clawlike roots, as if fearing to be dragged down to what might lurk in the lower reaches. Some of the ancient pines, long dead, lay partly fallen, caught by their brethren before they could topple to the ground.

The nearby trees embraced them, as if trying to help them up. Dead gray wood was visible in places under the covering of growth climbing up the tilted trunks. Many, though, had collapsed to the ground. One old tree lay across her way, as if it had melted there, conforming to every contour, every rise and fall of the ridge. The disintegrating wood was spongy underfoot, and teeming with insects.

Up in the branches, an owl watched as she scrambled ever downward. Ants marched along the ground, carrying bits of treasures from the damp forest. Roaches, big, hard, and glossy brown, skittered across the leaf litter. Things off in the dense undergrowth disturbed branches as they moved away from her.

Jennsen had spent a lifetime in forests and had seen everything from huge bears to newborn fawns, birds to bugs, bats to newts. There were things that worried her, like snakes and bears with cubs, but she knew the animals well. For the most part, they feared people and usually wanted only to be left alone, so they generally didn't frighten her. But she didn't know what animals might be lurking in this dark and damp place, what poison things with fangs. She didn't know what conjured beasts might prowl the nether reaches of this sorceress's lair, beasts that feared nothing.

She saw spiders, fat, dark, and hairy, their legs slowly raking the dank air, descending smoothly on threads anchored somewhere above. They vanished into the ferns growing in sprawling mats across the ground. As warm and humid as it was, Jennsen kept her cloak closed around her and the hood covering her head to better protect herself from the likes of spiders.

The bite of a spider could be as deadly as any animal. Dead was dead, no matter the cause. The Keeper of the dead gave no special dispensation because the deadly poison came from something small and seemingly insignificant. The Keeper of the dead embraced with eternal darkness those come into his domain – for whatever reason. No grace was granted for how you came to be dead.

As at home as Jennsen felt in the out-of-doors, and as hauntingly beautiful as the swamp was, the place still kept her eyes wide and her pulse racing. Every vine or green wisp she touched seemed threatening, and more than once made her jump.

The whole place felt as though death skulked nearby.

And then, before her, the spine of rock, her only path down, ended in a still, flat, rank, moldering, mossy place crisscrossed with a tangle of roots. It looked like the trees feared the murky wet, and tried to keep their roots up out of it. To the sides, the ground was grown over with every sort of spreading vegetation.

She spotted the distinctive shape of a leg bone sticking up from the muddy expanse to the side. The bone was covered with fuzzy green mold, but the general shape remained recognizable. What sort of animal it could be from, she didn't know. At least, she hoped it was an animal bone.

She was surprised to come upon muddy spots that actually looked as if the mud were boiling. Gooey bubbles of dark brown mud bubbled as if at a slow boil, throwing globs of the thick mud and releasing steam. Nothing grew in the sunken areas of bubbling mud. In some places, the mud had hardened into collections of short cones from which rose yellowish vapor.

As Jennsen carefully picked a path among the tangle of roots, between steaming vents and boiling mud, wending her way deeper into the shadows at the bottom, she saw that the muddy stretches began to be replaced by standing water. At first, it was pools and puddles that boiled and hissed and released plumes of acrid vapor. As she left the hot springs behind, the water grew in size to ponds surrounded by tall reeds reaching up toward clouds of tiny bugs flitting together in balls.

Stagnant water finally took over in earnest, a forest floor that was dark and liquid. Dead trunks stood in the black water, sentinels watching over a land reeking of rot. The whoops and calls of animals carried across the water from places darker still. Duckweed grew in some areas near the edges, under leafy banks, welcoming the unwary with the look of green ground to tread more easily across. Jennsen noticed eyes poked up through the duckweed, watching her pass near by.

The mossy ground became spongy, until it, too, gradually lowered beneath the motionless water. At first, she could see the bottom, just inches below the glassy surface, but it went deeper until she could see only darkness below. Through that darkness, she saw shapes, darker yet, glide by.

Jennsen stepped from root to root, trying to keep her balance without having to put her hands to the often slimy trunks of trees for support. By staying on the protruding curves of roots, she didn't have to step down into water. She feared the water might hide a hole that could swallow her.

With each step, as the roots standing above the surface of the water grew farther and farther apart, the knot in the pit of her stomach drew tighter. She hesitated, fearing she was going too far, that she would reach a place where she couldn't turn around. She couldn't really question her judgment that this was the best way in, because there had been no opportunity to make a choice; this had been the only way. She leaned down, squinting into the gloom, peering ahead past trailers of moss and leafy vines. Through the mist and shadows and undergrowth, she thought that not far ahead the ground rose up again, offering a drier path.

Taking a deep breath of the sultry air, Jennsen extended her leg to step across to the next fat root, but she couldn't reach it. She squatted slightly and stretched harder, trying to span the patch of still water, but it was just too far. She straightened to reconsider.

She was going to have to jump to the distant thick bulge of root. It was more of a hop, really, than a jump. She just didn't like what would be under her if she slipped and fell. She also didn't want to have to balance on the lone root out in the expanse of water. If she jumped with enough speed and hit the root just right, she could spring off it to the far bank.

She put her fingertips against the smooth but sticky trunk of a tree for support. At least it wasn't slimy, which could make her hand slip at the worst possible moment. She studied the distance. As much of a reach as it was, it was the closest place that offered a firm dry step. With enough momentum she could hop to the next root beyond on drier ground.

Jennsen took a deep breath and then with a grunt of effort shoved away from the tree, bounding out over the span of open water.

Just as she landed on the curve of tree root, the root moved underfoot. Her weight was committed – she couldn't reverse direction.

The root, thicker than her ankle, suddenly writhed beneath her and disappeared. In an instant, a thick coil twisted back around, grasping her calf as another length of cold scales whipped up to seize her around her knee.

It was all so fast that part of her was still going for the root that had grabbed her as another part of her was trying to recoil. Caught between where she'd left and where she was going, she had nothing to help her stay upright.

Instinctively, Jennsen grabbed for her knife, but as she did the thing twisted violently, flinging her down face-first. She threw her arms out to break her fall. Water frothed under her. She just caught the distant roots at the water's edge, real roots, wet but rough and woody under her clutching fingers.

But even as she broke her fall by desperately seizing the roots barely at the limit of her reach, she was welcomed into the embrace of an enormous snake surfacing from beneath her through the churning water.

Chapter 21

Jennsen strained with all her might, using the roots to try to pull herself free. She cried out as living coils wrenched her around, breaking her grip on the roots, and flipped her onto her back. She frantically reached behind, splashing, groping, trying to snatch for another handhold. She reached, then stretched again, catching hold of thick roots with first one hand and then the other just in time to prevent herself from being dragged under the water.

The head came out of the depths to slink up across her stomach, as if to inspect its stubborn prey. It was the biggest snake Jennsen had ever seen. The body, covered in iridescent green scales, shimmered in the weak light as muscles along the powerful trunk flexed. The light intermittently played gleaming stripes along the length of it. Black bands sweeping back across the fierce yellow eyes made it look as if it were wearing a mask. Red tongue flicking, the dark green head glided up between her breasts, coming for her face.

Crying out, she shoved the head aside. In response, the muscular body twisted and contracted, grappled with her, drawing her out into the deeper water. Jennsen's fingertips held fast to the roots. With all her might she tried to pull herself out of the water, but the snake was too heavy and too strong.

She tried to kick her legs, but the snake had them both, now. The coils compressed, tugged, and dragged her in deeper. Coughing up water, Jennsen fought panic that clawed at her, just as fiercely, just as tenaciously, as if it, too, were a thing alive.

She needed her knife. But to get the knife, she would have to let go of the roots. But if she let go, the beast would pull her down under the black water and drown her.

One hand, she told herself. That was all she needed, one hand. She could get her knife if she let go with one hand. But as the unrelenting snake undulated, steadily working itself up her body, gripping her now around the middle, her panic locked her fingers all the tighter to the root.

As the broad flat head of the snake emerged from the water and once again began slinking up along her body, Jennsen gripped the root as tight as she could in her left hand. With desperate resolve, she let her right hand go and thrust it in under her cloak. Wet cloth bunched as she pushed. She couldn't get under it. The snake's jaw pressed against her chest, as if to let her know that next it was going to compress her lungs so she couldn't breathe.

She sucked in her stomach and pushed with her fingers, trying to get them in under the snake, but the heavy body squeezed with paralyzing power against the length of her torso, preventing her from getting her hand in under her cloak to get her knife.

As she struggled madly to get to the weapon, wriggling, worming her fingers, the snake suddenly lurched, lifting heavy coils higher, pinning her arm to her body.

With her one hand, she still tightly gripped the root behind. The weight of the thing, though, felt as if it would pull her arm from the socket if she didn't let go. She was absolutely certain that letting go would be the worst thing she could do. But the weight was too much. The snake was pulling her so hard that she feared the skin was going to strip from her fingertips.

Despite her best effort, she felt her fingers slipping from the root. As tears of pain stung her eyes, she had no choice. She let go of the root.

She plunged into the dark depths of deeper water. Her feet at last contacted the bottom. She used her momentum to go where she was pulled, letting her legs bend, and then with strength powered by terror, she pushed off the submerged roots. As her body flicked around, she seized the roots on the far side.

The snake rolled with her, turning her on her back. She cried out as her shoulder twisted. But in all the movement, the splashing, the rolling, the choking on water, there was a brief opening in the snake's grip on her. She didn't waste it. She seized the silver handle.

As the broad head, with the thin red tongue flicking, was again coming toward her face, she brought her knife up, wedging the tip of the blade up under the snake's jaw. The snake paused, seeming to recognize the threat that the razor-sharp point represented. Both were still, staring at each other. She felt giddy relief to at last have her knife in hand, even if it was a deadlock.

She was on her back, lying in water with the heavy snake wrapped around her. She wouldn't be able to balance or use her weight to help her. Her arm was weak from the struggle and ached from being twisted. She was exhausted. With all that working against her, it would be no easy matter to dispatch an animal so big and powerful. Even if they were on dry land, such a task would be difficult.

The yellow eyes watched her. She wondered if it was a venomous snake. She hadn't yet seen its fangs. If it went for her face, she wondered if she could be quick enough to stop it.

'I'm sorry I stepped on you,' she said. She didn't actually believe the snake could understand her; she was, in a way, talking to herself, reasoning out loud. 'We've both scared each other.'

The snake remained stone still as it watched her. The tongue remained inside the mouth. Its head, lifted several inches by the tip of the knife, could probably feel the sharp point. Maybe it conceived the threat of the blade as a fang. Jennsen didn't know, she just knew that it would be better not to have to battle such a creature.

She was in the water, the snake's domain, and out of hers. Knife or no knife, the outcome was not certain. Even if she killed it, the weight of the creature, its coils locked around her in a death grip, could still drag her under and drown her. Better to part without a battle, if possible.

'Go, now,' she whispered with deadly seriousness. 'Or I will have to try to kill you.' She lifted the point of the knife to make herself understood in a language she was more confident the snake might possibly understand.

Her legs began to throb as she felt the constriction ease. Inch by inch, the head drew back. Scaled coils loosened and slipped away from her body and legs, leaving her to feel suddenly buoyant. Jennsen followed the head as it backed away, keeping the point of her knife under the thing's jaws, prepared at the slightest sign of threat to thrust with all her strength. Finally, it slipped back into the water.

As soon as she was free of the weight, she scrambled up onto solid ground. She rested on her hands and knees, knife gripped in her fist, gasping for air, getting her breath, letting her frayed nerves settle. She had no idea what the snake thought, or why, or if the same thing might work in another time and place, but this day it had and she whispered a prayer of thanks to the good spirits. If indeed they had anything to do with her deliverance from death's scaly grip, she didn't want to fail to express her gratitude.

With the back of her trembling hand, Jennsen wiped tears of fright from her cheeks before rising up on shaky legs. She turned and looked out at the still black water lying beneath the overhanging leaves and mosses. In retrospect, she recalled her feet touching submerged roots. Looking back at the expanse of water she had crossed, she could see that perhaps the water had risen a few feet to cover the ground there. Maybe the land had sunk. Either way, if she had just carefully walked through the shallow area, rather than tried to jump to the root-turned-snake, it might have proven much less troublesome.

On the way back, she planned to cut herself a walking stick to help her wade through the low place, to feel ahead, and she would take care not to step on a snake.

Still catching her breath, Jennsen turned back to the dark way ahead. She had yet to get to the sorceress's place, and she was wasting time standing around feeling sorry for herself. Sebastian needed her help, not for her to feel sorry for herself.

She struck out once more, soaked to the skin. Fortunately, though it was winter, it was warm in the swamp. At least she wouldn't freeze. She remembered being wet when she and Sebastian fled her house after the quad murdered her mother.

The ground was mere inches above the expanses of stagnant

water, but, with the profusion of roots woven through it, firm enough to hold her weight. Where the water came over the ground, it was only for short expanses and shallow. Even though the water was only inches deep, Jennsen stepped carefully, watching that the roots just below the surface were not lurking snakes. She knew that water snakes were some of the most dangerous. A poison snake, even if it was only a foot long, could kill a person. Like a spider, the size was immaterial if its venom was deadly.

She came to another area where steam rose from fissures in the ground. Colored deposits, mostly yellow, crusted around the openings where the vapor rose. The smell gagged her, and she had to seek a way around that would allow her to breathe. The brush was thorny and thick.

With her knife, she was able to cut several of the heavier branches and make it through to a shelf of rock against a rock wall. Following the narrow ledge, she skirted a dark pool of water. The surface moved with slow ripples as something beneath followed her movement. She kept her knife to hand, trying to watch her footing and keep an eye out for anything that might lunge at her out of the water. When she grabbed for a handhold and loose rock came away, almost making her lose her footing, she threw the rock in the water at the thing she couldn't see. It continued to follow her until she reached the far end, where she was able to climb up onto higher ground that took her into dense growth of tall shoots with broad leaves.

It reminded her of moving through a field of cornstalks. Off through the stalks, she could see slow movement. She didn't know what it could be, but by the size of it, she didn't want to find out, and picked up the pace. Before long, she was running through the thick growth, dodging stems and ducking under branches.

The trees grew in close again, and she was soon back to treading among the tangle of roots. They seemed endless, and progress was agonizingly slow. The day was wearing on. When she came to open areas, or at least open enough, she trotted to save time. She had been in the swamp for hours. It had to be close to the middle of the day.

Tom had told her that he thought it might be a day of travel in and back out of the swamp. But she had been at it so long that she began to worry that she might have missed the sorceress's house. After all, there was no telling how wide the swamp was. She could easily have passed it by and never have seen it. She began to worry that that was exactly what had happened.

What if she couldn't find the house? What would she do, then? She didn't relish the idea of spending the night in the swamp. There was no telling what manner of creature would come out at night. She didn't think there was any chance of making a fire. The thought of being in this place in the dark, with no hope of even the light of the moon or stars, gripped her with fear.

When she emerged at last on the shore of a broad lake, Jennsen paused to catch her breath. Trees, fat at the bottom where they emerged from the water, stood like a series of poles supporting a low roof of green. The light was slightly brighter over the lake. To the right side was a wall of rock that provided not so much as a handhold, much less a way to traverse it. It dropped straight down into the water, suggesting how deep that end might be.

Scanning the shore to the left, she was startled to see footprints. Jennsen ran over and went to one knee to inspect the depressions in the soft ground. By the size of them, they looked to be made by a man, but were not fresh. She followed the prints along the shore and in a few places found fish scales from a catch that had been cleaned on the spot. The growth beyond was thick and tangled, but the grass and dry ground at the edge of the lake provided a good path, and the footprints, hope.

At the far side of the still lake, she followed the footprints along a well-worn path through a dense stand of willow and up onto higher ground. When she peered through an open place in the vegetation, she spotted, off through the trees, beyond the tangled growth of brush and the veil of vines, up on a rise ahead, a distant house. Woodsmoke curled from a chimney to blend into the gray fog overhead, almost as if the smoke itself were creating the ashen overcast.

In the gray gloom of the dark swamp, the light coming from a window at the side of the house shone like a golden jewel, a beacon to welcome the lost, the desperate, the forsaken and defenseless. The sight of her journey's end, after so much terror and loss, brought tears of relief. The tears might have been joy, were it not for her dire need.

Jennsen hurried along the path among the willow and oak, up through the tangled undergrowth, past curtains of vines, and soon reached the house. It was set on a foundation of stone, painstakingly fit without mortar. The walls were made of cedar logs. The roof overhung a narrow porch running around the side, with steps down the back to the path to the nearby lake from where she had come.

Taking the steps two at a time up to the narrow porch and following it around the house brought her to a door flanked by pillars of stout logs supporting a simple but welcoming portico. From the door, down wide steps, was a broad and well-maintained path out through the swamp in front. That was the way people came when they were invited to visit the sorceress. After the way she had come in, it looked like a road.

Wasting no time, Jennsen knocked. Impatient, she rapped her knuckles again. Her knocking was interrupted when the door swung inward. An older man stood staring out at her in surprise. Gray hair was taking over from the dark brown and looked to have receded some, but it was still thick. He was neither lean nor stout, and average height. His clothes were not the clothes of a trapper or a man of a swamp, but those of a craftsman; his brown trousers, clean and well kept, were not coarse, but of a more expensive tightly woven fabric. Flecks of gold sparkled from his green shirt. He was the gilder, Friedrich.

His discerning face scrutinized her more carefully, taking in the red hair under her hood. 'What are you doing here?' he asked. His deep voice fit well with the rest of him, but it was none too friendly.

'I came to see Althea, if I may.'

His eyes turned to the path, then back to her. 'How did you get here?'

By his suspicious expression after checking, she reasoned that he had some way of knowing if someone had been up the path.

Jennsen knew of such telltales; she and her mother used them all the time to be sure that no one had sneaked up on them.

Jennsen gestured off around the house. 'I came in the other way. In the back. From beyond the lake.'

'No one can go beyond the lake, not even me.' His brow of wiry black and gray hairs drew down without so much as considering her words or questioning her further. 'You're lying.'

Jennsen was stunned. 'I'm not. I came the back way. It's urgent that I see your wife, Althea.'

'You have not been invited to come here. You must leave. You will not wander off the trail, this time, if you know what's good for you. Now, go away!'

'But it's a matter of life and death. I must—'

The door slammed shut in her face.

Chapter 22

Jennsen stood unmoving with the suddenly closed door inches from her face. She didn't know what to do. At that moment, she was too stunned for any other emotion to yet flood in.

From inside, she heard a woman's voice. 'Who is it, Friedrich?'

'You know who it was.' Friedrich's voice was nothing like it had been when he had spoken to Jennsen. It was now tender, respectful, familiar.

'Well, let her in.'

'But, Althea, you can't—'

'Let her in, Friedrich.' Her voice was scolding without being at all harsh.

Jennsen felt relief wash through her. The knot of arguments burgeoning inside her as she prepared to knock again melted away. The door opened, more slowly this time.

Friedrich gazed out at her, not as a man defeated or reprimanded, but as a man come to face fate with dignity.

'Please come in, Jennsen,' he said in a quieter, more kindhearted voice.

'Thank you,' Jennsen said in a small voice of her own, somewhat astonished and slightly troubled that he knew her name.

She took in everything as she followed him into the home. Despite how warm it was in the swamp, the small fire crackling in the stone fireplace gave the air a sweet smell along with a welcome, dry feel. That was the sense of it, more than heat – dryness. The furnishings were simple but well made and embellished with carved designs. The main room had only two small windows, on opposite side walls. There were rooms to the back and in one of them a workbench, lined with orderly tools, sat before another small window.

Jennsen didn't remember the house, if indeed this was the same place. Her memory of coming to Althea's home was more of an impression of friendly faces than an actual memory of a place. The walls, decorated with things for her eyes to feast upon, seemed familiar. As a child, she would have noticed such visual treats. There were carvings of birds, fish, and animals everywhere, either hanging by themselves, or grouped on small shelves. That would be the most captivating to a small child.

Some of the carvings were painted, some left plain, but the feathers, scales, and fur had been carved with such fine texture that they looked like animals magically turned to wood. Other carvings were more stylized and beautifully gilded. A mirror on one wall, down low, was framed with a starburst, each ray alternately gilded gold and silver.

Toward the fireplace, a large red and gold pillow sat on the floor. Jennsen's eye was drawn to a square board with a gilded Grace upon it sitting on the floor before the pillow. It was just like the Grace she often drew, but this one, she knew, was real. Small stones rested in a pile to the side.

In a beautifully made chair, with a high back and carved arms, sat a slight woman with big, dark eyes made all the more striking by golden hair flecked through with gray. The fall of hair surrounded her face and swept down to lie about her shoulders. Her wrists rested over the arms of the chair while her long slender fingers gracefully traced the curve of the spiral carved in the end.

'I am Althea.' Her voice was gentle, but carried a clear ring of authority. She didn't get up.

Jennsen curtsied. 'Mistress, please forgive my bursting in uninvited and unexpected like this.'

'Perhaps uninvited, but not unexpected, Jennsen.'

'You know my name?' Jennsen realized too late how foolish the question sounded. The woman was a sorceress. There was no telling what her powers could discern.

211

Althea smiled, and a pleasant look it was on her. 'I remember you. One does not forget meeting one like you.'

Jennsen wasn't sure what that meant, but said 'Thank you' anyway.

The smile on Althea's face widened, crinkling her eyes. 'My, but you look just like your mother. Were it not for the red hair, I would think I had flown back in time to when I saw her last, when she was just the age you are now.' She held a hand out level before her. 'And you were only this big.'

Jennsen felt her face going as red as her hair. Her mother had been beautiful, not just wise and loving. Jennsen didn't believe she could compare to such an attractive woman, or ever live up to the kind of example her mother set.

'And how is she?'

Jennsen swallowed. 'My mother . . . my mother is gone.' In anguish, Jennsen's gaze sank to the floor. 'She was murdered.'

'I'm so sorry,' said Friedrich, standing behind her. He put a hand to her shoulder in sympathy. 'I truly am. I knew her, some, from the palace. She was a good woman.'

'How did it happen?' Althea asked.

'They finally caught up with us.'

'Caught up with you?' Althea's brow twitched. 'Who?'

'Why, the D'Haran soldiers. Lord Rahl's men.' Jennsen drew her cloak back, showing them both the handle of the knife. 'This came from one of them.'

Althea's gaze took in the knife, then returned to Jennsen's face. 'I'm so sorry, dear.'

Jennsen nodded. 'But I have to warn you. I went to see your sister, Lathea—'

'Did you see her before she died?'

Jennsen stared in surprise. 'Yes, I did.'

Althea shook her head with a sad smile. 'Poor Lathea. How was she? I mean, did she have a good life?'

'I don't know. She had a nice house, but I only saw her briefly. I got the impression she lived alone. I went to her because I needed help. I recalled my mother mentioning the name of a sorceress who had helped us, but I guess I got the names wrong. I ended up at your sister's. She didn't even want to talk to me.

She said she could do nothing, that it had been you who had helped me before. That's why I had to come here.'

'How did you get in?' Friedrich asked as he gestured to the path out front. 'You must have wandered off the path.'

'Not that way. I came from the back way.'

Now, even Althea frowned. 'There is no back way.'

'Well, there was no path, as such, but I made my way through.'

'No one can come in from that side,' Althea insisted. 'There are things back there that ward that side.'

'I know. I had a run-in with a huge snake—'

'You saw the snake?' Friedrich asked.

Jennsen nodded. 'I stepped on it accidentally. I thought it was a root. We had a time of it and I had a swim.'

They were both peering at her in a way that made Jennsen nervous.

'Yes, yes,' Althea said, sounding unconcerned about the snake, waving a hand as if to brush away such petty news, 'but, surely, you had to see the other things?'

Jennsen looked from Friedrich's wide eyes to Althea's frown. 'I never saw anything but the snake.'

'The snake is just a snake,' Althea said, dismissing the fearsome beast with another impatient wave of her hand. 'There are dangerous things back there. Things that would let no one through. No one. How in the name of Creation were you able to get past them?'

'What sort of things?'

'Things of magic,' Althea said in a grim tone.

'I'm sorry, but all I can tell you is that I got through, and I never saw anything but the snake.' She frowned toward the ceiling as she thought again. 'Although, I did see things in the water – dark things under the water.'

'Fish,' Friedrich scoffed.

'And in the bushes – I saw things in the bushes. Well, I didn't see them, exactly, but I saw the bushes move and I know something was in there. They remained hidden, though.'

'These things,' Althea said, 'do not hide in bushes. They fear

213

nothing. They hide from nothing. They would have come out and torn you apart.'

'I don't know why they didn't,' Jennsen said. Her gaze darted out through the window at the side to the stagnant expanses of murky water beneath a shadowy tangle of vines, feeling a pang of worry about her return journey. With Sebastian's life at stake, she felt frustration at the sorceress's pointless talk about what was in the swamp. After all, she had made it through, so it wasn't as impossible as the two of them wished her to believe. 'Why do you live out here, anyway? I mean, if you're so wise and all, then why do you live out here in a swamp with snakes?'

Althea lifted an eyebrow. 'I prefer my snakes without arms and legs.'

Jennsen took a breath and started again. 'Althea, I came because I'm in desperate need of your help.'

Althea shook her head as if she didn't want to hear it. 'I can't help you.'

Jennsen was stunned to have her request dismissed so out of hand. 'But, you must.'

'Really.'

'Please, you helped me before. I need that help again. Lord Rahl is getting closer all the time. I've only just escaped with my life on more than one occasion. I'm at my wits' end and don't know what else to do. I don't even really know why my father wanted to kill me in the first place.'

'Because you are an ungifted offspring.'

'There. You've just spoken the very reason why it makes no sense: I'm ungifted. So, what possible threat could I represent? If he was a powerful wizard, what harm could I cause him? What threat could I possibly represent? Why did he want so badly to kill me?'

'The Lord Rahl destroys any offspring he discovers who are not gifted.'

'But why? That he does is the result, not a reason. There must be a reason. If I at least knew that much of it, I might be able to figure out how to do something about it.'

She shook her head again. 'I don't know. It isn't like the Lord Rahl came to discuss his business with me.'

'After I saw your sister and she wouldn't help me, I went back to ask her about that very thing, but she had been murdered by the same men who are after me. They must have feared she could tell me something, so they murdered her.' Jennsen smoothed her hair back over her head. 'I'm sorry about your sister, I really am. But don't you see? You're in danger, too, for what you know about it.'

'I can't imagine why they would harm her.' Frowning, Althea stared off as she considered. 'What you're saying, that she might know something, makes no sense. She was never involved in any of it. Lathea knew less than I. She wouldn't have known anything of why Darken Rahl would have wanted to rid the world of you. She could have told you nothing.'

'Well, even if he thought those of us born without the gift were inferior and just plain worthless – if he wanted to exterminate the runts of the litter, so to speak – why would his son, my half brother, want just as badly to kill me? I couldn't harm my father, and I can't harm his son, yet Richard, too, sends quads to hunt me.'

Althea still didn't looked convinced. 'Are you sure they are Lord Rahl's men doing this? I just don't see in the stones—'

'They came into my house. They killed my mother. I saw them – I fought them. They were D'Haran soldiers.' She drew the knife from its sheath at her belt and held the handle up for the woman to see. 'One was wearing this.'

Althea's gaze took it in with care, the way one would look upon anything deadly, but she said nothing.

'Why would Lord Rahl kill my mother? Why does the House of Rahl want me dead?'

'I don't know the answer.' Althea lifted her hands and let them fall back to her lap. 'I'm sorry, but that's the truth.'

Jennsen went to her knees before the woman. 'Althea, please, even if you don't know why, I still need your help. Your sister wouldn't help, she said only you could. She said that only you can see the holes in the world. I don't know what that means, but I know it has something to do with all this, with magic. Please, I need help.'

The sorceress appeared puzzled. 'And what is it you wish me to do?'

'Hide me. Like you did when I was little. Cast a spell over me so that they won't know who I am or where to find me – so they can't follow me. I just want to be left alone. I need the spell that will hide me from Lord Rahl.

'But it's not just for me. I need it to help a friend, too. I need the spell to hide my true identity so that I can go back into the People's Palace and get him out.'

'Get him out? What do you mean? Who is this friend?'

'His name is Sebastian. He helped me when the men attacked and murdered my mother. He saved my life. He brought me here, to see you. Your sister said we should ask at the palace where we could find you. He traveled all that way with me, helped me get here, so I could come to see you to get the help I need. We went to the palace to find Friedrich so I could know where you lived, and while we were there the guards took Sebastian prisoner.

'Don't you see? He helped me and, because of that, they have him. They will surely torture him. He was helping me – it's my fault he's in this trouble. Please, Althea, I need your help to get him out. I need a spell to hide me so I can go back in and rescue him.'

Incredulous, Althea stared. 'Why do you think a spell could accomplish this?'

'I don't know. I don't know anything about how magic works. I just know that I need its help – that I need a spell to hide my true identity.'

The woman shook her head, as if she were dealing with a complete lunatic. 'Jennsen, what you are envisioning is not how magic works. Do you think I can cast a web and you will then be able to walk into the palace and guards will somehow fall under this spell and start unlocking doors for you?'

'Well, I don't know—'

'Of course you don't. That is why I'm telling you that it doesn't work that way. Magic is not a key that opens doors for you. Magic is not something that – poof – spontaneously solves problems. Magic would only compound the problems. If you have a bear in your tent, you don't invite another in. Two bears will not be better than the one.'

'But Sebastian needs my help. I need the help of magic in order to get him that help.'

'Were you to go in there, as you think, and use some kind of' – she waved a hand around as if trying to think of a word to describe it – 'I don't know, magic dust or something, to open prison doors to get your friend out, what do you suppose would happen? That you two could then go off happily and that would be the end of it?'

'Well, I don't know ... exactly ...'

Althea leaned forward on an elbow. 'Don't you suppose that the people who run the palace would want to know how this happened, so they could prevent it from happening again? Don't you suppose that some perfectly innocent people whose job it is to guard doors there would be in a great deal of trouble for allowing a prisoner to escape and that they might suffer because of it? Don't you suppose that the palace officials would want their escaped prisoner back? Don't you suppose, since such measures were used to get him out, that whatever threat they feared this friend of yours might represent, after such an escape they would think that he must be even more dangerous than they originally believed? Don't you suppose that some perfectly innocent people might be hurt during the extreme measures taken to apprehend such an escaped prisoner? Don't you suppose they would send out an army and the gifted to comb the countryside before he could get far?

'Don't you even suppose,' the sorceress finally said in the gravest of tones, 'that a wizard as powerful as the Lord Rahl of all of D'Hara might have some decidedly nasty and painfully protracted fatal surprise in store for anyone daring to use a pitiful old sorceress's spell against him – and within his very own palace walls on top of it?'

Jennsen stared at the dark eyes fixed on her. 'I never thought of all that.'

'You are telling me something I already know.'

'But ... how can I get Sebastian back? How can I help him?'

'I would suppose you must figure a way to get him out – if he can be gotten out in the first place – but it must be done in a way that takes all that I have said, and more, into account. Breaking a hole in the wall for him to step through to freedom would bring out the hounds, now wouldn't it? It would bring you trouble much like magic would. You must instead think of a way that convinces them to turn him out on their own. Then they won't be chasing you to have him back.'

That all made sense to her. 'How can I accomplish such a thing?'

The sorceress shrugged. 'If it can be done, I would wager that you can do it. After all, you have so far lived to grow into a fine young woman, escaped quads, found me, and got yourself in here, now didn't you? You've accomplished much. You must only set your mind to it. But you don't start out by picking up a stick and whacking a hornet's nest.'

'But I can't see how I can do it without the help of magic. I'm a nobody.'

'A nobody,' Althea scoffed as she leaned back. She was becoming a teacher impatient with a student doing poorly on a lesson. 'You are somebody; you are Jennsen, a smart girl with a brain. You should not kneel before me and plead ignorance, telling me what you cannot do while asking instead for others to do for you.

'If you want to be a slave in life, then continue going around asking for others to do for you. They will oblige, but you will find the price is your choices, your freedom, your life itself. They will do for you, and as a result you will be in bondage to them forever, having given your identity away for a paltry price. Then, and only then, you will be a nobody, a slave, because you yourself and nobody else made it so.'

'But, maybe, in this case, it's different—'

'The sun rises in the east; there are no special exceptions, just because you wish it. I know of what I speak, and I am telling you, magic is not the answer. What do you think? If you had a spell that they didn't know you were Darken Rahl's daughter, then they would fall over themselves to open doors for you? They will open the door of your friend's cell for no one unless they think it should be opened. It would make no difference if

218

there were a spell to turn you into a six-legged rabbit – they would still not open the doors you want opened just because you were now a six-legged rabbit by the hand of magic.'

'But magic—'

'Magic is a tool, not a solution.'

Jennsen reminded herself to remain composed even though she wanted to seize the woman by the shoulders and shake her until she agreed to help. Unlike with Lathea, she did not intend to lose this chance for that help. 'What do you mean, magic is not a solution? Magic is powerful.'

'You have a knife. You showed it to me.'

'That's right.'

'And when you are hungry do you wave your knife in someone's face and demand their bread? No. You entice them to give you bread by giving them a coin in exchange.'

'You mean you think they can be bribed?'

Another sigh. 'No. Of all I know, I can tell you that they cannot be bribed – at least not in the conventional sense. However, the principle is not entirely without some parallel.

'When Friedrich wishes bread, he doesn't use his knife to take the bread from those who have it – at least not in the sense of how you wish to use magic. He uses his knife as a tool to carve figures and then he gilds them. He sells what he made with his knife, and then exchanges that coin for the bread.

'You see? If he would use the knife – the tool – to directly solve the problem of getting bread, it would do him more harm in the end. He would be a thief and hunted as such. He uses his head, instead, and uses the knife as a tool to create something with the aid of his mind, thus solving the problem of obtaining bread with his knife.'

'You mean, then, that I need to use magic indirectly? I must somehow use magic as a tool to help me?'

Althea sighed heavily. 'No, child. Forget magic. You must use your head. Magic is trouble. Use your head.'

'I did,' Jennsen said. 'It wasn't easy, but I used my head to come to you to get help. It's a spell I need now as a tool to help me – to hide me. In that way it will be a tool, as you suggest.'

Althea looked away into the hearth, watching the wavering flames. 'I cannot help you in that way.'

'I don't think you understand. I'm hunted by powerful men. I just need a spell to hide my identity – like you did when I was little, when I lived at the palace with my mother.'

Still, the old woman stared off into the hearth. 'I cannot do that. I don't have the power.'

'But you do. You've already done it, once.' A lifetime of frustration, fear, loss, and futility surfaced, bringing with it bitter tears. 'I didn't travel all this way, suffer all this hardship, to have you tell me no! Lathea told me no, told me that only you can see the holes in the world, and that only you could help me. I must have your help, your spell, to hide me. Please, Althea, I'm begging for my life.'

Althea would not look her in the eyes. 'I cannot cast a spell like that for you.'

Jennsen choked back the tears. 'Please, Althea, I just want to be left alone. You have the power.'

'I do not have what you've invented in your mind for me. I have helped you in the only way I can.'

'How can you sit here knowing that other people are suffering and dying – and not help? How can you be so selfish, Althea? How can you not help when I need it?'

Friedrich put a hand under Jennsen's arm, lifting her to her feet. 'I'm sorry, but you've asked what you would. You've heard what Althea has to say. If you're wise, you will use what you've learned to help yourself. Now, it's time for you to leave.'

Jennsen pulled away. 'All I want is the help of a spell! How can she be so selfish!'

Friedrich's eyes blazed with fury, even if his voice did not. 'You have no right to speak to us in that manner. You don't know anything about it, about the sacrifices she's made. It's time for you to—'

'Friedrich,' Althea said in a soft voice, 'why don't you make us some tea?'

'Althea, there is no reason you should have to explain any of it – least of all to her.'

Althea smiled up at him. 'It's all right.'

'Explain what?' Jennsen asked.

'My husband may sound harsh to you, but it's because he doesn't want me to burden you. He knows that some people leave here unhappy with the knowledge I give them.' Her dark eyes turned up to her husband. 'Make us some tea?'

Friedrich's face twisted with a long-suffering expression before he nodded in resignation.

'What do you mean?' Jennsen asked. 'What knowledge? What is it you aren't telling me?'

As Friedrich went to a cupboard and retrieved a kettle and cups, setting the cups on the table, Althea gestured for Jennsen to sit on the pillow before her.

Chapter 23

Jennsen made herself comfortable on the red and gold pillow on the floor in front of the sorceress.

'Many years ago,' Althea began, clasping her hands in her lap atop her black-and-white print dress, 'more than you might believe, I traveled with my sister to the Old World, beyond the great barrier to the south.'

Jennsen decided that, for the time being, it might be best just to keep quiet and learn what she could, rather than bring up what she already knew – that the new Lord Rahl, bent on conquest, had destroyed the great barrier to the south in order to invade the Old World, and that Sebastian had come up from the Old World to try to find a way to help the emperor, Jagang the Just, stop the invading D'Harans. She thought that maybe if she understood it all a little better, herself, then she might be able to come up with a way of convincing Althea to help her.

'I went to the Old World to go to a place called the Palace of the Prophets,' Althea said. This, too, Jennsen had heard of from Sebastian. 'I have a gift for a very primitive form of prophecy. I wanted to learn what I could about it, while my sister wished to learn about cures and such. I also wanted to learn things about people like you.'

'Me?' Jennsen said. 'What do you mean?'

'The ancestors of Darken Rahl were no different than he. They all eliminated any ungifted offspring they discovered had been born. Lathea and I were young and full of fire to help those in need, and also those we felt were unjustly persecuted. We wanted to use our gift to help change the world for the better.

While we each hoped to study different things, we both went for much the same reasons.'

Jennsen thought that seemed pretty close to how she felt and was just the kind of help she was talking about, but she also knew that right then was not the moment to say it. She asked, instead, 'Why did you have to travel all the way to the Palace of the Prophets to learn these things?'

'The sorceresses there are renowned to have experience with many things, with wizards, and magic, and most of all, with matters to do with this world and with the worlds beyond.'

'Worlds beyond?' Jennsen gestured to the space outside the outer gilded ring on the Grace setting not far away. 'You mean, the world of the dead?'

Althea leaned back as she reflected. 'Well, yes, but not exactly. You understand the Grace?' Althea waited for Jennsen's nod. 'The sorceresses at the Palace of the Prophets have knowledge about the interactions of the gift, the veil between worlds, and their interdependent relationships – how it all fits together. They are called the Sisters of the Light.'

Jennsen recalled with a jolt that Sebastian had said that the Sisters of the Light were with Emperor Jagang, now. Sebastian had offered to take Jennsen to the Sisters of the Light. He'd said he thought they might be able to help her. It had to be that they had something to do with the Creator's Light, and especially the gift, in the center of the Grace.

Another thought came to her. 'This has something to do with what Lathea said? That you could see the . . . holes in the world, as she called it?'

Althea smiled with the pleasure of a teacher seeing a student flirting with discovery. 'That's the tip of the tooth. You see, the ungifted offspring of the Lord Rahl – of every Lord Rahl going back thousands of years – are different than anyone else. You are holes in the world to those of us with the gift.'

'What does that mean, exactly – holes in the world?'

'We are blind to you.'

'Blind? But you see me. Lathea could see me, too. I don't understand.'

'Not blind with our eyes. Blind with our gift.' She swept an

223

arm out toward Friedrich at the fire with an iron kettle, and then toward the window. 'There are living things all around. You see them with your eyes – you see Friedrich and the trees and such – just as I do, just as everyone does.' She held up a finger to make her point. 'But through my gift, I also see them.

'While our eyes may perceive you, those of us with the gift cannot see you with that aspect of ourselves. Darken Rahl could not see you any more than I can. Neither can the new Lord Rahl. To those of us with the gift, you are a hole in the world.'

'But, but,' Jennsen stammered in confusion, 'that makes no sense. He's been hunting me. He sent men after me – they had my name on a piece of paper.'

'They may hunt you, but only in the conventional sense. They cannot find you with magic. His gift is blind to you. He has to use spies, bribes, and threats to locate you, in addition to his wits and cunning. Were it not so, he might send some magic beast to reap your bones for him and be done with it, instead of sending out men with your name written down on a piece of paper.'

'You mean, I'm already invisible to him?'

'No. I know you. I remember your red hair. I recognized you because I remember your mother, and you look like her. I know you in those ways – the ways anybody knows and recognizes someone. Darken Rahl, were he alive, might recognize you if he remembered your mother. Others who knew him might well see some of him in you, as I do, in addition to your mother's looks. He could know you in all those same ways common to one without the gift. He can find you by ordinary means. Of course, if he or one with the gift were to actually lay eyes on you, they would realize you are an ungifted offspring of a Rahl – because they could see you.

'But, he could not find you with magic. That he cannot do. To those of us with the gift, you are in many ways like everyone else, except that you are a hole in the world.'

Jennsen was frowning. She only realized it when Althea tapped her thumbs together, thinking, in response to that face.

'When I was at the Palace of the Prophets,' Althea finally said, 'I knew a woman there, a sorceress, like me, named Adie. She had traveled alone to the Old World from a far-off land in order to learn what she could. But Adie was blind.'

'Blind? She could travel alone when she was blind?'

Althea smiled at the memory of the woman. 'Oh yes. With the use of her gift, rather than her eyes. All sorceresses – all people with the gift – have unique abilities. On top of that, in some the gift is stronger, like people who have big muscles are stronger than me. Like Friedrich. He is stronger in muscles. You have hair like other people, but yours is red. Some have blond, or black, or brown. Despite what things people have in common, each person has different attributes.

'It's like that with the gift. It's not only different in its aspects, but the power of those aspects differ. With some, it's very strong, with some, weak. Each of us is an individual. We're all unique in our ability, our gift, the same as you are unique in other ways.'

'And what about your friend, Adie?'

'Ah, well, Adie's eyes were completely white – blind – but she had learned the trick of seeing with her gift. The gift told her more about the world around her than my eyes told me. Adie could see people better with her gift than I could with my eyes. Much like when people who don't have the gift go blind, they depend more on their hearing, so they learn to hear more than you or I.

'Adie did that with her gift. She saw by sensing that infinitesimal spark of the Creator's gift that everything has – life itself, and more: Creation.

'The point is that, to me, to Darken Rahl, to Adie, you do not exist. You are a hole in the world.'

For reasons Jennsen could not at first comprehend, terror washed through her. And then the sense of her terror began to take shape. She could feel her eyes filling with tears.

'The Creator didn't give me life, like everyone else? I came to exist in some other way? I'm some kind of . . . monster? My father wanted to have me killed because I'm some monstrosity of nature?'

'No, no, child,' Althea said as she leaned forward and stroked a comforting hand down Jennsen's hair, 'that is not at all what I mean.'

Jennsen tried mightily to contain the new shape of dread. Through watery vision, she saw Althea's concerned face gazing down at her. 'I'm not even part of Creation. That's why the gift can't sense me. The Lord Rahl only wanted to rid the world of an error of nature, an evil thing.'

'Jennsen, don't put words where I have not. Listen to me, now.'

Jennsen nodded as she wiped under her eyes. 'I'm listening.'

'Just because you're different, that doesn't make you evil.'

'Just what am I, then, if not a monster untouched by Creation?'

'My dear child, you are a pillar of Creation.'

'But you said—'

'I said that those with the gift cannot see you with it. I did not say that you don't exist, or that you are not as the rest of us, a part of Creation.'

'Then why am I one of those . . . things? One of those holes in the world?'

Althea shook her head. 'I don't know, child. But our lack of knowledge does not prove something evil. An owl can see at night. Does it make you evil because people can't see you while the owl can? One person's limitations don't confer wickedness on another. It shows only one thing: the existence of limitations.'

'But all the offspring of the Lord Rahl are like this?'

She considered carefully before answering. 'The genuinely ungifted ones, yes. Those who are born with at least some tiny aspect of the gift are not. That aspect can be so infinitesimal and unusable that it would not even be recognized to exist by anyone in any other way aside from this one. For all practical purposes, those offspring would be thought of as ungifted, except that they would have this quality that would keep them from being like you – holes in the world. It also makes them vulnerable. This kind of offspring can be found with magic and thus eliminated.'

'Could it be that most of the offspring of Lord Rahl are like that, and those like me, holes in the world, are actually the ones who are more rare?'

'Yes,' Althea admitted quietly.

Jennsen sensed an undercurrent of tension in the single word answer. 'Are you suggesting that there is something more to all of this than just that we are holes in the world to the gifted?'

'Yes. That was one of the reasons I went to study with the Sisters of the Light. I wanted to better understand the interrelationship of the gift with life as we know it – with Creation.'

'Did you discover anything? Were the Sisters of the Light able to help you?'

'Unfortunately, no.' Althea gazed off in reflection. 'Few if any would agree with me, but I have come to suspect that all people, with the single exception of those like you – offspring of a Lord Rahl born wholly without the gift – have this imperceptible spark of magic that, while intangible in every other way, connects them to the gifted, and thus to the greater world of Creation.'

'I don't understand what this would mean for me, or for anyone else.'

Althea slowly shook her head. 'There is more to this, Jennsen, than I know. I suspect there is something far more important involved.'

Jennsen couldn't imagine what that could be. 'How many offspring are born entirely without the gift?'

'As far as I've learned, it's exceedingly rare for more than one offspring of each Lord Rahl to be born with the gift, as we think of it – his seed conceives but one true heir.' Althea held up a finger as she leaned forward. 'But it is possible that, while the others are ungifted in the conventional sense, many have this otherwise invisible and sterile spark of the gift so that they are detected and destroyed before others, like me, know of them.

'It is entirely possible that those like you are the ones who are truly rare, as is the single formally gifted heir, and that's why you survived for those like me to notice, thus slanting our idea of which kind is rare, and which common. As I said, I think there is far more to this than I know or can understand. But of those truly like you, devoid of even this otherwise imperceptible glimmer of the gift, all are—'

'Pillars of Creation,' Jennsen said, sarcastically.

Althea chuckled. 'Perhaps that sounds better.'

'But to the gifted, we are holes in the world.'

Althea's smile withered. 'It is so. Were Adie here, blind as she

227

is with her eyes and seeing only with her gift, were you to stand before her she would see everything but you. She would be blind to you. To Adie, able to see with the gift only, you would truly be a hole in the world.'

'That doesn't make me feel very good about myself.'

Althea's smile returned. 'Don't you see, child? It proves only the limitation. To one who is blind, everyone is a hole in the world.'

Jennsen thought it over. 'Then, it's only a matter of perception. Some people are simply lacking the ability to perceive me in one narrow way.'

Althea gave her a single nod. 'That's right. But because those with the gift often use their ability without conscious thought, like you use your vision, it's very disturbing to those with the gift to encounter one such as you.'

'Disturbing? Why is it disturbing?'

'It's troubling when your senses do not agree.'

'But they can still see me, so why do I trouble them?'

'Well, imagine if you heard a voice but you could see no source for it.'

Jennsen didn't have to imagine that. She understood quite well how troubling that was.

'Or imagine,' the sorceress said, 'if you could see me, but when you reached out to touch me, your hand passed through me as if I wasn't here. Wouldn't that trouble you?'

'I suppose,' Jennsen conceded. 'Is there anything else about us that's different? Other than that we are holes in the world to those with the gift?'

'I don't know. It's exceedingly rare to come across one such as you who is still alive. While it's possible that others exist, and I once heard a rumor that one lived with the healers called the Raug'Moss, I only know of you for certain.'

When Jennsen had been very young, she had visited the healers, the Raug'Moss, with her mother. 'Do you know the name?'

'Drefan was the name whispered, but I don't know if it's true. Even if it is, the likelihood of him still being alive would be remote. The Lord Rahl is the Lord Rahl. He is his own law.

Darken Rahl, like most of his ancestors, probably fathered many children. Hiding the knowledge of such a child's paternity is dangerous. Few would risk it, so most of your kind were known and immediately put to death. The rest are eventually found.'

Thinking out loud, Jennsen asked, 'Could it be that we're like this as a form of protection? There are animals that have special traits when they're born that help them survive. Fawns, for example, have spots to hide them, to make them invisible to predators – make them holes in the world.'

Althea smiled at the notion. 'I suppose that could be as good an explanation as any. Knowing magic, though, I would expect the reason to be more complex. Everything seeks balance. The deer and the wolves strike a balance – the fawns' spots help them survive, but that threatens the existence of wolves who need food. Such things go back and forth. If the wolves ate all the fawns, then the deer would die out and the wolves, if they had no other source of food, would also die out because they had altered the balance between them and the deer. They coexist in a balance that allows both species to survive, but at the cost of some individuals.

'With magic, balance is critical. What on the surface may seem simple often turns out to have much more complex causes. I suspect that, with those like you, an elaborate form of balance is being struck, and that being a hole in the world is merely an ancillary indication.'

'And maybe some of the balance is that, like some fawns are caught despite their spots, some with the gift are able to see me? Your sister said you could see the holes in the world.'

'No, I can't really. I simply learned a few tricks with the gift, in much the same way Adie did.' Jennsen frowned, feeling bewildered again, so Althea asked, 'Can you see a bird on a moonless night?'

'No. If there's not even a moon, it's impossible.'

'Impossible? No, not entirely.' Althea pointed skyward, moving her hand as if suggesting something passing overhead. 'You will see the stars go dark where the bird passes. If you watch the holes in the sky, you will in a way be seeing the birds.'

'Just a different way of seeing.' Jennsen smiled at such a clever notion. 'So, that's how you see those like me?'

'That comparison is the easiest way I can explain it to you. Both, though, have limitations. It only works to see the bird at night if they're flying against a background of stars, if there are no clouds, and so on. With those like you, it's much the same. I simply learned a trick to help me see those like you, but it's very limited.'

'When you went to the Palace of the Prophets, did you learn about your ability for prophecy? Maybe that could somehow help with what I need to do?'

'Nothing in relation to prophecy would be of any use to you.'

'But why not?'

Althea tilted her head forward, as if to question whether or not Jennsen had been paying attention. 'Where does prophecy come from?'

'Prophets.'

'And prophets are strongly gifted with that ability. Prophecy is one form of magic. But the gifted cannot see you with their gift, remember? To them, you are a hole in the world. Therefore, prophecy, since it comes through prophets, cannot see you, either.

'I have a wisp of ability for prophecy, but I am no prophet. When I was with the Sisters of the Light, since such things were one of my fields of interest, I spent decades in their vaults studying prophecy. They had been written down by great prophets throughout the ages. I can tell you both from personal experience, and from all that I read, that the prophecies are as blind to you as would be Adie. As far as the prophecies are concerned, your kind never existed, do not exist now, and never will exist.'

Jennsen sat back on her heels. 'Hole in the world, indeed.'

'At the Palace of the Prophets, I met a prophet, Nathan, and, while I learned nothing about those like you, I learned some about my talent. Mostly, I only learned how limited it is. Eventually, the things I learned there came to haunt me.'

'What do you mean?'

'The Palace of the Prophets was created many thousands of

years ago and is like no other place that I know of. A unique spell surrounds the entire palace and grounds. It distorts the way in which those under the spell age.'

'It changed you, then, in some way?'

'Oh, yes. It changes everyone. Aging is slowed for those living under the spell of the Palace of the Prophets. While those outside the palace went about their lives and aged roughly ten to fifteen years, those of us in the palace aged only one year.'

Jennsen made a skeptical face. 'How could such a thing be?'

'Nothing ever stays the same. The world is always changing. The world back in the great war three thousand years ago was much different. The world has changed since then. When the great barrier to the south of D'Hara was put up, wizards were different. They had vast power, back then.'

'Darken Rahl had vast power.'

'No. Darken Rahl, as powerful as he was, was nothing compared to the wizards of that time. They could control powers Darken Rahl only dreamed of.'

'So, wizards like that, with that kind of vast power, all died out? There have been no wizards like them born since?'

Althea stared off as she answered in a grave tone. 'Not since that great war has there been one like that born. Even wizards themselves have come to be born less and less often. But for the first time in three thousand years, one has again been born. Your half brother, Richard, is such a man.'

It turned out her pursuer was far more fearsome than Jennsen had given him credit for, even in her all too vivid imagination. Small wonder that her mother had been murdered and Lord Rahl's men were so close on Jennsen's heels. This Lord Rahl was altogether more powerful and dangerous than had been their father.

'Because this was such an epochal event, some of those at the Palace of the Prophets knew of Richard long before he was born. There was much anticipation over this one, this war wizard.'

'War wizard?' Jennsen didn't like the sound of that.

'Yes. There was much controversy as to the meaning of the prophecy of his birth – even to the meaning of the term "war wizard." While at the palace, I had a chance on two brief

231

occasions to meet the prophet I mentioned, Nathan. Nathan Rahl.'

Jennsen's mouth fell open. 'Nathan Rahl? You mean, a real Rahl?'

Althea smiled not only at the memory, but at Jennsen's surprise. 'Oh yes, a real Rahl. Commanding, powerful, clever, charming, and inconceivably dangerous. They kept him locked away behind impenetrable shields of magic, where he could cause no harm, yet he sometimes managed it. Yes, a real Rahl. Over nine hundred years old, he was, too.'

'That's impossible,' Jennsen insisted before she had time to think better of it.

Friedrich, standing over her, harrumphed. He handed a steaming cup of tea to his wife and then passed one down to Jennsen. With the question in her eyes, Jennsen looked back at Althea.

'I am close to two hundred years old,' Althea said.

Jennsen just stared. Althea looked old, but not that old.

'In part, this business with my age and how the spell slowed my aging is how I came to have dealings with you and your mother when you were young.' Althea sighed heavily and took a sip of tea. 'Which brings me back to the story at hand, to what you wanted to know – why I cannot help you with magic.'

Jennsen sipped, then glanced up at Friedrich, who looked about as old as Althea. 'Are you that age, too?'

'No,' he gibed, 'Althea robbed the cradle for me.'

Jennsen saw the looks that passed between them, the kind of intimate glances between two people who were close. Jennsen could see in the eyes of these two that they could read each other's slightest expression. She and her mother had been like that, able to see thoughts in the slightest movement of the eyes of the other. It was the kind of communication she thought was facilitated not only through familiarity, but through love and respect.

'I met Friedrich when I returned from the Old World. I had aged only about the same as Friedrich. I had lived a much longer time, of course, but my body had not aged to show it because I had been under the spell of the Palace of the Prophets.

'When I came back, I became involved in a number of things, and one of them was how I might help those such as you.'

Jennsen hung on every word. 'That's when you met my mother?'

'Yes. You see, the spell at the palace, the spell that altered time, sparked an idea of how I might help those like you. I knew that regular means of casting webs – magic – around your kind never seemed to work out. Others had tried but failed; the offspring were killed. I struck on the idea, instead, to cast the web, not on you, but on those who came into contact with you and your mother.'

Jennsen leaned forward expectantly, feeling sure that she was finally getting to the core of what might prove to be the help she sought. 'What did you do? What sort of magic?'

'I used magic to alter people's perception of time itself.'

'I don't understand. What did that do?'

'Well, the only way Darken Rahl could search for you was as I've explained – by using regular means. I tinkered with those regular means. I made it so that those who knew of you perceive time differently.'

'I still don't understand. How – what – did you make them perceive? Time is time.'

Althea leaned forward with a cunning smile. 'I made them think you were just born.'

'When?'

'All the time. Whenever they found out some thread of news about you, as a child fathered by Darken Rahl, they perceived you, and reported you, as newborn. When you were two months, ten months, four years, five years, six years old, they were all still looking for a newborn, despite how long they had known of you. The spell slowed their perception of time, in relation to you alone, so that they were always looking for a newborn baby, rather than a girl growing up.

'In this way, until you were six, I hid you right under their noses. That threw everyone's calculations off by six years. To this day, anyone who suspected your existence would believe you to be around fourteen or so, when you are actually more than twenty, because they thought you were newborn when the spell ended, when you were six. That's when they began to mark your age.'

Jennsen rose up onto her knees. 'But that could work. You must only do it again. If you were to cast a spell like that for me now, like you did when I was little, it would work the same, wouldn't it? Then they wouldn't know I was grown up. They wouldn't be hunting me. They would be looking for a newborn. Please, Althea, just do that again. Do what you did once before.'

From the corner of her eye, Jennsen saw Friedrich, now sitting at his bench in a back room, turn away. By the look on Althea's face, Jennsen knew that she had somehow said the wrong thing, and precisely what the sorceress had planned on her saying.

Jennsen realized that this had been a trap of sorts, and she had just talked herself right into it.

'I was young and masterful in my skill with magic,' Althea said. In her dark eyes glimmered the spark of recollection of that grand time in her life. 'In thousands of years, few had been through the great barrier and back. I had. I had studied with the Sisters of the Light, had audiences with their Prelate, and with the great prophet. I had accomplished such things as few others had. I was well over a hundred years old and still young, with a handsome and charming new husband who believed I could walk to the moon and back if the fancy struck me.

'I was well over a hundred years of age, yet still youthful, with a full life ahead of me; wise with age, yet still young. I was clever, oh so clever, and powerful in my gift. I was experienced, knowledgeable, and attractive, with many friends and a circle of people who hung on my every worldly pronouncement.'

With long graceful fingers, Althea pulled up the hem of her skirt, uncovering her legs.

Jennsen drew back at the sight.

She saw, then, why Althea had not stood before; her legs were withered, deformed, shriveled bones covered with a dry veneer of pallid flesh, as if they had died years ago, but never been buried because the rest of her was still living. Jennsen didn't know how the woman could keep from screaming in constant anguish.

'You were six,' the sorceress said in a terribly calm and quiet voice, 'when Darken Rahl finally discovered what I had done. He was a very ingenious man. Much more shrewd, as it turned out, than a young sorceress of a hundred-odd years in age.

'I only had time to tell my sister to warn your mother, before he caught me.'

Jennsen remembered running. When she was little, she and her mother had fled the palace. It had been night. It had been shortly after a visitor had come to their door. In the dark hall, there had been whispering. And then they had fled.

'But, he ... he didn't kill you?' Jennsen swallowed. 'He showed you mercy – he spared your life.'

Althea chuckled without humor. It was an empty laugh at encountering a profoundly naive notion.

'Darken Rahl did not always believe in simply killing those who displeased him. He preferred, instead, that they should live a good long time; death would have been a release, you see. If they were dead, how could they regret, how could they suffer, how could they serve as an example to others?

'You cannot imagine, and I could not begin to tell you, the terror of such a capture, of the long walk to be taken before him, of what it was like being in the grip of that man, of what it was like to look up into his calm face, his cold blue eyes, and know you were at the mercy of a man who had none. You cannot imagine what it was like to know in that single terrible instant, that everything you were, everything you had, everything you had hoped for in life, was about to forever change.

'The pain was what you might expect, I suppose. Perhaps my legs can partly attest to it.'

'I'm so sorry,' Jennsen whispered through her tears, hands pressed over her heartache.

'But the pain was not the worst of it. Not the worst by far. He stripped me of everything I had, but took for granted. He did to my power, to my gift, worse than he did to my legs. You just cannot see it – you are blind to it. Every day, I see it. That hurt, I assure you, you cannot begin to imagine.

'Even all that, though, was not enough for Darken Rahl. His displeasure at what I had done to hide you had only begun. He banished me here, to this sunken, foul place of hot springs and sickening vapors. He imprisoned me here, filling in about me a swamp with monstrosities created by the very power he had stripped from me. He wanted me close, you see. Several times he visited, just to behold me in my prison.

'I'm at the mercy of those things out there that are given life by my own gift, a gift to which I no longer have access. I could never drag myself out by my arms alone, but even if I were to try, or if I had the help of another, those beasts, created from my own power, would rip me apart. I can't call them back even to save myself.

'He left a path, in the front, so that provisions and supplies could be brought in, so I would be sure to have the things I needed. Friedrich had to build a home for us, here, because I cannot ever leave. Darken Rahl wished me a long life – a life I could spend suffering for displeasing him.'

Jennsen trembled as she listened, unable to say anything. Althea lifted a hand to point with one long graceful finger toward the back room.

'That man, who loves me, had to witness it all. Friedrich was thus condemned to a life of tending to a crippled wife he loved, who could no longer be a wife to him in ways of the flesh.'

She ran a hand over her bony limbs, tenderly, as if seeing them as they they once were. 'I have never again had the joy of being with my husband as a woman is with a man. My husband never again was able to share and enjoy the intimate charms of the woman he loves.'

She paused to regain her composure before going on. 'As part of my punishment, Darken Rahl left me with the power to use my gift in the one way which would haunt me every day: prophecy.'

Jennsen could not help herself from asking, thinking that this must be one thread of possible comfort left to the woman. 'It's part of your gift – can't it bring you some joy?'

Dark eyes fixed on her again. 'Did you enjoy the last day with your mother – the day before she died?'

'Yes,' Jennsen finally said.

'Did you laugh and talk with her?'

'Yes.'

'What if you had known that the next day she was to be murdered? What if you saw it all, long before it happened? Days, weeks, or even years before? Knew what was to happen, when, every ghastly detail? Saw, by the power of your magic, the horrifying sight of it, the blood, the agony, the dying. Would that please you? Would you still have experienced that joy, that laughter?'

Jennsen answered in a small voice. 'No.'

'So you see, Jennsen Rahl, I cannot help you, not because I am selfish, as you put it, but because even if I were willing, I have no power left to cast you a spell. You must find within yourself the ability to help yourself, the free will to accomplish what you must. Only in that way can you truly succeed in life.

'I cannot give you a spell to solve your problems. I have spent a good deal of my life suffering for the last spell I cast for you. Were it only me, I would endure it willingly, for I was doing what I believe in; this is the fault of an evil man, not the fault of an innocent child. Yet I suffer each day because it was not just my life forfeit, but Friedrich's, too. He might have—'

'I might have nothing.' He had come up behind Jennsen. 'I have considered each day of my life a privilege because you are in it. Your smile is the sun, gilded by the Creator Himself, and brightens my small existence. If this is the price for all that I have gained, then I paid it willingly. Don't devaluate the quality of my joy, Althea, by minimizing it or trivializing it.'

Althea looked back down at Jennsen. 'You see? This is my daily torture: knowing what I have not been able to be, to do, for this man.'

Jennsen withered, sobbing, at the woman's feet.

'Magic,' Althea whispered from above, 'is trouble you don't need.'

Chapter 24

Jennsen's thoughts were lost in a forlorn fog. The swamp was only there because it was beneath her feet, around her, above her, but her mind was in a more confused and tangled jumble than all the twisted things around her. So much of what she believed had turned out to be wrong. That meant that not only were many of her hopes lost, but her solutions, too.

Worse yet, Jennsen had come face-to-face with the misery, hardship, and heartbreak her existence had ended up causing others who had tried to help her.

Through the tears she could hardly see her way. She moved almost blindly through the mire.

She stumbled at times, crawled when she fell, sobbing in racking agony when she paused, supported by the limb of an old, gnarled tree. It was like the day of her mother's murder all over again – the anguish, the confusion, the insanity of it all, the bitter despair – but this time for Althea's tortured life.

Staggering through the dense growth, Jennsen grasped vines for support as she wept. Since her mother's death, finding the sorceress and getting her help had given Jennsen's life a direction, a goal. She didn't know what to do, now. She felt lost, in the midst of her life.

Jennsen wound her way through an area where steam rose from fissures. All about her, angry vapor bellowed as it was unleashed from underground in billowing clouds. She plodded past the stench of the boiling vents and back into the thick growth. Thorny bushes scratched her hands, broad leaves slashed at her face. Reaching a dark pool she vaguely remembered,

Jennsen shuffled along the ledge, gripping rocks for handholds, weeping as she made her way along the brink. Rock crumbled and came away in her hand. She fought to keep her balance as she snatched for another handhold, catching on just in time to keep herself from falling.

She gazed over her shoulder, through blurry vision, at the dark expanse of water. Jennsen wondered if it might be better were she to fall, better to be swallowed into the depths and be done with it. It looked a sweet embrace, a gentle end to it all. It looked like the peace she sought. Peace at last.

If she could just die there, on the spot, the impossible struggle would be over. The heartache and sorrow would be ended. Maybe, then, she could be with her mother and the other good spirits in the underworld.

She doubted, though, that the good spirits took people who murdered themselves. To take a life, except to defend life, was wrong. If Jennsen were to give up, all that her mother had done, all her sacrifices, would be for nothing. Her mother, waiting in eternity, might not forgive Jennsen for throwing her life away.

Althea, too, had lost nearly everything to help her. How could Jennsen ignore such bravery – not just Althea's, but Friedrich's, too? Despite how miserably responsible she felt, she could not throw her only life away.

She felt, though, as if she had stolen Althea's chance at life. Despite what the woman had said, Jennsen felt a sense of burning shame for what Althea had suffered. Althea would be imprisoned in this miserable swamp forever, every day paying the price of having tried to hide Jennsen from Darken Rahl. Jennsen's mind might have been telling her that it was Darken Rahl's doing, but her own heart said otherwise. Althea would never have her own life back, be free to walk, free to go where she would, free to have the joy of her own gift.

What right had Jennsen to expect others to help her, anyway? Why should others forfeit their life, their freedom, for her sake? What gave her the right to ask such sacrifice of them? Jennsen's mother was not the only one to suffer because of her. Althea and Friedrich were chained to the swamp, Lathea had been murdered, and Sebastian was now held prisoner. Even Tom, waiting for her up in the meadow, had set aside earning his living to come to her aid.

So many people had tried to help her and paid a terrible price. Where had she ever gotten the idea that she could shackle others to her wishes? Why should they have to relinquish their lives and needs for hers? But how could she go on without their help?

Free of the ledge and deep pool, Jennsen trudged on through an endless tangle of roots. They seemed to deliberately catch her feet. Twice, she fell sprawling. Both times she got up and continued on.

The third time she fell, she hit her face so hard the pain stunned her. Jennsen ran her fingers over her cheekbone, her forehead, thinking something surely must be broken. She found no blood, nor protruding bone. Lying there among the roots like so many snakes coiled all about her, she felt shame for all the trouble she had brought to people's lives.

And then she felt anger.

Jennsen.

She recalled her mother's words: 'Don't you ever wear a cloak of guilt because they are evil.'

Jennsen pushed herself up on her arms. How many others might have tried to help those like Jennsen, the offspring of a Lord Rahl, and paid with their lives? How many more would? Why should they, like Jennsen, not have their own lives?

It was the Lord Rahl who bore the responsibility for lives ruined.

Jennsen. Surrender.

Would it never stop?

Grushdeva du kalt misht.

Sebastian was only the latest. Was he being tortured that very moment because of her? Was he paying with his life, too, for helping her?

Surrender.

Poor Sebastian. She felt a pang of longing for him. He had been so good to help her. So brave. So strong.

Tu vash misht. Tu vask misht. Grushdeva du kalt misht.

The voice, insistent, commanding, echoed around in her head, whispering the words that made no sense. She staggered to her feet. Could she never have her own life – not even her own mind? Must she always be pursued, by Lord Rahl, by the voice?

Jenn—

'Leave me be!'

She had to help Sebastian.

She was moving again, putting one foot in front of the other, pushing vines and leaves and branches aside, cutting through the underbrush. The thick mist and dense canopy of leaves made it dark as dusk. She had no idea how late in the day it was. It had taken a lot of time to reach Althea's place. She had been there a long time. For all Jennsen knew, it might be near dusk. At best, it could be no earlier than late afternoon. She had hours left before she made it back to the meadow where Tom waited.

She had come for help, but that help had been an illusion invented in her own mind. She had relied on her mother her whole life, and then she had expected Althea to help her. She had to accept that it was up to her to do what was necessary to help herself.

Jennsen. Surrender.

'No! Leave me alone!'

She was so very tired of it all. Now she was angry, too.

Jennsen plunged onward through the swamp, splashing through water, stepping along roots and rocks when they were available. She had to help Sebastian. She had to get back to him. Tom was waiting. Tom would take her back.

But what then? How was she going to get him out? She had depended on Althea to help her with some kind of magic. Now she knew there could be no such help.

Panting from the effort of running through the swamp, she halted when she came to the expanse of water where the snake had been before. Jennsen gazed out at the silent, still expanse of water, but didn't see anything. No roots that were really a snake protruded above the surface. It was getting gloomy. She couldn't tell if anything lurked in the dark shadows beneath leaves drooping over the banks.

Sebastian's life hung in the balance. Jennsen waded into the water.

Halfway in, she remembered that she had promised herself

that she was going to take a staff to help keep her balance when she returned through the open water. She paused, debating whether or not she should go back to cut a staff. Going back was just as far as going on, so she kept going. Feeling with her feet, she found a firm bottom of roots, real roots, and stepped carefully along them. Surprisingly, as long as she stayed on the roots the water came up only to her knees and she was able to hold up her skirts to keep them dry as she waded through the murky water.

Something bumped her leg. Jennsen flinched. She saw the flash of scales. Her foot slipped. She saw with heady relief that it was only a fish darting away.

Trying to get her balance, to regain her footing, Jennsen stepped heavily into the bottomless black depths. She only had time for a short gasp before she was under the water.

Darkness surrounded her. She saw a whirl of bubbles as she went under. Surprised, she kicked frantically, trying to find bottom, something, anything, to stop her descent. There was nothing. She was in deep water, weighted down by wet clothes. Rather than support her, now, her heavy boots dragged her under.

Jennsen flailed her arms, splashing at the surface just long enough to gasp a breath before she was under again. The shock of it was startling. With all her strength, she moved her arms, trying to swim to the surface, but her clothes were like a net around her, dampening and hampering any effective action. Eyes wide in fright, red hair floating, she could see shafts of the dim light wavering and glittering, piercing the murky depths around her.

It was all happening so shockingly fast. In spite of how she was trying to seize life, it was slipping through her fingers. It didn't seem real.

Jennsen.

Shapes moved closer around her. Her lungs aching for air, Althea said that no one could come through the swamp by the back way. There were beasts back here that would tear people apart. Jennsen had been lucky once. In the grip of terror, she saw a dark shape moving closer. She was not to be lucky twice.

She didn't want to die. She knew she had thought that she did, but she knew now that she didn't. It was her only life. Her precious life. She didn't want to lose it.

She tried to swim toward the surface, toward the light, but everything seemed so slow, so thick, so heavy.

Jennsen.

The voice sounded urgent.

Jennsen.

Something bumped her. She saw flashes of iridescent green. It was the snake.

Could she, she would have screamed. Struggling, but unable to get away, she could only watch as the dark length of the thing underneath rolled up around her.

Jennsen was too exhausted to fight. Her lungs burned for air as she saw herself sinking down through the shafts of light, getting farther and farther from the surface, from life. She tried to swim to that light and air, but her leaden arms merely waved, like weed drifting in the water. It was surprising to her, since she could swim.

Jennsen.

Now, she was going to drown.

Dark coils surrounded her.

With all her clothes on, her heavy cloak, her knife, her boots, and as weary as she had been, not to mention her surprise and her half breath before going under, her ability to swim had been overwhelmed.

It hurt.

She had thought drowning would be the sweet embrace of gentle waters. It was not. It hurt worse than anything had ever hurt. The feeling of helpless suffocation was horrifying. The pain crushing her chest was sharp and unbearable. She desperately wanted it to stop. She struggled in the water against the pain, the panic, consumed with the urgent need of air. Her throat was locked tight, terrified she might gasp in water, so badly did she need a breath.

It hurt.

Jennsen felt the coils of the snake under her, touching her, caressing her. She wondered if she should have tried to kill it when she'd had the chance. She supposed she could pull her knife, now. But she was so weak.

It hurt.

The coils pushed against her. In the silent darkness, she had stopped struggling. There was no reason.

Jennsen.

She wondered why the voice didn't ask her to surrender, the way it always did. She thought it ironic, since she was at last resigned, that the voice didn't ask, but only called her name.

Jennsen felt something bump her shoulder. Something hard. Another bumped her head. Then her thigh.

She was being pushed against the bank where the roots went down into the water. Almost without realizing what she was doing, she seized the roots and pulled with sudden desperation. The thing under her continued its gentle push up.

Jennsen broke the surface. Water sluiced off her head in a sudden rush of sound. Mouth open wide, she gasped wildly at the air. She pulled herself up enough to throw her shoulders up onto the knotted roots. She couldn't drag herself the rest of the way out of the water, but at least her head was up, and she could breathe. Her legs dangled, drifting, floating in the water,

Panting, with her eyes closed, Jennsen clung to the roots with trembling fingers to keep herself from slipping back into the water. The desperate pulls of air felt wonderful as they filled her lungs. With each breath, she could feel her strength returning.

Finally, inch by inch, hand over hand, pulling against the roots, she managed to drag herself up onto the bank. She flopped on her side, panting, coughing, shivering, watching the water lapping only inches away. She felt giddy with the simple joy of breathing air.

She saw then the snake's head break the surface, easily, gracefully, silently. Yellow eyes in the black band watched her. They stared at each other for a time.

'Thank you,' Jennsen whispered.

The snake, having seen her there on the bank, seen her breathing, seen her living, slipped back into the water.

Jennsen had no idea what it had thought, or why it hadn't tried to kill her, again, when it had an easy chance at it. Maybe, after the first time, it thought she might be too big to eat, or might suddenly fight back.

But why help her? Could it be a sign of respect? Maybe it simply viewed her as competition for food, and wanted her out of its territory but didn't want to fight her again. Jennsen had no idea why it had pushed her to the surface, but the snake had saved her life. She hated snakes, and this one had saved her from drowning.

One of the things that she had feared most had been her salvation.

Still trying to catch her breath, to say nothing of recovering her wits after coming so close to passing through the veil into death, she began moving again, on her hands and knees, crawling up higher. Water ran from her clothes and hair. She couldn't get to her feet, yet, didn't trust her legs, yet, so she crawled. It felt good just to be able to move. Before long, she had recovered enough to stagger to her feet. She had to keep going. Her time was running out.

Walking revived her further. She had always liked to walk. It made her feel alive again, like her old self. She knew she wanted to live. She wanted Sebastian to live, too.

Hurrying through the tangle of vines and thorny shrubs, over the twisted roots and among the trees, her worry eased when she came at last to the place where the rock began to rise up from the mossy ground. She started up the spine of rock, relieved to have found the landmark among the trackless swamp and to be climbing out of the wet boggy bottom. It was getting darker by the moment and she remembered that it was a long way up. Jennsen desperately didn't want to spend the night in the swamp, but she didn't want to be scaling the spine of rock in the dark, either.

Those fears spurred her on. While there was still light enough, she had to keep moving. When she stumbled, she recalled how in places the ground dropped off precipitously to the sides. She admonished herself to be more careful. No helpful snake would catch her if she plummeted off a cliff in the dark.

While she made her way up, she kept going over in her mind everything that Althea had told her, hoping that something in it might be helpful. Jennsen didn't know how she could get Sebastian out, but she knew she had to try – she was his only hope. He had saved her life, before; she had to help save his, now.

She wanted desperately to see his smile, his blue eyes, his spikes of white hair. She couldn't bear the thought of them torturing him. She had to get him out of their clutches.

But how was she to accomplish such an impossible task? First, she had to get back there, she decided. Hopefully, by then, she would think of a way.

Tom would get her back to the palace. Tom would be waiting, worrying. Tom. Why had Tom helped her? The nugget of that question stuck out in her mind like a landmark to an answer, like the spine of rock lead up and out of the swamp. She just didn't know where it led.

Tom had helped her. Why?

She focused her mind on that question as she trudged up the steep rise. He said he couldn't live with himself if he watched her go out onto the Azrith Plains alone, with no supplies. He said she would die and he couldn't let that happen. That seemed a decent enough sentiment.

She knew there was more, though. He seemed determined to help her, almost as if he was duty bound. He never really questioned what it was she had to do, only her method of going about it, then did what he could to assist her.

Tom said that she should tell Lord Rahl about his help, that he was a good man. That memory kept nagging at her. Even though it had been an offhand comment, he'd been serious. But what had he meant?

She kept turning it over in her mind as she ascended the rise of rock, up among the trees, among the limbs and leaves. Animals, distant strange creatures, called out through the humid air. Others, more distant, answered with the same echoing whoops and whistles. The smell of the swamp rose to her on hot waves of air.

Jennsen recalled that Tom had seen her knife when she'd been looking for her purse that had been stolen. She had pulled back her cloak only to find that the leather thong from her purse of coins had been cut. He had seen the knife then.

Jennsen paused in her climb and straightened. Could it be that Tom thought she was some kind of ... some kind of representative, or agent, of the Lord Rahl? Could it be that Tom thought she was on an important mission on behalf of Lord Rahl? Could it be that Tom thought she knew Lord Rahl?

Was it the knife that made him think she was someone special? Perhaps it had been her pressing determination to go on a seemingly impossible journey. He certainly knew how important she thought it was. Perhaps it was that she had told him it was a matter of life and death.

Jennsen moved on, ducking under heavy limbs drooping down close over the rock. On the other side, she stood and looked around, realizing that darkness was quickly descending. With a renewed sense of urgency, she scrambled up the steep slope.

She recalled how Tom had looked at her red hair. People were often worried about her because of her red hair. Many thought she had the gift because of it. She had often encountered people who feared her because of her red hair. She had used that fear deliberately to help herself stay safe. That first night, with Sebastian, she had made him think she had some kind of magical ability to protect her if he harbored hostile intent. She had used people's fear to ward the men at the inn.

All of those things churned together in Jennsen's mind as she climbed ever upward, gasping for breath at the strenuous effort. Darkness was enveloping her. She didn't know if she could still make it through in such conditions, but she knew she had to try. For Sebastian, she had to keep going.

Just then, something dark swept up, right at her face. Jennsen let out a clipped cry and nearly fell as the dark thing fluttered away. Bats. She put a hand over her racing heart. It was beating as fast as their wings. The little creatures had come out to snatch the bugs that were so thick in the air.

She realized, then, that in her surprise, she might easily have stepped back and fallen. It was frightening to think how a lapse of attention in the dark, a fright, a loose rock, or a slip, could put her over an edge from which there could be no return. She knew, though, that remaining in the swamp at night might be just as fatal.

Weary from the day's struggles, the sudden scares, she climbed, stumbling in the dark, feeling the rock, groping her way, trying to stay on the ridge and not wander off what she knew to be steep drops to either side. She worried, too, what creatures might still come out in the darkness to seize her just as she thought she was nearly free of the swamp.

Althea had said that no one could come into the swamp by the back way. A new worry gripped her: maybe after dark, Tom would be in danger. Under cover of night, one of the creatures might venture out of the swamp to snatch him. What if she reached the meadow only to discover Tom and his horses mauled by the monsters created out of Althea's magic? What would she do, then?

She had worries enough. She told herself not to come up with new ones.

Jennsen stumbled suddenly out into the open. There was a fire burning. She stared, trying to reconcile it.

'Jennsen!' Tom jumped up and rushed over. He put his big arm around her shoulders to steady her. 'Dear spirits, are you all right?'

She nodded, too exhausted to speak. He didn't see the nod – he was already running for the wagon. Jennsen sank down to sit heavily on the grassy ground, catching her breath, surprised to be there at last, and relieved beyond words to be free of the swamp.

Tom ran back with a blanket. 'You're soaking wet,' he said as he threw the blanket around her. 'What happened?'

'I went for a swim.'

He paused at mopping her face with the corner of the blanket to frown at her. 'I don't want to tell you your business, but I don't think that was a good idea.'

'The snake would agree with you.'

His frown tightened as his face drew closer to hers. 'Snake? What happened in there? What do you mean, the snake would agree with me?'

Still struggling to get her breath, Jennsen waved a hand, dismissing it. She had been so afraid of being caught down there in the dark that she had virtually been running up the steep hillside for the last hour, on top of the exertion of the rest of it. She was spent.

The fear of it all was catching up with her. Her shoulders began to tremble. She realized then that she was clutching Tom's muscular arm for dear life. He seemed not to notice, or if he did, he didn't comment on it. She drew back, despite how good it felt to feel his strength, his solid reliable form, his sincere concern.

Tom protectively bunched more of the blanket around her. 'Did you make it through to Althea's?'

She nodded, and when he handed her a waterskin, drank greedily.

'I swear, I've never heard of anyone ever making it back out of that swamp – except going in the other side when they were invited. Did you see any of the beasts?'

'I had a snake, bigger round than your leg, wrapped around me. I got a pretty good look at it – more of a look than I wanted, actually.'

He let out a low whistle. 'Did the sorceress help you, then? Did you get what you needed from her? Is everything all right, then?' He halted abruptly, and seemed to rein in his curiosity. 'Sorry. You're all cold and wet. I shouldn't be asking you so many questions.'

'Althea and I had a long talk. I can't say that I got what I needed, but just knowing the truth is better than chasing illusions.'

Concern showed in his eyes and the way he made sure the warm blanket was covering her. 'If you didn't get the help you needed, then what will you do now?'

Jennsen drew her knife, along with a breath to steel herself. Holding the knife by the blade, she held it up before Tom's face, so that the handle was lit by the firelight. The worked metal that made up the ornate letter 'R' glimmered as if it were covered in jewels. She held it out before her like a talisman, like an official proclamation cast in silver, like a demand from on high that could not be denied.

'I need to get back to the palace.'

Without pause, Tom scooped her up in his massive arms, as if she were no more weight than a lamb, and carried her to the wagon. He lifted her over the side and gently set her in the back, among the nest of blankets.

'Don't worry – I'll get you back there. You did the hard part. Now, you just rest in those warm blankets and let me get you back there.'

Jennsen was relieved to have her suspicions confirmed. In a way, though, it made her feel slimy, like falling into the swamp again. She was lying to him, using him. That wasn't right, but she didn't know what else to do.

Before he turned away, she seized his arm. 'Tom, aren't you afraid to be helping me, when I'm involved in something so . . .'

'Dangerous?' he finished for her. 'What I'm doing is nothing much compared to the risk you took in there.' He gestured to her matted red hair. 'I'm nothing special, like you, but I'm glad you allowed me to do the small part I could do.'

'I'm not nearly as special as you think I am.' She suddenly felt very small. 'I'm just doing as I must.'

Tom pulled blankets from the back up toward her. 'I see a lot of people. I don't need the gift to tell you're special.'

'You know that this is secret business, and I can't tell you what it is I'm doing. I'm sorry, but I can't.'

'Of course you can't. Only special people carry such a special weapon. I'd not expect you to say a word and I'd not ask.'

'Thank you, Tom.' Feeling even more detestable to be using him as she was, and when he was such a sincere man, Jennsen squeezed his arm in gratitude. 'I can tell you it's important, and you're a huge help in it all.'

He smiled. 'You wrap yourself in those blankets and get yourself dry. We'll soon be back out on the Azrith Plains. In case you forgot, it's winter out there. Wet as you are, you'll freeze.'

'Thank you, Tom. You're a good man.' Jennsen slumped back into the blankets, too exhausted from the ordeal to sit up any longer.

'I'm counting on you to tell Lord Rahl,' he said with his easy laugh. Tom quickly doused the fire and then climbed up into the wagon seat.

Without guile, he was helping her, at what he had to believe was at least some risk. She feared to think what they might do to him were he to be caught helping Darken Rahl's daughter. Here he thought he was helping the Lord Rahl, and he was doing the opposite without even knowing the chance he was taking.

Before it was over, she would put him at greater risk yet.

Despite her fear that they were racing back to the palace of the man who wanted to kill her, the stomach-churning anxiety of what lay ahead, the disappointment of failing to get the help she had hoped for, the heartbreak of learning all she had from Althea, the cold that was making her wet clothes feel like ice, and the bouncing wagon, Jennsen was soon fast asleep.

Chapter 25

Swaying atop the seat of the wagon, Jennsen watched the immense plateau gradually drawing closer. The morning sun lit the soaring stone walls of the People's Palace, warming them in a pastel glow. Although the wind had died down, the morning air remained bone-chilling cold. After the reeking rot of the swamp, she welcomed the flat, dry, stony scent of the open plain.

With her fingertips, Jennsen rubbed her forehead, trying to soothe her dull throbbing headache. Tom had driven all night and she had slept in the back of the bouncing wagon, but not well nor nearly long enough. At least she had slept some, and they had made it back.

'Too bad Lord Rahl isn't there.'

Shocked out of her private thoughts, Jennsen opened her eyes. 'What?'

'Lord Rahl.' Tom gestured off to the right, to the south. 'It's too bad he isn't here to help you.'

He had pointed south, the direction of the Old World. On occasion, Jennsen's mother had spoken of the bond connecting the D'Haran people with the Lord Rahl. Through its ancient and arcane magic, D'Harans were somehow able to sense where the Lord Rahl was. While the strength of the bond varied among D'Haran people, they all shared it to some degree.

What the Lord Rahl accrued from the bond, Jennsen didn't know. She thought of it as yet more chains of domination around his people. In her mother's case, though, it helped them avoid Darken Rahl's clutches.

From her mother's descriptions, Jennsen was aware of the

bond, but for some reason never felt anything of it. Perhaps it was so weak in her, as it was with some D'Haran people, that she simply couldn't feel it. Her mother said it had nothing to do with one's level of devotion to the Lord Rahl, that it was purely a link of magic, and, as such, it would be governed by criteria other than her feelings about the man.

Jennsen remembered times when her mother would stand in the doorway of their home, or at a window, or pause out in the forest, and stare off toward the horizon. Jennsen knew at those times that her mother was sensing Darken Rahl through the bond, where he was, and how close. It was a shame that it told her only where the Lord Rahl himself was, and not the brutes he sent after them.

Tom, being D'Haran, took that bond to the Lord Rahl for granted, and had just given Jennsen a valuable bit of information: Lord Rahl was not at his palace. That news buoyed her hopes. It was one less obstacle, one less thing to worry about.

Lord Rahl was off to the south, probably in the Old World making war on the people there, as Sebastian had told her.

'Yes,' she finally said, 'too bad.'

The marketplace below the plateau was already busy. Wisps of dust drifted above the crowds gathered there and over the road south. She wondered if Irma the sausage lady was there. Jennsen missed Betty. She wanted so much to see the goat's little tail wagging furiously, to hear her bleating with elation at being reunited with her lifelong friend.

Tom pointed his team toward the market, to where he had been set up selling his load of wine. Maybe Irma would go to the same place. Jennsen would have to leave Betty again in order to go up through the entrance and into the plateau. It would be a long climb up all those stairs, and then she had to find where Sebastian was being held.

As the wagon rumbled across the hardpan of the Azrith Plains, Jennsen stared at the empty road that wound its way up the side of the plateau.

'Take the road,' she said.

'What?'

'Take the road up to the palace.'

'Are you sure, Jennsen? I don't think that's wise. It's only for official business.'

'Take the road.'

In answer, he urged the horses to the left, away from their course toward the market, and toward the base of the road, instead. From the corner of her eye she saw him snatch glances at his inscrutable passenger.

Soldiers stationed at the base of the plateau, where the road began its ascent, watched them approach. As the wagon rolled closer, Jennsen drew out her knife.

'Don't stop,' she said to Tom.

He stared over at her. 'What? I have to. They have bows, you know.'

Jennsen continued to stare ahead. 'Just keep going.'

When they reached the soldiers, Jennsen held the knife out, holding it by the blade so that the handle stuck up above her fist. She kept her arm out straight and stiff, pointed down at the cluster of men, so that they might see what she was announcing. She didn't look at them, but watched the road ahead, showing them the knife as if she couldn't be bothered to talk to them.

Every pair of eyes watched that knife handle with the ornate letter 'R' upon it as it flashed past their eyes. None moved to stop the wagon, or to nock an arrow. Tom let out a low whistle. The wagon shook and rattled as it rolled onward.

The road switched back and forth as it made its way steadily up the plateau. In some places there was ample room, but occasionally the road narrowed, forcing the wagon to ride close to the dizzying drop. Each tight bend offered them a new vista, a new view of the expanse of the Azrith Plains spread out far below. Off in the distance the plains were rimmed by dusky blue mountains.

When they arrived at the bridge, they finally did have to stop; the bridge was pulled up. Her faith in herself, and her plan, faltered as she realized that this, and not her bold bluff, was probably the reason the soldiers below had let her pass so easily. They knew she couldn't get over the chasm unless the guards lowered the bridge. They knew she couldn't simply barge into the palace, and at the same time they didn't have to challenge a woman who had what very well might be an official pass, of sorts, from the Lord Rahl himself. Worse yet, she now saw how the soldiers had also isolated, in a place without escape or hope of rescue by reinforcements, people they deemed potential intruders. Any hostile foray would be stopped cold, here, and in all likelihood, the intruder captured or killed on the spot.

It was no wonder Tom had advised against using the road up.

Stimulated by the effort of the climb, the big horses tossed their heads at the interruption. One man stepped in front and took control of the horses' bits to keep them still. Soldiers approached the side of the wagon. Jennsen sat on the cliff side, and although she saw men guarding the rear quarter on her side, most of the men approached on Tom's side.

'Good day, Sergeant,' Tom called out.

The man scrutinized the inside of the wagon and, after finding it empty, looked up at the two in the seat. 'Good day.'

Jennsen knew that this was no time for her to become timid. If she failed here, everything would be lost. Not only would Sebastian have no hope, but she would likely join him in a dungeon. She could not afford to lose her nerve. When the soldiers were close enough, she reached past Tom to hold the knife down toward the sergeant of the guards, showing him the handle as if she were flashing a royal pass.

'Drop the bridge,' she said before he had a chance to ask them anything.

The sergeant took in the knife handle before meeting her glare. 'What's your business?'

Sebastian had told her how to bluff. He had explained how she had done it her whole life, that she was a natural at it. Now she had to do it with deliberate intent if she was to save him, and get out alive, herself. Despite how fast her heart pounded, she showed the man a stern but empty expression.

'Lord Rahl's business. Lower the bridge.'

She thought that he was taken back a bit by her tone, or possibly he was worried by her unexpected words. She could see his level of caution rise, tensing his features. Nevertheless, he stood his ground.

'I need a little more than that, ma'am.'

Jennsen twirled the knife, weaving it over and under and between her fingers, the polished metal flashing in the sunlight as it spun, until it came to an abrupt halt with the handle upright in her fist once more, the ornate letter 'R' showing to the soldier. In a deliberate manner, she pushed the hood of her cloak back, exposing her fall of red hair to the morning sunlight and the men's stares. She could see in their eyes that her implication had been clearly understood.

'I know you have a job to do,' Jennsen said with terrible calm, 'but so do I. I'm on official business for Lord Rahl. I'm sure you can appreciate how displeased Lord Rahl would be with me were I to discuss his business with everyone who asked about it, therefore, I have no intention of doing so, but I can tell you that I wouldn't be here were it not a matter of life or death. You are wasting my precious time, Sergeant. Now, lower the bridge.'

'And what might be your name, ma'am?'

Jennsen leaned farther past Tom in order to more directly scowl at the sergeant.

'Unless you lower that bridge, Sergeant, and right now, you will forever after remember me as Trouble, sent by Lord Rahl himself.'

The sergeant, backed by a few dozen men with pikes, along with crossbows, swords, and axes, didn't flinch. He looked at Tom.

'What's your part in this?'

Tom shrugged. 'Just driving the wagon. Were I you, Sergeant, this is one lady I'd not want to be delaying.'

'Is that so?'

'It is,' Tom said with conviction.

The sergeant gazed long and hard into Tom's eyes. Finally, he considered Jennsen again, then turned and rolled his hand, motioning a man to lower the bridge.

Jennsen gestured with her knife toward the palace up the road. 'How may I find the place where we hold prisoners?'

As the gears started clattering and the bridge began to descend, he turned back to Jennsen.

'Inquire with the guards at the top. They can direct you, ma'am.'

'Thank you,' Jennsen said with finality, sitting back up straight and putting her eyes ahead, waiting for the bridge to lower. Once it had thudded into place, the sergeant signaled them ahead. Tom nodded his thanks and flicked the reins.

Jennsen had to play the part through the whole way, if this were to have a chance of working. She found that her performance was aided by her very real anger. She was disturbed, though, that Tom had played some part in the success of the bluff. She wouldn't have his help for all of it. She decided that it would be wise to keep her anger out and in plain view of the other guards.

'You want to see the prisoners?' Tom asked.

She realized that she never had said why she had to return to the palace. 'Yes. They've taken a man prisoner by mistake. I've come to see that he's released.'

Tom checked the horses with the reins, keeping them wide to negotiate the wagon around a switchback. 'Ask for Captain Lerner,' he said at last.

Jennsen glanced over at him, surprised that he had offered a name rather than an objection. 'A friend of yours?'

The reins moved ever so slightly, with practiced precision, guiding the horses around the bend. 'I don't know if I'd call him a friend. I've dealt with him a time or two.'

'Wine?'

Tom smiled. 'No. Other things.'

He apparently didn't intend to say what other things. Jennsen watched the sweep of the Azrith Plains and distant mountains as they rode up the side of the plateau. Somewhere beyond those plains, those mountains, lay freedom.

At the top, the road leveled out before a great gate through the massive outer wall of the palace. The guards stationed before the gate there waved them through, then blew whistles in a short series of notes to others, unseen, beyond the walls. Jennsen realized that they had not arrived unannounced.

She nearly gasped as they cleared the short tunnel through the massive outer wall. Inside, expansive grounds spread out before them. Lawns and hedges bordered the road that curved toward a hill of steps well over a half mile away. The grounds inside the walls were teeming with soldiers in smart uniforms of leather and chain mail covered with wool tunics. Many, with pikes held upright at precisely the same angle, lined the route. These men were not loafing about. They weren't the kind to be surprised by what came up the road.

Tom took it all in casually. Jennsen tried to keep her eyes pointed ahead. She tried to look indifferent amid such splendor.

Before the hill of steps awaited a reception party of guards over a hundred strong. Tom pulled the wagon into the pocket they'd formed blocking the road. Jennsen saw, standing on the steps overlooking the soldiers, three men in robes. Two wore silver-colored robes. Between them, one step higher, stood an older man wearing white, both hands held in the opposite sleeves trimmed in golden-colored braiding that shimmered in the sunlight.

Tom set the brake on the wagon as a soldier took control of the horses to keep them from moving. Before Tom could begin climbing down, Jennsen put a hand on his arm to stop him.

'This is as far as you go.'

'But you—'

'You've done enough. You helped with the part I needed. I can handle it from here on out on my own.'

His measured, blue-eyed gaze swept over the guards standing around the wagon. He seemed reluctant to accede. 'I don't think it could hurt if I went along.'

'I'd rather you go back to your brothers.'

He glanced to her hand on his arm before looking up into her eyes. 'If that's your wish.' His voice lowered to little more than a whisper. 'Will I see you again?'

It sounded more like a request than a question. Jennsen could not bring herself to deny such a simple thing, not after all he had done for her.

'We'll need to go down to the market to buy some horses. I'll stop by your place, first, right after I'm done inside with getting my friend released.'

'Promise?'

Under her breath, she said, 'I have to pay you for your services – remember?'

His lopsided grin reappeared. 'I've never met anyone like you, Jennsen. I . . .' He noticed the soldiers, remembering then where he was, and cleared his throat. 'I'm thankful you let me do my small part, ma'am. I will hold you to your word on the rest of it.'

He had risked enough by bringing her this far – a risk he hadn't known he was taking. Jennsen fervently hoped that in her brief smile he would see how genuinely grateful she was for his help, since she didn't think she could afford to keep her promise to see him before they left.

With his powerful hand gripping her arm to halt her for a final word, he spoke in a low but solemn voice. 'Steel against steel, that he may be the magic against magic.'

Jennsen had absolutely no idea what he meant. Staring into his intense gaze, she answered with a single, firm nod.

Not wanting to let the soldiers suspect that she might really be mild-mannered, Jennsen turned away and climbed down from the wagon to stand before the man who looked to be in charge. She allowed him only a perfunctory look at the knife before replacing it in the sheath at her belt.

'I need to see the man in charge of any prisoners you're holding. Captain Lerner, if memory serves me.'

His brow drew together. 'You want to see the captain of the prison guards?'

Jennsen didn't know his rank. She didn't know much of anything about military matters, except that for most of her life soldiers like these had been trying to kill her. He could be a general, or, for all she knew, a corporal. As she considered the man, his dress, his age, his bearing, she reasoned that he definitely looked more than a corporal. She feared to make a mistake with his rank, though, and decided it would be healthier to ignore it.

Jennsen dismissed his question with a curt flick of her hand. 'I haven't got all day. I'll need an escort, of course. You and some of your men will do, I suppose.'

As she started up the steps, she glanced over her shoulder and saw Tom wink at her. It lifted her heart. The soldiers had parted to let his wagon leave, so he flicked the reins and urged his big horses away. Jennsen hated to see his comforting presence go. She turned her mind from her fears.

'You,' she said, gesturing to the man in the white robes, 'take me to where you hold prisoners.'

The man, the top of his head showing through his thinning gray hair, lifted a finger, sending most of the milling guards back to their posts. The officer of mysterious rank and a dozen of his soldiers remained behind her.

'May I see the knife?' the man in the white robes asked in a gentle voice.

Jennsen suspected that this man, able to dismiss guards of rank, must be someone important. Important people in Lord Rahl's palace might have the gift. It occurred to her that if he did have the gift, he would see her as a hole in the world. It also occurred to her that this was a very poor time to blurt out a confession, and an even worse time to try to bolt for the gate. She had to hope that he was a palace official and that he wasn't gifted.

Many of the soldiers were still watching. Jennsen casually pulled her knife from the sheath at her belt. Without a word, but showing a face that clearly said she was running out of patience, she held the knife up before the man's eyes so he could see the ornate 'R' on the handle.

He looked down his nose at the weapon before returning his attention to her. 'And this is real?'

'No,' Jennsen snapped, 'I smelted it while sitting around the campfire last night. Are you going to take me to where you hold prisoners, or not?'

Showing no reaction, the man graciously held out a hand. 'If you would follow me this way, madam.'

Chapter 26

The palace official's white robes flowed out behind him as he ascended the hill of steps, flanked by the two men in silver robes. Jennsen remained what she judged to be an imperious distance behind the men. When the man in white noticed how she had lagged behind, he slowed to allow her to catch up. She slowed her pace accordingly, maintaining the distance. He nervously checked behind, then slowed more. She slowed yet more, until the three robed men, Jennsen, and the soldiers behind her were all pausing ponderously on each step.

When they reached the next landing on the broad, sunlit marble steps, the man glanced over his shoulder again. Jennsen gestured impatiently. He finally understood that she had no intention of walking with him, but expected him to lead the procession. The man acceded, quickening his steps, allowing her to have the distance she demanded, resigned to being what amounted to her lowly crier.

The officer of unknown rank and his dozen soldiers climbed the stairs with mincing steps, trying to duplicate the distance she maintained in front of her. It was unanticipated and awkward for her escorts. She wanted it to be; like her red hair, the distraction gave them something to think about, something to worry about.

At intervals, the smooth ascent of marble stairs was broken by broad landings that gave the legs a rest before continuing up. At the top of the stairs, tall embossed brass doors were set back beyond colossal columns. The entire front of the palace looming over them was one of the grandest sights Jennsen had ever seen, but her mind was not on the intricate architecture of the entrance. She was thinking about what lay inside.

They passed the shadows of the towering columns and swept on through the doorway; the dozen soldiers still trailed in her wake, their weapons, belts, and mail jangling. The sound of their boots on the polished marble floor echoed off the walls of a grand entry lined with fluted pillars.

Deeper into the palace, people going about their business, or standing in twos and threes talking, or strolling the balconies, paused to watch the unusual procession, paused to see the officials in their white and silver robes and a dozen guards at a respectful distance escorting a woman with red hair. By her outfit, especially in comparison to the neat clean dress of the others, it was obvious that she had just traveled in. Rather than being embarrassed by her clothes, Jennsen was pleased that they added to the sense of urgent mystery. The reaction of the people, too, was bound to infect her escort.

After the man in white whispered to the two in silver robes, they nodded and ran on ahead, vanishing around a corner. The guards followed at her measured distance.

The procession wound through a maze of small passageways and funneled down narrow service stairs. Jennsen and her escorts made a number of turns through intersecting halls, along dim corridors to doors opening onto wide halls, and intermittently descended a variety of stairs, until she could no longer keep track of their route. By the dusty condition of some of the dingy stairs and musty-smelling, apparently little-used halls, she realized that the man in white robes was taking her on a shortcut through the palace in order to get her to where she wanted to go as swiftly as possible.

This, too, was reassuring, because it meant they took her seriously. That helped her confidence in playing the part. She told herself that she was important, she was a personal representative of Lord Rahl himself, and she was not going to be deterred by anyone. They were here for no other purpose but to assist her. It was their job. Their duty.

Since it was hopeless trying to keep track of all the turns and twists they took, she put her mind instead to the matter at hand, to what she would do and say, going over it all in her head.

Jennsen reminded herself that no matter what condition Sebastian was in, she had to keep to her plan. Acting surprised, bursting into tears, falling on him, wailing, would do neither of them any good. She hoped that when she saw him she could remember all that.

The man in white checked his charge before turning down a stone stairwell. Dull red rust showed through chipped paint on the iron railing. The uncomfortably steep flight of stairs twisted downward, finally ending in a lower passageway lit by the eerie wavering light from torches in short floor stands, rather than by lamps and reflectors that were used to light the way above.

The two men in silver robes who had gone on ahead were waiting for them at the bottom. Hazy smoke hung near the low beams of the ceiling, leaving the place reeking of burning pitch. She could see her breath in the cold air. Jennsen felt, viscerally, how deep they were in the People's Palace. She had a brief, unpleasant memory of what it felt like sinking down beneath the dark, bottomless water of the swamp. She felt a similar pressure on her chest in the depths of the palace as she imagined the inconceivable weight overhead.

Down the murky stone corridor to the right she thought she could see evenly spaced doors. In some of the doors, it looked like there might be fingers gripping the edge of small openings. From down that hall, in the darkness, came a dry, echoing cough. As she looked off toward the unseen source of the sound, she had the feeling that this was a place where men were sent not for punishment, but to die.

Before an ironbound door sealing off the corridor to the left stood a powerfully built man, feet spread, hands clasped behind his back, chin held high. His bearing, his size, the way his cut-stone gaze locked on her, made Jennsen's breath falter.

She wanted to run. Why did she think she could do this? After all, who was she? Just a nobody.

Althea said that wasn't true unless she made it so herself. Jennsen wished she had as much faith in her own abilities as Althea seemed to have in her.

Looking Jennsen in the eye, the man in white robes held a hand out in introduction. 'Captain Lerner. As you requested.' He turned to the captain and held his other hand out toward Jennsen. 'A personal envoy of Lord Rahl. So she says.'

The captain gave the man in white a grim smile.

'Thank you,' she said to the men who had escorted her. 'That will be all.'

The man in white opened his mouth to speak, then, as he met the look in her eyes, thought better of it and bowed. With his arms held out like a hen herding chicks, he ushered the other two in silver and then the soldiers away with him.

'I'm looking for a man I heard was taken prisoner,' she told the big man standing before the door.

'For what reason?'

'Someone messed up. He was taken prisoner by mistake.'

'Who says it was a mistake?'

Jennsen lifted the knife from its sheath at her belt and held it by the blade, nonchalantly showing the man the handle. 'I do.'

His iron eyes briefly took in the design on the handle. Still, he stood in the same relaxed stance, barring the iron door to the passageway beyond. Jennsen twirled the knife through her fingers, caught it by the handle, and returned it smoothly to its sheath at her belt.

'I used to carry one, too,' he said with a nod toward the knife she had returned to its sheath. 'Few years back.'

'But not any longer?' She applied gentle pressure to the crossguard until she felt the knife click home. The soft sound echoed back from the darkness behind her.

He shrugged. 'It gets wearing, having your life at risk for Lord Rahl all the time.'

Jennsen feared he might ask her something about the Lord Rahl, something she couldn't answer, but should be able to. She sought to block that possibility.

'You served under Darken Rahl, then. That was before my time. It must have been a great honor to have known him.'

'Obviously, you didn't know the man.'

She feared she had just failed her first test. She had thought that everyone who served would be a loyal follower. She thought it would be safe to go with that assumption. It wasn't.

Captain Lerner turned his head and spat. He looked back at her with challenge. 'Darken Rahl was a twisted bastard. I'd have liked to put his knife between his ribs and twisted it good.'

Despite her anxiety, she showed him no more than a cool expression. 'Then why didn't you?'

'When the whole world is crazy, it doesn't pay to be sane. I finally told them I was getting too old and took a job down here. Someone far better than I ever was finally sent Darken Rahl to the Keeper.'

Jennsen was thrown off by such an unexpected sentiment. She didn't know if the man had really hated Darken Rahl, or if he was only saying he did in front of her so as to show loyalty to the new Lord Rahl, Richard, who had killed his father and assumed power. She tried to gather her wits without being obvious.

'Well, Tom said you weren't stupid. I guess he knew what he was talking about.'

The captain laughed, a spontaneous, deep, rolling sound that unexpectedly made Jennsen smile at the incongruity of it coming from a man who otherwise looked like death's darling.

'Tom would know.' He clapped a fist to his heart in salute. His face softened to an easy smile. Tom had helped her again.

Jennsen clapped a fist to her heart, returning the salute. It seemed the right thing to do. 'I'm Jennsen.'

'Pleased, Jennsen.' He let out a sigh. 'Maybe if I'd have known the new Lord Rahl, like you do, I might still be serving with you. But I'd already given it up by then and come down here. The new Lord Rahl has changed everything, all the rules – he's turned the whole world upside down, I guess.'

Jennsen feared she was treading on dangerous ground. She didn't know what the man meant and feared to say anything in response. She simply nodded and forged ahead with her reason for being there.

'I can see why Tom said that you'd be the one to see.'

'What's this about, Jennsen?'

She took a deep, casual breath, preparing herself. She had

thought it out a hundred different ways, forward and backward. She was ready to come at it from any angle.

'You know that those of us who serve Lord Rahl in this capacity can't always allow everyone to know what we're doing, or who we are.'

Captain Lerner was nodding. 'Of course.'

Jennsen folded her arms, trying to look relaxed, despite how her heart pounded. She had made it past the riskiest assumption; she had guessed correctly.

'Well, I had a man working with me,' Jennsen went on. 'I heard he was taken prisoner. It wouldn't surprise me. The fellow sticks out in a crowd – but for what we were doing, that was what we needed. Unfortunately, the guards must have noticed him, too. Because of the mission and the people we were dealing with, he was well armed, so that would have put the men who stopped him on edge.

'He hasn't been here before, so he wouldn't know who to trust, and besides, it's traitors we're hunting.'

The captain was frowning in thought as he rubbed his jaw. 'Traitors? In the palace?'

'We don't know for certain. We suspect infiltrators are about – that's who we're hunting – so he wouldn't dare to trust anyone here. If the wrong ears heard who he really was, it would imperil the rest of us. I doubt he would even give you his real name, though he might have – Sebastian. With the danger we're in, he would know that the less he says, then the less risk there is to the others on our team.'

He stared off, seeming to be caught up in her story.

'No ... no prisoner has admitted to that name.' His brow bunched in earnest reflection. 'What's he look like?'

'A few years older than me. Blue eyes. Short white hair.'

The captain instantly recognized the description. 'That one.'

'My information was correct, then? You have him.'

She wanted to grab the man by his leather and shake him. She wanted to ask if they'd hurt Sebastian. She wanted to scream at him to let Sebastian out.

'Yes, we have him. If it's the same man you're talking about, that is. Matches your description, anyway.'

'Good. I need him back. I have urgent business for him. I can't afford to delay. We need to leave at once before the trail gets any colder. It would be best if we not make a big show of him being released. We need to slip out with as little notice as possible, as little contact with soldiers as possible. The ring of infiltrators might have managed to place themselves in the army.'

Captain Lerner folded his arms and sighed as he leaned down toward her a little, looking at her as a big brother might look at a little sister. 'Jennsen, are you sure he's one of your men?'

Jennsen feared to overplay the bluff. 'He was chosen for this assignment specifically because soldiers would not suspect he was one of us. Looking at him, you'd never guess. Sebastian has a proven knack for being able to get close to the infiltrators without them getting wind that he's one of our men.'

'But are you sure of this man's heart? Are you really sure he'd not bring Lord Rahl into harm's view?'

'Sebastian is one of mine – that much I know – but I'm not sure the man you have is my Sebastian. I guess I'd have to see him to be sure. Why?'

The captain stared off as he shook his head. 'I don't know. I spent a lot of years carrying the knife, like you're starting out doing, and going places where you can't carry the knife, so you won't be known for who you really are. I don't have to tell you how being in such danger all the time sometimes gives you a sense about people. Something about that fellow with the white hair makes mine stand on end.'

Jennsen didn't know what to say. The captain was twice the size of Sebastian, so it wasn't Sebastian's physical presence that would worry the man. Of course, size was no valid indicator of potential threat. Jennsen very well might be able to beat the captain in a knife fight. Maybe Captain Lerner sensed how deadly Sebastian was with weapons. The captain's eyes had been heedful of the way her fingers handled the knife.

Perhaps the captain was able to tell by various small things that Sebastian was not D'Haran. That could be troublesome, but Jennsen had thought out a plan to explain that, too, just in case.

'Tom still up to his trouble?' the man asked.

'Oh, you know Tom. He's selling wine, along with the help of Joe and Clayton.'

The captain stared incredulously. 'Tom – and his brothers? Selling wine?' He shook his head as a grin spread wide. 'I'd like to know what he's really up to.'

Jennsen shrugged. 'Well, that's just what he's selling at the moment, of course. The three of them travel around, buying goods, bringing them back to sell.'

He laughed at that, and slapped her shoulder. 'That sounds like he'd want it told. Small wonder he trusts you.'

Jennsen was completely confused and desperately didn't want to be dragged any further into a dangerous discussion about Tom, or she could soon be found out. She didn't really know much about Tom; this man apparently did.

'I guess I'd better see this fellow you have. If it is Sebastian, I need to kick his tail and get him on his way.'

'Right,' Captain Lerner said with a firm nod. 'If he is your man, at least I'll finally know his name.' He turned to the ironbound door as he rooted around in his pocket for a key. 'If it is him, he's lucky you came for him before one of them women in red showed up to ask him questions. He'd be spouting more than his name, then. He'd have saved himself and you a lot of trouble if he'd have told us what he was about in the first place.'

Jennsen felt giddy relief to hear that a Mord-Sith hadn't tortured Sebastian. 'When you're doing Lord Rahl's business, you keep your mouth shut,' she said. 'Sebastian knows the price of our work.'

The captain grunted his agreement as he turned the key. The latch unlocked with a cavernous clang. 'For this Lord Rahl, I'd keep my mouth shut – even if it was a Mord-Sith asking the questions. But you'd have to know the new Lord Rahl better than I, so I guess I don't need to tell you.'

Jennsen didn't understand, but didn't ask anything, either. As the captain tugged on the door, it slowly swung open, revealing a long hallway lit by a few candles along the length of the corridor. To each side were doors with small, barred openings. As they passed some of those openings, as many as half a dozen arms stretched out, imploring, reaching, grabbing. From the darkness through others came the clamor of voices calling out vile curses and oaths. From the reaching hands and the collection of voices, she knew that each room beyond held groups of men.

Jennsen followed behind the captain, deeper into the fortress prison. When eyes peered out and saw it was a woman, the men called out obscenely to her. She was shocked by the lewd and vulgar things yelled at her, the jeering laughter. She hid her feelings, her fears, and wore a calm mask.

Captain Lerner kept to the center of the passageway, occasionally batting aside a reaching hand. 'Watch yourself,' he cautioned.

Jennsen was about to ask why when someone threw something sloppy at her. It missed, splattering on the opposite wall. She was appalled to see that it was feces. Several more men joined in. Jennsen had to duck and dodge to miss it. The captain suddenly kicked a door of a man about to throw more. The bang of the kick echoed up and down the corridor, serving as warning enough to cause men to retreat back into the depths of their cells. Only when the glaring captain was sure his threat was understood did he start out once again.

Jennsen couldn't help but to ask in a whisper, 'What are all of these men accused of?'

The captain glanced back over his shoulder. 'Various things. Murder, rape – things like that. A few are spies – the kind of men you're hunting.'

The stench of the place gagged her. The raw hatred of the prisoners was understandable, she supposed, but no matter how much she sympathized with captives of Lord Rahl's soldiers, men fighting against his brutal rule, their behavior only served to support any accusations of perversity. Jennsen stayed close to Captain Lerner's heels as he turned down a side passageway.

From a shelf built into the stone, he collected a lamp, then lit it from a nearby candle. The light from the lamp only served to throw a little more light into a nightmare and make it all the more frightening. She had terrifying visions of being found out and ending up in this place. She couldn't keep from imagining being locked in a room with men like these. She knew what they would do to her. Jennsen had to remind herself to slow her breathing.

Another door had to be unlocked, taking them beyond to a low passageway with doors spaced much closer. She guessed that they were cells holding a single man. A grasping hand, grimy and covered with open sores, shot out of an opening to catch her cloak. She shrugged the hand off her and kept moving.

Captain Lerner unlocked another door at the end and they entered a space smaller yet, hardly wider than his shoulders. The twisting, cramped opening, like a fissure in the rock, made Jennsen's skin crawl. No hands reached out of the door openings in this place. The captain stopped and held up the lamp to look through the small hole in the door to the right. Satisfied with what he saw, he handed her the lamp and then unlocked the door.

'We put special prisoners in this section,' he explained.

He had to use both hands and all his weight to pull on the door. It moved with grating protest. Inside, Jennsen was surprised to see it was only a tiny, empty room with a second door. That was why there were no hands reaching in this hall. The cells had double doors, to make escape even more improbable. After unlocking the second door, he took back the lamp.

The captain ducked through the short doorway, pushing the light in before him, his bulk in the door momentarily throwing her into the darkness. Once through, he extended a hand out to help her so she wouldn't trip over the high sill. Jennsen held the man's big hand and stepped into the cell. It was larger than she expected, looking to be carved out of the solid stone of the plateau. Tooled gouges in the rock walls testified to how difficult the work had been. No prisoner was going to dig his way out of such a secure place.

On a bench carved in the opposite wall sat Sebastian. His blue eyes were on her from the instant she entered. In those eyes she thought she could see how much he wanted out. Nevertheless, he showed no emotion and said nothing. From outward appearances, no one would even know that he knew her.

He had neatly folded his cloak and used it as a cushion on the cold stone. Nearby sat a water cup. His clothes were orderly, showing no evidence that they abused him.

It was so good to see his face, his eyes, his spikes of white hair again. He licked his lips, his beautiful lips that so often had smiled at her. Now, though, he dared not smile. Jennsen had been right. She did want to fall on him, to throw her arms around him, to wail with her relief at seeing him alive and unhurt.

The captain gestured with his lamp. 'This him?'

'Yes, Captain.'

Sebastian's eyes were fixed on her as she stepped forward. She had to pause to be sure she had her voice under control. 'It's all right, Sebastian. Captain Lerner, here, knows you're one of my team.' She patted the handle of her knife. 'You can trust him to keep your identity confidential.'

Captain Lerner extended a hand. 'Glad to meet you, Sebastian. Sorry about the mix-up. We didn't know who you were. Jennsen explained your mission. I used to serve, so I understand the need for secrecy.'

Sebastian rose to his feet and clasped hands with the man. 'No harm done, Captain. I can't fault our men for doing their job.'

Sebastian didn't know her plan. He appeared to be waiting for her lead. She gestured impatiently and asked a question she knew he wouldn't be able to answer and, in that way, let him know what it was she intended him to say.

'Did you make contact with any of the infiltrators before you were stopped by the guards? Did you find out who any of them are and gain their confidence? Did you at least get any names?'

Sebastian took her lead and sighed convincingly. 'I'm sorry, no. I'd only just arrived and didn't have a chance before the guards . . .' His gaze drifted to the floor. 'Sorry.'

Captain Lerner's eyes shifted between the two of them.

Jennsen assumed a tone of forbearance. 'Well, I can't blame guards for not taking chances in the palace. We need to be on our way, though. I made some headway in our search and uncovered some important new contacts. It can't wait. These men are wary and I need you to approach them. They aren't likely to let a woman buy them drinks – they'd get the wrong idea – so I'm going to leave it to you. I've got other snares to set.'

Sebastian was nodding as if he were entirely familiar with the imaginary work. 'All right.'

The captain held an arm out. 'Let's get you both on your way, then.'

Sebastian, following Jennsen out, glanced back. 'I'll need my weapons, Captain. And all the coins that were in the purse. That's Lord Rahl's money, and I need it to do his bidding.'

'I have it all. Nothing is missing – my word on that.'

Outside, in the confining passageway, Captain Lerner pulled the cell door shut. He had the light, so Jennsen and Sebastian waited on him. As she started out, the captain gently reached past Sebastian to grasp her arm, stopping her.

Jennsen froze, fearing to breathe. She felt Sebastian's hand slip around her waist to the handle of her knife.

'Is it true what people say?' the captain asked.

Jennsen looked back into his eyes. 'What do you mean?'

'I mean, about Lord Rahl. About how he's . . . I don't know, different. I've heard men talk – men who have met him, fought with him. They talk about how he handles that sword of his, how he fights and all, but more than that, they talk about him as a man. Is it true what they say?'

Jennsen didn't know what he meant. She feared to move, to say anything, not knowing how to answer such a question. She didn't know what people, especially D'Haran soldiers, said about the new Lord Rahl.

She knew that she and Sebastian could kill this man, here, now. They would have the element of surprise. Sebastian, with his hand on her knife, was surely thinking that very thing.

But they would still have to make it out of the palace. If they killed him, it was likely that the body would soon be discovered. The D'Haran soldiers were anything but lax. Even if they hid the dead captain of the prison guards, a check of the prisoners would soon reveal that Sebastian was missing. Their chances of escaping, then, became remote.

Worse, though, she didn't think she could kill this man. Despite the fact that he was a D'Haran officer, she held no ill feeling for him. He seemed a decent sort, not a monster. Tom liked him, and the captain respected Tom. Stabbing a man who was trying to kill them was one thing. This would be entirely different. She couldn't do this.

'We would lay down our lives for the man,' Sebastian said in an earnest voice. 'I'd have let you torture and kill me before I would have said a word, for fear it would endanger Lord Rahl.'

'I, too,' Jennsen added in a soft voice, 'think of little else but Lord Rahl. I even dream about him.'

She had spoken the truth, but a truth calculated to deceive. The captain smiled, staring off with an inner satisfaction as his fingers released her arm.

Jennsen felt Sebastian's hand slip away from her knife.

'I guess that tells it plain,' the captain said in the near darkness. 'I've served a long time. I had lost hope of daring to dream such a thing.' He hesitated, then spoke again. 'And his wife? Is she really a Confessor, like they say? I've heard tales about the Confessors, from back before the boundaries, but I never knew if it was really true.'

Wife? Jennsen didn't know anything about Lord Rahl having a wife. Jennsen couldn't picture him with a wife, or imagine what such a woman would be like. Jennsen couldn't even conceive of why the Lord Rahl, a man who could possess any woman he wanted and then discard her at will, would bother to take a wife.

And what a 'Confessor' could be was a complete mystery to Jennsen, but the very title 'Confessor' certainly sounded ominous.

'Sorry,' Jennsen said. 'I've not met her.'

'Nor I,' Sebastian said. 'But I've heard much the same about her as you have.'

The captain smiled distantly. 'I'm glad I've lived to see a Lord Rahl like this finally come to command D'Hara as it should be commanded.'

Jennsen started out again, troubled by the man's words, troubled that he was pleased this new Lord Rahl was going to conquer and rule the whole world in the name of D'Hara.

Jennsen was eager to get out of the prison and out of the palace. The three of them moved quickly back through the narrow passageways, back through iron doors and past the reaching prisoners. The captain's growled warning silenced them, this time.

When they rushed through the last ironbound door before the stairs, they all came to an abrupt halt. A tall, attractive woman, with a single long blond braid, stood waiting for them, blocking their escape route. The look on her face was lightning waiting to strike.

She was wearing red leather.

It could be nothing other than a Mord-Sith.

Chapter 27

The woman's hands were clasped casually behind her back. Her expression was anything but casual. Boot strikes echoed off the stone walls as she stepped forward, a dark thundercloud approaching, a thundercloud that didn't know fear.

A wave of gooseflesh tingled up Jennsen's body from her knees to the nape of her neck where downy hair stiffened.

In a steady, measured pace, the woman strode one full turn around them, looking them up and down, a hawk circling, inspecting mice. Jennsen saw an Agiel, the weapon of a Mord-Sith, hanging from a fine chain at the woman's right wrist. Lethal as Jennsen knew such a weapon could be, it looked like nothing more than a thin leather rod not a foot in length.

'A very agitated official came to see me,' the Mord-Sith said in a quiet, silken voice. Her deadly glare moved very deliberately from Sebastian to Jennsen. 'He thought I needed to come down here and see what was going on. He mentioned a woman with red hair. He seemed to think she might be trouble of some sort. What do you think he was so worried about?'

The captain, who was behind Jennsen, stepped out to the side. 'There's nothing going on that you need concern yourself—'

With a flick of her wrist, the Agiel spun up into her fist and was pointing at the captain's face. 'I didn't ask you. I asked this young woman.'

The glare turned back to Jennsen. 'Why do you suppose he would say that I needed to come down here? Hmm?'

Jennsen.

'Because,' Jennsen said, unable to look away from the cold

275

blue eyes, 'he's a pompous dolt and he didn't like it that I wouldn't pretend he wasn't, just because he wore white robes.'

The Mord-Sith smiled. It was not humor, but grim respect for the veracity of what Jennsen had said.

The smile evaporated as she glanced at Sebastian. When her gaze returned to Jennsen, it looked as if it could cut steel. 'Pompous or not, that doesn't change the fact that there is a prisoner being released for no more cause than your word.'

Jennsen.

'My word is sufficient.' Jennsen irritably lifted the knife at her belt and flashed the handle at the woman. 'This backs my word.'

'That,' the Mord-Sith said in her silken hiss, 'means nothing.'

Jennsen could feel her face going red. 'It means—'

'Do you think we're stupid?' The Mord-Sith's skintight red leather creaked as she leaned closer. 'That if you come in here and merely wave that knife handle in our faces, that our faculty of reason will evaporate?'

The tight leather outfit revealed a body as shapely as it was powerful. Jennsen felt small and ugly before this flawless creature. Worse, she felt totally inadequate faking a story before a woman as confident as this woman was, a woman who seemed able to see right through their invented tale, but Jennsen knew that if she dared to waver now, she and Sebastian were as good as dead.

Jennsen put as much of an edge to her voice as she could manage. 'I carry this knife for Lord Rahl, in his name, and you will yield to it.'

'Really. Why?'

'Because this knife shows the trust Lord Rahl has placed in me.'

'Ah. So just because you happen to carry it, we're supposed to believe that Lord Rahl gave it to you? That he trusts you? How are we to know you didn't find the knife? Hmm?'

'Find it? Are you out of your—'

'Or perhaps you and this prisoner, here, ambushed the knife's true owner – murdered him – for no reason but to get your hands on a coveted object, hoping it would give you credibility.'

'I don't know how you can possibly believe such a—'

'Or maybe you're a coward and murdered the knife's owner in his sleep? Or maybe you didn't even have that much courage, and you bought it from cutthroats who murdered him. Is that what you did? Simply got it from the real murderer?'

'Of course not!'

The Mord-Sith leaned closer yet, until Jennsen could feel the woman's breath on her own face. 'Maybe you enticed the man it belonged to into lying between your sweet legs while your partner, here, stole it. Or maybe you're just a whore and it was the gift of a murderous thief in exchange for your womanly favors?'

Jennsen backed away. 'I – I wouldn't—'

'Showing us such a weapon proves nothing. The fact is, we don't know who the knife belongs to.'

Surrender.

'It's mine!' Jennsen insisted.

The Mord-Sith straightened and lifted an eyebrow. 'Really.'

The captain folded his arms. Sebastian, standing to Jennsen's side, didn't move. Jennsen fought to contain tears of panic trying to surface. She endeavored to show a defiant face, instead.

Jennsen. Surrender.

'I have important business on behalf of Lord Rahl,' Jennsen said through gritted teeth. 'I don't have time for this.'

'Ah,' the Mord-Sith mocked, 'business on behalf of Lord Rahl. Well, that does sound important.' She folded her arms. 'What business?'

'It's my affair, not yours.'

The cool smile returned. 'Magic business? That it? Magic?'

'It's not any of your concern. I'm doing Lord Rahl's bidding and you would do well to remember that. He'd not be pleased to know you were meddling.'

The eyebrow lifted again. 'Meddling? My dear young lady, it is impossible for a Mord-Sith to meddle. If you were who you say you are, you would know that much, at least. Mord-Sith exist only to protect Lord Rahl. It would be a dereliction of my duty, don't you think, were I to ignore such curious goings-on?'

'No – I told you—'

'And if Lord Rahl finds himself bleeding his life away, and asks me what happened, before he dies I can tell him that a girl with a pretty knife danced in here and demanded to have a very suspicious and tight-lipped prisoner released, and, well, we were so dazzled by the knife and by her big blue eyes that we all just thought we ought to let her have her way. That about it?'

'Of course you have to—'

'Do some magic for me.' The Mord-Sith reached out and tested some of Jennsen's red hair between a finger and thumb. 'Hmm? A bit of magic to prove yourself. A spell, a charm, a dazzling show of your craft. Call some lightning down, if you will. If not that, maybe then just a simple flame fluttering in midair?'

'I don't—'

'Do some magic, witch.' Her voice was a deadly command. *Surrender*.

Angry at the voice, but more so at the Mord-Sith, Jennsen slapped the hand away from her hair. 'Stop it!'

Faster than seemed possible, Sebastian went for the woman. Faster yet, her Agiel spun into her hand. She rammed the tip against Sebastian's shoulder as he was still flying at her.

Sebastian cried out as the weapon stopped him cold. The woman calmly pressed the Agiel against his shoulder, driving him to the ground. Sebastian screamed as he lay crumpled on the floor.

Jennsen rushed toward the Mord-Sith. In one swift movement, the woman stood and had the Agiel before Jennsen's face, halting her. At their feet, Sebastian writhed in agony.

Thinking only of Sebastian, only of getting to him, only of helping him, Jennsen grabbed the Agiel, pushing it and the woman's hand away. She went to one knee beside Sebastian. He had rolled to his side, holding himself, trembling, as if he'd been struck by lightning.

He calmed under her gentle touch as she told him to lie still. As he recovered somewhat and tried to sit up, Jennsen put an arm behind his shoulders and helped him. He leaned against her, panting, clearly suffering the lingering effect of the pain of the weapon. He blinked, trying to clear his watering eyes, struggling to focus his vision. Jennsen, horrified by what the touch of the Agiel could do, stroked a hand down Sebastian's face. She lifted his chin, trying to see if he recognized her, if he was all right. He could hardly sit up on his own, but he gave her a little nod.

'Stand up.' The Mord-Sith towered over them. 'Both of you.'

Sebastian couldn't, yet. Jennsen shot to her feet, defiantly facing the woman. 'I'll not tolerate this! When I tell Lord Rahl about this, he'll have you horsewhipped!'

The woman was frowning. She held the Agiel out. 'Touch it.'

Again, Jennsen seized the weapon and shoved it aside. 'Stop it!'

'It works,' the Mord-Sith muttered to herself, 'I know it does – I can feel it.'

She turned and experimentally pressed the awful thing to the captain's arm. He cried out and went to his knees.

'Stop it!' Jennsen caught hold of the red rod, pulling it back away from the captain.

The Mord-Sith stared. 'How do you do that?'

'Do what?'

'Touch it without being hurt? No one is immune to the touch of an Agiel – not even Lord Rahl himself.'

Jennsen realized then that something unprecedented had happened. She didn't understand it, but she knew that while the situation was confused, she had to seize the opportunity.

'You wanted to see magic – you saw it.'

'But how—'

'Do you think that Lord Rahl would allow me to carry the knife if I wasn't competent?'

'But an Agiel—'

The captain was coming to his feet. 'What's the matter with you? I fight for the same cause as you.'

'And that cause is protecting Lord Rahl,' the woman snapped. She held her Agiel up. 'This is my means of protecting him. I have to know what's wrong lest I fail him.'

Jennsen reached up and curled her fingers around the weapon, holding it tight as she met the Mord-Sith's gaze. She told herself that she had to remember who she was supposed to be and to maintain the pretense. She tried to think of what she would do if she really were one of Lord Rahl's elite.

'I understand your concern,' Jennsen said with resolve,

determined not to miss her unexpected chance, even if she didn't fully understand it herself. 'I know you want to protect Lord Rahl. We share that devotion and sacred duty. Our lives are his. I have vital business doing the same as you – protecting Lord Rahl. You don't know all that's involved in this and I don't have the time to even begin to explain it to you.

'I've had enough of this. Lord Rahl's life is in danger. I have no more time to spare. If you don't let me do my job of protecting him, then you are imperiling him and I will remove you as I would any threat to his life.'

The Mord-Sith considered Jennsen's words. What she could be thinking, Jennsen had no idea, but that very notion – thought – was one Jennsen had never ascribed to the Mord-Sith. She had always considered them to be mindless killers. In this woman's eyes, Jennsen could see cognition.

Finally, the Mord-Sith reached down and with a hand under Sebastian's arm, helped him to his feet. When he was standing steadily, she turned back to Jennsen.

'I'd gladly suffer the horsewhipping – and far worse – if it would help protect this Lord Rahl. Get going – and be quick about it.' She gave Jennsen a small but warm smile and then a firm clap on the side of the shoulder. 'May the good spirits be with you.' She hesitated. 'But, I need to know how it is that you don't feel the power of an Agiel. Such a thing is simply not possible.'

Jennsen was taken aback that a person this evil dared to invoke the name of the good spirits. Jennsen's mother was a good spirit, now. 'I'm sorry, but that's part of what I have no time to begin to tell you, and besides, Lord Rahl's safety hinges on me keeping it secret.'

The woman stared long and hard. 'I am Nyda,' she said at last. 'Swear to me, personally, that you will do as you say, and protect him.'

'I swear, Nyda. Now, I have to go. I can't spare any more time – not for anything.'

Before Jennsen could move, the Mord-Sith seized a fistful of her dress and cloak at her shoulder. 'This is one Lord Rahl we cannot afford to lose, or we all lose everything. If I ever find out you're lying to me, I promise you two things. First, there will never be a hole deep enough for you to hide in that I won't find you, and, second, your death will be beyond anyone's worst nightmare. Do I make myself clear?'

Jennsen could only nod dumbly at the look of fierce resolve in Nyda's eyes.

The woman turned and started up the steps. 'Get going, then.'

'Are you all right?' the captain asked Sebastian.

Sebastian brushed dirt off his knees as he headed for the steps. 'I'd have rather had the horsewhipping than that, but I guess I'll live.'

The captain grimaced his sympathy as he comforted his own arm. 'I have your things up there, locked away. Your weapons and your money.'

'Lord Rahl's money,' Sebastian corrected.

Jennsen wanted nothing so much as to be out of the palace. She hurried up the steps, forcing herself not to break into a dead run.

'Oh,' the Mord-Sith called back down the steps. She had paused, her hand on the rusty rail as they rushed up after her. 'I forgot to tell you.'

'Forgot to tell us what?' Jennsen asked. 'We're in a hurry.'

'That official who came to get me? The one in white robes?'

'Yes?' Jennsen asked as she reached the woman.

'After he came for me, he was going to go looking for Wizard Rahl, to bring him down to see you, too.'

Jennsen felt the blood drain from her face.

'Lord Rahl is far to the south,' the captain scoffed as he came up the stairs behind them.

'Not Lord Rahl,' Nyda said. 'Wizard Rahl. Wizard Nathan Rahl.'

Chapter 28

Jennsen remembered that name, Nathan Rahl. Althea had said she met him in the Old World, at the Palace of the Prophets. He was a real Rahl, she said. She said he was powerful and inconceivably dangerous, so they kept him locked away behind impenetrable shields of magic where he could cause no harm, yet he sometimes still managed it. Althea had said that Nathan Rahl was over nine hundred years old.

Somehow, the old wizard had escaped those impenetrable shields of magic.

Jennsen seized the Mord-Sith by the elbow. 'Nyda, what's he doing here?'

'I don't know. I've not met him.'

'It's important he not see us.' Jennsen nudged Nyda ahead, urging her to hurry. 'I don't have time to explain, but he's dangerous.'

At the top of the stairs, Nyda looked both ways before meeting Jennsen's gaze. 'Dangerous? Are you sure about this?'

'Yes!'

'All right. Come with me, then.'

'I need my things,' Sebastian said.

'Here.' The captain pointed at a door not far away.

While Nyda stood guard, Sebastian followed Captain Lerner inside. Jennsen, her knees trembling, stood in the doorway watching as the captain set the lamp down and unlocked a second door inside. He and Sebastian went into the room beyond, taking the lamp. Jennsen could hear brief words and the sounds of things being dragged off shelves.

With every passing moment, Jennsen could almost hear the wizard's footsteps bringing him ever closer. If he caught them, Sebastian's weapons would do them no good. If Wizard Rahl saw them, he would recognize Jennsen for what she was – a hole in the world, the ungifted offspring of Darken Rahl. There would be no bluffing her way out of that. They would have her at last.

Sebastian emerged ahead of the captain. 'Let's go.'

He simply looked like a man in a dark green cloak, the same as before. Few would suspect the collection of weapons he carried. His blue eyes and spikes of white hair made him look different from other people; maybe that was why the guards had stopped him.

The captain caught Jennsen by the arm. 'As she said' – he nodded toward the Mord-Sith – 'may the good spirits be with you always.'

He handed her the lamp. Jennsen whispered her sincere gratitude before rushing to follow the other two down the passageway, leaving the captain of the guards behind.

Nyda led them down dark halls and through empty rooms. They raced through a narrow cleft without a ceiling – at least, when Jennsen looked up she could see nothing but darkness above. The floor appeared to be bedrock. The wall to the right was rather unremarkable fitted stone. To the left, though, the passageway was lined with colossal, speckled pink granite blocks. Each smooth-faced block was larger than any house Jennsen had ever lived in, yet the joints were so tight that no blade could have slipped between them.

At the end of the passageway beside the huge stone blocks, they ducked through a low door and out onto a narrow walkway made of iron and laid with planks to cross on. The thread of a footbridge spanned a wide chasm in the bedrock of the plateau. Jennsen could see by the light of her lamp that the walls of sheer rock to each side dropped straight down, fading away far below. The light of the lamp wasn't enough for her to see the bottom. Standing there on the slender stretch of walkway suspended over the enormous void made her feel as tiny as an ant.

The Mord-Sith, a hand on the iron rail as she moved across the bridge, paused and looked back over her shoulder. 'Why is

Wizard Rahl dangerous?' It was obvious that the question had been playing on her mind.

'What trouble can he cause you?' The brittle tone of her voice reverberated off the surrounding rock walls.

Stopped there in the center of the walkway over the black abyss, Jennsen could feel the bridge swaying underfoot. It was making her dizzy. The Mord-Sith waited. Jennsen tried to think of something to say. A glance back at Sebastian's blank expression told her that he had no ideas. She quickly decided to mix in some of the truth, in case Nyda knew anything about the man.

'He's a prophet. He escaped from a place where he was held, a place where he couldn't hurt anyone. They had him there because he's dangerous.'

The Mord-Sith pulled her long blond braid over her shoulder, drawing her hand down its length as she considered Jennsen's words. She clearly didn't intend to move, yet. 'I've heard he's quite an interesting man.' In her eyes was awakened challenge.

'He's dangerous,' Jennsen insisted.

'Why?'

'He can harm my mission.'

'How?'

'I've already said it – he's a prophet.'

'Prophecy could be a benefit. It might help you in your mission to protect Lord Rahl.' The Mord-Sith's frown darkened. 'Why wouldn't you want such help?'

Jennsen recalled what Althea said about prophecy. 'He might tell me how I'll die, even the very day. What if you were the one who had to protect Lord Rahl against an approaching threat, and you knew that the very next day you were going to die in some horrifying fashion? Knew the exact hour, the agonizing details. It might put you in a state of paralyzing fear, and in that panic of knowing exactly when and how you were to die, you would naturally be ill suited to protect Lord Rahl's life.'

Nyda's frown eased only slightly. 'Do you really think that Wizard Rahl would tell you such a thing?'

'Why do you think they had him locked away? He's

284

dangerous. Prophecy could be dangerous for those like me who protect Lord Rahl.'

'Or maybe it could help,' Nyda said. 'If you knew that something bad was going to happen, you could stop it.'

'Then it wouldn't be prophecy, now would it?'

Nyda ran her hand down her braid as she considered the implications. 'But if you knew of some dire foretelling, then maybe you could turn the prophecy aside and avert the disaster.'

'If you could turn prophecy aside, that would make it wrong. If it were wrong, if it were prophecy unfulfilled, then it would just be the foolish empty words of an old man, wouldn't it? Then how could prophecy be distinguished from the ranting of any lunatic who claimed he was a prophet?'

'But it's not empty ranting,' Jennsen insisted. 'It's prophecy. If this prophet wanted to harm my mission, he might tell me something terrible about my future. If I knew something terrible, I might fail Lord Rahl.'

'You mean,' Nyda asked, 'that you think it would be like if I were to jab my Agiel at someone? It would make them flinch?'

'Yes. Only if we know a prophecy, and flinch, as it were, it's Lord Rahl who would be put at risk because of our weakness and fear.'

Nyda released her braid and put her hand back on the railing. 'But I would not flinch, knowing how I was to die, especially if it was Lord Rahl's life I was saving. As a Mord-Sith, I'm always prepared to die. Every Mord-Sith wishes to die fighting for the Lord Rahl, not old and toothless in bed.'

Jennsen wondered if the woman was mad, or if she could really be that dedicated.

'A brave boast,' Sebastian put in. 'But are you willing to bet Lord Rahl's life on it?'

Nyda looked him in the eye. 'If it were my life on the line? Yes. I would not flinch knowing how and when I was to die.'

'Then I admit that you're a better woman than I,' Jennsen said.

Nyda nodded grimly. 'I would not expect you to be the same as I. You may carry the knife, but are not Mord-Sith.'

Jennsen wished Nyda would move on. If she couldn't convince the woman, and had to fight her, this would be a very bad place to have to do it. The Mord-Sith was strong and quick. With Sebastian behind, he could be little help. Besides that, hanging on to the swaying bridge over the chasm, Jennsen's head was spinning. She didn't like high places, and had never prided herself in her sense of balance.

'I'd do my best not to fail Lord Rahl in a situation like that,' Jennsen said, 'but I can't swear I wouldn't. I'd not like Lord Rahl's life to hang on the answer.'

Nyda nodded in resignation. 'That's wise.' She finally turned and started out once more across the footbridge. 'I would still try to change the prophecy, though.'

Jennsen let out a silent sigh as she shuffled along, following close behind. In some manner she didn't understand, her words were swaying the Mord-Sith more than seemed possible.

She glanced over the edge but still saw no bottom. 'Prophecy can't be changed, or it would cease to be prophecy. Prophecy comes from prophets, who are gifted with it.'

Nyda had her braid over her shoulder again, stroking it. 'But if he's a prophet, then he knows the future, and, like you said, that can't be changed or it wouldn't be prophecy – so he would only be telling you what is going to happen. He can't change it, you can't change it. It's already going to happen whether he tells you or not. If telling you would make you fail to protect Lord Rahl, then he would already see such an event, so it is preordained to happen and would be part of the prophecy to begin with.'

Jennsen pulled a strand of her hair out of her eyes as she advanced along the bridge, gripping the rail tightly. In her mind, she furiously raced to come up with a logical answer. She had no idea if the things she was saying were true or not, but she thought they sounded convincing and seemed to be working. The problem was, Nyda kept asking questions Jennsen had more and more trouble answering. She felt almost as if she were descending into the void below, each attempt to climb out only letting her slip deeper. She did her best to keep any trace of desperation out of her voice.

'But don't you see? Prophets don't see everything about everyone, as if the whole world and every single thing that happens is some grand play to be acted out according to a script the prophet has already read. A prophet would only see some things – maybe even some things of his choosing. But other things, things he doesn't see, he might try to influence.'

Nyda frowned back at them. 'What do you mean?'

Jennsen sensed that her only safety was to keep Nyda worried for her Lord Rahl. 'I mean, if he wanted to harm Lord Rahl, he might tell me something that would make me flinch, just to make me flinch, even if he didn't see such an event.'

Nyda's frown grew more serious. 'You mean he might lie?'

'Yes.'

'But why would Wizard Rahl want to harm Lord Rahl? What possible reason would he have?'

'I told you, he's dangerous. That's why they had him locked away in the Palace of the Prophets. Who knows what other things they knew about him that we don't, things that made them feel it was necessary to lock such a man away.'

'That still doesn't answer why Wizard Rahl would wish to harm Lord Rahl.'

Jennsen felt as if she were in a knife fight – trying to protect herself from this woman's razor-sharp verbal blade. 'It's not just prophecy – he's a wizard. He's gifted. I don't know if he's interested in harming Lord Rahl – maybe he's not – but I don't want to risk Lord Rahl's life to find out. I know enough about magic to know I don't like messing around with things of magic that are beyond me. I have to put Lord Rahl's life first. I'm not saying that I believe Nathan Rahl is bent on harm, I'm just saying that it's my job to protect Lord Rahl and I don't want to take the chance with such magic, magic I can't ward.'

The woman shouldered open the door at the end of the foot bridge. 'I can't argue that. I don't like anything to do with magic. But if Lord Rahl is in danger from this prophet of a wizard, maybe you had better stay here so we can look into it.'

'I don't know if Nathan Rahl represents a threat, but I have pressing business that I know for certain is a grave danger to Lord Rahl. My responsibility is to tend to that.'

Nyda tried a door but found it locked. She continued on down the dingy hallway. 'But if your suspicions about Nathan Rahl are correct, then we must—'

'Nyda, I'm hoping you can keep your eye on this Nathan Rahl for me. I can't do it all myself. Watch him for me?'

'Do you wish me to kill him?'

'No.' Jennsen was surprised at how ready the Mord-Sith seemed to be to commit to such an act. 'Of course not. I'm just saying to pay attention, keep an eye on him, that's all.'

Nyda reached another door. This time the lever lifted. Before she opened it, she turned back to the two of them. Jennsen didn't like the look in her eyes as her gaze shifted between them.

'This is all crazy,' Nyda said. 'Too much of it makes no sense. Too many things don't fit. I don't like it when things don't make sense.'

This was a dangerous creature who could at any moment turn on them. Jennsen had to find a way to close the subject for good. She remembered what Captain Lerner had said, how filled with conviction he had been, and spoke the words softly to Nyda.

'The new Lord Rahl has changed everything, all the rules – he's turned the whole world upside down.'

Nyda finally let out a deep breath. A wistful smile came to her lips.

'Yes, he has,' she said in a soft voice. 'Wonder of wonders. That's why I would lay down my life to protect him, why I worry so.'

'Me too. I need to do my job.'

Nyda turned away and led them to a dark spiral of stairs tunneling down through the rock. Jennsen knew that the tale she was spinning wasn't entirely convincing. She was perplexed that it worked anyway.

A long journey down seemingly endless stairs and along dark corridors, occasionally cutting through passageways crowded with soldiers, took them ever lower in the plateau below the People's Palace. Sebastian's hand on her back for much of the journey was a reassuring comfort, and a relief. Jennsen could hardly believe that she had managed to get him free. Soon, they would be out of the palace and safely away.

Somewhere within the interior of the plateau, they emerged into the central public area. Nyda had taken them down a more direct route and saved them time. Jennsen preferred staying within the hidden passageways, but, apparently, those shortcuts ended at this place within the common area. They would have to finish their descent among the crowds.

Small stands selling food lined the way along the route as throngs of people shuffled past on their long ascent to the palace above. Jennsen recalled passing the vendors opposite the stone balusters overlooking the level below on her first visit to the palace. The smells, after the dusty places they had been, were temptation almost beyond endurance.

Soldiers patrolling nearby noticed them on their way down, moving against the crowds. Like all the soldiers she had seen in the palace, these were big men, muscular, fit, eyes alert. In their leather and chain mail, weapons hanging from their belts, they were an intimidating sight. As soon as they realized that Nyda was escorting them, the soldiers turned their scrutiny to other people.

When Jennsen saw Sebastian pull up his hood, she realized it would be a good idea to hide her hair and followed suit. The air inside the plateau was frosty and a number of people had their heads covered with hoods or hats, so it wouldn't raise suspicions.

As they reached the far end of a long landing in the lower reaches inside the plateau, just as they turned to descend the next flight of stairs, Jennsen looked up. At the opposite end of the landing, a tall older man with a full head of straight white hair hanging to his broad shoulders was just coming down off the stairs. Even though he was old, he was still a strikingly handsome man. Despite his age, he moved with vigor.

He looked up. His gaze met Jennsen's.

The world seemed to stop in the man's dark azure eyes.

Jennsen froze. There was something about him that looked vaguely familiar, something in those eyes that seized her attention.

Sebastian had stopped two steps below her. Nyda was at her side. The Mord-Sith's gaze followed Jennsen's.

The man's hawklike glare was fixed on Jennsen, as if they were the only two people in the entire palace.

'Dear spirits,' Nyda whispered. 'That has to be Nathan Rahl.'

'How do you know?' Sebastian asked.

She stepped up beside Jennsen, her attention fixed on the man. 'He has the eyes of a Rahl, of Darken Rahl. I've seen those eyes in enough nightmares.'

Nyda's gaze slid to Jennsen. Her brow drew together.

Jennsen realized where she had seen the man's eyes – in the mirror.

Chapter 29

In the distance, across the landing, Jennsen saw the wizard's eyes going wide. His hand came up, pointing across the throng of people.

'Stop!' He called out in a deep, powerful voice. Even above the racket around her, Jennsen could clearly hear that voice ring out. 'Stop!'

Nyda was staring at her, as if the spark of recognition was but an instant away. Jennsen seized her arm.

'Nyda, you have to stop him.'

Nyda broke the gaze to look over her shoulder at the man rushing toward them. She looked back at Jennsen.

Jennsen remembered Althea saying that she could see some Rahl in Jennsen's looks, and that others who knew Darken Rahl might recognize her.

Jennsen gripped red leather in her fist. 'Stop him! Don't listen to anything he says!'

'But he might only—'

Gripping the fistful of red leather tightly, Jennsen shook the woman. 'Haven't you heard anything I've said? He might keep me from helping Lord Rahl. He might try to trick you. Stop him. Please, Nyda – Lord Rahl's life is in grave danger.'

Invoking the name of Lord Rahl tipped the balance back.

'Go,' Nyda said. 'Hurry.'

Jennsen nodded and dashed down the steps. She only had time for a brief look. She saw the prophet's long legs striding toward them, his hand held out, calling for them to stop. Nyda, Agiel in her fist, ran for him.

Jennsen scanned the area for soldiers, then turned back for a look, trying to see if Nathan Rahl was still coming, trying to see if Nyda was stopping him. Sebastian snatched her hand, pulling her in a headlong rush down the steps. Jennsen didn't get a chance for another glimpse of her wizard kin.

She hadn't realized how it would affect her to see someone who was related to her. She hadn't expected to see it in his eyes. There had only been her mother and her, before. It was the strangest feeling – a kind of pensive longing – seeing this man who was in some way her blood.

But if he caught her, her doom would be sealed.

Together, she and Sebastian raced down the steps, dodging people who were on their way up. Some people grumbled at them to watch where they were going, or cursed them for running. At each landing, she and Sebastian skirted the crowds and flew down the next flight of stairs.

When they reached a level where soldiers were stationed, they slowed. Jennsen pulled her hood up a little tighter, making sure that her hair was hidden, along with some of her face, fearing people might recognize her for being the daughter of Darken Rahl. Anxiety knotted her insides at having discovered that there was that, too, she now had to worry about.

Sebastian's arm around her waist held her close as he wound his way through the flowing river of people. To avoid soldiers on patrol moving by near the balusters, he had to guide Jennsen to the side with benches, taking them closer among the stands, weaving through lines of people.

The landing was choked with people buying trinkets and treasures of their visit to the People's Palace. The air was filled with the aroma of meats and spices from some of the stands. Couples sat on benches eating, drinking, smiling, talking excitedly. Others simply watched people pass. There were shadowy spaces between stands and pillars where some couples sat tight together on short benches or, where there were no benches, stood close in the dark, cuddling, kissing.

When Jennsen and Sebastian reached the edge of the landing, about to head down, they spotted a large patrol of soldiers coming up the steps. Sebastian hesitated. She knew he had to be thinking about the last time soldiers took notice of him. This was a large group; it would be impossible to pass them without being within an arm's length. As they marched up the steps, the men looked carefully at everyone.

Jennsen doubted that she would ever again be able to talk Sebastian out of a prison cell. It was likely, since she was with him, that this time they might take her in to be questioned. If they detained her, Nathan Rahl would seal her fate. She felt the sense of panic, of doom, closing in on her.

Jennsen, not wanting to separate from Sebastian, instead grabbed his arm and pulled him back across the landing, past couples on benches, past those in lines at counters, past people standing back in the shadows, embracing, and into one of the dark empty niches. Panting from the effort of their long run, she put her shoulders into the narrow nook back between the rear of a stand and a pillar. She drew Sebastian around in front of her, so that his back would be to the soldiers.

With his hood up as it was, they wouldn't see much of him. If they noticed them at all, they would only see enough to notice she was a woman. They would look like nothing more than a couple of completely unremarkable people. Jennsen put her arms around Sebastian's waist so they would look like any of the other ordinary couples spending a few moments alone with each other.

It was quieter back in their small sanctuary. The sound of their heavy breathing drowned out the voices not far away. Most people couldn't see them, and the ones who could have were turned to other things. It had made Jennsen uncomfortable and awkward to watch couples snuggled together as she and Sebastian were now, so she imagined it would be the same for other people. It looked to her that she was right; no one paid any attention to a young couple embracing and obviously wanting to be by themselves.

Sebastian's hands were on her waist. Her hands held his back, so that they would look the part as they waited for the soldiers to pass. She was grateful beyond words that the good spirits had helped her get Sebastian out.

'I never thought I'd see you again,' he whispered, for the first time alone with her since he'd been released, for the first time able to say what he wanted.

Jennsen looked away from the passing people, into his eyes, and saw how earnest he was. 'I couldn't leave you there.'

He shook his head. 'I can't believe what you did. I can't believe how you talked your way into that place. You had them wrapped around your will. How did you manage such a thing?'

Jennsen swallowed, feeling at the edge of tears from the rush of emotion, the fear, the elation, the panic, the triumph. 'I had to, that's all. I had to get you out.' She checked to be sure that no one was near before she went on. 'I couldn't stand the thought of you being in there, or of what they might do to you. I went to Althea, the sorceress, for help—'

'That's how you managed it, then? Her magic?'

Jennsen shook her head as she gazed up into his eyes. 'No. Althea couldn't help me – it's a long story. She told me how she's been to your homeland, to the Old World.' She smiled. 'Like I said, it's a long story for another time. It has to do with the pillars of Creation.'

One eyebrow lifted. 'You mean, she's actually been there?'

'What?'

'The Pillars of Creation – she really went there when she was in the Old World?' His gaze followed a distant soldier for a moment. 'You said it has something to do with how she helped you. She actually saw the place?'

'What . . .? No . . . she couldn't help me. She said that I had to do it on my own. I was terrified for you. I didn't know what to do. Then, I remembered what you told me about bluffing.'

Jennsen frowned with a curious squint. 'What do you mean about her seeing the . . .'

But then her words, her very thought, trailed off as he gazed into her eyes and smiled that wonderful smile of his.

'I've never seen anyone pull off anything like that.'

It felt unexpectedly wonderful knowing that she had surprised him – pleased him.

His arms felt so good, so powerful. Pressed back into the shadows, he was holding her close. She could feel his warm breath on her cheek.

'Sebastian . . . I was so afraid. I was so afraid I'd never see you again. I was so afraid for you.'

'I know.'

'Were you afraid, too?'

He nodded. 'I could only think about how I'd never see you again.'

His face was so close she could feel the warmth radiating from his skin. She could feel the entire length of his body, his legs, his torso, pressed against her as his lips gently brushed hers. Her heart pounded at a furious pace.

But then he pulled back, as if having second thoughts. She was thankful for his arms because, realizing that he had almost kissed her, she wasn't sure her legs would hold her up, just then. What a heady notion a kiss stolen in the shadows like this would have been. Almost a kiss.

Feet shuffled past nearby, but the people seemed miles away. Jennsen felt completely alone with Sebastian, weak in his arms. Safe in his arms.

He drew her closer, then, as if overcome, as if he was in the grip of something he could no longer control. She saw in his eyes a kind of helpless surrender.

He kissed her.

Jennsen stood rock still, surprised that he was actually doing it, kissing her, holding her in his arms, just like she had seen lovers doing.

And then her arms tightened and she was holding him, too, kissing him back.

She had never imagined that anything could feel so wonderfully intoxicating.

In all her life, Jennsen had never thought such a thing could happen to her. She had dreamed of it, of course, but she knew it was only a fantasy, something for other people. She never thought it could happen to her. To Jennsen Rahl.

And now, magically, it was.

A helpless moan escaped her throat as he held her tight, hugging her fiercely, kissing her with passionate abandon. She was acutely aware of his arm encircling the small of her back, his other arm behind her shoulders, her breasts mashed against the hard muscles of his chest, his mouth pressed to hers, his own needful moan in answer to hers.

Unexpectedly, it ended. It was almost as if he had recovered his composure and forced himself back. Jennsen panted, catching her breath. She liked the way it felt to be held by him. Inches apart, they gazed into each other's eyes.

It was all so startling, so quick, so unexpected. So confusing. So right.

She wanted to melt into another embrace, another delicious kiss, but when he checked who was around, who might be watching, she gathered herself, remembering where they were and why they were pressed back into the dark niche.

Nathan Rahl was after them. Only Nyda stood between them. If he told her who Jennsen was, and she believed him, then the entire army would be after them.

They had to get out of the palace.

When Sebastian pulled away from her, doubts washed into the void.

His gaze swept the crowd as he looked to make sure no one was watching them. 'Let's go.'

His hand found hers and he was suddenly pulling her away from the sanctuary of the shadowy fold in the palace.

Jennsen felt light-headed with a flood of confusing emotions, everything from fear and shame to giddy excitement. He had kissed her. A real kiss. A man-woman kiss. Her, Jennsen Rahl, the most hunted woman in D'Hara.

She almost didn't notice the steps as they descended. She tried to look normal, to look like any other person simply leaving the palace after a visit. She didn't feel normal, though. She felt as if everyone who looked at her would know that he had just kissed her.

When a soldier unexpectedly turned their way, she held Sebastian's arm in both hands, pressing her head to his shoulder, and smiled at the man as if in casual greeting. It was enough of a distraction that they passed him and were away before he even thought to look at Sebastian.

'That was quick thinking,' Sebastian whispered, letting out a breath.

Once past the soldier, they picked up their pace again. The sights she had seen on the way in were now a blur. She didn't care about any of it. She just wanted out. She wanted away from the place where they had imprisoned Sebastian, where the two of them were in constant danger. She was more exhausted from the unremitting tension of being in the place than she had been from the dangers in the swamp.

At last, the stairs finally ended. The light coming in the huge maw of the grand entrance made it difficult to see, but the opening out of the plateau was a welcome sight. Together, hand in hand, they rushed toward the light.

Crowds of people milled about, stopping at stands, watching passersby, gawking at the size of the place, while still others flowed past on their way up to the stairs. Soldiers near the sides watched people going in, so she and Sebastian moved toward the middle. The soldiers didn't seem as interested in those leaving as those entering.

Cold daylight greeted them outside the tower of rock. The marketplace below the plateau was a bustle of activity, just as it had been before. The makeshift streets past the tents and stands teemed with people looking or sometimes stopping to make a purchase. Others moved toward the entrance to the People's Palace, with business, with hopes, with small goods, with money. Hawkers strolled among the visitors, calling out the wonders of their wares.

She had told him that the horses and Betty were missing, so Sebastian led her instead to a nearby enclosure filled with horses of every variety. The man watching the horses was sitting on a crate that made up part of the rope fence, rubbing his arms in the cold. Saddles sat in a line along the edge of the makeshift fence.

'We'd like to buy some horses,' Sebastian said as he approached, checking the condition of the animals.

The man looked up, squinting in the sunlight. 'Good for you.'

'Well, are you selling or not?'

'Not,' the man said. He turned and spat. With the back of his hand he wiped his chin. 'These horses belong to people. I'm paid to watch them, not to sell them. I go selling someone's horse, I'm liable to be skinned alive.'

'Do you know who might sell horses?'

'Sorry, can't say as I do. Check around.'

They thanked him and moved down the makeshift streets, looking for open areas where horses might be picketed. Jennsen didn't mind walking – that was usually how she and her mother traveled – but she understood Sebastian's urgency to find a horse. With such a narrow escape, and then with the wizard, Nathan Rahl, trying to stop them, they needed to get far away from the People's Palace as fast as they could.

At a second place, they got the same answer as the first. Jennsen was hungry, and wished she could get something to eat, but she knew that they would be better off making good their escape than lingering to have a meal and end up dying on a full stomach. Sebastian, holding her hand tight, pulled her between stands, cutting across the crowded streets toward horses picketed in a dusty enclosure.

'You able to sell horses?' Sebastian asked a man watching over them.

The man, his arms folded, was leaning against a post. 'No. I've none to sell.'

Sebastian nodded. 'Thanks anyway.'

The man caught Sebastian's cloak before they moved on. He leaned closer. 'You be leaving the area?'

Sebastian shrugged. 'Going back south. Thought we'd like to pick up a horse while we were visiting the palace.'

The man leaned out a little and checked both ways. 'After dark, come see me. Plan on being around that long? I may be able to help you.'

Sebastian nodded. 'I have some business that will keep me here the day. I'll be back after it's dark.'

He took Jennsen's arm and moved her down the crowded street. They had to step out of the way of two sisters fawning over necklaces they'd bought as the father walked behind with a load of goods they had purchased. The mother watched her girls as she pulled a couple of sheep along behind. It gave Jennsen a pang of heartache for Betty.

'Are you crazy?' she whispered at Sebastian, confused as to

why he would tell the man that they would be back after dark. 'We can't stay here all day.'

'Of course we can't. The man is a cutthroat. Since I had to ask if he was selling horses, he knows I have the money to buy one and would like to relieve me of it. If we go back there after dark he'll likely have friends hiding in the shadows waiting to do us in.'

'He's a thief? Are you serious?'

'This place is full of thieves.' Sebastian leaned in with a stern look. 'This is D'Hara – a land where the greedy and perverse prey on the weak, where people care nothing about the welfare of their fellow man, and even less about the future of mankind.'

Jennsen understood what he meant. On their way to the People's Palace, Sebastian had told her about Brother Narev and his teachings, his hope for a future where mankind's lot was not suffering, a future where there was no starvation or sickness or cruelty. Where every man cared for his fellow man. Sebastian said that, along with the help of Jagang the Just and the will of good and decent people, the Fellowship of Order would help to bring it about. Jennsen had trouble imagining such a wonderful world, a world away from Lord Rahl.

'But, if that man was a thief, why would you tell him that you'll come back?'

'Because if I didn't, if I told him I couldn't wait, then he might signal his partners. We wouldn't know who they are but they would know us and likely find a spot they could surprise us.'

'You really think so?'

'Like I said, the place is full of thieves. Watch yourself or you might get your purse cut right off your belt without even knowing it.'

She was just about to confess that that very thing had already happened when she heard her name being called.

'Jennsen! Jennsen!'

It was Tom. Big as he was, he stood out like a mountain among foothills, yet he was holding up his hand, waving for her, as if he feared she would have trouble spotting him.

Sebastian leaned closer. 'You know him?'

'He helped me get you out.'

Jennsen had no time to explain any more than that before smiling her acknowledgment to the big man waving his arm at her. Tom, happy as a puppy at seeing her, rushed out to meet her in the middle of the street. She saw his brothers back at their table.

Tom wore a wide grin. 'I knew you'd come, just like you promised. Joe and Clayton said I was nuts to think you would, but I told them you would keep your promise to stop before you left.'

'I . . . I just came from the palace, just now.' She patted her cloak where it concealed the knife. 'I'm afraid that we're in a rush and need to be on our way.'

Tom nodded knowingly. He seized Sebastian's hand and pumped it as if they were friends long separated.

'I'm Tom. You must be the friend Jennsen was helping.'

'That's right. I'm Sebastian.'

Tom tilted his head in gesture toward Jennsen. 'She's something, isn't she?'

'I've never seen anyone like her,' Sebastian assured him.

'A man couldn't want for more than a woman like this on his side,' Tom said. He stepped between them, putting an arm around their shoulders, preventing any escape, and guided them back to his stand. 'I've got something for you both.'

'What do you mean?' Jennsen asked.

They didn't have time for any delay. They needed to get away before the wizard came out looking for them – or sent troops after them. Now that Nathan Rahl had seen her, he could describe her to guards. Everyone would know what they looked like.

'Oh, something,' Tom said, cryptically.

She smiled up at the big blond man. 'What do you have?'

Tom reached into his pocket and came up with a purse. He held it out to her. 'Well, first off, I got this back for you.'

'My money?'

Tom grinned as he watched the astonishment in her eyes as her fingers touched her familiar worn leather purse. 'You'll be pleased to know that the gentleman who had it was reluctant to

300

part with it, but since it wasn't his, in the end he saw the light of reason, along with a few stars.'

Tom nudged her shoulder as if to say she could figure out what more he meant by that.

Sebastian's gaze followed as she pulled back her cloak and tied the purse around her belt. His expression said that he had no trouble figuring out what had happened to it.

'But how did you find him?' Jennsen asked.

Tom shrugged. 'The place looks big to those visiting, but when you're here often, you learn who the regulars are and know what their business is. I recognized your description of the cutpurse. Early this morning he breezed by, talking his line, trying to gull a woman out of her money. About the time he passed, I saw his hand below her packages, slipping into her shawl, so I snatched him by the collar. My brothers and I had a long talk with the fellow about returning things he'd "found" that didn't belong to him.'

'This place is full of thieves,' Jennsen said.

Tom shook his head. 'Don't judge a place by one man. Don't get me wrong – they're around. But most folks here are honest enough. The way I see it, wherever you go there will always be thieves. Always has been, always will be. The man I fear most is the one who preaches virtue and a better life while using people's good intentions to shade their eyes from the light of truth.'

'I guess so,' she said.

'Maybe virtue and a better life is a goal worthy of such means,' Sebastian said.

'From what I've seen in life, a man who preaches a better way at the cost of the truth is a man who wants nothing more than for himself to be the master and you the slave.'

'I see what you mean,' Sebastian conceded. 'I guess I'm fortunate not to have had dealings with such people.'

'Count your blessings,' Tom said.

At his table, Jennsen took the hand of both Joe and Clayton. 'Thank you for helping. I can't believe you got my purse back.'

Their grins had much in common with Tom's.

'Most fun we've had in a while,' Joe said.

'Not only that,' Clayton added, 'but we can't thank you enough for keeping Tom busy so we could spend a couple days visiting the palace. About time Tom gave us a break.'

Tom put a hand against Jennsen's back, urging her around the table, to his wagon beyond. Sebastian followed the two of them between the wine barrels and the stand beside them selling leather goods, where, before, Irma had sold her sausages.

Behind Tom's wagon, Jennsen saw his big horses. Then, beyond them, she saw the others.

'Our horses!' Jennsen's jaw dropped. 'You got us our horses?'

'Sure did,' Tom said, beaming with pride. 'Found Irma this morning when she came to the market with another load of sausages. She had the horses with her. I told her you'd promised to come see me today before you left, so she was glad to have a chance to get them back to you. All your supplies are there with them.'

'That's good luck,' Sebastian said. 'We can't thank you enough. We're in a hurry to get going.'

Tom gestured to Jennsen's waist, where she kept the knife under her cloak. 'I figured.'

Jennsen looked around, feeling a rising flood of dismay. 'Where's Betty?'

Tom frowned. 'Betty?'

Jennsen swallowed. 'My goat, Betty.' It was a mighty effort to keep her voice steady. 'Where's Betty?'

'I'm sorry, Jennsen. I don't know anything about a goat. Irma only had the horses.' Tom's face sagged. 'I never thought to ask about anything else.'

'Do you know where Irma lives?'

Tom's head hung. 'Sorry, no. She showed up this morning and she had your horses and things. She sold her sausages and waited around for a while before she said she had to get on home.'

Jennsen seized his sleeve. 'How long ago?'

Tom shrugged. 'I don't know. Couple hours ago?' He glanced over his shoulder at his brothers. They both nodded.

Jennsen's jaw trembled. She feared to test her voice again. She knew that she and Sebastian couldn't hang around waiting. With the wizard so close, trying to stop her, she knew they would be lucky to get away with their lives. Returning would be out of the question.

A glance to Sebastian's face confirmed it.

Tears stung her eyes. 'But . . . didn't you find out where she lived?'

Tom's gaze sank as he shook his head.

'Didn't you ask if she had anything else belonging to us?'

He shook his head again.

Jennsen wanted to scream and pound her fists against his chest. 'Did you even think to ask when she would be back?'

Tom shook his head.

'But we promised her money for watching our horses,' Jennsen said. 'She would say when she would be back so she could be paid.'

Still looking at his feet, Tom said, 'She told me she was owed money for watching the horses. I paid her.'

Sebastian pulled out money, counted out silver coins, and held them out to Tom. Tom refused it, but Sebastian insisted, finally tossing the money on the table to settle the debt.

Jennsen choked back her desperation. Betty was gone.

Tom looked heartbroken. 'I'm sorry.'

Jennsen could only nod. She wiped her nose as she watched Joe and Clayton saddling their horses for them. The sounds of the market seemed distant. In a numb state, she hardly felt the cold. When she saw the horses she had thought . . .

Now, she could think only of Betty bleating in distress. If Betty was even still alive.

'We can't stay,' Sebastian answered softly to the pleading look she gave him. 'You know that as well as I. We have to be on our way.'

She looked back to Tom. 'But I told you before, about Betty.' Desperation drove into her voice. 'I told you that Irma had our horses and my goat, Betty. I told you – I know I did.'

Tom couldn't meet her eyes. 'You did, ma'am. I'm sorry, but I just forgot to ask her. I can't lie to you and tell you anything else or make an excuse. You told me. I forgot.'

Jennsen nodded and put a hand on his arm. 'Thank you for

303

getting our horses, and all the other help. I couldn't have done it without you.'

'We have to get going,' Sebastian said, checking his saddlebags and securing the flaps. 'It's going to take time to work our way through the crowds and out of here.'

'We'll give you an escort,' Joe said.

'People get out of the way of our big draft horses,' Clayton explained. 'Come on. We know the quickest way out. Follow us and we'll get you through the crowds.'

Both men pulled a horse over so they could step up on a barrel and mount up bareback. They deftly guided the huge horses out of the narrow way between the stands and barrels without so much as jostling anything. Sebastian stood waiting for her, holding the reins to their horses, Rusty and Pete.

On her way past, Jennsen paused and gazed up into Tom's eyes, sharing with him a private, wordless moment among all the people around. She stretched up and kissed his cheek, then held her own cheek against his for a moment. His fingertips just touched her shoulder. As she drew away, his wistful gaze stayed on her face.

'Thank you for helping me,' she whispered. 'I'd have been lost without you.'

Tom smiled then. 'My pleasure, ma'am.'

'Jennsen,' she said.

He nodded. 'Jennsen.' He cleared his throat. 'Jennsen, I'm sorry—'

Jennsen, holding back her tears, touched her fingers to his lips to silence him. 'You helped me save Sebastian's life. You were a hero for me when I needed one. Thank you from the depths of my heart.'

He stuffed his hands in his pockets as his gaze sank to the ground once more. 'Safe journey to you, Jennsen, wherever you may go in your life. Thank you for letting me join you for a small part of it.'

'Steel against steel,' she said, not even understanding why, but it somehow sounded right. 'You helped me in that.'

Tom smiled then, with a look of intense pride and gratitude.

304

'That he may be the magic against magic. Thank you, Jennsen.'

She patted Rusty's muscular neck before putting a boot into a stirrup and boosting herself up onto the saddle. She cast the big man a last look over her shoulder. Staying with his things, Tom watched as Jennsen and Sebastian followed Joe and Clayton out into the sea of people. Their two big escorts, yelling and whistling, moved people out of the way, creating a clear path ahead. People stopped and looked when they heard the commotion coming, then stepped aside at the sight of the huge horses.

Sebastian, flashing a heated scowl, leaned toward her. 'What was the big ox babbling about magic?' he whispered over at her.

'I don't know,' she said in a low voice. She let out a sigh. 'But he helped me get you out.'

She wanted to tell him that Tom might be big, but he was no ox. She didn't though. For some reason, she didn't want to talk about Tom to Sebastian. Even though Tom had been helping her to rescue Sebastian, what they had done together for some reason felt very private to her.

When they finally reached the edge of the marketplace, Joe and Clayton waved them a farewell as Jennsen and Sebastian urged their horses ahead at a gallop, out onto the cold, empty Azrith Plains.

Chapter 30

Jennsen and Sebastian rode north and west, across the Azrith Plains, not far from where only that morning she had ridden back with Tom in his wagon from the swamp around Althea's place. Her visit to Althea only the day before, along with the treacherous journey through the swamp, seemed remote to her, now. She had spent most of the day getting up into the palace, talking her way past guards and officials, getting Sebastian released, bluffing the Mord-Sith, Nyda, into helping them, and getting down and out of the plateau with Wizard Rahl at their heels. With so much of the day already gone, they weren't able to travel a great distance before darkness descended and they had to make camp out in the open plain.

'With those cutthroats not all that far away, we don't dare make a fire,' Sebastian said when he saw her shivering. 'They could spot us from miles away and if we're night-blinded by a fire we would never know they were sneaking up on us.'

Overhead, the moonless sky was a vast glittering mantle of stars. Jennsen thought about what Althea said, that a bird could be seen on a moonless night by noting the stars it blocked out as it passed overhead. She said that was how she could see one who was a hole in the world. Jennsen saw no bird, just three coyotes in the distance, trotting along on a night patrol of their territory. In the flat, empty land, they were easy enough to spot by starlight alone as they went on their hunt for small nocturnal animals.

With numb fingers, Jennsen untied her bedroll from the back of the saddle and pulled it down. 'And where would you propose we get the wood to make a fire, anyway?'

Sebastian turned and stared at her. A smile stole onto his face. 'I never thought of that. I guess we couldn't have a fire even if we wanted one.'

She scrutinized the empty plain as she dragged the saddle off of Rusty's back and laid it on the ground near Sebastian. Even with only the cold starlight, she could make out things well enough. 'If anyone approached, we could see them coming. Do you think one of us should keep watch through the night?'

'No. Without a campfire and not moving, they'd never find us out in this great dark expanse. I think it would be better to get some sleep so we can make good time tomorrow.'

With the horses picketed, she used her saddle for a seat. As she unfurled her bedroll, Jennsen found two white cloth bundles inside. She knew she hadn't put any such things in her bedroll. She undid the knot at the top of one bundle and discovered a meat pie inside. She saw, then, Sebastian making the same discovery.

'Looks like the Creator has provided for us,' he said.

Jennsen smiled as she stared down at the meat pie in her lap. 'Tom left these.'

Sebastian didn't ask how she knew. 'The Creator has provided for us through Tom. Brother Narev says that even when we think someone has provided for us, it is actually the Creator working through them. We in the Old World believe that when we give to someone in need, we are really doing the Creator's good works. That's why the welfare of others is our sacred duty.'

Jennsen said nothing, fearing that if she did, he might think she was criticizing Brother Narev, or even the Creator. She couldn't dispute the word of a great man like Brother Narev. She had never done any good works like Brother Narev had. She had never even left anyone meat pies or done anything else helpful. It seemed to her that she brought only trouble and suffering to people – her mother, Lathea, Althea, Friedrich, and who knew how many others. If any force worked through her, it certainly wasn't the Creator.

Sebastian, perhaps seeing something of her thoughts in her expression, spoke softly. 'That's why I'm helping you – I believe it's what the Creator would want me to do. That's how I know

307

Brother Narev and Emperor Jagang would approve of me helping you. This is the very thing we're fighting for – to have people care about others by sharing their burdens.'

She smiled not just her appreciation, but also at the notion of such noble intentions. Noble intentions, though, which, for reasons she didn't even fully understand, felt to her like a knife in the back.

Jennsen looked up from the meat pie in her lap. 'So, that's why you're helping me, then.' Her smile was forced. 'Because it's your duty.'

Sebastian looked almost as if he'd been slapped. 'No.' He came closer, going down on one knee. 'No. I ... in the beginning, of course, but ... it's not just duty.'

'You make it sound like I'm a leper you think you have to—'

'No – that's not it at all.' As he searched for words, that radiant smile of his came to his face, that smile that made her heart ache. 'I've never met anyone like you, Jennsen. I swear, I've never laid my eyes on a woman as beautiful as you, or as smart. You make me feel like I'm ... like I'm a nobody. But then when you smile at me, I feel like I'm someone important. I've never met anyone who made me feel this way. At first it was duty, but now, I swear ...'

Jennsen sat in shock at hearing him say such things, at hearing the tender sincerity, the earnest pleading, in his voice.

'I never knew.'

'I should never have kissed you. I know it was wrong. I'm a soldier in the army against oppression. My life is devoted to the cause of helping my people – all people. I don't have anything to offer a woman like you.'

She couldn't imagine why he would think he had to offer her something. He had saved her life. 'Then, why did you kiss me?'

He gazed into her eyes, looking as if he had to pull words up from some great painful depth. 'I couldn't help myself. I'm sorry. I tried not to. I knew it was wrong, but when we were that close, and I was looking into your beautiful eyes, and your arms were holding me, and I was holding you ... I'd never wanted anything so much in my life ... I just couldn't help myself. I had to. I'm sorry.'

Jennsen's gaze fell away. She stared down at the meat pie. Sebastian pulled the familiar mask of composure around himself and sat back down on his saddle.

'Don't feel sorry,' she whispered without looking up. 'I liked the kiss.'

He sat forward expectantly. 'You did?'

Jennsen nodded. 'I'm glad to hear that it wasn't done out of duty.'

That made him smile and eased the tension.

'No duty ever felt that good,' he said.

Together, they laughed – something she couldn't even remember doing. It felt good to laugh.

As Jennsen devoured one of the meat pies, relishing the flavorful spices and savory chunks of meat, she felt good again. She hoped she hadn't been too hard on Tom for forgetting about Betty. She had let her frustrations, fear, and anger come out at him. He was a good man. He had helped her when she needed it most.

Her thoughts lingered on Tom, on how good she had felt when she was around him. He made her feel important, feel confident in herself, whereas Sebastian often made her feel humble. Tom had a handsome smile – a different kind of handsome than Sebastian's smile. Tom had a hearty smile. Sebastian had an inscrutable smile. Tom's smile made her feel secure and strong. Sebastian's smile made her feel defenseless and weak.

After she had eaten every crumb of the meat pie, Jennsen wrapped herself in blankets over the top of her cloak. Still shivering, she remembered how Betty had kept them warm at night. In the silence, her sense of gloom returned to haunt her, refusing to allow her to fall asleep, despite her exhaustion from everything she had been through the last couple of days.

She didn't look forward to the forlorn prospect of what the future might hold for her. She could foresee only an endless hunt until Lord Rahl's men finally caught her. She felt empty without her mother, without Betty. She realized that she didn't have any idea where she would go, now, other than to keep running. She had been intent on Althea's help, but even that had proved to be an empty dream. In some distant corner of her mind, Jennsen had held out a spark of irrational hope that going to her childhood home of the People's Palace might somehow hold a favorable resolution.

She shivered not only with the cold, but with the bleak prospect of what the future held.

Sebastian inched his back up close to her, protecting her from the wind. The idea of it being more than duty to him was a comfort. She thought about what it felt like to have his body pressed against the length of her. She thought about the intoxicating feel of his mouth against hers.

His words that had so surprised her, 'I've never laid my eyes on a woman as beautiful as you,' still echoed around in her head. She wasn't sure that she believed him. Maybe she was afraid to believe him.

The first day she had met him he made several complimentary remarks, the first about how people might say the dead soldier saw a beautiful young woman strutting along and thus tripped and fell to his death, and then 'Sebastian's rule,' as he called it, giving her the dead soldier's ornate knife, saying beauty belonged with beauty. She had never trusted words offered so effortlessly.

She thought again about the sincerity in his eyes, this time, and how surprisingly tongue-tied and awkward he'd seemed. Insincerity was often smoothly delivered, but matters of the heart were more difficult to express because so much was at stake.

It surprised her to hear that her smile made him feel important. She hadn't suspected that he might feel the same kinds of emotions she felt. She hadn't suspected how good it would feel to have a man like Sebastian, a man of the world, an important man, think she was beautiful. Jennsen always felt graceless and plain compared with her mother. She liked knowing that someone thought she was beautiful.

She wondered what it would be like if he rolled over, right there, and embraced her again, kissed her again, this time with no one around. She could feel her heart pounding at the very prospect.

'I'm sorry about your goat,' he whispered in the silence, his back still to her.

'I know.'

'But with Wizard Rahl after us and still this close, the goat would only slow us down.'

As much as she loved Betty, Jennsen knew she had to put other things first. Still, she would give almost anything to hear that singular bleat of Betty's voice, or see her little upright tail wagging in a blur as her whole body wiggled with the excitement of Jennsen's greeting. Jennsen could feel the lumps of carrots under her head in the pack she was using as a pillow.

She knew they couldn't stay and search for Betty, but that didn't make it any easier to know they were leaving her for good. It broke her heart.

Jennsen looked back over her shoulder in the darkness. 'Did they hurt you? I was so worried that they would hurt you.'

'That Mord-Sith would have. You came just in time.'

'What did it feel like when she touched you with the Agiel?'

Sebastian thought a moment. 'Like being hit by lightning, I suppose.'

Jennsen laid her head back down on the pack. She wondered why she had felt nothing from the power of Mord-Sith's weapon. He had to be wondering that same thing, but if he was, he didn't ask. She would have had no answer for him, anyway. Nyda had been astonished, too, and said that her Agiel worked on everyone.

Nyda was wrong.

For some reason, Jennsen found that strangely worrisome.

Chapter 31

Stiff and sore from the cold night on the ground, Jennsen woke just as the sky was beginning to take on a faint pink glow. The western sky still displayed a sweep of stars. She hadn't slept much, and wished she could sleep more, but they could not afford to linger. It could be fatal to be caught out in the open like they were, where they could be spotted from miles away.

Stretching her arms over her head, the first thing Jennsen laid her eyes upon was the black shape of the plateau against the faint blush of the eastern sky. As she watched, the People's Palace atop it took on a glow around the edges as the first golden rays of the morning sun, still beyond the horizon, touched it from behind. Standing there, looking at the palace, Jennsen felt a peculiar longing. This was her homeland. She wanted so much to have some sense of her place in the world. But her homeland harbored only terror and death for her.

Fearing how near they yet were to the palace and Wizard Rahl, they quickly gathered their belongings and saddled the horses. Climbing up onto a frigid saddle was a miserable experience. Jennsen spread a blanket across her lap so that Rusty's heat would help warm her. She patted and rubbed her horse's neck, both out of affection and to warm her fingers. Rusty's body heat would keep her second meat pie, wrapped in her bedroll tied to the back of the saddle, from freezing.

They rode hard, walking at times to give the horses a rest, but their effort rewarded them, when, later in the day, the country began to bear evidence that they were reaching the edges of the Azrith Plains. Their goal was to escape into the wall of mountains rimming the western horizon. Their clear view back across the plains revealed no pursuers, so far, anyway.

By late in the afternoon they rode into an area of low hills, ravines, scraggly vegetation, and stunted trees. It was as if the unbroken hardpan of the Azrith Plains could no longer keep itself flat and out of boredom had to finally roll and heave into a featured terrain.

The hungry horses tore at the shrubs and thick clumps of dry grasses on the way past. Even though the horses had bits in their mouth, Jennsen didn't have the heart to deny them a bite to eat. She was hungry, too. The meat pies had provided them a good breakfast but were long ago finished off.

Before dark, they reached foothills leading up into more rugged country, where they made camp in the lee of a rock outcropping. At the base of a cut of rock Jennsen found a place that would provide them shelter from the wind and, for the horses, at last enough grasses to graze on. As soon as the horses were unsaddled, they eagerly began browsing on the clumps of tough stalks.

Jennsen pulled out some of their gear and supplies while Sebastian hunted around, coming up with remnants of some of the stunted little trees, long dead and dried to a silver gray. He used his battle-axe to cut down the dry wood and built a small fire up close to the cut of rock, where it wouldn't easily be seen. While she waited for the fire to get hot, he gently laid a blanket around her shoulders. Sitting before the fire, with Sebastian close at her side, Jennsen worked salt pork onto sticks and rested them across rocks so the pork could cook over the fire.

'Was it hard to get to Althea's place?' he asked at last.

She realized that, being preoccupied with everything that had happened, she hadn't told him much at all about what had taken place while he was being held prisoner.

'I had to go through a swamp, but I made it.'

She didn't really want to complain about her difficulties, her fears, her battle with the snake, or nearly drowning. That was past. She had survived. Sebastian had all the while been sitting in a prison, knowing that at any moment they might put him to death, or torture him. Althea was forever a prisoner in the swamp. Others had it worse than she.

'The swamp sounds wonderful. It had to be better than this wretched cold. I've never seen anything like it in all my life.'

'You mean it isn't cold where you come from? In the Old World?'

'No. Winters have cold spells – nothing like this, of course – and sometimes it's rainy, too, but we never have that dreadful snow and it's not like this miserable cold of the New World. I don't know why anyone would want to live here.'

She was startled at the idea of a winter without snow and cold. She had trouble even imagining it.

'Where else could we live? We have no choice.'

'I guess,' he admitted with a sigh.

'Winter is wearing on. Spring will arrive before you know it. You'll see.'

'I hope so. I'd even rather be in that place you mentioned before, the Keeper's Furnace, than in this frozen wasteland.'

Jennsen frowned. 'The place I mentioned? I never mentioned any place called the Keeper's Furnace.'

'Sure you did.' Sebastian used his sword to move the logs together so that the flames could build. Sparks swirled up into the darkness. 'Back at the palace. Just before we kissed.'

Jennsen held her hands out, warming her fingers before the glorious heat. 'I don't remember.'

'You said Althea had been there.'

'Where?'

'The Pillars of Creation.'

Jennsen drew her hands back inside her cloak and stared over at him. 'No, I never said that. She was talking about something else – not anywhere she'd been.'

'What was she talking about, then?'

Jennsen dismissed his question with an impatient wave of her hand. 'It was just idle talk. It's not important.' She pulled a ringlet of red hair away from her face. 'The Pillars of Creation is a place?'

He nodded as he banked the white-hot coals together with his sword. 'Like I said, the Keeper's Furnace.'

Frustrated, she folded her arms. 'What does that mean?'

He looked up, puzzled by her tone. 'You know, hot. Like, when someone says, "it's as hot today as the Keeper's furnace." That's why people will occasionally refer to the place as the Keeper's Furnace, but its name is the Pillars of Creation.'

'And you've been there?'

'Are you kidding? I don't even know of anyone who has gone there. People fear the place. Some think it really is the Keeper's province, and that only death exists there.'

'Where is it?'

He gestured south with his sword. 'In a desolate place down in the Old World. You know how it is – people are often superstitious about remote places.'

Jennsen stared back into the flames, trying to reconcile it all in her head. There was something about it that wasn't exactly right. Something about it that alarmed her.

'Why is it called that? The Pillars of Creation?'

Sebastian shrugged, frowning again at her tone. 'Like I said, it's a deserted place, hot as the Keeper's furnace, so that's why some people call it that, the heat of the place. As for the actual name, the place is said to be—'

'If no one goes there, then how does anyone know all this?'

'Over time there have been some people who have gone there, or rather, gone near there, and they've told others about it. Word spreads, knowledge is accumulated. It's in a place kind of like the plains here—'

'The Azrith Plains?'

'Yes, deserted like the Azrith Plains, but much bigger. And it's always hot there. Dry, and deathly hot. There are a few trade routes that cross the barren fringes. Without proper clothing to protect you from the broiling sun and blistering winds, you would bake alive in no time. Without enough water you won't last long.'

'And this place is called the Pillars of Creation?'

'No, that's just the land you must go through, first. Near the center of this vast empty land, there is said to be a low place, a broad valley, that's even hotter yet – deadly hot, hot as the Keeper's furnace. That's the Pillars of Creation.'

'But why is it called the Pillars of Creation?'

Sebastian mounded sand with his boot to contain the red-hot coals that dropped from the logs down into the wavering heat. 'It's said that down the cliffs, down the surrounding rugged rock walls and slopes, down in that vast valley, there are towering rock columns. It's for those soaring rock formations that the place is named.'

Jennsen turned the sticks with the salt pork. 'That would make sense. Rock pillars.'

'I've seen towers something like that before, in other places, where rock is stacked up like disorderly columns of coins on a table. These are said to be more extraordinary than any others, as if the world itself were reaching up in homage toward the Creator, so some consider it a sacred place. But it's a place of deadly heat, too, so while it is thought of by some as the Creator's Forge, it's also associated with the Keeper – so some call it the Keeper's Furnace. In addition to the heat, everyone has reason enough to fear going there. It remains for everyone a place of otherworldly conflict best left alone.'

'Creation and destruction – life and death – together?'

The firelight danced in his eyes as he looked over at her. 'That's what people say.'

'You mean, some think this is a place where death itself is trying to consume the world of life?'

'Death is always stalking the living. Brother Narev teaches that man's own evil is what brings the Keeper's shadow to darken the world. If we give in to evil ways, that gives evil power in the world of life, then the Keeper will be able to topple the very Pillars of Creation, and the world will end.'

The words chilled Jennsen to the bone, as if the hand of death itself had touched her. It would be just like a sorceress to practice sly wiles with words. Jennsen's mother had warned her that sorceresses never told what they knew, but often held back important things.

What had been Althea's true intent when she had so casually named Jennsen one of 'the pillars of Creation'? Although Jennsen didn't understand it, it now seemed all too clear that

316

Althea might have had some hidden motive for planting the seed of that name in Jennsen's mind.

'So, what happened with Althea? Why couldn't she help you?'

Jennsen was startled out of her thoughts by his voice. She turned the sticks with the salt pork, seeing that it still needed more cooking, as she considered how to answer the question simply.

'She told me that she tried to help me, once, when I was little. Darken Rahl found out and crippled her for it. He twisted her gift, too, so she can't use her own magic. Now, she couldn't cast me a spell even if she had wanted to.'

'Maybe, without even knowing it, Darken Rahl was doing the Creator's work.'

Jennsen frowned in astonishment. 'What do you mean?'

'The Imperial Order wants to eliminate magic from the world. Brother Narev says it's the Creator's work we do, because magic is evil.'

'And what do you think? Do you really think the gift of the Creator could be evil?'

'How is magic used?' His hooded gaze fixed on her, anger clearly evident in his eyes. 'Is it used to help people? Help the Creator's children in this life? No. It's used for selfish reasons. You have only to look at the House of Rahl. They've used the gift, for thousands of years, to rule D'Hara. And what has that rule been? Has it been to the help or benefit of the people? Or has it been one of torture and death.'

The last of it was not a question, but a statement, and one Jennsen could not argue.

'Maybe,' Sebastian added, 'the Creator was working through Darken Rahl to lift the taint of magic from Althea – to mercifully free her from it.'

Jennsen rested her chin on her knees as she watched the meat sizzling. Althea said that she was left with only the gift of prophecy, complaining that it was torturous to her.

Jennsen's mother had taught her to draw a Grace and told her that the gift was given by the Creator. In the proper hands, a Grace *was* magic. Even though Jennsen had no magic, that magical symbol had on several occasions protected her. While

317

she knew that people could do evil, Jennsen didn't like the idea of thinking that the gift was evil. Even though she couldn't do magic, she knew that it could be a wondrous thing.

She gently sought to try a different approach. 'You said that Emperor Jagang has sorceresses with him, the Sisters of the Light, who might be able to help me. They use magic. If magic is evil—'

'They use magic in our cause, so that magic might one day be eliminated from the world.'

'How can that make sense? If you truly believe magic to be evil, then how could you think to ally yourselves with what you profess to be evil?'

Sebastian checked the salt pork when she held one of the sticks out to him, then pulled a piece off on the point of his knife. He held up the knife and waggled it for her to see.

'People kill other people with knives and swords. If we wanted to eliminate knives and swords so that the killing would stop, we could hardly do so with words alone. We would have to take away people's knives and swords by force in order to stop the madness of violence for the good of everyone. People cling to evil. We would have to use knives and swords in that fight to rid the world of those evil things. Then the world would be at peace. Without the means of murder, people's passions would cool and the Keeper would flee their hearts.'

Jennsen carved off a chunk of sizzling meat and blew on it to cool it a little. 'And so you use magic in that way?'

'That's right.' Sebastian chewed, giving a moan of approval to the taste before he swallowed and went on. 'We want to eliminate the evil of magic, but to do so we have to use magic in the fight, or else evil would win.'

Jennsen took a juicy bite of the pork, moaning her agreement with his opinion of the taste. It was wonderful having something hot to eat.

'And do Brother Narev and the Emperor Jagang think that knives and swords are evil, too?'

'Of course, because their sole purpose is to maim and kill – naturally we don't mean tools like bread knives, but weapons, certainly, are evil things. People will eventually be free of their

318

scourge, though, and then the plague of murder and death will be a thing of the past.'

'You mean to say that even soldiers won't have weapons?'

'No, soldiers will always have to be armed in order to defend a free and peaceful people.'

'But, then how can people protect themselves?'

'From what? Only the soldiers will carry deadly weapons.'

Jennsen tilted her head toward him in admonition. 'Were it not for the knife I carry, soldiers would have easily murdered me along with my mother.'

'Evil soldiers. Our soldiers fight only for good, for the defense and security of the people, not to enslave them. When we defeat the D'Haran forces, then there will be peace.'

'But even then—'

He leaned toward her. 'Don't you see? Eventually, with magic eliminated, weapons will no longer be needed. It's the corrupt passions of people which are made lethal because they have access to weapons that result in crimes and murders.'

'Soldiers have passions.'

He dismissed the thought with a wave of a hand. 'Not if they're trained properly and are under supervision of good officers.'

Jennsen gazed off at the sparkling dome of stars. The world he envisioned certainly sounded inviting. But if what he claimed were true, then magic, as they used it, was being used for a good end, so that would mean it could be neither good nor bad, but that, much like her knife, the intent of the person wielding magic actually carried the moral condition, not the magic itself. Rather than say so, she asked another question.

'What would a world without magic be like?'

Sebastian smiled wistfully. 'Everyone would be equal. No one would have an unfair advantage.' He stabbed another piece of meat and pulled it off the stick on the point of his knife. 'Everyone would work together, then, because we would all be the same. No one would have the unfair use of magic and be able to take advantage of others. You, for example, would be free to live your life without Lord Rahl hunting you with his magic.'

Althea said that Richard Rahl had been born with powers of

the gift not seen in thousands of years. He had, after all, gotten closer to her than Darken Rahl ever had. He had sent those men who had murdered her mother. But Althea had also said that Jennsen was a hole in the world to those with the gift; Lord Rahl could hunt her, but not with magic.

'You will never be free,' Sebastian finally added in a quiet voice, 'until you eliminate Richard Rahl.'

Her eyes turned toward him. 'Why me? With all those fighting against him, why do you say until I eliminate him?'

But even as she was asking the question, she began to see the terrible answer.

'Well,' he said, leaning back. 'I guess what I really meant to say was that you won't be free until Lord Rahl is eliminated.'

He turned away and pulled a waterskin closer. She watched him take a long drink, then changed the subject.

'Captain Lerner said that Lord Rahl was married.'

'To a Confessor,' Sebastian confirmed. 'If Richard Rahl was looking to find a wife who was his match in evil, he found her.'

'You know about her, then?'

'Only the little I've heard from the emperor. I can tell you what I know, if you want.'

Jennsen nodded. With a finger and thumb, she pulled some more salt pork off one of the long sticks, eating while she watched the firelight dance in his eyes as he spoke.

'The barrier between the Old World to the south and the New World to the north stood for thousands of years – until Lord Rahl destroyed it so that he might conquer our people. Probably not long before your mother would have been born, I think, the New World was itself divided up into three lands. To the far west was Westland. D'Hara is to the east. After killing his father and seizing rule, Richard Rahl destroyed these boundaries separating the three lands of the New World.

'Between Westland and D'Hara is the Midlands, an evil place where magic is said to hold sway and where the Confessors live. The Midlands is ruled by the Mother Confessor herself. Emperor Jagang told me that, while she is young, maybe my age, she is as smart as she is deadly.'

Jennsen was given pause by his chilling words. 'Do you know what a Confessor is? What "Confessor" means?'

Holding the waterskin, Sebastian draped a forearm over his bent knee. 'I don't know, except that she's gifted with frightening power. Her mere touch burns away a man's mind, making him into her mindless slave.'

Jennsen listened, rapt, appalled by such a notion. 'And they really do anything she says – simply because she touched them?'

Sebastian handed her the waterskin. 'Touched them with her evil magic. Emperor Jagang told me that her magic is so powerful that if she tells a man so enslaved that she wants him to die on the spot, he will do so.'

'You mean . . . he would kill himself right before her eyes?'

'No. I mean he would simply drop dead because she commanded it. His heart would stop, or something. He would just drop dead.'

Shaken by the very idea, Jennsen set the waterskin aside. She drew her blanket up around herself. She was exhausted, and she was weary of learning new things about Lord Rahl. Every time she learned something new, it was more terrible than the last thing. Her monster half brother, after he had killed their father, seemed to have wasted no time in assuming the family duty of hunting her.

After they'd eaten and seen to the horses, Jennsen curled up under a blanket and her cloak. She wished she could go to sleep and wake to find it had all been a bad dream. She almost wished she would never wake to have to face the future.

Because they had a fire, Sebastian didn't sleep with his back to hers. She missed the comfort of that. With anguishing thoughts cascading through her mind, she stared into the flames, eyes wide open, as Sebastian fell asleep.

Jennsen wondered what she could do, now. Her mother was dead, so she had no real home. Home had been with her mother, wherever they were. She wondered if her mother was watching her from the world of the dead, along with all the other good spirits. She hoped her mother was at peace, and had happiness at last.

Jennsen felt an empty, desolate sorrow for Althea. There could be no help from the sorceress, and none wanted. Jennsen felt shame at the trouble she had brought to others who tried to help her. Her mother had died for the crime of giving birth to Jennsen. Althea's sister, Lathea, had been murdered by Jennsen's relentless hunters. Poor Althea was stuck forever in that awful swamp for the crime of trying to protect Jennsen when she had been but a child. Friedrich was almost as much a prisoner as Althea, his life robbed of many joys.

Jennsen remembered the thrill of Sebastian's kiss. Althea and Friedrich had lost the pleasure of sharing passion. It was as if there had been that kiss for Jennsen, the awakening discovery, the spark of possibility, and then there could be no more, ever. She was in her own kind of swamp, also a prison of Lord Rahl's making, trapped in the endless flight from killers.

She thought about what Sebastian had said, that she would never be free until she eliminated Richard Rahl.

Jennsen watched Sebastian as he slept. He had come unexpectedly into her life. He had saved her life. She could never have imagined, the first time she saw him, or the first night when she looked up into his eyes from across the fire after she had drawn the Grace at the cave entrance, that he would one day end up kissing her.

His spikes of white hair had a soft golden glow from the firelight. His face was such a pleasure for her.

What more was there for them? She didn't know the answer to that. She didn't know what that kiss had meant, or where it could lead them, if anywhere. She wasn't sure she wanted it to. She wasn't sure he did. She feared he didn't.

Chapter 32

The more open ground closer to the plains was soon behind them, and they began a difficult journey through deepening snow and rugged terrain taking them slowly but inexorably up into mountainous country. Sebastian had agreed to take her where she wanted to go, to the Old World. There, she hoped to be safe, to be free, for the first time in her life. Without Sebastian, such a dream would not even have been possible.

He told her that the rugged range of mountains they were entering, along with their vast tracks of forests, skirted the western edge of D'Hara, safely out of the way of most people, and would eventually lead them down toward the Old World. As they entered the sheltering solitude among the shadows of the towering peaks, they finally began to work their way more to the south, following the mountains toward a distant liberty.

The weather was brutal in the mountains. For several days they had to walk, lest they kill the poor horses. Rusty and Pete were hungry, and the heavy snow cover made it difficult for them to get at any vegetation. Their thick winter coats were getting mangy. At least they were still sound, if weak. The same could be said for her and Sebastian.

As the heavy overcast darkened ominously and a light snow began to fall late one afternoon, they were fortunate to find a small village. They spent the night there, letting the horses stay in the small stable, where they had good oats and clean bedding. There was no inn in the town. Sebastian and Jennsen paid a few copper pennies to sleep in the hayloft. After having been out in the open so long, Jennsen felt it was a palace.

The morning brought a storm with wind and snow, but even worse, the snow was interspersed with a heavy wet sleet that came in gales. Traveling in such conditions would be not only miserable, but dangerous. She was glad, especially for the horses, that it kept them at the stable an extra day and another night. The horses ate and rested while Sebastian and Jennsen told each other lighthearted stories from their youth. She loved to see the gleam in his eyes when he told her some of his misadventures of fishing as a boy. The next day dawned blue, but with a wind. Still, they dared not linger longer.

They made their way along roads or trails, since people were few and far between. Sebastian was ever cautious, but quietly confident that they would be safe enough. With the ever-present comfort of the knife at her belt, Jennsen, too, felt that it was better to risk the roads and trails rather than attempt to strike out across remote and unknown territory covered in a thick blanket of snow. Traveling cross-country was always difficult, from time to time dangerous, and with the barrier of towering mountains all about, frequently impossible. Winter only made such travel all the more difficult, but worse, hid perils lurking beneath the snow. They feared to have a horse break a leg attempting it needlessly.

That night, as she started building them a shelter by loosely weaving together a dozen saplings and covering them with balsam boughs, Sebastian stumbled back to their camp, panting from effort. His hands were slick with blood.

'Soldier,' he said, trying to catch his breath.

Jennsen knew what soldiers he meant. 'But how could they have followed us? How could they!'

Sebastian looked away from her fury, her frantic demand. 'It's Lord Rahl's gifted chasing us.' He pulled a deep breath. 'Wizard Nathan Rahl saw you, back at the palace.'

That made no sense. She was a hole in the world to the gifted. How could any gifted follow a hole in the world?

He saw her dubious expression. 'Not too hard to track through snow.'

Snow. Of course. She nodded in resignation, her fury turning to fear. 'One of the quad?'

'I'm not sure. It was a D'Haran soldier. He came out of nowhere at me. I had to fight for my life. I killed him, but we must hurry and get out of here in case there were others nearby.'

She was too frightened to argue. They had to keep moving. The thought of men coming out of the darkness at them lent swiftness to her actions as they saddled the horses. They were quickly mounted and soon riding hard while there was still enough light to see by. They had to dismount, then, and walk to let the horses rest. Sebastian was sure they would have put distance on anyone after them. The snow helped them see, so that, even with clouds scudding past a partial moon, they were able to follow the road.

By the next night, they were so exhausted that they had to stop, even at the risk of being captured. They slept sitting up, leaning together before a small fire with their backs to a deadfall.

They made slow but steady progress in the days following and saw no sign of anyone following them. Jennsen took little comfort in that. She knew that they would not give up.

A stretch of sunny days allowed them to make good time. It was no comfort to her because they left clear tracks and the soldiers pursuing them would be able to make equally good time. They stayed to roads that had been traveled, whenever they came across them, so as to throw off and delay anyone who followed.

But then the storms returned. They pushed onward for five days despite near-blizzard conditions. As long as they could see the paths and narrow roads, and were able to put one foot in front of the other, they couldn't afford to stop, because the wind and snow covered their tracks almost as soon as they made them. Jennsen had spent enough of her life outdoors to know that tracking them would be impossible in such conditions. It was their first real hope of slipping the noose from their necks.

They selected roads or trails randomly. Each time they came to a cross-roads or fork, Jennsen was relieved to see it, because it meant another chance for their pursuers to choose wrong. Several times they cut cross-country, the drifting snow making it impossible for anyone to know where they had gone. Despite how weary she was, Jennsen began to breathe easier.

It was exhausting traveling in such conditions and it seemed like the foul weather would never relent, but then it did. Late in the afternoon, as the wind finally died, allowing the quiet of winter to settle back in, they came across a woman struggling along one of the roads. As they rode up behind her, Jennsen saw that the woman was carrying something heavy. Even though the weather had begun to break, fat snowflakes still drifted in the air. Sun shone through an orange slash in the clouds, lending the gray day a peculiar gilding.

The woman heard them coming and stepped aside. As they reached her, she held one arm up.

'Help me, please?'

It looked to Jennsen like the woman was carrying a small child all bundled up in blankets.

By the look on Sebastian's face, Jennsen feared that he intended to pass on by. He would say that they couldn't stop when they had killers and maybe even Wizard Rahl at their heels. Jennsen felt confident that, for the time being at least, they had succeeded in slipping away from their hunters.

When Sebastian cast her a sidelong glance, she spoke softly before he had a chance to say anything. 'Looks like the Creator has provided for this needy woman by sending us to help her.'

Whether Sebastian was convinced by her words, or dared not challenge the Creator's intentions, Jennsen didn't know, but he drew his horse around to a halt. As he dismounted and took the reins to both horses, Jennsen slid down off Rusty. She struggled through heavy knee-deep snow to reach the woman.

She held out her bundle, apparently hoping it would explain everything. She looked as if she were ready to accept help from the Keeper himself. Jennsen drew back the flap of bleached wool blanket and saw a boy, maybe three or four, with a blotchy red face. He was still. His eyes were closed. He was burning up with fever.

Jennsen lifted the burden from the woman's arms. The woman, about Jennsen's age, looked exhausted. She hovered close, worry creasing her face.

'I don't know what's taken him,' the woman said, on the verge of tears. 'He just came down sick.'

'Why are you out here in the weather?' Sebastian asked.

'My husband went off hunting two days ago. I don't expect him back for several days more. I couldn't just wait there with no help.'

'But what are you doing out here?' Jennsen asked. 'Where are you going?'

'To the Raug'Moss.'

'The what?' Sebastian asked at Jennsen's back.

'Healers,' Jennsen whispered to him.

The woman's fingers traced their way along her boy's cheek. Her eyes rarely left his little face, but she finally looked up.

'Can you help me get him there? I fear he's getting worse.'

'I don't know if we—'

'How far are they?' Jennsen asked, cutting Sebastian off.

The woman pointed down the road. 'That way, the way you're going. Not far.'

'How far?' Sebastian asked.

The woman, for the first time, began to weep. 'I don't know. I had hoped to make it by tonight, but it will be dark before long. I fear it's farther than I can manage. Please, help me?'

Jennsen rocked the sleeping boy in her arms as she smiled at the woman. 'Of course we'll help you.'

The woman's fingers clutched Jennsen's arm. 'I'm sorry to trouble you.'

'Hush, now. A ride is no trouble.'

'We can't leave you out here with a sick child,' Sebastian agreed. 'We'll take you to the healers.'

'Let me get up on my horse, and then hand your boy up to me,' Jennsen said as she returned the child to his mother's arms.

Once mounted, Jennsen stretched her arms down. The woman hesitated, fearing to part with her child, but then quickly handed him up. Jennsen settled the sleeping boy in her lap, making sure he was well balanced and secure, as Sebastian clasped arms with the woman and helped lift her up behind him. As they started out, the woman held Sebastian tight around the waist, but her eyes were on Jennsen and the boy.

Jennsen took the lead to give the woman the assurance of being able to see the stranger who now held her baby, and her hopes. She urged Rusty ahead through the deep snow, worried that the child was not really sleeping, but unconscious with fever.

The wind billowed snow around them as they raced along the road in the fading light. Concern for the boy, wanting to get him to help, made the road seemed endless. Each rise revealed only more forest ahead, each curve in the road yet another sweep of empty woods. Jennsen was concerned, too, that their horses couldn't be pushed so hard through deep snow without a rest or they would drop. Sooner or later, despite the fading light, they would have to slow to give the struggling horses a rest.

Jennsen looked back over her shoulder when Sebastian whistled.

'That way,' the woman called, gesturing toward a cutoff to a smaller trail.

Jennsen urged Rusty to the right, up the trail. It rose abruptly, switching back and forth to ascend the sharp rise. The trees on the mountainside were huge, with trunks as big around as her horse, rising to a great height before branches spread overhead to close off the leaden sky. The snow was unbroken by anyone before them, but the lay of the trail, the dish in the surface of the snow, the undulating but smooth line it took up through the forest, among rocks and snow-crusted brush, and the way it followed beneath steep overhangs of rock wall and along ledges made it easy enough to follow.

Jennsen checked the boy asleep at her lap and found him the same. She watched the forest around them for any sign of people, but saw none. After being at the palace, in Althea's swamp, and out on the Azrith Plains, it was comforting to again be in the forest. Sebastian didn't especially like the woods. He didn't like the snow, either, but she found it peaceful the way the snow lent the woods a sacred silence.

The smell of woodsmoke hanging in the air told her that they were close. A look over her shoulder at the mother's face told her the same. Breaking over the top of a ridge revealed several small wooden buildings along a gently rising wooded slope. In a clearing behind was a small barn with a fenced paddock. A horse at the fence rail, its ears alert, watched them approaching. The horse lifted its head, tossing a whinny their way. Rusty and Pete both snorted a brief greeting in return.

Jennsen put two fingers between her teeth and whistled as Rusty plowed through the drifts toward the small cabin at the upper end, the only one with smoke rising from the chimney.

The door opened as she reached the building. A man threw on a flaxen cloak on his way out to greet them. He wasn't old. He could be the right age. He pulled up the cloak's broad hood against the cold before she could get a good look at his face.

'We have a sick boy,' Jennsen said as the man took hold of Rusty's reins. 'Are you one of the healers known as the Raug'Moss?'

The man nodded. 'Bring him inside.'

The mother had already slid down off Sebastian's horse and was standing beside Jennsen to receive her boy into her waiting arms. 'Thank the Creator you're here, today.'

The healer, laying a reassuring hand on the woman's back, urging her toward the door, tilted his head in gesture to Sebastian. 'You're welcome to put your horses in the back with mine and then come inside.'

Sebastian thanked him and led the horses away while Jennsen followed the other two toward the door. In the failing light, she still hadn't been able to get a good look at the man's face.

It was too much to hope, she knew, but at the very least, this man was a Raug'Moss and could answer her question.

Chapter 33

Inside the cabin, a large hearth made of rounded rocks took up most of the wall to the right. Crude burlap curtains hung to the sides of the two doorways to rear rooms. A rough-hewn mantel held a lamp, as did the plank tabletop, neither lamp lit. Oak logs crackled and popped in the hearth, lending the room a smoky but inviting aroma, as well as the soft flicker of firelight. An iron arm, black with soot, held a lidded kettle off to the side of the fire. After so long out in the weather, Jennsen felt it was almost too hot inside.

The healer laid the boy on one of several pallets along the wall opposite the hearth. The mother knelt on one knee, watching as he drew back the folds of the blanket. Jennsen left them to examine the child as she casually checked the place, making sure there were no surprises lurking. There hadn't been any chimney smoke coming from the other cabins, and she hadn't seen any tracks through the fresh snow, but that didn't mean there couldn't be people in those other cabins.

Jennsen moved across the room, past the trestle table in the center, to warm her hands at the hearth. It gave her the chance to cast a glance into the two rooms at the rear. Each was tiny, with a sleeping pallet and a few items of clothing hanging on pegs. There was no one else in the place. Between the doorways stood simple pine cabinets.

As Jennsen held her hands up before the heat of the fire and the boy's mother sang him soft songs, the healer hurried to the cabinet and pulled out a number of clay jars.

'Bring a flame for the lamp, please?' he asked as he set his armload of items on the table.

Jennsen pried a long splinter from one of the logs stacked to the side, then held it in the wavering flames until it caught. While she lit the lamp and then replaced the tall glass chimney, he took pinches of fine powders from several of the jars and added them to a white cup.

'How is the boy?' she asked in a whisper.

He glanced across the room. 'Not good.'

'What can I do to help?' Jennsen asked after she had adjusted the wick.

He wiggled the stopper from a jar. 'Well, if you wouldn't mind, bring over the mortar and pestle from the center cupboard.'

Jennsen retrieved the heavy gray stone mortar and pestle for him and set it on the table beside the lamp. He was adding a mustard-colored powder to the cup. So intent was he on his task that he hadn't removed his cloak, but when he pushed the hood back out of his way she could finally get a good look at him.

His face didn't rivet her, the way Wizard Rahl's so unexpectedly had. She saw nothing in this man's round eyes, straight brow, or the pleasant enough line of his mouth that looked at all familiar to her. He gestured to a bottle made of wavy green glass.

'If you would, could you please grind one of those for me?'

While he hurried to the corner to lift a brown crockery pot down from a high shelf, Jennsen unfastened the wire hold-down and removed the glass lid from the jar. She was astonished to see the strangest little things inside. It was the shape that so surprised her. She turned one over with a finger. It was dark, flat, and round. She could see by the light of the lamp that it was something that had been dried. She jiggled the jar. They all looked the same – like a jar full of little Graces.

Just like the magical symbol, these things had an outer circle, parts that suggested a square inside that, and a smaller circle inside the square. Overlaying it all, tying it together, was another structure rather like a fat star. While not exactly a Grace, the way she had always seen it drawn, it bore a remarkable resemblance.

'What is this?' she asked.

The healer cast off his cloak and pushed up the sleeves of his simple robes. 'Part of a flower – the dried base of the filament from a mountain fever rose. Pretty little things, they are. I'm sure you must have seen them before. They come in a variety of colors, depending on where they grow, but they're best known for the common blush color. Hasn't your husband ever brought you a nosegay of mountain fever roses?'

Jennsen felt her face flush. 'He's not – we're just traveling together. We're friends, is all.'

'Oh,' he said, sounding neither surprised nor curious. He pointed. 'See there? The petals are attached to it here, and here. When the petals and stamen are removed and this selected part of the head is dried, they end up looking like this.'

Jennsen smiled. 'It looks like a little Grace.'

He nodded, returning her smile. 'And like the Grace, it can be beneficial, but it can also be deadly.'

'How is it possible to be both beneficial and deadly?'

'One of those dried flower heads, ground up and added to this drink, will help the boy sleep deeply so he can fight off the fever, help drive it from him. More than one, though, actually causes fever.'

'Really?'

Looking as if he had anticipated her question, he held up a finger as he leaned closer. 'If you were to take two dozen, thirty for certain, there would be no cure. Such a fever is swiftly fatal. It's for this effect that the plant is named.' He showed her a sly smile. 'In many ways an apt name for a flower so associated with love.'

'I suppose,' she said, thinking it over. 'But if you ate more than one, but less than a couple dozen, would you still die?'

'If you were foolish enough to crush up ten or twelve and add them to your tea, you would come down with a fever.'

'And then you would eventually die, just as if you ate more?'

He smiled at the earnest concern on her face. 'No. If you ate that many, it would cause a mild fever. In a day or two you would be over it.'

Jennsen peered carefully in at the whole collection of the deadly little Grace-like things and then set down the jar.

'It's not going to harm you to touch one,' he said, seeing her reaction to the jarful. 'You'd have to eat them to be affected. Even then, as I said, one in conjunction with other things will help the boy's fever.'

Jennsen smiled her embarrassment and reached in with two fingers to retrieve one. She dropped it in the bottom of the mortar, where it looked like nothing so much as a Grace.

'If it was for an adult who was awake, I'd just crush it between my thumb and finger,' the healer said as he drizzled honey into the cup, 'but he's little and asleep besides. I need to get him to drink it down easily, so grind it to a dust.'

When he was finished, he added the dark dust of the little fever rose flower head Jennsen had crushed for him. Like the Grace it resembled, it could be lifesaving, or lethal.

She wondered what Sebastian would think of such a thing. She wondered if Brother Narev would want such mountain fever roses eradicated because they could potentially be lethal.

Jennsen put away the jars for the healer while he took the honeyed drink to the boy. Along with the mother's help, they put the cup to his little lips and gently worked at getting him to drink. Drop by precious drop, they coaxed the sleeping boy to suckle and swallow each little bit they dribbled into his mouth. They weren't able to rouse him, so they had to drip it into his mouth a little at a time, waiting until he swallowed as he slept, then urge him to drink a little more.

While they worked, Sebastian returned from the barn. Before he closed the door, she saw stars outside. A wave of cold air rolled past her legs, sending a shiver through her shoulders. When the wind died like this as the sky cleared, it often meant a bone-chilling cold night.

Sebastian made for the fire, eager to warm himself. Jennsen put another log on, using the poker to position it askew so it would catch well. The healer, his hand lying gently on the woman's shoulder, nodded his assurance to her as she slowly gave the drink to her sick child. He left her to do the work, and, after hanging his cloak on a hook just inside the door closest to the hearth, joined Jennsen and Sebastian at the fire.

'Are this woman and child kin?' he said.

'No,' Jennsen said. With the warmth of the fire, she removed her cloak, too, and laid it over the bench at the table. 'We saw her on the road, and she needed help. We just gave her a ride here.'

'Ah,' he said. 'She will be welcome to sleep here with her boy. I need to keep my eye on him through the night.' She had forgotten about the singular nature of the knife she wore at her belt until he noticed it. 'Please,' he said, 'help yourself to the stew I have cooking; we always have plenty at hand for those who may come here. It's late to be traveling. You both are welcome to use the cabins for the night. They're all empty at present, so you may each have your own for the night.'

'That would be a kindness,' Sebastian said. 'Thank you.'

Jennsen was about to say that they could share one cabin, when she realized that he had said that because she had told him that Sebastian wasn't her husband. She realized how it would look if she said anything to change the plan, so she didn't.

Besides, the idea of sleeping with Sebastian outdoors was only natural and innocent enough. Together in a cabin seemed somehow different. She recalled that several times on their long journey north to the People's Palace they had taken shelter at inns. But that was before he had kissed her.

Jennsen gestured to include the general area. 'Is this the place of the Raug'Moss?'

He smiled at her question, as if he found it amusing but didn't want to mock her ignorance. 'By no means. This is just one of several small outposts we use when we travel – shelter – and a place where people who need our services can come to us.'

'The boy is lucky you were here, then,' Sebastian said.

The Raug'Moss studied Sebastian's eyes for a moment. 'If he lives, I will be pleased that I was here to help him. We frequently have a brother at this station.'

'Why is that?' Jennsen asked.

'Outposts such as this help provide the Raug'Moss with income from serving the needs of people with no other access to healers.'

'Income?' Jennsen asked. 'I thought that the Raug'Moss helped people out of charity, not for profit.'

'The stew, the hearth, the roof we offer, they do not appear magically because there is a need. People who come to us for the knowledge we've spent a lifetime acquiring are expected to contribute something in exchange for that help. After all, if we starve to death, how can we then help anyone else? Charity, if you have the means, is a personal choice, but charity which is expected or compelled is simply a polite word for slavery.'

The healer hadn't been speaking about her, of course, but Jennsen still felt stung by his words. Had she always expected others to help her, feeling entitled to their help simply because she wanted it? As if her wish for their assistance took precedence over the best interest of their own lives?

Sebastian fished around in a pocket, coming up with a silver mark. He held it out to the man. 'We would like to share what we have in return for your sharing what you have.'

After the briefest of glances at Jennsen's knife, he said, 'In your case, that isn't necessary.'

'We insist,' Jennsen said, feeling uncomfortable knowing that this money wasn't even really hers, something she had earned in exchange for the food, shelter, and care of their horses, but was taken from dead men.

With a bow of his head, he accepted the payment. 'There are bowls in the cupboard on the right. Please help yourselves. I must tend to the boy.'

Jennsen and Sebastian sat on a bench at the trestle table and ate two bowls each of the hearty lamb stew from the big kettle. It was the best meal they had had since – since the meat pies Tom had left for them.

'This turned out to our advantage,' Sebastian said in a low voice.

Jennsen glanced to the side of the room to see the healer and the mother bent over the boy. She leaned closer as he stirred a spoon through his stew.

'How so?'

His blue eyes turned up to her. 'Gives the horses good feed and a good rest. Us too. That gives us an advantage over anyone chasing us.'

'Do you really think they could have any idea where we are? Or even be close?'

Sebastian shrugged as he ate more of his stew. He checked across the room before he spoke. 'I can't see how they could, but they've surprised us before, haven't they?'

Jennsen admitted the truth of it with a nod and went back to eating her own meal in silence.

'Anyway,' he said, 'this gives us and the horses needed food and rest. It can only help us put more distance on them. I'm glad that you reminded me of how the Creator helps those in need.'

Jennsen was warmed by his smile. 'I hope it helps that poor boy.'

'Me too,' he said.

'I'm going to clean up and see if they need any help.'

He nodded as he scooped up the last piece of lamb into his spoon. 'You take the next to last cabin. I'll take the one after, on the end. I'll go start you a fire first while you finish up, here.'

After he put his spoon in his empty bowl, Jennsen put a hand over his. 'Sleep well.'

She basked in his private smile for her and then watched as he whispered to the healer. By the man's nod, she guessed that Sebastian had thanked him and wished him a good night. The mother, sitting beside her boy, stroking his brow, also thanked Sebastian for the help, and hardly noticed the icy air that rushed in as he went out the door.

Jennsen carried a steaming bowl of stew over to the woman. She accepted it politely, but absently, her attention on her small worry asleep at her hip. At Jennsen's urging, the healer sighed in agreement and sat at the table while she served him a bowl of his stew.

'Quite good, even if I made it,' he said with good humor as she brought him a mug of water.

Jennsen chuckled, assuring him that she shared his conviction. She let him eat, occupying herself with cleaning the dirty bowls in a wooden wash bucket and then adding several logs to the fire. The burning logs shot showers of sparks. Oak made a good fire, but it was messy without a screen. As she arranged the logs, sparks anew swirled up the chimney amid billowing smoke.

With a broom from the corner, she swept the dead ashes back into the hearth.

When she saw that the healer was nearly finished with his meal, she sat on the bench, close to him, so that she could speak privately. 'We must be leaving early, so in case I miss you in the morning, I wanted to thank you for all your help this evening, not only for the boy, but for us as well.'

Although he didn't look down, she knew by the expression on his face that he interpreted her need to be away early as having to do with the knife at her belt. She said nothing to dissuade that notion.

'We appreciate the generous contribution to our sect. It will help in our efforts to help our people.'

Jennsen knew he was just marking time until she said what was really on her mind, so she finally did. 'I would like to inquire about a man that I've learned is living with the Raug'Moss. He may even be a healer, I'm not sure. I'd like to know if you know anything about him.'

He shrugged. 'Ask. I will tell you what I know.'

'His name is Drefan.'

For the first time that night, the man's eyes revealed the fire of emotion. 'Drefan was the evil spawn of Darken Rahl.'

Jennsen had to force herself not to show any reaction at the power of his words. She reminded herself that he had seen her knife with the symbol of the House of Rahl, and that might be coloring his words. Still, he sounded emphatic.

'I know that much. I still need very much to find him.'

'You're too late.' A satisfied smile ghosted across his face. '"Master Rahl protect us,"' he quoted from the devotion.

'I don't understand.'

'Lord Rahl, the new Lord Rahl, killed him – spared us all from that bastard son of Darken Rahl.'

Jennsen.

Jennsen sat stunned, feeling almost as unseen talons were coming out of a dark sky toward her throat.

'You're sure' was all she could think to say. 'I mean, you're sure that Lord Rahl was the one who did it.'

'While there were polite words spoken about Drefan's death,

about how he had died in service of the people of D'Hara, I believe, as do the rest of the Raug'Moss, that Lord Rahl killed Drefan.'

Jennsen.

Polite words. Polite words for murder. Jennsen imagined that one did not just come right out and call it murder to Lord Rahl's face. Ordinary people were murdered. Lord Rahl's victims died in service to the people of D'Hara.

Jennsen felt her chest tightening at the fright of Lord Rahl being one murder closer to her. Darken Rahl had not found Drefan. Richard Rahl had. Richard Rahl would find her, too.

She gripped her trembling hands together in her lap, under the table. She hoped her face didn't show anything. This man was obviously loyal to the Lord Rahl. She dared not reveal her true revulsion, her true terror.

Surrender.

Her true anger.

Surrender.

That single word echoed around in her head behind the tumbling thoughts, her frustration, her hopeless gloom, her burgeoning anger.

Chapter 34

Jennsen sat alone on the floor before the robust fire Sebastian had made for her, staring into the flames, her unblinking gaze absently fixed on the glowing yellow-orange coals that now and again dropped from the checkering logs. She only dimly recalled the farewells to the healer and the boy's mother. She was hardly aware of the slow shuffle through the snow and cold that had gotten her to the empty cabin.

She didn't know how long she sat there, staring at nothing, as somber thoughts glided unceasingly through her mind. In his unrelenting effort to get to her, Richard Rahl had taken Jennsen's mother from her, leaving her with no sense of family or home. Jennsen missed her mother to the marrow of her bones, missed her so much that the agony seemed unendurable, yet she had no choice but to endure it. There were no tears left. At times, even the pain of the loss seemed to grow distant.

Ever since Althea had told her about Drefan, Jennsen had thought that if she could find this other child of Darken Rahl, her half brother, a hole in the world like her, she might find strength through that connection. She thought that they might possibly have a sense of kinship and, in their common struggle, together come up with a solution to their shared station in life. Whether or not any of that might have come to pass, she would never know, now.

It had been her hope that it would. That hope was dead. Richard Rahl had killed Drefan. Richard Rahl would surely kill her when he found her. And he would find her. She knew that, now. Really knew it. He would find her.

Jennsen.

A mad torrent of thoughts cascaded through her mind, everything from hope to despair, terror to rage.

Tu vash misht. Tu vask misht. Grushdeva du kalt misht.

The voice, too, was there, beyond the churning thoughts, beyond the turmoil of emotions, beyond the jumble of disorder, whispering to her in those strangely seductive words.

In the end, all other thoughts melted away in the glowing heat of her anger.

Jennsen. Surrender.

She had tried everything else. She had no options left. The Lord Rahl had cut her off from any other hope. She had no choice.

She knew what she had to do, now.

Jennsen rose up, feeling the strange sensation of inner peace at having made the decision. She threw her cloak around her shoulders and marched out into the still, frigid, quiet night. The air was so cold that it hurt to breathe it. The snow crunched as she made her way through the fresh tracks.

Shivering with the cold, or maybe the enormity of what she had decided, she knocked gently on the door to the last cabin. Sebastian pulled the door in enough to see it was her, and then, quickly, opened it to admit her. She hurried in though the opening, into the firelight and cocoon of warmth. Delicious heat embraced her.

Sebastian was without a shirt. By his clean scent and the towel thrown over his shoulder, she realized that she must have caught him at the washbowl. He had probably filled a washbowl in her cabin, too, though she hadn't noticed.

Concern creased Sebastian's brow as he stood, posture tense, waiting to see what had brought her there. Jennsen stepped up close to him, so close that she could feel the heat of him. Fists at her sides, she met his eyes boldly.

'I intend to kill Richard Rahl.'

He studied her face, accepting her determined words calmly, as if he had known all along that she would someday come to see the inescapable need. He remained silent, waiting to hear the rest of what she had to say.

'I know, now, that you were right,' she said. 'I have to eliminate him or I'll never be safe. I'll never be free to live my own life. I'm the only one to do it – the one who must do it.'

She didn't tell him why it had to be her.

His hand came up to grip her upper arm. His intense gaze never left hers. 'It will be difficult getting near such a man in order to do as you must. I've told you that we have sorceresses with the emperor, sorceresses fighting to end the reign of Lord Rahl. Let me take you to them, first.'

Jennsen had been focused on the decision rather than the details of how to go about it. She had given no thought to the approach or dealing with all the layers of people who would be protecting him. She would have to get in close enough for the killing itself. She had only pictured in her mind hitting him with her fist clutching her knife, yelling at him, screaming how much she hated him, how much she wanted him to suffer for all he had done. She had only fixed on the deed, not on how she would come to be standing that close before him. There were practical matters she needed to take into account if she was to succeed.

'Do you think these women could help me with what you said – magic used to end magic. Do you think they might be able to provide me with the means to go after him?'

Sebastian nodded. 'I wouldn't suggest it if I didn't. I know the destructive power of the magic on Lord Rahl's side – I've seen it with my own eyes – and I know how our sorceresses have been able to help us fight back. Magic can't do it all, but I think they can provide valuable help.'

Jennsen held herself erect, her chin up. 'I would appreciate it. I will gladly accept any assistance they can offer.'

A small smile curved the line of his mouth.

'But know this,' she added. 'With or without their help, I intend to kill Richard Rahl. If I must go alone and bare-handed, I intend to kill him. I will not rest until I do, because I have no life until I kill him – by his choice, not mine. I'm at the end of running. I will run no more.'

'I understand. I will take you to our sorceresses, then.'

'How far do you think it is to the Old World? Until we can reach them?'

'We won't be going to the Old World for now. In the morning we'll need to start looking for a pass to the west, over the mountains. We have to begin looking for a way into the Midlands.'

Jennsen pulled a ringlet of her hair back off her face when she noticed him looking at it. 'But, I thought that the emperor and the Sisters of the Light were in the Old World.'

Sebastian's expression twisted with a sly smile. 'No. We cannot allow Lord Rahl to bring war to our people without answering his aggression, without making him pay a price. We intend to fight, and win – the same as you have finally decided. Emperor Jagang is with our troops, laying siege to their seat of rule in the Midlands, the city of Aydindril. That's where the Confessors' Palace is – Lord Rahl's wife's palace. We're cleaving the New World. When spring arrives, we will take Aydindril and break the back of the New World.'

'I had no idea. Have you known all along that Emperor Jagang would try something so bold?'

Sebastian half laughed. 'I'm his strategist.'

Jennsen's jaw dropped. 'You? You thought of it?'

He dismissed her wide-eyed astonishment. 'Emperor Jagang came to the rule of the Old World because he is a genius. He had two alternatives in this, two different recommendations – to attack the Midlands, or to attack D'Hara first. Brother Narev advised that right is on our side, and that the Creator would grant us victory either way, so he had no preference, no military advice to offer.

'The emperor himself already had the goal of Aydindril in mind, though he kept silent on it until he heard the recommendations. My recommendation decided it for him. Emperor Jagang does not always use my strategy, but I was pleased that in this he saw what I saw – that taking the city and palace of Lord Rahl's wife would not only be a momentous military victory, but will also strike a great blow at our enemy's very heart.'

Jennsen was seeing him again as she had at first, in awe at how important he truly was. This was a man who, in part, directed the very course of history. The fate of nations, and countless lives, hung on Sebastian's word.

'You don't think the emperor may have taken the Confessors' Palace by now?'

'No,' he said with certainty. 'We will not waste our brave men trying to take such an important objective until the weather is with us. We will seize Aydindril in the spring, when this wretched winter is over. I think we can yet reach them in time to be there for the great event.'

Jennsen was enthralled by the very idea of seeing such a momentous event – the forces of a free people striking a mighty blow against Lord Rahl. At the same time, she knew it meant the beginning of the end of D'Hara. But it really only meant the end of evil rule.

In the crackling firelight, it seemed a remarkable night in more ways than one. The world was changing and she was going to be a part of it. She had changed this night, too.

The fire was warm on the side of her face. She realized that she had never seen Sebastian without a shirt. She liked the sight.

His other hand came up to gently grasp her other arm. 'Emperor Jagang will like to meet you.'

'Me? But, I'm no one important.'

'Oh, yes, Jennsen, Jagang the Just will be eager to meet you, I can promise you that, to meet the brave woman who wishes to strike such a blow for our courageous people, for the future of a free mankind, and finally bring an end to the scourge of the House of Rahl. For such an historic event as the taking of Aydindril and the Confessors' Palace, Brother Narev himself intends to travel up from the Old World to witness the great victory on behalf of our people. I'm sure he, too, would be most pleased to meet you.'

'Brother Narev . . . '

Jennsen thought about the sweep of events that, until now, she had no idea were taking place. Now she was a part of those momentous events. She felt a kind of thrill that she would meet Jagang the Just – a real emperor – and maybe even Brother Narev, who Sebastian said was just about the most important spiritual leader ever to have lived.

Without Sebastian, none of it would be possible. He was such a remarkable man – everything from his wonderful blue eyes and his exotic spikes of white hair, to his handsome smile and extraordinary intellect.

'Since you had a hand in planning the campaign, I'm happy that you'll be there to see your strategy triumph. I admit, too, that I would be honored to be in the presence of such great and noble men.'

Even though Sebastian seemed as modest as always, she still thought she saw a spark of pride in his eyes, but then he turned serious. 'When we meet with the emperor, you mustn't be alarmed by what you see.'

'What do you mean?'

'Emperor Jagang has been marked by the Creator with eyes that see more than ordinary men can see. Foolish people are frightened by his looks. I wanted to forewarn you. You mustn't be frightened of such a great man simply because he looks different.'

'I won't be.'

'It's settled, then.'

Jennsen grinned. 'I agree to your new strategy. We can leave for the Midlands, the emperor, and the Sisters of the Light in the morning.'

It seemed he hardly heard her. His gaze wandered her face, her hair, returning at last to her eyes.

'You're the most beautiful woman I've ever met.'

Jennsen felt his fingers tighten on her arms, pulling her closer. 'You favor me with such words,' she heard herself say. He was a trusted advisor to an emperor. She was just a girl who grew up in the woods. He influenced history; she simply ran from it. Until now.

And yet, he was just Sebastian. A man she talked with, traveled with, ate with. She had seen him yawn from exhaustion and fall asleep countless times.

He was a fascinating mix of nobility and commoner. He seemed to chafe at being held in awe, yet by his manner he seemed to court it, if not demand it.

'I'm sorry at how inadequate those words sound,' he whispered, looking very humble. 'I mean so much more than that you're merely beautiful.'

'You do?' Her words were more than a question. They were expectant wonder.

Sebastian's mouth met hers in a rush. His arms surrounded her. She held her hands out to the side, afraid to hug him because if she did she would have to touch his naked flesh. She stood in his arms, her own arms held out stiffly, her spine arched back under the press of him.

His mouth felt luscious against hers. His arms did more than encircle her; they sheltered her. Her eyes closed as she sagged into his kiss. His whole body felt so hard against hers. His fist seized her hair at the nape of her neck, holding her as he moaned against her lips, as his warm tongue unexpectedly filled her mouth. Jennsen's head was spinning with the delicious sensations.

The world seemed to be tipping, and she felt as if she were hanging in his arms. She felt the sudden press of the bedding against her. The shock of being on her back, with him atop her, had her suddenly confused and not knowing what to do or how to react.

She wanted to stop him before he went any further. At the same time, she feared to do anything that would cause him to stop, to believe she was spurning him.

It occurred to her how very alone they were. Such isolation worried her. Yet, it excited her, too. With the two of them so completely alone, only she could stop him. The choices that she made not only decided her own path, but also held sway over Sebastian's heart. It gave her a comforting sense of power.

But it was just a kiss. More of a kiss than in the palace, but still, just a kiss. A head-spinning, heart-pounding kiss.

She surrendered herself into his embrace, daring to use her tongue as he did his, and was exhilarated by his ardent response. She felt like a woman – a desirable woman. Her hands ran up the smooth skin of his back, feeling the landscape of his bone and muscle, unhindered by a veil of cloth, feeling him flex as he pressed against her. She could hardly get her breath with the wonder of such feelings.

'Jenn,' he whispered breathlessly into her ear, 'I love you.'

Jennsen was stunned speechless. It didn't seem real. It felt like she had to be dreaming it, or living in someone else's body. She knew she'd heard him say it, but it just didn't seem real to her.

Her heart was racing so fast that she feared it might burst. Sebastian's breath, too, came in desperate pulls, as if his lust for her were driving him mad. She clung to him, eager to feel the warm breath of his words in her ear again.

She feared to believe him, though, to allow herself to believe him, to know if it was real, if this was really happening to her, or if she was only imagining it.

'But . . . you can't mean it.' Her words were a wall to protect her.

'I do,' he panted. 'I do. I can't help myself. I love you, Jennsen.'

His warm breath tickled her in a way that ran a scrumptious shiver up through the core of her.

For some reason, the memory of Tom came into her mind. She saw him, in her mind's eye, smiling at her in that way of his. This would not be Tom's manner. She didn't know how she knew that, but she did. Tom would not approach the subject of love in this fashion.

For some reason, she felt a stab of ache for Tom.

'Sebastian—'

'Tomorrow, we leave to carry out our destiny . . ..'

Jennsen nodded against his shoulder, marveling at how those words sounded somehow passionate. Their destiny. She held on tight, feeling the slick warmth of his back, feeling him push himself against her leg, feeling his arm lying across her belly as his hand caressed her hip, in a way hoping he would say something to thrill her, to frighten her, at the same time praying he wouldn't.

'But this night is ours, Jenn, if you will only seize it.'

Jennsen.

'Sebastian—'

'I love you, Jennsen. I love you.'

Jennsen.

She wished the image of Tom would leave her mind.

'Sebastian, I don't know what—'

'I never wanted to. It wasn't my intention to allow myself to feel this way, but I do. I love you, Jenn. I didn't expect it. Dear Creator, I can't help myself. I love you.'

Her eyes closed as he kissed her neck. It felt so good feeling his intimate whispers in her ear, a whisper that in a way sounded close to a painful confession, laced with regret, anger, yet thick with desperate hope.

'I love you,' he whispered again.

Jennsen.

Jennsen shuddered with the pleasure of the sensation, with the pleasure of feeling like a woman, of knowing that her mere existence thrilled a man. She had never felt particularly attractive before. Right then, she felt more than beautiful – she felt seductively beautiful.

Surrender.

She kissed his neck as he shifted his weight. She kissed his ear and ran her tongue along it as he had done to her. His whole body felt afire.

She froze when his hand slid up under her dress. His fingers glided over her bare knee, over her bare thigh. It was her choice to make, she told herself. It was.

She gasped, eyes wide, staring up at the dark rafters. His mouth covered hers before she could say the word wanting to come out. Her fist pounded his shoulder, once, in frustration at not being able to say that one, short, important word.

She gripped his face to push him away, to allow her to say it. But this was the man who had saved her life. If not for him, she would have been killed along with her mother that rainy night. She owed him her very life. Letting him touch her in such a way was nothing in exchange for that. What harm was it? It was a small thing compared to the way he had opened his heart to her.

Besides, she cared for him. He was a man any woman would desire. He was handsome, smart, and important. Moreover, she was excited that he cared so for her. She was. What more could she want?

She forcefully banished the unwanted image of Tom from her mind by focusing all her attention on Sebastian and what he was doing to her. His touch weakened her in a way that made her ache.

His fingers felt so good that tears ran down her cheeks. She forgot the word, wondering why she would ever have wanted to say it.

Her fingers clutched the back of his head, holding on for dear life. Her other fist pressed against the sides of his ribs as she cried out at what he was doing to her. All she could do was pant as she squirmed, helpless, at the indecent delight of it.

'Sebastian—' she gasped. 'Oh, Sebastian—'

'I love you so much, Jenn.' He forced her knees farther apart. He pushed himself between her trembling legs. 'I need you, Jennsen. I need you so. I can't live without you. I swear I can't.'

It was supposed to be her choice. She told herself that it was.

'Sebastian—'

Surrender.

'Yes,' she breathed. 'Dear spirits, forgive me, yes.'

Chapter 35

Oba leaned a shoulder against the red-painted side of a wagon set back out of the way. Hands in his pockets, he casually surveyed the busy marketplace. People crowding among the open-air stands seemed in a festive mood, possibly because at long last spring was nearly at hand, even if winter was not yet ready to relinquish its harsh grip. Despite the biting chill, people chatted and chuckled, bargained and bickered, purchased and perused.

Little did the shuffling crowds braving the cold wind know that someone important was among them. Oba grinned. A Rahl was among them. A member of the ruling family.

Since he had decided to become invincible, and over the course of his long journey north, Oba had become a new man, a man of the world. At first, after the death of the troublesome sorceress and his lunatic mother, he was aswirl in newfound liberty, and hadn't given any thought to coming to the People's Palace, but the more he considered the pivotal events that had taken place and all the new things he had learned, the more he had come to realize that the journey was vital. There were still bits missing, bits that could lead to trouble.

That Jennsen woman had said that quads hunted her. Quads only hunted important people. Oba was concerned that they might turn to hunting him, too, since he was important. Like Jennsen, he was also one of those holes in the world. Lathea hadn't explained to him what that meant, but it made Oba and Jennsen both special in some way. It somehow linked them.

It was possible that Lord Rahl had learned about Oba, maybe

from the treacherous Lathea, and he feared having a rightful rival who could challenge him. Oba was, after all, also a son of Darken Rahl. An equal, in many ways. Lord Rahl had magic, but Oba was invincible.

With all the potential trouble brewing, Oba thought it best to look after his own interests by traveling to his ancestral home to learn what he could.

Even before he had decided to travel north, Oba had had his concerns. Still, he enjoyed his visits to new places, and had learned many new things. He kept lists of them in his head. Places, sights, people. Everything meant something. In quiet moments he would go over those mental lists, seeing what things fit together, what revelations he could divine. It was important to keep the mind active, he always said. He was a man on his own, now, making his own decisions, choosing his own road, doing as he pleased, but he still had to learn and grow.

But no more did Oba have to feed the animals, tend the garden, mend fences and barns and houses. No longer did he have to haul and fetch and obey every foolish whim of his lunatic mother. No more did he have to endure the troublesome sorceress's loathsome cures, her furtive glances. No more did he have to listen to his mother's tirades, her taunts, or be subjected to her venomous humiliation.

To think, she had once had the gall to order him to pick away at a frozen mound of muck – him, the son of Darken Rahl himself. How Oba put up with it, he didn't know. He supposed that he was a man of remarkable patience, one of his many stellar traits.

Since his maniacal mother had always been so harshly adamant that he never spend money on women, Oba had celebrated his freedom from her tyranny, once he reached a good sized city, by visiting the most expensive whore he could find. He understood, then, why his mother had always been so dead set against him being with women – it was enjoyable.

He had found, though, that those women, too, could be cruel to a man of his sensitivity. They, too, would sometimes try to make him feel small and unimportant. They, too, would fix him with that calculating, callous, condescending gaze he so hated.

Oba suspected that it was his mother's fault. He suspected that even from the world of the dead, she might still manage to reach into this world, through a whore's cold heart, to vex him in his most triumphant moments. He suspected that her dead voice whispered vicious things in the women's ears. It would be just like her to do that; even in her eternal rest, she would not be content to let him have any peace or satisfaction.

Oba wasn't a spendthrift – not by any means – but the money that had so rightly been his did bring him some well-deserved pleasures, like clean beds, good food and drink, and the company of attractive women. He tended his money carefully, though, lest he end up without it. People, he knew, were only too covetous of his wealth.

He had learned that just having money, though, brought him favors, especially from women. If he bought them drinks or small gifts – a pretty piece of cloth for a scarf, a trinket for their wrist, a shiny pin for their hair – they were more likely to cozy up to him. They often took him somewhere quiet, where they could be alone with him. Sometimes it was an alley, sometimes it was a deserted wood, sometimes it was a room.

He suspected that some of them just wanted to get at his money. Still, it never failed to amaze him what entertainment and satisfaction he could derive from a woman. Frequently with the aid of a sharp knife.

Being a man of the world, Oba knew about women, now. He had been with many. Now, he knew how to talk to women, how to treat women, how to satisfy women.

There were a number of women still waiting, hoping, praying he would one day return to them. Several had even deserted their husbands, expecting they might win his heart.

Women couldn't resist him. They fawned over him, delighted over his looks, marveled at his strength, moaned at the way he pleasured them. They especially enjoyed it when he hurt them. Anyone less sensitive than he would fail to recognize their tears of joy for what they really were.

While Oba enjoyed the company of women, he knew he could always have another, so he didn't become entangled in long love affairs. Most were brief. Some very brief. For now, he had more important matters on his mind than women. Later, he would have all the women he could ever want. Just like his father had.

Now, at last, he could look upon the soaring stone splendor of his true home: the People's Palace. Someday, it would be his. The voice had told him so.

A hawker pushed in close beside him, disturbing Oba's pleasant thoughts, his imagining of what lay ahead for him.

'Charms, for you, sir? Magic charms. Good luck for sure.'

Oba frowned down at the hunched hawker. 'What?'

'Special charms with magic. Can't go wrong for a silver penny.'

'What do they do?'

'Well, sir, the charms are magic, sure. Wouldn't you like a bit of magic to ease the terrible struggles of life? Make things go your way for a change? Only a silver penny.'

Things did go his way, now that his lunatic mother wasn't around to pester him and keep him down. Still, Oba did like to learn new things.

'What will this magic do? What kinds of things?'

'Great things, sir. Great things. Give you strength, it will. Strength, and wisdom. Strength and wisdom beyond any normal mortal man.'

Oba grinned. 'I already have that.'

The man was at a loss for words for only a moment. He looked over each shoulder, making sure no one was close before he leaned in closer, pushing against Oba's side, in order to speak confidentially. He winked up at Oba.

'These magic charms will help win the girls for you, sir.'

'Women already can't get enough of me.' Oba was losing interest. This magic promised only what he already had. The man might as well say that the charms would give Oba two arms and two legs.

The filthy little man cleared his throat, thick with phlegm, as he leaned close again. 'Well, sir, no man can have enough wealth or the most beautiful—'

'I'll give you a copper penny if you can tell me where I can find the sorceress Althea.'

352

The man's breath stank. Oba pushed him back. The hawker lifted a crooked finger. His wiry eyebrows rose as well.

'You, sir, are a wise man, just as you said. I knew I saw something keen about you. You, sir, have ferreted out the one man in this market who can tell you what you need.' He thumped his chest. 'Me. I can tell you all you need to know on the subject. But, as a man of your wisdom will no doubt realize, such obscure and privileged information will of necessity cost you a great deal more than a copper penny. Yes, sir, a great deal more, and worth it.'

Oba frowned. 'How much more?'

'A silver mark.'

Oba grunted a laugh and started walking away. He had the money, but he didn't appreciate being played for a fool.

'I'll ask around. Decent people can offer such simple help as directions to the sorceress and they will expect nothing more than a tip of my cap.'

The hawker scurried along at Oba's side, eager to renegotiate, speaking hurriedly as he struggled to keep up. Loose ends of his ragged outfit flapped like flags in the breeze as he dodged people dodging Oba.

'Yes, I can see you're a wise man indeed. I'm afraid I'm no match for you, sir. You've bested me – that's the simple truth of it. But there are more knotty matters you don't know about, matters a man of your rare sensitivity should know, things which could very well mean your safety in such a dangerous venture as I think you may be about to undertake, things which not many folks can tell you true.'

Oba was sensitive, that much was true. He gazed down at the man shuffling along sideways, like a dog begging for a scrap. 'A silver penny, then. That's all I'm offering.'

'A silver penny, then,' he conceded with a sigh, 'for the valuable information you need, sir, which I warrant you will hear nowhere else.'

Oba halted, satisfied that the man had caved in to the superior intellect. Hands on his hips, he stared down at the hopeful fellow licking his cracked lips. It was against Oba's nature to part with money so easily, but he had plenty, and something about this intrigued him. He fished around in his pocket, slipping two fingers into the leather purse he kept there, and drew out a silver penny.

He flipped it to the scruffy fellow. 'All right, then.' As the man caught the coin, Oba caught the hawker's bony wrist. 'I will give you the price you ask. But if I don't think you're telling it true, or if I suspect that you're holding back on me, I'll take back the coin, and I'll have to wipe your blood off it before I return it to my pocket.'

The man swallowed at the dangerous look on Oba's face. 'Sir, I'd not cheat you – especially not once my word is given.'

'You'd best not. So, where is she? How can I find Althea?'

'In a swamp, she lives. But I can tell you how to get in to her, for only—'

'Do you think I'm a stupid oaf!' Oba twisted the wrist. 'I've already heard that people go to see this sorceress, that she receives visitors in her swamp, so something more than the way in to her place had better be included in the fair price I've given you.'

'Yes!' The hawker gulped in pain. 'Of course it is.' Oba eased up. Still wincing, the man was quick to go on. 'I was going to say that I will tell you the secret way to get to her through her swamp for the generous price you've already paid. Not just the regular way in, which folks know, but the secret way in, as well. Few, if any, know of it. All included in the price. I'd not hold anything back from a fair man like you, sir.'

Oba glared. 'Secret way in? If there is a regular way, a way people use to see Althea, why would I care about this other way?'

'People go in to see the sorceress Althea for a telling. She's a powerful one, this sorceress.' He leaned closer. 'But you must be invited before you can go see her for a telling. None dare to go without being invited. People all go in the same way, so as she can see them coming – after she's invited them in and withdrawn her bloodthirsty beasts that guard the path.' A sly smile spread on the man's twisty face. 'It seems to me that if you were invited in, you wouldn't need to ask people how to get there. Have you been invited, sir?'

Oba gently pushed the reeking hawker back. 'So, there is another way in?'

'There is. A back way in. A way to sneak up on her, if you're of a mind, while her beasts guard the front door, as it were. A smart man might not choose to approach a powerful sorceress on her terms.'

Oba glanced to the sides, checking that people weren't listening. 'I don't need to go in a secret back way. I'm not afraid of the sorceress. But as long as I've already paid for it all, I'll hear it all told. Both ways in, and everything else about her, too.'

The man shrugged. 'If you're of a mind, you can simply ride due west, as the folks who was invited to Althea's place do. You travel west across the plains until you come to the largest snowcapped mountain. Beyond the mountain, you turn north and follow along the base of the cliffs. The land goes lower until it finally enters the swamp. Just follow the well-kept path on in through the swamp. Stay on that path – don't wander off. It leads to the home of the sorceress Althea.'

'But the swamp would be frozen, this time of year.'

'No, sir. This is the wicked place of a sorceress and her menacing magic. Althea's swamp does not bow to winter.'

Oba twisted the man's wrist until he cried out. 'Do you think me a fool? No place is a swamp in winter.'

'Ask anyone!' the man squealed. He swept his other arm around. 'Ask anyone and they'll tell you Althea's place doesn't bow to the Creator's winter, but is hot and boggy all year round.'

Oba let up on the man's wrist. 'You said there was a back way in. Where is it?'

For the first time, the man hesitated. He licked his weather-cracked lips. 'It's difficult to find. There are few landmarks, and they're hard to spot. I could tell you how to find the place, but you might miss it, and then you'll think I lied to you when it's only that it's tricky to find by directions alone if you're not familiar with the land in these parts.'

'I'm already thinking about having my coin back.'

'I'm only looking to your safety, sir.' He flashed a quick, apologetic smile. 'I don't like giving a man like you only part of what he needs, for fear I might live to regret it. I believe in giving the full measure of my word.'

'Go on.'

The hawker cleared his wet throat and then spat to the side. He wiped his mouth with the back of his filthy sleeve. 'Well, sir, the best way to find it is if I take you there.'

Oba checked an older couple passing nearby, then pulled the man by his wrist. 'Fine. Let's go.'

The hawker dug in his heels. 'Now hold on there. I agreed to tell you, and I can do that. Like I said, though, it's hard to find. But I can't be expected to give up my business to go off as a guide. It's a number of days I'd be away from an income.'

Scowling, Oba leaned down. 'And how much is it you want to guide me there?'

The man took a heavy breath as he considered, muttering to himself as if toiling at tallying up numbers in his head.

'Well, sir,' he said at last, lifting a finger on his free hand that stuck up through a short stub of a knit glove. 'I guess I could be gone for a few days if I were to be paid a gold mark.'

Oba laughed. 'I'm not giving you a mark – gold nor even silver – for the work of guiding me for a few days. I'd be willing to pay you another silver penny, but that's all. Take it or give me back my first silver penny and be gone.'

The hawker shook his head as he mumbled to himself. Finally, he squinted up at Oba with a look of resignation.

'My charms aren't selling well, of late. To tell the truth, I could use the money. You have the best of me again, sir. I'll guide you, then, for a silver penny.'

Oba released the man's wrist. 'Let's go.'

'It's across the Azrith Plains. We'll need horses.'

'Now, you want me to buy you a horse? Are you out of your mind?'

'Well, walking is no good. But I know folks, here, who will give you a good deal on a couple of horses. If we treat the animals right, I'm sure they'd agree to buy them back once we return – less a small fee for their use.'

Oba thought it over. He wanted to go up into the palace to

have a look around, but he thought it best if he visited Lathea's sister, first. There were things to learn.

'That sounds fair.' Oba gave the hunched hawker a nod. 'Let's go get some horses and be off, then.'

They moved out of the quieter side route into a main road thick with milling throngs. There were a number of attractive women about. Some of them looked Oba's way, the invitation and longing clear in their eyes. They met his gaze, hungry for him. Oba gave them smiles, a token suggesting the possibility of more, later. He could see that even that much thrilled them.

It occurred to him, though, that these women roaming the market were probably lowly peasants. Up in the palace were likely to be the kind of women Oba wanted to meet: women of station. He deserved no less. After all, he was a Rahl, practically a prince, or something comparable. Maybe even something more than that.

'What's you name, anyway?' Oba asked. 'Seeing as we'll be traveling together.'

'Clovis.'

Oba didn't offer his name. He liked being called 'sir.' It was, after all, only fitting.

'With all the people,' Oba said as his gaze swept the crowds, 'how is it that your charms aren't selling? Why is it that you're having hard times?'

The man sighed in apparent misery. 'It's a sad tale, but it's not your burden, sir.'

'Simple enough question, I think.'

'I suppose it is.' He shielded his eyes from the sunlight with a hand, partly covered in a knitted fingerless glove, as he peered up at Oba. 'Well, sir, a time ago, back in the thick of winter, I met a beautiful young woman.'

Oba looked over at the hunched, wrinkled, disheveled man shuffling along beside him. 'Met her?'

'Well, sir, truth be told, I was offering her a charm ...' Clovis's brow twisted curiously – as if he'd suddenly come across something quite unexpected. 'It was her eyes that seized you. Big blue eyes. Blue like you rarely see ...' Clovis ogled up at Oba. 'The thing is, sir, her eyes looked very much like yours.'

It was Oba's turn to frown. 'Like mine?'

Clovis nodded earnestly. 'They did, sir. She had eyes like yours. Imagine that. Something about her – about you as well – that looks . . . somehow, familiar. Can't say as I know what it is, though.'

'What does this have to do with your hard times? Did you give her all your money and fail to get between her legs?'

Clovis seemed shocked by the very notion. 'No sir, nothing like that. I tried to sell her a charm – so she would have good fortune. Instead, she stole all my money.'

Oba grunted skeptically. 'I'd bet she was batting her eyelashes and smiling at you while she had her arm in your pocket to her elbow, and you were too eager to suspect what she was really doing.'

'Nothing like that, sir. Nothing like that at all.' His voice turned bitter. 'She set a man upon me and he took it all for her. He did it, but it was at her word – I'm sure of it. The two of them stole all my money. Robbed me of everything I had earned all year.'

Something tickled Oba's memory. He scanned his mental lists of odd and unrelated things. Some of those things began to come together.

'What did this woman with the blue eyes look like?'

'Oh, she was beautiful, sir, with thick ringlets of red hair.' Even if this woman had robbed the man of his savings, the distant look in his eye told Oba that he was still clearly taken by her. 'Her face was like a vision of a good spirit, it was, and her figure was enough to take your breath away. But I should have known, by that bewitchingly evil red hair, that there was something more devious to her than her beauty.'

Oba halted and seized the man by the arm. 'Was her name Jennsen?'

Clovis offered only a regretful shrug. 'Sorry, sir. She never gave me her name. But I don't imagine there are many women that look like her. Not with those blue eyes, her exquisite looks, and those ringlets of red hair.'

Oba didn't think so, either. The description fit Jennsen perfectly.

Well, wasn't that just something.

Clovis pointed. 'There, sir. Down there is the man who can sell us horses.'

Chapter 36

Oba squinted into the gloom under the thick vegetation. It was hard to believe how dark it was in under the towering trees, down at the bottom of the crooked spine of rock, when it had been such a bright sunny morning up in the meadow above. It looked wet ahead, too.

He turned from the way leading in under the vines and hanging trailers of moss, to look back up the steep rocky incline, toward where he had left Clovis by a warm fire, watching their horses and gear. Oba was glad to finally be free of the jumpy little man. He was wearing, like a pesky fly buzzing around all the time. All the way across the Azrith Plains, the man jabbered on and on at length about everything and nothing. Oba would have rather been rid of the hawker and gone alone, but the man had been right about how difficult it would have been to have found this place down into the back of Althea's swamp.

At least the man had no intention of going into the swamp with Oba. Clovis had seemed nervous and edgy about making sure that his customer went in, though. He was probably worried that Oba wouldn't believe him and was eager to prove himself. He waited at the top, watching, shooing with hands covered in tattered, fingerless gloves, impatient for Oba to go in and see that he was being given his money's worth.

Oba sighed and started out again, slogging ahead through the underbrush, stooping beneath low branches. He tiptoed across roots where he could, and waded through standing water where he had to. The air was still and as stagnant as the water. It felt wet, too, besides smelling foul.

Strange birds called from far off through the trees, back in the shadows where light probably never reached, back beyond vines, thick clumps of leaves, and rotting trunks leaning drunkenly against stalwart companions. Creatures moved through the water, too. What they could be, fish or reptile or conjured beast, there was no telling. Oba didn't like the place. Not one bit.

He reminded himself that there would be a myriad of new things to learn once he got to Althea's place. Not even that cheered him. He thought about the strange bugs and weasels and salamanders he'd seen so far, and the ones he was likely yet to see. That, too, failed to cheer him; he still didn't like the place.

Ducking under branches, he swept spiderwebs aside. The fattest spider he'd ever encountered fell to the ground and darted for a hiding place. Oba, quicker yet, squashed it good. Hairy legs clawed the air in death before going still. Oba grinned as he moved on. He was beginning to like the place better.

His nose wrinkled. The farther in he went, the worse it smelled, reeking with a strange, pungent, dank rot. He saw steam rising off through the trees, and began to detect an odor something like rotten eggs, but more acidic. Oba was beginning not to like the place, again.

He plowed onward, unsure if it had been a good idea to go to see Althea, especially by the route suggested by the hand-wringing hawker. Oba sighed as he slogged through thick brush. The sooner he got in and had a chat with Althea, the sooner he could be out of the disgusting place.

Besides, the voice had stirred, restless that he continue.

The sooner he was finished with Lathea's sister, the sooner he could visit his ancestral home, the People's Palace. It would be wise to learn what he could, first, so that he might know what to anticipate from his half brother.

Oba wondered if Jennsen had been to see Althea, yet, and if she had, what she had found out. Oba was more and more convinced that his fate was somehow linked to the Jennsen woman. Too many things kept leading back to her for it to be a meaningless connection. Oba was very careful about how things on the lists he kept connected. Other people weren't so observant, but they didn't have to be – they weren't important.

Both he and Jennsen were a hole in the world. Possibly even more interesting, they both had something in their eyes that Clovis had noticed. What it was, exactly, the man wasn't sure. Oba had pressed him, but he couldn't say.

As the morning wore on, Oba made the best time he could along the twisted tangle of roots that passed for a path, until it sank lower ahead of him into an expanse of still, dark water. Oba paused, panting, sweat streaming down his face, checking to the sides, searching for another way across to where the ground looked to rise up again. It appeared that the way ahead tunneled on through the thick, steamy growth. But first, he had to get across the water. Hot as he was, that didn't sound half bad.

He saw no vines hanging down that might steady him, so he quickly cut a stout limb and stripped it of branches to make himself a staff to help him balance as he crossed the low place.

Staff in hand, Oba waded out into a stretch of water. It wasn't as much of a cooling relief as he had hoped; it smelled awful and was full of brown leeches. As he moved through the water, trailing a wake that dislodged debris from the banks, he had to keep brushing the clouds of biting bugs from his face. He kept checking, but unless he backtracked to look for another way, he saw that it was the only way to dry land beyond. That thought alone convinced him to keep going.

There were roots enough under the surface for footing, but Oba soon found himself in up to his chest and he wasn't yet to the middle. As deep as it was, the water made him buoyant, which meant his footing wasn't as good. The roots at the bottom were slippery and poor support for the staff, but it at least helped him keep his balance.

He was a good swimmer, but didn't like the thought of what else might be swimming with him, and preferred to keep on his feet. Almost to the far bank, Oba was just about to discard the staff and swim the rest of the way to wash the sweat off, when something heavy brushed against his leg. Before he could think what to do about it, the thing bumped him hard enough to push him from his feet, dumping him into the water. As soon as he plunged into the deeper water, the thing enveloped his legs.

He instantly thought of the monsters that were said to dwell in the swamp. Throughout their long ride, Clovis had regaled him with stories of the beasts, warning him to be careful, but Oba had scoffed, confident in his own strength.

Now, Oba cried out in fright of the monster that had him. He struggled frantically, in gasping panic, trying to shake his legs free, but the fire-breathing beast had him fast and wouldn't let go. It reminded him of being locked in the pen when he was little, trapped and helpless. Oba's cry echoed out across the frothing water, returning threefold from the darkness beyond. The only clear thought that came to him was that he was too young to die – especially in so awful a fashion. He had so much ahead of him to live for. It wasn't fair that this should happen to him.

He cried out again as he splashed and fought to escape. He wanted away, just as he had wanted out of the terrible trapped feeling of being locked in the pen. His screams never helped then, and they didn't help now; their echo was empty companionship.

The thing suddenly and forcefully twisted him around, spinning him, and dragged him under.

Oba gasped a breath just in time. As he went under, eyes wide in fright, he saw for the first time the scales of his captor. It was the biggest snake he had ever seen, but he was also struck with relief because it was still a snake. It might be big, but it was just an animal – not a fire-breathing monster.

Before his arm could be pinned, Oba snatched the knife in a sheath at his belt and yanked it free. He knew that in water it would be difficult to use the same force as on dry land. Still, stabbing the thing would be his only chance, and he had to do it before he drowned.

With his neck stretching for air, but the life-giving surface getting farther and farther away as the weight around him continued to drag him deeper, his feet unexpectedly found something solid. Rather than continue to fight to reach the surface for air, he let his legs bend as he sank. When his legs were folded like a bullfrog ready to spring, he tensed his powerful leg muscles and pushed with a mighty shove off the bottom.

Oba exploded from the water, coils of snake wrapped around him. He landed on his side, halfway out of the water, up on twisted roots. The snake, its body cushioning Oba's weight when they crashed to the ground, clearly didn't appreciate it. Iridescent green scales shimmered in the weak light as the reeking water sluiced from both combatants.

The snake's head rose over Oba's shoulder. Yellow eyes peered at him through a dark mask. A red tongue flicked out, feeling along its troublesome prey.

Oba grinned. 'Come closer, my pretty friend.'

The snake undulated along his body as the eyes fixed him with a menacing stare. If a snake could get angry, this one was. Lightning quick, Oba snatched the thing behind the dark green head, gripping it in his brawny fist. It reminded him of the wrestling he had done before on rare occasions. He liked wrestling. Oba never lost at wrestling.

The snake paused to hiss. With powerful muscles, each held back the other. The snake tried to enfold Oba in yet more coils and gain the advantage by constricting. It was a mighty struggle of strength as each tried to wrestle the other into submission.

Oba recalled that ever since he had listened to the voice, he had been invincible. He remembered how his life used to be ruled by fear, fear of his mother, fear of the powerful sorceress. Most everyone feared the sorceress, just as most everyone feared snakes. Except Oba had stood up to her dangerous magic. She had sent fire and lightning at him, magic able to blast its way through walls and vanquish any opposition, yet he had been invincible. What was a lowly snake in the face of that kind of opponent? He felt a bit chagrined that he had cried out in fright. What had he, Oba Rahl, to fear, least of all from a mere snake?

Oba rolled farther up onto solid ground, taking the snake with him. He grinned as he brought the knife up under the scaled jaw. The huge animal went still.

With deliberate care, gripping the thing behind the head with one hand, Oba pressed the blade upward with his other. The tough scales, like pale white armor, resisted penetration. The snake, now under threat from Oba's deadly blade, suddenly began struggling – not to dominate, this time, but to escape.

364

Muscular coils unwrapped from Oba's legs, sweeping across the ground, trying for purchase against roots and saplings, searching for anything to latch on to. With his foot, Oba pulled a length of the shimmering green body back toward him, preventing any escape.

The razor-sharp blade, with Oba's powerful muscles pushing it, suddenly popped through the thick scales under the jaw. Oba watched, fascinated, as blood ran down his fist. The snake went wild with fear and pain. Any thoughts of conquest were long forgotten. Now, it wanted desperately to get away. The animal put all its considerable strength to that effort alone.

But Oba was strong. Nothing ever escaped him.

Straining with the effort, he dragged the twisting, turning, writhing body up onto higher, drier ground. He grunted as he lifted the heavy beast. Holding it aloft, screaming with fury, Oba ran forward. With a mighty lunge, he drove his knife into a tree, pinning the snake there with the blade through its lower jaw and roof of its mouth, like a long, third fang.

The snake's yellow eyes watched, helpless, as Oba drew another knife from his boot. He wanted to see the life go out of those wicked yellow eyes as they watched him.

Oba made a slit in the pale underbody, in the fold between rows of scales. Not a long slit. Not a slit that would kill. Just a slit big enough for his hand.

Oba grinned. 'Are you ready?' he asked the thing. It watched, unable to do anything else.

Oba pushed his sleeve up his arm as far as he could, then wormed his hand in through the slit. It was a tight fit, but he wriggled his hand, then his wrist, then his arm into the living body, farther and farther as the snake whipped side to side, not just in its futile effort to escape, but now in agony. With a knee, Oba pinned the body to the trunk of the tree and with a foot held down the thrashing tail.

For Oba, the world seemed to vanish around him as he felt what it was like to be a snake. He imagined he was becoming the animal, in its living body, feeling its skin around his own as he pushed his arm in. He felt its warm wet insides compressed around his flesh. He slithered his hand in deeper. He had to stand closer, so that he could get his arm down in farther, until his eyes were only inches from the snake's.

Looking into those eyes, he was wildly exhilarated at seeing not just brutal pain, but the most marvelous terror.

Oba felt his destination pulsing through the slippery viscera. Then, he found it – the living heart. It beat furiously in his hand, throbbing and jumping. As they gazed deeply into each other's eyes, Oba squeezed with his powerful fingers. In a thick, warm, wet gush, the heart burst. The snake thrashed with the sudden, wild strength of death. But as Oba held the quivering burst heart, each of the snake's movements became progressively more labored, more sluggish, until with one last rolling flip of its tail, it went still.

The whole time, Oba stared into the yellow eyes, until he knew they were dead. It wasn't the same as watching a person die, because it lacked that singular connection of human identity – there were no complex human thoughts with which he could relate – but it was still thrilling to see death enter the living.

He was liking the swamp better all the time.

Victorious and blood-soaked, Oba squatted at the water's edge, washing himself and his knives clean. The entire encounter had been unexpected, rousing, and satisfying, although he had to admit that it was nowhere near as exciting with a snake as it was with a woman. With a woman, there was the thrill of sex added in to the experience, the thrill of having more than his hand inside her as death entered her, too, to share her body with him.

There could be no greater intimacy than that. It was sacred.

The dark water was turned red by the time Oba had finished. The color made him think of Jennsen's red hair.

As he straightened, he checked to make sure he had all his belongings and hadn't lost anything in the struggle. He patted his pocket for the reassuring presence of his hard-earned wealth.

His money purse wasn't there.

In cold panic, he thrust his hand in his pocket, but the purse was gone. He realized that he had to have lost it in the water while struggling with the snake. He kept the purse on the end of a thong he tied to a belt loop so as to be sure it was safe and couldn't be accidentally lost. He didn't see how it was possible, but the knot in the leather thong must have come loose in the struggle.

He turned a scowl on the dead thing slumped in a heap at the base of the tree. In a screaming rage, Oba lifted the snake by the throat and pounded the lifeless head against the tree until the scales started sloughing off.

Panting and drained from the effort, Oba finally halted. He let the bloody mass slip to the ground. Despondent, he decided he would have to dive back into the water and search for his missing money. Before he did, he made one last despairing check of his pocket. Looking closer, he saw, then, that the leather thong he kept tied to his belt loop was still there. It hadn't come undone, after all. He pulled the short length of leather out in his fingers.

It had been cut.

Oba turned, looking back the way he had come. Clovis.

Clovis was always pushing up close, yammering away, like a pesky fly buzzing around him. When Oba had bought the horses, Clovis had seen the money purse.

With a growl, Oba glared back through the swamp. A light rain had begun to fall, making but a whisper against the living canopy of leaves. The drops felt cool on his heated face.

He would kill the little thief. Slowly.

Clovis would no doubt feign innocence. He would beg to be searched to prove he didn't have the missing money purse. Oba figured the man would likely have buried the money somewhere, intending to come back later and retrieve it.

Oba would make him confess. There was no doubt in his mind about that. Clovis thought he was clever, but he had not met the likes of Oba Rahl before.

Striking out back through the swamp to wring the hawker's neck, Oba didn't get far before he stopped. No. It had taken him a good long time to get this far. He had to be close to Althea's by now. He couldn't let his anger rule him. He had to think. He was smart. Smarter than his mother, smarter than Lathea the sorceress, and smarter than a scrawny little thief. He would act out of deliberate intent, not out of blind anger.

He could deal with Clovis when he was finished with Althea.

In a dark mood, Oba started out again toward the sorceress.

Chapter 37

Watching from a distance through the slow fall of rain, Oba didn't see anyone outside the cedar log house that lay beyond the tangled undergrowth and trees. There had been tracks – the boot prints of a man – around the shore of a small lake. The tracks weren't fresh, but they had led Oba up a path to the house. Smoke from the chimney curled lazily in the stagnant humid air.

The house up ahead, almost hidden under trailers of moss and vines, had to be the home of the sorceress. No one else would be fool enough to live in such a miserable place.

Oba crept lightly on the balls of his feet, up the back steps, up onto the narrow porch. Around in front, columns made of thick logs supported a low, overhanging roof. Out beyond the wide front steps lay a broad path – no doubt the way visitors timidly approached the sorceress for a telling.

In the grip of rage, and well beyond any pretense of being polite enough to knock, Oba threw open the door. A small fire burned in the hearth. With only the fire and two little windows, the place was rather dimly lit. The walls were covered with fussy carvings, mostly of animals, some plain, some painted, and some gilded. It was hardly the way Oba chose to carve animals. The furnishings were better than any he had ever grown up with, but not nearly as nice as he had become accustomed to.

Near the hearth, a woman with big dark eyes sat in an elaborately carved chair – the finest of the furnishings – like a queen on her throne, quietly watching him over the rim of a cup as she sipped. Even though her long golden hair was different and she didn't have that hauntingly austere cast to her face, Oba still recognized her features. Looking into those eyes, there could be no doubt. It was Lathea's sister.

Eyes. That was something on one of the mental lists he kept.

'I am Althea,' she said, taking a cup away from her lips. Her voice wasn't at all like her sister's. It conveyed a sense of authority, as did Lathea's voice, yet it didn't have the haughty ring that went with it. She didn't rise. 'I'm afraid you've arrived much sooner than I expected.'

Seeking to quickly nullify any potential threat, Oba ignored her and hurried to the rooms at the rear, checking first the room where he saw a workbench. Clovis had told him that Althea had a husband, Friedrich, and, of course, there had been a man's boot prints outside. Chisels, knives, and mallets were laid out in an orderly fashion. Each could be a deadly weapon in the right hands. The place had the tidy look of work put up for a time.

'My husband is gone to the palace,' she called from her chair by the fire. 'We're alone.'

He checked for himself anyway, looking in the bedroom, and found it empty. She was telling the truth. But for the rain on the roof, the place was quiet. The two of them were indeed alone.

Finally confident that they would not be disturbed, he returned to the main room. Without a smile, without a frown, without worry, she watched him coming toward her. Oba thought that if she had any brains, she should at least be worried. If anything, she looked resigned, or maybe sleepy. A swamp, with its heavy humid air, could certainly make a person drowsy.

Not far from her chair, on the floor off to the side, rested a square board with an elaborate gilded symbol on it. It reminded him of something on one of his lists of things. A pile of small, smooth, dark stones sat to the side on the board. A large red and gold pillow lay near her feet.

Oba paused, suddenly realizing the connection between one of the things on his lists and the gilded symbol on the board. The symbol reminded him of the dried base of a mountain fever rose – one of the herbs Lathea used to put in his cures. Most of Lathea's herbs were already ground up, but that one never was. She would crush a single one of the dried flowers only just before she added it to his cure. Such an ominous conjunction could only be a warning sign of danger. He had been right; this sorceress was the threat he had been concerned she might be.

Fists flexing at his side, Oba towered over the woman as he glared down at her.

'Dear spirits,' she whispered to herself, 'I thought that I would never again have to stare up into those eyes.'

'What eyes?'

'Darken Rahl's eyes,' she said. Her voice carried a thread of some distant quality, maybe regret, maybe hopelessness, maybe even terror.

'Darken Rahl's eyes.' A grin stole onto Oba's face. 'That's very generous of you to mention.'

Not a trace of a smile visited her. 'It was not a compliment.'

Oba's smile curdled.

He was only mildly surprised that she knew he was the Darken Rahl's son. She was a sorceress, after all. She was also Lathea's sister. Who knew what that troublesome woman might have tattled from her eternal place in the world of the dead.

'You're the one who killed Lathea.'

Her words were not so much question as condemnation. While Oba felt confident, because he was invincible, he remained wary. Though he had feared the sorceress Lathea his whole life, she had in the end turned out to be less formidable than he had reckoned.

But Lathea was not the equal of this woman, not by any means.

Rather than answer her accusation, Oba asked a question of his own.

'What's a hole in the world?'

She smiled a private smile, then held a hand out. 'Won't you sit and have some tea with me?'

Oba guessed that he had the time. He would have his way with this woman – he was sure of that. There was no rush to be done with it. In a way he regretted having rushed right into it with Lathea, before he'd thought to get answers to everything, first. Done was done, he always said.

Althea, though, would answer all his questions. He would take his time and be sure if it. She would teach him many new things before they were finished. Such long-anticipated gratification should be savored, not rushed. He cautiously sank into the chair. A pot sat on the simple little table between the two chairs, but there was no second cup.

'Oh, I'm sorry,' she said when she noticed his eyes searching and realized the omission. 'Please go to the cupboard over there and get a cup?'

'You're the hostess of this tea party, why don't you go get it for me?'

The woman's slender fingers traced the spiral curves at the ends of the chair's arms. 'I'm afraid that I'm a cripple. I can't walk. I'm only able to drag my useless legs around the house and do a few simple things for myself.'

Oba stared at her, not knowing if he believed her. She was sweating profusely – a sure sign of something. She was sure to be terrified in the presence of the man powerful enough to do away with her sorceress sister. Maybe she was trying to distract him, hoping to make a run for it as soon as he turned his back.

Althea took her skirt between forefingers and thumbs and lifted the hem in a dainty manner, allowing him to see her knees and a little higher. He leaned over for a look. Her legs were mangled and withered. They looked like they had died ages ago and not been buried. Oba found the sight fascinating.

Althea lifted an eyebrow. 'Crippled, as I said.'

'How?'

'Your father's work.'

Well, wasn't that just something.

For the first time, Oba felt a very tangible connection to his father.

He had had a difficult and trying morning and was entitled to a leisurely cup of tea. In fact, he found the notion provocative. What he had in mind for her would be thirsty work. Oba crossed the room and retrieved the biggest cup from among the collection he found on a shelf. When he set the cup down, she poured it full of a dark thick tea.

'Special tea,' she explained when she noticed the frown on his face. 'It can be terribly uncomfortable here in the swamp, what with the heat and humidity. This helps clear the head, too, after the onus of a morning's difficult tasks. Among other things, it will sweat the weariness from tired muscles – such as from a long walk.'

His head was pounding after his tough morning. Although his clothes were finally dry after his swim, and the blood had all been washed off, he wondered if she could somehow sense the difficult time he'd had. There was no telling what this woman could do, but he wasn't worried. He was invincible, as Lathea's end had proved.

'Your tea will help all that?'

'Oh yes. It's a very powerful tonic. It will cure many problems. You'll see for yourself.'

Oba saw that she was drinking the same thick tea. She was sweating, sure, so he figured she was right about that. She downed the rest of her cupful and poured herself another.

She held her cup up in toast. 'To sweet life, while we have it.'

Oba thought it an odd toast. It sounded almost as if she was admitting that she knew she was about to die.

'To life,' Oba said, lifting his cup to tap against hers. 'While we have it.'

Oba took a gulp of the dark tea. He grimaced at recognizing the taste. It was what the symbol on the board represented – the mountain fever rose. He had learned to identify the bitter taste from the times when Lathea crushed one and added it to his cure.

'Drink up,' his companion said. Her breathing seemed labored. She took a few long swallows. 'As I said, it will solve a lot of problems.' She drained the rest in her cup.

He knew that Lathea, despite her mean streak, sometimes mixed up cures to help sick people. While he'd waited on her to make cures for him and his mother, he had seen her crush up a mountain fever rose in many a concoction she mixed for others. Now, Althea was downing it by the cupful, so she obviously had faith in the distasteful herb, too. Such heavy humidity always gave Oba a headache. Despite the bitter taste, he took another sip, hoping it would help his sore muscles in addition to clearing his head.

'I have some questions.'

'You mentioned that,' Althea said, peering at him from over the rim of her cup. 'And you expect me to provide answers.'

'That's right.'

Oba took another swallow of the heavy tea. He grimaced again. He didn't know why the woman called it 'tea.' There was no 'tea' about it. It was just ground dried mountain fever rose in a little hot water. Her dark-eyed gaze followed as he set the big cup on the table.

The wind had picked up, beating the rain in against the window. Oba guessed he'd made it to her house just in time. Foul swamp. He turned his attention back to the sorceress.

'I want to know what a hole in the world is. Your sister said that you could see holes in the world.'

'Did she now? I don't know why she would say such a thing.'

'Oh, I had to convince her,' Oba said. 'Am I going to have to convince you, too?'

He hoped so. He tingled with the anticipation of getting to the blade-work. But he was in no rush. He had time. He enjoyed playing games with the living. It helped him understand how they thought, so that when the time came and he looked into their eyes, he was better able to imagine what they were thinking as death hovered close.

Althea tilted her head in gesture to the table between them. 'The tea won't help if you don't have enough. Drink up.'

Oba waved off her concern and leaned closer on an elbow. 'I've traveled a long way. Answer my question.'

Althea finally looked away from his glare and used her arms to lower her weight from her chair down onto the floor. It was quite a struggle. Oba didn't offer to help. It fascinated him to watch people struggle. The sorceress pulled herself to the red and gold pillow, dragging her useless legs behind. She worked herself into a sitting position and folded her dead legs up before herself. It was difficult, but she managed with precise and efficient moves that looked well practiced.

All the effort puzzled him. 'Why don't you use your magic?'

She peered up at him with those big dark eyes so filled with silent condemnation. 'Your father did the same to my magic as he did to my legs.'

Oba was stunned. He wondered if his father had been invincible, too. Perhaps Oba had always been meant to be his father's true heir. Perhaps fate had finally stepped in and rescued Oba for better things.

'You mean, you're a sorceress, but you can't do magic?'

As distant thunder rumbled through the swamp, she gestured to a place on the floor. While Oba sat down before her, she dragged over the board with the gilded symbol and placed it between them.

'I was left with only a partial ability to foretell things,' she said. 'Nothing else. If you wished to, you could strangle me with one hand while finishing your tea with the other. I could do nothing to stop you.'

Oba thought that might take some of the fun out of it. Struggle was part of any genuinely satisfying encounter. How much could a crippled old woman struggle? At least there was still the terror, the agony, and witnessing death's arrival to look forward to.

'But, you can still do prophecy? That was how you knew I was coming?'

'In a way.' She sighed heavily, as if the effort of pulling herself to her red and gold pillow had left her exhausted. As she turned her attention to the board before her, she seemed to shrug off her weariness.

'I want to show you something.' She was speaking now like a confidant. 'It may finally explain some things for you.'

He leaned forward expectantly, pleased that she had at last wisely decided to reveal secrets. Oba liked to learn new things.

He watched as she sorted through her little pile of stones. She inspected several carefully before she found the one she wanted. She set the others to the side, apparently in some order she understood, though he thought they all looked the same.

She turned back to him and lifted the single stone up before his eyes. 'You,' she said.

'Me? What do you mean?'

'This stone represents you.'

'Why?'

'It chose to.'

'You mean that you decided it would represent me.'

'No. I mean that the stone decided to represent you – or, rather, that which controls the stones decided.'

'What controls the stones?'

He was surprised to see a smile spread on Althea's face. It grew to a dangerous grin. Not even Lathea had ever managed a look as chillingly malevolent.

'Magic decides,' she hissed.

Oba had to remind himself that he was invincible. He gestured, trying to look unconcerned.

'What about the others? Who are they, then?'

'I thought you wanted to learn about yourself, not others.' She leaned toward him with a countenance of supreme self-confidence. 'Other people don't really matter to you, now do they?'

Oba glared at her private smile. 'I guess not.'

She rattled the single stone in her loose fist. Without looking away from his eyes, she cast the stone down at the board. Lightning flickered. The stone tumbled across the board, rolling to a stop out beyond the outer gilded circle. Thunder rumbled in the distance.

'So,' he asked, 'what does it mean?'

Rather than answer, and without looking down, she scooped up the stone. Her gaze didn't move off his face as she rattled his stone again. Again, and without a word, she cast it at the board. Lightning flashed. Amazingly, the stone came to rest in the same place as it had the first time – not just close to the same place, but in the exact same place. Rain drummed against the roof as a stutter of thunder crackled through the swamp.

Althea quickly swept up the stone and cast it a third time, again accompanied by a flash of lightning, only this time the lightning was closer. Oba licked his lips as he waited for the fall of the stone that represented him.

Goose bumps ran up his arms as he saw the dark little stone roll to a stop in the same place on the board as it had the two previous times. The instant it had halted, thunder boomed.

Oba put his hands on his knees and leaned back. 'Some trick.'

'Not a trick,' she said. 'Magic.'

'I thought you couldn't do magic.'

'I can't.'

'Then how are you doing that?'

'I told you, I'm not doing it. The stones are doing it themselves.'

'Well, then, what's it supposed to mean about me when it stops, there, in that place?'

He realized that somewhere during the stone-rolling, her smile had gone away. One graceful finger, lit by the firelight, pointed down to where his stone lay.

'That place represents the underworld,' she said in a grim voice. 'The world of the dead.'

Oba tried to look only mildly interested. 'What does that have to do with me?'

Her big dark eyes wouldn't stop boring into his soul. 'That's where the voice comes from, Oba.'

Goose bumps flitted up his arms. 'How do you know my name?'

She cocked her head, casting half her face in deep shadow. 'I made a mistake, once, long ago.'

'What mistake?'

'I helped save your life. Helped your mother get you away from the palace before Darken Rahl could find out that you existed and kill you.'

'Liar!' Oba snatched up the stone from the board. 'I'm his son! Why would he want to kill me!'

She hadn't taken her penetrating gaze from him. 'Maybe because he knew you would listen to the voices, Oba.'

Oba wanted to cut out her terrible eyes. He would cut them out. He thought it best, though, if he found out more, first, if he gathered his courage, first.

'You were a friend of my mother?'

'No. I didn't really know her. Lathea knew her better. Your mother was but one young woman among several who were in trouble and a great deal of danger. I helped them, that's all. For that, Darken Rahl crippled me. If you choose not to believe the truth about his intentions toward you, then I leave it to you to please yourself with a different answer of your own devising.'

Oba considered her words, checking them for any connection

they might have to anything on his lists. He didn't find any links right off.

'You and Lathea helped the children of Darken Rahl?'

'My sister Lathea and I were at one time very close. We were both committed, each in our own way, to helping those in need. But she came to resent those like you, offspring of Lord Rahl, because of the agony it caused me to have tried to help. She could not bring herself to witness my punishment and pain. She left.

'It was a weakness on her part, but I knew she could not help having such feelings. I loved her, so I would not beg her to visit me, here, like this, despite how terribly I missed her. I never saw her again. It was the only kindness I could do her – let her run away. I would imagine she did not look kindly upon you. She had her reasons, even if they were misdirected.'

Oba was not about to be talked into any sympathy for that hateful woman. He inspected the dark stone for a time and then gave it back to Althea.

'Those three were just luck. Do it again.'

'You wouldn't believe me if I did it a hundred times.' She handed the stone back. 'You do it. Cast it yourself.'

Oba defiantly rattled the stone in his loose fist, as he had seen her do. She leaned back against her chair as she watched him. Her eyes were getting droopy.

Oba threw the stone down at the board with enough force to be certain that it would roll well beyond the board and prove her wrong. As the stone left his hand, lightning flashed so hard that he flinched and looked up, fearing it was blasting through the roof. Thunder crashed on its heels, shaking the house. The strike felt like it rattled his bones. But then it was over and the only sound was the rain drumming against the undamaged roof and windows.

Oba grinned in relief and looked down, only to see the cursed stone sitting in the exact same place it had come to rest the three times before.

He jumped up as if he'd been bitten by a snake. He rubbed his sweating palms against his thighs.

'A trick,' he said. 'It's just a trick. You're a sorceress and you're just doing magic tricks.'

'You are the one who has done the trick, Oba. You are the one who invited his darkness into your soul.'

'And what if I have!'

She smiled at his admission. 'You may listen to the voice, Oba, but you are not the one. You are merely his servant, no more. He must choose another if he is to bring darkness upon the world.'

'You don't know what you're talking about!'

'Oh, but I do. You may be a hole in the world, but you are missing a necessary ingredient.'

'And what would that be?'

'*Grushdeva.*'

Oba felt the hair at the back of his neck stiffen. While he didn't recognize the specific word, the source was indisputable. The idiosyncratic nature of the word belonged solely to the voice.

'A senseless word. It means nothing.'

She regarded him for a time with a look that he feared because it seemed to hold a world of forbidden knowledge. By the cast of iron resolve in her eyes, he knew that no mere blade would gain that knowledge for him.

'A long time ago, in a faraway place,' she said in her quiet voice, 'another sorceress revealed to me a bit of the Keeper's tongue. That is one of his words, in his primordial language. You would not have heard it unless you were the right one. *Grushdeva*. It means "vengeance." You are not the one he has chosen.'

Oba thought she might be taunting him. 'You don't know what words I've heard or anything about it. I'm the son of Darken Rahl. A rightful heir. You don't know anything about what I hear. I will have power you can only imagine.'

'Free will is forfeit when dealing with the Keeper. You have sold what is yours alone and priceless . . . for nothing but ashes.

'You have sold yourself into the worst kind of slavery, Oba, in return for nothing more than the illusion of self-worth. You have no say in what is to be. You are not the one. It is another.' She wiped the sweat from her brow. 'And, that much of it is yet to be decided.'

'Now you presume to think you can alter the course of what I have wrought? Dictate what shall be?' Oba's own words surprised him. They'd seemed to come out before he thought to say them.

'Such things are not amenable to the likes of me,' she admitted. 'I learned at the Palace of the Prophets not to meddle in that which is above me and ungovernable. The grand scheme of life and death are the rightful province of the Creator and the Keeper.' She seemed contented behind a sly expression. 'But I am not above exercising my free will.'

He'd heard enough. She was only trying to stall, to confuse him. For some reason, he couldn't make his racing heart slow.

'What are holes in the world?'

'They are the end of the likes of me,' she said. 'They are the end of everything I know.'

It was just like a sorceress to answer with a senseless riddle. 'Who are the other stones?' he demanded.

At last, she turned her formidable eyes from him to look down at the other stones. Her movements seemed oddly jerky. Her slender fingers selected one of the stones. As she lifted it, she paused to put her other hand across her middle. Oba realized that she was in pain. She was trying her best to cover it, but she couldn't cover it now. The sweat beading her brow was from pain. The agony came out in a low moan. Oba watched with fascination.

Then, it seemed to ebb some. With great effort she straightened her posture and returned her attention to what she had been doing. She held out her hand, palm up, with the stone sitting in the center.

'This one,' she said, her breathing labored, now, 'is me.'

'You? That stone is you?'

She nodded as she cast it at the board without even looking. The stone tumbled to a stop, this time, without the accompaniment of lightning and thunder. Oba felt relieved, even a little foolish, that he had been so rattled by that before. He smiled, now. It was just a silly board game, and he was invincible.

The stone had come to rest at one corner of the square that lay within the two circles.

He gestured. 'So, what does that mean?'

'Protector,' she managed through a shallow pant.

Her trembling fingers gathered up the stone. She lifted her hand up before him and opened her slender fingers. The stone, her stone, rested in the center of her palm. Her eyes were fixed on his.

As Oba watched, the stone crumbled to ash in her palm.

'Why did it do that?' he whispered, his eyes going wide.

Althea didn't answer. Instead, she slumped and then toppled over. Her arms sprawled out before her, her legs to the side. The ash that had been a stone scattered in a dark smear across the floor.

Oba leaped to his feet. His goose bumps were back. He had seen enough people die to know that Althea was dead.

Rending slashes of thunderous lightning ignited, lacing the sky with violent flashes of light that lanced in through the windows, throwing blinding white light across the dead sorceress. Sweat trickled down his temple and over his cheek.

Oba stood staring at the body for a long moment.

And then he ran.

Chapter 38

Panting and nearly spent from the effort, Oba stumbled out of the thick vegetation into the meadow. He squinted around in the sudden bright light. He was spooked, hungry, thirsty, weary, and in a mood to tear the little thief limb from limb.

The meadow was empty.

'Clovis!' His roar came back to him in an empty echo. 'Clovis! Where are you!'

Only the moan of the wind between the towering rock walls answered. Oba wondered if the thief might be nervous, might be reluctant to come out, worried that Oba might have discovered his fortune missing and suspect the truth of what happened.

'Clovis, come here! We need to leave! I must get back to the palace at once! Clovis!'

Oba waited, his chest heaving, listening for an answer. With fists at his sides, he again bellowed the little thief's name into the cold afternoon air.

When no answer came, he fell to his knees beside the fire Clovis had started that morning. He thrust his fingers into the powdery gray ash. It hadn't rained up in the meadow, but the ashes were ice cold.

Oba stood, staring up the narrow defile through which they had ridden in early that morning. The cold breeze blowing across the empty meadow ruffled his hair. With both hands, Oba ran his fingers back through his hair, almost as if to keep his head from bursting as the awful truth settled in.

He realized that Clovis had not buried the money purse he'd stolen. That had never been his plan. He'd taken the money and run as soon as Oba had gone down into the swamp. He'd run with Oba's fortune, not buried it.

With a sick, empty, sinking feeling, Oba understood, then, the full extent of what had really happened. No one ever went in the swamp by this back way. Clovis had talked him into it and guided him there because he believed Oba would perish in the treacherous swamp. Clovis had been confident that Oba would become lost and the swamp would swallow him, if the monsters supposedly guarding Althea's back didn't snare him first.

Clovis had felt no need to bury the money – he figured Oba was dead. Clovis was gone, and he had Oba's fortune.

But Oba was invincible. He had survived the swamp. He had bested the snake. No monsters had dared come out to challenge him after that.

Clovis had probably thought that even if the swamp didn't finish his benefactor, there were two other mortal dangers he could count on. Althea hadn't invited Oba in; Clovis had probably figured that she would not take kindly to uninvited guests – sorceresses rarely did. And, they had deadly reputations.

But Clovis had not anticipated Oba being invincible.

That left the thief only one safeguard against Oba's wrath, and that one was a problem – the Azrith Plains. Oba was stranded in a desolate place. He had no food. Water was nearby, but he had no means to take it with him. He had no horse. He had even left his wool jacket, unnecessary in a swamp, with the underhanded little hawker. Walking out of this place, without supplies, exposed to winter's weather, would finish anyone who had somehow managed to survive the swamp and Althea.

Oba couldn't make his feet move. He knew that, given his situation, if he struck out and tried to walk back, he would die. Despite the cold, he could feel sweat running down his neck. His head was pounding.

Oba turned and stared back down into the swamp. There would be things back at Althea's house – food, clothing, and surely something in which he could carry water. Oba had spent his life making do. He could make a pack, at least a pack good enough to get him back to the palace. He could put together a supply of food from the sorceress's house. She wouldn't be there alone and crippled without food on hand. Her husband would be back, but maybe not for days. He would have left food.

Oba could wear layers of clothes to keep himself warm enough to make the trek across the bitterly cold plains. Althea said her husband went to the palace. He would have warm clothes to cross the Azrith Plains, and might have left extra clothes at the house. Even if they didn't fit, Oba could make do. There would be blankets he could take in a pack and wear as a cloak.

There was always the possibility, though, that the husband might come back sooner. By the lack of a trail on this side, he would most likely come in the wide path from the other side of the swamp. He could already be there and have discovered his wife's body. Oba wasn't really concerned about that, though. He could deal with the nuisance of a grieving husband. Maybe the man would even be pleased to be out from under the obligation of having to care for a petulant crippled wife. What good was she, anyway? The man should be glad to be rid of her. He might offer Oba a drink to help him celebrate his liberation.

Oba didn't feel like celebrating, though. Althea had pulled some evil trick and denied him the pleasure he had so looked forward to – the pleasure he deserved after his long and difficult journey. Oba sighed at how trying sorceresses could be. At least she could provide him with what he needed in order to get back to his ancestral home.

But when he got back to the People's Palace, he would have no money, unless he could find Clovis. Oba knew that was a thin hope. Clovis had Oba's hard-earned fortune, now, and might well have decided to travel to fine places, wantonly spending his ill-gotten gain. The little thief was likely to be long gone.

Oba didn't have a copper penny. How was he to survive? He couldn't go back to that pauper's life, a life like the one he had had with his mother, not now, not after he had discovered that he was a Rahl – almost royalty.

He couldn't go back to his old life. He wouldn't.

Simmering with anger, Oba plunged back down the spine of rock. It was getting late in the day. He had no time to waste.

*

Oba didn't touch the corpse.

He wasn't at all queasy about the dead. Quite the contrary, the dead fascinated him. He had spent a great deal of time with dead bodies. But this woman gave him the shivers. Even dead, she seemed to watch him as he searched her house, throwing clothes and supplies in a pile in the center of the room.

There was something profane – sinful – about the woman sprawled on the floor. Even the flies buzzing around the room didn't light on her. Lathea had been troublesome, but this woman was different. Althea had pulled some evil trick and denied him the answers he deserved after his long and difficult journey.

Oba fumed at how trying sorceresses could be. At least she could provide him with what he needed in order to get back to his ancestral home. There was something unholy about this woman. She had been able to look right into him. Lathea had never been able to do that. Of course, he had once thought she could, but she couldn't. Not really. This woman could.

She could see the voice in him.

Oba wasn't sure if he was safe around her, even if she was dead. Since he was invincible, it was probably only his fertile imagination, he knew, but a person couldn't be too cautious.

In the bedroom, he found warm wool shirts. They were not nearly large enough, but by ripping out some of the seams a little here, or a little there, he could get them on. Once he was satisfied with his alterations, he threw the item of clothing on the pile. They would be good enough to keep him warm. He added blankets and shirts to the pile in the center of the main room.

Annoyed that the tardy husband hadn't returned, and to distract his mind from the smug dead woman who just lay there watching him work, Oba laid plans to kill someone before he went crazy. Maybe a catty woman. One who had those vicious scowl lines around her eyes like his mother had. He needed to make someone pay for all the trouble he had been through. It wasn't fair. It wasn't.

It was already dark outside. He had to light an oil lamp in order to continue his search. Oba was in luck; in a lower cupboard he found a waterskin. On his hands and knees, he rummaged through a collection of odd scraps of cloth, cups with cracks, broken cooking tools, and a supply of wax and wick. From the back he pulled out a small roll of canvas. He tested its strength and decided he could stitch a pack from it. There was material from clothes around he could use to make straps. A sewing kit was handy enough on a low shelf nearby.

He had noticed that such useful things were on low shelves, where the crippled sorceress with the evil eyes could get to them. A sorceress without magic. Not likely. She was jealous because the voice chose him and not her. She was up to something.

He knew it would take him some time to collect everything and stitch together a pack for his supplies. He couldn't leave at night. It would be impossible to make it out through the swamp at night. He was invincible, not stupid.

With the oil lamp close by, he sat at the workbench and started in on sewing himself a pack. Althea watched him from the floor in the main room. She was a sorceress, so he knew it would do no good to throw a blanket over her head. If she could watch him all the way from the world of the dead, a mere blanket wasn't going to blind her dead eyes. He would just have to be satisfied to have her watch while he worked.

When he had the pack finished and tested to his satisfaction, he set it on the bench and started packing it with food and clothing. She had dried fruit and jerky, along with sausages and cheese. There were biscuits that would be easy enough to carry. He didn't bother with pots or food that had to be cooked because he knew there was nothing on the Azrith Plains from which to build a fire, and he certainly wasn't going to be able to lug firewood along. He'd travel light and swiftly. He hoped it would only take him a few days to reach the palace.

What he would do once he reached the palace, how he would survive without money, he didn't know. He briefly considered stealing it, but rejected the idea; he wasn't a thief and wouldn't lower himself to being a criminal. He wasn't sure how he would get by at the palace. He only knew he had to get there.

When he had finished putting together what he would take, his eyes were drooping and he was yawning every few minutes. He was sweating from all his work, and from the heat of the foul swamp. Even at night the place was miserable. He didn't know how the know-it-all sorceress could stand to live in such a place. No wonder her husband went off to the palace. The man was probably downing ales and moaning to his chums about having to go back to his swamp-wife.

Oba didn't like the idea of sleeping in the same house with the sorceress, but she was dead, after all. He still didn't trust her, though. She might be up to some trick. He yawned again and wiped sweat from his brow.

There were two well-stuffed sleeping pallets close together on the floor in the bedroom. One was neatly made, the other was less orderly. Judging from the tidy workbench, the neatly made bed was likely the husband's, and the other Althea's. Since she was dead on the floor way in the other room, he didn't feel quite so uneasy about sleeping on a nice soft pallet.

The husband wasn't going to be coming home in the dark, so Oba wasn't worried about waking to a madman at his throat. Still, he thought it best if he wedged a chair against the door lever before he retired for the night. With the house all secured, he yawned, ready for bed. On his way by, Oba gave Althea the cold shoulder.

Oba fell right off to sleep, but it was a fitful slumber. Dreams haunted him. It was hot in the swamp house. Since it was winter everywhere else, he hadn't gotten accustomed to such sudden sultry heat. Outside, bugs kept up a steady buzzing while night animals hooted and called. Oba tossed and turned, trying to get away from the sorceress's haunting gaze and knowing smile. They seemed to follow him no matter which way he turned, watching him, not letting him sleep soundly.

He woke for good just after it had begun to get light out

He was in Althea's bed.

In a rush to untangle himself from the covers and escape her bed, he rolled over onto his hands and knees. His weight abruptly pushed his hand through the stuffed bedding. In wild alarm, Oba threw back the bedding and overturned the pallet to see what vile trick she had planted for him. She had known he was coming to see her. She was up to something.

Under where her pallet had been resting, he saw that a floorboard was loose. That was all it was – a floorboard that had pivoted. Oba frowned in suspicion. A close inspection revealed that the plank had pins in the middle so it would seesaw.

With one careful finger, he pushed the sunken end farther down. The other end of the board rose up. A compartment under the board contained a wooden box. He lifted out the box and tried to open it, but it was locked, somehow. There was no hole for a key, and no readily apparent lid, so there was probably some trick to opening it. It was heavy. When he shook it, it made only a muffled sound from inside. It might have simply been a weighted weapon the crippled woman kept under her bed in case she was attacked in the night by a snake or something.

With the box in his meaty hand, Oba shuffled to the workbench. He sat on the stool and leaned close. As he selected a chisel and mallet, he noticed that the sorceress was still on the floor in the other room, watching.

'What's in the box?' he called to her.

Of course she didn't answer. She had no intention of being cooperative. If she had been cooperative, she would have answered all his questions, instead of dropping dead after performing her stone-to-ash trick. It gave him shivers just remembering it. Something about the entire encounter had been more than he wanted to contemplate.

Oba used the chisel to pry on the box. He tested every joint, but it wouldn't open. He hammered on it with the mallet, but he only succeeded in breaking the mallet's handle. He sighed, deciding that it was probably just a weighted weapon Althea kept for defense.

He rose from the bench to go gather his supplies and check that he had everything. He'd had enough of the odd goings-on and the puzzling things she'd left. He needed to be on his way.

Oba paused, then, and turned back at some inner urging. If the heavy box was a weapon, she would have kept it easily at hand. Something about this box was important, or it wouldn't be hidden under a floorboard. Something inside told him so.

Resolving to get into the box, he sat again at the bench and selected a narrower chisel and another mallet. He worked the sharp blade between a lengthwise joint, near the edge. Sweat dripping off the end of his nose, he grunted with the effort of

387

whacking at the end of the chisel handle, trying to open the joint to see if it was just lead weight inside.

All of a sudden, wood split with a loud snap and the box broke open. Gold and silver coins spilled out like guts from a carp. Oba stood staring at the glut of gold heaped on the bench. The box hadn't rattled only because it had been packed full. There was a fortune – a real fortune.

Well, wasn't that just something.

There had to be twenty times as much gold as the little weasel, Clovis, had stolen from him. Oba had thought that poverty had been inflicted upon him by the cowardly little thief, and it turned out he was richer than ever – richer even than his wildest dreams. He truly was invincible. He had suffered through adversity and misfortune that would have defeated a lesser man, and fate had justly rewarded him for all his struggles. He knew that this could be nothing other than divine direction.

Oba smiled across the room at the woman who lay there watching his triumph.

In the drawers of the bench, he found tools kept in pouches. There were three nice leather pouches containing finely crafted beading planes. The leather pouches were probably used to keep the sharp edges on the blades from being dinged and dulled. A cloth pouch held a set of dividers. Another pouch held rosin, while still others held various odd tools. The husband was exceptionally orderly. Life with his swamp-wife had probably driven him mad.

Oba wiped sweat from his eyes and then scooped all the coins together in the center of the bench. He divided them up into equal piles, carefully counting each pile out so he would know exactly how much money he had earned.

Finished counting, he filled the leather and cloth pouches, putting one in each pocket. For safety's sake, he tied each pouch with two thongs going in different directions to different belt loops. He tied a smaller purse around each leg, letting them rest inside the tops of his boots. He opened his trousers and secured several of the heaviest purses inside, where no one could get to them. He reminded himself that he would have to be cautious of passionate ladies with friendly hands, lest they come up with more than he wished to give them.

Oba had learned his lesson. From now on, he wouldn't keep his fortune all together. A man as wealthy as he had to protect his holdings. The world was full of thieves.

Chapter 39

Oba trudged at last into the outer fringes of the open-air market. After the isolation of the barren plains, the raucous swirl of activity was disorienting. Ordinarily, he would be intrigued by all the goings-on, but this time he paid little heed.

He had learned before that rooms could be rented up in the palace. That was what he wanted – to get up into the People's Palace and get himself a proper room. One that was quiet. After some good food and rest to recover his strength, he would buy some new clothes and then have a look around. But now, he only wanted the quiet room and the rest. For some reason, the thought of food sickened him.

It seemed somewhat inappropriate to him that a Rahl should lower himself to renting a room in his own ancestral home, but he would have to deal with that matter later. Now, he just wanted to lie down. His head was pounding. His eyes hurt every time he turned them to look at something, so, as he plodded along with his head hanging, he tried to limit his focus to the patch of dusty ground immediately before his feet.

He had made the long journey from the miserable swamp to the palace by sheer force of will. Despite the cold, he was sweating. He probably had been too wary of the cold weather he would encounter crossing the Azrith Plains and, with all the shirts he was wearing, had overdressed for it. After all, with spring getting closer, it wasn't as cold as it had been in the depths of winter when his lunatic mother had saddled him with the humiliating task of chipping away at mounds of frozen muck.

Oba dug at a wad of cloth bunching uncomfortably under his

armpit. The shirts had been too small for him, so he had had to rip out seams here and there to get them all on. Some of the sleeves had come apart on his long trek across the windswept plain, and had ridden up his arm under the outer layers that now hung like tattered flags. His canvas pack, made in such haste, was coming apart, too, so that the corners of the dark wool blanket hung down, flapping behind him as he walked.

With all the different colors of cloth showing through the various torn layers, and the brown woolen blanket he wore as a cloak, he mused that he must look like a beggar. He was probably wealthy enough to buy the entire market a dozen times over. He would buy some fine clothes later. First, he needed a quiet room and a good long rest.

No food, though. He definitely didn't feel like eating anything. He ached all over – even blinking was painful – but it was his gut that was in particular agony.

When he had been here before, the savory aromas of cooking had made his mouth water. Now the tendrils of smoke from cooking fires nauseated him. He wondered if it was because he had more refined tastes now. He thought that maybe if he went up into the palace, he could get himself something mild to eat. The thought failed to rally his appetite. He wasn't hungry, just tired.

Eyes drooping, Oba slogged onward through the makeshift streets of the open-air market. He aimed himself at the plateau towering over them. The pack on his back felt as if it weighed as much as three good-sized men. Probably some trick of the swamp-witch, some spell she had cast. Knowing he was on his way to her place, she had probably put some magic lead weights in her sausages. The thought of sausages made his stomach roil.

Peering up at the palace shining in the sunlight far overhead as he walked, he accidentally blundered into someone, driving a grunt from their lungs. Oba was just about to kick the annoying obstacle out of his path, when the hunched bundle of rags wheeled to growl a curse.

It was Clovis.

Before Oba could snatch him, Clovis scrambled out from underfoot and dove between two older men passing by. Oba, right behind him, but being wider, knocked the men aside. As the two men fell, Oba staggered through, fighting to keep his balance, and went for the little thief. Clovis skidded to a stop. He looked left then right. Seeing his chance, Oba lunged for the thief draped with tattered clothes, but the slight man was able to cut down another street just in time to slip out of Oba's reaching arms. Oba fell short, capturing only a faceful of dirt and a small flag of cloth from the man's sleeve.

As Oba clambered to his feet, he saw Clovis leap over a fire to the side where people were cooking strips of meat skewered on sticks, and run back between picketed horses. For such a stooped fellow, he could run like smoke in a gale. But Oba was big and strong – and quick. Oba had always prided himself on being light on his feet. He cleared the cook fire with room to spare and ran back between the horses, trying not to lose sight of his prey.

The horses spooked at having men racing recklessly between them. Several panicked animals reared, pulling up lines, and bolted. The man watching them, yelling curses and oaths Oba didn't really hear or care about, jumped out in front of him. His attention fixed on the man he was chasing, Oba clouted the irate fellow out of the way. More horses reared. Without pausing, Oba careered after the thief.

Oba didn't really need his money back. He had a fortune now. He had more money than he could probably ever spend – even if he was only halfway careful. But this was not about money. This was about a crime, a betrayal. Oba had paid the man, trusted him, and he had been cheated for it.

Worse, he had been played for a fool. His mother always told him that he was a fool. Oba the oaf, she always called him. Oba wasn't going to allow anyone to make a fool of him anymore. He wasn't going to allow his smug mother to be proven right.

That Oba had triumphed and come out of the swamp richer than ever was no thanks to Clovis. No, it was thanks only to Oba himself. Just when he thought he was a pauper again, he managed to find the secret to a fortune that was, after all, due him for any number of reasons, the least of which was his long and difficult journey to see Althea, only to have her, too, cheat him out of answers for no more reason than out-and-out meanness.

Clovis had plotted it all out and left him for dead. His intention had been to kill him. The fact that Oba had survived was no thanks to Clovis. The man was a murderer, when you thought about it. A killer. The people of D'Hara would owe Oba Rahl a debt of gratitude after he dealt out swift and just retribution to the wicked little outlaw.

Clovis darted around a corner stand displaying hundreds of items made from sheep's horn. Oba, being heavier, shot past the corner and, as he tried to turn, he slipped on horse manure. Through mighty effort and sheer skill, he managed to keep his balance and remain upright. Oba had spent years in such slop, carrying heavy loads, tending animals, and running when his mother yelled for him. He had had to do it in all kinds of conditions, too, including icy weather.

In a way, all those years of effort had been practice that had prepared Oba for making the corner when no other man his size and weight would have stood a chance. He made it, and in a smooth and swift fashion that was shocking to the thief. As Clovis glanced back with a mocking grin, apparently expecting that Oba was down for sure, he looked stunned to see instead Oba's full weight bearing down on him at full speed.

Clovis, obviously spurred on by the terror of knowing justice itself was descending on him, darted down another of the makeshift streets, a smaller and less peopled byway. But this time, Oba was right there behind him. He snatched the flapping rags at a shoulder, spinning Clovis around. The man stumbled. His arms windmilled awkwardly as he tried to keep his footing and escape at the same time.

Clovis's eyes went wide. First from surprise, and then from the pressure of the hand that had clamped around his throat. Whatever sort of squeal or plea was trying to make its way out didn't get past Oba's vise-like fingers.

Fatigue forgotten, Oba dragged the murderous little thief, kicking and twisting, back between two wagons. The wagons' canvas tops shaded the narrow space between. To the rear of the tight space was a tall wall of crates. Oba's back blocked the constricted opening between the wagon beds, closing off the cramped spot from view as effectively as a prison door.

Oba could hear people behind him going about their business, laughing and talking as they hurried by in the brisk air. Others, in the distance, argued and bargained with merchants over the price of goods. Horses clopped past, their tack jangling. Peddlers plied the streets, calling out the benefits of their wares in a high-pitched singsong, trying to entice buyers.

Only Clovis was silent, but not by choice. The hawker's lying little mouth opened wide trying to say something. But as Oba lifted him clear of the ground and the man's eyes rolled from side to side, it was clearly a scream for help trying unsuccessfully to escape. With his feet kicking only air, Clovis pried at the powerful fingers around his neck. His dirty fingernails broke backward as he clawed in desperation at the iron fist of justice. His eyes grew as big around as the gold marks he had stolen from Oba.

Holding him aloft with one hand, pressing him against one of the heavy wooden crates in the back, Oba searched the man's pockets, but found nothing. Clovis desperately pointed at his chest. Oba felt a lump under the tattered layers of rags and shirt. Ripping the shirt open, he saw his familiar fat purse hanging by a leather thong around the thief's neck.

A mighty pull burned the thong down into the man's flesh until the leather snapped.

Oba slipped his pouch safely back into a pocket. Clovis tried to smile, to make an apologetic face as if to say that everything was square, now.

Oba was long past forgiveness. His head pounded with rage unleashed. Holding Clovis's shoulders up against the heavy wooden crates, Oba rammed his fist up into the little man's gut. Clovis was turning purple. Oba threw a heavy punch into the dirty little face. He felt bone break. He whipped his elbow around and into the lying, conniving little mouth and broke all the front teeth out. Oba growled as he walloped the little weasel with three more rapid blows. With each blow, Clovis's head snapped back, his greasy hair throwing back blood each time the back of his skull whacked the crates.

Oba was furious. He had suffered the indignity of being a helpless victim of a thief who had left him for dead. He had been attacked by a giant snake. He had nearly been drowned. He had been taunted and tricked by Althea. She had looked into his soul without his permission. She had cheated him out of his answers, belittled him for making something of himself, and died before he could kill her besides. He had suffered through a long march across the Azrith Plains dressed in rags – he, Oba Rahl, practically royalty. The utter indignity was humiliating.

He was enraged and aptly so. He could hardly believe that he finally had the object of that rightful anger at hand. He would not be denied just retribution.

Holding Clovis down on the ground, with a knee pressed to the man's chest, Oba at last let the full and rightful rage of vengeance free. He didn't feel the blows any more than he felt the aches and pains he had come down with. He cursed the murderous little thief as he dealt out justice, turning Clovis to a bloody pulp.

Copious sweat poured down Oba's face. He gasped for air as he slugged away. His arms felt like lead. As he became worn out, he felt his head pounding as hard as his fists. He had trouble focusing on the target of his anger.

The ground was soaked with blood. What had been Clovis was no longer remotely recognizable. His jaw was shattered and hung completely unhinged to the side. One eye socket had been altogether caved in. Oba's knee had broken the man's sternum and crushed his chest. It was glorious.

Oba felt hands snatching his clothes and arms, pulling him back. He didn't have the strength left to try to stand. As he was dragged backward from between the wagons, he saw a crowd of people formed in a half circle – all stricken with horror. Oba was pleased by that, because it meant that Clovis had gotten what he deserved. Proper punishment for crimes should horrify people so as to serve as an example. That's what his father would have said.

Oba looked up, closer, at the men hauling him out from between the wagons. A wall of leather armor, chain mail, and steel had poured in to surround him. Pikes and swords and axes glinted in the sunlight. They were all pointing at him. He could only blink, too drained to lift a hand to wave them away.

Exhausted, out of breath, and soaked in sweat, Oba couldn't hold his head up. As he started to sag in the arms of the men holding him, blackness enveloped him.

Chapter 40

In a somber daze, Friedrich used the shovel to steady himself as he sank to his knees. Sitting back on his heels, he let the shovel topple to the cold ground. The chill wind ruffled his hair as well as the long grasses around the freshly turned soil.

His world was ashes.

Dazed with grief, his mind wouldn't focus on any other thought.

A sob overwhelmed him. He worried that he might not have done the right thing. It was cold, here. He worried that Althea would be cold. Friedrich didn't want her to be cold.

But it was sunny, too. Althea loved sunlight. She always said that she liked the feel of the sun on her face. Despite the heat in the swamp, the sunlight rarely made it down to the ground, at least anywhere near where she could see it from her confinement.

To Friedrich, though, her hair was golden sunlight. She would always scoff at such sentiment, but occasionally, if he hadn't mentioned it in a while, she would innocently ask if he thought her hair was brushed enough and looked all right for visitors due for a telling. She always could keep her face blameless when she was angling for what she wanted. Then, he would tell her that her hair looked like sunshine. She would blush like an adolescent girl and say, 'Oh, Friedrich.'

Now, the sun would never shine for him again.

He had considered what to do, and had decided this would be better for her – to be up here, in the meadow, out of the swamp. If he could never take her out of that place in life, at least he could take her out now. The sunny meadow was a better place to lay her to rest than in her former prison.

He would have given anything to have taken her out before, to show her beautiful places again, to see her smile, carefree, in the sunlight. But she could not leave. For everyone else, including him, only the path in the front could be safely traversed. There was no other way past the dark things created of her power. For her, there was not even that safe passage.

Friedrich knew that the dire consequences for anyone who ventured anywhere else in the swamp were not imaginary. Several times over the years, the unwary or the foolhardy had wandered off the path, or tried to make it through the back way, where not even he dared go. It had been torturous for Althea, knowing that her power had ended innocent lives. How Jennsen had made it in the back way unharmed, not even Althea knew.

For her last journey, Friedrich had carried Althea out that back way as a symbol of her freedom reclaimed.

Her monsters were gone. She was with the good spirits, now. Now, he was alone.

Friedrich bent forward in agony, sobbing over her fresh grave. The world was suddenly an empty, lonely, dead place. His fingers clutched at the cold ground covering his love. He felt crushing guilt that he had not been there to protect her. He was sure that if he had been there, she would still be alive. That was all he wanted. Althea alive. Althea back. Althea with him.

He had always delighted in returning home, such as it was, to tell her about any little thing he had seen – a bird skimming over a field, a tree with its leaves shimmering in the sunlight, a road lying like a ribbon over rolling hills, anything that would have brought a little of the world home to her in her prison.

In the beginning, he hadn't talked about the world beyond. He thought that if he told her about the things he had seen outside her swamp, about what was suddenly out of her reach, she would only feel more confined, more isolated, more heartsick. Althea smiled that special smile of hers and said that she wanted to hear every detail of what he saw, because in that way she could deny Darken Rahl his wish to confine her. She said that Friedrich was her eyes, and through them, she could escape her prison. With the descriptions Friedrich brought her, Althea's mind soared up and away from her confinement. In that way, Friedrich helped her deny that vile man his wish that she should never again see the world.

To that extent, Friedrich could feel good about leaving the swamp when she had to remain behind. He wasn't sure who was giving who the gift. Althea was like that – making him think he was doing something for her, when it was she who was really helping him live his life in the best way he could.

Now, Friedrich didn't know what he would do. His life seemed suspended. He had no life without Althea. She was a presence that had given him life, given him himself, made him whole. Without her in his life, life was pointless.

How her life had ended, Friedrich didn't know for sure. The things he'd found made little sense to him. She hadn't been touched, but the house had been ransacked. The strangest things had been taken; their entire lifetime of savings, along with food, a few odd supplies, and old clothing of little worth. Yet, other valuable items were left – gilded carvings, gold leaf, and tools. Try as he might, Friedrich could make no sense or order out of it.

The one thing he did understand was that Althea had poisoned herself. And, there had been another cup. She had tried to poison someone else. Maybe someone who had come for a telling, someone who hadn't been invited.

Friedrich realized, though, that Althea must have been expecting whoever it was and had kept that knowledge from him, encouraging him to make a trip to the palace to sell his gilded carvings. She had seemed somewhat insistent, and he had thought that, since she had invited no visitors, she must have wanted to be alone for a while, which wasn't entirely unusual, or perhaps she was just impatient for him to take a little journey out into the world and see some sights since he hadn't done so in a while. She had held his face in her hands as she kissed him that last time, savoring the feel of him.

Now he knew the truth. That long kiss had been her farewell. She had wanted him safely out of the way.

Friedrich reached in a pocket and pulled out the note she had left him. She sometimes wrote notes for him – things she thought

of while he was away, things she wanted to remember to tell
him. He had checked in the gilded cup he had carved for her,
which she kept down on the floor under her chair behind the
pillow she sat on, and was surprised to find a letter to him.

He carefully unfolded it and read it again, even though he had
read it so many times that he knew every word by heart.

> *My beloved Friedrich,*
>
> *I know that you can't understand right now, but I want
> you to know that I have not forsaken my duty to the
> sanctity of life – rather, I am fulfilling it. I realize it won't
> be easy for you, but you must trust me when I say that I
> had to do this.*
>
> *I am at peace. I have had a long life – longer by far
> than nearly any other person is fortunate enough to have.
> But the best of it was the part I lived with you. I have loved
> you almost since the day you walked into my life and
> awakened my heart. Do not let grief crush your heart; we
> will be together in the next world and for all time.*
>
> *But in this world, you, like me, are one of the four
> protectors – the four stones at the corners on my Grace.
> You remember. You asked who they were and I told you
> that Lathea and I were two of the stones in my last telling.
> I wish I could have told you then that you are one as well,
> but I dared not. I am blind to much of what is happening,
> but with what I do know, I must do what I can or the
> chance for others to live and love would be forever lost.*
>
> *Know that you are always in my heart, and will be even
> when I cross the veil to be with the good spirits.*
>
> *The world of life needs you, Friedrich. Your part in this
> has yet to begin. I beg of you that when you are called
> upon, you will fulfill that purpose.*
>
> *Yours for eternity, Althea.*

Friedrich wiped the tears from his cheeks and then read
Althea's words again. When he read, he could hear her voice in
his head, speaking to him, almost as if she were right there

beside him. He feared to let go of that voice, but at last, he carefully folded the note and returned it to his pocket.

When he looked up, a tall man was standing before him.

'I was an acquaintance of Althea's.' His powerful voice was solemn and earnest. 'I'm terribly sorry for your loss. I came to pay my respects and to offer my sympathy.'

Friedrich slowly rose to his feet, watching the older man's dark azure eyes. 'How could you know? How do you know what happened?' Friedrich's anger rose, too. 'What part have you played in this?'

'The part of a sad witness to that which I cannot change.' The man, much older but vigorous-looking, laid a hand on Friedrich's shoulder, squeezing in a gentle manner. 'I knew Althea from long ago, when she came to study at the Palace of the Prophets.'

'You didn't answer my question. How did you know?'

'I am Nathan, the prophet.'

'Nathan, the prophet . . . Nathan Rahl? Wizard Rahl?'

The man nodded as he took his hand away, letting his arm slip back under the edge of his open, dark brown cape. Friedrich dipped his head out of deference, but couldn't muster the concern to do more, to bow, even if he was in the presence of a wizard, even if this wizard was a Rahl.

The man wore brown wool trousers and high boots, not the robes of a wizard. For the most part, he didn't look like what Friedrich expected of a wizard, and he looked not at all like a man Althea had said was close to a thousand years old. His strong jaw was clean-shaven. His straight white hair was long enough to touch his broad shoulders. He was not stooped with age, but had the fluid posture of a swordsman, though he wore no sword, and the effortless bearing of authority.

His eyes, though, so piercing from under his hawkish brow, were what Friedrich would expect of such a man. They were the eyes of a Rahl.

Friedrich felt a twinge of jealousy. This man knew Althea long before Friedrich had met her, back when she was young and exquisitely beautiful, a sorceress at the prime of her power and ability, a woman sought after, a woman courted by many a great man. A woman who knew what she wanted and went after it with fierce passion. Friedrich wasn't so naive as to believe he was the first man in her life.

'I spoke with her briefly a few times,' Nathan said, as if in answer to questions unspoken, making Friedrich wonder if a man of this ability could also read minds. 'She had an exceedingly talented gift for prophecy – at least for a sorceress. Compared, though, to a true prophet, she was but a child trying to play at adult games.' The wizard softened his words with a kindly smile. 'That is not to discount at all her heart or intellect, but merely to put it into perspective.'

Friedrich looked away from the man's eyes, back to the grave. 'Do you know what happened?' When no answer came, he gazed back up at the tall man watching him. 'And if you knew, could you have stopped her?'

Nathan considered the question for a moment. 'Did you ever know Althea to be able to alter that which she saw when she cast her stones?'

'I guess not,' Friedrich admitted.

A few times, he had held her as she wept with the sorrow of wishing she could change something she saw. She had often told him when he asked about it, or asked what could be done, that such things were not as simple as they seemed to those without the gift. While Friedrich couldn't understand many of the complexities of her ability, he did know that at times the burden of prophecy nearly crushed her with anguish.

'Do you know why she would have done this?' Friedrich asked, hopeful for some explanation that might make the pain more bearable. 'Or who it was that brought her to it?'

'She made the choice of how she would die,' Nathan said in simple summation. 'You must trust that she made that choice of her own free will and for sound reasons. You must understand that what she did was not only done because it was the best for her, and for you, but for others as well.'

'Others? What do you mean?'

'You both know what love brings to life. By her choice, she was doing what she could so that others might have their chance to know life and love.'

'I still don't understand.'

Nathan gazed off distantly as he slowly shook his head. 'I know only bits of what is happening, Friedrich. In this, I feel blind in a way I have never felt before.'

'You mean, this has to do with Jennsen?'

Nathan's brow twitched as his eyes focused abruptly and intently on Friedrich. 'Jennsen?' His voice was laced with suspicion.

'One of the holes in the world. Althea said that Jennsen is a daughter of Darken Rahl.'

The wizard drew back his cape and propped a hand on his hip. 'So, that was her name. Jennsen.' His mouth turned up with a private smile. 'I've never heard that term, hole in the world, but I can see how apt it would seem to a sorceress's restricted gift.' He shook his head. 'Despite her talent, Althea couldn't begin to comprehend what is involved with those like Jennsen. The inability of the gifted to recognize aspects of their existence, and so referring to them as a hole in the world, is but the tail of the bull. The tail is the least important part. "Hole" is not even really accurate. I should think "void" would be better.'

'I'm not so sure you're right about her not comprehending. Althea was involved with those like Jennsen for a long time. She may have been more aware than you realize. She explained to Jennsen and me that she didn't know any more, but that the most important part was that the gifted were blind to them.'

Nathan grunted a short chuckle of respect for the woman buried before them. 'Oh, Althea knew more, much more. This hole-in-the-world business was but window dressing for what Althea knew.'

Friedrich dared not contradict the wizard, for he knew how sorceresses kept secrets, never revealing the true extent of what they knew. Althea did this, too. Even to Friedrich. He knew that it wasn't a lack of respect, or love, but just the way sorceresses were. He couldn't be offended by what was simply her nature.

'So, there is more about those like Jennsen, then?'

'Oh, yes. This bull has horns, not just a tail.' Nathan sighed. 'But despite the fact that I understand much of what Althea did not, even I don't begin to know enough to claim to grasp all of what is truly involved in the events beginning to unfold. This part of prophecy is obscured. I know enough, though, to know that this can alter the very nature of existence.'

'You're a Rahl. How could you not know of such things?'

'At a very young age I was taken away to the Old World by the Sisters of the Light and imprisoned there in the Palace of the Prophets. I am a Rahl, but in many ways I know little of my ancestral homeland of D'Hara. Much of what I know, I learned through books of prophecy.

'Prophecy is silent about those like Jennsen. I only recently have begun to discover why, and the dire consequences.' He clasped his hands behind his back. 'So, this girl, Jennsen, came to see Althea? How did she know of Althea?'

'Yes. Jennsen was the cause of . . .' Friedrich's gaze fell away from the man watching him, not knowing how he would feel about his kinsman, but then he decided to say it, even if it brought the man's wrath. 'When Jennsen was young, Althea tried to help protect her from Darken Rahl. Darken Rahl crippled Althea for it, and imprisoned her in the swamp. He stripped her of her power, except for that of prophecy.'

'I know,' Nathan whispered, clearly in sorrow. 'Although I never knew the causes behind it, I saw some of it foretold.'

Friedrich took a step forward. 'Then why would you not help her?'

This time, it was Nathan's gaze that broke away. 'Oh, but I did. I was imprisoned there at the Palace of the Prophets when she came to see me—'

'Imprisoned for what?'

'Imprisoned for the unjust fears of others. I am a rarity, a prophet. I am feared as an oddity, as a madman, as a savior, as a destroyer. All because I see things others don't. There are times when I cannot help but to try to change what I see.'

'If it's prophecy, how can it be changed? If you changed it, it would be untrue. Then it wouldn't be prophecy.'

Nathan stared off at the cold sky, the wind lifting his long hair back away from his face. 'I could never explain it adequately to one such as you, one ungifted, but I can explain a small part of it in this way. There are books of prophecy going back thousands of years. Those books contain events that have not yet happened.

In order for free will to exist, there must be questions left open. This is done partly through forked prophecies.'

'Forked prophecies? You mean that events could go one of two ways?'

Nathan nodded. 'At the least – often many ways. Key events, anyway. The books will often contain a line of prophecy for several outcomes that could result from free will. When a particular fork proves to be the one that actually takes place, one line of prophecy will be true while others, at that moment, become invalid. Up until then, they were all viable. Had another choice been made, that fork would have turned out to be the valid prophecy. Instead, that branch of prophecy withers and dies, even though the book with that line of prophecy remains. Prophecy is thus tangled with the deadwood of ages past, with all the choices not made, the things that never came to be.'

Friedrich's anger rose again. 'And so you knew what would happen to Althea? You mean you could have warned her?'

'When she came to me, I told her of a fork. I didn't know when she would reach it, but I knew that death waited down both paths. With the information I gave her, she would be able to know when the time was at hand. I had hoped that, somehow, she could find a way around what I saw. Sometimes there are shrouded forks that we are unaware of. I was hoping that was the case this time and she might find it, if it existed.'

Friedrich was incredulous. 'You could have done something! You might have prevented what happened!'

Nathan lifted a hand toward the grave. 'This is the result of trying to change what will be. It does not work.'

'But maybe if—'

Nathan's hawklike glare rose in warning. 'For your own peace of mind, I will tell you this, but no more. Down the other path was a murder so torturous, so bloody, so painful, so violent, that when you discovered what was left of her, you would have ended your own life rather than continue to live with what you had seen. Be thankful that did not happen. It did not happen – not because she feared that death more, but in part because she loved you and didn't want you to suffer that.' Nathan gestured to the grave again. 'She chose this path.'

'This was that fork you told her of, then?'

Nathan's glare softened. 'Not exactly. The fork she took was that she would die. She chose how.'

'You mean . . . she might have chosen another fork, a path in which she would live?'

Nathan nodded. 'For a time. But had she chosen that path, we would all soon be in the Keeper's clutches. Because of those involved, I know only that down that path everything ended. The choice she made was that there would still be a chance.'

'A chance? A chance for what?'

Nathan sighed. Friedrich suspected that the sigh reflected things more grave, more sweeping, than anything Althea had ever seen.

'Althea bought us all time that others might make the right choices when the time comes for them to act of their free will. This knot of forks in prophecy is obscured unlike any other, but most of the threads lead to nothing.'

'To nothing? I don't understand. What could that mean?'

'Existence is at stake.' Nathan's eyebrow lifted. 'Most of those prophecies end in a void, in the world of the dead – for everything.'

'But you can see the way though?'

'The tangle ahead is a mystery to me. In this, I feel helpless. In this, I know what it feels like to be ungifted and blind. In this, I might as well be. I can't even see all of those who are making the critical choices.'

'It must be Jennsen. Maybe if you found her . . . but Althea said the gifted are blind to the ungifted offspring of Darken Rahl.'

'Of any Rahl. The gift is of no use in locating such truly ungifted offspring. There is no telling where they are. Unless you could gather all the people in the entire world and parade them before the gifted, there would be no practical way to detect them with the gift. Physical proximity is the only means for the gift to tell you who they are – because your eyes and your gift don't agree – like when I saw Jennsen by accident.'

'You think, then, that Jennsen is somehow involved in this?'

Nathan threw his cape closed against the bitter wind. 'As far as the prophecies are concerned, those like Jennsen don't even exist. I have no way of telling if there are others, and if there are, how many there might be. I have no idea what part any of them play in this. I know only that they somehow play a pivotal role.

'I know some of what is involved, and some of those who will stand at critical forks in prophecy. As I said, though, many of those forks in prophecy are obscured.'

'But you're a prophet – a true prophet, according to Althea; how could you not know what prophecy says if the prophecy exists?'

Nathan gauged him from behind intent azure eyes. 'Try to understand what I will tell you. It's a concept that few people can grasp. Perhaps it can help you in your grief, for it is the point at which Althea found herself.'

Friedrich nodded. 'Tell me, then.'

'Prophecy and free will exist in tension. They exist in opposition. Yet, they interact. Prophecy is magic, and all magic needs balance. The balance to prophecy, the balance that allows prophecy to exist, is free will.'

'That makes no sense. They would cancel each other.'

'Ah, but they don't,' the prophet said with a sly, knowing smile. 'They are interdependent and yet they are antithetical. Just as Additive and Subtractive Magic are opposite forces, they both exist. They each serve to balance the other. Creation and destruction, life and death. Magic must have balance to function. Prophecy functions by the presence of its counter: free will.'

'You're a prophet, and you're telling me that free will exists, making prophecy invalid?'

'Does death invalidate life? No, it defines it, and in so doing creates its value.'

In the silence, none of it seemed to matter. It was too hard for Friedrich to fathom just then. Besides, it changed nothing for him. Death had come to take Althea's precious life. Her life was all the value he had had. His anguish poured back in to flood everything else. For Friedrich, it had already all ended. There was nothing ahead but blackness.

'I came for another reason,' Wizard Rahl said in a quiet voice. 'I must call upon you to help in this struggle.'

Too tired to stand anymore, too grief-stricken to care, Friedrich sank back to the ground beside Althea's grave. 'You have come to the wrong person.'

'Do you know where Lord Rahl is?'

Friedrich looked up, squinting against the bright sky. 'Lord Rahl?'

'Yes, Lord Rahl. You are D'Haran. You should know.'

'I guess I can feel the bond.' Friedrich gestured off to the south. 'He's that way. But it's weak. He must be a great distance. Greater than I've ever felt of a Lord Rahl in all my life.'

'That's right,' Nathan said. 'He's in the Old World. You must go to him.'

Friedrich grunted. 'I've no money for a journey.' It seemed the easiest reason.

Nathan tossed down a leather pouch. It hit the ground before Friedrich with a heavy muffled clunk. 'I know. I'm a prophet, remember? This is more than was taken from you.'

Friedrich tested the weight of the bag. It was indeed heavy. 'Where did all this come from?'

'The palace. This is official business, so D'Hara will supply you with the money you will need.'

Friedrich shook his head. 'I thank you for coming and offering your sympathy. But I'm the wrong man. Send another.'

'You are the man who is to go. Althea would have known it. She would have left you a letter, telling you that you are needed in this struggle. She would have asked you to accept when called upon. Lord Rahl needs you. I am calling upon you.'

'You know of the letter?' Friedrich asked as he rose to his feet once more.

'It's one of the precious few things I know about in this matter. From prophecy, I know you are the one to go. But you must do so of your own free will. I am calling upon you to do so.'

Friedrich shook his head, this time with more conviction. 'I'm not the one to do this. You don't understand. I'm afraid that I just don't care anymore.'

Nathan drew something out from under his cloak. He held it out. Friedrich saw then that it was a small book.

'Take it,' the wizard commanded, his voice suddenly full and rich with authority.

Friedrich did so, letting his fingers roam the ancient leather cover as he inspected words embossed with gold leaf. There were four words on the cover, but Friedrich had never seen the language before.

'This book is from the time of a great war, thousands of years ago,' Nathan said. 'I only just discovered it in the People's Palace after a frantic search among the thousands of tomes there. As soon as I located it, I rushed here. I haven't had time to translate it, so I don't even know what's written in it.'

'It's all written in a different language.'

Nathan nodded. 'High D'Haran, a language I helped teach Richard. It's vitally important he get this book.'

'Richard?'

'Lord Rahl.'

The way he said those two words gave Friedrich a chill. 'If you've not read it, how do you know it's the right book?'

'By the title, there, on the front.'

Friedrich ran his fingers lightly over the mysterious words. The gilding was still good after all this time. 'May I ask the book's title?'

'*The Pillars of Creation.*'

Chapter 41

Oba opened his eyes, but for some reason that didn't seem to help; he couldn't see. Dismay stiffened him. He was lying on his back, on something like rough cold stone. It was a complete mystery to him as to where he could be or how he had gotten there, but his first and most important concern was that he had somehow gone blind. Trembling from head to foot, Oba blinked, trying to clear his vision, but still he could not see.

A thought worse by far was what really ignited his panic: he wondered if he was back in the pen.

He feared to move and prove the suspicion true. He didn't know how they had done it, but he despaired that those three conniving women – the troublesome sorceress sisters and his lunatic mother – had somehow managed to once again lock him in his dark, childhood prison. They had probably been plotting from beyond the grave, and in his sleep, they had pounced.

Paralyzed by his plight, Oba couldn't gather his wits.

But then, he heard a noise. He turned his eyes toward the sound and saw movement. He realized as things came into focus that it was only some dark room and not his pen, after all. Relief washed through him, followed by chagrin. What had he been thinking? He was Oba Rahl. He was invincible. It would serve him well to remember that.

Though he was relieved to know it wasn't what he had at first feared, prudence kept him cautious; the place felt strange and dangerous. He concentrated, trying to recall what had taken place and how he could have come to be in such a cold dark place, but it wouldn't come to him. His memory was all foggy, just a

410

collection of random impressions; dizzying illness, pounding headache, profound weakness and nausea, being carried, hands everywhere on him, light hurting his eyes, darkness. He felt battered and bruised.

Someone nearby coughed. From another direction, a man grumbled at him to shut up. Oba lay still as a mountain lion, his muscles tensed. He worked at gathering his senses, letting his gaze carefully roam the dark room. It wasn't completely dark, as he had feared at first. On the wall opposite him a weak light, possibly wavering candlelight, came in through a square opening. There were two dark vertical lines in the opening.

Oba's head still pounded, but it was much better than it had been before. He remembered, then, how sick he had been. Looking back on it, he realized that he hadn't even grasped at the time how truly ill he had been. As a youngster he'd had a fever, once. This had been like that, he supposed, a fever. He had probably gotten it visiting Althea, the awful swamp-witch.

Oba sat up, but that made him feel light-headed, so he leaned back against the wall. It was rough stone, like the floor. He rubbed his cold, stiff legs, and then stretched his back. He wiped his knuckles across his eyes, trying to banish the lingering haze in his head. He saw rats, whiskers twitching, nosing along the edge of the wall. Oba was starving, despite the rank stench of the place. It smelled of sweat and urine and worse.

'Look, the big ox is awake,' someone across the room said. The voice was deep and mocking.

Oba peered up and saw men looking at him. Altogether, there were five others in the room with him. They looked a scruffy lot. The man who had spoken, off in the corner to the right, was the only other man beside Oba sitting. He leaned back into the corner as if he owned it. His humorless grin showed that what teeth weren't missing were crooked as could be.

Oba looked around at the other four men standing watching him. 'You all look like criminals,' he said.

Laughter echoed around the room.

'We're all being wrongly persecuted,' the man in the corner said.

'Yeah,' someone else agreed. 'We were minding our own

business when those guards snatched us up and threw us in here for nothing at all. They locked us up like we was common criminals.'

More laughter rang out.

Oba didn't didn't think he liked being in a room with criminals. He knew he didn't like being locked in a room. That felt too much like his pen. A cursory inspection proved his suspicion true, his money was gone. From across the room, under the crack of the door, a rat watched with beady little rat eyes.

Oba looked up from the rat, to the opening with the light. He saw then that the two lines were bars.

'Where are we?'

'In the palace prison, you big ox,' crooked-teeth said. 'Does it look like a proper whorehouse to you?'

The other men all laughed at his joke. 'Maybe the kind he visits,' one of them said, and the rest laughed all the louder. Over to the side, another rat watched.

'I'm hungry. When will they feed us?' Oba asked.

'He's hungry,' one of the standing men said in a taunting voice. He spat in disgust. 'They don't feed us unless they feel like it. You might starve, first.'

Another man squatted in front of him. 'What's your name?'

'Oba.'

'What did you do to get yourself thrown in here, Oba? Rob an old maid of her virginity?'

The men guffawed with him.

Oba didn't think the man was funny. 'I didn't do anything wrong,' he said. He didn't like these. They were criminals.

'So, you're innocent, eh?'

'I don't know why they would put me in here.'

'We heard different,' the man squatting before him said.

'Yeah,' the keeper of the corner agreed. 'We heard the guards talking, saying that you beat a man to death with your bare hands.'

Oba frowned in true bewilderment. 'Why would they put me in here for that? The man was a thief. He left me out in a desolate

412

place to die after he'd robbed me. He only got what was coming to him.'

'Says you,' crooked-teeth said. 'We heard you was probably the one robbing him.'

'What?' Oba was incredulous, as well as indignant. 'Who said that?'

'The guards,' came the answer.

'They're lying, then,' Oba insisted. The men started in laughing again. 'Clovis was a thief and a murderer.'

The laughter cut off. Rats stopped and looked up. They sniffed the air, their noses twitching.

The keeper of the corner sat up straight 'Clovis? Did you say Clovis? You mean the man who sold charms?'

Oba ground his teeth at the memory. He wished he could pound on Clovis some more.

'That's the one. Clovis the hawker. He robbed me and left me for dead. I didn't kill him, I measured out justice. I should be rewarded for it. They can't imprison me for administering justice to Clovis – he deserved it for his crimes.'

The man in the corner rose up. The other men closed in.

'Clovis was one of us,' crooked-teeth said. 'He was a friend of ours.'

'Really?' Oba said. 'Well, I pounded him to a bloody pulp. If I'd have had time, I'd have cut some tender pieces off of him before I mashed his head.'

'Pretty brave, for a big fellow, when it comes to beating a hunched little man who's all alone,' one of the men said under his breath.

Another of the men spat at him. Oba's anger sprang to life. He reached for his knife, but found it missing.

'Who took my knife? I want it back. Which one of you thieves stole my knife?'

'The guards took it.' Crooked-teeth snickered. 'You really are a dumb oaf, aren't you?'

Oba glared up at the man standing in the center of the room, fists at his sides, his crooked teeth making his lips look lumpy. The man's powerful barrel chest rose and fell with each seethed

413

breath. His shaved head made him look to be a troublemaker. He took another step toward Oba.

'That's what you are – a big oaf. Oba the oaf.'

The others laughed. Oba simmered as he listened to the voice counseling him. He wanted to cut the tongues out of these men and then go to work on them. Oba preferred doing such things to women, but these men were earning it, too. It would be fun to take his time and watch them squirm, to make them cry, to watch the look in their eyes as death entered their convulsing bodies.

As the men closed in around him, Oba remembered that he didn't have his knife, so he couldn't have the kind of fun he would have liked to. He needed to get his knife back. He was tired of this place. He wanted out.

'Stand up, Oba the oaf,' crooked-teeth growled.

A rat scurried across in front of him. Oba slapped a hand down on its tail. The rat tugged and twisted, but couldn't get away. Oba snatched the furry thing up in his other hand. It wriggled, wrenching this way and that, trying to escape, but Oba had a good grip on it.

As he stood, he bit off the rat's head. When he had reached his full height, a good head taller than crooked-teeth, he glared into the eyes of the men around him. The only sound was bones crunching as Oba chewed the rat's head.

The men backed away.

Oba, still chewing, went to the door and peered out the barred opening. He saw two guards standing at the intersection of a nearby hall, talking quietly.

'You there!' he called out. 'There has been a mistake! I need to speak with you!'

The two men paused in their conversation. 'Oh yeah? What's the mistake?' one asked.

Oba's gaze moved between the two, but it was not just his gaze. The gaze of the thing that was the voice also watched from within him.

'I am brother to Lord Rahl.' Oba knew that he was saying aloud what he had never said to a stranger before, but he felt compelled to do so. He was somewhat surprised to hear himself go on as everyone watched him. 'I am falsely imprisoned for measuring out justice to a thief, as is my duty. Lord Rahl will not stand for this false imprisonment. I demand to see my brother.' Oba glared at the two guards. 'Go get him!'

Both men blinked at what they saw in his eyes. Without further word, they left.

Oba glanced back at the men locked in with him. As he met each man's eyes in turn, he gnawed a hind leg off the limp rat. They moved aside for him to pace as he chewed, little rat bones crunch, crunch, crunching. He looked out the opening again, but saw no one else. Oba sighed. The palace was immense. It might be some time before the guards returned to let him out.

The men in the room with him silently backed out of the way as Oba went back to his spot against the wall opposite the door and sat down. They stood watching him. Oba watched back as he tore another chunk off the rat with the teeth at the side of his mouth.

They were all fascinated by him, he knew. He was almost royalty. Maybe he was royalty; he was a Rahl. They had probably never seen anyone as important as him before, and were in awe.

'You said they don't feed us.' He waved what was left of the limp rat at their silent stares. 'I'll not starve.' He pulled off the tail and discarded it. Animals ate rat tails. He was hardly an animal.

'You're not just an oaf,' crooked-teeth said in a quiet voice filled with contempt, 'you're a crazy bastard.'

Oba exploded across the room and had the man by the throat before anyone could so much as gasp in surprise. Oba lifted the squealing, kicking, crooked-toothed criminal up to where he could glare eye to eye. Then, with a mighty shove, Oba rammed him against the wall. The man went as limp as the rat.

Oba looked back and saw that the others had backed against the far wall. He let the man slip to the floor, where he moaned as he comforted the back of his shaved head. Oba lost interest. He had more important things to think about than bashing this man's brains out, even if he was a criminal.

He went back to his place and lay down on the cold stone. He had been ill and might not be fully recovered; he had to take care of himself. He needed his rest.

Oba lifted his head. 'When they come for me, wake me up,' he told the four men still silently watching him. It amused him to see how fascinated they were by having nobility in their midst. Still, they were common criminals; he would have them executed.

'There's five of us and only one of you,' one of the men said. 'What makes you think you'll ever wake up again after you close your eyes?' There was no mistaking the threat in his voice.

Oba grinned up at him.

The voice grinned with him.

The man's eyes widened. He swallowed and backed away until his shoulders smacked the wall; then he shuffled sideways. When he reached the far corner, he slid down and pulled his knees up close to himself. Whimpering, tears running down his cheeks, he turned his face away and hid his eyes behind a trembling shoulder.

Oba laid his head down on his outstretched arm and went to sleep.

Chapter 42

Faint footsteps coming from beyond the door woke Oba from his nap. He opened his eyes, but he didn't move or make a sound. The men were peeking out the opening in the door.

When the distant footsteps sounded like they began coming closer, all but one man moved back. The single man remained at the door, standing watch. He stretched up on his toes, gripped the bars, and pressed his face close, trying to get a better look down the hall. Off in the distance, Oba could hear the metallic clangs and echoing squeals of doors being unlocked and pulled opened. The man at the door remained motionless for a time as he watched, then he suddenly stepped back.

'They turned this way – they're coming this way,' he whispered to the others.

All five of the men huddled closer on the far side of the room. Whispers passed among them.

'But what if a Mord-Sith comes in, instead,' one of the men whispered.

'Makes no difference to us,' another man said. 'I know some about their kind. Their magic works to capture those with the gift. It makes them safe from magic, not muscle.'

'But their weapon will still work on us,' the first said.

'Not if we all overpower her and take it away from her,' came the insistent whisper in answer. 'There are five of us. We're stronger and we outnumber her.'

'But what if—'

'What do you think they're going to do with us?' one of the others whispered in a heated voice. 'If we don't take this chance, we're as good as dead in here. I don't see what other chance we have. I say we do it and get away.'

There were nods in turn from each man. Satisfied, they straightened and moved off to different parts of the room, making it appear as if they wanted nothing to do with one another. Oba knew they were up to something.

One man took a quick check out the opening again, then moved away from the door. One of the other men came closer and jostled Oba with the side of his foot.

'They're back. Wake up. You hear?'

Oba moaned, feigning sleep.

The man nudged with his foot again. 'You wanted us to tell you when they came back. Wake up, now.' He stepped away when Oba stirred, yawning and stretching to pretend he was just then waking. The men, all except the one who had already seen more than he wanted to see in Oba's eyes, glanced his way before they settled on a spot to stand. While they waited, they struck slouching poses, trying hard to appear detached and disinterested.

Down the passageway, two people spoke in words Oba couldn't quite make out, but he could hear their voices well enough to tell that their brief conversation was no more than businesslike. The footsteps finally stopped just outside the door. A key turned in the lock. The clang from the bolt as it snapped back echoed through the hall. The men cast quick glances to the door. Outside, a man grunted with the effort of a strong tug. The door grated as it yielded, admitting more light.

Oba was astonished to see a woman silhouetted in the doorway.

Outside, in the hall, the big guard with her used the candle from a holder on the wall to light his lamp. While the woman stood just inside the door, casually appraising the men to each side, the guard brought the lamp into the room and hung it on the wall to the side. The lamp threw harsh light across the men's faces and revealed the grim impenetrable reality of the confines of the rough-hewn stone room.

Oba saw then, too, what a truly mean and nasty-looking lot the men were. With cunning animal eyes glinting out from the shadows, they all watched the woman.

In the bleak lamplight, Oba saw that she was wearing the strangest outfit he had ever seen – skintight red leather. Tall and shapely, she wore her long blond hair in a single braid. Something dangled from a thin chain around her right wrist as her hand rested on her hip. Though she was not taller than the men, her commanding presence alone made her seem to tower, like some austere fury come to judge the living in their last hours.

Her scowl was as dark with displeasure as any Oba's mother had ever worn.

But Oba was even more astonished to see her signal with a casual flip of her hand, dismissing the guard who had unlocked the door. If it surprised Oba, it didn't faze the guard. After a last glance around at the men, he pulled the heavy door closed behind himself and locked it. Oba could hear the guard's boots against the stone floor as he departed back down the hall.

The woman's cool scrutiny swept over the men around her, appraising each, dismissing each, until at last her glare descended on Oba. Her piercing stare carefully studied his face.

'Dear spirits . . .' she whispered to herself at what she saw in his eyes.

Eyes.

Oba grinned. He knew she recognized that he was telling the truth about his paternity. She could see in his eyes that he was the son of Darken Rahl.

Eyes.

Understanding suddenly clicked into place for him like a knife into its sheath.

And then, bellowing like animals, the men all leaped toward her. Oba expected her to cry out in fright, or scream for help, or at least flinch. Instead, she stood her ground and casually met their attack.

Oba saw some kind of red rod, the one he had seen before hanging near her hand, spin up into her fist. As the first man reached her, she rammed the rod against his chest, pushing him back with a twist of her wrist. He dropped like a hay bale out of the loft – thud, onto the stone floor.

Nearly at the same time, the others pounced from all directions in a flurry of flailing arms and fists. The woman sidestepped, effortlessly avoiding the trap of meaty arms as it snapped shut. As the men lurched around, hastily trying to renew their attack, she moved with cold grace, meeting each man swiftly and methodically, and with staggering violence.

Without turning, she drove her elbow back into the face of the closest man as he tried to seize her from behind. Oba heard bone crack as his head snapped back, throwing a long string of blood against the wall.

The third man, to the side, was checked by her strange red rod against his neck. He crumpled, holding his throat, crying out in a choking gurgling blubber. Blood frothed at his mouth as he twisted on the floor, reminding Oba of nothing so much as the way the snake in the swamp had wriggled in death. Eluding another lunge, the woman spun away, past and over the man on the floor. As she did so, she hammered the heel of her boot down, smashing his face to finish him.

As she swung around, she delivered three rapid strikes to the neck of the fourth man. His eyes rolled back in his head before he slowly started corkscrewing down. Her leg swept his feet from under him, pitching him face-forward. His forehead smacked the stone floor with a sickening crack.

Her economy of motion, the easy flowing evasion followed by a swift and brutal counterattack, was fascinating to watch.

The last man flew at her with his full weight behind the lunge. She wheeled around, backhanding him across the face so hard that it spun him around like a top. She snatched him by the hair at the back of his head, jerked him from his feet, and with a thrust of that strange red rod into his back, drove him to his knees.

It was crooked-teeth. He shrieked louder than Oba had ever been able to get anyone to shriek. Oba was amazed by her ability to inflict pain. She held crooked-teeth by the hair, on his knees before her, as he screamed in desperate agony, begging for release as he tried without effect to twist away from her. With a knee in his back, along with the red rod, she bent his head back to control him as easily as if he were a child.

And then, as she looked up very deliberately into Oba's eyes, she pressed the red rod against the base of the man's skull. His arms thrashed out in a crazy fashion as his entire body convulsed as violently as if he'd been struck by lightning. He went limp, blood running from his ears. Finished with him, the woman released her fist from his hair and let him pitch forward to the stone floor. It was clear to Oba by the boneless way he fell that he was already dead and didn't feel the heavy impact against the unyielding stone.

It was all over in what seemed like no more than five heartbeats, one for each man killed. Blood everywhere glistened in the light from the lamp. All five men lay sprawled in awkward positions around the room. The woman in red leather wasn't even breathing hard.

She stepped closer. 'Sorry to disappoint you, but you won't escape that easily.'

Oba grinned. She wanted him.

He reached out and grabbed her left breast.

With a grimace of rage, she lashed her strange red rod down on the top of his shoulder, beside his neck.

Oba reached out with his other hand and grabbed her other breast. He gave them a both a firm squeeze as he grinned at her.

'How could you not—' She fell silent as some profound inner understanding suddenly filled her expression.

Oba liked her breasts. They were as nice as any he had ever held. Still, she was quite the unusual woman. He had a feeling that he would learn many new things with her.

Her fist came out of nowhere with deadly speed.

Oba caught it in the palm of his hand. He closed his fingers tight around her fist, squeezing as he twisted it back, turning her around so that her back was arched and her shoulders pressed against him. She rammed her free elbow toward his middle, but he was expecting it and snatched her forearm, using the momentum to wrench it up behind her so he could gather it up with the fingers of his other hand already holding her other arm.

That left him a hand to feel the delights of her feminine form.

He slid his free hand around the front of her waist, in under the leather. She twisted with all her strength, trying to get free. She knew how to use leverage to try to wrench out of an opponent's grip, but her strength wasn't anywhere near up to the task. Oba slipped his hand down the front of her skintight leather pants, feeling her taut flesh.

The vixen drove her heel into his shin. Oba recoiled, crying out, just managing to hold on to her. But then she spun around, ducked under his arms, and broke his grip. Quick as a blink, she was free.

Rather than run, she used her momentum to strike at the side of his neck.

Oba was able to partially deflect the blow at the last possible instant, but it still hurt. More than that, it angered him. He was tired of playing gentle games. He caught her arm, twisting it around until she cried out. He swept his leg around to knock her feet out from under her first, then threw his full weight into her. Oba roughly wrestled her around as they crashed to the floor, landing on top of her, driving the wind from her lungs. Before she could get a breath, he slammed a good punch into her middle. He could see in her eyes how much it hurt her.

He was going to see much more in her eyes before he was done with her.

As they struggled on the floor, Oba had the clear advantage, and used it. He began tearing at her clothes. She had no intention of making it easy, and fought with everything she had. Her fighting, though, was unexpected in Oba's experience. She didn't fight to get away, as other women did. She fought, instead, to hurt him.

Oba knew, then, how desperately she wanted him.

He intended to give her the satisfaction she craved, to give her what she had never been able to get from any man before.

His powerful fingers pulled up on the top of her leather outfit, but it was cinched tight around her middle with a thick overbelt. The back of the outfit was crisscrossed with a web of tight straps and buckles. It was too strong to rip. Oba managed, instead, to strip it up past her ribs. The sight of her flesh ignited him. He fought her hands, her feet, even her head as she tried to butt his face.

Despite her best efforts, he managed to yank and tug the bottom of her tight outfit partway down over the curve of her hips. She struggled ever more violently, trying every move she could to hurt him. He could sense that she wanted him so badly she was hardly able to control herself.

As he was devoting his attention to trying to get her bottom off, her teeth seized his other forearm. The shock of pain stiffened him. Instead of pulling back, he rammed the arm in her teeth at her, smacking the back of her head against the stone. The second whack against the stone floor took a lot of the fight out of her and he was able to free his arm.

Oba didn't want her unconscious. He wanted her awake. He watched her eyes as he rolled on top of her, forcing his knee between her thighs, and was pleased to see by the way she gritted her teeth, the way her eyes tracked his, that she was indeed aware of him.

Cognition was integral to the experience. It was important that she be aware of what was happening to her, of the transformations that would take place in her living body. Aware of death stalking near, waiting, watching. It was essential to Oba that he see all her primal emotions and sensations through her expressive eyes.

He licked the side of her neck, back behind her ear where the fine little hairs felt soft on his tongue. His teeth raked their way back down. Her neck tasted delightful. He knew she liked the feel of his lips and teeth on her, but she had to fight to keep up the pretense, lest he think her promiscuous. It was all part of her game. By the way she struggled, though, he knew how much she itched for him. As he nuzzled her neck, he worked with his other hand to unbuckle his trousers.

'You've always wanted it like this,' he whispered hoarsely, nearly delirious with his lust for her.

'Yes,' she answered, breathlessly. 'Yes, you understand.'

This was new. He had never been with a woman before who was comfortable enough with her own needs to admit them aloud – except through the show of moans and cries. Oba realized that she must be frantic with desire to cast off pretense and confess her true feelings. It drove him crazy with hunger for her.

'Please,' she panted against the shoulder he had pressed to her jaw, holding her head against the floor, 'let me help you.'

This was definitely new. 'Help me?'

'Yes,' she confided urgently up toward his ear. 'Let me help you unfasten your trousers so that you'll be free to touch me where I need it most.'

Oba was eager to oblige her brazen desires. Leaving her to the treasured task of opening his trousers left him free to grope her. She was a delightful creature – a fitting mate to a man like him, a Rahl, almost a prince. He had never had such a wonderfully unexpected and intimate experience. Apparently, knowing that he was royalty drove women delirious with uncontrollable yearnings.

Oba grinned at her shameless need while her covetous fingers fumbled at unbuttoning his trousers. He shifted his weight to give her a little room for her work as he leisurely explored her feminine secrets.

'Please,' she breathed in his ear again as she finally got his trousers undone, 'let me hold you down there? Please?'

She was so hot for him that she had completely abandoned her dignity. He had to admit, though, that it didn't put him off. Biting her neck, he grunted his permission for her to go ahead.

Oba lifted his hips so she could get at the objects of her lewd desire. He moaned with pleasure as she stretched her lithe body to reach down under him. He felt her long cool fingers gathering up his most private parts into her lovely hand.

Driven by his unrestrained passion for her, Oba bit into her sumptuous neck again. She moaned with the feel of his teeth as she urgently collected his sac together in her greedy hand. He would reward her with the slowest death he could give her.

She suddenly wrenched her handful around with such abrupt violence that as Oba jerked up, he went blind with the shock.

The lightning jolt of pain was so acute that he couldn't draw a breath. While he was momentarily immobilized by the trauma, she lunged lower and seized him in a more tenacious grip. Without pause, she mercilessly wrung him even more forcibly the second time. His eyes bulged as he convulsed but once, tenting over her, the spasm fixing his muscles into stiff, stark rigidity. His thinking scrambled. He couldn't hear, see, breathe, or even cry out. He was paralyzed, ironbound in pure agony.

Everything was one long, fiery-sharp, twisting pang. It went on without end. His mouth rounded, trying to scream, but no sound came out. It seemed forever before blurred vision started to return, along with jumbled sounds that filled his ringing ears.

The room suddenly spun wildly. Tumbling across the stone floor, Oba realized he had been kicked in his side hard enough to drive the remaining wind from him. It was a complete mystery to him. He slammed into the wall and flopped to a stop. He had to pull hard several times before he could draw a breath. The pain lancing his side felt like a cow had kicked him, but it was nothing compared to the searing inferno in his groin.

Then Oba saw the guard. The man had come back. That was who had kicked him in the side. Him, not her. She was still sprawled on the floor, her lovely flesh exposed in a teasing manner.

The guard had a sword to hand. He went to one knee near the woman, checking her with quick glances.

'Mistress Nyda! Mistress Nyda, are you all right?'

She groaned as she tottered haltingly to her hands and knees while the man, in a crouch, feet spread, watched Oba. He looked like he feared to help her, to even look at her, but he didn't look to fear Oba. Oba lay back against the wall, gathering his wits as he watched the two of them.

She didn't try to cover her hips, her exposed breasts. Oba knew that she was still game for him, but with the guard there, she couldn't show her feelings. She must be insane with lust for him to have provoked him so by what she had done.

Oba pushed himself up a bit, getting his wind back, as the feeling began returning to his tingling extremities. He watched the woman – Mistress Nyda, the guard had called her – staggering to her feet.

Oba lay still, listening to the voice whispering to him, as he watched sweat run across her skin. She was divine. He still had much to learn from a woman like this. There were pleasures untold yet to come.

Still recovering his strength, Oba rose up, leaning against the wall, watching as she provocatively used the back of one hand to wipe blood from her mouth. With her other hand, she tugged at her leather outfit, trying to cover herself. She was dazed, no doubt by her heady brush with lust, and was unable to get her trembling hands to work right. Having trouble balancing, she staggered sideways a couple of steps. It appeared as if it was all she could do to stand. Oba was surprised that her bones weren't broken, considering their brief but vigorous love tussle. There would be time for that.

Blood trickled from the love bites on her neck. He noticed that her blond hair was matted with blood from when he had banged her head against the stone floor. Oba reminded himself to be mindful of his strength, lest he end it prematurely. That had happened before. He had to be careful; women were delicate.

Oba, still panting to catch his breath, still hobbled by the throbbing ache between his legs, fixed his gaze on the guard. The man had remarkable control to stand there so confidently, considering that he was in the presence of a Rahl.

Their gazes met. The man took a step forward.

The eyes of the voice opened to look at him, too.

The man froze.

Oba grinned.

'Mistress Nyda,' the guard whispered, his eyes staring, fixed on Oba, 'I think you'd better get out of here.'

She frowned at him as she tried to pull her leather up over her shapely hips. She was still having trouble balancing, and trying to tug her outfit back into place wasn't helping.

'We don't want her to leave,' Oba said.

The guard's wide eyes stared.

'We don't want her to leave,' Oba said again, in unison with the voice. 'We can both enjoy her.'

'We don't want her to leave . . .' the guard repeated.

Pausing in her attempt to cover herself, Mistress Nyda looked from the guard to Oba.

'Bring her to me,' Oba commanded, amazed at what the voice

426

could think of, and delighted by the very notion. 'Bring her over here, and we will both have her.'

The woman, still unsteady, followed Oba's gaze to the guard. When she saw his face, she tried to snatch her dangling red rod. The guard seized her wrist, preventing her from getting at it. His other hand swept around her waist. She fought him, but he was a big man, and she was already woozy.

Oba grinned as he watched the guard dragging the struggling Nyda closer. The man's fingers roamed over her exposed flesh as Oba's had done.

'She feels delightful, don't you think?' Oba asked.

The guard smiled and nodded as he wrestled the woman toward the back of the prison cell where Oba and the voice waited.

When they were close enough, Oba reached for her. It was time he finished what he had started. Finished it good.

She seized the guard's clothes in her fists for support. With stunning speed, her whole body twisted in midair. From nowhere, for just an instant, Oba saw the bottom of the heel of her boot flying at his face like a bolt of lightning. Before he could react, the world went black amid a stunning crash of pain.

Chapter 43

Oba opened his eyes to darkness. He was lying on his back, on a stone floor. His face throbbed in pain. He drew his knees up and comforted his aching groin.

That vixen, Nyda, had proven as troublesome as any woman he had ever known. It seemed like he was always being tormented by troublesome women. They were all jealous of him, of his importance. They were all trying to keep him down.

Oba was getting weary of waking up in cold dark places, too. He had hated the way, throughout his life, he was always waking up in some confined place. They were always hot or cold. No place he had ever been locked in was ever comfortable.

He wondered if his lunatic mother, or the troublesome sorceress, Lathea, or her swamp-witch sister had something to do with this. They were selfish, and certain to be bent on revenge. This had all the markings of a vindictive act by that pompous trio.

But they were dead. Oba wasn't entirely certain that death protected him from those three harpies. They were devious in life; death wasn't likely to have reformed them.

The more he thought about it, though, he had to admit that this was most likely entirely the doing of that vixen in red leather, Nyda. She had cleverly pretended to be dizzy and disoriented until the guard had brought her close enough to strike, and then she had kicked him. She was something. It was hard to hold a grudge against a woman who wanted him so badly. The thought of not having Oba exclusively probably drove her to it. She wanted to be alone with him. He supposed he couldn't blame her.

Now that he had publicly acknowledged his royal standing, Oba had to recognize that there would be women of such intense passions who would want what he had to offer. He had to be prepared to live up to the demands of being a true Rahl.

Groaning in pain, Oba rolled over. With the aid of his hands, pushing first against the floor and then a wall, he was finally able to lever himself upright. His own discomfort would only heighten the pleasures of the eventual conquest of his concubine. He had learned that somewhere. Maybe the voice had told him.

He saw a small slit of light, much smaller than the opening in the door in the last place, but it at least helped him get his bearings. Feeling along the cold stone walls, he began to take stock of the room. Almost immediately he came to a corner. He moved his hand sideways from the corner, along the rough stone of the wall, and was alarmed when he shortly come to another corner. With increasing urgency, he traced the walls and was horrified to discover how tiny the room was. He must have been lying corner to corner, for it wasn't large enough for him to lie down any other way.

The suffocating terror of such a small place welled up, threatening to smother him. He couldn't get his breath. He pressed a hand to his throat, trying mightily to pull a breath. He was certain he would go mad being confined in such a small pen.

Maybe it wasn't Nyda, after all. This did have all the marks of his insidious mother's doing. Perhaps she had been watching from the world of the dead, gleefully conniving, plotting how she could harass him. The troublesome sorceress had probably helped her. The swamp-witch had no doubt butted in to offer her assistance. Together, the three women had managed to reach out from the world of the dead and help the vixen Nyda lock him back in a tiny place.

He raced around the cramped little room, feeling the walls, terrified that they were shrinking in toward him. He was too big to be in such a small room where he couldn't even breathe. Fearing he might use up all the air in the room and then slowly suffocate, Oba threw himself against the door and pressed his face up against the opening, trying to suck in the outside air.

Weeping with self-pity, Oba wanted nothing so much at that moment as to bash his lunatic mother's head in all over again.

After a time, he listened to the voice counseling him, reassuring him, calming him, and began gathering his wits. He was smart. He had triumphed over all those who had conspired against him, despite how evil they were. He would get out. He would. He had to pull himself together and act up to his station in life.

He was Oba Rahl. He was invincible.

Oba put his eyes up to the slit to peer out, but he could see little more than another dim space beyond. He wondered if maybe he was in a box inside a box, and for a time he pounded at the door, screaming and crying at the terror of such a sinister torture.

How could they be so cruel? He was a Rahl. How could they do this to an important person? Why would they treat him this way? First, they locked him up as a common criminal, in with the scum of humanity, for doing the right thing and dispensing justice to rid the land of a lawless thief, and now this wicked persecution.

Oba concentrated, putting his mind to something else. He remembered then the look on Nyda's face when she had first gazed into his eyes. She had recognized him for who he was. Nyda had known the truth, that he was the son of Darken Rahl, just by looking into his eyes. Small wonder she had wanted him so badly. He was important. Selfish people were like that; they wanted to be near those who were great, and then they wanted to keep them down. She was jealous. That was why he was locked up – petty jealousy. It was as simple as that.

Oba pondered that look in Nyda's eyes when she had first seen him. The look of recognition on her face had sparked memories that enabled him to put odd bits together. He mulled over the new thing he had learned.

Jennsen was his sister. They were both holes in the world.

It was too bad she was kin; she was seductively beautiful. He thought her ringlets of red hair were quite bewitching even if he

430

worried that they might signify some magical ability. Oba sighed as he pictured her in his mind. He was too principled to consider her as a lover. They shared the same father, after all. Despite her ravishing looks and the way thinking of her made his groin wake, if painfully, his integrity wouldn't allow such a breach of decency. He was Oba Rahl, not some rutting animal.

Darken Rahl had fathered her, too. That was a wonder. Oba wasn't sure what he thought about that. They shared a bond. The two of them stood against a world of jealous people who wanted to keep them from greatness. Lord Rahl sent quads to hunt her, so she would have no loyalty there. Oba wondered if it could be that she might be a valuable ally.

On the other hand, he recalled the anxiety in her eyes when she looked at him. Maybe she recognized in his eyes who he was – that he, too, was the son of Darken Rahl, like she was. Maybe she already had plans of her own that didn't include him. Maybe she was upset that he existed. Maybe she, too, would be an adversary, intent on having it all for herself.

Lord Rahl – their own brother – wanted to keep them down because they were both important, that much seemed likely. Lord Rahl didn't want to share all the riches that rightfully belonged to Jennsen and Oba. Oba wondered if Jennsen would be as selfish. After all, such selfish tendencies seemed to run in the family. How Oba had avoided that wicked aspect of heritage was a wonder.

Oba felt his pockets, recalling as he did so that he had done the same thing when he had been in the other room with the criminals, but his pockets were empty. Lord Rahl's people had stripped him of his wealth before locking him away. They had probably taken it for themselves. The world was full of thieves, all after Oba's hard-earned wealth.

Oba paced, as best he could in such a confined place, trying not to think of how small it was. All the while he listened to the voice advising him. The more he listened, the more things made sense to him. More and more items on the mental lists he kept began falling into place. The grand tapestry of lies and deception that had so afflicted him knitted itself together into a broader picture. And, solutions began to solidify.

His mother had known all along, of course, how important Oba really was. She had wanted to keep him down from the first. She had locked him in his pen because she was jealous of him. She was jealous of her own little boy. She was a sick woman.

Lathea had known, too, and had conspired with his mother to poison him. Neither had the bold nerve to simply do away with him. They weren't that kind. They both hated him for his greatness, and enjoyed making him suffer, so their plan from the first appeared to have been to poison him slowly. They called it a 'cure' so as to soothe their guilty consciences.

All along, his mother wore him down with menial chores, treated him with contempt, heaped endless scorn on him, and then sent him to Lathea to retrieve his own poison. Loving son that he was, he had gone along with their devious plans, trusting in their words, their instructions, never suspecting that his mother's love was a cruel lie, or that they might have a secret plan.

The bitches. The conniving bitches. They had both gotten what they deserved.

And now Lord Rahl was trying to hide him, to deny to the world that he existed. Oba paced, thinking it through. There was too much he still didn't know.

After a time, he calmed and did as the voice told him; he went to the door and put his mouth near the opening. He was, after all, invincible.

'I need you,' he spoke into the darkness beyond.

He didn't shout the words – he didn't have to, because the voice inside added to his own would make it carry.

'Come to me,' he said into the quiet emptiness outside the door.

Oba was surprised by the calm confidence – the authority – in his own voice. His endless talents amazed him. It was only to be expected that those less endowed would resent him.

'Come to me,' he and the voice spoke into the empty darkness beyond.

They had no need to yell. The darkness effortlessly bore their voices, like shadows traveling on wings of gloom.

432

'Come to me,' he said, bending unsuspecting inferior minds to his will.

He was Oba Rahl. He was important. He had important things to do. He couldn't stay in this place and play their petty games. He had had enough of this nonsense. It was time to assume the mantle of not just his birthright, but his special nature.

'Come to me,' he said, their voices oozing through the dark cracks of the deep dungeon.

He kept calling, not loudly, for he knew they could hear him, not urgently, for he knew they would come, not desperately, for he knew they would obey. Time passed, but did not matter, for he knew they were on their way.

'Come to me,' he murmured into the still darkness, for he knew that a softer voice yet would draw them in.

Off in the distance, he heard the faint answer of footsteps.

'Come to me,' he whispered, enthralling those beyond to listen.

He heard a door in the distance grate open. The footsteps grew louder, closer.

'Come to me,' he and the voice cooed.

Closer still, he heard men shuffling along a stone floor. A shadow in the dim light fell across the small opening in the door beyond.

'What is it?' a man asked, his echoing voice tentative.

'You must come to me,' Oba told him.

The man hesitated at so pure and innocent a declaration.

'Come to me, now,' Oba and the voice commanded with deadly authority.

As Oba listened, the key in the far lock turned. The heavy door rasped open. A guard stepped into the space between the doors. The shadow of the other guard filled the outer doorway. The guard edged closer to the small slit where Oba waited on the other side. Wide eyes peered in.

'What do you want?' the man asked in a hesitant voice.

'We wish to leave, now,' Oba and the voice said. 'Open the door. It is time for us to go from here.'

The man bent forward and worked at the lock until the bolt snapped back with a metallic clang that echoed in the darkness.

The door pulled back, squeaking on rusty hinges. The other man stepped up behind him, looking in with the same lifeless expression.

'What would you like us to do?' the guard asked, his eyes unblinking as he stared into Oba's eyes.

'We must leave,' Oba and the voice said. 'You two will guide us out of here.'

Both guards nodded and turned to lead Oba away from the dark pen. He would never again be locked in confining little places. He had the voice to help him. He was invincible. He was glad that he had remembered that.

Althea had been wrong about the voice; she was just jealous, like all the others. He was alive, and the voice had helped him. She was just dead. He wondered how she liked that.

Oba told the two guards to lock the doors of his empty cell. That would make it more likely that it would be a while before he was discovered missing. He would have a small head start to escape Lord Rahl's greedy grasp.

The guards led Oba through a labyrinth of narrow, dark passageways. The men moved with unerring steps, avoiding those halls where Oba could hear men talking in the distance. He didn't want them to know he was leaving. Better if he simply slipped away without a confrontation.

'I need my money back,' Oba said. 'Do you know where it is?'

'Yes,' one of the guards said in a dead voice.

They went through iron doors and onward through passageways lined with coarse stone blocks. They turned down a passageway where there were men in cells to each side, coughing, snickering, cursing through the openings in the doors. When they approached the row of doors, filthy arms reached out, clawing the air.

As the somber guards, carrying lamps, led the way down the center of the wide hall, men grabbed for them, or spat at them, or cursed them. As Oba passed, the men all fell silent. The arms drew back in through the openings. Shadows trailed behind Oba like a dark cape.

The three of them, Oba and his escort of two guards, reached a small room at the bottom of narrow twisting stairs. One guard led Oba up the stairs while the other followed. At the top, they took him into a locked room, and then through another locked door.

The lamps the guards carried in cast angular shadows through the rows of shelves heaped with things; clothing, weapons, and various personal possessions, everything from canes to flutes to puppets. Oba scanned the shelves crammed with odd things, stooping to look low, stretching up on his tiptoes to check the upper shelves. He guessed that all these things were taken from prisoners before they were locked away.

Near the end of one row, he spotted the handle of his knife. Behind the knife was a mound of the tattered clothes that he had taken from Althea's house so that he could make it across the Azrith Plains. His boot knife was there, too. Piled in front were the cloth and leather pouches containing his considerable fortune.

He was relieved to have his money back. He was even more relieved to once again curl his fingers around the smooth wooden handle of his knife.

'You two will be my escorts,' Oba informed the guards.

'Where shall we escort you?' one asked.

Oba mulled over the question. 'This is my first visit. I wish to see some of the palace.' He restrained himself from calling it his palace. That would come in time. For now, there were other matters that must come first.

He followed them up stone stairwells, through corridors and past intersections and myriad flights of stairs. Patrolling soldiers, off in the distance, saw his guards and paid little attention to the man between them.

When they came to an iron door, one of his guards unlocked it and they stepped through into a corridor beyond with a polished marble floor. Oba was taken by the splendor of the hall, the fluted columns to the sides, and the arched ceiling. The three of them marched onward, around several corners lit by dramatic silver lamps hung in the center of marble panels.

The hall turned again to open into a grand courtyard of such staggering beauty that it cast the hall they had been in, that had been the finest place Oba had ever seen, as little more than a pigsty by contrast. He stood motionless, his mouth hanging, as he stared out at a pool of water open to the sky, with trees – trees – growing on the other side, as if it were a woodland pond. Except that this was indoors, and the pond was surrounded by a low benchlike enclosure of polished rust-colored marble, and the pond was lined with blue glazed tiles. There were orange fish gliding through the pond. Real fish. Real orange fish. Indoors.

In his whole life Oba had never been so struck dumb by the grandeur, the beauty, the sheer majesty of a place.

'This is the palace?' he asked his escorts.

'Only a tiny part of it,' one answered.

'Only a tiny part,' Oba repeated in astonishment. 'Is the rest as nice as this?'

'No. Most places are much more grand, with soaring ceilings, arches, and massive columns between balconies.'

'Balconies? Inside?'

'Yes. People on different levels can look down on lower levels, down on grand courtyards and quadrangles.'

'On some levels vendors sell their wares,' the other man said. 'Some areas are public areas. Some places are quarters for soldiers, or staff. There are some places where visitors may rent rooms.'

Oba took this all in as he stared at the well-dressed people moving through the place, at the glass, marble, and polished wood.

'After I've seen some more of the palace,' he announced to his two big, uniformed D'Haran escorts, 'I will want a quiet and very private room – luxurious, mind you, but someplace out of the way where I won't be noticed. I will first want to purchase some decent clothes and some supplies. You two will stand watch and make sure that no one knows I'm here while I have a bath and get a good night's rest.'

'How long will we be watching you?' the other man asked. 'We will be missed if we're away for too long. If we're gone even longer, they will search for us and find your cell empty. Then they will come looking for you. They will soon know you are here.'

Oba considered. 'Hopefully, I can leave tomorrow. Will you be missed by then?'

'No,' one of the two said, his eyes empty of everything but the desire to do Oba's bidding. 'We were just leaving at the end of our guard watch. We shouldn't be missed before tomorrow.'

Oba smiled. The voice had chosen the right men. 'By then, I'll be on my way. But until then, I should enjoy my visit and see some of the palace.'

Oba's fingers glided over the handle of his knife. 'Maybe tonight, I might even like the company of a woman at dinner. A discreet woman.'

Both men bowed. Before he left, Oba would leave the two as nothing more than a stain of ashes on the floor of a lonely passageway. They would never tell anyone why his cell was empty.

And then . . . well, it was nearly spring, and in spring, who could tell where his fancy might turn?

One thing for sure, he was going to have to find Jennsen.

Chapter 44

Jennsen's astonishment was wearing off. She was becoming numb to the sight of the endless expanse of men, like some dark flood of humanity across the bottomland. The vast army had churned the broad plain between the rolling hills to a drab brown. Inestimable numbers of tents, wagons, and horses were crowded in among the soldiers. The drone of the horde, cut through with yelling, hoots, calls, whistles, the rattle of gear, the clatter of hooves, the rumble of wagons, the ringing rhythm of hammers on steel, the squeals of horses, and even occasional odd cries and screams of what almost sounded to Jennsen like women, could be heard for miles.

It was like gazing down on some impossibly huge city, but without buildings or pattern, as if all of man's ingenuity, order, and works had magically vanished, with the people left behind reduced to near savages under the gathering dark clouds, trying to make do against the forces of nature and having a grim time of it.

Nor was this the worst of the conditions Jennsen had seen. Several weeks before and farther to the south, she and Sebastian had passed through the very place where the army of the Imperial Order had wintered. An army of this size wore heavily on the land, but she had been shocked at how much worse it was when they stopped for any length of time. It would be years before that vast, festering wound in the landscape healed.

Worse still, throughout the long harsh winter, men by the thousands had fallen ill. That dismal place would be forever haunted by an endless expanse of haphazardly placed graves marking those left behind when the living had marched on. It was horrifying to see such a staggering loss of life to sickness; Jennsen feared to imagine the far worse carnage to come in the battle for freedom.

With the frost finally out of the ground, the muddy soil had dried and firmed enough that the army had at last been able to strike out from those befouled winter quarters, to start their drive toward Aydindril, the seat of power in the Midlands. Sebastian had told her that the force they brought up from the Old World was so huge that while the leading edge was stopping here to set up camp, it would be hours before those at the tail end caught up and halted for the night. In the morning, the head of the great army would have to start off, stretching itself out, long before the end could have room to begin to move.

While their spring march north was not yet swift, their advance was inexorable. Sebastian said that once the men smelled their prey, their pulse, and their pace, would quicken.

It was a terrible shame that Lord Rahl's greed for conquest and rule made this all necessary, that such a peaceful valley should be given over to men at war. With spring, the grasses were at last coming back to life, so that the hills rising up to each side of the valley looked as if they were covered in living green velvet. Forests took over on the steeper slopes beyond the hills. In the distance, off to the west and north, stone peaks still wore heavy mantles of snow. Headwaters swollen with the snowmelt roared down the rocky slopes, and, farther to the east, emptied into a mighty river that meandered out into a great, lush plain. The dirt there was so black, so fertile, that Jennsen imagined even rocks planted there might sprout roots and grow.

Before she and Sebastian had come upon the vast stain of the army, the land had been as beautiful as any Jennsen had seen in all her life. She longed to explore those enchanting forests, and fancied she could contentedly spend the rest of her life among such timber. It was hard for her to cast the Midlands as a place of evil magic.

Sebastian had told her that those woods were dangerous places where beasts roamed, and where those who wielded magic lurked. With the things she was learning, she was almost tempted

439

to risk it. She knew, though, that even in those trackless and seemingly endless forests, Lord Rahl would still find her. His men had already demonstrated their ability to locate her in even the most remote areas; her mother's murder was only the first proof of that. Ever since that terrible day, his merciless assassins had somehow been able to hound her up through D'Hara and halfway across the Midlands.

If Lord Rahl's men caught her, they would take her back to the dungeons where Sebastian had been held, and then Lord Rahl would have her tortured endlessly before he granted her a slow, agonizing death. Jennsen could have no safety, no peace, as long as Lord Rahl pursued her. She intended to catch him, instead, and seize a life for herself.

Another clot of sentries spotted her and Sebastian riding over the open ground and moved down the slope from their observation post at the top of a hill to intercept them. When she and Sebastian were closer, and the men saw his spikes of white hair and the casual salute he gave them, they turned and swarmed back up the hill to their campfire and cooking their dinner.

Like the rest of the Imperial Order army she had seen, the men were a rough-looking lot, in tattered clothes, furs, and hides. Down in the broad valley, many sat around small campfires outside little tents made of hides or oiled canvas. Most looked to have been set up wherever their owners had found enough space, rather than to any order. Randomly set among the tents were local command centers, mess tables, arms stockpiles, supply wagons, paddocks packed with livestock or horses, tradespeople laboring, and even blacksmiths working at transportable forges. Scattered here and there were small trading markets where men gathered to barter or buy small goods.

There were even agitated, angry, rawboned men standing among the throngs preaching to smatterings of vacant onlookers. What exactly the men were preaching, Jennsen couldn't hear, but she had seen men preach before. According to her mother, the tempestuous body language prophesying doom and proselytizing salvation was as unmistakable as it was unchanging.

As they rode closer in to the immense encampment, she saw

men at their tents occupied with everything from laughing and drinking to working at cleaning weapons and gear. Some men stood in crooked lines, arms thrown over the next fellow's shoulders, singing songs together. Others cooked by themselves, while still others crowded around mess areas, waiting to be fed. Some men were occupied with chores and tending animals. She saw some men gambling and arguing. The entire place was dirty, smelly, noisy, and frighteningly confusing.

As uncomfortable as she had always felt around crowds, this looked more terrifying even than a fevered nightmare. Descending toward the churning mass of humanity, she wanted to run in the opposite direction. Only her single, burning reason for being there, and nothing else, kept her from doing so.

She had reached the brink within, and crossed over. She had embraced the need to kill and resolved with cold deliberate calculation to do it. There could be no turning back.

The uniforms the soldiers wore were not that – uniform – but seemed to be a mismatched collection of leather set with spikes, fur, chain mail, wool cloaks, hides, and filthy tunics. Almost all the burly men she saw were unshaven, grimy, grim. It was readily apparent why Sebastian was so easily recognized and why no one ever challenged him, yet she remained awed at how, without fail, every man who laid eyes on him gave him a salute. Sebastian stood out like a swan among maggots.

Sebastian had explained how difficult it was to amass a huge army to defend their homeland and what an arduous undertaking it was to send them on such a long journey. He said that they were men far from home with a grisly job to do; they couldn't be expected to look presentable for womenfolk or pause in their life-and-death battles to be mannerly and make tidy camps. These were fighting men.

So were D'Haran soldiers. These men certainly didn't look anything like D'Haran soldiers looked, nor were they as disciplined, but she didn't say so.

Jennsen could understand, though. As hard as she and Sebastian had been traveling, all the while taking precautions to evade Lord Rahl's men by riding until they nearly dropped with exhaustion, often backtracking and working hard at making false trails, she had little time to worry about looking her best. Added to that, it had been a long and difficult journey across mountains in winter. It often rankled her that Sebastian should see her with her hair all tangled, when she was as filthy and sweaty as her horse and smelling no better. Still, he never seemed fazed by her all too often unkempt appearance. Rather, he usually seemed ignited by the mere sight of her, and often wanted nothing so much as to do whatever he could to please her.

The previous day they had taken a shorter route across hill country in order to make their way toward the head of the army, and had come across an abandoned farmhouse. Sebastian had indulged her wish to stay there for the night, even though it was early to make camp. After bathing and washing her long hair in the old tub in the tiny washroom, she put the water to use to wash out her clothes. Sitting before the warm fire Sebastian had built in the hearth, Jennsen brushed her hair as it dried. She was nervous about meeting the emperor and wanted to look presentable. Sebastian, leaning back on an elbow, watching her before the flickering glow of flames, had smiled that wonderful smile of his and said that even if she went unwashed and with tangled hair, she would be the most beautiful woman Emperor Jagang had ever seen.

Now, as they rode along the fringes of the Imperial Order encampment, her stomach was in knots, even if her hair was not. From the looks of the turbulent clouds moving in past the mountains to the west, a spring storm would be on them before long. Off above distant valleys, lightning flickered through the dark clouds. She hoped the rain didn't arrive to drench her hair and dress right before meeting the emperor.

'There,' Sebastian said, leaning forward in his saddle to point. 'Those are the emperor's tents, and those of his important advisors and officers. Not far beyond, up the valley, will be Aydindril itself.' He looked over with a grin. 'Emperor Jagang hasn't moved to take the city yet. We've made it in time.'

The huge tents were an imposing sight. The largest was oval, its tripeaked roof pierced by three lofty center poles. The tent's sides bore brightly colored panels. Standards and tassels hung from the eaves. High atop the three poles, colorful yellow and red banners flapped in the gusty wind, while long pennants streamed out, undulating like airborne serpents. The emperor's congregation of tents stood out among the drab little quarters of the regular soldiers the way a king's palace towered over surrounding huts.

Jennsen's heart raced as they urged their horses down into the thick of the encampment. Both Rusty and Pete, their ears alert, snorted their misgivings about entering such a noisy and busy place. She urged Rusty ahead in order to take Sebastian's hand when offered it.

'Your hand is all sweaty,' he said, smiling. 'You aren't nervous, are you?'

She was water at a boil, a horse at a gallop. 'Maybe a little,' she said.

But her purpose stiffened her will.

'Well, don't be. Emperor Jagang will be the one to be nervous, meeting such a beautiful woman.'

Jennsen could feel her face heat. She was about to meet an emperor. What would her mother think of such a thing? As she rode, she considered how her mother, as a young servant girl on the palace staff – a nobody – must have felt when she met Darken Rahl himself. Jennsen could, for the first time, truly begin to empathize with the enormity of such an event in her mother's life.

As she and Sebastian trotted their horses into camp, men everywhere peered Jennsen's way. Mobs of men crowded closer to see the woman riding in. She saw that there were a number of soldiers with pikes forming a rough line along their route, holding back the press of men. She realized that the guards were clearing the way and preventing any of the more celebratory men from getting too close.

Sebastian watched her as she took note of the way the soldiers opened a clear path for them.

'The emperor knows we're coming,' he told her.

'But how?'

'When we encountered scouts a few days ago, and then sentries this morning as we got closer, they would have sent runners on ahead to inform Emperor Jagang that I've returned, and that I'm not alone. Emperor Jagang would want to insure the safety of any guest I would bring.'

It appeared to Jennsen that the guards were meant to keep the great mass of regular soldiers away from the two of them. She thought it an odd thing to do, but by the drunken nature of some of the soldiers, and the rough looks and leering grins of others, she couldn't say that she was sorry about it.

'The soldiers look so . . . I don't know . . . brutish, I guess.'

'And as you are about to plunge your knife into Richard Rahl's heart,' Sebastian said without pause, 'do you intend to curtsy and say please and thank you so that he will see how well mannered you are?'

'Of course not, but—'

He turned his halting blue eyes on her. 'When those brutes came into your house and butchered your mother, what sort of men would you have wished were there to protect her?'

Jennsen was taken aback. 'Sebastian, I don't know what that has to do—'

'Would you trust dressy soldiers with polished leather and polite manners – like some pompous king would have at a fancy dinner party – to be the ones to make a desperate last stand protecting your beloved mother against the onslaught of vicious killers? Or would you want men even more brutish to be the ones to stand before your mother, protecting her life? Wouldn't you want men steeped in the most brutal traditions of combat, to be the ones standing between her and those savage men intent on killing her?'

'I guess I see what you mean,' Jennsen admitted.

'These men are serving in that role for all their loved ones back in the Old World.'

The unexpected encounter with that terrible memory was so chilling, so painful, that she had to work at putting it out of her mind. She felt humbled, too, by Sebastian's heated words. She was here for a reason. That reason was all that mattered. If the men arrayed against Lord Rahl's forces were tough and mean, so much the better.

It wasn't until they reached the heavily defended compound around the emperor's tents that Jennsen saw other women. They were an odd mix, from young-looking to some who were stooped with age. Most peered curiously, some frowned, and a few even appeared alarmed, but all watched as Jennsen rode closer.

'Why do the women all have rings through their lower lip?' she whispered to Sebastian.

His gaze swept the women near the tents. 'As a sign of loyalty to the Imperial Order, to Emperor Jagang.'

Jennsen thought it not just a strange way to show loyalty, but disquieting. Most of the women wore drab dresses, most had unkempt hair. Some were dressed a little better, but only a little.

Soldiers took the horses when they dismounted. Jennsen stroked Rusty's ear and whispered reassuringly to the nervous animal that it was all right to go with the stranger. Once Rusty was calmed, Pete contentedly followed her toward the stable area. Parting from her constant companion of so long unexpectedly reminded Jennsen of how she missed Betty.

The women moved farther into the background as they watched, as if fearing to get too close. Jennsen was used to such behavior; people feared her red hair. It was a rare warm spring day, and it had intoxicated Jennsen with the promise of more such days. She had forgotten to put her hood up as they came close to the encampment. She started, then, to put it up, but Sebastian's hand stayed her arm.

'It's not necessary.' With a tilt of his head, he indicated the women.

'Many of them are Sisters of the Light. They don't fear magic, only strangers entering the emperor's compound.'

Jennsen realized then the reason for the strange looks from a number of the women; they were gifted and saw her as a hole in the world. Their eyes were seeing her, but their gift was not.

Sebastian wouldn't be aware of that. She had never told him exactly what Althea had explained about the gifted and the offspring of a Lord Rahl. Sebastian had, on more than one occasion, shown a condescending disgust in the details of magic. Jennsen had never felt entirely comfortable talking to him about the specifics of what she had learned from the sorceress, and the even more important things she had figured out on her own. It was all difficult enough for her to reconcile in her own mind, and

445

seemed too personal to reveal to him unless the time and circumstances were right. They never seemed to be.

Jennsen forced a smile at the women watching from the shadows of the tent. They stared back.

'Why is the emperor insulated from his men, and guarded?' she asked Sebastian.

'With this many men, you can never be absolutely certain that one isn't an infiltrator, or even a deranged madman, who might try to make a name for himself by harming Emperor Jagang. Such a foolish act would deprive us all of our great leader. With so much at risk, we have to take precautions.'

Jennsen supposed she could understand. After all, Sebastian himself had been an infiltrator in the People's Palace. Had he come across an important man there, he could have done harm. The D'Harans were troubled by such a threat. They had even arrested the right man.

Fortunately, Jennsen had been able to get him out. *How* she had been able to accomplish such a thing was part of what she had finally come to terms with, but could never find the right time to share with Sebastian. She didn't think he would understand, anyway. He probably wouldn't even believe such a far-fetched notion.

Sebastian's arm circled her waist and drew her onward toward two huge, silent men standing guard outside the emperor's tent. Stepping between the two after they bowed their heads to him, Sebastian lifted aside a heavy doorway curtain covered with gold and silver medallions.

Jennsen had never even imagined, much less seen, such a lavish tent, but what she saw as she stepped inside was far more opulent than even the outside suggested. The ground was entirely covered with a variety of rich carpets laid every which way. An assortment of woven hangings decorated with exotic scenes and elaborate designs defined the space. Delicate glass bowls, fine pottery, and tall painted vases sat on the polished tables and chests around the room. To the side there was even a tall glass-fronted bureau filled with painted plates displayed on stands. Colorful pillows in a variety of sizes rimmed the floor. Overhead, openings covered with sheer silk let in muted light.

Scented candles shimmered everywhere, while all the carpets and hangings imposed a quiet hush to the air. The place felt sacred.

There were women inside, each wearing the ring through her lower lip, busily going about duties. While most appeared absorbed in their work, one of the women, polishing a collection of tall, delicate vases in a measured, methodical manner, coolly watched Jennsen out of the corner of her eye. She was middle-aged, broad shouldered, and wore a simple floor-length dark gray dress buttoned to her neck. Her gray and black hair was loosely tied back. For the most part, she appeared unremarkable, except for the knowing, self-satisfied smirk that seemed enduringly etched in her face. That look gave Jennsen pause.

As their eyes met, the voice stirred, calling Jennsen's name in that haunting, dead whisper, calling for her to surrender. For some reason, Jennsen was momentarily suffused with the icy sense that the woman knew that the voice had spoken. Jennsen dismissed the odd notion, deciding that it was merely due to the woman's expression, which exuded a demeanor of stark superiority.

Another woman busied herself brushing at the carpets with a small hand broom. Yet another was replacing candles that had guttered. Other women – some sure to be Sisters of the Light – hurried in and out of rooms beyond, tending to the collection of pillows, lamps, and even flowers in vases. One thin young man wearing only baggy cotton trousers worked with a comb ordering the fringe of the carpets set before openings into back rooms. Except for the brown-eyed woman polishing the tall vases, they were focused on their work and none paid any particular notice that visitors had entered the emperor's tent.

Sebastian's arm held her securely as he guided her deeper into the dimly lit room. The walls and ceiling moved and billowed slightly in the wind. Jennsen's heart could have pounded no harder were she being led to her own execution. When she realized that her fingers were tightening around the hilt of her knife to check if it was clear in its scabbard, she forced herself to let her hand drop away from it.

Near the back of the room sat an ornately carved and gilded

447

chair draped with streamers of red silks. Jennsen swallowed when she finally made herself look at the man sitting there, his elbow on the arm of the chair, his chin held by his thumb, his forefinger resting along the side of his face.

He was a thick-necked bull of a man. Flickering candlelight reflecting off his shaved head lent the illusion that he wore a crown of tiny flames. Two long, thin braids of mustache grew down from the corners of his mouth, and another braid grew from the center of his chin. Fine gold chain connected the gold rings through his left nostril and ear, while a collection of much heavier, jeweled chains rested in the cleft of muscles on his powerful chest. Each meaty finger was studded with a large ring. The lamb's-wool vest he wore had no sleeves, revealing his hefty shoulders and brawny arms. While he didn't appear tall, his muscled mass was nonetheless imposing.

But it was his eyes that, despite Sebastian's cautionary description, had her holding her breath. No words could have prepared her for being in the presence of the real thing.

His inky eyes had no whites, no irises, no pupils, leaving only glistening dark voids. Yet somber shapes shifted across those dark voids, like thunderclouds at midnight. Despite his having no irises or pupils, she was certain beyond any doubt that he was looking directly and intently at her.

Jennsen thought her knees might buckle.

When he smiled at her, she was sure of it.

Sebastian's arm tightened, helping hold her up. He bowed slightly from the waist.

'Emperor, I am thankful that the Creator has watched over you and kept you safe.'

The smile widened. 'And you, Sebastian.' Jagang's voice matched the look of him, husky, powerful, menacing. He sounded as if he were a man who brooked no weakness or excuses. 'It has been a long time. Far too long. I'm glad to have you back with me.'

Sebastian bowed his head toward Jennsen. 'Excellency, I have brought an important guest. This is Jennsen.'

Despite Sebastian's arm around her waist, holding her, she slipped free and went to her knees of her own accord and before trepidation imposed it. She used the occasion to bow forward until her head nearly touched the floor. Sebastian hadn't told her that she was supposed to do so, but she felt an overwhelming fear that it was what she must do. If nothing else, it momentarily relieved her of the obligation of looking into those nightmare eyes.

She supposed that a man like this, a warrior who hoped to prevail against the invading force from D'Hara, had to be a man of brute strength, iron command, and grim tenacity. Being the emperor of a people hoping to be saved from the threatening shadow of enslavement was a job for a man no less than the one she knelt before.

'Your Excellency,' she said in a trembling voice toward the floor. 'I am at your service.'

She heard a booming laugh. 'Come, now, Jennsen, no need for that.'

Jennsen felt her face going scarlet as she rose with Sebastian's jovial insistence and help. Neither the emperor nor Sebastian took note of her embarrassment.

'Sebastian, where did you ever find such a lovely young woman?'

Sebastian's blue eyes beheld her with pride. 'It's a long story for another time, Excellency. For now, you must know that Jennsen has come to an important determination, one that will bear on us all.'

Jagang's inky gaze returned to Jennsen in a way that made her heart seem to rise up into her throat. He wore the slightest smile, the smirk of an emperor looking down indulgently on a nobody.

'And what would that determination be, young lady?'

Jennsen.

An image of her mother lying on the floor of their house, bleeding, dying, flashed into Jennsen's mind. She would never forget her mother's last precious moments of life. The agonizing grief of having to flee without even being able to care for and bury her mother's body still burned unabated in her soul.

Jennsen.

Rage flooded in to overwhelm any nervousness at answering an emperor's question.

'I intend to kill Lord Rahl,' Jennsen said. 'I have come to ask for your help.'

In the dead silence, any trace of mirth evaporated from the Emperor Jagang's face. He watched her with cold, dark, merciless eyes, his brow set in warning. This was clearly a subject that tolerated no humor. Lord Rahl had invaded this man's homeland, killed untold thousands of his people, and set the whole world to war and suffering.

Emperor Jagang the Just, the muscles in his jaw flexing, waited, clearly expecting her to explain herself.

'I am Jennsen Rahl,' she said in answer to his dark glare. She drew her knife, gripped the blade in her rock-steady fist, and thrust the handle up before him on his throne, showing him the ornate letter 'R,' the symbol of the House of Rahl.

'I am Jennsen Rahl,' she repeated, 'Richard Rahl's sister. I intend to kill him. Sebastian told me that you may be able to provide me some help to that end. If you can, I would be eternally in your debt. If you cannot, then tell me now, for I still intend to kill him and will need to be on my way.'

Elbows on the arms of his red-silk-draped throne, he leaned toward her, holding her in his nightmare gaze.

'My dear Jennsen Rahl, sister to Richard Rahl, for a task such as this, I would lay the world at your feet. You have but to ask, and anything within my power shall be yours.'

Chapter 45

Jennsen sat close to Sebastian, drawing comfort from his familiar presence, yet wishing they could instead be alone by a campfire frying up fish or cooking beans. She felt more alone at the emperor's table, with servants hovering all about, than she'd ever felt by herself in the silence of a forest. Without Sebastian there, laughing and talking, she didn't know what she would have done, how she would have behaved. She was uncomfortable enough around regular people; this was far more unnerving.

Emperor Jagang was a man who, without effort, fluidly dominated the room. Although he never broke his gracious, courtly manner with her, in some inscrutable way, he made her feel that every breath she took had been granted her only by his grace. He referenced momentous matters offhandedly, without realizing he was doing it, so common were such responsibilities, so sure his unflinching rule. He was a mountain lion at rest, sleek and poised, tail swishing lazily, licking his chops.

This was not an emperor who was content to sit safely by, back in some remote palace, and receive reports; this was an emperor who led his men into the thick of battle. This was an emperor who dug his hands down into the bloody muck of life and death and pulled out what he wanted.

Though it seemed an extravagant dinner for what was, after all, an army on the march, it was still the emperor's tent and table, and reflected that fact. There was food and drink in abundance, everything from fowl to fish, beef to lamb, wine to water.

As servants, focused on their tasks, rushed in and out with

steaming platters of beautifully prepared food, treating her like royalty, Jennsen was struck with a sudden gut-wrenching glimpse of how her mother, as a lowly, obscure, humble young woman, must have felt as she sat at Lord Rahl's table, as she saw such tempting variety and abundance as she had never imagined, while at the same time trembling at being in the presence of a man with the power to sentence death, without pausing his meal.

Jennsen had little appetite. She pulled dainty strips of meat off of the succulent piece of pork sitting before her on a thick slab of bread, and nibbled as she listened to the two men talk. Their conversation was trivial. Jennsen sensed that when she was not around, the two men would have much more to say to each another. As it was, they spoke of acquaintances and caught up on inconsequential matters that had taken place since Sebastian had left the army the previous summer.

'What of Aydindril?' Sebastian asked at last as he stabbed a slice of meat on the point of his knife.

The emperor twisted a leg off a crispy goose. He planted his elbows on the edge of the table as he leaned forward and gestured vaguely with his prize. 'I don't know.'

Sebastian lowered his knife. 'What do you mean? I remember the lay of the land. You are but a day or two away.' His voice was respectful, but clearly concerned. 'How can you march in without knowing what awaits in Aydindril?'

Jagang tore a big bite off the fat end of the goose leg, the bone spanning the fingers of both hands. Grease dripped from the meat, and from his fingers.

'Well,' he said at last, waving the bone over his shoulder before casting it aside on a plate, 'we sent scouts and patrols to have a look, but none returned.'

'None of them?' Concern put an edge on Sebastian's voice.

Jagang picked up a knife and sliced off a chunk of lamb from a platter to the side. 'None,' he said as he stabbed the piece of meat.

With his teeth, Sebastian eased the bite off his knife and then set the blade down. He rested his elbows on the edge of the table and folded his fingers together as he considered.

'The Wizard's Keep is in Aydindril,' Sebastian said at last in a quiet voice. 'I saw it, when I scouted the city last year. It sits on the side of a mountain, overlooking the city.'

'I remember your report,' Jagang answered.

Jennsen wanted to ask what a 'Wizard's Keep' was, but not enough to break her silence while the men talked. Besides, it seemed somewhat self-evident, especially by the ominous tone in Sebastian's voice when he said it.

Sebastian rubbed his palms together. 'Then may I ask your plan?'

The emperor flicked his fingers in command. All the servants vanished. Jennsen wished she could go with them, go hide under her blanket and be a proper nobody again. Outside, thunder rumbled and occasional gusts of wind drove fits of rain against the tent. The candles and lamps set about the table lit the two men and the immediate area, but left the soft carpets and walls in near darkness.

Emperor Jagang glanced briefly at Jennsen before directing his inky gaze to Sebastian. 'I intend to move in swiftly. Not with the whole army, as I believe they will expect, but with a small enough force of cavalry to be maneuverable, yet large enough to maintain control of the situation. Of course we will take a sizable contingent of the gifted.'

In the span of those brief words, the mood had turned deadly serious. Jennsen sensed that she was silent witness to the pivotal moments of a momentous event. It was frightening to think of the lives that hung in the balance of the words these two men spoke.

Sebastian weighed the emperor's words for a time before speaking. 'Do you have any idea how Aydindril wintered?'

Jagang shook his head. He pulled a chunk of lamb off the point of his knife and spoke as he chewed.

'The Mother Confessor is many things; stupid is not one of them. She would have known for a long time, by the direction of our push, by the movements she's observed, by the cities that have already fallen, the path we have chosen, by all the reports and information she would have gathered, that with spring I will move on Aydindril. I've given them a good long time to sweat as they ponder their fate. I suspect that by now they're all shaking in their boots, but I don't think she has the heart to flee.'

'You think that Lord Rahl's wife is there?' Jennsen blurted out in astonishment. 'In the city? The Mother Confessor herself?'

Both men paused and gazed at her. The tent was silent.

Jennsen shrank. 'Forgive me for speaking.'

The emperor grinned. 'Why should I forgive you? You've just stuck a knife in the prize goose and called it true.' With his blade, he gestured toward Sebastian. 'You brought a special woman, a woman with a good head on her shoulders.'

Sebastian rubbed Jennsen's back. 'And a pretty head, at that.'

Jagang's black eyes gleamed as he watched her. 'Yes, indeed.' His fingers blindly scooped olives from a glass bowl to the side. 'So, Jennsen Rahl, what is your thinking about all this?'

Since she had already spoken, she couldn't now decline to answer. She gathered herself and considered the question.

'Whenever I was hiding from Lord Rahl, I would try not to do anything that would let him know where I was. I tried to do everything I could to keep him blind. Maybe that's what they are doing, too. Trying to keep you blind.'

'That's what I was thinking,' Sebastian said. 'If they're terrified, they might try to eliminate any scout or patrol in order to make us think that they're more powerful than they are and to conceal any defensive plans.'

'And keep at least some element of surprise on their side,' Jennsen added.

'My thought, too,' Jagang said. He grinned at Sebastian. 'Small wonder you would bring me such a woman – she is a strategist, too.' Jagang winked at Jennsen, then rang a bell to the side.

A woman, the one in the gray dress and tied-back gray and black hair, appeared at a distant opening. 'Yes, Excellency?'

'Bring the young lady some fruits and sweetmeats.'

As she bowed and left, the emperor turned serious again. 'That's why I believe it best to take a smaller force than they are sure to expect, one able to maneuver quickly in response to what defenses they try to catch us up in. They may be able to overpower our small patrols, but not a sizable force of cavalry and gifted. If need be, we can always pour men into the city. After a winter of sitting on their behinds, they would be more than happy to be unleashed. But I'm reluctant to start out with what those in Aydindril are expecting.'

Sebastian was idly poking a thick slab of roast beef with his knife as he considered. 'She might be in the Confessors' Palace.' He redirected his gaze to the emperor. 'The Mother Confessor very well might have decided to make her stand at long last.'

'I think so, too,' Emperor Jagang said. Outside, the spring storm had picked up, the chill wind moaning among the tents.

Jennsen couldn't restrain herself. 'You really think she will be there?' she asked both men. 'You honestly think she would remain there when she knows you're coming with an enormous army?'

Jagang shrugged. 'I can't be sure, of course, but I've battled her all the way up through the Midlands. In the past, she had options, choices, tough though they sometimes were. We drove her army into Aydindril just before winter, then sat at her doorstep. Now, she and her army have run out of choices, and, with the mountains all around, places to flee. Even she knows that a time comes when the choice you are given must be faced. I think this may be where she chooses to at last stand and fight.'

Sebastian stabbed a portion of meat. 'It sounds too simple.'

'Of course it does,' Jagang said, 'that's why I must consider that she may have decided to do it.'

Sebastian gestured north with the red piece of meat on the point of his blade. 'She may have pulled back into the mountains, and left only enough men to take out scouts and patrols, to keep you blind, as Jennsen suggested.'

Jagang shrugged. 'Possibly. She is a woman who is impossible to predict. But she's running out of places to pull back to. Sooner or later there will be no ground left. This may not be her plan, but, then again, it might be so.'

Jennsen hadn't realized that the Old World had made such progress at throwing back the enemy. Sebastian, too, had been away a long time. Matters, for the Old World, were not nearly so bleak as she had thought. Still, it sounded a great risk to take based on such thin conjecture.

'And so you're willing to gamble your men on such a battle, hoping she will be there?'

'Gamble?' Jagang sounded amused by the suggestion. 'Don't you see? It isn't really a gamble at all. Either way, we have nothing to lose. Either way, we will have Aydindril. In so doing, we finally cleave the Midlands, thus cleaving the entire New World in two. Cleave and conquer is the path to victory.'

Sebastian licked the blood from his knife. 'You know her tactics better than I and are better able to predict what her next will be. But, as you say, whether she decides to stand with her people, or leaves them to their fate, we will have the city of Aydindril and the seat of power in the Midlands.'

The emperor stared off. 'That bitch has killed hundreds of thousands of my men. She has always managed to stay one step ahead of me, to stay out of my grip, but all the while she was backing toward the wall – this wall.' He looked up in cold rage. 'May the Creator grant that I have her at last.' His knuckles were white around the handle of his knife, his voice a deadly oath. 'I will have her, and I will settle the score. Personally.'

Sebastian measured the look in the emperor's dark eyes. 'Then perhaps we are near to the final victory – in the Midlands, at least. With the Midlands won, the fate of D'Hara will be sealed.' He held his knife up. 'And if the Mother Confessor is there, then Lord Rahl very well might be, too.'

Jennsen, thoughts tumbling through her mind, looked from Sebastian to the emperor. 'You mean, you think that her husband, Lord Rahl, is there, too?'

Jagang's nightmare gaze turned toward her as he grinned wickedly. 'Exactly, darling.'

Jennsen felt a chill run up her spine at the murderous look in his eyes. She was grateful to the good spirits that she was on this man's side, and not his enemy. Still, she had to voice the vital information Tom had told her. She felt a stab of anguish, wishing it had been someone other than Tom who had confirmed it for her, but it was Sebastian who was really the first one to have told her about it.

'Lord Rahl can't be there, in Aydindril.' Both men stared at her. 'Lord Rahl is far to the south.'

Jagang frowned. 'To the south? What do you mean?'

'He's in the Old World.'

'Are you sure?' Sebastian asked.

Jennsen puzzled at him. 'You told me so yourself. That he led his army of invasion into the Old World.'

A look of recollection came over Sebastian's face. 'Yes, of course, Jenn, but that was long before I even met you – way back before I left our troops – that I had heard those reports. That was a long time ago.'

'But I know he was in the Old World after that.'

'What do you mean?' Jagang asked in a gravely growl.

Jennsen cleared her throat. 'The bond. The D'Haran people feel a bond to the Lord Rahl—'

'And do you feel the bond?' Jagang asked.

'Well, no. It just isn't strong enough in me. But when Sebastian and I were at the People's Palace, I met people there who said that Lord Rahl was far to the south, in the Old World.'

The emperor considered her words as he glanced over at a woman who had come in with platters of dried fruits, sweetmeats, and nuts. She worked at a distant side table, apparently not wanting to come any closer and disturb the emperor and his guests.

'But Jenn, you heard that last winter when we were at the palace. Have you heard anyone with the bond confirm it since then?'

Jennsen shook her head. 'I guess not.'

'If the Mother Confessor intends to make her stand in Aydindril,' Sebastian said, thoughtfully, 'then it's possible, since we last had this report of him to the south, that he's come north to stand by the Mother Confessor.'

Jagang leaned in low over the bloody meat before him. 'Those two are like that. Evil to the end. I've dealt with them both for a long time, now. I know from experience that if there's any way for them to be together, they will be – even if it's in death.'

The implications were staggering. 'Then ... we might have him,' Jennsen whispered, almost to herself. 'We might have Richard Rahl, too. The nightmare might be close to over. We could be on the eve of victory for all of us.'

Jagang leaned back, drumming his fingers on the table, looking from one to the other. 'While I find it hard to believe Richard Rahl would also be there, from what I know about him, he could well decide to stand and lose with her, rather than live to see it all slip away from him bit by bloody bit.'

Jennsen felt an unexpected pang at the thought of the two of them standing together as the end came. It was completely out of character for a Lord Rahl to care for any woman, much less to stand by one as she was about to lose the war for her homeland, and her life as well. Lord Rahl would be more concerned about preserving his own life and land.

Still, the thought of him being this close was too tantalizing to dismiss, and had her pulse racing. 'If he is this close, then I wouldn't need the help of the Sisters of the Light. I wouldn't need a spell. I would only have to get a little closer, to be with you when you make your drive into the city.'

Jagang's grim, humorless smile was back. 'You will ride with me; I will deliver you to the Confessors' Palace.' His knuckles were white around his knife again. 'I want them both dead. I will see to the Mother Confessor, personally. I grant you permission to be the one to plunge your knife into Richard Rahl.'

Jennsen felt a wild swing of emotion, from giddy elation that the deed was close at hand, to sickening horror. For an instant, she doubted that she could really carry out such a grisly, cold-blooded act.

Jennsen.

But then she remembered her mother lying in a pool of blood on the floor of their home, bleeding to death from those awful ripping stab wounds, her severed arm not far away, a house full of Lord Rahl's brutes standing over her. Jennsen remembered her mother's eyes, as she lay dying. She remembered how helpless she felt as her mother's life slipped away. The horror of it was as fresh as ever. The rage was as white-hot as ever. Jennsen lusted to plunge her knife into her bastard brother's heart.

That was all she wanted.

In the searing haze of righteous anger, as she saw herself

slamming the knife into Richard Rahl's chest, she only distantly heard Jagang speak.

'But why is it you wish to kill your brother? What is your reason, your purpose?'

'*Grushdeva*,' she hissed.

Behind her, Jennsen heard a glass vase hit the floor and shatter. The sound startled her back to where she was.

The emperor frowned at the woman off in the shadows. Her brown eyes were fixed on Jennsen.

'I apologize for Sister Perdita's clumsiness,' Jagang said as he glared at the woman.

'Forgive me, Excellency,' the woman in the dark gray dress said as she backed out between the hangings, bowing all the way.

The emperor's frown turned back to Jennsen.

'Now, what was it you said?'

Jennsen hadn't the slightest idea. She knew she'd said something, but she wasn't sure what. She thought that maybe her grief had tied her tongue in knots right when she went to answer. Her sorrow returned, like a great, grim weight on her shoulders.

'You see, Excellency,' Jennsen said as she stared down at her uneaten dinner, 'all my life, my father, Darken Rahl, has been trying to murder me because I was his ungifted offspring. When Richard Rahl killed him and assumed rule over D'Hara, he took up in his father's place, and part of that place was to murder his ungifted siblings. But in this duty, he was even more vicious than his father had been.'

Jennsen looked up through watery vision. 'Just after I met Sebastian, my brother's men finally caught up with us. They brutally murdered my mother. If not for Sebastian being there, they would have had me, too. Sebastian saved my life. I intend to kill Richard, because, if I don't, I can't ever be free. He will always send men to hunt me. Besides saving my life, Sebastian helped me to see that.

'Perhaps even more importantly, I must avenge the murder of my mother if I am ever to be at peace.'

'Our purpose is the welfare of our fellow man. Your story saddens me, and is the very reason we fight to eradicate the blight of magic.' The emperor finally shifted his gaze to

Sebastian. 'I am proud of you for helping this fine young woman.'

Sebastian had turned moody. She knew how ill at ease he felt under the weight of praise. She wished he could feel proud about his accomplishments, his importance, his stature with the emperor.

He laid his knife down across the scraps of his meal. 'Just doing my job, Excellency.'

'Well,' Jagang said with an encouraging smile, 'I'm glad you've returned in time to see the culmination of your strategy.'

Sebastian leaned back, nursing a mug of ale. 'Don't you want to wait for Brother Narev? Shouldn't he be here to witness it, if this turns out to be the blow that ends it?'

With a thick finger, Jagang pushed an olive around in a little circle on the table. It was a time before he spoke quietly without looking up.

'I've not heard from Brother Narev since Altur'Rang fell.'

Sebastian came up against the table. 'What! Altur'Rang fell? What do you mean? How? When?'

Jennsen knew that Altur'Rang was the emperor's homeland, the city he came from. Sebastian had told her that Brother Narev and the Fellowship of Order were there, in that great shining city of hope for mankind. A great palace would be built there in homage to the Creator and as a symbol to solidify the unity of the Old World.

'I received reports not long ago that enemy forces overran the city. Altur'Rang is very distant, and it was cut off. Partly because of winter, the reports were a very long time in reaching me. I await news.

'Given this inauspicious turn of fate, I don't think it wise to wait for Brother Narev to make it up here. He will be busy throwing the invaders back. If the Mother Confessor and Richard Rahl are in Aydindril, we must not wait; we must strike back swiftly, and with withering force.'

Jennsen laid a sympathetic hand on Sebastian's forearm. 'That must have been what you told me about. When I first met you and you told me that Lord Rahl was invading your homeland, that must have been what he was after – Altur'Rang.'

Sebastian stared at her. 'It may be that he isn't in Aydindril. It may turn out that he's still to the south, Jenn, in the Old World. You have to keep that in mind. I don't want you to invest all your hopes only to have them dashed.'

'I hope he is here and it can finally be ended, but, as His Excellency said about moving on Aydindril, there is nothing to lose. I didn't expect to find him here. If he isn't in Aydindril, then I'll still have the help for which you brought me here in the first place.'

'And what is the nature of that help?' Jagang asked.

Sebastian answered for her. 'I told her that the Sisters might be able to help with a spell – so that she can get past all of Lord Rahl's protection and get close enough to him to act.'

'One way or another, then. If he is in Aydindril, you shall have him.' Jagang plucked up the olive he had been rolling around and popped it in his mouth. 'If not, then you shall have the sorceress at your disposal. Whatever help you need from the Sisters is yours. You have but to ask, and they will provide it – my word on that.'

His raven eyes were deadly serious.

Outside, thunder rumbled. The rain had picked up. Lightning flickered, lighting the tent from the outside with eerie light that made the candlelight seem all the darker when each flash of lightning ended, leaving them again in near darkness, waiting for the roll of thunder.

'I just need them to cast me a spell to divert those protecting him, so I can get close enough to him,' Jennsen said after the thunder had died out. She drew her knife from its sheath and held it up to look at the ornate letter 'R' engraved in the silver handle. 'Then I can put my knife through his evil heart. This knife – his own knife. Sebastian explained how important it is to use what is closest to an enemy to strike back at them.'

'Sebastian has spoken wisely. That is our way, and why, with the Creator's guidance, we will prevail. Let us pray that we at last have them both and it can finally be ended, that the scourge of magic will finally be ended, and that mankind will at last be allowed to live in peace as the Creator intended.'

Jennsen and Sebastian both nodded at the invocation.

'If we catch them in Aydindril,' Jagang said, looking her in the eyes, 'I promise that you will be the one to put your blade through his heart, so that your mother may finally rest in peace.'

'Thank you,' Jennsen whispered in gratitude.

He didn't ask how she could accomplish such a task. Maybe the conviction in her voice had betrayed the fact that there was more to this than he knew – that she had some special advantage that would enable her to accomplish such a thing.

And there was more to this than he knew, or Sebastian knew.

Jennsen had been thinking long and hard about it, putting all the various elements together. Her whole life had been devoted to thinking about this problem. But in the past, her thoughts always revolved around how insoluble it was, how it was only a matter of time until Lord Rahl caught her and the nightmare began in earnest.

She had always been focused on the problem.

Now, since meeting Sebastian and the death of her mother, events had accelerated at a breathtaking pace, but those events had also added, bit by bit, to her understanding of the larger picture. Questions were beginning to have answers, answers that seemed so simple, now, looking back on them. She almost felt as if, deep down inside, she must have known all along.

Now, she was turning her focus away from the problem; she was beginning to think in terms of the solution.

Jennsen had learned a great deal from Althea – as it turned out, more, even, than the sorceress knew she was revealing. A sorceress of Althea's power would not be trapped there all those years unless what she said about the beasts in the swamp were true. The snake was different. Friedrich had said that the snake was just a snake.

But the beasts were magic.

Those beasts kept even a sorceress of Althea's power locked in her prison. Friedrich said that no one, not even he, could come in by the back way. Tom had also said that he had never heard of anyone going in the back way and returning to tell about it. No one used the meadow, either, because of the things that came out of that swamp. The things in the swamp were real and they were

462

deadly. All the facts but one were consistent in supporting that.

Jennsen had gone in and come out again without ever being approached, much less attacked or harmed. She had seen nothing of any beasts created from the very substance of the gift. That was the one piece that hadn't fit, at the time. It did, now.

There had been other indications, too, such as in the People's Palace, when Jennsen had touched Nyda's Agiel without it harming her. It had certainly harmed both Sebastian and Captain Lerner. Nyda had been dumbstruck. She said that not even Lord Rahl was immune to the touch of an Agiel. Jennsen was.

And, Jennsen had been able to bend Nyda's will to helping, rather than what, by all rights, she should have done, which was to stop this stranger who couldn't be touched with the power of an Agiel, stopped a woman who raised so many unanswered questions, until it all could be sorted out and confirmed. Even when Nathan Rahl tried to stop her, Jennsen had been able to get Nyda to help protect her – from a gifted Rahl. Jennsen knew now that it was more than just a good bluff. A bluff might have been the kernel, but there was much more wrapped around it.

All of those things and more, over the course of the long and difficult journey to Aydindril, had at last come together, so that Jennsen finally saw the true extent of her unique status and why she was the one to kill Richard Rahl.

Jennsen had come to understand that she was the only one able to do this – that she was born to do this – because, in a central, critical, cardinal way . . . she was invincible.

She knew, now, that she had always been invincible.

Chapter 46

From atop Rusty, the chill, gusty breeze ruffling her hair, Jennsen gazed off at the splendor of the Confessors' Palace crowning a distant rise. Sebastian sat beside her on a nervous Pete. Emperor Jagang, his magnificent dappled gray stallion pawing the road, waited on the other side of Sebastian, a cadre of officers and advisors huddled close, but silent. Jagang's forbidding scowl was fixed on the palace. Dark, menacing shapes, like a gathering storm, drifted across the surface of his black eyes.

The advance into Aydindril had, so far, been unlike anything anyone had expected, leaving everyone tense and on edge.

Arrayed behind was a contingent of Sisters of the Light who kept to themselves, apparently concentrating on matters of magic. Although none of the Sisters, as of yet, had had the chance to speak to Jennsen, they were all acutely aware of her, and kept a close eye on her. Yet more of them had ridden off in various directions as the emperor had led the detachment of Imperial Order cavalry, like some dark floodwater, across farms, roads, and hills, around buildings and barns, ever onward up roads and then in around buildings, to seep into the outermost fringes of Aydindril. The great city now lay spread out before them, silent and still.

The night before, Sebastian had slept fitfully. Jennsen knew, because, on the eve of such a momentous battle, she had slept hardly at all. Yet, with the thought of finally being able to use the knife sheathed at her belt, she was wide awake.

Behind the Sisters, more than forty thousand of the Imperial Order's elite cavalry waited, some with pikes and lances poised at the ready, some with swords or axes in hand. Each wore a ring through his left nostril. While most wore beards, and some had long, dark, greasy hair, with good luck charms tied in, there were quite a few with shaved heads, apparently out of open fealty to Emperor Jagang. They were all a tightly coiled spring, destroyers, poised to storm into the city.

Besides being elite members of the cavalry, trusted officers, or Sisters of the Light, every person there, except Jennsen and Sebastian, had one essential thing in common: they knew the Mother Confessor by sight. From what Jennsen was able to gather, the Mother Confessor had led raids on the Order's camp and had been at battles where she had been seen by a number of the men, as well as the Sisters. All those chosen to ride into Aydindril with the emperor had to know the Mother Confessor by sight. Jagang didn't want her slipping out of their snare by hiding in crowds of people, or escaping by pretending to be a lowly washwoman. Such a worry had evaporated in the light of what they had so far found.

Chilled not only by the breeze, but by the lust for battle gleaming in the soldiers' eyes, Jennsen gripped the horn of her saddle tight in an attempt to make her hands stop trembling.

Jennsen.

For the hundredth time that morning, she checked that her knife was clear in its scabbard. After reassuring herself, she pressed it back down, feeling the satisfying metallic click as it seated. She was there with the army because she was a part of this, with a job to do.

Surrender.

She thought about the irony of how this was the very knife that Lord Rahl had given a man he sent to kill her, and now she was bringing that same knife, a thing close to him, back to defeat him.

At last, she was the hunter, and not the hunted.

Whenever she felt her courage waver, she had but to think of her mother, or Althea and Friedrich, or Althea's sister, Lathea, or even Jennsen's unknown half brother, the Raug'Moss healer, Drefan. So many lives had been ruined or forfeit because of the

House of Rahl, because of Lord Rahl – first her father, Darken Rahl, and now her half brother, Richard Rahl.

Surrender your will, Jennsen. Surrender your flesh.

'Leave me be,' she snapped, annoyed that the voice wouldn't leave her alone and at having to repeat it so often when she had important things on her mind.

Sebastian frowned over at her. 'What?'

Chagrined that she had inadvertently said it aloud this time, Jennsen simply shook her head as if to say it was nothing. He turned back to his own thoughts as he watched the city spread out before them, studying the imposing maze of tight buildings, streets, and alleyways. There was only one thing missing from the city, and that had everyone tense and jumpy.

From the corner of her eye, Jennsen saw the Sisters all whispering among themselves. All except one, Sister Perdita, the one in the dark gray dress and the salt and pepper hair loosely tied back. When their eyes met, the woman smiled in that knowing, self-satisfied smirk of hers that seemed able to look right into Jennsen's soul. Jennsen thought that it probably looked different to her than the woman intended, so she bowed her head slightly in acknowledgment and smiled all the smile she could muster before turning away.

Along with everyone else, Jennsen watched the palace in the distance, on a hill overlooking the city. It was hard not to look at it, the way it stood out against the gray walls of mountains like snow on slate. Tall windows fronted the building between towering white marble columns topped with gold capitals. To the rear, at the center, a domed roof with a belt of windows rose up well clear of the high walls. Jennsen had trouble reconciling the splendor of such a beautiful building with the wicked rule of the Mother Confessor.

The sinister specter of the Wizard's Keep, high up on a mountain behind the palace, seemed like it would be more fitting for the Mother Confessor. Jennsen noticed that no one liked looking up at that baleful place; their eyes were always quick to turn to less unnerving sights.

The Keep watching down on them was larger than any man-made thing Jennsen had ever seen, save the People's Palace in

D'Hara. Ragged gray clouds floated past dark stone exterior walls that soared to staggering heights. The Keep itself, behind those lofty walls, appeared to be a complex collection of battlements, ramparts, crenellated walls, towers, spires, and connecting bridges and walkways. Jennsen had never imagined that anything made of stone could look so alive with menace.

In the quiet, her gaze sought solace in Sebastian's spikes of white hair, his knowing eyes, the familiar contours of his face. His handsome features were comforting to her, even if he didn't look her way. What woman wouldn't be honored to have the love of a man like him? If not for him being there with her since her mother's death, Jennsen didn't know what she would have done, how she would have gotten by.

Sebastian wore his cloak laid back to expose some of his weapons. He surveyed the scene with studied calm. She wished she could feel so calm. It frightened her, unexpectedly, to contemplate him having to draw those weapons, of him having to fight for his life.

'What do you think?' she whispered as she leaned closer to him. 'What could it mean?'

He gave her a brief shake of his head along with a harsh glance. He didn't want to discuss it. That curt gesture told her that she was supposed to be quiet. She had known, of course, by the silence of tens of thousands of men right behind her that she was supposed to be quiet, but the anxiety was twisting her insides into a knot. She had only wanted a small token of reassurance. Instead, his abrupt snub cut her down, making her feel like a small nobody.

She knew that he had important things on his mind, but his brusque dismissal still stung like a slap, especially after the night before when he had so desperately wanted her comfort, wanted her as fiercely as he had ever wanted her. She had understood. She hadn't turned him away, even though she found it distressing that they weren't alone, but had guards standing right outside who she suspected could hear everything.

Of course, she knew that this was not the time or place he could afford to give her comfort; they were all on the brink of battle. Still, it hurt.

Over the sound of the wind moaning through the bare branches of majestic, mature maple trees lining the road, she picked up the sound of hooves at a gallop. All eyes turned to watch bearded, long-haired men, streamers of fur and hides trailing out behind as they hunched forward over their horses' withers, charging in from the road on the right. Jennsen recognized them by the lead horse's patchy white, pied coloration. They were one of the small reconnoitering parties the emperor had sent ahead hours before. In the distance to the west, their counterpart was returning from the opposite direction, but they were yet tiny specks riding down out of the far foothills.

As the first group of horsemen came storming in before the emperor and his advisors, Jennsen covered her mouth with the edge of her cloak to mask her coughing on the cloud of dust.

The husky man at the lead of the riders pulled his pied horse around. His greasy strings of hair whipped around like the horse's white tail. 'Nothing, Excellency.'

Jagang, looking in a foul mood and near the end of patience, shifted his weight in his saddle. 'Nothing.'

'No, Excellency, nothing. No sign of troops anywhere to the east, or on the far side of the city, or all the way up the slopes of the mountains. Nothing. The roads, the trails – all deserted. No people, no tracks, no horse dung, no wagon ruts . . . nothing. We could find no sign that anyone has been here for a good long time.'

The man went on with a detailed account of where they had looked, but without result, as the other knot of men thundered in from the west, their horses lathered and in a high state of excitement.

'No one!' the man at the front called out as he hauled in on the reins, laying his horse's head over. The horse, eyes wild and keyed up from the hard ride, pivoted around to a halt before the emperor, snorting through flared nostrils. 'Excellency, there are no troops – or anyone – to the west.'

Jagang glared at the Confessors' Palace. 'What about the road up to the Keep?' he asked in a quiet growl. 'Or are you going to tell me that my scouts and patrols were ambushed by the ghosts of all the vanished people!'

The brawny man, layered in hides, looked as fierce as anyone Jennsen had ever seen. His top teeth were missing, adding to his savage aspect. He cast a cautious look back up at the wide ribbon of road that wound its way up from the city toward the Wizard's Keep. He turned back to the emperor.

'Excellency, there were no tracks on the road up to the Keep, either.'

'Did you go all the way up to the Keep to check?' he asked, his dark gaze turning on the man.

The man swallowed under the hot scrutiny of Jagang's glower. 'There is a stone bridge, not far from the top, that crosses a great crevasse. We went that far, Excellency, but still saw no one, nor any tracks. The portcullis was lowered. Beyond, the Keep showed no sign of life.'

'That means nothing,' a woman not far behind scoffed.

Jennsen turned, along with Sebastian, most of the advisors, officers, and Jagang, to look at her. It was Sister Perdita who had spoken. At least she managed to keep most of the superior smirk off her face as everyone stared at her.

'It means nothing,' she repeated. 'I'm telling you, Excellency, I don't like this one bit. Something is wrong.'

'Something? Like what?' Jagang asked, his voice low and surly.

Sister Perdita left the company of several dozen Sisters of the Light and walked her horse forward to speak more privately to the emperor.

'Excellency,' she said only after she was close, 'have you ever walked into a wood, and realized that there were no sounds, when there should be? That it had suddenly gone quiet?'

Jennsen had. She was struck by how accurately the Sister had hit upon the peculiar, uneasy feeling she was having – a kind of portent to doom, yet without definable cause, that made the fine hairs at the back of her neck stand on end like when she would be lying in her bedroll, almost asleep, and every insect, all at once, went silent.

Jagang glared at Sister Perdita. 'When I walk into a wood, or anywhere, it always goes silent.'

The Sister didn't argue, but simply started over. 'Excellency, we have fought these people long and hard. Those of us with the gift know their tricks with magic. We know when they are using their gift. We've learned to know if they've used magic to set traps, even if those traps are not themselves magic. But this is different. Something is wrong.'

'You still have not told me what,' Jagang said with restrained, impatient irritation, as if he didn't have time for someone who wouldn't come to the point.

The woman, noting his annoyance, bowed her head. 'Excellency, I would tell you if I knew. It is my duty to advise you of what I know. We can detect no magic being used – none. We sense no traps that have ever been touched by the gift.

'But that knowledge still does not set my mind at ease. Something is wrong. I'm telling you, now, my warning, even though I admit that I don't know the cause of my concern. You have but to search my mind for yourself and you will see I'm speaking the truth.'

Jennsen had no idea what the Sister meant, but after staring at her for a moment, Jagang visibly cooled. He grunted dismissively as he looked back toward the palace. 'I think you're just nervous after a long idle winter, Sister. As you said, you know their tactics and tricks with magic, so if it was something real, you and your Sisters would know it and know the cause.'

'I'm not sure that's true,' Sister Perdita pressed. She cast a quick, troubled glance at the Wizard's Keep up on the mountain. 'Excellency, we know a great deal about magic. But the Keep is thousands of years old. Being from the Old World, that place is outside my experience. I know next to nothing about the specific kinds of magic which are likely to be kept in that place, except that whatever magic is kept there will be dangerous in the extreme. That is one purpose of a Keep – to safeguard such things.'

'That's why I want the Keep taken,' Jagang shot back. 'Those dangerous things must not be left in the enemy's hands to later deal us murder.'

With her fingertips, Sister Perdita patiently rubbed the creases in her brow. 'The Keep is strongly warded. I can't tell how; the wards were set by wizards, not sorceresses. Such wards could easily have been left untended – no one needs stand guard. Such wards can be triggered by simple trespass – much as with any trap without magic. Such wards can be cautionary, but, just as likely, they can be deadly. Even if the place is deserted, those wards could easily kill anyone – anyone – who so much as tries to get close, much less take the place. Such defensive measures are timeless; they do not wear away. They are just as effective whether they've been there for a month or millennia. The attempt to take a place so warded could deal us the murder we are trying to avoid.'

Jagang nodded as he listened. 'We still must untangle those wards so we can gain the Keep.'

Sister Perdita glanced over her shoulder at the dark stone Keep far up on the mountainside before she spoke. 'Excellency, as I have often tried to explain, our degree of ability and aggregate power doesn't mean we can untangle or defeat those wards. Such a thing is not directly relational. A bear, strong as he is, can't open a lock on a strongbox. Strength isn't necessarily the key to such things. I'm telling you that I don't like this, that something is wrong.'

'You have told me only that you are afraid. Of all those with magic, the Sisters are exceptionally well armed. That is the reason you're here.' Jagang leaned toward the woman, his patience appearing to be at an end. 'I expect the Sisters to stop any threat from magic. Must I make it any more clear?'

Sister Perdita paled. 'No, Excellency.' After a bow from her saddle, she pulled her horse around to rejoin her Sisters.

'Sister Perdita,' Jagang called after her. He waited until she turned back. 'As I've told you before, we must gain the Wizard's Keep. I don't care how many of you it takes, only that it gets done.'

As she returned to her Sisters to discuss the matter, Jagang, along with everyone else, caught sight of a lone rider racing toward them from the city. Something about the look on the man's face had everyone checking their weapons. They all waited in tense silence until his horse skidded to a stop before the emperor. The man was drenched in sweat and his narrow-set eyes were wide with excitement, but he kept his voice under control.

'Excellency, I saw no one – no one – in the city. But I smelled horses.'

Jennsen saw apprehension etched on the faces of the officers at this further confirmation of their disbelief of the preposterous notion that the city was deserted. The Order had driven the enemy forces to Aydindril as winter had descended, trapping not only the army but the people of the city as well. How a place this large could be evacuated – in the dead of winter – was beyond their imagination. Yet no one seemed willing to voice that conviction too strongly to the emperor as he stared out upon an empty city.

'Horses?' Jagang frowned. 'Maybe it was a stable.'

'No, Excellency. I could not find them, nor hear them, but I could smell them. It was not the smell of a stable, but horses. There are horses there.'

'Then the enemy is here, just as we thought,' one of the officers said to Jagang. 'They're hiding, but they're here.'

Jagang said nothing as he waited for the man to go on.

'Excellency, there is more,' the burly soldier said, nearly bursting with excitement. 'As I searched, I could not find the horses anywhere, so I decided to return for more men to help ferret out the cowardly enemy.

'As I was returning, I saw someone in a window of the palace.'

Jagang's gaze abruptly turned to the man. 'What?'

The soldier pointed. 'In the white palace, Excellency. As I rode out from behind a wall at the edge of the city, before the palace grounds, I saw someone on the second floor move away from a window.'

With an angry yank on the reins, Jagang checked his stallion's impatient sidesteps. 'Are you sure?'

The man nodded vigorously. 'Yes, Excellency. The windows there are tall. On my life, just as I came out from behind the wall and looked up, someone saw me and moved back from a window.'

The emperor peered intently up the road lined with maple trees, toward the palace, as he considered this new development.

'Man or woman?' Sebastian asked.

The rider paused to wipe sweat from his eyes and to swallow in an effort to catch his breath. 'It was the briefest look, but I believe it was a woman.'

Jagang turned his dark glare on the man. 'Was it her?'

The maple branches clattered together in the gusts as all eyes watched the man.

'Excellency, I could not tell for certain. It might have been a reflection of the light on the window, but in that brief look, I thought I saw that she was wearing a long white dress.'

The Mother Confessor wore a white dress. Jennsen thought it was pretty far-fetched to believe it could be a coincidence that there would be a reflection on the glass right as a person moved away from the window, a reflection that made it look like they were wearing the white dress of the Mother Confessor.

Yet, it made no sense to Jennsen. Why would the Mother Confessor be alone in her palace? Making a last stand was one thing. Making it alone was quite another. Could it be, as the man suggested, that the enemy was cowardly and hiding?

Sebastian idly tapped a finger against his thigh. 'I wonder what they're up to.'

Jagang drew his sword. 'I guess we'll find out.' He looked, then, at Jennsen. 'Keep that knife of yours handy, girl. This may be the day you've been praying for.'

'But Excellency, how could it possibly—'

The emperor stood in his stirrups and flashed a wicked grin back to his cavalry. He circled his sword high in the air.

The coiled spring was unleashed.

With a deafening roar, forty thousand men loosed a pent-up battle cry as they charged away. Jennsen gasped and held on to Rusty for dear life as the horse leaped into a gallop ahead of the cavalry racing toward the palace.

Chapter 47

Nearly out of breath, Jennsen bent forward over Rusty, stretching her arms out to each side of the horse's neck to give her all the reins she needed as they charged at a full gallop out of the fringes of the countryside toward the sprawling city of Aydindril. The roar of forty thousand men yelling battle cries along with the thundering hooves was as frightening as it was deafening.

Yet, the rush of it all, the heart-pounding sensation of wild abandon, was also intoxicating. Not that she didn't grasp the enormity, the horror, of what was happening, but some small part of her couldn't help being swept up with the intense emotion of being a part of it all.

Fierce men with blood lust in their eyes fanned out to the sides as they raced ahead. The air seemed alive with light flashing off all the swords and axes held high, the sharpened points of lances and pikes piercing the muted morning air. The scintillating sights, the swell of sounds, the swirling passions, all filled Jennsen with the hunger to draw her knife, but she didn't; she knew the time would come.

Sebastian rode near her, making sure she was safe and didn't become lost in the crazy, headlong, willful stampede. The voice rode with her, too, and would not remain silent, despite how she tried to ignore it, or begged in her mind for it to leave her be. She needed to focus on what was happening, on what might soon happen. She couldn't afford the distraction. Not now.

As it called her name, called for her to surrender her will, to surrender her flesh, called to her in mysterious but strangely seductive words, the surrounding roar of masking sound gave Jennsen the anonymity to finally scream at the top of her lungs 'Let me be! Leave me alone!' without anyone noticing. It was a heady purification to be able to banish the voice with such unrestrained force and authority.

In what seemed an instant, they suddenly plunged into the city, leaping over fences, skirting poles, and flying past buildings with bewildering speed. With the way they had been in the open and then abruptly had to deal with all the things around them, it reminded her of racing into a stand of woods.

The wild charge was not what she had imagined it would be – an ordered marshaled run across open ground – but instead was a mad dash through a great city; along wide thoroughfares lined with magnificent buildings; then veering suddenly down dark canyonlike alleys made of tall stone walls that in some places bridged the narrow slice of open sky overhead; and then abruptly impetuous dashes through warrens of narrow twisting side streets among ancient, windowless buildings laid out to no design. There was no slowing for deliberation or decision, but, rather, it was one long, reckless, relentless rush.

It was made all the more surreal because there were no people anywhere. There should have been crowds scattering in wild panic, diving out of the way, screaming. In her mind's eye, she overlaid scenes she had seen in cities before: peddlers pushing carts with everything from fish to fine linen; shopkeepers outside their businesses tending tables of bread, cheese, meat, wine; craftsmen displaying shoes, clothes, wigs, and leather goods; windows filled with wares.

Now, all those windows were strangely empty – some boarded up, some just left as if the owner would be opening any minute. All the windows lining their route stood empty. Streets, benches, parks, were mute witness to the onslaught of cavalry.

It was frightening to charge at full speed through the convoluted maze of streets, cutting around buildings and obstacles, dashing down dirt alleyways, flying at full speed along curving cobblestone roads, cresting rises only to plummet down the far side, like some bizarre, headlong, out-of-control snow sled ride plunging down an icy hill through the trees, and just as dangerous. Sometimes, as they galloped half a dozen abreast, the way suddenly narrowed with a wall or a corner of a building that stuck out. More than one rider went down with calamitous results. Buildings, colors, fences, poles, and intersecting streets flashed by in dizzying array.

Without the resistance of an enemy force, the unbridled rush felt to Jennsen like it was out of all control, yet she knew that these were the elite cavalry, so a wanton charge was their specialty. Besides, Emperor Jagang looked in complete control atop his magnificent stallion.

The horses kicked up a shower of sod as they suddenly broke past a wide opening in a wall to find themselves charging up the expansive lawns of the Confessors' Palace. The fury of yelling riders spread out to each side, their horses tearing up the picturesque setting, the crude and filthy bloodthirsty invaders defiling the deceptively serene beauty of the grounds. Jennsen rode beside Sebastian, not far behind the emperor and several of his officers, between wide-spread flanks of howling men, straight up the wide promenade lined with mature maple trees, their bare branches, heavy with buds, laced together overhead.

Despite everything she had learned, everything she knew, everything she held dear, Jennsen couldn't understand why she felt such a sense of being a participant in a profane violation.

The impression melted away as she focused her attention instead on something she spotted ahead. It stood not far from the wide marble steps leading up to the grand entrance of the Confessors' Palace. It looked like a lone pole with something atop it. A long red cloth tied near the top of the shaft of the pole flew and flapped in the breeze, as if waving to them, calling for their attention, giving them all, at last, a destination. Emperor Jagang led the charge directly toward that pole with its red flag flying.

As they raced across the lawns, she concentrated on the heat of Rusty's obedient and powerful muscles flexing beneath her, finding reassurance in her horse's familiar movements. Jennsen couldn't help gazing up at the white marble columns towering above them. It was a majestic entrance, imposing, yet elegant and welcoming. This day, the Imperial Order was at last to own the place where evil had, for so long, ruled unopposed.

Emperor Jagang held his sword high, signaling the cavalry to halt. The cheering, yelling, screaming battle cries died out as tens of thousands of men, all at once, brought their excited horses down from a charge to a stop. It amazed her, what with so many men with weapons out, that it all happened in seconds and without carnage.

Jennsen patted the sweaty side of Rusty's neck before sliding down off her horse. She hit the ground among a confusion of men, mostly officers and advisors, but regular cavalry, too, all swarming in to protect the emperor. She had never been this close in among the regular soldiers before. They were intimidating as they eyed her in their midst. They all seemed impatient for an enemy to fight. The men were a filthy, grimy lot, and smelled worse than their horses. For some reason, it was that suffocating, sweaty, foul stink that frightened her the most.

Sebastian's hand seized her arm and pulled her close. 'Are you all right?'

Jennsen nodded, trying to see the emperor and what had stopped him. Sebastian, trying to see as well, pulled her along with him as he stepped through a screen of burly officers. Seeing it was him, they made way.

She and Sebastian halted when they saw the emperor standing several paces ahead, alone, his back to them, his shoulders slumped, his sword hanging from his fist at his side. It appeared that all his men were afraid to approach him.

Jennsen, with Sebastian quickly moving to catch up, closed the distance to reach Emperor Jagang. He stood frozen before the spear planted butt end in the ground. He stared with those completely black eyes as if seeing an apparition. Tied beneath the long, barbed, razor-sharp metal point of the spear, the long red cloth flapped in the otherwise complete silence.

Atop the spear was a man's head.

Jennsen winced at the arresting sight. The gaunt head, severed cleanly at mid-neck, looked almost alive. The dark eyes, beneath a deeply hooded brow, were fixed in an unblinking stare. A dark, creased cap rested halfway down the forehead. Somehow, the austere cap pressed down on the head seemed to match the severe countenance of the man. Wisps of wiry hair curled out from above his ears to ruffle in the wind. It seemed as if the thin lips, at any moment, might give them a forbidding smile from the world of the dead. The face looked as if the man, in life, had been as grim as death itself.

The way Emperor Jagang stood stupefied, staring at the head right before him impaled on the point of the spear, and the way not one of the thousands of men so much as coughed, had Jennsen's heart hammering faster than when she had been riding Rusty at a reckless gallop.

Jennsen cautiously peered over at Sebastian. He, too, stood stunned. Her fingers tightened on his arm in sympathy for the look in his wide, tearful eyes. He finally leaned closer to her in order to whisper in a choked voice.

'Brother Narev.'

The shock of those two barely audible words hit Jennsen like a slap. It was the great man himself, the spiritual leader of the entire Old World, Emperor Jagang's friend and closest personal advisor – a man who Sebastian believed was closer to the Creator than any man who had ever been born, a man whose teachings Sebastian religiously lived by, dead, his head impaled on a spear.

The emperor reached out and pulled free a small, folded piece of paper that was stuck in the side of Brother Narev's cap. As Jennsen watched Jagang's thick fingers open the carefully folded small piece of paper, it reminded her unexpectedly of the way she had unfolded the paper she had found on the D'Haran soldier that fateful day she had discovered him lying dead at the bottom of the ravine, the day she had met Sebastian. The day before Lord Rahl's men had finally located her and killed her mother.

Emperor Jagang lifted the paper out to silently read what it said. For a frightening long time, he just stared at the paper. At last, his arm lowered to his side. His chest heaved with a terrible, burgeoning wrath as he stared once more at Brother Narev's head on the end of the spear. In a smoldering voice, bitter with indignation, Jagang repeated the words from the note just loud enough for those standing close to hear.

'Compliments of Richard Rahl.'

The stiff wind moaned through a stand of nearby trees. No one said a word as they all waited on Emperor Jagang for direction.

Jennsen's nose wrinkled at a foul smell. She looked up to see the head, so perfect only moments before, beginning to putrefy before her very eyes. The flesh sagged heavily. The bottom eyelids drooped, revealing their red undersides. The jaw sank. The thin line of the mouth opened, almost looking as if the head were letting out a scream.

Jennsen, along with everyone else, including Emperor Jagang, took a step back as the flesh of the face decayed in sudden ghastly ruptures, revealing festering tissue beneath. The tongue swelled as the jaw dropped lower. The eyeballs sank forward out of their sockets as they shriveled. Reeking flesh fell away in clumps.

What would have been long months of decomposition took place in a matter of seconds, leaving the skull beneath that creased cap grinning at them through tattered bits of hanging flesh.

'It had a web of magic around it, Excellency,' Sister Perdita said, almost sounding as if she were answering a question unspoken. Jennsen hadn't heard her come up behind them. 'The spell preserved it in that condition until you pulled the note from the cap, triggering the dissolution of the magic preserving it. Once that magic was withdrawn, the . . . remains went through the decomposition that would ordinarily have taken place.'

Emperor Jagang was staring at her with cold dark eyes. What he might be thinking, Jennsen couldn't be sure, but she could see the fury building within those nightmare eyes.

'It was a very complex and powerful ward that preserved it until the right person touched it – to pull the note free,' Sister Perdita said in a quiet voice. 'The ward was likely keyed to your touch, Excellency.'

For a long, terrifying moment, Jennsen feared that Emperor Jagang might suddenly swing his sword with a wild cry and behead the woman.

To the side, an officer suddenly pointed up at the Confessors' Palace.

'Look! It's her!'

'Dear Creator,' Sebastian whispered as he, too, looked up and saw someone in the window.

Other men yelled that they saw her, too. Jennsen rose up on tiptoes, trying to see around the tall soldiers rushing forward, and the officers pointing, past the reflections on the glass, to the person she saw back within the dark interior. She shielded her eyes, trying to see better. Men whispered excitedly.

'There!' another officer on the other side of Jagang cried out. 'Look! It's Lord Rahl! There! It's Lord Rahl!'

Jennsen froze from the jolt of those words. It didn't seem real. She ran the man's words through her mind again, so shocking were they to hear that she felt she had to check again if it really was what she thought she had heard.

'There!' another man yelled. 'Moving down that way! It's both of them!'

'I see them,' Jagang growled as he tracked the two fleeing figures in his black glare. 'I'd recognize that bitch in the farthest reaches of the underworld. And there! – Lord Rahl is with her!'

Jennsen could catch only fleeting flashes of two figures racing away past windows.

Emperor Jagang sliced the air with his sword, signaling his men. 'Surround the palace so they can't escape!' He turned to his officers. 'I want the assault company to come with me! And a dozen Sisters! Sister Perdita – stay with the Sisters out here. Don't let anyone get by you!'

His gaze sought Sebastian and Jennsen. When he found them among those standing close he fixed Jennsen in his hot glare.

'If you want your chance, girl, then come with me!'

Jennsen realized, as she and Sebastian raced away after Emperor Jagang, that she had her knife clenched in her fist.

Chapter 48

Close on Jagang's heels, in the shadows of towering marble columns, Jennsen raced up the wide expanse of white marble steps. Sebastian's reassuring hand was on the small of her back the whole way. Fierce determination etched the faces of the savage men bounding up the steps all around her.

The men of the assault company, sheathed in layers of leather armor, chain mail, and tough hides, wielded short swords, huge crescent axes, or wicked flails in one hand, while on their other arm they all carried round metal shields for protection, but the shields were also set with long center spikes to make them weapons as well. The men were even swathed with belts and straps set with sharpened studs to make grappling with them in hand-to-hand combat treacherous, at best. Jennsen couldn't imagine anyone with the nerve to go against such vicious men.

Storming up the steps, the burly soldiers growled like animals, crashing through the carved double doors as if they were made of sticks, never checking to see if the doors might be unlocked. Jennsen shielded her face with an arm as she flew through the shower of splintered wood fragments.

The thunder of the men's boots echoed through the grand hall inside. Tall windows of pale blue glass set between polished white marble pillars threw slashes of light across the marble floor where the assault force stormed through. Men hooked the marble railing with big hands and swooped up the first stairway, going for the upper floors where they had seen the Mother Confessor and Lord Rahl. The sound of the soldiers' boots on stone echoed up through the high-ceilinged stairwell decorated with ornate moldings.

Jennsen couldn't help being wildly excited that this might be the day it all ended. She was but one mighty thrust of her knife from freedom. She was the one to do it. She was the only one who could. She was invincible.

The fact that she was going to kill a man was only dimly important to her. As she raced up the steps, she thought only about the horror Lord Rahl had brought to her life and the lives of others. Filled with righteous rage, she intended to end it once and for all.

Sebastian, racing right along with her, had his sword out. A dozen of the big brutes were in front of her, led by Emperor Jagang himself. Behind were hundreds more of the grim assault force, all determined to deliver merciless violence to the enemy. Between her and those charging soldiers behind, Sisters of the Light ran up the steps, without weapons but for their gift.

At the top of the flight of stairs, they all bunched to a halt on a slick oak floor. Emperor Jagang looked both ways down the hall.

One of the panting Sisters pushed through the men. 'Excellency! This makes no sense!'

His only answer was a glare as he caught his breath, before his gaze moved, searching for his prey.

'Excellency,' the Sister insisted, if more quietly, 'why would two people – so important to their cause – be alone here in the palace? Alone without even a guard at the door? It doesn't make sense. They would not be here alone.'

Jennsen, as much as she wanted Lord Rahl under her knife, had to agree. It made no sense.

'Who says they're alone?' Jagang asked. 'Do you sense any conjuring of magic?'

He was right, of course. They might go through a door and encounter a surprise of a thousand swords waiting for them. But that chance seemed remote. It seemed more logical that a protecting force, if there was one here, would not have wanted to allow them to all get inside.

'No,' the Sister answered. 'I sense no magic. But that doesn't mean it can't be called in an instant. Excellency, you are endangering yourself needlessly. This is dangerous to go chasing after such people when there are so many things about it that make no sense.'

She stopped short of calling it foolish. Jagang, seeming to pay minimal attention to the Sister as she spoke, signaled to his men, sending a dozen racing off in each direction down the hall. A snap of his fingers and a quick gesture sent a Sister with each group.

'You're thinking like a green army officer,' Jagang said to the Sister. 'The Mother Confessor is far more sly and ten times as cunning as you give her credit for. She is smarter than to think in such simple terms. You've seen some of the things she's pulled off. I'll not let her get away with this one.'

'Then, why would she and Lord Rahl be here alone?' Jennsen asked when she saw that the Sister feared to speak up further. 'Why would they allow themselves to be so vulnerable?'

'Where better to hide than in an empty city?' Jagang asked. 'An empty palace? Any guards would tip us to their presence.'

'But why would they even hide here, of all places?'

'Because they know that their cause is in jeopardy. They're cowards and want to evade capture. When people are desperate and in a panic, they often run for their home to hide in a place they know.' Jagang hooked a thumb behind his belt as he analyzed the layout of halls around him. 'This is her home. In the end, it's only their own hides that they think of, not that of their fellow man.'

Jennsen couldn't help herself from pressing, even as Sebastian was pulling her back, urging her to be quiet. She threw her arm out toward the expanse of windows. 'Why would they allow themselves to be seen, then? If they're trying to hide, as you suggest, then why would they let themselves be spotted?'

'They're evil!' He leveled his terrible eyes at her. 'They wanted to watch me find Brother Narev's remains. They wanted to see me discover their profane and heinous butchery of a great man. They simply couldn't resist such sick delight!'

'But—'

'Let's go!' he called to his men.

As the emperor charged off, Jennsen seized Sebastian's arm in exasperation, holding him back. 'Do you really think it could be them? You're a strategist – do you honestly think that any of this makes sense?'

He noted which way the emperor went, followed by a flood of men charging after him, then turned a heated glare on her.

'Jennsen, you wanted Lord Rahl. This may be your chance.'

'But I don't see why—'

'Don't argue with me! Who are you to think you know better!'

'Sebastian, I—'

'I don't have all the answers! That's why we're in here!'

Jennsen swallowed past the lump in her throat. 'I'm only worried for you, Sebastian, and Emperor Jagang. I don't want your heads to end up on the end of a pike, too.'

'In war, you must act, not only by careful plan, but when you see an opening. This is what war is like – in war people sometimes do stupid or even seemingly crazy things. Maybe she and Lord Rahl have simply done something stupid. You have to take advantage of an enemy's mistakes. In war, the winner is often the one who attacks no matter what and presses any advantage. There isn't always time to figure everything out.'

Jennsen could only stare up into his eyes. Who was she, a nobody, to try to tell an emperor's strategist how to fight a war?

'Sebastian, I was only—'

He snatched a fistful of her dress and yanked her close. His red face twisted in anger. 'Are you really going to throw away what might turn out to be your only chance to avenge your mother's murder? How would you feel if Richard Rahl really is crazy enough to be here? – Or if he has some plan we can't even conceive of? – And you just stand here arguing about it!'

Jennsen was stunned. Could he be right? What if he was?

'There they are!' came a cry from far down the hall. It was Jagang's voice. She saw him among a distant clot of his soldiers, pointing his sword as they all scrambled to turn a corner. 'Get them! Get them!'

Sebastian seized her arm, spun her around, and shoved her on down the hall. Jennsen caught her footing and ran with wild abandon. She felt ashamed for arguing with people who knew what war was all about when she didn't. Who did she think she was, anyway? She was a nobody. Great men had given her a chance, and she stood around on the doorstep of greatness, arguing about it. She felt a fool.

As they ran past tall windows – the very windows where the Mother Confessor and Lord Rahl had only moments before been seen – something outside caught her eye. A collective groan went up from beyond the panes of glass. Jennsen slid to a stop, her hands out, gathering up Sebastian to stop him, too.

'Look!'

Sebastian glanced impatiently toward the others racing away, then stepped closer to look out the window as she shook her hand, frantically pointing.

Tens of thousand of cavalry men had formed up into a huge battle line out across the palace grounds, stretching all the way down the hill, appearing to charge the enemy in a great battle. They all brandished swords, axes, and pikes as they rushed as a single mass, yelling bloodcurdling battle cries.

Jennsen watched in stunned silence, seeing nothing yet for them to fight. Still, the men, raising a great cry, ran forward with weapons raised. She expected to see them run down the hill toward something out beyond the wall. Perhaps they could see an enemy approaching that she could not from her angle up in the palace.

But then, in the middle of the grounds, with a mighty shock all along the line, there was a resounding crash as they met the wall of an enemy that was not there.

Jennsen couldn't believe her eyes. Her mind groped to reconcile it, but the terrifying sight outside made no sense. She wouldn't have believed what she was seeing, were it not for the shock of sudden carnage. Bodies, man and horse, were rent open. Horses reared. Others went down, tumbling over broken legs. Men's heads and arms spun through the air, as if lopped off by sword and axe. All along the line, blood filled the air. Men were driven back by blows that exploded through their bodies. The dark and grimy force of Imperial Order cavalry was suddenly bright red in the muted daylight. The slaughter was so horrific that the green grass was left red in a swath down the hill.

Where there had been battle cries, now there were piercing

screams of appalling suffering and pain as men, hacked to pieces, limbs severed, mortally wounded, tried to drag themselves to safety. Out in that field, there was no such place, there was only confusion and death.

Horrified, Jennsen looked up into Sebastian's baffled expression. Before either could say a word, the building shook as if struck by lightning. Following close on the heels of the thunderous boom, the hall filled with billowing smoke. Flames boiled toward them. Sebastian snatched her arm and dove with her into a side hall opposite the window.

The blast roared down the hall, driving chunks of wood, whole chairs, and flaming drapery before it. Fragments of glass and metal shrieked by, slicing through walls.

As soon as the smoke and flames had rolled past, Jennsen and Sebastian, both with weapons to hand, raced out into the hall, running in the direction Emperor Jagang had gone.

Whatever questions or objections she had were forgotten – such questions were suddenly irrelevant. It only mattered that – somehow – Richard Rahl was there. She had to stop him. This was finally her chance. The voice, too, urged her on. This time, she didn't try to put the voice down. This time, she let it fan the flames of her burning lust for vengeance. This time, she let it fill her with the overwhelming need to kill.

They raced past tall doors lining the hall. Each of the deep-set windows that flashed by had a small window seat. The walls were faced with frame and panel wood painted a shade of white warmed with a bit of rose color to it. As they came to the intersection of corridors and rounded the corner, Jennsen didn't really notice the elegant silver reflector lamps centered in each of those panels; she saw only the bloody handprints smeared along the walls, the long splashes of blood on the polished oak floor, the disorderly tangle of still bodies.

There were at least fifty of the burly assault soldiers scattered haphazardly down the hall, each burned, many ripped open by flying glass and splintered wood. Most of the faces weren't even recognizable as such. Shattered rib bones protruded from blood-soaked chain mail or leather. Along with the weapons that lay scattered, the hall was awash with gore and loose intestines, making it look like someone had spilled baskets of bloody dead eels.

Among the bodies was a woman – one of the Sisters. She had been nearly torn in two, as had been a number of the men, her slashed face set in death with a fixed look of surprise.

Jennsen gagged on the stench of blood, hardly able to draw a breath, as she followed Sebastian, jumping from one clear space to another, trying not to slip and fall on the human viscera. The horror of what Jennsen was seeing was so profound that it didn't register in her mind; at least, it didn't register emotionally. She simply acted, as if in a dream, not really able to consider what she was seeing.

Once past the bodies, they followed a trail of blood down a maze of grand halls. The distant sound of men shouting drifted back to them. Jennsen was at least relieved to hear the emperor's voice among them. They sounded like hounds locked on the scent of a fox, baying insistently, refusing to lose their prey.

'Sir!' a man called from far back through a doorway to the side. 'Sir! This way!'

Sebastian paused to look at the man and his frantic hand signals, then pulled Jennsen into a resplendent room. Across a floor covered with an elegant carpet of gold and rust-colored diamond designs, past windows hung with gorgeous green draperies, a soldier stood at a doorway into another hall. There were couches like none Jennsen had ever seen, and tables and chairs with beautifully carved legs. While the room was elegant, it was not imposingly so, making it seem like a place where people might gather for casual conversations. She followed Sebastian as he ran for the soldier at the door on the opposite side of the room.

'It's her!' the man called to Sebastian. 'Hurry! It's her! I just saw her pass by!'

The hulking soldier, still trying to catch his breath, sword hanging in his fist, peeked out the doorway again. Just before they reached him, as he peered down the hall, Jennsen heard a dull thump. The soldier dropped his sword and clutched at his chest, his eyes going wide, his mouth opening. He fell dead at their feet, no sign of any wound.

Jennsen pushed Sebastian up against the wall before he could go through the doorway. She didn't want him encountering whatever had just dropped the soldier.

Almost at the same time, from the way they had come, she heard the snapping hiss of something otherworldly. Jennsen dropped to the floor, stretching out over Sebastian, holding him against the edge of floor and wall, as if he were a child to be protected. She closed her eyes tight, crying out with fright at the thunderous blast behind her that shook the floor. A barrage of rubble shrieked through the room.

When it finally went still and she opened her eyes, dust drifted through the destruction. The wall around them was peppered with holes. Somehow, she and Sebastian were not hurt. It only served to confirm what she already believed.

'It was him!' Sebastian's arm shot out from under her to point across the room. 'It was him!'

Jennsen turned but saw no one. 'What?'

Sebastian pointed again. 'It was Lord Rahl. I saw him. As he ran past the door he cast in a spell of some kind – a pinch of sparkling dust – just as you pushed me against the wall. Then it exploded. I don't know how we survived in a room filled with such flying debris.'

'I guess it all missed us,' Jennsen said.

The room had been turned inside out. The draperies were shredded, the walls holed. The furniture that only moments before had been so beautiful was now a wreck of splinters and ripped upholstery. The rumpled carpet was covered in white dust, pieces of plaster, and splintered wood.

A hanging chunk of plaster broke away and crashed to the floor, raising yet more dust as Jennsen made her way through the wreckage of the room, toward the door they had come through, the door where Sebastian had pointed, the door where only moments before Lord Rahl had been. Sebastian retrieved his sword and quickly followed her out.

The hall, its woodwork so tastefully painted, was now smeared with blood. The body of another Sister lay crumpled not far away. When they reached her, they saw her dead eyes staring up at the ceiling in surprise.

'What in the name of Creation is going on?' Sebastian whispered to himself. Jennsen thought, by the look on the dead Sister's face, that she must have wondered the same thing in the last instant of her life.

A glance out the window showed a killing ground littered with thousands of bodies.

'You have to get the emperor out of here,' Jennsen said. 'This isn't the simple thing it appeared.'

'I'd say it was a trap of some kind. But we might still be able to carry out our objective. That would make it a success – make it worth it.'

Whatever was happening was outside her experience and beyond her ability to comprehend. Jennsen only knew that she intended to carry out her objective. As they raced down halls, chasing the sounds and following the trail of bodies, they worked their way deeper into the mysterious Confessors' Palace, away from any outside windows to where the air was hushed and gloomy. The deep shadows in the halls and rooms, where little light penetrated, added a frightening new dimension to the terrifying events.

Jennsen was well past shock, horror, or even fear. She felt as if she were watching herself act. Even her own voice sounded remote to her. In some distant way, she marveled at the things she did, at her ability to carry on.

As they cautiously rounded an intersection, they encountered a few dozen soldiers hunched in the shadows just inside a small room – bloodied, but alive. Four Sisters were there, too. Jennsen spotted Emperor Jagang leaning against a wall as he panted, his sword gripped tightly in a bloody fist. As she rushed up, he met her gaze, his black eyes filled not with the fear or sorrow she expected but with rage and determination.

'We're close, girl. Keep that knife out and you'll get your chance.'

Sebastian moved off to check other doorways, securing the immediate area, several men moving at his direction when he gave them silent hand signals.

She could hardly believe what she was hearing, or seeing. 'Emperor, you have to get out of here.'

He frowned at her. 'Are you out of your mind?'

'We're being cut to pieces! There are dead soldiers everywhere. I saw Sisters back there, ripped open by something—'

'Magic,' he said with a wicked grin.

She blinked at that grin. 'Excellency, you have to get out of here before they have you, too.'

His grin vanished, replaced by red-faced anger. 'This is a war! What do you think war is? War is killing. They've been doing it, and I intend to do it back twice over! If you don't have the guts to use that knife, then put your tail between your legs and run for the hills! But don't ever ask me to help you again.'

Jennsen stood her ground. 'I'll not run. I'm here for a reason. I only wanted you out of here so the Order would not lose you, too, after they've already lost Brother Narev.'

He huffed in disgust. 'Touching.' He turned to his men, checking that they were paying attention. 'Half take the room on the right, just ahead. The rest stay with me. I want them flushed out into the open.' He swept his sword before the faces of the four Sisters. 'Two with them, two with me. Don't disappoint me, now.'

With that, the men and Sisters split up and quickly moved off, half through the room at the right, half charging after the emperor. Sebastian gestured urgently for her. Jennsen joined him, running at his side, as they raced out into the smoky hall after the emperor.

'There he is!' she heard Jagang call from up ahead. 'Here! This way! Here!'

And then there was a thunderous blast so violent it took Jennsen's feet from under her, sending her sprawling. The hall was suddenly filled with fire and fragments of every sort rebounding off the walls as it all came flying toward them. Snatching her arm, Sebastian yanked her up and into a recessed doorway just in time to miss the bulk of the flying objects that came careening past.

Men up the hall let out screams of mortal pain. Such unbridled wails sent shivers up Jennsen's spine. Following Sebastian, Jennsen ran through thick smoke, toward the screams. The dark, in addition to the smoke, made it difficult to see very far, but they soon encountered bodies. Beyond the dead, there were still some men alive, but it was clear by the ghastly nature of their wounds that they would not live long. The last moments of their lives were to be spent in horrifying agony. Jennsen and Sebastian scrambled past the dying, through the carnage and rubble piled knee-deep from wall to wall, looking for Emperor Jagang.

There, among the splintered wood, leaning boards, overturned chairs and tables, glass shards, and fallen plaster, they spotted him. Jagang's thigh was laid open to the bone. A Sister stood beside him, her back pressed to the wall. A huge, splintered oak board had been driven through her just below her breastbone, pinning her to the wall. She was still alive, but it was evident that there was nothing to be done for her.

'Dear Creator forgive me. Dear Creator forgive me,' she whispered over and over through quivering lips. Her eyes turned to watch them approach. 'Please,' she whispered, blood frothing from her nose, 'please, help me.'

She had been close to the emperor. She had probably shielded him with her gift, deflecting whatever power had been unleashed, and saved his life. Now she was shivering in mortal agony.

Sebastian lifted something from under his cloak, behind his back. With a mighty swing, he brought his axe around. The blade slammed into the wall with resounding thunk, and stuck. The Sister's head tumbled down, bouncing through the dusty rubble.

Sebastian yanked once, freeing his axe. As he replaced it in the hanger at the small of his back, he turned and came face-to-face with Jennsen. She could only stare in horror into his icy blue eyes.

'If it were you,' he said, 'would you want me to let you endure such suffering?'

Trembling uncontrollably, unable to answer him, Jennsen turned away and fell to her knees beside Emperor Jagang. She imagined he had to be in frightening pain, but he hardly seemed to notice the gaping wound, except that he knew his leg wouldn't work. He held the two sides of the wound closed as best he could with one hand, but he was still losing a lot of blood. With his other hand, he had managed to drag himself to the side, where he leaned against the wall. Jennsen was no healer, and didn't really know what to do, but she did realize the urgent need to do something to stop the gushing blood.

His face streaked with sweat and soot, Jagang pointed with his sword down a side hall. 'Sebastian, it's her! She was just right here. I almost had her. Don't let her get away!'

Another Sister, wearing a dusty brown wool dress, came clambering over the rubble, stumbling toward them in the darkness, passing all the groaning soldiers. 'Excellency! I heard you! I'm here. I'm here. I can help.'

Jagang nodded his acknowledgment, one hand resting on his heaving chest. 'Sebastian – don't let her get away. Move!'

'Yes, Excellency.' Sebastian took note of the Sister climbing awkwardly over a broken side table, then pressed a hand to Jennsen's shoulder. 'Stay here with them. She'll protect you and the emperor. I'll be back.'

Jennsen snatched for his sleeve, but he had already dashed away, collecting all the remaining men on his way past. He led them off down the hall, disappearing into the darkness. Jennsen was suddenly alone with the wounded emperor, a Sister of the Light, and the voice.

She snatched up the end of a strip of a sheer curtain and pulled it out from under the rubble. 'You're losing a lot of blood. I need to close this as best I can.' She looked up into Emperor Jagang's nightmare eyes. 'Can you help hold it closed while I wrap it?'

He grinned. Sweat coursed down his face, leaving streaks through the dusty grime. 'It doesn't hurt, girl. Do it. I've had worse than this. Be quick about it.'

Jennsen started threading the filthy curtain under his leg, wrapping it around and under again as Jagang held the gaping wound closed as best he could. The fine fabric almost immediately turned from white to red with all the thick blood flowing across it. The sister put a hand to Jennsen's shoulder as she knelt down to help. As Jennsen continued wrapping, the Sister laid her hands flat on each side of the massive gash in the meat of his thigh.

Jagang cried out in pain.

'I'm sorry, Excellency,' the Sister said. 'I have to stop the bleeding or you'll bleed to death.'

'Do it, then, you stupid bitch! Don't talk me to death!'

The Sister nodded tearfully, clearly terrified by what she was doing, yet knowing she had no choice but to do it. She closed her eyes and once more pressed trembling hands to Jagang's hairy, blood-soaked leg. Jennsen pulled back to give her room to work, watching in the dim light as the woman apparently wove magic into the emperor's wound.

There was nothing to see, at first. Jagang gritted his teeth, grunting in pain as the Sister's magic began to do its work. Jennsen watched, spellbound, as the gift was actually being used to help someone, instead of cause suffering. She wondered briefly if the Imperial Order believed that even this magic, used to save the life of the emperor, was evil. In the murky light, Jennsen saw the blood pumping copiously from the wound abruptly slow to an oozing trickle.

Jennsen leaned closer, frowning, trying to see in the shadows, as the Sister, now that the bleeding was nearly stopped, moved her hands, probably to start the work of closing the emperor's terrible wound. Leaning close as she watched, Jennsen heard Jagang suddenly whisper.

'There he is.' Jennsen looked up. He was staring off down the hall. 'Richard Rahl. Jennsen – there he is. It's him.'

Jennsen followed Emperor Jagang's gaze, her knife gripped in her fist. It was dark in the hallway, but there was smoky light down at the far end, silhouetting the figure standing in the distance, watching them.

He lifted his arms. Between his outstretched hands, fire sprang to life. It wasn't fire like real fire, like the fire in a hearth, but fire like that out of a dream. It was there, but somehow not there; real, but at the same time unreal. Jennsen felt as if she were standing in a borderland between two worlds, the world that existed, and the world of the fantastic.

Yet, the lethal danger that the wavering flame represented was all too clear.

Frozen in dread, squatted down beside Emperor Jagang, Jennsen could only stare as the figure at the end of the hall lifted his hands, lifted the slowly turning ball of blue and yellow flame. Between those steady hands, the rotating flame expanded, to look frighteningly purposeful. Jennsen knew that she was seeing the manifestation of deadly intent.

And then he cast that implacable inferno out toward them.

Jagang had said that it was Richard Rahl down at the end of the hall. She could see only a silhouetted figure casting out from his hands that awful fire. Oddly enough, even though the flame illuminated the walls, it left its creator in shadow.

The sphere of seething flame expanded as it flew toward them with ever-gathering speed. The liquid blue and yellow flame looked as if it burned with living intent.

Yet, it was, in some strange way, nothing, too.

'Wizard's fire!' the Sister shrieked as she sprang up. 'Dear Creator! No!'

The Sister ran down the dark hall, toward the approaching flame. With wild abandon, she threw her arms up, palms toward the approaching fire, as if she were casting some magic shield to protect them, yet Jennsen could see nothing.

The fire grew as it shot toward them, illuminating the walls, ceiling, and debris as it wailed past. The Sister cast out her hands again.

The fire struck the woman with a jarring thud, silhouetting her against a flare of intense yellow light so bright that Jennsen threw an arm up before her face. In a heartbeat, the flame enveloped the woman, smothering her scream, consuming her in a blinding instant. Blue heat wavered as the fire swirled a moment in midair, then winked out, leaving behind only a wisp of smoke to hang in the hall, along with the smell of burnt flesh.

Jennsen stared, thunderstruck by what she had just seen, by a life so cruelly snuffed out.

Off down at the end of the hall, Lord Rahl again conjured a ball of the terrible wizard's fire, nursing it between his hands, urging it to grow and expand. Again he cast it outward from lifted arms.

Jennsen didn't know what to do. Her legs wouldn't move. She knew she couldn't outrun such a thing.

The howling sphere of roiling flame tumbled down the hall, wailing toward them, expanding as it came, illuminating the walls it passed, until the burning death spanned from wall to wall, from floor to ceiling, leaving no place to hide.

Lord Rahl started away, leaving them to their fate, as death roared down on Jennsen and Emperor Jagang.

Chapter 49

The sound was horrifying. The sight of it was paralyzing.

This was a weapon conjured for no reason but to kill. This was deadly magic. Lord Rahl's magic.

This time, there was no Sister of the Light to intercept it.

Magic. Lord Rahl's magic. There, but not.

In the last instant before it was on her, Jennsen knew what she had to do. She threw herself over Emperor Jagang. In that fraction of a second before the fire was upon her, she covered him with her body where he lay at the edge of the floor against the wall, protecting him as she would a child.

Even through her tightly closed eyes, she could see the brilliant light. She could hear the terrible wail of the tumbling flames howling around her.

But Jennsen felt nothing.

She heard it roaring past her, thundering off down the hall. She opened one eye to peek out. At the end of the corridor, the orb of living fire exploded through the wall, coming apart in a shower of liquid flame, sending a hail of blazing wood out onto the lawn far below.

With the wall gone, the hall was better lit. Jennsen pushed herself up.

'Emperor – are you alive?' she whispered.

'Thanks to you. . ..' He sounded stunned. 'What did you do? How could you not—'

'Hush,' she whispered urgently. 'Stay down, or he'll see you.'

There was no time to waste. It had to be ended. Jennsen sprang up and ran down the hall, knife in hand. She could now see the man standing there in the smoky light at the end of the hall. He had stopped and turned to stare back at her. As she raced toward him, she realized that it couldn't be her half brother. This was an old man, a collection of bones in dark maroon and black robes with silver bands at the cuff of the sleeves. Wavy white hair stuck out in disarray, but did not diminish his air of authority.

Yet he stared in shock at seeing her racing toward him, as if hardly believing it, hardly believing she had survived his wizard's fire. She was a hole in the world to him. She could see understanding flooding his hazel eyes.

Despite his kindly look, this was a man who had just killed countless people. This was a man doing Lord Rahl's bidding. This was a man who would kill more people unless stopped. He was a wizard, a monster. She had to stop him.

Jennsen held her knife high. She was almost there. She heard herself screaming in rage, like the battle cries she had heard from the soldiers, as she plunged forward. She understood those battle cries, now. She wanted his blood.

'No ...' the old man called to her. 'Child, you don't understand what you're doing. We don't have time – I don't have a moment to spare! Stop! I can't delay! Let me—'

His words were no more to her than those of the voice. She ran through the rubble littering the hall as fast as her legs would carry her, feeling the same sense of wild but deliberate fury she had in her house, when the men had attacked her mother, and then her – that same fierce commitment.

Jennsen knew what she had to do, and knew she was the one to do it.

She was invincible.

Before she reached him, he cast one hand out toward her, but lower than he had before. This time, no fire erupted. She didn't care if it did. She would not be stopped. She could not be stopped. She was invincible.

Whatever he did caused the debris at her feet to suddenly shift, as if he'd given the whole lot of it a mighty shove. Before she could jump clear, one foot tangled in the debris, breaking through the jumble of broken plaster and lath. Rumpled carpeting and wreckage of furniture ensnared her ankle. With a surprised gasp, Jennsen pitched violently forward. Pieces of wood and plaster flipped dust and debris up in the air as she crashed to the floor. Her face hit hard, stunning her.

Small chunks and scraps rained down on her back. Dust slowly rolled away. Her face stung with dizzyingly intense pain.

Jennsen listened to the voice calling to her to get up, to keep moving. But her vision had narrowed down to a tiny spot, as if she were looking through a soft fuzzy tube. The world looked dreamlike through that tunnel of sight. She lay still, breathing the settling dust until it coated her throat, unable even to cough.

Groaning, Jennsen was at last able to push herself up. Her vision was rapidly returning. She began coughing, hacking, trying to clear her windpipe of the choking dust. Her leg was jammed down among the tangle of debris. She was finally able to pry a board to the side, giving her room to pull her foot free. Fortunately, her boot had prevented the splintered wood from slicing her leg.

Jennsen realized her hands were empty. Her knife was gone. On her hands and knees, she rummaged madly through the wreckage of wood, plaster, and tangled fabric of draperies, throwing things aside, searching for her knife. She thrust her arm under a nearby overturned table, groping blindly.

With the tips of her fingers, she felt something smooth. She groped along it until she touched the ornately engraved letter 'R.' Grunting with the effort, she shouldered the leg of the overturned table until the whole mess grated as it moved a little. At last, she was able to reach in far enough to pull her knife free.

When Jennsen was finally able to scramble to her feet, the man was long gone. She went after him anyway. When she reached the intersection of passageways, a quick look revealed only empty halls. She ran down the corridor she thought he had taken, looking in rooms, searching alcoves, making her way ever deeper into the murky palace.

She could hear people in the distance, soldiers, yelling for others to follow them. She listened for Sebastian's voice, but didn't hear him. She heard, too, the sound of magic being unleashed, like the crack of lightning, only indoors. It sometimes shook the entire palace. Sometimes, too, the screams of dying men could be heard.

Jennsen chased after the sounds, trying to find the man who had loosed the wizard's fire, but found only more empty rooms and passageways. Some places were littered with dead soldiers. She couldn't tell if they had been there from the first, or had been left in the wake of the fleeing wizard.

Jennsen heard the sound of running soldiers, their boots rumbling through corridors. And then, she heard Sebastian's voice call out, 'That way! It's her!'

Jennsen raced for an intersection and turned down a hall running off in the direction she had heard Sebastian's voice. Her footfalls were muted by a long green carpet with gold fringe running the length of a grand corridor. It was all the more startlingly beautiful after coming out of ruined areas. A window overhead lit the variegated brown-and-white marble columns that supported arches to each side, like silent sentinels watching her race by.

The palace was a maze of corridors and exquisite chambers. Some of the rooms Jennsen cut through were lavishly furnished in muted tones, while yet others were decorated with carpets, chairs, and draperies in a riot of colors. She dimly noted that the grand sights were astoundingly beautiful as she concentrated on not getting lost. She imagined the place as a vast forest, and noted landmarks along the way so as to find her way back. She had to help get Emperor Jagang to safety.

Racing down the wide passageway lined with granite recesses in the walls to each side, each holding a delicate object of one kind or another, Jennsen burst through double gold-bound doors into an enormous chamber. The sound of the doors rebounding echoed back from the room beyond. The size of place, the splendor of the sight, caught her up short. Overhead, rich paintings of figures in robes swept across the inside of the huge dome. Below the majestic figures a ring of round windows let in ample light. A semicircular dais sat off to the side, along with chairs behind an imposing carved desk. Arched openings around the room covered stairways up to curving balconies edged with sinuous, polished mahogany railings.

Jennsen knew by the imposing architecture that this must be the place from where the Mother Confessor ruled the Midlands. All the seating up in the balconies must have provided visitors or dignitaries a view of the proceedings.

Jennsen saw someone making their way among the columns on the other side of the chamber. Just then, Sebastian burst through another door not far to Jennsen's right. A company of soldiers funneled through the doors after him.

Sebastian lifted his sword, pointing. 'There she is!' He was nearly out of breath. Rage flashed in his blue eyes.

'Sebastian!' Jennsen ran to his side. 'We have to get out of here. We need to get the emperor to safety. A wizard came and the Sister was killed. He's alone. Hurry.'

The men were fanning out, a jangling dark mass clad in chain mail and armor and gleaming weapons spreading around the edge of the vast chamber like wolves stalking a fawn.

Sebastian heatedly pointed his sword across the room. 'Not until I have her. Jagang will at last have the Mother Confessor.'

Jennsen peered off to where he pointed and saw, then, the tall woman across the room. She wore simple, coarsely woven flaxen robes decorated at the neck with a bit of red and yellow. Her black and gray hair was parted in the middle and cut square with her strong jaw.

'The Mother Confessor,' Sebastian whispered, transfixed by the sight of her.

Jennsen frowned back at him. 'Mother Confessor ...?' Jennsen couldn't envision the Lord Rahl wedding a woman as old as his great-grandmother. 'Sebastian, what do you see?'

He flashed a smug look. 'The Mother Confessor.'

'What does she look like? What's she wearing?'

'She's wearing that white dress of hers.' His heated expression was back. 'How can you miss her?'

'She's a beautiful bitch,' a soldier on the other side of Sebastian said with a grin, unable to take his eyes from the woman across the room. 'But the emperor will be the one to have her.'

The rest of the men, too, started across the room with that

same disturbing, lecherous look. Jennsen seized Sebastian by the arm and yanked him around.

'No!' she whispered harshly. 'Sebastian, it's not her.'

'Are you out of your mind?' he asked as he glared at her. 'Do you think I don't know what the Mother Confessor looks like?'

'I've seen her before,' the soldier beside him said. 'That's her all right.'

'No, it's not,' Jennsen whispered insistently, all the while tugging at Sebastian's arm, trying to get him to pull back. 'It must be a spell or something. Sebastian, it's an old woman. This whole thing is going terribly wrong. We have to get out—'

The soldier on the other side of Sebastian grunted. His sword clattered to the marble floor as he clutched his chest. He toppled, like a tree that had been felled, and crashed to the floor. Another soldier, then another, then another fell. Thump, thump, thump they hit the floor. Jennsen put herself in front of Sebastian, throwing her arms around him to protect him.

The room exploded with a blinding flash of lightning. The sizzling arc twisted through the air, yet it unfailingly found its mark, raking down the line of men running out around the edge of the room, cutting them down in an instant. Jennsen looked over her shoulder and saw the old woman cast a hand out to the other side, toward men, and a Sister, charging across the room straight toward her. The soldiers, struck down by an invisible power, dropped in their tracks, one at a time. Their heavy crumpled bodies slid across the slick floor a short distance when they collapsed in mid-stride.

The Sister cast out her hands, Jennsen assumed to protect herself with magic of some kind, although she could see nothing of it. But when the Sister again thrust out an arm, Jennsen not only saw but could hear light forming at the tips of her fingers.

With all the soldiers down – all but Sebastian dead – the old sorceress turned her full attention on the attacking Sister. With weathered hands, the old woman warded the attack, sending the thrumming light back on the Sister.

'You know you have but to swear allegiance, Sister,' the old woman said in a raspy voice, 'and you will be free of the dream walker.'

Jennsen didn't understand, but the Sister surely did. 'It won't work! I'll not risk such agony! May the Creator forgive me, but it will be easier for us all if I kill you.'

'If that be your choice,' the old woman rasped, 'then so be it.'

The younger woman started to cast her magic again, but fell to the floor with a sudden cry. She clawed at the smooth marble, trying to whisper prayers between grunts of terrible agony. She left a smear of blood on the marble, but before getting far, she stilled. Her head sank to the floor as she expelled one long last rattling breath.

Knife in hand, Jennsen ran for the murderous old woman. Sebastian followed, but had taken only a few steps when the woman wheeled and cast a shimmering light at him just as Jennsen stepped into her line of sight. Only that prevented the streak of glimmering light from hitting him square. The light glanced off his side in a shower of sparks. Sebastian fell with a cry.

'No! Sebastian!' Jennsen started for him. He pressed his hands to the side of his ribs, clearly in pain. If hurt, at least he was alive.

Jennsen swung back to the old woman. She stood immobile, her head cocked, listening. There was confusion in her manner, and a curious kind of awkward helplessness.

The sorceress wasn't looking at her, but instead had an ear turned to her. Being a little closer, now, Jennsen noticed for the first time that the old woman had completely white eyes. Jennsen stared, at first from surprise, and then with sudden recognition.

'Adie?' she breathed, not having intended to say it aloud.

Startled, the woman cocked her head the other way, listening with her other ear. 'Who be there?' the raspy voice demanded. 'Who be there?'

Jennsen didn't answer, for fear of giving away her exact location. The room had gone silent. Worry wore heavily on the old sorceress's weathered face. But determination, too, set her jaw as her hand lifted.

Jennsen gripped her knife in her fist, not knowing what to do. If this really was Adie, the woman Althea had told her about, then, according to Althea, she would be completely blind to

Jennsen. But she was not blind to Sebastian. Jennsen crept a step closer.

The old woman's head turned to the sound. 'Child? Do you be a sister of Richard? Why would you be with the Order?'

'Maybe because I want to live!'

'No.' The woman shook her head with stern disapproval. 'No. If you be with the Order, then you have chosen death, not life.'

'You're the only one intent on bringing death!'

'That be a lie. All of you came to me with weapons and murderous intent,' she said. 'I did not come to you.'

'Of course! Because you defile the world with your taint of magic!' Sebastian called from behind. 'You would smother mankind – enslave us all – with your wicked ancient ways!'

'Ah,' Adie said, nodding to herself. 'It be you, then, who has deluded this child.'

'He's saved my life! Without Sebastian I would be nothing! I would have nothing! I would be dead! Just like my mother!'

'Child,' Adie said in a quiet rasp, 'that, too, be a lie. Come away from them. Come with me.'

'You'd love that, wouldn't you!' Jennsen shrieked. 'My mother died in my arms because of your Lord Rahl. I know the truth. The truth is that you'd love to deliver the prize plum to Lord Rahl, at last.'

Adie shook her head. 'Child, I don't know what lies be filling your head, but I do not have the time for this. You must come away with me, or I cannot help you. I cannot wait a moment longer. Time be in short supply and I have used all I have.'

As the woman spoke, Jennsen used the opportunity to take small quiet steps forward. She had to take this chance to end the threat. She knew she could take this woman out. If it was only a matter of muscle and skill with a knife, then Jennsen would have the distinct advantage. A sorceress's magic was useless against someone who was invincible – against a pillar of Creation.

'Jenn, take her! You can do it! Avenge your mother!'

Jennsen was still only a quarter of the distance from Sebastian to Adie. Knife held tight, she took another step.

'If that be your choice,' Adie rasped at hearing the whisper of the footstep, 'then so be it.'

When the sorceress lifted her hand out toward Sebastian, Jennsen realized with horror what she meant: the price of her choice was that Sebastian would be forfeit.

Chapter 50

Sebastian was on the floor, not far away, leaning to the side, propping himself up on one arm. Jennsen saw blood on the marble floor under him. Since Adie couldn't stop Jennsen, she intended to finish him as the price. The appalling reality of seeing Sebastian in pain, of knowing he was about to be murdered, shook Jennsen to her very soul.

Sebastian was all she had.

The sorceress was but a blink away from loosing lethal magic on him. Jennsen was a great deal closer to Sebastian than to the sorceress. Jennsen knew she would never reach the sorceress in time to stop her, but she might make it to Sebastian in time to protect him. She could only kill the sorceress if she were willing to forfeit Sebastian to do it. That was the choice Adie had given her.

Jennsen abandoned her attack and instead dove for Sebastian, putting herself in the woman's line of sight, making a hole in the world where she was trying to aim her terrible conjured fire. The magic the sorceress loosed missed Sebastian, raking crackling lightning across the polished marble floor, ripping it up in a line right beside him. The air was filled with a burst of flying stone shards.

Jennsen scooped Sebastian protectively into her arms as she fell to his side. 'Sebastian! Can you move? Can you run? We have to get out of here.'

He nodded. 'Help me up.' His voice was labored, his breathing shallow.

Jennsen ducked her head under his arm and strained with the

505

effort of lifting him to his feet. With her help, they hurriedly worked their way toward the door. Behind, Adie lifted her hands again, her white eyes tracking Sebastian's movements, if not Jennsen's. Jennsen twisted sideways, putting herself in the way. A blast of lightning laced past, missing them by inches, blowing the heavy metal-clad door off its hinges. The door went skittering down the hall.

Jennsen and Sebastian scuttled through the smoking opening and hastened down the wide hall. Jennsen realized, as she watched the heavy doors crashing down the hall, bouncing off walls, tearing out great chunks of stone, that if something like that hit her, she would be crushed. She noticed, too, that her arm was bleeding from small cuts from the stone shards that had struck her. It wasn't magic that had done it, but sharp stone, even if the sharp stone had been sent flying by magic.

She might be in some ways invincible, but if magic toppled a massive stone column on her, she would be just as dead as if it had been pushed over by brute strength instead. Dead was dead.

Jennsen suddenly didn't feel so invincible.

At the first intersection, she took them to the right, getting Sebastian out of the line of sight of Adie's gift, and her weapons of magic, as quickly as possible. Jennsen could feel his warm blood running over the arm she had around him. Despite his injury, Sebastian didn't ask her to slow to spare him any pain. Together, they rushed through halls and rooms as fast as he was able, crossing the palace, going back toward where Jennsen had left the emperor.

'Are you hurt bad?' she asked, fearing the answer.

'Not sure,' he said, nearly out of breath and clearly in pain. 'Feels like there's a fire burning in my ribs. If you wouldn't have prevented her from hitting me square on, I'd be dead for sure.'

As they moved through the palace, they came across a squad of their men. Jennsen collapsed next to them, panting, exhausted, unable to hold Sebastian up another step. Her leg muscles trembled from the exertion.

'We're leaving,' Sebastian told the men, his breathing labored with pain. 'We have to get out. The emperor is hurt. We have to get him out of here.' He motioned in different directions. 'Some of you go each way. Collect all our men. We need to get everyone we can to protect the emperor and then we have to get him back to safety. You two, you'll have to help me.'

The bulk of the men immediately rushed off to their tasks. The two remaining behind threw Sebastian's arms over their shoulders and easily lifted him. He winced in pain. Jennsen led them through the palace, watching for the landmarks she remembered, desperate to reach Emperor Jagang and to get out of the death trap of a palace.

The Confessors' Palace was a confusion of halls, passageways, and rooms. Some of the rooms were huge, but when they came to such places, they went around, staying to the maze of passageways; Sebastian said they didn't want to be caught in one of those big rooms where they would be an easier target. Intermittently, Jennsen heard the awful thump of magic. Each time, the entire palace shuddered with the concussion.

'This way,' she said, recognizing the yawning breach in the wall at the corner of a passageway strewn with rubble. That gaping hole through the outer wall, looking out to daylight and overlooking the lawns far below, was where the wizard's fire, meant for her and Emperor Jagang, had blasted through.

Five soldiers made their way down the hall from the other direction, climbing over the tangled debris, bringing a Sister of the Light with them. From behind, nearly a dozen more men appeared. Two Sisters, their faces streaked with soot, came through a nearby room to the side, followed by yet more of the assault force. Half the men were bleeding, but all of them were able to move under their own power.

Emperor Jagang was sitting up against the wall where Jennsen had left him. The deep jagged gash was partly being held together by the curtain Jennsen had wrapped around his leg, but the meat of his muscle wasn't aligned properly and the terrible wound clearly needed attention. It appeared that the healing magic performed by the Sister, just before she had been killed, still held, and at least the emperor wasn't still losing blood the way he had been.

The blood the emperor had lost left him weak-looking and

507

pale, but not as pale as the faces of those who for the first time saw the seriousness of his injury.

One of the Sisters knelt down to check his wound. Jagang winced when she tried to better align the two halves of his split leg.

'There's no time to heal it now,' she said. 'We'll need to get him to safety, first.'

She immediately set to tightening the bandage of blood-soaked curtain that Jennsen had started to apply. She snatched up more cloth from the rubble.

'Did you get her?' Jagang asked as the Sister worked at pulling the injury closed with the filthy strip of cloth. 'Where is she? Sebastian!' He used a board to lever himself upright, peering this way and that around the company of soldiers as they helped Sebastian make his way through to the emperor. 'There you are. Where's the Mother Confessor? Did you get her?'

'It isn't her,' Jennsen answered in his place.

'What?' The emperor glanced around angrily at the people watching him. 'I saw the bitch. I know the Mother Confessor when I see her! Why didn't you get her!'

'You saw a wizard and a sorceress,' Jennsen told him. 'They were using magic to make you think you were seeing Lord Rahl and the Mother Confessor. It was a trick.'

'I think she's right,' Sebastian put in before Jagang could scream at her. 'I was standing right beside her and while I saw the Mother Confessor, Jennsen didn't.'

Jagang turned a dark scowl on her. 'But if the others saw her, how could you not . . .'

Understanding seemed to come over him. For some reason that Jennsen couldn't exactly fathom, he suddenly recognized the truth in her words.

'But why?' the Sister tending the emperor's injury asked, looking up from her work of bandaging the wound.

'Both the wizard and the sorceress seemed to be in a hurry,' Jennsen said. 'They must be up to something.'

'It's a diversion,' Jagang whispered, staring off down the empty hall littered with rubble. 'They wanted to keep us occupied. Keep us away, and busy thinking about something else.'

'Keep us away from what?' Jennsen asked.

'The main force,' Sebastian said, catching Jagang's line of thought.

Another Sister, casting surreptitious glances to the other Sisters after inspecting Sebastian's wound, worked quickly at pressing a padded bandage against his ribs and then wrapping a long strip of cloth around his chest to hold it in place.

'This will only help for a short time,' she muttered, half to herself. 'This is not good.' She glanced again to the other Sister. 'We're going to need to tend to this. We can't do it here.'

Sebastian winced in pain, ignoring her, then spoke. 'It's a trick. They keep us here, puzzling over where they could be, kept us chasing after illusions, while they attack our main force.'

Jagang growled a curse. He looked off out the hole the wizard's fire had blasted in the wall, peering out toward the army they had left a long ride back down the river valley. He clenched his fist and gritted his teeth.

'That bitch! They wanted us busy so our main force would be sitting in place while they attack. That filthy scheming bitch! We have to get back!'

The small force moved quickly through the halls. Jagang was carried with a man under each arm, as was Sebastian, so that they could make quick progress back out of the Confessors' Palace. Sebastian was looking worse.

Along the way, they gathered up more of their men. Jennsen was astounded that there were still any others alive. Compared with the force they had come in with, though, they had been cut to pieces. Had they all stayed together, rather than the way the emperor and Sebastian continually divided them up, they might have all been killed at once. As it was, the Order would still have to leave behind a great many dead.

Once on the lower level, they worked their way along service halls, toward the side of the palace, Sebastian advising that it would be best not to go out by the main entrance, where they had entered, for fear that such a move might be expected and they very well could be struck down before they could get away.

Everyone moved as silently as possible through the empty kitchens, emerging to a gray day in a side courtyard. It was secluded, with a wall screening it off from the city.

The sight as they came around the side of the palace was horrifying. It looked like the entire force had been cut down, that none of the cavalry could possibly still be alive. Jennsen couldn't stand the sight of so much carnage, yet it was so overwhelming that she could not look away. The dead, horses as well as men, lay tangled in a ragged line down the hillside, fallen in the place where they met the foe head-on at a full charge. In the distance, near the trees, a few scattered horses, their riders no doubt dead, nibbled at the grass.

'There are no enemy dead,' Jagang said, surveying the sight as he limped along with the aid of a pike a soldier had handed him. 'What could have done this?'

'Nothing living,' a Sister said.

As they moved quickly down the hill, making their way past the silent battle line, not far in front of the heaps of corpses, others of the cavalry, far down the slope on the other side of a wall in an area among small garden buildings and trees, spotted the emperor and raced out to protect him. Soldiers on horseback – numbering less than a thousand out of the over forty thousand they started with – swept in to surround the company returning from the palace. A number of the Sisters rode in, pulling in close to the emperor to provide an inner circle of defense.

Rusty, trailed by Pete, trotted across the lawns, accompanying the tattered remnants of the cavalry. When Jennsen whistled, Rusty recognized the call and rushed in to be close to her. The mare, nuzzling Jennsen's shoulder, voiced a plaintive whinny, eager for comfort. Rusty and Pete weren't cavalry horses, trained to be accustomed to the terrors of war. Jennsen ran a soothing hand over the horse's trembling neck and rubbed her ears. She gave similar comfort to Pete when he pressed his forehead against the back of her shoulder.

'What happened!' Jagang called out in a rage. 'How could you let yourselves be taken like this?'

The officer leading the men on horseback looked around in

dismay. 'Excellency, it was ... out of the clear air. It wasn't anything we could fight.'

'Are you trying to tell me it was ghosts!' Jagang bellowed.

'I think it was the horses the scout smelled,' another officer said. His arm was bandaged up high but soaked in blood.

'I want to know what's going on,' Jagang said as he glared around at the faces watching him. 'How could this have happened?'

As men brought extra horses, Sister Perdita dismounted close by. 'Excellency, it was some kind of attack involving magic – phantom horsemen invoked by wizardry is the only explanation I have.'

His menacing eyes were leveled at her in a way that made even Jennsen quail. 'Then why didn't you and your Sisters stop it?'

'It wasn't anything like the conjured magic we ordinarily encounter. I believe it had to be a form of constructed magic, or we would have not only detected it, but been able to stop it. At least, that's what I assume. I've never actually seen any constructed magic, but I've heard of it. Whatever this was that attacked us would not respond to anything we tried.'

The emperor was still frowning darkly at her. 'Magic is magic. You should have stopped it. That's what you were here for.'

'Constructed magic is different than conjured, Excellency.'

'Different? How?'

'Rather than using the gift on the spot, constructed magic has already been made up in advance. It can be preserved for a great period of time – thousands of years, maybe even forever. When it's needed, the spell is triggered and the magic is loosed.'

'Triggered by what?' Sebastian asked.

Sister Perdita shook her head in frustration. 'By just about anything, as I've heard it told. It just depends on how it was constructed. No wizard now is able to construct such a spell. We know little about those ancient wizards or what they could do, but from what little we do know, a constructed spell could be something kept dry that comes to life when you get it wet – for example something to help fertilize crops when the spring rains come. It could be triggered by heating, like a cure taken for a fever – the cure carries a construction in and the fever triggers it. Others are triggered by a little magic, some by an elaborate application of incredibly intricate wizardry and great power.'

'So,' Jennsen reasoned, 'someone with magic must have unleashed something so powerful as these phantom horsemen? A wizard, or a sorceress, or something?'

Sister Perdita shook her head. 'It could be that kind of constructed magic, but it could just as easily be a spell – albeit an incredibly powerful one – kept in a thimble, and triggered by exposing the construction to . . . anything – horse dung, even.'

Emperor Jagang waved off the very notion. 'But something that small and easily triggered wouldn't be this powerful.'

'Excellency,' the Sister said, 'in this, you can't equate the apparent material size of the construction or its trigger with the result – they have no relational value, at least not in the terms in which most people think. The trigger has no bearing on the power of the construction. Even the construction and its trigger are not necessarily relational. There is simply no rule by which to judge a construction.'

The emperor swept an arm out before the tens of thousands of men and horses tangled in death. 'But, surely, something of this magnitude had to have been something more.'

'The army of phantom horsemen who carried out this attack might have been triggered by a wizard drawing spells in magic dust while speaking an incredibly complex invocation, or it could just as easily have been a book containing a cavalry counter that is simply opened to the proper page and held out before the attacking force – even from miles away. Even the simple fear of a person holding out such a construction could be the trigger.'

'You mean, anyone might accidentally trigger one, then?' Jennsen asked.

'Of course. That's what makes them so dangerous. But from what I've read, that kind is exceedingly rare. Because they can be so dangerous, most are layered in complex precautions and fail-safe mechanisms involving the most profound knowledge of the application of magic.'

'But,' Jennsen asked, 'once a person – a wizard – with that

advanced knowledge removes those layers of precautions and fail-safe mechanisms, then they might be set off by one final, simple trigger?'

Sister Perdita gave Jennsen a meaningful look. 'Exactly.'

'So,' Jagang said, gesturing around at the thousands of bodies, 'this force of phantom cavalry might be sent out again at any moment to finish us off.'

The Sister shook her head. 'As I understand it, a constructed spell is usually good only once. It's used up by doing what it was constructed to do. That's one reason they're rare; once used, they're gone forever, and there are no longer any wizards alive who can make more.'

'Why haven't we encountered such constructed spells before?' Sebastian asked with growing impatience. 'And why now, all of a sudden?'

Sister Perdita stared at him for a moment, a picture of bottled anger that Jennsen knew she would never have dared direct at the emperor, even though the attack on the Confessors' Palace, which he ordered, against her warning, had resulted in the deaths of many of her Sisters of the Light.

With a show of deliberate care, Sister Perdita pointed up at the dark Keep hard against the mountain above them. 'There are a thousand rooms in the Wizard's Keep if there's one,' she said in a low voice. 'A good many of them will be stuffed full of nasty things. It's likely that when we drove them here for the winter, that wizard of theirs – Wizard Zorander – finally had the good long time he needed to search through the Keep, looking for just the kinds of things he hitherto lacked, so as to be ready for us when spring arrived and we advanced toward Aydindril. I fear to think what catastrophic surprises he yet has in store for us. That Keep has stood invincible for thousands of years.'

Sebastian's glare turned as dark as Jagang's 'Why haven't you warned us about this? I never heard you say anything.'

'I did. You were gone.'

'You've also advised against many other things, as well, and we've overcome them,' Jagang growled at her. 'When you fight a war, you must expect to take risks and to take casualties. Only those who dare, win.'

Sebastian gestured up at the Keep. 'What other things might we expect?'

'Constructed spells are only one of the dangers in fighting these people. None of us Sisters really considered constructed spells a great threat because they're so rare, but, as you can see, even one constructed spell is profoundly perilous. Who knows what even more deadly things might be waiting to be unleashed.

'What's more, there's a whole world of dangers we can't even begin to conceive of. Their winter weather, alone, has killed hundreds of thousands of our men without the enemy having to lift a finger or risk a single man. That, alone, has done more damage to us than almost any battle or calamity of magic. Did we expect such losses from something so simple as snow and cold weather? Did our size and strength protect us from it? Are those hundreds of thousands any less of a loss because they died of fever rather than some fancy application of magic? What difference does it make to the dead – or those left to fight?

'I admit, to a soldier, winning because your enemy falls ill might not seem very glamorous or heroic, but dead is dead. Our army outnumbers these people many times over, yet we lost those hundreds of thousands to fever because of simple weather – not the magic you are so worried about us protecting you from.'

'But in a real fight,' Sebastian scoffed, 'then our numbers really mean something and will win out.'

'Tell that to those who died of fever. Numbers don't always determine the winner.'

'That's outlandish,' Sebastian shot back.

Sister Perdita pointed at the line of dead. 'Tell it to them.'

'We must take risks if we're to win,' Jagang said, settling the matter. 'What I want to know is if the enemy can be expected to throw more of these constructed spells at us?'

Sister Perdita shook her head, as if to say she had no idea. 'I doubt that Wizard Zorander knows much about the constructed spells kept there. Such magic is no longer understood well.'

'He apparently understood one of them pretty well,' Sebastian said.

'And, that might have been the only one he understood well

514

enough to use. As I said before, once used, constructed spells are used up.'

'But it's also possible,' Jennsen interrupted, 'that there are more constructed spells he does understand.'

'Yes. Or, for all anyone knows, this could have been the last constructed spell in existence. On the other hand, he might be sitting in there with a hundred of them in his lap, all much worse than this one. There is simply no way to know.'

Jagang's black eyes gazed out at his fallen cavalry elite. 'Well, he certainly used this one to cut—'

There was a sudden blinding flash off at the horizon.

The world around them lit with the intensity of a flash of lightning, but the flash didn't die out as lightning did. Jennsen seized the reins just under Rusty and Pete's bits to keep them from bolting. Other horses spooked, rearing up.

White-hot light flared up from the river valley down over the hills – in the direction of the army. The light was so white, so pure, so hot, that it lit the clouds from underneath all the way to the opposite horizon. It was a light of such power, such intensity, that many of the men dropped to a knee in alarm.

The incandescent glow expanded outward with incredible speed, dwarfing the hills, yet it was so distant that they heard nothing. The rocky slopes of the mountains ringing the city were all illuminated in the harsh glare.

And then Jennsen heard at last a deep rumbling boom that vibrated in her chest. It shook the ground beneath their feet. The powerful, resonant boom stretched out into a growing, clacking roar.

A dark dome expanded up through the light. Jennsen realized that, because of the distance, what looked to her like a spreading dome of dust had to be debris at least as big as trees. Or wagons.

As the dark cloud expanded upward through the light, it dissipated, as if evaporating in the might of that consuming heat and light. Jennsen could see a wave, like the rings made by tossing a rock in a pond, radiating outward, except this was a single wave racing across the ground.

As everyone stood transfixed, gripped in fright, a sudden wall of wind, driving dirt and sand before it, blasted up the hill toward them. It was the shock of the wave that had finally reached them. It was so abrupt and so powerful that if the branches were not already bare, they would have been stripped of leaves right then and there. Limbs snapped as trees shuddered under the concussion of wind.

More horses panicked, bucking and bolting. Men dropped to the ground to protect themselves from what might come next. Jennsen, staggered by the blast of wind, shielded her eyes with a hand while huge soldiers recited prayers learned in childhood, begging the Creator for salvation.

Jagang stood facing the sight with angry defiant challenge.

'Dear spirits,' Jennsen finally said, squinting, blinking the dust from her eyes as the aftermath seemed to abate. 'What could that have possibly been?'

Sister Perdita had gone ashen. 'A light web.' Her voice was low and heavy with what Jennsen had never detected from her before: dread.

'Impossible!' Emperor Jagang roared. 'There are Sisters down there warding for light spells!'

Sister Perdita said nothing. She couldn't seem to take her gaze from the arresting sight.

Jennsen could tell that the pain was wearing heavily on Sebastian, but he spoke forcefully. 'I've been told that a light web can't do any more damage than' – he gestured back at the palace – 'perhaps to destroy a building.'

Sister Perdita said nothing, and with that silence offered the evidence to the contrary that was clearly before his eyes.

Jennsen took the reins to both horses in one hand and put the other to Sebastian's back in sympathy. She ached for him and wanted him to be somewhere safe where his injury could be tended to. The Sisters had said that it was serious and needed their attention. Jennsen suspected that the wound he suffered at the hands of the sorceress needed the intervention of magic.

'How can it be a light web!' Jagang demanded. 'There's not even anyone here! No troops, no army, no force – except maybe a couple of their gifted.'

'That's all it would take,' Sister Perdita said. 'Such a thing needs no supporting troops. I told you that something was wrong. With the Keep here, in Aydindril, there's no telling what even a lone wizard might be able to do to hold off an army – even our army.'

'You mean,' Sebastian asked, 'it's like the way a small force in a high pass, for example, can hold off a whole army?'

'That's right.'

Jagang looked incredulous. 'You mean to say that you think that even that one skinny old wizard, in a place like the Keep, might be able to do all that?'

Sister Perdita's gaze shifted to the emperor. 'That one skinny old wizard, as you call him, has just managed to do the impossible. He has not only found what was probably a light web constructed thousands of years ago, but, even more inconceivable, he somehow managed to ignite it.'

Jagang turned to stare off to where the light was finally dying. 'Dear Creator,' he whispered, 'that's right where the army is.' He wiped a hand back across his shaved head as he considered the frightening implications. 'How could they ignite a light web among our army? We're warded for that! How!'

Sister Perdita's eyes turned toward the ground. 'There is no way for us to tell, Excellency. It could be something as simple as a box containing an ancient light web from which he removed all the fail-safes and then left it for us to come across. As our men set up camp, maybe a man found it, wondered what was in the innocent-looking little box, opened it, and the light of day was the final trigger. It could be something else entirely that we could never begin to dream up or imagine, much less forestall. We'll never know. Whoever triggered it is now part of that cloud of smoke hanging over the river valley.'

'Excellency,' Sebastian said, 'I urgently advise that we get the army out of here – move them back.' He paused to wince in pain. 'If they're able to unleash such a defense – with all the gifted and their protection we have – then taking the Keep might be impossible.'

'But we must!' Jagang roared.

Sebastian sagged forward, waiting for a stitch of pain to pass. 'Excellency, if we lose the army, then Lord Rahl will triumph. It's as simple as that. Aydindril is not worth the risk it has proven

517

itself to be.' This was not so much the Sebastian Jennsen knew, as it was Sebastian, the Order's strategist, speaking. 'Better for us to withdraw and fight another day on our terms, not theirs. Time is our ally, not theirs.'

In silent fury, the emperor stared off toward his imperiled army as he considered Sebastian's advice. There was no telling how many men had just died.

'This is Lord Rahl's doing,' Jagang finally whispered. 'He has to be killed. In the Creator's name, he must be killed.'

Jennsen knew that she was the only one who could accomplish such a thing.

Chapter 51

Jennsen paced in the dimly lit tent, her footsteps silent across the emperor's opulent carpets. A Sister stood vigil near the outer entry, making sure that no one could come into the tent to disturb the emperor, or, more important, to harm him. Outside, a massive contingent of guards, including more Sisters, patrolled the area. Occasionally, the Sister over by the outer entry glanced at Jennsen as she paced.

Pacing was all she could do. Her insides were a painful knot of worry over Sebastian. He had lost consciousness on the long ride back to the encampment. Sister Perdita said that he was in danger of losing his life. Jennsen couldn't bear the thought of losing him. He was all she had.

Emperor Jagang was also in grave condition after having lost so much blood and then having to endure the long hard ride back with the tattered remnants of the elite cavalry, but he'd refused to delay his return for any reason, even his own well-being. He never thought of himself, only of getting back to his army. Both men were at last now secure in the confines of the emperor's tents, being attended to by Sisters of the Light. Jennsen had wanted to stay with Sebastian, but the Sisters chased her out.

The emperor had been made worse by the sight of the army. He'd been fit to kill anyone who gave him an excuse. Jennsen could understand his rage of emotion.

The light web had ignited close to the center of the encampment. Even this many hours after the event, the place was still mass confusion.

Many units had scattered, preparing for the possibility of an imminent attack. Others, it was suspected, had simply run for the hills. In the area where the light web had ignited there was nothing but a vast depression of blackened ground. In the ensuing chaos, no one had been able to determine how many men had been killed. It was next to impossible, with so many either killed or scattered, to get an accurate count of units, much less individuals, but there was no argument that the devastation was staggering.

Jennsen had overheard whispers of over half a million men turned to dust in an instant, and maybe as many as twice that number. In the end, the number killed might prove to be much higher; there were inestimable numbers of seriously injured soldiers – men burned or blinded, men severely cut or with limbs taken off by flying debris, men partially crushed by heavy wagons and equipment toppling on them, men made deaf, men so insensate, so stupefied, that they could only stare unblinking at nothing. There were not enough army surgeons or Sisters of the Light to even begin to attend to the tiniest fraction of the wounded. With every hour that passed, thousands of those who survived the initial blast died of their injuries.

As staggering a blow as it was, it was not fatal to the great beast of the Imperial Order army. The encampment was immense, and precisely because it was so vast, much of it had survived. According to the emperor, it was only a matter of time before they replaced the dead with fresh troops, and then he would unleash his men to seek vengeance on the people of the New World.

Jennsen was beginning to understand why Sebastian had always been so adamant that all magic must eventually be eliminated. There was no good that she could think of that could offset such wickedness. She hoped magic could at least spare his life.

Despite Emperor Jagang's conviction that their forces would soon recover, there were difficult times ahead for them. Much of the food had been destroyed, along with vast amounts of equipment and weapons. Every tent in the entire encampment had been at least knocked down. It was a cold night and many men would be exposed to the elements. Fortunately, even though the emperor's tent had been flattened, men had been able to erect it again for the injured emperor and Sebastian.

Jennsen paced, burning, not only with worry, but with rage. She doubted that a greater monster than Richard Rahl had ever lived. Surely, no single man had ever been the cause of so much suffering in the world. It was inconceivable to her that anyone could have such a lust for power that they would lead a cause that could murder so many people. She didn't see how Richard Rahl could be a part of Creation; surely, he was the Keeper's disciple.

Tears ran down Jennsen's cheeks at her gnawing apprehension. She prayed fervently to the good spirits that Sebastian would not die, that the Sisters could heal him.

In agonizing worry, she halted in her pacing and leaned on a table she had not seen the last time she had been in the tent. When the tent had fallen, it had been hastily erected, and this table, probably from the emperor's private quarters, apparently hadn't been replaced in its proper location. There was a small bookcase at the rear of the top.

Looking for something that might divert her mind from the ache of anxiety while she waited for word of Sebastian, Jennsen idly scanned the old books. She didn't understand the words on any of them. For some reason, though, one in particular drew her attention – something about the rhythm of the foreign words. She pulled the book out and turned it toward the candlelight, trying to read the title. She ran her fingertips over the four gilded words on the cover. They made no sense to her, yet they seemed somehow almost familiar.

Jennsen gasped in surprise when the Sister, who had been over by the door, lifted the book from her hands. 'These belong to Emperor Jagang. Besides being very old and very fragile, they are quite valuable. His Excellency doesn't like anyone to touch his books.'

Jennsen watched the woman inspect the book for any damage. 'I'm sorry. I meant no harm.'

'You are a very special guest, and we have been instructed to accord you every privilege, but these are His Excellency's most prized works. He is a man of great learning. He collects books.

As a guest, I think you should respect his wishes that no one but he touch them.'

'Of course. I didn't know. I'm sorry.' Jennsen chewed her lower lip as she looked back at the curtain drawn across the doorway to the back, where Sebastian was being seen to. She wished there would be some word. She turned back to the Sister. 'I was only puzzled because I've never seen such words.'

'These are in the tongue of the emperor's homeland.'

'Really?' Jennsen gestured to the book the Sister was returning to its place. 'Do you know what it says?'

'I don't know the language very well, but . . . let me see if I might be able to tell.' In the dim light, the Sister squinted at the book for a time, her lips moving silently as she worked at the translation, before finally sliding the volume back in place.

'It says, *The Pillars of Creation*.'

'*The Pillars of Creation* . . . What can you tell me about such a book?'

The woman shrugged. 'There's a place in the Old World called by that name. I would guess the book must be about that.'

Before Jennsen could ask anything else, Sister Perdita suddenly emerged from behind the rear partition of the tent, the candles casting harsh shadows across her somber face.

Jennsen rushed to meet her. 'How are they?' she asked in an urgent whisper. 'They're both going to be all right, aren't they?'

Sister Perdita's gaze shifted to the Sister who had just replaced the book. 'Sister, you are needed by the others. Please go help them.'

'But His Excellency told me to guard—'

'His Excellency is the one who needs the help. The healing is not going well. Go and help the Sisters.'

At that, the woman nodded and rushed off to the back.

'Why isn't the healing going well?' Jennsen asked after the Sister had vanished behind the heavy curtain.

'A healing that is started and then interrupted, as Emperor Jagang's was, creates unique problems – especially since the Sister who started it is dead. Each person brings unique ability to the task, so to go in later and try to unravel exactly how it was started, much less build on it, makes the healing much more difficult and delicate.' She offered a small smile. 'But we're confident that His Excellency will be fine. It's just a matter of some concentrated work by the Sisters of the Light. I imagine they will be at it most of the night. By morning, I'm sure everything will be under control and the emperor will be as strong as ever.'

Jennsen swallowed. 'What about Sebastian?'

Sister Perdita appraised her with a cool, unreadable look. 'I would say that depends on you.'

'On me? What do you mean? What do I have to do with healing him?'

'Everything.'

'But, what is it you could possibly need from me? – You have but to ask. I'll do anything. Please, you must save Sebastian.'

The Sister pursed her lips as she clasped her hands. 'His recovery hinges on your commitment to eliminating Richard Rahl.'

Jennsen was baffled. 'Well, yes, of course, I want to eliminate Richard—'

'I said commitment, not words. I need more than mere words.'

Jennsen stared a moment. 'I don't understand. I've traveled a long and difficult journey to come here so that I might secure the help of the Sisters of the Light so that I can get close enough to Lord Rahl to put my knife in his heart.'

Sister Perdita smiled that terrible smile of hers. 'Well then, if that's true, then Sebastian should have nothing to worry about.'

'Please, Sister, just tell me what it is you want.'

'I want Richard Rahl dead.'

'Then we share the same goal. If anything, I'd venture that I feel more strongly about it than you ever could.'

One of the Sister's eyebrows lifted. 'Really. Emperor Jagang said that the Sister who was trying to heal him, up in the palace, was killed by wizard's fire.'

'That's right.'

'And did you see the man who did it?'

Jennsen thought it strange that Sister Perdita didn't ask how it was that she wasn't also killed by the wizard's fire. 'He was an old man. Skinny, with wavy white hair sticking out in disarray.'

'First Wizard Zeddicus Zu'l Zorander,' the Sister said in a venomous hiss.

'Yes,' Jennsen said, 'I heard someone call him Wizard Zorander. I don't know him.'

Sister Perdita glared. 'Wizard Zorander is Richard Rahl's grandfather.'

Jennsen's jaw dropped. 'I didn't know.'

'Yet here was a wizard doing all this damage, nearly killing Emperor Jagang, and you – who claim to be so committed – failed to kill him.'

Jennsen held her hands out in frustration. 'But, but, I tried, I did. He got away. There was so much going on—'

'And you think it will be easier to kill Richard Rahl? Words are easy. When it comes to true commitment, you couldn't even stop the threat from his doddering old grandfather!'

Jennsen refused to allow herself to fall to tears. It was a struggle. She felt foolish and shamed. 'But I—'

'You came here for the help of the Sisters. You said you wanted to kill Richard Rahl.'

'I do, but what does that have to do with Sebastian—'

Sister Perdita held up a finger, commanding silence. 'Sebastian is in grave danger of dying. He was struck by a dangerous form of magic cast by a very powerful sorceress. Those shards of magic are still in him. Left alone, they will shortly kill him.'

'Please, you must hurry then—'

An incensed expression silenced Jennsen. 'That magic is also dangerous to us, to those trying to heal him. For us Sisters to attempt to remove those embedded shards of magic endangers our lives, as well as his. If we are to risk the lives of Sisters, then I want in return your commitment to kill Richard Rahl.'

'How could you place a condition on the life of a man!'

The Sister straightened with contempt. 'We will have to let many others die in order to devote the necessary numbers and time to healing this one man. How dare you ask that of us? How dare you ask us to let others die so that your lover might live?'

Jennsen had no answer to such a terrible question.

'If we are to do this, then it must be for something worth more than those lives that will be lost without our help. Helping this one man must count for something. Would you expect less? Would you not want the same? In return for us saving this man so dear to you—'

'He's dear to you, too! To the Imperial Order! To your cause! To your emperor!'

Sister Perdita waited to see if Jennsen would now be silent. When Jennsen's angry gaze faltered, and finally sank, the Sister continued.

'No one individual is important except for what value he can contribute to others. Only you can provide that value for him. For us saving this man so dear to you, I must have in return your unqualified commitment to stopping Richard Rahl, once and for all. Your material commitment to killing him.'

'Sister Perdita, you have no conception of how much I wish to kill Richard Rahl.' Jennsen's hands fisted at her sides. 'He ordered the murder of my mother. She died in my arms. His rule resulted in Emperor Jagang nearly being killed. Richard is responsible for hurting Sebastian! For suffering beyond any imagining! For murders beyond estimate! I want Richard Rahl dead!'

'Then let us free the voice.'

Jennsen stepped back in shock. 'What?'

'*Grushdeva*.'

Jennsen's eyes went wide at encountering that word aloud. 'Where did you hear that?'

A self-satisfied smirk settled comfortably on Sister Perdita's face. 'From you, dear.'

'I never—'

'At dinner with His Excellency. He asked you why it was you wished to kill your brother, what was your reason, your purpose. You said *Grushdeva*.'

'I never said any such thing.'

The smirk soured to condescension. 'Oh, but you did. Are you going to lie to me? To deny that word has been whispered in your mind?' When Jennsen stood silent, Sister Perdita went on. 'Do you know what it means? That word, *Grushdeva*?'

'No,' Jennsen said in a very small voice.

'Vengeance.'

'How do you know?'

'I know that tongue.'

Jennsen stood rigid, her shoulders drawn up. 'What is it, exactly, you are proposing?'

'Why, I'm proposing to save Sebastian's life.'

'But, what else?'

Sister Perdita shrugged. 'Some of us Sisters will take you out to a quiet place, where we can be alone, while some of us stay here and save Sebastian's life, like you want. In the morning, he will be better, and then you and he can be on your way to kill Richard Rahl. You came here for our help. I am proposing to give you that help. With what we do for you, you will be able to accomplish your task.'

Jennsen swallowed. The voice was strangely silent. Not a word. It was somehow more awful that it was silent, right then.

'Sebastian is dying. He has only moments before it will be too late for us to save him. Yes, or no, Jennsen Rahl?'

'But, what if—'

'Yes, or no! Your time has run out. If you want to kill Richard Rahl, if you want to save Sebastian, then utter but one word. Do it now, or forever wish you had.'

Chapter 52

After they picketed their horses, Jennsen gave Rusty a rub on the forehead. With trembling fingers, she smoothed her other hand along the underside of the jaw as she pressed the side of her face against the horse's nose.

'Be a good girl until I get back,' she whispered.

Rusty neighed softly in response to the gentle words. Jennsen liked to imagine that the horse could understand her words. From the way her goat, Betty, had always cocked her head and stilled her little upright tail as Jennsen confided her innermost fears, she had firmly believed that her hairy four-legged friend could understand every word.

Jennsen peered overhead at the clawlike branches swaying in the muted light of a full moon occulted by a milky veil of ethereal clouds drifting across the sky, as if gathering to bear silent witness.

'Are you coming?'

'Yes, Sister Perdita.'

'Hurry, then. The others will be waiting.'

Jennsen followed the woman up the side of a bank. The mossy ground was littered with leathery dried oak leaves and a layer of small branches. Roots emerging here and there from the loose loam provided enough footing to climb the steep rise. At the top, the ground leveled out. The Sister's dark gray dress made her nearly vanish as she moved into the thick brush. For a woman with such big bones, Jennsen noticed that the Sister moved with disturbing grace.

The voice remained silent. In tense times like this the voice always whispered to her. Now it was silent. Jennsen had always wanted the voice to leave her be. She had come to understand just how frightening such silence could be.

The full moon, being only thinly obscured, provided enough light to make their way. Jennsen could see her breath in the cold air as she followed the Sister into the thick of the woods back between the low spreading boughs of balsams and spruce. She had always felt at home in the woods, but, somehow, following a Sister into the woods didn't give her the same comforting feeling.

She would rather be alone than in the company of the stern woman. Ever since Jennsen had given her the only word that would save Sebastian's life, Sister Perdita had settled into a demeanor of blunt superiority devoid of any tolerance. She was now firmly in command, and was certain that Jennsen knew it.

At least she had kept her word. As soon as Jennsen had given hers, Sister Perdita had urgently set other Sisters to saving Sebastian's life. While other Sisters were sent on ahead to prepare whatever it was they had to prepare, Jennsen was allowed to briefly look in on Sebastian to reassure her that everything possible to save him was being done.

Before she had left his side, Jennsen had bent and softly kissed his beautiful lips, run her hand tenderly back over his white spikes of hair, and gently brushed her lips across both his closed, sky blue eyes. She had whispered a prayer for her mother, with the good spirits, to watch over him.

Sister Perdita had not stopped her, or hurried her, until at the end when she pulled Jennsen back and whispered that the Sisters, huddled all around him, had to be left to do their work.

On her way out, Jennsen had been allowed to put her head into the private chamber of the emperor, and saw four Sisters bent close over his injured leg. The emperor was unconscious. The four Sisters working feverishly on the emperor seemed to be in pain themselves, sometimes putting their hands to their heads in agony. Jennsen hadn't known, until she saw the four and Sister Perdita explained, just how unpleasantly difficult healing could be. The Sisters were not concerned, though, about the life of the emperor being in immediate danger, as they were about Sebastian.

Jennsen held a balsam bough back out of her way as she followed the Sister deeper into the forbidding wood.

'Why do we have to go so far from the camp?' Jennsen whispered. The horseback ride had taken what seemed hours.

Sister Perdita's tail of hair fell forward over her shoulder when she looked back, as if it were a particularly inane question. 'So we can be alone to do what must be done.'

Jennsen wanted to ask what must be done, but she knew the Sister wouldn't tell her. The woman had turned away all questions with answers that were no more than general. She said that Jennsen had given her word, and now it was her duty to uphold her end of the bargain – to do as she was told until it was finished.

Jennsen tried not to think about what might be ahead. She put her mind, instead, to thinking about leaving in the morning with a healthy Sebastian, about being back out on the trails, out in the countryside, away from all the people. Away from the grim-looking soldiers of the Imperial Order.

She knew that the soldiers were doing an invaluable job fighting against Lord Rahl, but, still, she just couldn't help the way those men made her skin crawl. She felt as nervous as a fawn being watched by a pack of drooling wolves. Sebastian just didn't understand whenever she'd tried to put it into words for him. He was a man; she supposed he couldn't understand what it felt like to be leered at. How could she make him understand that it was especially daunting to be watched by men such as those, men with such lecherous grins and savage eyes?

If she just did as Sister Perdita said, then, by morning, she and Sebastian could leave. With whatever help the Sisters were planning, they had at least assured her that she would be better able to kill Richard Rahl. That was all Jennsen cared about, now. If she could at last kill Lord Rahl, then she would be free. Her life would be her own. And if that much never came to be for herself, at least the rest of the world would be safe from a butcher of momentous proportions.

They had left the horses among trees with bare branches –

oaks, mostly. Since the trees had yet to leaf out, the forest had at first been open, but they moved steadily into thicker woods of balsam, spruce, and pine, many with thick boughs skirting their trunks all the way to the ground. Although the soaring pines had no lower branches, their spreading crowns sealed off the weak moonlight. Jennsen followed behind the Sister, watching her glide deeper into the silent, gloomy wood.

Jennsen had spent much of her life in forests. She could follow the trail left by a chipmunk. Sister Perdita was moving with all the certainty of someone following a road, yet there was no trail Jennsen could detect. The ground was covered with the typical forest litter; none of it had been moved by anyone's passing. She saw twigs lying undisturbed, dried leaves intact, delicate mosses that were untouched by any boot. For all Jennsen could tell, she and the Sister were making their way through virgin woods without any reason or destination, yet she knew by the deliberate way the Sister moved that she had to have one, even if only she saw it.

And then, Jennsen caught a faint sound drifting through the thick woods. She saw a blush of light on the underside of branches ahead. The chill air had an odd, unpleasant cast like the faint scent of rot, but with a sickening sweet trace to it.

As she followed Sister Perdita through thick, tightly spaced evergreens, Jennsen began to hear the individual voices joined in a low, rhythmic, guttural chant. She couldn't understand the words, but they resonated deep in her chest, and, the unusual cadence being disturbingly familiar, in the back of her mind. Even without her hearing the individual words, the cant of them almost seemed to be what lent the stench to the air. The words, peculiar yet hauntingly intimate, cramped her stomach with nausea.

Sister Perdita paused to look back, to make sure that her charge wasn't flagging. Jennsen could see the faint moonlight reflecting off the ring through the Sister's lower lip. All the Sisters wore one. Jennsen found the custom revolting, even if it was to show loyalty.

When Sister Perdita held a low balsam bough aside for her, Jennsen stepped through. Hearing the voices in chant beyond had her heart hammering. She could see, through the gap, a clearing in the forest, allowing an open view of the sky and moon overhead.

Jennsen glanced at the Sister's stern expression, then continued on to the brink of the clearing. Before her lay a broad circle of candles. The candles were placed so close together that it almost looked like a ring of fire invoked to hold back demons. Just inside the candles, a circle had been made on the bare ground with what looked like white sand that glimmered in the moonlight. All around just inside the circle, made with the same strange white sand, were geometric symbols Jennsen didn't recognize.

Seven women sat in a circle inside the sparkling sand. There was one place where it looked like someone belonged but was missing, no doubt Sister Perdita. The women had their eyes closed as they chanted in the strange language. Moonlight reflected off the rings through their lower lips as they spoke the grating guttural words.

'You are to sit in the center of the circle,' Sister Perdita said in a low voice. 'Leave your clothes here.'

Jennsen looked over into her hard eyes. 'What?'

'Remove your clothes and sit in the center facing the breach in the circle.'

The command was spoken with such cold authority that Jennsen knew that she had no choice but to obey. The Sister took her cloak, then watched silently. After her dress slipped to the ground, Jennsen hugged her goose-bump-covered shoulders. Her teeth chattered, but it was more than from just the cold. Seeing the Sister's silent glare, Jennsen swallowed in revulsion and then hurriedly took off the rest of her things.

Sister Perdita prodded her with a finger. 'Go.'

'What is it I'm doing?' Jennsen's own voice sounded surprisingly powerful to her.

Sister Perdita considered the question for a moment before finally answering. 'You are going to kill Richard Rahl. To help you, we are breaching the veil to the underworld.'

Jennsen shook her head. 'No. No, I'm not doing any such thing.'

'Everyone does it. When you die, you cross the veil. Death is part of life. In order for you to kill Lord Rahl, you are going to need help. We are giving you that help.'

'But the underworld is the world of the dead. I can't—'

'You can and you will. You have already given your word. If you don't do this, then how many more will Lord Rahl go on to murder? You will do this, or you will have the blood of each of those victims on your hands. By refusing, you will be invoking the death of countless people. You, Jennsen Rahl, will be aiding your brother. You, Jennsen Rahl, will be throwing open the doors of death and allowing all those people to die. You, Jennsen Rahl, will be the Keeper's disciple. We are asking you to have the courage to reject that, and to turn death, instead, on Richard Rahl.'

Jennsen shivered, tears running down her face, as she considered Sister Perdita's terrible challenge, her terrible choice. Jennsen prayed to her mother, asking what she should do, but no sign arrived to help her. Even the voice was silent.

Jennsen stepped over the candles.

She had to do this. She had to end the rule of Richard Rahl.

Thankfully, the center of the whole careful arrangement at least looked dark. Jennsen was mortified being naked in front of strangers, even if they were women, but that was the least of her fears at the moment.

As she stepped across the circle of glimmering white sand, it felt frighteningly colder, as if she were stepping into the grip of living winter. She shivered and shook, hugging herself, as she made her way to the center of the circle of women.

In the middle was a Grace made of the same white sand, sparkling in the moonlight. She stood staring down at it, a symbol she herself had drawn many times, but her hand was not guided by the gift.

'Sit,' Sister Perdita said.

Jennsen started with a gasp. The woman was standing right behind her. When she pressed on Jennsen's shoulders, Jennsen sank to the ground, sitting cross-legged in the center of the eight-pointed star in the center of the Grace. She noticed, then, that each of the Sisters sat at the extension of a ray coming from each point of the star, save one directly in front. That spot was empty.

Jennsen sat naked, shivering, in the center of the circle as the Sisters of the Light began their soft chanting again.

The woods were dark and gloomy, the trees bare of leaves. The branches clacked together in the wind like the bones of the dead Jennsen feared the Sisters were calling forth.

The chanting suddenly halted. Rather than sit in the single empty spot remaining in the circle of Sisters, as Jennsen had expected, Sister Perdita stood behind her and spoke short, sharp words in the strange language.

At points in the long, singsong speech, Sister Perdita stressed a word – *Grushdeva* – and cast her arm out over Jennsen's head, flinging out dust. The dust ignited with a roaring whoosh that made Jennsen jump each time she did it, the harsh light bathing the Sisters briefly in the light of the rolling flame.

As the fire ascended, the seven Sisters spoke as if with one voice. *'Tu vash misht. Tu vask misht. Grushdeva du kalt misht.'*

Not only were those words she knew, but Jennsen realized that the voice was speaking the words in her head along with the Sisters. It was both frightening and comforting to have the voice back. The anxiety when the voice had gone strangely silent had been unbearable.

'Tu vash misht. Tu vask misht. Grushdeva du kalt misht.'

Jennsen was lulled by the sound of the chanting, and as it went on, calmed, too. She thought about what it was that had brought her to this point, about the terror her life had been, from the time when she was six and she fled the People's Palace with her mother, to all the times that Lord Rahl had come close and they'd run for their lives, to that awful rainy night when Lord Rahl's men were in her house. Jennsen felt tears coursing down her cheeks as she thought about her mother there on the floor dying. As she thought about Sebastian fighting valiantly. As she thought about her mother's last words, and having to run and leave her mother there on the bloody floor. Jennsen cried out with the terrible anguish of it.

'Tu vash misht. Tu vask misht. Grushdeva du kalt misht.'

Jennsen cried in racking sobs. She missed her mother. She was afraid for Sebastian. She felt so terribly alone in the world. She had seen so many people die. She wanted it to end. She wanted it to stop.

'Tu vash misht. Tu vask misht. Grushdeva du kalt misht.'

When she looked up, through her watery vision, she saw something dark sitting in the spot before her that had moments before been empty. Its eyes glowed like the candlelight. Jennsen stared into those eyes, as if staring into the voice itself.

'Tu vash misht, Jennsen. Tu vask misht, Jennsen,' the voice before her and in her head said in a low, growling voice. 'Open yourself to me, Jennsen. Open yourself for me, Jennsen.'

Jennsen could not move in the glowing glare of those eyes. That was the voice, only not in her head. It was the voice in front of her.

Sister Perdita, behind her, cast out her dust again, and this time, when it ignited, it lit the person sitting there with the glowing eyes.

It was her mother.

'Jennsen,' her mother cooed. *'Surangie.'*

'What?' Jennsen whimpered in shock.

'Surrender.'

Tears flooded forth in an uncontrollable torrent. 'Mama! Oh, Mama!'

Jennsen started to rise, started to go to her mother, but Sister Perdita pressed down on her shoulders, keeping her in place.

As the rolling flames lifted and evaporated, as the light faded, her mother vanished into the darkness, and before her was the thing with the glowing candlelight eyes.

'Grushdeva du kalt misht,' the voice growled.

'What?' Jennsen wept.

'Vengeance is through me,' the voice growled in translation. *'Surangie,* Jennsen. Surrender, and vengeance will be yours.'

'Yes!' Jennsen wailed in inconsolable agony. 'Yes! I surrender to vengeance!'

The thing grinned, like a door to the underworld opening.

It rose up, a wavering shadow, leaning forward toward her. Moonlight glistened on knotted muscles as it stretched out, coming toward her, almost catlike, smiling, showing those heart-stopping fangs.

Jennsen was beyond knowing what to do, except that she had had all she could take, and wanted it to end. She could take none of it any longer. She wanted to kill Richard Rahl. She wanted vengeance. She wanted her mother back.

The thing was right before her, shimmering power and form that was there, but not, partly in this world and partly in another.

Jennsen saw then, beyond the ring, beyond the ring of Sisters and sparkling white sand and candles, huge shapes out in the shadows – things on four legs. There were hundreds of them, their eyes all glowing yellow in the darkness, breath steaming up from snarls. They looked like they could have come from another world, but were most definitely now wholly in this one.

'Jennsen,' the voice hovering close over her whispered, 'Jennsen,' it cooed, 'Jennsen.' It smiled a smile as dark as Emperor Jagang's eyes, as dark as a moonless night.

'What . . .' She whispered through her tears. 'What are those things out there?'

'Why, the hounds of vengeance,' the voice whispered intimately. 'Embrace me, and I shall unleash them.'

Her eyes widened. 'What?'

'Surrender to me, Jennsen. Embrace me, and I shall unleash the hounds in your name.'

Jennsen couldn't blink as she sank back away from the thing. She could hardly breathe. A low sound, a kind of purring rattle, came from the throat of the thing as it stretched over her, looking down into her eyes.

She was trying to think of that little word, that important little word. It was somewhere in her mind, but as she stared up into those glowing eyes, she couldn't think of it. Her mind felt frozen. She wanted that word, but it wasn't there.

'*Grushdeva du kalt misht,*' the voice cooed in that throaty, echoing growl. 'Vengeance is through me.'

'Vengeance,' Jennsen whispered numbly in answer.

'Open yourself to me, open yourself for me. Surrender. Avenge your mother.'

The thing passed a long finger over her face, and she could

feel where Richard Rahl was – as if she could feel the bond that told others where he was. To the south. Distant, to the south. She could find him, now.

'Embrace me,' the voice breathed, inches from her face.

Jennsen was flat on her back. The realization both surprised and alarmed her. She didn't recall lying back. She felt like she was watching someone else do these things. She realized that the thing that was the voice was kneeling between her open legs.

'Surrender your will, Jennsen. Surrender your flesh,' the voice cooed, 'and I will release the hounds for you. I will help you kill Richard Rahl.'

The word was gone. Lost. Just like her . . . lost.

'I . . . I,' she stammered as tears ran from her wide eyes.

'Embrace me, and vengeance will be yours. Richard Rahl will be yours to kill. Embrace me. Surrender your flesh, and with it, your will.'

She was Jennsen Rahl. It was her life.

'No.'

The Sisters in the circle wailed in sudden pain. They held their hands to their ears, crying in agony, howling like hounds.

The glowing candlelight eyes peered down at her. The smile returned, this time vapor hissing from between wet fangs.

'Surrender, Jennsen,' the voice rumbled with such terrible command that Jennsen thought it might crush her. 'Surrender your flesh. Surrender your will. And then you will have vengeance. You will have Richard Rahl.'

'No,' she said, shrinking back as the thing stretched closer to her face. Her fingers dug into the dirt. 'No! I will surrender my flesh, my will, if that is the price, if that is what I must do to rid the world of life of the murdering bastard Richard Rahl, but I will not do so until you give me that, first.'

'A bargain?' the voice hissed. The glow in the eyes went red. 'You wish to bargain with me?'

'That is my price. Release your hounds. Help me kill Richard Rahl. When I have vengeance, then I will surrender.'

The thing grinned a nightmare grin.

A long thin tongue snaked out, licking her, in terrible intimate promise, from her naked crotch all the way up to between her breasts. It sent a violent shudder through her to her very soul.

'Bargain struck, Jennsen Rahl.'

Chapter 53

Friedrich wove his way between the fat clumps of grasses at the edge of the small lake, trying not to think about how hungry he was. With the way his stomach grumbled, he was not having much success. Fish might be nice for a change, but fish had to be cooked, and first he had to catch one. He gazed along the water's edge. Frog legs would be good, too. A meal of dried meat, though, would be quicker. He wished he had gotten a hard biscuit out of his pack the last time he'd stopped for a respite. At least if he had, he would have something to suck on.

In some places, shorter grass bowed over to line the lake's edge like a green pelt. In other places there were hushed stands of tall reeds. As the sun sank behind the low hills beyond the lake, it began to turn gloomy in among the imposing trees, contorted by great age, on the other side of the path. The air was dead still, leaving the mirrored surface of the water gilded with the golden glow of the western sky.

Friedrich paused to stand at ease, stretching his back, as he peered into the shadows among the trees. He needed a brief break to rest his tired legs as he considered whether or not he should stop for the night to set up a shelter, or at least get out a biscuit. He could see dark stretches of standing water in among trees draped with long strands of gauzy moss.

The hilly countryside was easy enough traveling, when the path stayed up out of the low places. Down in the depressions it tended to be swampy and hard going. He didn't like the swampy places; they brought back painful memories.

Friedrich swished at a small cloud of gnats flitting around his face, then shifted the shoulder straps of his pack as he tried to decide what to do – make camp, or push on. Even though he was tired and sore from an arduous day of traveling, he had grown stronger over the course of such a long journey and was now better able to stand the rigors of his new life – at least, much more so than he had been at first.

As he walked along, Friedrich often talked, in his mind, to Althea. He would describe to her all the sights he was seeing, the terrain, the vegetation, the sky, hoping that in the world beyond she was able to hear him and smiled her golden smile.

With the day drawing to an end, he had to decide what to do. He didn't want to be traveling when it grew too dark. It was a new moon, so he knew that, once the afterglow of dusk receded, the darkness would be nearly total. There were no clouds, so at least the starlight would stave off the kind of smothering, total blackness he hated most, the kind where he couldn't even see up from down – that was the worst. That was when he was most lonely.

Even with the stars out, it was difficult to travel unknown regions by starlight alone. In darkness it was easy to wander off the path and end up getting lost. Getting lost would mean that in the morning he would likely have to backtrack to find a way through an impassable area, or find the trail, and in the end it accomplished nothing but to waste time.

It would be wise to set up camp. It was warm, so he wouldn't really need a fire, although for some reason he felt as if he wanted one. Still, with a fire, he might attract notice. He had no real way to know who might be around, and a campfire could be spotted for miles. Best not to have a fire, as much comfort as it would provide, in exchange for the security. At least there would be stars overhead.

He considered, too, the possibility that if he kept going the trail might shortly lift out of the boggy lowlands and he would come across a better place for a campsite – a place not as likely to be rife with snakes. Snakes, seeking warmth, would slither up to be close to a person sleeping on the ground. He'd not like to wake to find a snake cuddled up to him under his blanket.

Friedrich hiked his pack up higher on his back. There was still enough light to push on for a while.

Before he could start out again, he heard a small sound. Even though it wasn't loud, the inexplicable nature of it made him turn and look back up the trail to the north, the direction from which he had come. He couldn't quite put the sound to anything that came to mind, to any frog or squirrel or bird. As he listened, it was again dead quiet.

'I'm getting too old for this sort of thing,' he muttered to himself as he started out once more.

The other reason nagging at him to keep going, the reason that was actually the most important, was that he hated to stop when he was this close. Of course, it could still be distant enough to require a walk of several days – it was hard for him to tell with any precision – but it was also possible that he was much closer. If that was the case, stopping for the night would be foolish. Time was of the essence.

He could walk for a little longer, at least. There was still time to make camp, if he had to, before it was too dark. He supposed he could push on until he couldn't see the trail well enough to follow it and then make himself a place to sleep in the grass beside the lake, but Friedrich didn't really relish the notion of sleeping out in the open right beside a trail, either, not when he was so deep into the Old World, and not when he knew there could be night patrols about. He'd been seeing more of the Order's patrolling troops in recent days.

He'd avoided cities and towns, for the most part sticking as close as he could to a straight course down through the Old World. Several times he'd had to change that course when the destination had changed. As he traveled, Friedrich had gone to great pains to avoid troops. Being near any of the Order soldiers meant there was always the potential of being detained for questioning. While he wasn't as free of suspicion as a farmer in his own home might be, he knew that an older man traveling alone didn't look very threatening to big young soldiers and wasn't likely to raise suspicions.

However, he also knew, from bits of conversation he'd overheard when he had been in towns, that the Imperial Order had no qualms about torturing people when the fancy struck them. Torture had the great advantage of always eliciting a confession of guilt, which proved the questioner's wise judgment in having suspicions in the first place, and, if desired, could produce the names of more conspirators with 'wrong thoughts,' as he had heard told. A cruel questioner never ran out of work or guilty people needing punishment.

At a snapping sound, Friedrich turned around and stood still as a stump, listening, watching. The sky and lake were mirrored violet. Tree limbs stood out still and silent, hanging out over sections of the path like claws waiting to snatch travelers when it became dark enough.

The woods were probably full of creatures just coming out from a long day's sleep to hunt at night. Owls, voles, opossum, raccoons, and other creatures became more active as it got dark. He watched, waiting to see if he heard the sound again. Nothing moved in the hush of twilight.

Friedrich turned back to the trail and hurried his steps. It must be some creature, searching through the forest litter, looking for a grub. His breathing quickened with his increased effort. He tried to wet his mouth by working his tongue, but it wasn't really doing much good. Despite his thirst, he didn't want to stop to have a drink of water.

He was just imagining things, he knew. He was in a strange land, by a strange wood, and it was getting dark. He wasn't usually so susceptible to being spooked by the little noises in the woods that frightened most people. He'd lived in the swamp with Althea a good long time, and he knew about truly terrifying beasts; he also knew a great deal about the variety of those creatures that were innocent enough, just going about their own lives. This was undoubtedly innocent. Still, he no longer felt tired or wanted to stop for the night.

Friedrich turned to look over his shoulder as he hurried along the faintly lit trail. He had the uncanny feeling that there was something behind him. Something watching him. The thought of being watched made the hair at the nape of his neck stand on end.

He kept looking but he saw nothing. It remained quiet behind him. He knew that either it was too quiet, or else his imagination was too active.

Breathing hard, his heart pounding, Friedrich quickened his pace. Maybe if he hurried, he would finally get there, and not have to be all alone in the night out in the woods.

He glanced back over his shoulder again.

Eyes were watching him.

It startled him so much that he tripped over his own feet and fell sprawling to the ground. He scrambled around to sit up and face back down the trail as he crabbed backward on his hands and feet.

The skulking eyes were still there. He hadn't imagined it. Twin, glowing, yellow eyes watching from back in the dark gloom of the woods.

In the still hush, he heard a low growl as the beast stole out of the shadows into the somber light between the forest and the lake. It was huge – maybe twice the size of a wolf, with a massive chest and bull neck. It took careful steps, the head hovering low to the ground as it advanced, glowing eyes never leaving him.

The thing was stalking.

With a cry, Friedrich scrambled to his feet and took off running as fast as his legs would fly. His age mattered little when powered by such a fright. A quick glance over his shoulder revealed the beast bounding down the trail behind him, easily closing the distance.

Worse yet, in that brief glance back, Friedrich saw more pairs of glowing yellow eyes emerging from the woods to join in the pursuit.

They were coming out for the night's hunt.

Friedrich was their prey.

The howling beast hit his back with such force that it drove the wind from his lungs. He pitched face-first to the ground, hitting with a grunt, sliding through the dirt. As he tried to scramble away, the powerful beast pounced on him. Raging with snarling snapping teeth, it lunged, caught his backpack, tearing it open in a mad effort to get at his bone and muscle.

Friedrich vividly envisioned being torn apart.

He knew he was about to die.

542

Chapter 54

Friedrich screamed in terror as he struggled frantically to escape. Right over his shoulder the thing howled with vicious fury as snapping teeth tore though his backpack, trying to rip him apart. His backpack, stuffed full of his things, was now a bulwark between Friedrich and the huge teeth tearing at him. The weight of the savage beast held him down, and the clutching forelegs kept him from being able to wriggle away, much less get up and run.

With desperate urgency, Friedrich forced his hand under himself, trying to reach his knife. His fingers caught the handle and pulled it free. Immediately, he struck out, slamming his blade into the beast. It hit hide-covered shoulder bone, doing little damage. He stabbed again, but failed to make contact. Fighting for all he was worth, he slashed as he rolled, missing the beast, trying to get away when it ducked his blade.

Just as he was about to escape to the side, if only to spare himself momentarily, more of the beasts bounded into the fray. Friedrich screamed again, slashing with his knife, trying to protect his face with his other arm at the same time. He managed to get up on his hands and knees, only to have another of the beasts pounce and knock him sprawling.

Friedrich saw the book tumble out of the inner pocket he'd stitched into his pack. Their teeth had ripped open the sealed compartment. The beasts lunged for the book. The one that snatched it up in its jaws snarled and shook its head like a hound with a hare.

Just as another of the howling creatures roared toward him,

wet fangs stretching wide, the head abruptly spun crazily away. Hot blood splashed across the side of Friedrich's face and neck. It was totally unexpected and completely disorienting.

'In the water!' a man yelled at him. 'Jump in the water!'

It was all Friedrich could do to roll and twist, trying to keep himself from the snapping snarling beasts. He certainly had no intention of going into the water; he had no desire to be set upon by such ferocious animals in water. That was a favorite trick of beasts in the swamp – get you in the water, then they had you. Going in the water was the last thing Friedrich wanted.

The world seemed to go mad with steel flashing by his face, just over his head, up along the side of him, whistling through the air, slicing beasts apart with each mighty swing, defending him just before they were on him. Reeking, slippery innards spilled across the ground, slopped across his legs.

The man above stepped over Friedrich, straddling him. His sword slashed and stabbed with swift, fluid grace that Friedrich found spellbinding. The stranger stood his ground over Friedrich, cutting through the creatures as they charged, seemingly dozens of them, all snarling and howling.

Friedrich saw yet more of the wild beasts bound out of the woods. With frightening speed and terrifying determination, they leaped at the man standing over him, throwing themselves at him with wild abandon. Friedrich saw another swordsman to the side slice into the onslaught. He thought he saw a third person behind, but with all the furious activity, he wasn't sure how many rescuers there might be. The strident snarling, ringing howls, and roaring growls, all so close, were deafening. When one of the heavy beasts crashed sideways into him, Friedrich stabbed it, only to see that it was already headless.

As the second person raced in close to join the fray, the man standing over Friedrich stepped to the side, reached down with one hand, snatched a fistful of his shirt, lifted him to his feet, and, with a grunt, heaved him out into the lake. Friedrich had no time to get his balance and only an instant to gasp a breath before he hit the water. He plunged under, unable to tell up from down in the dark depths.

Breaking the surface, gasping for air, splashing for the shore,

Friedrich finally found footing on the muddy bottom and was just able to keep his head above the surface of the water. To his surprise, none of the beasts came in after him. Several raced to the shore, but stopped short, unwilling to enter the water despite how much they hungered to have him. When they saw he was out of reach, they returned to the attack and were killed as soon as they joined the others charging the big man.

The beasts leaped at the three from all sides, the fierce battle raging on with frightening intensity. As fast as the animals attacked, they were dispatched decisively – beheaded, stabbed, or rent open with mighty swings of a sword.

With sudden finality, the dark figure swung upward, lopping the head off a beast as it leaped through the air toward the second person. The night finally fell silent, but for the heavy breathing of the three people up on the trail.

The three stepped out of the pile of unmoving carcasses, to sit wearily on the bank, exhausted, heads hanging as they caught their breath.

'Are you all right?' the first of the three, the one who had saved Friedrich's life, asked. His voice was still filled with the terrible rage of battle. His blood-slick sword, still in his hand, glinted in starlight.

Friedrich, stunned and shivering, suddenly weak with relief, took several steps toward the shore, water sluicing off him, until he was standing waist-deep in the lake before the man.

'Yes, thanks to you. Why'd you throw me in the water like that?'

The man raked his fingers back through thick hair. 'Because,' he said between deep breaths pulled not just from exertion, but driven by wrath, 'heart hounds won't go in water. It was the safest place for you.'

Friedrich swallowed as his gaze played over the dark heaps of hounds. 'I don't know how to thank you. You saved my life.'

'Well,' the man said, still catching his breath, 'I happen not to like heart hounds. They've scared the wits out of me on more than one occasion.'

Friedrich feared to ask where the man would have seen such fearsome creatures before.

'We were way back up the trail when we saw them come out after you.' It was a woman's voice. Friedrich stared at the figure in the middle who had spoken as she caught her breath. He could just make out her long fall of hair. 'We were worried that we wouldn't reach you before the heart hounds had you,' she added.

'But ... what are heart hounds?'

The three figures stared at him.

'The more important question,' the first man said at last in a quiet, measured, but commanding voice, 'is why were heart hounds here at all. Do you have any idea why they might have been after you?'

'No, sir. I've never seen such creatures before.'

'It's been a long while since I've seen heart hounds,' the man said, sounding troubled. Friedrich almost thought that he'd been going to say more about the hounds, but instead he asked, 'What's your name?'

'Friedrich Gilder, sir, and you have my undying gratitude – all of you do. I haven't been that scared since – well, since I don't know when.' He looked to the three faces watching him, but it was too dark to clearly make out their features.

The first man put an arm around the woman, in the middle, and in a whisper asked if she was all right. She answered with the kind of nod against his shoulder that Friedrich knew conveyed true concern and intimate familiarity. When his fingers reached past, touching the shoulder beyond her, the third figure nodded.

These weren't at all likely to be Imperial Order soldiers. Still, there were always other risks in such a strange land. Friedrich took a chance.

'May I ask your name, sir?'

'Richard.'

Friedrich took a cautious step closer, but, for some reason, by the way the silent third person watched him, he feared to step up out of the water any closer to Richard and the woman.

Richard swished his blade clean in the water, then stood. After wiping both sides dry on his leg, he slid the sword home into its scabbard at his hip. In the dim light, Friedrich could see that the lustrous silver-and-gold wrought scabbard was secured with a baldric over Richard's right shoulder. Friedrich was pretty sure that he remembered the look of that baldric and scabbard. Friedrich had carved for nearly his whole life and also recognized a certain effortless grace with a blade – no matter what kind of blade. Artful control was required to wield edged steel with mastery. When it was in Richard's hands, he truly seemed in his element. Friedrich well remembered the sword the man was wearing that day. He wondered if this could possibly be that same remarkable weapon.

With a foot, Richard prodded at parts of heart hounds, searching. He bent and lifted a severed hound head. Friedrich saw then that the beast had something clenched in its teeth. Richard tugged at it, but it was impaled on the fangs. As he worked it out of the hound's mouth, off the fangs, Friedrich's eyes went wide when he realized that it was the book. The hound had torn it out of the backpack.

'Please.' Friedrich lifted a hand, reaching. 'Is it . . . is it all right?'

Richard tossed the heavy head aside, where it thumped down and rolled into the trees. He peered closely at the book in the dim light. His hand lowered and he looked over at Friedrich standing in waist-deep water.

'I think you had better tell me who you are, and why you're here,' Richard said. The woman rose up at the dark tone in Richard's voice.

Friedrich cleared his throat and swallowed back his worry. 'Like I said, I'm Friedrich Gilder.' He took a terrible chance. 'I'm looking for a man related to a very old fellow I know named Nathan.'

Richard stood staring for a moment. 'Nathan. Big man? Tall, long white hair to his shoulders? Thinks a lot of himself?' He sounded not just surprised, but suspicious as well. 'Born-for-mischief Nathan?'

Friedrich smiled at the last part, and with relief. His bond had served him well. He bowed, as best he could standing in the water.

'Master Rahl guide us. Master Rahl teach us. Master Rahl protect us. In your light we thrive. In your mercy we are

547

sheltered. In your wisdom we are humbled. We live only to serve.
Our lives are yours.'

Lord Rahl watched as Friedrich finally straightened, and then extended a hand down. 'Come out of the water, Master Gilder,' he said in a gentle voice.

Friedrich was somewhat confounded to be offered a helping hand by Lord Rahl himself, and yet didn't know how he could refuse what could be judged an order. He took the hand and pulled himself up out of the water.

Friedrich went to a knee, bowing forward. 'Lord Rahl, my life is yours.'

'Thank you, Master Gilder. I'm honored by your gesture, and value the sincerity, but your life is your own, and belongs to no one else. That includes me.'

Friedrich stared up in wonder. He had never heard anyone say anything so remarkable, so unimaginable, least of all a Lord Rahl. 'Please, sir, would you call me Friedrich?'

Lord Rahl laughed. It was a sound as easy and pleasant as any Friedrich had ever heard. It made a smile well up through him, too.

'If you'll call me Richard.'

'I'm sorry, Lord Rahl but . . . I'm afraid that I just couldn't bring myself to do such a thing. I've spent my whole life with a Lord Rahl, and I'm too old to change it, now.'

Lord Rahl hooked a thumb behind his wide belt. 'I understand, Friedrich, but we're deep in the Old World. If you utter the words "Lord Rahl" and anyone hears you, we're all likely to have a great deal of trouble on our hands, so I would greatly appreciate it if you would do your best to learn to call me Richard.'

'I'll try, Lord Rahl.'

Lord Rahl held out an introductory hand. 'This is the Mother Confessor, Kahlan, my wife.'

Friedrich went to a knee again, bowing his head. 'Mother Confessor.' He wasn't sure how to properly greet such a woman.

'Now, Friedrich,' she said with as much of a scolding tone as Lord Rahl's, but in a voice that he thought revealed a woman of rare grace, command, and heart, 'that title, too, will serve us ill, here.' It was as lovely a voice as Friedrich had ever heard, its lucid quality holding him spellbound. He had seen the woman once, in the palace; the voice fit his memory of her perfectly.

Friedrich nodded. 'Yes, ma'am.' He thought he might be able to learn to call Lord Rahl 'Richard,' but he was almost positive that he would never be able to call this woman anything other than 'Mother Confessor.' The familiar name Kahlan seemed a privilege beyond him.

Lord Rahl gestured past the Mother Confessor. 'And this is our friend, Cara. Don't let her scare you – she'll try. Besides being a friend, first, she is a valued protector, who remains always concerned for our safety above all else.' He glanced over at her. 'Although, lately, she has been causing more trouble than help.'

'Lord Rahl,' Cara growled, 'I told you that wasn't my fault. I had nothing to do with it.'

'You're the one who touched it.'

'Well . . . how was I supposed to know!'

'I told you to leave it be, but you had to touch it.'

'I couldn't very well just leave it, now could I?'

Friedrich didn't understand a word of the exchange. But even in the near darkness, he could see the Mother Confessor smile and pat Cara on the shoulder.

'It's all right, Cara,' she whispered reassuringly.

'We'll figure something out, Cara,' Lord Rahl added in a sigh. 'We still have time.' He turned suddenly solemn and switched his line of thought as swiftly as he changed direction with that sword of his. He waggled the book. 'The hounds were after this.'

Friedrich eyebrows went up in astonishment. 'They were?'

'Yes. You were just the treat for doing a good job.'

'How do you know?'

'Heart hounds would never attack a book. They would have fought to the death over your heart, first, had they not been sent for another reason.'

'So that's why they're called heart hounds,' Friedrich said.

'That's one theory. The other is that with those big round ears, they can find their victim by the sound of their beating heart.

Either way, I've never heard of a heart hound going for a book when a human heart was there for the taking.'

Friedrich gestured to the book. 'Lord – sorry, Richard – Nathan sent me with this book. He thought it was very important. I guess he was right.'

Lord Rahl turned back from staring at the hounds sprawled across the ground. If it had not been dark, Friedrich was sure he would have seen a frown, but he certainly could hear repressed anger in the man's voice. 'Nathan thinks a lot of things are important – usually prophecies.'

'But Nathan was sure about this.'

'He always is. He's helped me before, I don't deny that.' Lord Rahl shook his head with determination. 'But, from the beginning, prophecy has been the cause of more trouble for us than I care to think about. Heart hounds mean we suddenly have immediate, deadly danger on our hands. I don't need Nathan's prophecies adding to my problems. I know some people think prophecy is a gift, but I regard it as a curse best avoided.'

'I understand,' Friedrich said with a wistful smile. 'My wife was a sorceress. Her gift was prophecy. She sometimes called it her curse.' His smile faltered. 'I sometimes held her as she wept over some foretelling she saw, but could not change.'

Lord Rahl watched him in the awkward silence. 'She's passed away, then?'

Friedrich could only nod as he sagged under the pain of the memories.

'I'm sorry, Friedrich,' Lord Rahl said in a quiet voice.

'So am I,' the Mother Confessor whispered in sad, sincere sympathy. She turned to her husband, clasping his upper arm. 'Richard, I know we don't have time for Nathan's prophecies, but we can hardly ignore what heart hounds mean.'

Distress sounded heavily in Lord Rahl's sigh. 'I know.'

'What are we going to do?'

Friedrich saw him shake his head in the dim light. 'We'll have to hope they can handle it, for now. This is more urgent. We'll need to find Nicci, and fast. Let's just hope she has some ideas.'

The Mother Confessor seemed to accept what he'd said as sensible. Even Cara was nodding silent agreement.

'I'll tell you what, Friedrich,' the Mother Confessor said in a voice steady with mettle. 'We were about to set up camp for the night. With the heart hounds loose, you had better stay with us until we meet up with some of our friends in a day or two and have better protection. At camp you can tell us what this is all about.'

'I'll listen to what Nathan wants,' Lord Rahl said, 'but that's all I can promise. Nathan is a wizard; he's going to have to solve his own problems; we have enough of our own. Let's make camp, first, somewhere safe. I'll at least take a look at this book – if it's still readable. You can tell me why Nathan thinks it's so important. Just spare me the prophecies.'

'No prophecies, Lord Rahl. In fact, the lack of prophecy is the real problem.'

Lord Rahl gestured around at the carcasses. 'This is the immediate problem. We'd better find a spot down there in the swamp, surrounded by water, if we want to live to see morning. There will be more where these came from.'

Friedrich peered nervously around in the darkness. 'Where do they come from?'

'The underworld,' Lord Rahl said.

Friedrich's jaw dropped. 'The underworld? But how is such a thing possible?'

'Only one way,' Lord Rahl said in a low voice filled with terrible knowledge. 'Heart hounds are, in a way, the guardians of the underworld – the Keeper's hounds. They can only be here because the veil between life and death has been breached.'

Chapter 55

The four of them started down the path, heading toward the dark expanse of low-lying forest, as Friedrich contemplated the staggering significance of the veil between the world of life and the world of the dead being breached. The latter part of Althea's life revolved around the Grace she used in her tellings, so he certainly knew about the veil between worlds. Over the years, Althea had often spoken to him about it. In particular, preceding her death, she had told him much of what she had come to believe about the interaction of those worlds.

'Lord Rahl,' Friedrich said, 'I think what you said about the veil between the world of the living and the dead being torn might be tied in with why Nathan thought it was so vital that I reach you with this book. He doesn't want you to help him – that's not why he sent me with this book – he meant this to help you.'

Lord Rahl snorted a laugh. 'Right. That's the way he always puts it – that he only wants to help you.'

'But I think this is about your sister.'

Everyone froze in their tracks.

Lord Rahl and the Mother Confessor spun around, hovering close to him. Even in the darkness, Friedrich could see how wide their eyes were open.

'I have a sister?' Lord Rahl whispered.

'Yes, Lord Rahl,' Friedrich said, taken by surprise that he didn't know. 'Well, a half sister, actually. She, too, is the offspring of Darken Rahl.'

Lord Rahl seized him by the upper arms. 'I have a sister? Do you know anything about her?'

'Yes, Lord Rahl. A little, anyway. I've met her.'

'Met her! Friedrich, that's wonderful! What's she like? How old is she?'

'Not many years younger than you, Lord Rahl. Early twenties, I'd say.'

'Is she smart?' he asked with a grin.

'Too smart for her own good, I'm afraid.'

Lord Rahl laughed in delight. 'I can't believe it! Kahlan, isn't that wonderful? I have a sister.'

'It doesn't sound wonderful to me,' Cara growled before the Mother Confessor could answer. 'It doesn't sound wonderful at all!'

'Cara, how can you say that?' the Mother Confessor asked.

Cara leaned toward them. 'Need I remind you both of the trouble we had when Lord Rahl's half brother, Drefan, showed up?'

'No ...' Lord Rahl said, clearly troubled by the mention.

Everyone fell silent. 'What happened?' Friedrich finally dared to ask.

He gasped when Cara snatched him by the collar and jerked him close to her hot glare. 'That bastard son of Darken Rahl nearly killed the Mother Confessor! And Lord Rahl! He nearly killed me! He did kill a lot of other people. He nearly got everyone killed. I hope the Keeper of the dead put Drefan Rahl in a cold dark hole for all of eternity. If you only knew what he did to the Mother Confessor—'

'That's enough, Cara,' the Mother Confessor said in quiet command as she put a hand on the woman's arm, gently urging her to release Friedrich's collar.

Cara complied, but, in the heat of anger, only with great reluctance. Friedrich could clearly see why this woman was a guard to the Lord Rahl and the Mother Confessor. Even though he could not see her eyes, he could feel them, like a hawk's, locked on him even in the dark. This was a woman whose penetrating judgment could weigh a man's soul, and decide his fate. This was a woman not only with the authority, but with the ability, to act on what she decided was necessary.

Friedrich knew, because he had seen women like this often in the People's Palace. When her hand came out from under her cloak to snatch him by the collar, he'd seen her Agiel dangling on a chain from her wrist. This was a Mord-Sith.

'I'm sorry about your half brother,' Friedrich said. 'But I don't think Jennsen means you harm.'

'Jennsen,' he whispered, testing his first encounter with the name of someone he never knew existed.

'As a matter of fact, Jennsen is terrified of you, Lord Rahl.'

'Terrified of me? Why would she be afraid of me?'

'She thinks you're after her.'

Lord Rahl stared incredulously. 'After her? How can I be after her? I've been stuck down here in the Old World.'

'She thinks you want to kill her, that you send men to hunt her down.'

He was stunned to silence for a moment, as if each new thing he was hearing was even more incredible than the last. 'But . . . I don't even know her. Why would I want to kill her?'

'Because she is ungifted.'

Lord Rahl stepped back, trying to understand what Friedrich was telling him. 'What difference does that make? Lots of people are ungifted.'

Friedrich pointed to the book in Lord Rahl's hand. 'I think Nathan sent that book to explain it.'

'Prophecy won't help explain anything.'

'No, Lord Rahl. I don't think this has to do with prophecy so much as with free will. You see, I know some about prophecy from my wife. Nathan explained how prophecy needs free will, and that's why you react so strongly against prophecy, because you are a man who brings free will to balance the magic of prophecy. He said that prophecy had not proclaimed it to be me who was to bring this book to you, but that I had to bring it of my own free will.'

Lord Rahl stared at the book in the darkness. His tone softened. 'Nathan can be trouble at times, but I know he's a friend who has helped me before. His help can sometimes cause me considerable trouble, but even if I don't always agree with the things he chooses to do, I know he chooses to do them for good reason.'

'I loved a sorceress for most of my life, Lord Rahl. I know how complex such things as this can be. I would not have come all this way if I didn't believe Nathan in this.'

Lord Rahl appraised him for a moment. 'Did Nathan say what was in this book?'

'He told me the book is from the time of a great war, thousands of years ago. He said he discovered it in the People's Palace after a frantic search among the thousands of tomes there, and that as soon as he'd located it he brought it to me, to ask that I take it to you. He said time was so urgently short that he dare not take any more to translate the book. Because of that, he didn't know what was in it.'

Lord Rahl looked down at the book with considerably more interest. 'Well, I don't know how much good it's going to be able to do us. The hounds did a lot of damage to it. I'm beginning to fear why.'

'Richard, do you know at least what it says on the cover?' the Mother Confessor asked.

'I only saw it in the light long enough to see that it was in High D'Haran. I didn't try to translate it. It says something about Creation.'

'You're right, Lord Rahl. Nathan told me the title.' Friedrich tapped the book. 'It says, there, on the cover, in gilded letters, *The Pillars of Creation*.'

'Great,' Lord Rahl muttered, seemingly in unhappy recognition of the title. 'Well, let's get to a safe place and set up camp. I don't want the heart hounds to catch us out in the open in the dark. We'll make a small fire and maybe I can see if the book will tell us anything useful.'

'You know about the pillars of Creation, then?' Friedrich asked, following after the three of them as they started off down the trail.

'Yes,' Lord Rahl said back over his shoulder in a troubled tone. 'I've heard of them. Nathan came from the Old World, so I guess he would know about them, too.'

Friedrich scratched his jaw in confusion as they crested a small rise in the trail. 'What do the pillars of Creation have to do with the Old World?'

'The Pillars of Creation are in the center of a forsaken wasteland.' Lord Rahl pointed ahead, to the south. 'It's not all that far from here, off that way. We went past there not long ago. We had to cross the fringes of the place; some very unpleasant people were after us.'

'Their bloody bones are drying in the wasteland,' Cara said with obvious pleasure.

'Unfortunately,' Lord Rahl said, 'it cost us our horses, too; that's why we're on foot. At least we escaped with our lives.'

'Wasteland . . . but, Lord Rahl, the pillars of Creation are also what my wife called—'

Friedrich halted when something beside the path caught his eye. Even in the dim light, the hauntingly familiar dark shape silhouetted against the light color of the dusty trail drew him up short.

He squatted down to touch it. To his surprise, it felt like what he thought. When he picked it up, he was sure of it. It had the same crooked opening for the drawstring, the same notch in the supple leather where he had once accidentally nicked it with a sharp gouge when he had been in a hurry.

'What's the matter?' Lord Rahl asked in a suspicious voice as he scanned the near-dark landscape. 'Why did you stop?'

'What did you find?' the Mother Confessor asked. 'I didn't see anything there when I walked past.'

'Neither did I,' Lord Rahl said.

Friedrich swallowed as he placed the leather pouch in the palm of his hand. It felt like there were coins inside, and, by the weight, it felt like they were gold.

'This is mine,' Friedrich whispered in stunned amazement. 'How could it possibly be here?'

He couldn't claim the gold was his, though it certainly could be, but he'd handled the leather pouch nearly every day for decades. He used it to hold one of his tools – a small gouge he used often.

'What's it doing here?' Cara asked as her gaze swept the

surrounding countryside. Her Agiel was gripped tightly in her fist.

Friedrich stood, still staring at his tool pouch. 'It was stolen by the man who I believe caused the death of my wife.'

Chapter 56

Well, wasn't that just something.

Oba could hardly believe that he had dropped his money purse. He was always so careful. He huffed in exasperation. If it wasn't one thing, it was another. Either it was a scheming little cutpurse, or some thieving woman, always after his money. Was that all that the small-minded little people cared about? Money? After all his troubles, all the envious covetous conniving people trying to get at his hard-earned fortune, Oba had learned that a man of his standing had to always be careful. He could hardly believe that, this time, he had done it to himself.

He hurriedly checked his pockets, inside his shirt, down in his trousers. All his pouches full of his considerable wealth were there, right where they belonged. He supposed that the one out on the path might not be his, but what were the odds that someone else would drop a purse right there?

When he checked the top of his boots, he found that one of his money purses was missing. Fuming, Oba checked the leather thong he always kept tied around his ankle, and found it had come untied.

Someone had untied his money purse.

He peered out through the trees, watching the touching scene. His brother, Richard, and his precious wife turned to the man who had found the purse – Oba's purse, full of his money.

'It was stolen by the man who I believe caused the death of my wife.' Oba heard the man exclaim.

Oba's jaw dropped. It was the husband of the swamp-witch –

the obnoxious selfish sorceress who wouldn't answer Oba's questions.

Oba knew better than to think that this could all be some comical coincidence. He just flat knew better.

'Don't touch it!' Richard Rahl and the Mother Confessor yelled at the same time.

'Run!' the other woman yelled.

Oba watched them bolt like frightened deer. He realized that the voice was up to something. He knew that the voice used what belonged to people to reach out to them. Oba looked to each side, to the glowing yellow eyes watching with him, and grinned.

The very air shook as if the ground right there where the money purse hit had been struck by lightning. The hounds whined and backed away. Oba plugged each ear with a finger and squinted as he watched the violet concussion spread outward in a circle like the rings in a pond when he threw in a dead animal.

In a brutal instant, quicker than thought, the people were flattened as the ring of violet light raced outward faster than his eye could follow. Oba's hair was blown back as the undulating circle swept past him. In its wake the ground was left covered with a still, cottony bed of eerie violet smoke.

Oba's suspicions had been proven right; the voice was planning something grand. He wondered with delight what it could be.

The scene had gone still, but Oba watched for a time to be sure the four people wouldn't get up. Only after he was confident that it was safe did he finally rise up from his secret watching place, the place where the voice had told him to wait.

The voice urged him on, now. The hounds stayed well behind, watching, as Oba hurried across the smoke-covered ground. It was the strangest smoke he had ever seen – a softly glowing bluish violet, but most odd of all, it didn't swirl as Oba ran through it. His legs passed through the still vapor without causing it to stir, as if it were in another world altogether and he wasn't there with it, but just walking in the same place in this world.

The four lay sprawled on the ground right where they had

fallen. Oba cautiously leaned closer, while trying to stay at a safe distance, and found them all breathing, if slowly. Their eyes weren't closed. He wondered if they could see him. When he waved his arms, none of the four reacted.

Oba bent over Richard Rahl, peering into his still face. He waved a hand low, right before his brother's unblinking eyes. There was no response.

It was hard to see in the starlight, but Oba was sure he could make out in those eyes a bit of the fascinating family resemblance. It was a spooky feeling seeing a man who had a trace of similarity in his looks. Oba looked more like his mother, though. That would be just like her to want him to look more like her than his father. The woman was completely self-centered. She had tried to deny him his rightful place at every turn, even in his looks. The selfish bitch.

But Richard was the man cheating Oba from his rightful place, now, the place their father would have wanted Oba to have. After all, Oba and Darken Rahl shared special qualities that Oba was sure his brother didn't have.

A check showed that the old husband of the swamp-witch was breathing, too. Oba recovered his money purse from nearby and shook it over the man's staring eyes, but he, too, showed no response. Oba tied the purse back around his ankle, now that the voice was finished with it.

Oba wasn't thrilled about the voice using his money for such tricks, but with all the voice had done for him, making him invincible and all, he guessed he couldn't begrudge a favor now and again. As long as it didn't became a habit.

The woman with them had a single long braid lying out across the grassy ground. She wore one of those strange rods on a chain around her wrist. He realized that she was a Mord-Sith. He squeezed her breasts. She didn't react. He grinned as he lingered at doing it again. With her so willing, and all, he considered what else he might do. The idea was startlingly arousing.

Oba realized, then, there was someone handy who was even better than a Mord-Sith. He peered over at her. His brother's wife, the woman they called the Mother Confessor, was lying there close by for the taking. What better justice than to have her?

Oba crawled over to her, his grin fading with awed reverence when he saw how beautiful she was. She lay on her back, one arm thrown out to the side, her fingers open and slack, as if pointing the way south. Her other arm lay casually across her stomach. Her eyes, too, stared up at nothing.

Oba carefully reached out and ran the back of a finger down her cheek. It was as soft as the silken petal of a rose. He pushed a long strand of hair back from her face to better see her features. Her lips were slightly parted.

Oba bent over her, putting his lips close to hers, running his hand up her body, feeling her luscious form. His hand glided up the mound of her breast. He fondled it gently in his big hand, just to show her that he could be gentle. He reached over and squeezed her other breast, but still she refused to acknowledge how excited she was by his gentle, tantalizing touch.

Quick as a fox, Oba blew in her parted mouth. She didn't react at all. He suspected that she was playing a game with him, teasing him. The haughty bitch.

She was going nowhere, now. She could not run, now. The voice had apparently given him a gift. Oba threw his head back and laughed at the sky. As the hounds far back in the shadows watched, he howled his delight at the stars.

Smiling, Oba bent back over Lord Rahl's wife, staring into her eyes. She was probably by now bored with her Lord Rahl husband, and was ready for an adventuresome romp. The more Oba thought about it, the more he realized that this woman should be his. She belonged to the Lord Rahl. By all rights, Oba should keep her as his wife when he became the new Lord Rahl.

And, he would be the Lord Rahl; the voice had told him that such things were within his reach.

Oba gazed at the sweep of her features, the curve of her body. He wanted his woman. He'd been doing favors for the voice, and hadn't had time to be with a woman for ages. The voice had been prodding him ever onward at a breakneck pace. It was about time Oba had the pleasure of a woman. His hand roamed lightly over the Mother Confessor's body as he contemplated the satisfaction to come.

But he didn't like the others watching him. They all refused to close their eyes and give him and the lady some privacy. Busybodies – all of them. Oba grinned. He supposed it might be a thrill to have her husband watch his wife's new master. The grin faded. What business was it of Richard's if she wanted a new man – a better man?

Oba bent over his brother and pushed his eyelids closed. He did the same for the old man. He paused, deciding to let the other woman watch. It would undoubtedly arouse her to see Oba in action. Such arousal was a small favor, but Oba was inclined to do such favors for attractive women.

Trembling with anticipation, knowing he could grant her the thrill he knew she craved, Oba bent to rip open the Mother Confessor's clothes. Before his fingers could touch her, a violent flash of violet light threw him back. Oba sat up, stunned, confused, pressing his hands to the nerve-shredding agony shrieking through his head. The voice was crushing his mind with punishing pain.

Oba shoved at the ground with his feet, backing away from the Mother Confessor, and at last the pain eased. He sagged, panting with exhaustion after the brief bout. He felt downhearted that the voice would punish him so, dejected that the voice would be so cruel as to deny him so simple a pleasure, and after all the good things he had done.

The voice changed, then, cooing to him, whispering about the important calling it had for him – important works that only Oba was qualified to do. Through his melancholy, Oba listened.

Oba was important, or the voice would not rely on him. Who else but Oba could accomplish such things as the voice asked of him? Who else could the voice depend on to set things right?

Now, in the silence of the still night, the voice made clear what it was Oba was to do. If he did as he was asked, then there would be rewards. Oba grinned at the pledges. First, he had to do the favor; then the Mother Confessor would be his. That wasn't so hard. Once she was his, he could do with her whatever he wanted, with the voice's blessing, and no one would interfere.

Pictures of it – along with the smells, the feel, the cries of her pleasure – came into his mind, and he nearly fainted with the promise of such rapture. Oba could wait for an encounter such as this would be.

He glanced over at the Mord-Sith. She could provide him some entertainment in the meantime. A man such as he, a man of action, great intellect, and heavy responsibilities, had to have a release of his pent-up tensions. Such diversions were a necessary outlet for a man of Oba's importance.

He bent over the Mord-Sith, grinning into her open eyes. She was to be honored to be the first to have him. The Mother Confessor would have to wait her turn. He reached out to pull off her clothes.

Oba's head suddenly flared with howling, blinding agony. He pressed his hands to his ears until it stopped – after he agreed.

The voice was right. Of course it was; he could see that, now. Only when Richard Rahl was dead could Oba take his rightful place. That made sense. It would be best to do things right. In fact, it would be wrong to bring pleasure to these women before he had done what needed doing. What had he been thinking? They didn't deserve him, yet. They should first see him as the important man he was shortly to become, and then they would have to beg to have him. They didn't deserve him until they begged.

He had to be quick. The voice said they would wake soon – that Lord Rahl would soon figure out how to break the spell of sleep.

Oba pulled his knife and crawled to his brother. Lord Rahl was still staring dumbly at the stars.

'Who's the big oaf, now?' he asked his brother.

Lord Rahl had no answer. Oba put the knife to Richard's throat, but the voice warned him back, and filled his mind instead with what he must do. He had to do it right. He had to hurry. There was no time for such common retribution. There were much better ways to do such things – ways that would punish the man for all the years he had kept Oba from his rightful place. Yes, that was what Richard Rahl needed: proper punishment.

Oba put his knife away and ran back over the nearby hill as

fast as his legs would carry him. When he returned with his horse, the four were still lying there in the blue fog, staring up at the stars.

Oba did as the voice asked, and scooped up the Mother Confessor in his arms. She had now been promised to him. He would have her when the voice was done borrowing her. Oba could wait. The voice had promised him delights that Oba would never have dreamed up on his own. This was turning out to be a very beneficial partnership. For the paltry work involved, and the small delay, Oba would have everything that rightfully belonged to him: the rule of D'Hara and the woman who would be his queen.

Queen. Oba puzzled at that as he heaved her body over the back of the saddle. Queen. If she was a queen, then he would have to be a king. He supposed that would be better than 'Lord' Rahl. King Oba Rahl. Yes, that made better sense. He worked quickly to lash her down.

Before he mounted up, Oba peered down at his brother. He couldn't kill him. Not yet. The voice had plans. If Oba was anything, he had always been accommodating; he would oblige the voice. He put a foot in the stirrup. The voice tickled at him. He turned back, looking.

He wondered . . .

He cautiously returned to Richard's side. Carefully, Oba reached out and experimentally touched the sword. The voice murmured indulgently.

A king should have a proper sword. Oba grinned. He deserved a small reward for all his hard work.

He pulled the baldric off over Richard Rahl's head. He lifted the scabbard close, inspecting his gleaming new sword. The wire-wound hilt had a word woven into each side.

'TRUTH'

Well, wasn't that just something.

He lifted the baldric over his head and placed the scabbard at his hip. He patted his new wife's bottom before he mounted up. From the saddle, Oba grinned out at the night. He circled his horse around until the voice pointed him in the right direction.

Hurry hurry, before Lord Rahl woke. Hurry hurry, before he could be caught. Hurry hurry, away with his new bride.

He thumped his heels to the horse's ribs and off they charged. The hounds bounded out of the woods, a king's faithful escort.

Chapter 57

Standing outside the squat buildings made of sun-dried bricks, Jennsen idly surveyed the barren landscape broiling under a brutally blue sky. The rocks, the seemingly endless expanse of flat hardpan to her right, and the rugged range of mountains plummeting into the shimmering valley in the distance to her left, were all stained with variations of the same ruddy gray color as the sparse collection of square structures huddled nearby.

The bone-dry air was so hot that it reminded her of nothing so much as bending over a bonfire and trying to breathe. Blistering heat radiated from the rocks and buildings around her and rose from the ground beneath her feet as if there were a blast furnace below. Using bare hands to touch anything baking under the ruthless sun was a painful experience. Even the hilt of her knife, shaded by her body, was so warm that it felt feverish.

Jennsen leaned a hip wearily against a low wall, nearly numb from the long and difficult journey. She patted Rusty's neck and then stroked an ear when the horse neighed gently and put her head close. At least Jennsen was nearly at her journey's end. She felt as if she had lost sight of how it had all begun that day so long ago when she had found the dead soldier at the bottom of the ravine and Sebastian had happened by.

What a long and tortured journey fate would deal her, she could never have guessed that day. She hardly knew herself anymore. Back then, she could never have guessed how much her life would change, or how much she would change.

Sebastian, pulling Pete behind, reached out and gripped her

arm. 'You all right, Jenn?' Pete nudged Rusty's flanks, as if to ask the same question of the mare.

'Yes,' Jennsen said. She smiled for him and then gestured to the knot of black-robed men in the doorway of a nearby building. 'Any luck?'

'He's asking the others.' Sebastian sighed in annoyance. 'They're a strange people.'

Despite being part of the Old World, and a part of the domain of the Imperial Order, the traders who traveled the vast deserted land, sometimes using the desolate trading outpost where Sebastian had found them, were an independent lot. Apparently, there were not enough of them to worry about, so the Order didn't bother.

Sebastian leaned against the wall beside her as he gazed out at the silent wasteland. He was weary, too, from the long journey back to his homeland of the Old World. But at least he was well, now, just as Sister Perdita had promised.

The journey, though, had been nothing like what Jennsen had thought it would be. She had imagined that she and Sebastian would be off on their own again, as they had been before traveling to the army of the Imperial Order. But behind them stretched a column of Imperial Order soldiers a thousand strong. A small escort, Sebastian had called them. She had told him that she wanted to go alone, but he said that there were more important considerations.

With a thumbnail, Jennsen idly picked at the leather reins while watching the figures in black. 'The men are afraid of all the soldiers,' she told Sebastian. 'That's why they don't want to talk to us.'

'What makes you think so?'

'I can just tell by the way they keep peeking out. They're trying to decide if telling us anything will somehow get them in trouble with all the soldiers.'

She understood the way the small band of traders felt to be under the scrutiny of so many brutish men sitting up on their big cavalry horses – how it felt to be watched by such grim soldiers layered with leather and chain-mail armor and bristling with weapons. The black-robed men, with their pack mules, were traders, not soldiers, nor were they used to dealing with soldiers. They feared for their safety, feared that if they said something wrong these warriors might decide to slaughter them out here in this wasteland. At the same time, while vastly outnumbered, the traders seemed reluctant to be cowed, lest they set a precedent for how they were treated thereafter. They were debating, now, trying to figure out the balance where their safety lay.

Sebastian pushed away from the wall. 'Maybe you're right. I'll go in and talk to them alone – in their building, instead of out here under the eyes of the army.'

'I'll go with you,' she said.

'What is it? What do you think?' Sister Perdita asked Sebastian as she marched up from behind.

With a casual flip of his hand, Sebastian dismissed her concern. 'I think they just want to bargain. They're traders. That's what they do – bargain. It might be counterproductive to try to force them.'

'I will go in and change their minds,' the Sister said with dark intent.

'No,' Sebastian said. 'Now is not the time to complicate a simple matter. We can always apply more pressure if we need to. Just let Jennsen and me go in and talk to them, first.'

Jennsen walked away from a scowling Sister Perdita, sticking close to Sebastian's side, pulling Rusty along behind. The other thing about the journey that had been unexpected – in addition to the escort of the thousand troops – had been that Sister Perdita had decided to come along. She said that it was necessary, in case Jennsen needed any more help in getting close to Lord Rahl.

Jennsen just wanted to plunge her knife into that murderous bastard son of Darken Rahl and be done with it all. She had long since given up any hope of it freeing her to have her own life. After that night in the woods with Sister Perdita and the seven other Sisters, everything had changed. Jennsen had made a bargain that she knew would mean she would have no life after she finally killed Richard Rahl. But at least everyone else would have their lives back. The world would at last be free of her half brother and his evil rule.

And she would have vengeance. Her mother, who had been

denied even a proper burial, could at last rest in peace knowing that her murderer had finally been visited with justice. That was all Jennsen could do for her mother.

Jennsen and Sebastian led Rusty and Pete to where the Sister's horse was waiting, in a small side paddock. Rusty and Pete welcomed the shade and the water trough.

After closing the small rickety gate to the paddock, Jennsen followed Sebastian into the shadow of the doorway of the squat building. The jabbering voices of the men echoing inside the single room fell silent. All the men were swathed in the traditional black robes of the nomadic traders who lived in this part of the world.

'Leave us, then,' the lead man said, waving his fellows out at seeing Sebastian and Jennsen enter.

The men, their eyes peering out at her from gaps in the black cloth they were pulling back up across their mouths and noses, nodded as they filed by. By their crinkled exposed eyes, the men seemed to be smiling congenially at her from beneath the masks, but she couldn't be sure. Just in case, and considering what was at stake, she smiled back as she returned a bow of her head.

The stagnant air inside the room was sweltering, but at least the shade was a relief. The one man remaining inside hadn't pulled the loose wraps of black cloth back up, so they sagged around his neck, away from his smiling, weathered, leathery face.

'Please,' he said to Jennsen, 'come in. You look fiery.'

'Fiery?' she asked.

'Hot,' he said. 'You are not dressed for this place.' He shuffled over to the rough plank shelves at the side and returned with one of the black bundles stored there. 'Please to wear this.' He lifted it toward her several times, urging her to take it. 'It will make you better. It will cover you from the sun and hold in your sweat so you don't dry like rock.'

Jennsen again bowed her head toward the small wiry man and smiled her appreciation. 'Thank you.'

'Well?' Sebastian asked when the man turned away from Jennsen. Sebastian wearily pulled his pack off his back. 'Any luck finding out anything from those other men?'

The black-robed figure hesitated, clearing his throat. 'Well, they say that maybe . . .'

Sebastian impatiently rolled his eyes when he caught the man's veiled meaning, and then fished around in his pocket until he came up with a silver coin. 'Please accept this gesture of my appreciation for the efforts of your men.'

The man took it respectfully, but it was clear the silver coin was not the price he was hoping for. He seemed hesitant, though, to say that he found the amount inadequate. Jennsen couldn't believe that Sebastian was quibbling about money at a time like this. She pulled a heavy gold coin from her pocket and, without bothering to ask Sebastian if it was all right, simply flipped it to the man. The man caught the gold in midair, then opened his fist just enough for a peek of confirmation. He grinned his appreciation at her. Sebastian shot her a look of displeasure.

It was Lord Rahl's blood money, the money he had given the men sent to kill her and her mother. She could think of no better use for it.

'I don't need it,' she said before he could lecture her. 'Besides, aren't you the one who said it was your way to use what was close to the enemy to get back at him?'

Sebastian withheld any comment and turned to the man. 'What about it?'

'Late yesterday,' the man said, finally more forthcoming, 'some of our men spotted two people going down into the Pillars of Creation.' He went to a small, uncovered window beside shelves stocked with simple supplies along with more of the black outfits. He pointed. 'Down that way. There is a trail of sorts.'

'Did your men talk to them?' Jennsen asked, stepping forward impatiently. 'Do your men know who it was?'

The man looked from her to Sebastian, hesitating, apparently not comfortable answering such direct questions from a woman, even if she had been the one who had paid his price. Sebastian gave her a look that said she should let him handle it. Jennsen stepped back toward the doorway, peering out, acting disinterested so that Sebastian could get the answers they needed.

Jennsen's heart hammered as she pictured in her mind

stabbing Lord Rahl. The shadow of the awful price of luring her brother to this place where she was to kill him loomed over the scene in her mind of the act itself.

Sebastian wiped sweat from his brow and tossed his heavy pack to the side of the floor. The pack hit with a hard clank and fell over. Some of the things spilled out. Annoyed, he made to pick it up, but Jennsen intercepted him.

'I'll tend to this,' she whispered, waving him back to the questioning of the small fellow in black.

Sebastian leaned against the heavy, ancient-looking plank table and folded his arms. 'So, did your men have a chance to talk to these two people?'

'No, sir. The men were not close enough, but stood at the rim and watched the horse pass below.'

Jennsen retrieved a cake of lye soap and replaced it in the pack. She folded the razor and put it back in, along with an extra waterskin that had tumbled out. She picked up small items – a flint, strips of dried meat wrapped in cloth, and a whetstone. A tin she had never seen before had rolled out of the pack and under a low shelf.

'What did these two people on horseback look like, then?' Sebastian was asking as he tapped a finger on the table.

As she reached under the shelf, Jennsen listened carefully, waiting to hear if this might be Richard Rahl. She couldn't really imagine who else it could be. She didn't believe such a thing could be coincidence.

'It was a man and a woman. But they came on only one horse.'

Jennsen thought that was strange, that both would be riding one horse. It sounded likely that it was what she expected, Lord Rahl and his wife, the Mother Confessor, but it was odd that they were on one horse. Something could have happened to the other horse. In this dangerous land such a thing wasn't hard to imagine.

'The woman, she . . .' The man made a face, uncomfortable with what he had to say. 'She was not upright, but lying flat' – he gestured as if draping something over the horse – 'across the back. She was tied up with rope.'

As Jennsen pulled the tin out in a rush of surprise, the lid caught a jagged edge of the wooden shelf and popped off. The contents spilled out across the floor in front of her.

'What did the man look like?' Sebastian asked.

A short piece of wood wound with twine and fastened down with fishing hooks had fallen out of the top of the tin. Jennsen stared down at a dark pile of dried mountain fever roses that had spilled out after the twine. They looked like dozens of little Graces.

'The man was big, and young. He had a very grand sword, my men say, its shining scabbard held on with a baldric across his shoulder.

'That sounds like Richard Rahl,' Sister Perdita said from the doorway, startling Jennsen.

'Other men use a baldric for their sword,' Sebastian said.

While she couldn't fathom a reason for him to have his wife tied across his horse, at the heady thought of Richard Rahl being spotted, Jennsen hurriedly scooped up the dried mountain fever roses in her trembling fingers and stuffed them back in the tin followed by the twine. She replaced the lid and quickly shoved the tin back into the pack along with the few remaining items that had fallen out.

She checked her knife in its sheath at her belt as she hastily stood next to Sebastian, waiting to hear what else the wiry man in black might have to say. Sister Perdita had stepped outside and was wrapping herself in the protective black clothes.

'Come on,' the Sister called. 'We have to get down there.'

Jennsen wanted to follow after her, but Sebastian was still questioning the man. She didn't want to leave Sebastian and go alone with Sister Perdita, but the woman was already heading off in the direction of the trail the man had pointed out.

From outside, on the other side of the buildings, came the sound of the traders jabbering excitedly. Jennsen peered around the side of the building and saw them pointing out across the flat, baked ground.

'What is it?' Sebastian asked as he followed the man out the door.

'Someone approaches,' the man said.

'Who could it be?' Jennsen whispered to Sebastian as he came up beside her.

'I don't know. Could just be another trader arriving at the post.'

The wiry little man, having answered the questions, bowed and wanted to depart to be with his men where they huddled together in the shade beside another building. Sebastian made him wait as he went back in and pulled a black bundle off the shelf.

'We best catch up with Sister Perdita,' he said as he watched the woman vanish over the rim of the trail down into the wavering landscape of the Pillars of Creation. 'She'll protect you from Richard Rahl's magic and help you do what you need to do.'

Jennsen wanted to say that she didn't need Sister Perdita's protection, that Lord Rahl's magic couldn't hurt her, but it was not the time to go into the whole subject with him, to explain the whole thing to him. Somehow, it never seemed the time. It didn't really matter, anyway, what Sebastian believed about how she could get close to Richard Rahl, it only mattered that she did.

Together, the two of them stood in the sweltering sun, watching the tiny speck racing across the endless flat landscape. In the withering heat, the distant ground undulated like the rippling surface of a faraway lake. A thin plume of dust rose behind the lone rider. Their escort of a thousand men restlessly checked their weapons.

'Is it one of your men?' Sebastian asked the wiry leader of the black-robed figures.

'The ground here plays tricks with your eyes,' he said. 'He is still far off; the heat only makes him look closer. It will be some time before the rider reaches us and we can tell who it is.' He smiled at Jennsen, gesturing encouragement. 'Put the clothing on, and you will be covered from the sun.'

Rather than argue, Jennsen threw the gauzy, capelike garment around her shoulders. She wrapped the long scarf over and around her head, as she had seen the men doing, pulling it across her nose and mouth and then tucking the tail under the side. She was immediately surprised at how the black cloth cut the hot glare of the sun. It felt a relief, almost like standing in shade.

The man's eyes smiled at seeing the look on her face. 'Good, yes?' he asked through his own thin black mask.

'Yes,' Jennsen said. 'Thank you for your help. But we must pay you for these things you gave us.'

With a twinkle in his eye, he said, 'You already have.'

The man turned to Sebastian, still pulling his black scarf over his head. 'I have told you all I can, all we know. My men and I go, now.'

Before Sebastian could answer, the man was already hurrying across the parched ground toward the dark knot of men waiting with their dusty mules. The men started away, pulling their mules after on lead lines, eager to be away from the soldiers.

They were headed south, in the opposite direction of the approaching rider.

'If it might be one of their men,' Sebastian said, almost to himself, 'then why are they leaving?'

He looked impatiently to the small trail where Sister Perdita had disappeared, and then signaled to his column of men still waiting on horseback. The grim-looking force of men advanced across the hard ground, raising a lazy fog of dust.

'We have to go down there,' Sebastian said as he gestured toward the valley that held the Pillars of Creation. 'Wait up here until we get back.'

The officer at the head of the column folded his wrists across the horn of his saddle. 'What do you want us to do about that?' he asked. His greasy strings of hair fell forward over his shoulder as he pointed with his chin toward the yet distant rider.

Sebastian turned and watched the far-off horse galloping toward them. 'If he turns out to be suspicious for any reason at all, kill him. This is too important to risk trouble, now.'

The officer gave Sebastian a single nod. Jennsen could see in the hungry eyes and humorless grins of the men behind him that they were pleased by the orders.

'Let's go,' Sebastian said. 'I want to catch up with Sister Perdita before she gets too far ahead of us.'

'Don't worry,' Jennsen said, 'I want Lord Rahl more than Sister Perdita does.'

Chapter 58

The heat had been withering up on the barren plain, but venturing down the trail felt like descending into a blast furnace. Every breath drew the torrid air into her lungs, making Jennsen feel as if she were being cooked from the inside, too. The air rising before the steep walls wavered like heat shimmering above a fire.

There were places where the trail simply vanished crossing loose rock, or perhaps went under it. In other places, a depression had been worn into the soft sandstone to show the way. In some places, the track went along natural pathways, so it was largely self-evident, with little choice to make a mistake. Occasionally, they had to cross slides of scree that had buried any trace of a trail, and hope they could pick it up farther along. Jennsen knew enough about trails to know that this one was ancient and unused.

Although nothing could make the scorching heat any less, the black garments that the traders had given them were at least an improvement. The black cloth around her eyes cut the painful glare, absorbing the bright light, making it easier to see. It was a relief to have the dark cloth shading her face. Instead of making her hotter, as she thought, the thin cloth covering the exposed skin of her arms and neck stopped the sun from burning her, and somehow seemed to keep some of the heat out.

As she and Sebastian hurried to follow the trail ever downward, she soon found, to her dismay, that it led them up, again, over one of the fingers of ridges that extended down into the valley. The rocky ground was so rugged that it would be difficult, if not impossible, to simply go right down, so the trail cut across the ridges so it wouldn't drop so precipitously. The trade-off was that it made it necessary to descend the back side of one ridge only to have to climb the face of the next. They had no choice but to follow it as it made a harrowing descent, then rose again. The strain on the muscles of her thighs and shins was fatiguing, but then to have to climb up again in such heat was agonizing.

Jennsen remembered well that Sebastian had once told her that no one ever risked going into the valley that held the Pillars of Creation. She could see why. By the unused nature of the trail, she knew that it was true – at least in this one place. She recalled, too, that he'd said that if anyone did go into the central valley, they had never returned to talk about it. She guessed that she didn't have to worry about that.

As they went lower, yawning fissures and deep cuts opened in the craggy terrain, giving rise to rock walls that stood alone, as if cast off and abandoned. As they moved along the edges of vast cliffs, some of the spires made up of those splits rose up from below almost to their height at the valley rim. Looking down on such soaring towers of rock was dizzying. There were places where she and Sebastian were forced to make leaps across deep clefts. To see in places where they were going to have to follow the trail below was heart-stopping.

Sister Perdita stood at the top of one of the prominent ridges along the trail's tortuous descent, waiting for them, watching them with silent displeasure set enduringly in the lines of her implacable face. The growing shadows cast across the landscape added a strange new dimension to the place. The lowering sun highlighted the rugged features in a way that only helped to make clear how formidable the land truly was. Sebastian put a hand to Jennsen's back and hurried her along an open, level place in the trail as they moved in among the eerie rock columns that stood like imposing dead trunks of tree that had lost their crowns and all their limbs.

Ever since they'd left the traders, something had felt wrong to Jennsen, but as Sebastian spurred her along, she couldn't bring to mind precisely what it was that was bothering her. Sister Perdita scowled as she waited.

Jennsen checked that her knife was still there, as she had done countless times before. She sometimes simply brushed her fingertips across the silver handle. This time, she lifted it to make sure it was clear in its sheath, then pressed it back down until it seated with the reassuring metallic click.

The first time she had seen the knife, when she found the dead D'Haran soldier, she had thought it a remarkable weapon. She still thought so. That first time, seeing the ornate letter 'R' had terrified her – with good reason – but now the touch of the engraved handle reassured her, giving her hope that she could at long last end the threat. This was the day she was finally about to accomplish what Sebastian had told her that first night. She was going to use something close to her enemy to strike back.

Sebastian had been through a difficult time, too, since that first night when he'd had to fight those men even though he had been stricken with a fever. She could never forget how brave he had been that day, and how he had fought, despite having a fever. Far worse than being stricken with fever, though, he had been struck down by Adie's sorceress magic and nearly killed. Jennsen was thankful that he had recovered, and that he was well, and that he would have a life, even if it was to be without her.

'Sebastian . . . ' she said, suddenly realizing that she had never said her good-bye to him. She didn't want to say it in front of Sister Perdita. She halted, turning back, pulling the black scarf away from her mouth. 'Sebastian, I just want to thank you for all you've done to help me.'

He laughed a little through the mask of black fabric. 'Jenn, you sound like you're about to die.'

How could she tell him that she was?

'We can't know what will happen.'

'Don't worry,' he said, cheerfully. 'You'll be fine. The Sisters helped you with their magic while they were healing me, and now Sister Perdita will be there with you. I'll be there, too. You'll at last avenge your mother.'

He didn't know what price the Sisters had placed on their

help, and on vengeance. Jennsen couldn't bear to tell him, but she had to find a way to say something.

'Sebastian, if anything happens to me—'

'Jenn,' he said, taking hold of her arms, looking into her eyes, 'don't talk like that.' He turned suddenly morose. 'Jenn, don't say such a thing. I couldn't stand the thought of life without you. I love you. Only you. You don't know what you mean to me, how you've made my life different than I ever thought it would be – so much better than I ever thought life could be. I couldn't go on without you. I couldn't ever again endure life without you. You make the world right for me as long as I have you. I'm hopelessly, helplessly in love with you. Please don't torture me with the thought of ever being without you.'

Jennsen stared into his blue eyes, blue like her murdering father's eyes were said to have been, and she was unable to bring forth any words to explain, to say how she felt, to tell him that she was going to be taken from him and he would have to face life alone. She knew how awful it was to feel alone. She simply nodded as she turned back to the trail and veiled the black scarf back across her face.

'Hurry,' she said, 'Sister Perdita is waiting.'

The woman scowled at Jennsen through her own dark mask as she stood waiting in the wind atop a broad flat rock. Jennsen could see that the trail beyond the Sister descended steeply among the shadows, down into the very Pillars of Creation. As they approached, Jennsen realized that Sister Perdita wasn't frowning at her, but looking past her, staring back the way they had come.

Before they reached her, up on the flat rock where her black robes lifted in the sweltering gusts, they, too, turned to see what she was watching so intently. Jennsen could see, from their high vantage point, that in their efforts they had reached the top of a divide in the trail from where it dropped rapidly down, following the side of the ridge, to take them to the bottom. But looking back across the wide gorges and rocky ridges they had already crossed, she saw that they were almost as high again as the valley rim. There, she could see the small cluster of squat buildings, looking tiny in the distance.

The rider was almost there, charging in on his horse, following an arrow-straight route toward the trail. The company of a thousand men had gathered in a thick line not far from the trailhead, waiting for him. Dust rose in a long plume behind the galloping horse.

As the lathered animal raced in at full speed, before it reached the men, Jennsen detected a falter in its gait. The horse's front legs abruptly crumpled. The poor beast went down, crashing to the rocky ground, dead from exhaustion.

The man atop the horse smoothly stepped off the animal as it collapsed to the ground. Without seeming to lose momentum or stride, he continued to advance toward the trail. He was dressed in dark clothes, although not like those of the nomadic traders. A golden-colored cape billowed behind him. And, he appeared to be a lot bigger than the traders.

As he made straight for the trail, the commander of the cavalry cried out for the man to halt. He didn't challenge them, or seem to even say a word. He simply ignored them as he marched resolutely past the buildings on his way to the trailhead. The thousand men raised a shrill battle cry and charged.

The poor man brandished no weapon, made no threatening move toward the soldiers. As the Order cavalry raced down on him, he lifted an arm toward them, as if warning them to halt. Jennsen knew, from both Sebastian's orders and from the way they charged toward the lone man, that they had no intention of stopping for anything short of his head.

Jennsen watched with dread as a man was about to be killed, watched, spellbound, as the thousand men crashed in toward him.

The valley rim abruptly lit with a thunderous explosion. Despite the dark head wrap, Jennsen shielded her eyes as she gasped in surprise. The violent rope of lightning and its terrible counterpart had twined together – a blazing white-hot bolt of lightning twisted together with a crackling black line that looked to be a void in the world itself, terrible power joined and discharged in an explosive instant.

In the space of a heartbeat, it seemed as if all the glaring brightness of the barren plain, the fierce heat of the Pillars of

Creation, had been gathered at a single point and unleashed. In an instant, the ignition of that explosive lightning annihilated the force of a thousand in a brilliantly lit red cloud. When the blinding light, the thunderous roar, the violent concussion were suddenly gone, so were the thousand men – all of them leveled.

Among the smoking remains of horse and man, the lone man marched ever onward toward the trail, appearing not to have lost a step.

In that man's determined movement, even more than in the way he had loosed havoc, Jennsen saw the true depths of his terrible rage.

'Dear spirits,' Jennsen whispered. 'What just happened?'

'Salvation comes only through self-sacrifice,' Sister Perdita said. 'Those men died in service to the Order and thus the Creator. That is the Creator's highest calling. No need to mourn for them – they have gained salvation through loyal duty.'

Jennsen could only stare at her.

'Who is that?' Sebastian asked as he watched the lone man reach the rim of the valley of the Pillars of Creation and start down without pause. 'Do you have any ideas?'

'It isn't important.' Sister Perdita turned back to the trail. 'We have a mission.'

'Then we had better hurry,' Sebastian said in a worried tone as he stared back at the distant figure advancing down the trail at a swift, measured, relentless pace.

Chapter 59

Jennsen and Sebastian rushed to follow after Sister Perdita, who had disappeared over the top of the ridge. As they reached the edge, they saw her, already far below them. Jennsen looked back, in the direction of the trailhead, but didn't see the lone man. She did see, though, that a bank of dark clouds had rolled in over the expanse of barren plains.

'Hurry!' Sister Perdita called back up to them.

With Sebastian's hand at the small of her back, urging her on, Jennsen dashed down the steep trail. The Sister moved as swiftly as the wind, the black robes flying out behind her as she raced along a trail cut into the slope of steep rock. Jennsen had never worked so hard to keep up with anyone. She suspected that the woman was using magic to aid her.

Whenever Jennsen started to lose her footing on the loose scree and reached out for support, the rough rock rasped the skin on her fingers and the palms of her hands. The trail was as arduous as any she had ever climbed down. Loose rock atop layers of solid ledge constantly slipped and gave way underfoot, and she knew that if she grabbed the wrong handhold, the rock, in many places as sharp as shattered glass, would slice her hands open.

Jennsen was soon panting and trying to catch her breath, as well as the distant Sister. Sebastian, right behind, sounded just as winded. He, too, lost his footing a number of times and, once, Jennsen cried out and grabbed his arm just before he went over the edge of a precipitous drop of thousands of feet.

The look in his eyes expressed the relief that he was too winded to voice.

Finding herself closer to the bottom, after a seemingly unending, arduous descent, Jennsen was at least relieved to note that the walls and towers were blocking the broiling sunlight. She glanced up at the sky, something she hadn't had the luxury to do for quite a while, and realized that it wasn't just the shadows cast by rock darkening the day. The sky, that only hours before had been so clear and bright blue, was now roofed with churning gray clouds, as if the entire valley of the Pillars of Creation were being sealed off from the rest of the world.

She forged onward, rushing to keep up with Sister Perdita. There was no time to worry about clouds. As exhausted as Jennsen was, she knew that when the time came, she would find the strength to plunge her knife into Richard Rahl. That time was almost at hand. She knew that her mother, with the good spirits, would inspire her and thus help give her the strength. She knew, too, that other strength had been promised.

Rather than filling her with dread, knowing that the end of her life was so close left Jennsen with an odd, numb sense of calm. It seemed almost sweet, that promise of the end of struggle, the end of fear, the end of needing to care about anything. Soon, there would be no exhaustion, no insufferable heat, no pain, no sorrow, no anguish.

At the same time, when, for only an instant here or a moment there, she actually comprehended the staggering reality that she was about to die, her mind blanked out with overwhelming terror. It was her life, her only precious life, that was inexorably dwindling away, that would soon end with the cold embrace of death itself.

Flickering lightning skipped across a darkening sky, traveling under the clouds. Distant, intense flashes came again, lacing though the heavy clouds, lighting them from within with spectacular green light. Distant thunder boomed, rumbling out across the vast deserted valley. The hesitant rolling sound of the thunder seemed to match the way the landscape wavered in the heat.

As they descended, the towering rock columns became larger,

at first growing up from splits along the ridges, until down at the bottom they seemed rooted in the floor of the valley itself. Now, as the three of them moved at last ever farther away from the cliffs and out into the valley, those columns rose up like an ancient stone forest. Jennsen felt like an ant moving among them.

As their footsteps echoed among the rock walls, chambers, and tiers, she couldn't help marveling at the smooth, rippled sides of the pillars, that looked as if the rock had been worn smooth, like stones in a river. Different layers within the vertical rock appeared to be of varying density, making them wear at different rates, leaving the stone towers rippled up along their entire length. In places, huge sections of the columns perched atop narrow necks.

All the while, the heat felt like a great weight pressing down on her as her feet dragged through the jagged gravel at the bottom. The light among the columns cast eerie shadows, leaving dark places lurking farther back in among the towers. In other places, light seemed to come from behind the stone. As she looked up, it was like looking up from the depths of the world, seeing the rock itself, lit green at times by the flickering lightning within the clouds, reach up as if beseeching salvation.

Sister Perdita glided among the maze of rock, like a spirit of the dead, her black robes billowing out behind. Even Sebastian's presence behind was not a comfort for Jennsen among such silent sentinels to the power of Creation itself.

Lightning arced across above their heads, above the tops of towering rock, as if searching the forest of stone. Thunder shook the valley with violent shudders that brought crumbling rock down on them so that they had to run or dodge to the side to avoid being stoned. Jennsen saw, here and there, where some of the enormous pillars had previously come crashing down. They lay toppled, now, like fallen giants. In places they had to pass beneath the monumental stone lying across the path, walking through passages left where the colossal pieces spanned weathered gaps. She hoped the lightning that was streaking all across the sky didn't decide to hit a stone pillar right above them and send unimaginable weight crashing down on them.

Just when Jennsen thought that they would be forever lost in among the tight spaces among soaring rock, she saw an opening between the towers that revealed the expanse of the rest of the valley floor. Winding their way along the bottom, among the crowded stone columns, they began to wend their way out into more open ground, where the pillars stood as individual monuments rather than being tightly crammed together.

Down at the bottom, the valley, that had looked so flat from above, was a jumble of rolling low rock and scree, cut through with jagged rock formations and lifted slabs of smooth stone that ran for miles. Out from the fingers of tapering ridges coming in from the sides stood lofty pillars both separated, and in small clusters.

The thunder was becoming unnerving as it boomed and shuddered and rumbled almost continually through the forest of stone. The sky had lowered until the boiling clouds brushed along the surrounding walls of rock. Off at the far end of the valley, the darkest clouds threw out almost constant flickers and flashes, some startlingly bright, spawning jarring thunderclaps.

Coming past a broad stone spire, Jennsen was startled to see a wagon in the distance making its way across the valley floor.

Jennsen turned to tell Sebastian about the wagon, and there, behind them, towered the stranger.

Her gaze took in his black shirt, his black, open-sided tunic decorated with ancient symbols snaking along a wide gold band running all the way around its squared edges. The tunic was cinched at his waist with a wide, multilayered leather belt with leather pouches attached along each side. The small, gold-worked leather compartments on the belt bore silver emblems of linked rings, matching those on wide, leather-padded silver bands at each wrist. His trousers and boots were black. In contrast, his broad shoulders bore a cape that appeared to be made of spun gold.

He had no weapon but a belt knife, but he needed none to be the embodiment of threat itself.

Looking into his gray eyes, Jennsen knew instantly and unequivocally that she was staring into the raptor gaze of Richard Rahl.

It felt as if a fist of fear seized her heart, and squeezed. Jennsen pulled her knife free. She clutched it so tightly that her knuckles were white around the silver hilt. She could feel the ornately engraved letter 'R,' for the House of Rahl, biting into her palm and fingers as the Lord Rahl himself stood right there before her.

Sebastian spun around and saw him, then moved around behind her.

Her emotions in a jumble, Jennsen stood paralyzed before her brother.

'Jenn,' Sebastian whispered from behind, 'don't worry. You can do this. Your mother is watching. Don't let her down.'

Richard Rahl scrutinized her, not seeming to notice Sebastian, or even Sister Perdita, farther back. Jennsen stared at her brother, equally oblivious of the other two.

'Where is Kahlan?' Richard said.

His voice was not what she expected. It was commanding, to be sure, but it was so much more, so full of emotion, everything from cold fury, to unwavering resolve, to desperation. His gray eyes, too, reflected the same sincere and terrible determination.

Jennsen could not take her eyes from him. 'Who is Kahlan?'

'The Mother Confessor. My wife.'

Jennsen could not move, so conflicted was she in what she was seeing, in what she was hearing. This was not a man looking for a monster cohort, a brutal Confessor who ruled the Midlands with an iron will and an evil hand. This was a man motivated by love for this woman. Jennsen could clearly see that little else mattered to him. If they did not get out of his way, he would go through them like he went through those thousand men. It was as simple as that.

Except, unlike those thousand men, Jennsen was invincible.

'Where is Kahlan?' Richard repeated, his patience at an end.

'You killed my mother,' Jennsen said, almost defensively.

His brow twitched. He seemed truly puzzled. 'I only just learned that I have a sister. Friedrich Gilder just told me, and that your name is Jennsen.'

Jennsen realized she was nodding, unable to take her eyes off his, seeing her own eyes in his.

'Kill him, Jenn!' Sebastian whispered urgently in her ear. 'Kill him! You can do it. His magic can't hurt you! Do it.'

Jennsen felt a kind of tingling dread working its way up her legs. Something was wrong. Gripping the knife, she gathered her courage of purpose as the voice filled her head, until there was no room for anything else.

'The Lord Rahl has been trying to murder me my whole life. When you killed your father, you took his place. You sent men after me. You've hounded me just like your father. You sent the quads after us. You bastard, you sent those men who murdered my mother!'

Richard listened without argument, and then spoke in a calm, deliberate voice. 'Don't lay a cloak of guilt around my shoulders because others are evil.'

Jennsen was jolted, realizing that was very close to the words her mother had used the night before she died. *Don't you ever wear a cloak of guilt because they are evil.*

The muscles in his jaw flexed as he gritted his teeth. 'What have you done with Kahlan?'

'She's my queen, now!' came a voice echoing through the columns.

Jennsen vaguely recognized the voice. As she looked around, she didn't see Sister Perdita anywhere.

Richard passed her, already moving toward the voice, like a shadow moving by, and then he was suddenly gone. She had missed her chance to stab him. She couldn't believe that he had been standing right in front of her, and she had missed her chance.

'Jenn!' Sebastian called, pulling at her arm. 'What's the matter with you? Come on! You can still get him!'

She didn't know what was wrong. Something was. She pressed her hands to her head, trying to stop the drone of the voice. She no longer could. She had made a bargain, and the voice was mercilessly demanding that she hold to it, crushing her mind with pain unlike any she had ever suffered.

When Jennsen heard laughter echoing through the forest of stone pillars, she moved swiftly, the heat and her exhaustion forgotten. She and Sebastian ran toward the sound, weaving their way among the disorder of towering rock. She no longer knew where she was, which way was which. She raced through stone passageways that opened up to others, along their twisting course, under archways of rock, among columns, and through shadows and light. It was like moving through a strange and confusing combination of corridors and woods, except that these walls were stone, not plaster, and the trees were rock.

As they came around an immense pillar, there, among others standing like sentinels, was an open area of undulating smooth rock in a jumble of curves, with smaller stone columns as thick around as ancient pines.

A woman was tied to one of the columns.

There was no doubt in Jennsen's mind that this was Richard's wife, Kahlan, the Mother Confessor.

Off in another direction came the echoing laughter, teasing, leading Richard away from what he sought.

The Mother Confessor didn't look like the monster Jennsen had pictured. She looked in bad shape, limp in the ropes around the pillar. She was not bound securely, but simply, with rope around her middle, as a child might tie a playmate to a tree.

She was apparently unconscious, some of her long mass of hair pendent around her hanging head, her arms swinging free. She wore simple traveling clothes, though neither they nor the partial veil of hair hid what a beautiful woman she was. She looked only a few years older than Jennsen. She didn't look like she would live to be any older.

Sister Perdita appeared suddenly beside the woman, lifting the Mother Confessor's head by her hair, taking a look, then letting her head drop again.

Sebastian ran up, pointing. 'That's her. Come on.'

As Jennsen followed, she didn't need the voice in her head to tell her that this was the bait that had been provided in order to draw Richard Rahl in for the killing. The voice had done its part.

Girding her resolve, gripping her knife tightly, Jennsen ran over beside the Sister. She turned her back to the unconscious woman, not wanting to think about her, or to have to look at her, putting her mind instead to the task at hand. This was her chance to finish it.

The laughing man suddenly popped out from behind a pillar not far away, no doubt to help draw in the prey. Jennsen recognized his awful grin. It was the man she had seen the night the sorceress Lathea had been murdered. It was the man that had so frightened Betty, her goat. The man Jennsen thought she recognized from her nightmares.

'I see you have found my queen,' the nightmare man said.

'What?' Sebastian asked.

'My queen,' the man said, still with that terrible grin. 'I am King Oba Rahl. She shall be my queen.'

Jennsen recognized, then, that there was a small resemblance in the eyes to Nathan Rahl, to Richard, to her. He didn't have the strong likeness that Jennsen saw of herself in Richard's eyes, but she saw enough to know that he was telling the truth – he, too, was the son of Darken Rahl.

'Here he comes,' he said, turning, holding out an introductory arm, 'my brother, the old Lord Rahl.'

Richard strode out of the shadows.

'Don't be afraid, Jenn,' Sebastian whispered in her ear, 'he can't hurt you. You can get him, now.'

Now was her chance; she would not again waste it.

Off to the side, through the thicket of columns, she caught glimpses of a wagon rolling up. She thought she recognized the horses – both gray with black manes and tails. They were horses as big as any she'd ever seen. From the corner of her eye, she saw that the driver was big and blond-headed.

Jennsen turned, staring in disbelief at the wagon when she heard Betty's familiar bleat. The goat stood and put its front hooves up on the seat beside the driver. The big blond man gave her ears a quick affectionate rub. It looked like Tom.

'Jennsen,' Richard said, 'step away from Kahlan.'

'Don't do it, sis!' Oba yelled. He roared with laughter.

Knife in hand, Jennsen backed closer to the unconscious woman hanging from the pillar rising up behind. Richard would try to come through her to get at Kahlan; then Jennsen would have him.

'Jennsen,' Richard said, 'why would you side with a Sister of the Dark?'

She shot a brief puzzled frown at Sister Perdita. 'Sister of the Light,' she corrected.

Richard slowly shook his head as his gaze went beyond to Sister Perdita. 'No. She is a Sister of the Dark. Jagang has Sisters of the Light, but he also has the others as well. They are both slaves to the dream walker; that's why they have that ring through their lower lip.'

Jennsen had heard that name before – dream walker. She frantically tried to remember where. She recalled, too, what the Sisters had invoked that night in the woods. Everything was tumbling through her mind in a frantic rush. It wasn't helping that the voice was there, incessantly urging her on. She was screaming inside with the need to kill this man, but something was keeping her from moving. She knew it couldn't be his magic.

'You will have to come through Jennsen if you want to save Kahlan,' Sister Perdita said in her cool, disdainful voice. 'You have run out of time, and options, Lord Rahl. You had better at least save your wife, before her time is up, as well.'

Off in the distance to the side, Jennsen caught sight of the brown goat bounding through the forest of stone, outpacing Tom by a wide margin.

'Betty?' Jennsen whispered through choking tears as she unwrapped the black veil from her head so the goat would recognize her.

The goat bleated at the sound of her name, her little upright tail wagging in a blur as she ran. Something else, smaller, was coming from behind, back by Tom. Before the goat could reach her, it reached Oba. Spotting him as it came around the pillar, Betty let out a plaintive cry and sidestepped away. Jennsen knew well Betty's cry of distress and terror, her plea for help and comfort.

Overhead, the sky went wild with lightning and thunder, further frightening the poor animal.

'Betty?' Jennsen called, hardly able to believe what she was seeing, wondering if it could be an illusion, some cruel deception. But Lord Rahl's magic couldn't do that to her.

At the sound of her voice, the goat bounded toward Jennsen,

her beloved lifelong friend. Not a dozen strides away, Betty looked up at Jennsen and froze in her tracks. The wagging tail stopped dead. Betty bleated in distress. The bleats turned to terror at what she was seeing.

'Betty,' Jennsen cried, 'it's all right. Come – it's me.'

Trembling in fear as it gazed up at her, Betty backed away. The goat was reacting the same way it had to Oba, just now, and the same way it had that first night she saw him.

Betty turned and ran.

Right for Richard.

He crouched down as the goat, clearly in distress, came running, seeking comfort, and found it under a sheltering hand.

Stunned, Jennsen then heard other little bleats. Small little twin white goats came capering into the midst of all the people, into the middle of a deadly confrontation. They spooked at the sight of the man, turned, and at the sight of Jennsen, shrank back, crying out for their mother.

Betty bleated, calling to them. They spun and raced for her protection. With their mother there, they felt safe, and jumped up on Richard, eager for the reassuring touch their mother was getting.

Tom had stopped well back, waiting near a pillar as he watched, obviously intending to stay clear.

Jennsen thought that, surely, the world must have gone mad.

Chapter 60

'Betty, what are you doing?' Jennsen asked, unable to reconcile in her mind what was happening.

'Magic,' Sister Perdita whispered from behind, in answer to Jennsen's puzzled tone. 'It's his doing.'

Could it be that Richard Rahl had bewitched even her goat – turned it against her?

Richard took a step toward her. Betty and her twins romped around his legs, having no conception of the life-and-death events taking place before them.

'Jennsen, use your head,' Richard said. 'Think for yourself. You have to help me, now. Step away from Kahlan.'

'Kill him!' Sebastian whispered with vicious determination. 'Do it, Jenn! Magic can't hurt you! Do it!'

Jennsen lifted her knife as Richard calmly watched her. She felt herself stepping toward him. When she killed him, then his magic would die, too, and Betty would know her once again.

Jennsen froze. Something was wrong. She turned to Sebastian.

'How do you know? How do you know that? I never told you that magic can't harm me.'

'You too?' Oba called. He'd come closer. 'We're both invincible, then! We can rule D'Hara together – but I'll be the king, of course. King Oba Rahl. I'm not greedy, though. You could be a princess, maybe. Yes, I could let you be a princess, if you're good.'

Jennsen's eyes turned back toward Sebastian's surprised face. 'How do you know?'

'Jenn – I just – I thought,' he stammered, trying to find an answer.

'Richard . . .' It was Kahlan, waking, but groggy. 'Richard, where are we?' She winced in pain, and cried out, even though no one touched her.

When Richard took a step toward her, Jennsen stepped back before her, brandishing her knife.

'If you want her, you must come through Jennsen,' Sister Perdita said. Richard watched her without emotion for a long moment. 'No.'

'You must!' the Sister growled. 'You will have to kill Jennsen, or Kahlan will die!'

'Are you crazy!' Sebastian yelled at the Sister.

'Get ahold of yourself, Sebastian,' the Sister snapped. 'Salvation comes only through sacrifice. All of mankind is corrupt. One individual is unimportant – one life is meaningless. It matters not what happens to her – only her sacrifice matters.'

Sebastian stared at her, unable to answer, unable to find a reason to argue for Jennsen's life.

'You'll have to kill Jennsen!' Sister Perdita shrieked as she turned back to Richard. 'Or I will kill Kahlan!'

'Richard . . .' Kahlan moaned, clearly not understanding where she was or what was happening.

'Kahlan,' Richard said in a calm voice, 'stay still.'

'Last chance!' Sister Perdita screamed. 'Last chance to save the Mother Confessor's precious life! Last chance before the Keeper has her! Stop him, Jennsen, while I kill his wife!'

Jennsen was staggered that the Sister would be encouraging him to kill her. It made no sense. It was Lord Rahl that the Sister wanted dead. It was Lord Rahl they all wanted dead.

Jennsen knew she had to end it. She couldn't be hurt by his magic. How Sebastian knew that, she couldn't fathom, but she had to end it, now, while she had the chance. Why the Sister was doing this, though, was a mystery.

Unless Sister Perdita was trying to anger Richard so that he would lash out with his magic, strike with his power at Jennsen, thus giving her the opening she finally needed.

That had to be it. Jennsen dared not wait.

Unleashing a cry of fury filled with a lifetime of hate, filled with the burning agony of her mother's murder, filled with the howling rage of the voice in her head, Jennsen launched herself at Richard.

She knew he would hurl his magic at her in order to save himself, unleash magic at her as he had unleashed it at the thousand men. He would be shocked that it didn't work, shocked as she burst through his deadly conjuring at the last instant to suddenly plunge her knife through his evil heart. He would know too late that she was invincible.

Screaming her rage, Jennsen flew at him.

She expected a horrific blast, expected to fly through the lightning, thunder, smoke, but it never came. He caught her wrist in his fist. Simple as that. He used no magic. He cast no spell. He invoked no wizardly power.

Jennsen had no immunity to muscle, and he had plenty of that.

'Calm down,' Richard said.

She fought him furiously, an angry storm throwing all her hate and pain into her onslaught. He securely held her knife-wielding fist as she raged, her other fist pounding against his chest. He could have snapped her in two with his bare hands, but he instead let her scream and strike out at him, then let her yank herself back away to stand in the center of everyone, panting, knife held up, tears of anger and hate streaming down her cheeks.

'Kill her or Kahlan dies!' Sister Perdita shrieked again.

Sebastian shoved the Sister back. 'Have you lost your mind! She can do it! He isn't even armed!'

Richard pulled a small book from one of the pouches at his belt and held it up.

'Oh, but I am.'

'What do you mean?' Jennsen asked.

His raptor gaze settled on her. 'This is an ancient text titled *The Pillars of Creation*. It was written by some of our ancestors, Jennsen – those among the first to be Lord Rahl, among the first who came to understand the full extent of what had been engendered by the first of the line, Alric Rahl, who created the bond, among other things. It's very interesting reading.'

'I suppose it says that as Lord Rahl you should kill those like me,' Jennsen said.

Richard smiled. 'You're right. It does.'

'What?' She could hardly believe that he would admit it. 'It really says that?'

He nodded. 'It explains why all the truly ungifted offspring of the Lord Rahl – the Lord Rahl who carries down the gift of the bond to his people – must be killed.'

'I knew it!' Jennsen cried. 'You tried to lie! But it's true! It's all right there!'

'I didn't say that I would take the advice. I only said that the *book* says that your kind are to be killed.'

'Why?' Jennsen asked.

'Jenn, it doesn't matter,' Sebastian whispered. 'Don't listen to him.'

Richard gestured to Sebastian. 'He knows why. That's why he knew you couldn't be harmed by my magic. He knew because he knows what's in the book.'

Jennsen spun to Sebastian, her eyes wide with sudden understanding. 'Emperor Jagang has that book.'

'Jenn, you're just talking nonsense, now.'

'I saw it, Sebastian. *The Pillars of Creation*. I saw it in his tent. It's an ancient book, in his old tongue. It's one of his prized books. He knew what it says. You are one of his prized strategists. He told you. You knew all along what it said.'

'Jenn . . . I—'

'It was you,' she whispered.

'How can you doubt me? I love you.'

Then, over the terrible tumult of the voice, the whole thing began unravelling in her mind. The crushing pain of it all came crashing in on her. The true dimensions of the betrayal became horrifyingly clear.

'Dear spirits, it was you all along.'

Sebastian, his face going nearly as white as his white spikes of hair, turned deadly calm. 'Jenn, that doesn't change anything.'

'It was you,' she whispered, wide-eyed. 'You took a single mountain fever rose—'

'What! I don't even have any such thing.'

'I saw them in a tin in your pack. There was twine on top of them, hiding them. They spilled out.'

'Oh, those. I – I got them from the healer – the one we visited.'

'Liar! You had them all along. You took one to give yourself a fever.'

'Jenn, now you're just acting crazy.'

Trembling, Jennsen pointed at him with her knife. 'It was you, all along. That first night, you told me, "Where I come from, we believe in using what is closest to an enemy, or what comes from him, as a weapon against him." You wanted me to have this knife. You wanted me because I was closest to your enemy. You wanted to use me. How did you get it on that soldier?'

'Jenn—'

'You claim to love me. Prove it! Don't lie to me! Tell me the truth!'

Sebastian stared a moment before finally holding his head up and answering. 'I only wanted to gain your trust. I thought that if I had a fever you would take me in.'

'And the dead soldier I found?'

'He was one of my men. We captured the man who carried that knife. I gave it to one of my men, had him dress in a D'Haran uniform, then, after we saw you pass below, I pushed him over the cliff.'

'You killed your own man?'

'Sacrifice for the greater cause is sometimes necessary. Salvation comes through sacrifice,' he added in defiant defense.

'How did you know where I was?'

'Emperor Jagang is a dream walker. He learned about your kind through the book years ago. He used his ability to search for any who might know of your existence. Over time, he put together evidence in order to track you down.'

'And the note I found?'

'I planted it on him. Jagang found out through his ability that you once used that name.'

'The bond prevents the dream walker from entering a person's mind,' Richard said. 'He must have searched for a long time, looking for those who aren't bonded to the Lord Rahl.'

Sebastian nodded with satisfaction. 'That's right. And we succeeded, too.'

Jennsen, burning with blinding anger, with the agony of such monumental betrayal, swallowed. 'And the rest? My . . . mother? Was that one of your necessary sacrifices, too?'

Sebastian licked his lips. 'Jenn, you don't understand. I didn't really know you then—'

'They were your own men. That's why it was so easy for you to kill them. They weren't expecting you to attack them – they thought you were there to fight alongside them. And that's why you were confused when I told you about the quads, about how many more men I thought there were. They weren't really quads. You had to kill some innocent people along the way in order to make me think it was the other member of a quad. All those times you went out at night to scout and came back saying they were right behind us, and we kept running through the night – you made it all up.'

'To a good cause,' Sebastian said, quietly.

Jennsen gasped in her tears, her fury. 'A good cause! You killed my mother! It was you all along! Dear spirits . . . to think that I . . . oh, dear spirits, I slept with my mother's murderer. You filthy—'

'Jenn, get ahold of yourself. It was necessary.' He pointed at Richard. 'This is the cause of it all! We have him now! This was all necessary! Salvation only comes through selfless sacrifice. Your sacrifice – your mother's sacrifice – has captured us Richard Rahl, the man who has hunted you your whole life.'

Tears of rage poured down her face. 'I can't believe you could have done such things to me and claimed to love me.'

'But I do, Jenn. I didn't know you, then. I told you – I never intended to fall in love with you, but I did. It just happened. You are my life, now. I love you, now.'

She pressed her hands to the voice screaming in her head. 'You are evil! I could never love you!'

'Brother Narev teaches that all of mankind is evil. We can have no moral existence because mankind is a taint on the world of life. At least Brother Narev is at last in a better place. He's with the Creator, now.'

'You mean to say that even Brother Narev is evil, then? Because he is part of mankind? Even your precious, sacred Brother Narev was evil?'

Sebastian glared at her. 'The one who is truly evil is standing right there' – he pointed – 'Richard Rahl, for killing a great man. Richard Rahl must be put to death for his crimes.'

'If mankind is evil, and if Brother Narev is in a better place – with the Creator – then Richard has done a kindness by killing Brother Narev, by sending him into the Creator's arms, hasn't he? And if mankind is evil, then how could Richard Rahl be evil for killing men of the Order?'

Sebastian's face had gone red. 'We are all evil, but some are more evil than others! As least we have the humility before the Creator to recognize our own wickedness, and to glorify only the Creator.' He paused and cooled visibly. 'I know it's a sign of weakness, but I love you.' He gave her a smile. 'You have become my only reason for being, Jenn.'

She could only stare at him. 'You don't love me, Sebastian. You don't have any idea what love really is. You can't love anyone or anything until you love your own existence, first. Love can only grow out of a respect for your own life. When you love yourself, your own existence, then you love someone who can enhance your existence, share it with you, and make it more pleasurable. When you hate yourself and believe your existence is evil, then you can only hate, you can only experience the shell of love, that longing for something good, but you have nothing to base it in but hatred. You taint the very concept of love, Sebastian, with your corrupted longing for it. You want me only to justify your hatred, to be your partner in self-loathing.

'To truly love someone, Sebastian, you must revel in their existence because they make life all the more wonderful. If you think existence is corrupt, then you are sealed off from the fruition of such a relationship, from what love really is.'

'You're wrong! You just don't understand!'

'I understand all too well. I only wish I had sooner.'

'But I do love you, Jenn. You're wrong. I do love you!'

'You can only wish you did. They are the empty words of a barren shell of a man. There is nothing there for me to love –

nothing worth loving. You are so empty of humanity that it's even difficult for me to hate you, Sebastian, except in the sense of the way one would hate an open sewer.'

Lightning crashed down on the pillars all around. The voice in Jennsen's head felt as if it would tear her apart.

'Jenn – you don't mean any of that. You can't. I can't live without you.'

Jennsen turned her cold fury on him. 'The only thing in the whole world that you could do that would please me, Sebastian, would be to die!'

'I've listened to this touching lovers' spat long enough,' Sister Perdita growled. 'Sebastian, be a man and shut your mouth or I'll shut it for you. Your life means just as little as anyone else's. Richard, you have a choice. Jennsen or the Mother Confessor.'

'You don't have to serve the Keeper, Sister,' Richard said. 'You don't have to serve the dream walker, either. You have a choice.'

Sister Perdita pointed at him. 'You have a choice! I make you this offer, once! Your time is up! Kahlan's time is up! Jennsen or Kahlan – choose!'

'I don't like your rules,' Richard said. 'I choose neither.'

'Then I choose for you! Your precious wife dies!'

Even as Jennsen dove at her to stop her, Sister Perdita seized Kahlan by the hair and lifted her head. The Mother Confessor's face was blank of all expression.

Jennsen caught Sister Perdita's arm, swinging the knife with the ornate letter 'R' as fast as she could, with as much power as she could apply, hoping against hope that she was fast enough to save Kahlan's life, yet knowing even as she made the attempt that she was already too late.

There was a crystal-clear instant when the world seemed to stop, to freeze in place.

And then, there was a violent concussion to the air, thunder without sound.

The terrible shock drove a ring of dust and rock away from the Mother Confessor in an ever-expanding circle. The shock to the columns so close all around shook the towering pillars. Some, that were so precariously balanced, toppled. As they fell, they hit others, bringing them down as well. It seemed to take forever for the huge sections of rock to plunge through the sweltering air, trailing dust as they disintegrated, plummeting down like thunder made of stone. As the rock came crashing to ground it seemed the entire valley shook under the tremendous blows. Blinding dust swirled up into the air.

The world went black, as if all light had been taken away, and in that terrifying instant, in the total blackness, it seemed that there was no world, no anything.

The world came back, like a shadow lifting.

Jennsen found herself holding the arm of a dead woman. The Sister toppled to the ground like one of the stone pillars. Jennsen saw her knife jutting from the Sister's chest.

Richard was already there, holding Kahlan in his arms, slicing through the rope, easing her down. She looked drained, but other than her weakness, she looked fine.

'What happened?' Jennsen asked in wonder.

Richard smiled at her. 'The Sister made a mistake. I warned her. The Mother Confessor unleashed her power into Sister Perdita.'

'Did you have to warn her?' Kahlan asked, suddenly quite coherent-sounding. 'She might have listened to you.'

'No, it only encouraged her to do it.'

Jennsen realized that the voice was gone. 'What happened? Did I kill her?'

'No. She was dead before your knife touched her,' Kahlan said. 'Richard was distracting her so I could use my power. You tried, but you were an instant too late. She was already mine.'

Richard put a comforting hand on Jennsen's shoulder. 'You didn't kill her, but you made a choice that saved your own life. That shadow that passed over us as the Sister died was the Keeper of the dead taking one who had sworn herself to him. Had you made the wrong choice, you would have been taken with her.'

Jennsen's knees were trembling. 'The voice is gone,' she whispered aloud. 'It's gone.'

'The Keeper inadvertently revealed his intent,' Richard said.

'Since the hounds were loose, that meant the veil – the conduit between worlds – was open.'

'I don't understand.'

Richard gestured with the book before he tucked it back into one of the pouches at his belt. 'Well, I haven't had time to read it all, but I've read enough to learn a little. You are an ungifted offspring of a Lord Rahl. That makes you the balance to the gifted Rahl – to magic. You not only have none, but you're not touched by it. In a time of a great war, the House of Rahl was created to give birth to a line of powerful wizards, but in so doing, it also sowed the seeds of the end of magic for the world. It may be the Imperial Order that wants a world without magic, but it is the House of Rahl that may eventually deliver it.

'You, Jennsen Rahl, are potentially the most dangerous person alive, because you, like any truly ungifted Rahl, are the seed that could spawn a new world without magic.'

Jennsen stared into his gray eyes. 'Then why would you not want me dead, like every Lord Rahl before you?'

Richard smiled. 'You have as much right to your life as anyone else – as any Lord Rahl has ever had to their life. There is no right way for the world to be. The only right is that people be allowed to live their own life.'

Kahlan pulled the knife from Sister Perdita's chest and cleaned it on the black robes before handing it to Jennsen. 'Sister Perdita was wrong. Salvation is not through sacrifice. Your responsibility is to yourself.'

'Your life is your own,' Richard said, 'and not anyone else's. You made me proud, hearing everything you said to Sebastian.'

Jennsen stared down at the knife in her hand, still dazed and confused by everything that was happening. She looked around in the gathering darkness, but didn't see Sebastian anywhere. Oba was gone, too.

As she looked around, Jennsen was startled to see a Mord-Sith standing not far away. 'This is just great,' the woman complained to the Mother Confessor, throwing her hands up. 'The girl sounds like Lord Rahl. Now I'm going to have to listen to two of them.'

Kahlan smiled and sat down, leaning back against the pillar

where she had been tied, watching Richard, listening, stroking the ears of Betty's twin kids.

Betty watched her two young ones, then, seeing them safe, peered hopefully up at Jennsen. Her little tail started wagging in a blur.

'Betty?'

Betty happily jumped up on her, eager for a reunion. Jennsen tearfully hugged the goat before standing to face her brother.

'But why would you not do as your ancestors? Why? How can you risk everything in that book?'

Richard hooked his thumbs behind his belt and took a deep breath. 'Life is the future, not the past. The past can teach us, through experience, how to accomplish things in the future, comfort us with cherished memories, and provide the foundation of what has already been accomplished. But only the future holds life. To live in the past is to embrace what is dead. To live life to its fullest, each day must be created anew. As rational, thinking beings, we must use our intellect, not a blind devotion to what has come before, to make rational choices.'

'Life is the future, not the past,' Jennsen whispered to herself, considering all that life now held for her. 'Where did you ever hear such a thing?'

Richard grinned. 'It's the Wizard's Seventh Rule.'

Jennsen gazed up at him through her tears. 'You have given me a future, a life. Thank you.'

He embraced her, then, and Jennsen suddenly didn't feel alone in the world. She felt whole again. It felt so good to be held as she wept with tears for her mother, and tears for the future, for the joy that there was life, and a future.

Kahlan rubbed Jennsen's back. 'Welcome to the family.'

When Jennsen wiped her eyes, and laughed at everything and nothing while she used her other hand to scratch Betty's ears, she saw, then, Tom standing nearby.

Jennsen ran to him and fell into his arms. 'Oh, Tom. You can't know how glad I am to see you! Thank you for bringing me Betty.'

'That's me. Goat delivery, as promised. Turns out that Irma, the sausage lady, only wanted your goat to get herself a kid. She has a billy and wanted a young one. She kept one and let you have the other two.'

'Betty had three?'

Tom nodded. 'I'm afraid that I've become very fond of Betty and her two little ones.'

'I can't believe that you did that for me. Tom, you're wonderful.'

'My mother always said so, too. Don't forget, you promised to tell Lord Rahl.'

Jennsen laughed in delight. 'I promise! But, how in the world did you ever find me?'

Tom smiled and pulled a knife from behind his back. Jennsen was astonished to see that it was identical to the one she had.

'You see,' he explained, 'I carry the knife in service to Lord Rahl.'

'You do?' Richard asked. 'I've never even met you.'

'Oh,' the Mord-Sith said, 'Tom, here, is all right, Lord Rahl. I can vouch for him.'

'Why, thank you, Cara,' Tom said with a twinkle in his eye.

'And you knew all along, then,' Jennsen asked, 'that I was making it all up?'

Tom shrugged. 'I wouldn't be a proper protector to Lord Rahl if I let such a suspicious person as you roam around, trying to do harm, without doing my best to find out what you were up to. I've kept tabs on you, followed you a goodly part of your journeying.'

Jennsen swatted his shoulder. 'You've been spying on me!'

'As a protector to Lord Rahl, I had to see what you were up to, and to make sure you didn't harm Lord Rahl.'

'Well,' she said, 'I don't think you were doing a very good job of it then.'

'What do you mean?' Tom asked with exaggerated indignation.

'I could have really stabbed him. You just stood way over there the whole time, too far away to do anything about it.'

Tom smiled that boyish grin of his, but this time it was a little more mischievous than usual.

'Oh, I'd not have let you hurt Lord Rahl.'

Tom turned and heaved his knife. With blinding speed such as she had never seen, the blade flew across the valley, embedding itself with a thunk in one of the faraway fallen stone pillars. Jennsen squinted and saw that it had been driven through something dark.

She followed Tom, Richard, Kahlan, and the Mord-Sith between towering columns and stone rubble to where the knife was stuck. To Jennsen's astonishment, it had impaled a leather pouch – right through the center – being held up by a hand coming from beneath the huge section of fallen stone.

'Please,' came a muffled voice from under the rock, 'please let me out. I'll pay you. I can pay. I have my own money.'

It was Oba. The rock had fallen on him when he ran. It had landed on boulders that kept the main section of stone, big enough that twenty men couldn't have joined hands around it, from collapsing to the ground, leaving a tiny space, trapping the man alive under the tons of rock.

Tom pulled his knife from the soft stone and retrieved the leather pouch. He waved it in the air.

'Friedrich!' he called toward the wagon. A man sat up. 'Friedrich! Is this yours?'

Jennsen was astonished yet again, in this astonishing day, to see Friedrich Gilder, the husband of Althea, climb down from the wagon and make his way over to them.

'That's mine,' he said. He looked under the rock. 'You have more.'

After a moment, the hand began passing out more leather and cloth purses. 'There, you have all my money. Let me out, now.'

'Oh,' Friedrich said, 'I don't think I could lift that rock. Especially not for the man who is responsible for the death of my wife.'

'Althea died?' Jennsen asked in shock.

'I'm afraid so. My sunshine has gone from my life.'

'I'm so sorry,' she whispered. 'She was a good woman.'

Friedrich smiled. 'Yes, she was.' He pulled a small smooth stone from his pocket. 'But she left me this, and that much is a pleasure.'

'Isn't that odd,' Tom said in wonder. He fished around in his pocket until he came up with something. He opened his hand to reveal a small smooth stone sitting in his palm. 'I have one of those, too. I always carry it as a good-luck charm.'

Friedrich eyed him suspiciously. He grinned at last. 'She has smiled on you, too, then.'

'I can't breathe,' came a muffled voice from under the rock. 'Please, it hurts. I can't move. Let me out.'

Richard held his hand out toward the rock. There came a grinding sound and a sword floated from under the rock. He bent and pulled his scabbard out, dragging the baldric out behind. He wiped the dust off and placed the baldric over his shoulder, the scabbard at his hip. The sword was magnificent, a proper weapon for the Lord Rahl.

Jennsen saw the gleaming gold word 'TRUTH' on the hilt.

'You faced all those soldiers, and you didn't even have your sword,' Jennsen said. 'I guess your magic was better defense.'

Richard smiled as he shook his head. 'My ability works through need and anger. With Kahlan taken, I had plenty of need, and a ready rage.' He lifted the hilt clear of the scabbard until she could again see the word spelled out in gold. 'This weapon works all the time.'

'How did you know where we were?' Jennsen asked him. 'How did you know where Kahlan was?'

Richard burnished a thumb over the single gold word on the hilt of his sword. 'My grandfather gave me this. King Oba, there, stole it when, with the Keeper's help, he captured Kahlan. This sword is rather special. I have a connection to it; I can sense where it is. The Keeper no doubt induced Oba to take it in order to entice me here.'

'Please,' Oba called, 'I can't breathe.'

'Your grandfather?' Jennsen asked, ignoring Oba's distress, his weeping. 'You mean, Wizard Zorander?'

Richard's whole face softened with a splendid grin. 'You've met Zedd, then. He's wonderful, isn't he?'

'He tried to kill me,' Jennsen muttered.

'Zedd?' Richard scoffed. 'Zedd's harmless.'

'Harmless? He—'

The Mord-Sith, Cara, poked at Jennsen with the red rod she had – the Agiel.

'What are you doing?' Jennsen asked. 'Stop that.'

'That doesn't do anything to you?'

'No,' Jennsen said, scowling. 'No more than it did when Nyda did it.'

Cara's eyebrow went up. 'You've met Nyda?' She looked up at Richard. 'And she can still walk. I'm impressed.'

'She's immune to magic,' Richard said. 'That's why your Agiel won't work on her, either.'

Cara, with a sly smile, looked over at Kahlan.

'Are you thinking what I'm thinking?' Kahlan asked.

'She might just be able to solve our little problem,' Cara said, her wicked grin growing.

'Now, I suppose,' Richard said in ill humor, 'you're going to have her touch it, too.'

'Well,' Cara said defensively, 'someone has to. You don't want me to do it again, do you?'

'No!'

'What are you three talking about?' Jennsen asked.

'We have some urgent problems,' Richard said. 'If you'd like to help, I think you just might have the special talent it takes to get us out of a serious bind.'

'Really? You mean you want me to go with you?'

'If you're willing,' Kahlan said. She leaned on Richard, looking like she was at the end of her strength.

'Tom,' Richard said, 'might we—'

'Of course!' Tom said, dashing over to offer his arm to Kahlan. 'Come on over. I have some nice blankets in back where you can lay down – just ask Jennsen, they're real comfortable. I'll drive you back up the easy way.'

'That would be much appreciated,' Richard said. 'It's just about dark. We'd better stay here for the night and ride out as soon as it's light enough. Hopefully, before it gets too hot.'

'The rest of them will want to sit back there with the Mother Confessor, I expect,' Tom whispered to Jennsen. 'If you don't mind, you could ride up on the seat with me.'

'First I want to know something – the truth, now,' Jennsen

said. 'If you're a defender to Lord Rahl, what would you have done, standing over there, if I had harmed Lord Rahl?'

Tom looked down at her with a serious expression. 'Jennsen, if I really thought that you would or could, I'd have put this knife in you before you had the chance.'

Jennsen smiled. 'Good. I'll ride with you, then. My horse is up there,' she said pointing up past the Pillars of Creation. 'I've become good friends with Rusty.'

Betty bleated at the sound of the horse's name. Jennsen laughed and scratched Betty's fat middle. 'You remember Rusty?'

Betty bleated that she did as her kids frolicked near by.

In the distance behind, Jennsen could hear the murdering Oba Rahl demanding to be let out. She stopped and looked back, realizing that he, too, was a half brother. A very evil one.

'I'm sorry I thought such terrible things about you,' she said, looking up at Richard.

He smiled as he held Kahlan close with one arm, and then pulled Jennsen close with the other. 'You used your head when confronted with the truth. I couldn't ask for any more than that.'

The weight of the rock that had fallen was slowly crushing the sandstone boulders holding up the pillar trapping Oba. It was only a matter of hours until Oba was crushed to death in his inescapable prison, or, if not, until he died of thirst.

After such a defeat, the Keeper wasn't going to reward Oba with any help. The Keeper would have eternity to make Oba suffer for failure.

Oba was a killer. Jennsen suspected that Richard Rahl had no shred of mercy for someone like that, or anyone who hurt Kahlan. He showed Oba none.

Oba Rahl would be buried forever with the Pillars of Creation.

Chapter 61

In the morning, Tom gave them a ride out among the towering Pillars of Creation. The view in the early morning, with the sun throwing long shadows and lending striking colors to the landscape, was spectacular. It was a sight that no one else had ever come out of the valley to report.

Rusty was happy to see Jennsen, and turned positively frisky when she saw Betty and her two kids.

Jennsen, with Richard and Kahlan at her side, went into the squat building and discovered that Sebastian, unable to reconcile his beliefs and his feelings, had granted Jennsen her last wish.

He had taken all the mountain fever roses he'd had in the tin. He sat dead at the table.

Jennsen, sitting beside Tom, listened to Richard and Kahlan explain the whole story of how they came to be together. Jennsen could hardly believe that he was so much different than she had ever thought. His mother, having been raped by Darken Rahl, had run away with Zedd to protect Richard. Richard grew up far away in Westland, not knowing anything at all about D'Hara, or the House of Rahl, or magic. Richard had ended the evil rule of Darken Rahl. Kahlan, having been hunted by real quads, had killed their commander. With Richard as Lord Rahl, there were no more quads.

Jennsen felt proud and honored, now, that Richard had asked her to keep the knife with the ornate letter 'R' on it. He said she had earned the right to carry it. She intended to keep it and hold sacred its true purpose. Now, she truly was a protector, just like Tom.

As they rode along, Betty stood in the wagon beside Friedrich, with her front hooves up on the seat between Tom and Jennsen, each holding a sleeping little goat. Rusty was tied behind, where Betty frequently went back to visit. Richard, Kahlan, and Cara rode along at the side.

Jennsen turned to her brother after having considered what he'd just told her. 'So, you're not making that up, then? It really said that about me in that book – *The Pillars of Creation*?'

'It was speaking about those like you: "The most dangerous creature walking the world of life is the ungifted child of a Lord Rahl, because they are completely immune to magic. Magic can't harm them, can't affect them, and even prophecy is blind to them." But I guess you turned out to prove the book wrong.'

She thought it over. Some of it still didn't make sense to her. 'I don't understand why the Keeper was using me. Why was his voice in my head?'

'Well, I only had time to translate a small bit of the book, and other parts are damaged. But, from some of what I did read, I guess that the ungifted child, since he has no magic, is what the book calls a "hole in the world,"' Richard explained, 'so they're also a hole in the veil – making you potentially a conduit between the world of life and the world of the dead. In order for the Keeper to consume the world of life, he needed such a gateway. The need for vengeance was the final key. Your surrender to his wishes – when you went out in the woods with the Sisters of the Dark – had to be consummated by you being slain, by you completing the bargain with death by dying.'

'So, if anyone had killed me – Sister Perdita, for example – after I went out in the woods with those Sisters of the Dark, wouldn't that have opened such a gateway?'

'No. The Keeper needed a protector of the world of life. It took the balance to your lack of the gift. It took a gifted Rahl – the Lord Rahl, to accomplish such a thing,' Richard said. 'If I had killed you to save myself, or Kahlan, then the Keeper would have been loosed into this world through the breach created. I had to force you to choose life, not death, if you were to live, and if the Keeper was to be kept in the underworld.'

'I might have . . . destroyed life,' Jennsen said, shaken at truly understanding how close she'd come to unleashing cataclysmic destruction.

'I'd not have let you,' Tom said, good-naturedly.

Jennsen put her hand on his arm, realizing that she had never had feelings before like she had for him. The man positively made her heart sing. His smile made her life worth living. Betty stuck her nose in, wanting attention, and to see her sleeping babies.

'There is no greater treason to life than delivering the innocent to the Keeper of the dead,' Cara said.

'But she didn't,' Richard said. 'She used reason to discover the truth, and truth to embrace life.'

'You sure know a lot about magic,' Jennsen said to Richard.

Kahlan and Cara laughed so hard that Jennsen thought they might fall off their horses.

'I don't see what's so funny,' Richard grumbled.

The two of them laughed all the harder.

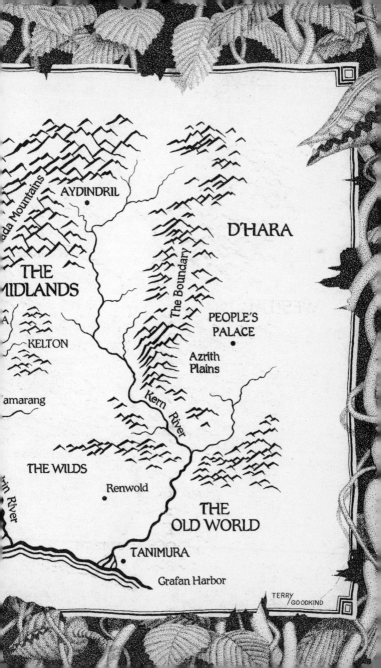